The Complete Dr. Thorndyke

Volume VI:
A Certain Dr. Thorndyke
As a Thief in the Night
Mr. Pottermack's Oversight

The Complete Dr. Thorndyke

Volume VI:
A Certain Dr. Thorndyke
As a Thief in the Night
Mr. Pottermack's Oversight

by

R. Austin Freeman

Edited by
David Marcum

ISBN Hardback 978-1-78705-677-0
ISBN Paperback 978-1-78705-678-7
AUK ePub ISBN 978-1-78705-679-4
AUK PDF ISBN 978-1-78705-680-0

These works are in the Public Domain in Great Britain
Portrait of Dr. Thorndyke by H.M. Brock (1908)

Published in the UK by
MX Publishing
335 Princess Park Manor, Royal Drive,
London, N11 3GX
www.mxpublishing.co.uk

David Marcum can be reached at:
thepapersofsherlockholmes@gmail.com

Cover design by Brian Belanger
www.belangerbooks.com and *www.redbubble.com/people/zhahadun*

CONTENTS

Introductions

Adventures

A Certain Dr. Thorndyke

Book I: *The Ishmaelite*

Book II: *The Investigator*

(Continued on the next page . . . .)

As a Thief in the Night

Mr. Pottermack's Oversight

The
Complete
Dr. Thorndyke

Volume VI:
A Certain Dr. Thorndyke
As a Thief in the Night
Mr. Pottermack's Oversight

Dr. John Thorndyke

5A King's Bench Walk
in the late 1890's when
Thorndyke would have moved in

5A King's Bench Walk
Photographed by the Editor
during his
Sherlock Holmes Pilgrimage No. 3
(September 8th, 2016)

Meet Dr. Thorndyke
by R. Austin Freeman

My subject is Dr. John Thorndyke, the hero or central character of most of my detective stories. So I'll give you a short account of his real origin – of the way in which he did in fact come into existence.

To discover the origin of John Thorndyke I have to reach back into the past for at least fifty years, to the time when I was a medical student preparing for my final examination. For reasons which I need not go into I gave rather special attention to the legal aspects of medicine and the medical aspects of law. And as I read my text-books, and especially the illustrative cases, I was profoundly impressed by their dramatic quality. Medical jurisprudence deals with the human body in its relation to all kinds of legal problems. Thus its subject matter includes all sorts of crime against the person and all sorts of violent death and bodily injury: Hanging, drowning, poisons and their effects, problems of suicide and homicide, of personal identity and survivorship, and a host of other problems of the highest dramatic possibilities, though not always quite presentable for the purposes of fiction. And the reported cases which were given in illustration were often crime stories of the most thrilling interest. Cases of disputed identity such as the Tichbourne Case, famous poisoning cases such as the Rugeley Case and that of Madeline Smith, cases of mysterious disappearance or the detection of long-forgotten crimes such as that of Eugene Aram. All these, described and analysed with strict scientific accuracy, formed the matter of Medical Jurisprudence which thrilled me as I read and made an indelible impression.

But it produced no immediate results. I had to pass my examinations and get my diploma, and then look out for the means of earning my living. So all this curious lore was put away for the time being in the pigeon-holes of my mind – which Dr. Freud would call the *Unconscious* – not forgotten, but ready to come to the surface when the need for it should arise. And there it reposed for some twenty years, until failing health compelled me to abandon medical practice and take to literature as a profession.

It was then that my old studies recurred to my mind. A fellow doctor, Conan Doyle, had made a brilliant and well-deserved success by the creation of the immortal Sherlock Holmes. Considering that achievement, I asked myself whether it might not be possible to devise a

1

detective story of a slightly different kind – one based on the science of Medical Jurisprudence, in which, by the sacrifice of a certain amount of dramatic effect, one could keep entirely within the facts of real life, with nothing fictitious excepting the persons and the events. I came to the conclusion that it was, and began to turn the idea over in my mind.

But I think that the influence which finally determined the character of my detective stories, and incidentally the character of John Thorndyke, operated when I was working at the Westminster Ophthalmic Hospital. There I used to take the patients into the dark room, examine their eyes with the ophthalmoscope, estimate the errors of refraction, and construct an experimental pair of spectacles to correct those errors. When a perfect correction had been arrived at, the formula for it was embodied in a prescription which was sent to the optician who made the permanent spectacles.

Now when I was writing those prescriptions it was borne in on me that in many cases, especially the more complex, the formula for the spectacles, and consequently the spectacles themselves, furnished an infallible record of personal identity. If, for instance, such a pair of spectacles should have been found in a railway carriage, and the maker of those spectacles could be found, there would be practically conclusive evidence that a particular person had travelled by that train. About that time I drafted out a story based on a pair of spectacles, which was published some years later under the title of *The Mystery of 31 New Inn*, and the construction of that story determined, as I have said, not only the general character of my future work but of the hero around whom the plots were to be woven. But that story remained for some years in cold storage. My first published detective novel was *The Red Thumb-mark*, and in that book we may consider that John Thorndyke was born. And in passing on to describe him I may as well explain how and why he came to be the kind of person that he is.

I may begin by saying that he was not modelled after any real person. He was deliberately created to play a certain part, and the idea that was in my mind was that he should be such a person as would be likely and suitable to occupy such a position in real life. As he was to be a medico-legal expert, he had to be a doctor and a fully trained lawyer. On the physical side I endowed him with every kind of natural advantage. He is exceptionally tall, strong, and athletic because those qualities are useful in his vocation. For the same reason he has acute eyesight and hearing and considerable general manual skill, as every doctor ought to have. In appearance he is handsome and of an imposing presence, with a symmetrical face of the classical type and a Grecian nose. And here I may remark that his distinguished appearance is not

2

merely a concession to my personal taste but is also a protest against the monsters of ugliness whom some detective writers have evolved.

These are quite opposed to natural truth. In real life a first-class man of any kind usually tends to be a good-looking man.

Mentally, Thorndyke is quite normal. He has no gifts of intuition or other supernormal mental qualities. He is just a highly intellectual man of great and varied knowledge with exceptionally acute reasoning powers and endowed with that invaluable asset, a scientific imagination (by a scientific imagination I mean that special faculty which marks the born investigator, the capacity to perceive the essential nature of a problem before the detailed evidence comes into sight). But he arrives at his conclusions by ordinary reasoning, which the reader can follow when he has been supplied with the facts, though the intricacy of the train of reasoning may at times call for an exposition at the end of the investigation.

Thorndyke has no eccentricities or oddities which might detract from the dignity of an eminent professional man, unless one excepts an unnatural liking for Trichinopoly cheroots. In manner he is quiet, reserved and self-contained, and rather markedly secretive, but of a kindly nature, though not sentimental, and addicted to occasional touches of dry humour. That is how Thorndyke appears to me.

As to his age. When he made his first bow to the reading public from the doorway of Number 4 King's Bench Walk he was between thirty-five and forty. As that was thirty years ago, he should now be over sixty-five. But he isn't. If I have to let him *"grow old along with me"* I need not saddle him with the infirmities of age, and I can (in his case) put the brake on the passing years. Probably he is not more than fifty after all!

Now a few words as to how Thorndyke goes to work. His methods are rather different from those of the detectives of the Sherlock Holmes school. They are more technical and more specialized. He is an investigator of crime but he is not a detective. The technique of Scotland Yard would be neither suitable nor possible to him. He is a medico-legal expert, and his methods are those of medico-legal science. In the investigation of a crime there are two entirely different methods of approach. One consists in the careful and laborious examination of a vast mass of small and commonplace detail: Inquiring into the movements of suspected and other persons, interrogating witnesses and checking their statements particularly as to times and places, tracing missing persons, and so forth – the aim being to accumulate a great body of circumstantial evidence which will ultimately disclose the solution of the problem. It is an admirable method, as the success of our police proves, and it is used

3

with brilliant effect by at least one of our contemporary detective writers. But it is essentially a police method.

The other method consists in the search for some fact of high evidential value which can be demonstrated by physical methods and which constitutes conclusive proof of some important point. This method also is used by the police in suitable cases. Finger-prints are examples of this kind of evidence, and another instance is furnished by the Gutteridge murder. Here the microscopical examination of a cartridge-case proved conclusively that the murder had been committed with a particular revolver, a fact which incriminated the owner of that revolver and led to his conviction.

This is Thorndyke's procedure. It consists in the interrogation of things rather than persons, of the ascertainment of physical facts which can be made visible to eyes other than his own. And the facts which he seeks tend to be those which are apparent only to the trained eye of the medical practitioner.

I feel that I ought to say a few words about Thorndyke's two satellites, Jervis and Polton. As to the former, he is just the traditional narrator proper to this type of story. Some of my readers have complained that Dr. Jervis is rather slow in the uptake. But that is precisely his function. He is the expert misunderstander. His job is to observe and record all the facts, and to fail completely to perceive their significance. Thereby he gives the reader all the necessary information, and he affords Thorndyke the opportunity to expound its bearing on the case.

Polton is in a slightly different category. Although he is not drawn from any real person, he is associated in my mind with two actual individuals. One is a Mr. Pollard, who was the laboratory assistant in the hospital museum when I was a student, and who gave me many a valuable tip in matters of technique, and who, I hope, is still to the good. The other was a watch- and clock-maker of the name of Parsons – familiarly known as Uncle Parsons – who had premises in a basement near the Royal Exchange, and who was a man of boundless ingenuity and technical resource. Both of these I regard as collateral relatives, so to speak, of Nathaniel Polton. But his personality is not like either. His crinkly countenance is strictly his own copyright.

To return to Thorndyke, his rather technical methods have, for the purposes of fiction, advantages and disadvantages. The advantage is that his facts are demonstrably true, and often they are intrinsically interesting. The disadvantage is that they are frequently not matters of common knowledge, so that the reader may fail to recognize them or grasp their significance until they are explained. But this is the case with all classes of fiction. There is no type of character or story that can be made sympathetic and acceptable to every kind of reader. The personal equation affects the reading as well as the writing of a story.

R. Austin Freeman
(1862-1943)

5A King's Bench Walk
in the early 1900's when
Thorndyke was in practice

Dr. Thorndyke: In the Footsteps
of Sherlock Holmes
by David Marcum

When Sherlock Holmes began his practice as a "Consulting Detective", his ideas of scientific criminal investigations caused the London police to look upon him as a mere "theorist". He was perceived as an amateur to be tolerated, often with amusement – until, that is, his assistance was required. Then they were more than willing to come knocking upon his door, asking for whatever help that they could receive. And usually this help took the form of brilliant solutions to bizarre and otherwise insoluble problems.

Holmes espoused methods and ideas that were considered ludicrous in the late 1800's. For instance, his frustration knew no bounds when a crime scene was disturbed. Holmes realized that so much could be determined from the physical evidence – footprints, fibers, and spatters. The police were happy to trod into and disturb the evidence as if they were herds of field beasts, with the equivalent level of intelligence.

However, Holmes's methods, and the science behind catching criminals, eventually won out and became so important that it's hard to now imagine the world without them. Many of the exact same techniques and methods that he advocated are now standard practice. From being an amateur with unusual ideas, Holmes is now recognized around the world as The Great Detective. In 2002, Holmes received a posthumous Honorary Fellowship from the British Royal Society of Chemistry, based on the fact that he was beyond his time in using chemistry and chemical sciences as a means of solving crimes.

And before that, in 1985, Scotland Yard introduced *HOLMES* (*Home Office Large Major Enquiry System*), an elaborate computer system designed to process the masses of information collected and evaluated during a criminal investigation, in order to ensure that no vital clues are overlooked. This system, providing total compatibility and consistency between all the police forces of England, Scotland, Wales, and Northern Ireland, as well as the Royal Military Police, has since been upgraded by the improved *HOLMES 2* – and like the first version, there is absolutely no doubt as to who is being honored and memorialized for his work in dragging criminology out of the dark ages.

Many famous Great Detectives followed in Holmes's footsteps – Nero Wolfe and Ellery Queen, Hercule Poirot and Solar Pons – each with their own methods and techniques, but before they began their careers, and while Holmes was still in practice in Baker Street, another London consultant – Dr. John Thorndyke – opened his doors, using the scientific methods developed and perfected by Holmes and taking them to a whole new level of brilliance.

Meet Dr. Thorndyke

Dr. John Evelyn Thorndyke was born on July 4th, 1870. We don't know about where he was raised, or if he has any family. At no point will we be introduced to a more brilliant brother who sometimes *is* the British Government. He was educated at the medical school of St. Margaret's Hospital in London, and while there, he met fellow student Christopher Jervis. They became friends but, after completing school in 1895, they lost touch with one another. Over the next six years, Thorndyke remained at St. Margaret's, taking on various jobs, hanging "about the chemical and physical laboratories, the museum and *post mortem* room," and learning what he could. He obtained his M.D. and his Doctor of Sciences, and then was called to the bar in 1896.

He'd prepared himself with the hope of obtaining a position as a coroner, but he learned of the unexpected retirement of one of St. Margaret's lecturers in medical jurisprudence. He applied for the position and, rather to his own surprise, it was awarded to him. (He would continue to maintain his association with the hospital, going on to become the Medical Registrar, Pathologist, Curator of the Museum, and then Professor of Medical Jurisprudence, all while maintaining his own private consulting practice.

It was when Thorndyke was named lecturer that he obtained his chambers at 5A King's Bench Walk, in the Inner Temple, that amazing and historic area between Fleet Street and the River. Founded over eight-hundred years ago by the Knights Templar, it is one of the four Inns of Court, (along with the Middle Temple, Lincoln's Inn, and Gray's Inn.) The buildings along King's Bench Walk, and particularly No.'s 4, 5, and 6, have a great deal of historical significance – and not just because Dr. John Thorndyke practiced at 5A for a number of years.

Thorndyke was quite fortunate to obtain a suite of rooms on multiple floors at this location, which leads to speculation about his influence and resources – a question which has no answer. In any case, it was there that he opened his practice and began to wait for clients and cases. He also made the acquaintance of elderly Nathaniel Polton, that man-of-all-work with the crinkly smile who ran the household, as well as Thorndyke's upstairs laboratory.

Like Sherlock Holmes during those early years in the 1870's when he had rooms in Montague Street next to the British Museum and spent his vast amounts of free time learning his craft, Thorndyke also found a way to make the empty hours more useful. He had the unique idea of imagining increasingly complex crimes – often a murder or series of them, for instance – and then, when he had planned every single aspect of the crime, he would turn around and work out the solution from the other side. While doing this, he made extensive notes of each of these theoretical exercises, and retained them for their later usefulness when encountering real-life crimes.

His first legal case was *Regina v Gummer* in 1897. Sadly, no further information about this affair is ever revealed to us, but we may be certain that Thorndyke used his considerable skills to bring it to a satisfactory conclusion, adding to his reputation as he did so.

In the meantime, Jervis had a more unfortunate story. As his time at school ended, his funds ran out rather unexpectedly, and after paying his various fees, he was left with earning his living as a medical assistant, or sometimes serving as a *locum tenens*, moving from one low-paying and temporary job to another, with no prospects of improvement.

Jervis is unemployed on the morning of March 22nd, 1901 when he encounters Thorndyke a few doors up from 5A King's Bench Walk. The two friends are happy to see one another, and before long, Jervis is involved in an investigation that will change his life in several ways, as recounted in *The Red Thumb Mark*.

But it should not be assumed that every Thorndyke adventure is narrated by Jervis in a typical Watsonian manner. In fact, the very next book, *The Eye of Osiris*, is instead told from the perspective of one of Thorndyke's students, Dr. Paul Berkeley. It is one of several that provide a look at Thorndyke – and Jervis – from a different perspective. But Jervis returns as narrator in the third novel, *The Mystery of 31 New Inn*, and we see Thorndyke through his eyes for a good many of both the novels and short stories.

Here a word might be mentioned about the Chronology of the Thorndyke stories. For some this is an irrelevant factor, but for others – like me – understanding the correct chronological placement of the stories is very important. Like the volumes that make up the Sherlock Holmes Canon, the Thorndyke stories aren't published in chronological order – a case set in 1907 (such as "Percival Bland's Proxy") might be collected before one that occurs in 1908, ("The Missing Mortgagee"), or it might not. For instance, *The Red Thumb Mark* (1907) is set in March and April 1901. (This chronological placement, by the way, is determined by noticing that a specific date is given three times in the book – in the British fashion of day before month – *9.3.01* – or *March 9th, 1901*. The dates for the events of the rest of the book can be carefully worked out from this fixed point.)

The next book, *The Eye of Osiris* (1911) is primarily set in the summer of 1904 (with Chapter 1, something of a prologue, taking place in late 1902.) Then, the next book to follow, *The Mystery of 31 New Inn* (1912), jumps back to the spring of 1902, about a year after the events of *The Red Thumb Mark*, and before *The Eye of Osiris*. And one of the short stories, "The Man With the Nailed Shoes" occurs in September and October 1901, between the first two books. Clearly, there is a great deal of material for the chronologicist in the Thorndyke Chronicles.

As Jervis becomes a part of Thorndyke's world, following their reacquaintance in March 1901, he meets others in Thorndyke's circle, including policemen such as Superintendent Miller and Inspector Badger, lawyers like Robert Anstey, Marchmont, and Brodribb, and other physicians like Dr. Paul Berkeley and Dr. Humphrey Jardine. He also has more opportunity to learn from his friend as he begins his own studies in order to become a similar specialist in the medico-legal practice – although he'll never be another Thorndyke.

Through Jervis's eyes – as well as others along the way – we build up our knowledge of Dr. Thorndyke. In appearance, he is tall and athletic, just under six feet in height, slender, and weighing around one-hundred-and-eighty pounds. He is exceptionally handsome – and has been called the handsomest detective in literature. He has no vices, except – perhaps – that he enjoys a Trichinopoly cigar upon occasion when he is feeling especially triumphant – although there is one time when the criminal's knowledge of this fact leads to a clever attempt at Thorndyke's murder . . . .

There are several instances where Thorndyke displays a marked resemblance to Sherlock Holmes – and not just in his scientific approach to crime. The two men sometimes say similar things – such as when Holmes says "*It is quite a pretty little problem,*" (in "A Scandal in Bohemia") or "*. . . there are some pretty little problems among them*" (in "The Musgrave Ritual"). Thorndyke mimics this in *Felo de Se?* ("*There, Jervis,*" said he, "*is quite a pretty little problem for you to excogitate*") or "*Ah, there is a very pretty little problem for you to consider*" (in *The Eye of Osiris*).

And who can forget the many instances when Holmes refers to *data*:

- *"It is a capital mistake to theorize before one has data. Insensibly one begins to twist facts to suit theories, instead of theories to suit facts."* – "A Scandal in Bohemia"
- *"I had,"* said he, *"come to an entirely erroneous conclusion which shows, my dear Watson, how dangerous it always is to reason from insufficient data."* – "The Speckled Band"
- *"No data yet,"* he answered. *"It is a capital mistake to theorize before you have all the evidence. It biases the judgment."* – A Study in Scarlet
- *"The temptation to form premature theories upon insufficient data is the bane of our profession."* – The Valley of Fear
- *"Still, it is an error to argue in front of your data."* – "Wisteria Lodge"

Thorndyke's version? *". . . believe me, it is a capital error to decide beforehand what data are to be sought for."* – from *The Mystery of 31 New Inn*. There are others.

Then there is Holmes's quote from "The Man With the Twisted Lip":

"You have a grand gift of silence, Watson," said he. *"It makes you quite invaluable as a companion."*

Here's the Thorndyke equivalent:

"It has just been borne in upon me, Jervis," said he, *"that you are the most companionable fellow in the world. You have the heaven-sent gift of silence."*

And then there is the time, in "The Anthropologist at Large", that a client – expecting a Holmes-like performance as based on "The Blue Carbuncle" – presents Thorndyke with an object for examination:

"I understand," said he, *"that by examining a hat it is possible to deduce from it, not only the bodily characteristics of the wearer, but also his mental and moral qualities, his state of health, his pecuniary position, his past history, and even his domestic relations and the peculiarities of his place of abode. Am I right in this supposition?"*
The ghost of a smile flitted across Thorndyke's face as he laid the hat upon the remains of the newspaper. "We must

11

not expect too much," he observed. "Hats, as you know, have a way of changing owners . . . ."

Another area of intersection between Holmes and Thorndyke is the assembly of information. Recall Holmes's *"ponderous commonplace books in which he placed his cuttings"* as mentioned in "The Engineer's Thumb". We find, also in "The Anthropologist at Large", that Thorndyke does the same thing:

> *[H]is method of dealing with [the morning newspaper] was characteristic. The paper was laid on the table after breakfast, together with a blue pencil and a pair of office shears. A preliminary glance through the sheets enabled him to mark with the pencil those paragraphs that were to be read, and these were presently cut out and looked through, after which they were either thrown away or set aside to be pasted in an indexed book.*

No doubt and examination of Thorndyke's lodgings at 5A King's Bench Walk would reveal – in addition to a series of indexed commonplace books filled with clippings – a number of other items and aspects that would remind one of 221b Baker Street.

Like many locations where the detective's residence is almost a character in and of itself – Sherlock Holmes's London address at 221 Baker Street, and the New York homes of Ellery Queen on West 87th Street and Nero Wolfe's Brownstone on West 35th Street – Thorndyke's rooms at 5A King's Bench Walk are a living and vibrant place – from the entry way, where a heavy door known as "The Oak" leads visitors into a most comfortable wood-paneled sitting room, located on the (British) first floor, one flight up from the ground floor. On the next floor up, Polton has his laboratory and workshop, containing everything that is needed (or what might be manufactured) in order to solve the case.

On the next floor, underneath the attic, are bedrooms belonging to Thorndyke, Jervis, and Polton. Even after Jervis has married – and now you know that he does get married! – he continues to reside a good deal of the time in King's Bench Walk. As he explains in *When Rogues Fall Out* (1932, with the U.S. title of *Dr. Thorndyke's Discovery*):

> *Here, perhaps, since my records of Thorndyke's practice have contained so little reference to my own personal affairs, I should say a few words concerning my domestic habits. As the circumstances of our practice often made it*

12

desirable for me to stay late at our chambers, I had retained there the bedroom that I had occupied before my marriage; and, as these circumstances could not always be foreseen, I had arranged with my wife the simple rule that the house closed at eleven o'clock. If I was unable to get home by that time, it was to be understood that I was staying at the Temple. It may sound like a rather undomestic arrangement, but it worked quite smoothly, and it was not without its advantages. For the brief absence gave to my homecomings a certain festive quality, and helped to keep alive the romantic element in my married life. It is possible for the most devoted husbands and wives to see too much of one another.

Thorndyke's Other Appearances

Through the years, Thorndyke's reputation continues to grow, as presented through a number of adventures. Surprisingly, in light of the tens of thousands of Post-Canonical Sherlock Holmes that have come to light over the years, as discovered by latter-day Literary Agents taking over Watson's first Literary Agent, Sir Arthur Conan Doyle, stopped literary-agenting, there have been almost no additional Thorndyke cases brought to the public's attention. The few exceptions to this statement are *Goodbye, Dr. Thorndyke* (1972) by Norman Donaldson, and *Dr. Thorndyke's Dilemma* (1974) by John H. Dirckx. Both narratives deal with Thorndyke and Jervis in their latter years, and each is written by an expert in the field of Thorndyke scholarship.

Donaldson also wrote what might be the final scholarly word on the subject, *In Search of Dr. Thorndyke* (1971). In fact, he had intended his pastiche, *Goodbye, Dr. Thorndyke*, to be published as the conclusion to this book, but it ended up appearing separately.

To my knowledge, "The Great Fathomer", as Thorndyke is sometimes known, has rarely appeared in other locations. He is mentioned in the Solar Pons tale "The Adventure of the Proper Comma" by August Derleth, which finds Dr. Parker returning "from Thorndyke & Polton with an analysis of the capsules Mrs. Buxton had carried with her . . . ."

In my own book of authorized Solar Pons stories, *The Papers of Solar Pons* (2017), Thorndyke makes two appearances. "The Adventure of the Additional Heirs" has Pons and Parker visiting King's Bench Walk:

At 5A, we learned that our friend Thorndyke, the medical juris-practitioner, was out on some investigation or other, but Pons handed the papers, sans photograph, into the care of Polton, his crinkly-faced laboratory technician, with a detailed explanation of what he wished to learn. The man nodded and smiled, and without any extraneous chit-chat, shut the door, freeing us to return to Fleet Street. We paused at the edge of the walk to look at the photograph, still in Pons's hand.

Later Thorndyke sends Pons a detailed report that helps toward the solution of the problem. And in "The Affair of the Distasteful Society", set in July 1921, Pons and Parker attend the first meeting of a group gathered to honor Sherlock Holmes, where the following conversation occurs:

"I see that you invited Thorndyke, and that little Belgian over on Farraway Street," said Rath.
"And Sexton Blake as well," replied Sir Amory.
"Sexton Blake is a fictional character, Sir Amory," said Pons with a smile.

In my story, "The Adventure of the Two Sisters", included in *The New Adventures of Solar Pons*, Dr. Parker writes:

Pons was not the only detective who offered his services to the London populace, although he might have been the most well-known. We were friends with several others, including the former Belgian policeman who lived in Farraway Street, and another rather mysterious fellow in nearby Bottle Street. And of course, Pons went way back with Thorndyke, whose chambers were across town. It wasn't unusual for Pons and the others to regularly confer on investigations, or simply to sit down and share a few drinks and professional anecdotes.

Thorndyke doesn't just appear in some of my Solar Pons adventures. He's also been referenced off-stage in a couple of Sherlock Holmes adventures that I've pulled from Watson's Tin Dispatch Box – and it's more than likely that others will follow. In "The "London Wheel", contained in *The MX Book of New Sherlock Holmes Stories* –

Part IV: 2016 Annual (2016), Holmes, looking through some documents, states:

> *"I believe," said Holmes, "that I have enough amateur legal training that I can get a sense of the implications of the clauses in question in both of these documents." He pulled the folded pages from his pocket. "I thought about sending a message to my* protégé *Thorndyke in King's Bench Walk for his opinion, as he could have been here very quickly, should he be at home at all and not out on his own business. However, I don't believe that will be necessary.*

Perhaps it is a point of interest that Thorndyke is referred to Holmes's protégé. Possibly more information will be forthcoming, such as that which is hinted in my story, "The Coombs Contrivance" (in *The Irregular Adventures of Sherlock Holmes!*). Set in 1889, when Thorndyke was nineteen years old, Holmes and Watson are discussing a precocious Baker Street Irregular:

> *[Holmes] pinched the bridge of his nose. "Do you trust Levi's judgment, Watson?"*
> *I considered. "For an eight-year-old, he's remarkably perceptive – as much as any of the other Irregulars who have assisted you. The Wiggins family, or the Peakes, or Thorndyke, before he went away to university."*

So was Thorndyke, perhaps, a gifted Irregular who learned from The Master, and then went on to create his own successful practice, taking what he learned to a next very successful level? Possibly. In my story "The Inner Temple Intruder", to be found in *Sherlock Holmes and the Great Detectives*, such an origin story is posited. As Robert Downey, Jr. succinctly stated when playing Holmes in 2009's *Sherlock Holmes*: "Food for thought!"

Thorndyke is also mentioned in Bob Byrne's Holmes story, "The Adventure of the Parson's Son" (*The MX Book of New Sherlock Holmes Stories – Part III: 1896-1929*), wherein Holmes, examining a piece of evidence, cries:

> *"Ha! I believe we have discredited the coat entirely. Though I wish I could get Thorndyke to examine it. Would that we were back in London."*

And it isn't just Thorndyke who has appeared elsewhere. His lawyer friend Marchmont has assisted Holmes and Watson in a small way a couple of my own: "The Coombs Contrivance" and the forthcoming adventure *Sherlock Holmes and The Eye of Heka.*

Although I have encouraged these Thorndyke cameos in my own stories or in Holmes and Pons books that I edit, his appearances elsewhere are much more fleeting. In the 2015 BBC radio series *The Rivals*, Inspector Lestrade, Holmes's most frequent associate at Scotland Yard, is placed into the events of the Thorndyke short story "The Moabite Cipher". And Thorndyke has only had a handful of other media appearances. In 1964, the BBC produced seven episodes (now lost) of *Thorndyke*, starring Peter Copley. The episodes were:

- "The Case of Oscar Brodski'
- "The Old Lag"
- "A Case of Premeditation"
- "The Mysterious Visitor"
- "The Case of Phyllis Annesley" – Adapted from "Phyllis Annesley's Peril"
- "Percival Bland's Brother" – Adapted from "Percival Bland's Proxy"
- "The Puzzle Lock"

From 1971 to 1973, Thames TV aired *The Rivals of Sherlock Holmes*, and two stories were adapted: "A Message from the Deep Sea" starring John Neville (who had also played Holmes in 1965's *A Study in Terror*), and "The Moabite Cipher" starring Barrie Ingram. Except for a 1963 BBC Radio adaption of *Mr. Pottermack's Oversight*, and a few on-air readings by a single performer, there have been no other Thorndyke adaptations – which is a terrible shame, as the stories certainly lend themselves to visual and audible interpretations. Perhaps a new generation will discover Thorndyke, Jervis, and the rest, and they will find popularity once again, as they did more than a century ago.

Copley, Neville, and Ingram as Thorndyke

A Few (Hundred) Words About R. Austin Freeman
Thorndyke's Chronicler

Richard Austin Freeman was born on April 11, 1862 in the Soho district of London. He was the son of a skilled tailor and the youngest of five children. As he grew, it was expected that he would become a tailor as well, but instead he had an interest in natural history and medicine, and so he obtained employment in a pharmacist's shop. While there, he qualified as an apothecary and could have gone on to manage the shop, but instead he began to study medicine at Middlesex Hospital.

Austin Freeman qualified as a physician in 1887, and in that same year he married. Faced with the twin facts of his new marital responsibilities and his very limited resources as a young doctor, he made the unusual decision to join the Colonial Service, spending the next seven years in Africa as an Assistant Colonial Surgeon. This continued until the early 1890's, when he contracted Blackwater Fever, an illness that eventually forced him to leave the service and return permanently to England.

For several years, he served as a *locum tenens* for various physicians, a bleak time in his life as he moved from job to job, his income low, and his health never quite recovered. (These experiences were reflected in the narratives of Doctors Jervis and Berkeley.) However, he supplemented his meager income and exercised his creativity during these years by beginning to write. His early publications included *Travels and Live in Ashanti and Jaman* (1898), recounting some of his African sojourns.

In 1900, Freeman obtained work as an assistant to Dr. John James Pitcairn (1860-1936) at Holloway Prison. Although he wasn't there for very long, the association between the two men was enough to turn Freeman's attention toward writing mysteries. Over the next few years, they co-wrote several under the pseudonym *Clifford Ashdown*, including *The Adventures of Romney Pringle* (1902), *The Further Adventures of Romney Pringle* (1903), *From a Surgeon's Diary* (1904-1905), and *The Queen's Treasure* (written around 1905-1906, and published posthumously in 1975.) The specifics of the two men's writing arrangement are unknown to the present day, although much research was carried out by Freeman scholar Percival Mason ("P.M.") Stone, who was actually able to confirm Pitcairn's involvement and influence. Following this association, which apparently helped to train Freeman to be a better writer and to focus on a recurring character, his luck changed, and he was able, within just a few years, to abandon the practice of medicine, which had never been successful, and become a professional author.

In approximately 1904, Freeman began developing a mystery novella based on a short job that he had held at the Western Ophthalmic Hospital. This effort, "31 New Inn", was published in 1905, and it is the true first Dr. Thorndyke story. In it, we meet narrator Dr. Christopher Jervis, working as a *locum tenens*, moving from practice to practice in the same bleak existence that Freeman had experienced. Jervis becomes involved with a patient that may or may not be in danger. Unsure what to do, he recalls his former classmate, the brilliant Dr. John Thorndyke.

Curiously, this novella, (included in Volume II of this newly reissued collection *The Complete Dr. Thorndyke*), has numerous references to the events of the first Thorndyke novel, *The Red Thumb Mark*, which would not be published until 1907. Much of Freeman's life is obscure and unknown, including his writing processes and milestones, but clearly, with so much already clearly defined in this novella about Thorndyke and Jervis, he had firmly established not only fixed aspects of their histories, but the plot of *The Red Thumb Mark* as well, several years before the book's publication. One wonders why he chose to first publish "31 New Inn", since it occurs chronologically a whole year *after* the events of *The Red Thumb Mark*.

Interestingly – at least to a chronologicist such as myself – the original novella of "31 New Inn" is specifically set in April 1900, as indicated internally. However, when it was later revised to become the third Thorndyke novel, *The Mystery of 31 New Inn*, (1912, and included in Volume I of *The Complete Dr. Thorndyke*), the narrative's date is changed to 1902 – which fits, since the events definitely occur after *The Red Thumb Mark*, which takes place in March and April 1901.

Like Rex Stout's Nero Wolfe, who seemed to have sprung fully formed from his creator's brow, Thorndyke and his world are well-defined and immediately real. Although certain characters are added to the circle through the years, the basic layout – with Thorndyke, Jervis, and Polton (the man-of-all-work crinkly-smiled assistant) are always at 5A, ready to spring into action when Jervis – or one of the other varied narrators who show up throughout the series – arrive with a curious problem.

Freeman had found his voice with the Thorndyke books and short stories, and he was able to make use of his lifelong interest in medicine and natural science – often conducting extensive experiments to work out exactly how the solutions in his stories could be discovered. And in Thorndyke's early days, Freeman was able to turn the literary form inside out with the creation of the "Inverted Mystery Story", wherein the criminal is known from the beginning – the motive is explained, the planning and execution of the crime are observed, and the miscreant is left to believe that all is well and that he'll never be caught. And then, in the second part of the story, Thorndyke enters to inexorably follow the trail that is completely invisible to everyone else, scraping away, layer by layer and point by point, until the truth is inevitably revealed.

As Freeman explained:

> *Some years ago I devised, as an experiment, an inverted detective story in two parts. The first part was a minute and detailed description of a crime, setting forth the antecedents, motives, and all attendant circumstances. The reader had seen the crime committed, knew all about the criminal, and was in possession of all the facts. It would have seemed that there was nothing left to tell. But I calculated that the reader would be so occupied with the crime that he would overlook the evidence. And so it turned out. The second part, which described the investigation of the crime, had to most readers the effect of new matter.*

This format went on to be used by a great many authors through the years. For example several of the Lord Peter Wimsey narratives come close to being this type of story, and television's *Columbo* used this type of story-telling as its basis.

While these volumes are an attempt to reintroduce the modern reader to Thorndyke, and are a celebration of him and his world, it must be discussed at some point that Freeman held views that are unacceptable. Unlike Sir Arthur Conan Doyle, who spent his last decades championing spiritualism but never allowed it to creep into the Sherlock Holmes stories, Freeman sometimes did let his own prejudices make their way into the Thorndyke tales. In his book *Social Decay and Regeneration* (1921), he expressed his rather nationalistic view that England had become an "homogenized, restless, unionized working class". Worse, he inexcusably and detestably supported the eugenics movement, arguing that people with "undesirable" traits should not be allowed to reproduce by means such as "segregation, marriage restriction, and sterilization". He referred to immigrants as "Sub-Man", and argued that society needed to be protected from "degenerates of the destructive type."

Some have attempted to excuse his beliefs as being a product of his times. For instance, it has been written that he had a distrust of Jews because of the competition that his father, a tailor, had faced when Freeman was a boy. Later, he served in the Colonial Service in Africa during some of the worst years in terms of treatment of natives by the British, and as an older man, he existed in the Great Britain between the two wars when great upheavals disrupted much of what he had known and expected.

Sadly, there are occasional racial stereotypes and references in the Thorndyke books. As I explain in the *Editor's Caveat*, some of these stereotypes had to be unfortunately maintained within the story in order to accurately reflect the plot and the characters of those times. However, there are some words or phrases that were used in the original stories – vile racial epithets that have no business being repeated or perpetuated anywhere – that I have cheerfully and happily removed. (There weren't many of them, but any are too many.)

These books are intended to bring Dr. Thorndyke and his adventures to a new generation – and not to be an untouchable and sacred literary artifact, with every nasty stain preserved and archived for the historical record. As I warn in the *Caveat*, if readers find that they want to experience the original versions as they were first written, with those hateful words included, then they would be advised to go and seek out the original books, because you won't find that filth here. These versions celebrate Dr. Thorndyke and Dr. Jervis – who do not use the awful stereotyped language, I'm glad to say! – and as such, I felt no need whatsoever to include and perpetuate the objectionable and offensive material

From Thorndyke's creation until 1914, Freeman wrote four novels and two volumes of short stories. Then, with the commencement of the First World War, he entered military service. In February 1915, at the age of fifty-two, he joined the Royal Army Medical Corps. Due to his health, which had never entirely recovered from his time in Africa, he spent the duration of the war involved with various aspects of the ambulance corps, having been promoted very early to the rank of Captain. He wrote nothing about Thorndyke during this period, but he did publish one book concerning the adventures of a scoundrel, *The Exploits of Danby Croker* (1916).

Following the war, he resumed his previous life, writing approximately one Thorndyke novel per year, as well as three more volumes of Thorndyke short stories and a number of other unrelated items, until his death on September 28th, 1943 – likely related to Parkinson's Disease, which had plagued him in later years.

Upon learning the news, *Chicago Tribune* columnist Vincent Starrett wrote:

> *When all the bright young things have performed their appointed task of flatting the complexes of neurotic semi-literates, and have gone their way to oblivion, the best of the Thorndyke stories will live on – minor classics on the shelf that holds the good books the world.*

Raymond Chandler wrote in his famous essay, which initially appeared in a couple of magazines and then was published in the book of the same name, *The Simple Art of Murder* (1950):

> *This man Austin Freeman is a wonderful performer. He has no equal in his genre, and he is also a much better writer than you might think, if you were superficially inclined, because in spite of the immense leisure of his writing, he accomplishes an even suspense which is quite unexpected . . . There is even a gaslight charm about his Victorian love affairs, and those wonderful walks across London.*

In the introduction to *Great Stories of Detection, Mystery, and Horror* (1928), Dorothy L. Sayers, Chronicler of Lord Peter Wimsey, stated:

> *Thorndyke will cheerfully show you all the facts. You will be none the wiser . . . .*

Discovering Dr. Thorndyke

I first encountered Dr. Thorndyke in a rather backwards way – in passing only – and it took several decades to correct that mistake. In approximately 1980, my dad gave me Otto Penzler's *The Private Lives of Private Eyes, Spies, Crime Fighters, and Other Good Guys* (1977). This wonderful oversized book has biographies of twenty-five well-known heroes, along with lists of the original books featuring each one.

My dad bought it for me because it had a chapter about Sherlock Holmes. There were a few others in there that I recognized or had already read about– Ellery Queen and Perry Mason – and soon I would become fanatical about a few more – Nero Wolfe and Hercule Poirot. Over the next few years I would also find the chapters on James Bond and Lew Archer indispensable, and later than that I would come to appreciate the entries about Philip Marlowe, Sam Spade, Miss Marple, Philo Vance, and Lord Peter Wimsey. But there were a few that, to this day, I've never bothered to read – such as Modesty Blaise or Mr. Moto – and a few others that I skimmed but otherwise ignored. And one of these was the biography of Dr. Thorndyke.

That fact was easily understandable, as throughout the entire time that I was growing up in eastern Tennessee – and in the years since as well – I've never come across a Thorndyke book for sale here in the wild, either in a new bookstore or in a used one. If I'd found one, I might have bought and read it, liked it, and then sought out others. Instead, I was bound to discover Thorndyke by way of Sherlock Holmes.

I've been collecting traditional Sherlock Holmes pastiches since the same time that I discovered the Sherlockian Canon, when I was ten years old in 1975. Since that time, I've collected, read, and chronologicized literally thousands of them. It never gets old, and I'm constantly looking for more – and that means checking Amazon to see what new releases are on the horizon.

In 2012, someone – and I've never determined who – began releasing a variety of Holmes stories for Kindle under the author name *Dr. John H. Watson.* This wasn't too unusual – there have been a number of pastiches that officially list Watson as the author, rather than putting the editor of Watson's papers first. Of course, after determining that these latest entries weren't going to be available as real books, I bought the e-versions, and then printed them on real paper. (I cannot stand e-books – ephemeral electronic blips that you lease instead of buy. I'll only buy those titles if they aren't going to be released as legitimate books – and in this case, it's a good thing that I did, as each of these Kindle stories that I found and paid for were soon withdrawn.)

As I read these latest "Holmes" stories, I noticed that each had a definite style that captured the writing from the late 1800's or early 1900's. (No matter how modern pasticheurs try to achieve that, they never quite pull it off.) But in one of the first two or three titles that I read, I caught a couple of mistakes. In one story, Holmes and Watson leave 221 Baker Street and are immediately in the area around The Temple and Fleet Street, rather than in Marylebone, where Baker Street is properly located. On another occasion, the story's policeman – who had been identified up to that point as Inspector Lestrade – was inexplicably named *Superintendent Miller* – but only in one instance. And in another place in one of the stories, Holmes's address was stated to be *5A King's Bench Walk.*

It was then that some vague memory triggered in my head, and I realized why these stories had captured the style of the late Victorian and early Edwardian eras: *It was because they had actually been written then*. I recalled – from reading Otto Penzler's book of biographies so long ago - that 5A King's Bench Walk belonged to Dr. Thorndyke, and not Sherlock Holmes. Someone was taking the original Thorndyke stories, which I had never before read, and simply changing names: Dr. Thorndyke, Dr. Jervis, and Superintendent Miller became Sherlock Holmes, Dr. Watson, and Inspector Lestrade, respectively.

Between 2012 and 2014, the anonymous author continued to load new Kindle editions on Amazon of Thorndyke-converted to-Holmes stories, and I continued to buy them. As soon as I had one, I would read it, and then try to figure out the original Thorndyke story from which it was taken. When I'd done so, I'd post a review, identifying what this editor was doing, from where he or she was taking the story, and urging that person, whoever it was, give credit to R. Austin Freeman instead of listing the author as Dr. John H. Watson.

Soon after each of my reviews would appear, the story would be withdrawn. I don't know if it was because the editor had made enough money from the initial sales, or if my reviews alerted him or her that they're game had been uncovered. In any case, I still have the printed copies of each of these converted stories – possibly the only copies that are still in existence.

For the record, over that two year period, this editor produced sixteen converted tales – four of the original Thorndyke novels, and twelve short stories. One of the original short stories, "The Mandarin's Pearl", was converted twice, with slight variations – initially published as "The Dragon Pearl", withdrawn, and later revised and reloaded as "The Oriental Pearl":

- "The Bloodied Thumbprint" – Originally the first Thorndyke novel, *The Red Thumb Mark*;
- "The Eye of Ra" – Originally the second Thorndyke novel, *The Eye of Osiris*;
- "The Cat's Eye Mystery" – Originally the sixth Thorndyke novel, *The Cat's Eye*;
- "The Julius Dalton Mystery" – Originally the ninth Thorndyke novel, *The D'Arblay Mystery*;
- "The Green Jacket Mystery" – Originally "The Green Check Jacket";
- "Mr. Crofton's Disappearance" – Originally "The Mysterious Visitor";
- "The Coded Lock" – Originally "The Puzzle Lock";

23

- "The Duplicated Letter" – Originally "The Stalking Horse";
- "The Bullion Robbery" – Originally "The Stolen Ingots";
- "The Talking Corpse" – Originally "The Contents of a Mare's Nest";
- "The Blue Diamond Mystery" – Originally "The Fisher of Men";
- "The Dragon Pearl" – Originally "The Mandarin's Pearl". (This story was also reworked and published again as a Holmes story under the title "The Oriental Pearl");
- "The Ingenious Murder" – Originally "The Aluminium Dagger";
- "The Bloodhound Superstition" – Originally "The Singing Bone"; *and*
- "The Magic Box" – Originally "The Magic Casket".

For quite a while, I was happy to have these as Holmes stories, and I even considered converting the rest of the Thorndyke adventures into additions to the extended Holmes Canon as well. (For at that time I cared nothing for Dr. Thorndyke.) It was partly with these converted stories in mind that I was motivated to go ahead and publish *Sherlock Holmes in Montague Street* (2014, 2016), which did the same thing to the Martin Hewitt stories, making them early adventures of Holmes before he met Watson and moved to Baker Street. I had long before decided to my own satisfaction that Martin Hewitt *was* a young Sherlock Holmes, with his identity changed through the preparations of a different literary agent than Sir Arthur Conan Doyle.

The taking of old public-domain stories featuring other detectives as the main protagonists and switching them so that Holmes is the main character has also been done by Alan Lance Andersen for his collection *The Affairs of Sherlock Holmes* (2015, 2016), wherein various non-series Sax Rohmer stories from nearly a hundred years ago were reworked as Holmes tales. Other non-Holmes authors have sometimes done the same thing. Raymond Chandler revised some of his early short stories so that the original characters' names were changed to Philip Marlowe. Ross MacDonald – (Kenneth Millar) also rewrote his old stories as well, making them into Lew Archer cases instead. More recently, the British

ITV series *Marple* has taken non-Miss Marple Agatha Christie stories and converted them into episodes featuring that character.

So I had no problems with this type of change – and still don't. In fact, in my foreword to *Sherlock Holmes of Montague Street*, I wrote that I would rather have these converted Thorndyke stories as Holmes adventures, because I would rather read about Holmes than Thorndyke. But gradually my mind began to change, and I became more curious about Thorndyke, as presented in the proper fashion.

In 2013, I was able to go to London, as well as other places in England and Scotland, on the first (of three so far) Holmes Pilgrimages. For the most part, if a location wasn't related to Holmes, I didn't visit it. There were a few exceptions – I did intentionally visit Solar Pons's house at 7B Praed Street, Hercule Poirot's two residences, James Bond's flat in Chelsea – but everything else was pretty much pure Holmes.

One day, during my Holmesian rambles, I was making my way east down Fleet Street, and I visited both of the possible locations of "Pope's Court" (as featured in "The Red-Headed League"), Poppin's Court and Mitre Court. (The latter is also one of the locations where Denis Nayland Smith and Dr. Petrie had quarters in some of the Fu Manchu books.) I decided that Mitre Court was certainly the original of "Pope's Court", and I passed through it to find myself unexpectedly in The Temple.

That's the amazing thing about a Holmes Pilgrimage to London – one travels to a site and finds two more very close by. I had planned to visit The Temple, but hadn't realized that I was so close. And now here I was – and more interesting was the fact that I was walking along King's Bench Walk, which runs downhill from the Miter Court passage. I recalled that Thorndyke had lived at 5A, so I made my way there – but without too much awe on that day, because I hadn't actually read any Thorndyke adventures yet – just some converted Holmes stories.

After I returned home, the thought of that side-trip to Thorndyke's front door stuck in my mind, and I sought out and read the first novel in the series, *The Red Thumb Mark.* I was so impressed that I kept going, and discovered a wonderful series of books and stories – fascinating characters and mysteries, and very evocative descriptions of both the London and the countryside of those times.

When I returned on my second Holmes Pilgrimage in 2015, I took the second Thorndyke book with me, reading it while there – while also reading Holmes stories too, of course! This one, *The Eye of Osiris*, has a great deal of London atmosphere, and I spent part of one late afternoon tracking down locations in this book – or what's now left of them – in the area around Fetter Lane to the north of Thorndyke's home in The Temple. It was truly unforgettable.

And of course I made an intentional stop at King's Bench Walk on that 2015 trip, and again on Holmes Pilgrimage No. 3 in 2016. By that point I was a Thorndyke fan, and I took the trouble to write to the current occupiers of 5A before I traveled to see if I could step inside and perhaps spend a moment in Thorndyke's old quarters. Sadly, they did not respond – either because it was simply beneath them to do so, or possibly because they get too many people like me who want to make a literary pilgrimage to what is a functioning and thriving business location.

While making photographs at Thorndyke's old doorway, I had several chances to go inside when someone else would enter or leave – My ever-present deerstalker and I could have simply been bold enough to slip in and then talk my way onward. It worked at other places on my Holmes Pilgrimages – the laboratory at Barts where Holmes and Watson met, for instance, and the site of the (former?) Diogenes Club at No. 78 Pall Mall, where they acted just oddly enough to make me think that the club is still there. But for some reason, barging into Thorndyke's old chambers without proper permission didn't feel quite right. But if or when I make Holmes Pilgrimage No. 4, I'll definitely make an even greater effort to see the doctor's former rooms.

The Editor and his Deerstalker at 5A King's Bench Walk
September 2016

With many thanks . . . .

These last few years have been an amazing ride, and I've been able to play in the Sherlockian sandbox more than I'd ever imagined. (And subsequently, the Solar Pons sandbox, and now Thorndyke, too! Along the way, I've been able to meet some incredible people, both in person and in the modern electronic way, and also I've been able to read several hundred new Holmes adventures, as well as to be able to share them with others.

Still, what is most important is my amazingly wonderful wife (of over thirty years!) Rebecca, and our truly awesome son and my friend, Dan. I love you both, and you are everything to me! I am the luckiest guy in the world.

I have all the gratitude in the world for everyone that I've encountered along the way – It's an undeniable fact that Sherlock Holmes authors are the *best* people! I'd like to thank those who offer support, encouragement, and friendship, sometimes patiently waiting on me to reply as my time is directed in many other directions. Many many thanks to (in alphabetical order): Brian Belanger, Derrick Belanger, Bob Byrne, Roger Johnson, Mark Mower, Denis Smith, Tom Turley, Dan Victor, and Marcia Wilson.

In particular, I'd also like to especially thank Steve Emecz, who is always supportive of every idea that I pitch. It's been my particular good fortune that he crossed my path – it changed my life in a way that would have never happened otherwise, and I'm grateful for every opportunity!

I hope that these books will provide pleasure to those discovering Dr. Thorndyke for the first time, and to others who have known him for a long time. As always, I approach these matters from a Sherlockian perspective, so of course these stories, to me, are a peripheral extension of Holmes's world, and as such they are just more tiny threads woven into the ongoing Great Holmes Tapestry. However, they are wonderful on their own, and however one reads them, I wish great joy upon the journey.

David Marcum
(Revised October 2020)

Questions, comments, and story submissions
may be addressed to David Marcum at
thepapersofsherlockholmes@gmail.com

5A King's Bench Walk
in the late 1890's when
Thorndyke was in residence

Editor's *Caveat*

These stories have been prepared using modern text-converting software, and as such, occasional deviations in punctuation have occurred. Those who absolutely must have the original version, down to each jot and dash, should understand that this version was created in order to present Dr. Thorndyke's adventures to a modern audience, and not to preserve an absolute pristine model for the historical archives.

Similarly, these stories were written in a time when racial prejudice and stereotypes were much more common than today. While some of these stereotypes must be unfortunately maintained within the story in order to accurately reflect the plot and the characters of those times, there are some words that were used in the original stories – vile racial epithets that have no business being repeated or perpetuated anywhere – that I have cheerfully removed. (There weren't many of them, but *any* are *too many*.)

If readers find that they want to experience the original versions as they were first written, with those hateful and ignorant words included, then they would be advised to seek out the original books. These versions celebrate Dr. Thorndyke and Dr. Jervis – who do *not* use the awful stereotyped language, I'm glad to say! – and as such, I felt no need whatsoever to include objectionable and offensive material simply for the sake of honoring or archiving the historical record.

David Marcum
Editor

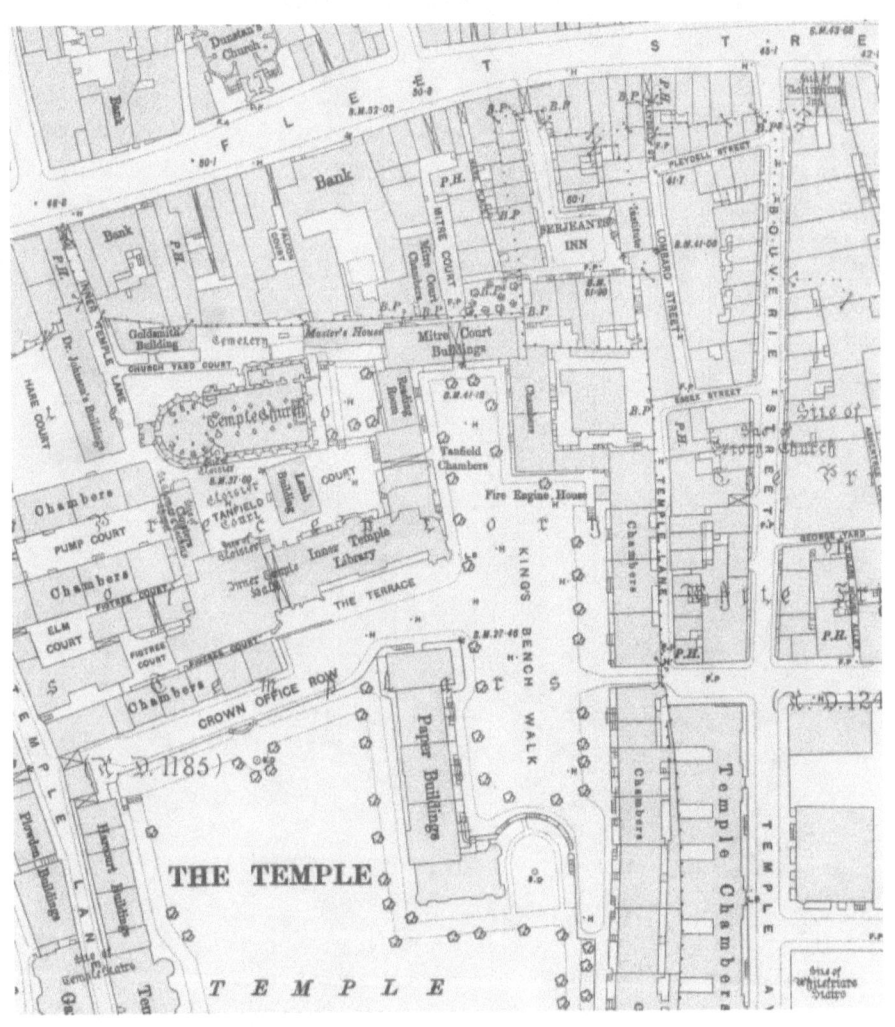

King's Bench Walk and the Temple, London
around 1900

33

A CERTAIN DR.THORNDYKE

R·AUSTIN FREEMAN

The Ace of Detectives

1927 Hodder & Stoughton, London Cover

Book I – The Ishmaelite

Chapter I
The Fugitive

The tropic moon shone brightly on the village of Adaffia in the Bight of Benin as a fishing-canoe steered warily through the relatively quiet surf of the dry season towards the steep beach. Out in the roadstead, an anchored barque stood up sharply against the moonlit sky, the yellow spark of her riding light glimmering warmly, and a white shape dimly discernible in the approaching canoe hinted of a visitor from the sea. Soon the little craft, hidden for a while in the white smother of a breaking wave, emerged triumphant and pushed her pointed nose up the beach, the occupants leaped out and, seizing her by her inturned gunwales, hauled her forthwith out of reach of the following wave.

"You know where to go?" the Englishman demanded, turning a grim, hatchet face towards the "headman". "Don't take me to the wrong house."

The headman grinned. "Only one white man live for Adaffia. Me sabby him proper." He twisted a rag of cotton cloth into a kind of turban, clapped it on his head and, poising on top a battered cabin-trunk, strode off easily across the waste of blown sand that separated the beach from a forest of coconut palms that hid the village. The Englishman followed less easily, his shod feet sinking into the loose sand, and as he went, he peered with a stranger's curiosity along the deserted beach and into the solemn gloom beneath the palms, whence came the rhythmical clamour of drums and the sound of many voices joining in a strange, monotonous chant.

Through the ghostly colonnade of palm trunks, out into the narrow, tortuous alleys that served for streets, between rows of mud-built hovels roofed with unkempt grass thatch, where all was inky blackness in the shadow and silvery grey in the light, the stranger followed his guide, and ever the noise of the drums and the melancholy chant drew nearer. Suddenly the two men emerged from an alley into a large open space and in an instant passed from the stillness of the empty streets into a scene of the strangest bustle and uproar. In the middle of the space was a group of men, seated on low stools, who held between their knees drums of various sizes, which they were beating noisily, though by no means

37

unskillfully, some with crooked sticks, others with the flat of the hand. Around the musicians a circle of dancers moved in an endless procession, the men and the women forming separate groups, and while the former danced furiously, writhing with starting muscles and streaming skins, in gestures grotesque and obscene, the latter undulated languorously with half-closed eyes and rhythmically moving arms.

The Englishman had halted in the black shadow to look on at this singular scene and to listen to the strange chant that rang out at intervals from dancers and spectators alike, when his guide touched him on the arm and pointed.

"Look!" said he. "There! You see?"

The stranger looked over the heads of the dancers and, sure enough, in the very midst of the revellers, he espied a fellow-countryman seated on a green-painted gin-case, the sides of which he was pounding with his fists in unsuccessful emulation of the drummers. He was not a spectacle to engender undue pride of race. To begin with, he was obviously drunk, and as he drummed on the case and bellowed discordantly at intervals, he was not dignified. Perhaps to be drunk and dignified at one and the same time is not easy, and assuredly the task is made no easier by a costume consisting of a suit of ragged pyjamas, the legs tucked into scarlet socks, gaudy carpet slippers, and a skullcap of plaited grass. But such was the garb of this representative, and the final touch was given to a raffish ensemble by an unlit cigar that waggled from the corner of his mouth.

The stranger stood for a minute or more watching, in silence and with grim disapproval, this unedifying spectacle, when a sudden interruption occurred. One of the dancers, a big, powerful ruffian, in giving an extra flourish to his performance, struck his foot against the gin-case and staggered on to the seated white man, who, with a loud, foolish laugh, caught him playfully by the ankle. As a result, the big man toppled over and fell sprawling amongst the drummers. In an instant all was confusion and uproar. The drummers pummelled the fallen man, the women howled, the men shouted, and the drunken man yelled with idiotic laughter. Then the big man leaped to his feet with a roar of fury, and rushing at the drunken man, closed with him. The gin-case turned turtle at the first onset, the two combatants flew off gyrating amongst the legs of the crowd, mowing down a little lane as they went, and for some moments nothing could be distinguished save a miscellaneous heap of black bodies and limbs with a pair of carpet slippers kicking wildly in the air. But the white man, if lacking in dignity and discretion, was not deficient in valour. He was soon on his feet and hitting out right and left with uncommon liveliness and spirit. This, however, could not, and did not, last long, a simultaneous rush of angry natives soon bore him to the

38

ground and there seemed every prospect of his being very severely mauled.

It was at this moment that the stranger abandoned his role of a neutral spectator. Taking off his helmet and depositing it carefully in the angle of a mud wall, he lowered his head, thrust forward his shoulder, and charged heavily into the midst of the shouting mob. Now, the Slave Coast native is a sturdy, courageous fellow and truculent withal, but he does not play the Rugby game and he is a stranger alike to the subtler aspects of pugilism and the gentle art of ju-jitsu. Consequently, the tactics of the new assailant created quite a sensation among the Adaffia men. Their heels flew up unaccountably, their heads banged together from unknown causes, mysterious thumps, proceeding from nowhere in particular with the weight of a pile-monkey, stretched them gasping on the earth, and when they would have replied in kind, Behold! The enemy was not there! They rushed at him with outstretched hands and straightway fell upon their stomachs, they grabbed at his head and caught nothing but a pain in the shoulder or a tap under the chin, and the sledge hammer blow that was to have annihilated him either spent itself on empty air or, impinging upon the countenance of an ally, led to misunderstanding and confusion. Hampered by their own numbers and baffled by the incredible quickness of their elusive adversary, they began to view his strange manoeuvres as feats of magic. The fire of battle died down, giving place to doubt, bewilderment, and superstitious fear. The space widened round the silent, swiftly-moving figure, the more faint-hearted made off with their hands clapped to their mouths, screeching forth the hideous *Efé* alarm cry, the panic spread, and the remainder first backed away and then fairly broke into a run. A minute later the place was deserted, save for the two Europeans and the headman.

The stranger had pursued the retreating mob for some distance, tripping up the stragglers or accelerating their movements by vigorous hammerings from behind, and he now returned, straightening out his drill jacket and dusting the grimy sand from his pipe-clayed shoes with a silk handkerchief. The other white man had by this time returned to the gin-case, on which he was once more enthroned with one of the abandoned drums between his knees, and, as his compatriot approached, he executed a martial roll and would have burst into song but that the cigar, which had been driven into his mouth during the conflict, now dropped into his throat and reduced him temporarily to the verge of suffocation.

"Many thanks, dear chappie," said he, when he had removed the obstruction. "Moral s'pport most valuable, uphold dignity of white man, congratulate you on your style, do credit to Richardsons. Excuse my not

39

rising, reasons excellent, will appear when I do." In fact his clothing had suffered severely in the combat.

The stranger looked down at the seated figure silently and with tolerant contempt. A stern-faced, grim-looking man was this new-comer, heavy-browed, square-jawed, and hatchet-faced, and his high-shouldered, powerful figure set itself in a characteristic pose, with the feet wide apart and the hands clasped behind the back as he stood looking down on his new acquaintance.

"I suppose," he said, at length, "you realize that you're as drunk as an owl?"

"I s'spected it," returned the other gravely. "Not's an owl, though. Owls very temp'rate in these parts."

At this moment the headman rose from the cabin-trunk, on which he had seated himself to view the conflict, and, picking up the stranger's helmet, brought it to him.

"Look," said he, earnestly, "you go for house one time. This place no good. Them people be angry too much, he go fetch gun."

"You hear that?" said the stranger. "You'd better clear off home."

"Ver' well, dear boy," replied the other, suavely. "Call a hansom, we'll both go."

"Whereabouts do you live?" demanded the stranger.

The other man looked up with a bland smile. "Grosvenor Square, ol' fellow, A1, brass knocker 'stinguishers on doorstep. Tell cabby knock three times and ring bottom bell." He picked up the cigar and began carefully to wipe the sand from it.

"Do you know where he lives?" asked the stranger, turning to the headman.

"Yass, me sabby. He live for factory. You make him come one time. You hear that?"

The sound of the strange and dismal *Efé* alarm cry (produced by shouting or screaming continuously and patting the mouth quickly with the flat of the hand) was borne down from the farther end of the village. The headman caught up the trunk and started off up the street, while the stranger, having hoisted the seated man off the gin-case with such energy that he staggered round in a half-circle, grasped him from behind by both arms and urged him forward at a brisk trot.

"Here, I say!" protested the latter. "Nosso fast, d'ye hear? I've dropped my slipper. Lemme pick up my slipper."

To these protests the stranger paid no attention, but continued to hustle his captive forward with undiminished energy.

"Lemme go, confound you! You're shaking me all to bits!" exclaimed the captive, and, as the other continued to shove silently, he continued, "Now I un'stand why you boosted those men so neatly. You're a bobby, that's what you are. I know the professional touch. A blooming escaped bobby. Well, I'm jiggered!" He lapsed, after this, into gloomy silence, and a few minutes' more rapid travelling brought the party to a high palm-leaf fence. A primitive gate was unfastened, by the simple process of withdrawing a skewer from a loop of cord, and they entered a compound in the middle of which stood a long, low house. The latter was mud-built and thatched with grass like the houses in the village, from which, indeed, it differed only in that its mud walls were whitewashed and pierced for several windows.

"Lemme welcome you to my humble cot," said the proprietor, following the headman, who had unceremoniously walked into the house and dumped down the cabin-trunk. The stranger entered a small, untidy room lighted by a hurricane-lamp and, having dismissed the headman with a substantial "dash", or present, turned to face his host.

"Siddown," said the latter, dropping into a dilapidated Madeira chair and waving his hand towards another. "Less' have a talk. Don't know your name, but you seem to be a decent feller – for a bobby. My name's Larkom, John Larkom, agent for Foster Brothers. This is Fosters' factory."

The stranger looked curiously round the room – so little suggestive of a factory in the European sense – and then, as he seated himself, said, "You probably know me by name: I am John Walker, of whom you have – "

He was interrupted by a screech of laughter from Larkom, who flung himself back in his chair with such violence as to bring that piece of furniture to the verge of dissolution.

"Johnny Walker!" he howled. "My immortal scissors! Sh'ld think I do know you, more senses than one. I've got a letter about you – I'll show it to you. Where is that blamed letter?" He dragged out a table-drawer and rooted among a litter of papers, from which he at length extracted a crumpled sheet of paper. "Here we are. Letter from Hepburn. You 'member Hepburn? He and I at Oxford together. Merton, y'know. Less see what he says. Ah! Here you are, I'll read it: *'And now I want you to do me a little favour. You will receive a visit from a pal of mine who, in consequence of certain little indiscretions, is for the moment under a cloud, and I want you, if you can, to put him up and keep him out of sight. His fame I am not permitted to disclose, since being, as I have said, sub nube, just at present, and consequently not in search of fame or notoriety, he elects to travel under the modest and appropriate name of Walker."*

41

At this point Larkom once more burst into a screech of laughter. "Funny devil, Hepburn! Awful rum devil," he mumbled, leering idiotically at the letter that shook in his hand. Then, wiping his eyes on the gaudy "trade" tablecloth, he resumed his reading. "'*He need not cause you any inconvenience, and you won't mind his company as he is quite a decent fellow – He entered at Merton just after you went down – and he won't be any expense to you. In fact, with judicious management, he may be made to yield a profit, since he will have some money with him and is, between ourselves, somewhat of a mug.*' Rum devil, awful rum devil," sniggered Larkom. "Doncher think so?" he added, grinning foolishly in the other man's face.

"Very," replied the stranger, stolidly. But he did not look particularly amused.

"'*I think that is all I have to tell you*,'" Larkom continued, reading from the letter. "'*I hope you will be able to put the poor devil up, and, by the way, you need not let on that I have told you about his little misfortunes*'." Larkom looked up with a ridiculous air of vexation. "There now," he exclaimed, "I've given old Hepburn away like a silly fool. But no, it was he that was a silly fool. He shouldn't have told me."

"No, he should not," agreed Walker.

"'Course not," said Larkom with drunken gravity. "Breach o' confidence. However, 's all right. 'Pend on me. Close as a lock-jawed oyster. What'll you drink?"

He waved his hand towards the table, on which a plate of limes, a stone gin jar, a bottle of bitters with a quill stuck through the cork, and a swizzle-stick, stained purple by long service, invited to conviviality.

"Have a cocktail," said Larkom. "Wine of the country. Good old swizzle-stick. I'll mix it. Or p'rhaps," he sniggered, slyly, "p'raps you'd rather have a drop of Johnny Walker – Ha! Ha! Hallo! Here they are. D'ye hear 'em?" A confused noise of angry voices was audible outside the compound and isolated shouts separated themselves now and again from the general hubbub.

"They're callin' us names," chuckled Larkom. "Good thing you don't un'stand the language. They can be rude. Personal abuse as a fine art. Have a cocktail."

"Hadn't I better go out and send them about their business?" asked Walker.

"Lor' bless you, they haven't got any business," was the reply. "No, siddown. Lerrum alone and they'll go home. Have a cocktail." He compounded one for himself, swizzling up the pink mixture with deliberate care and pouring it down his throat with the skill of a juggler, and when Walker had declined the refreshment and lit his pipe, the pair sat and listened to the threats and challenges from the outer darkness. The attitude of masterly inactivity was justified by its results, for the noise subsided by degrees, and presently the rumble of drums and the sound of chanting voices told them that the interrupted revels had been resumed.

After the third application to the stone bottle, Larkom began to grow sleepy and subsided into silence, broken at intervals by an abortive snore. Walker meanwhile smoked his pipe and regarded his host with an air of gloomy meditation. At length, as the latter became more and more somnolent, he ventured to rouse him up.

"You haven't said what you are going to do, Larkom," said he. "Are you going to put me up for a time?"

Larkom sat up in the squeaking chair and stared at him owlishly. "Put you up, ol' f'ler?" said he. "Lor bless you, yes. Wodjer think? Bed been ready for you for mor'n a week. Come'n look at it. Gettin' damn late. Less' turn in." He took up the lamp and walked with unsteady steps through a doorway into a small, bare room, the whitewashed walls of which were tastefully decorated with the mud-built nests of solitary wasps. It contained two bedsteads, each fitted with a mosquito net and furnished with a mattress, composed of bundles of rushes lashed together, and covered with a grass mat.

"Thash your doss, ol' f'ler," said Larkom, placing the lamp on the packing-case that served for a table, "this is mine. Goo' night!" He lifted the mosquito-curtain, crept inside, tucked the curtain under the mattress, and forthwith began to snore softly.

Walker fetched in his trunk from the outer room and, as he exchanged his drill clothes (which he folded carefully as he removed them) for a suit of pyjamas, he looked curiously round the room. A huge, hairy spider was spread out on the wall as if displayed in a collector's cabinet, and above him a brown cockroach of colossal proportions twirled his long antennae thoughtfully. The low, bumpy ceiling formed a promenade for two pallid, goggle-eyed lizards, who strolled about, defiant of the laws of gravity, picking up an occasional moth or soft-shelled beetle as they went. When he was half undressed an enormous fruit-bat, with a head like that of a fox-terrier, blundered in through the open window and flopped about the room in noisy panic for several minutes before it could find its way out again.

At length he put out the lamp, and creeping inside his curtain, tucked it in securely, and soon, despite the hollow boom of the surf, the whistle of multitudinous bats, the piping of the mosquitoes, and the sounds of revelry from the village, he fell asleep and slept until the sun streamed in on to the whitewashed wall.

43

Chapter II
The Legatee

Larkom appeared to have that tolerance of alcohol that is often to be observed in the confirmed soaker. As he sat with his guest in the living room, taking his early tea, although he looked frail and broken in health, there was nothing in his appearance to suggest that he had quite recently been very drunk. Nor, on the other hand, was his manner very different from that of the previous night, save that his articulation and his wits were both clearer.

"What made you pick out this particular health-resort for your little holiday?" he asked. "It isn't what you would call a fashionable watering-place."

"No," replied Walker. "That was the attraction. I had heard about you from Hepburn – he is my brother-in-law, you know – and as it seemed, from what he said, that your abode was on the very outside edge of the world, I marked it down as a good place to disappear in."

Larkom grinned. "You are not a bad judge, old chappie. Disappearing is our speciality. We are famous for it. Always have been. How does the old mariners' ditty run? You remember it? '*Oh, the Bight of Benin, the Bight of Benin, One comes out where three go in.*' But perhaps that wasn't exactly what was in your mind?"

"It wasn't. I could have managed that sort of disappearance without coming so far. But look here, Larkom, let us have a clear understanding. I came here on spec, not having much time to make arrangements, on the chance that you might be willing to put me up and give me a job. But I haven't come to fasten on to you. If my presence here will be in any way a hindrance to you, you've only got to say so and I will move on. And I shan't take it as unfriendly. I quite understand that you have your principals to consider."

"Principals be blowed!" said Larkom. "They don't come into it, and as to me, I can assure you, J. W., that this is the first stroke of luck I've had for years. After vegetating in this God-forgotten hole with nobody to speak to, you can imagine what it is to me to have a pukka white man – and a gentleman at that – under my roof. I feel like chanting '*Domine, non sum dignus*', but if you can put up with me, stay as long as you care to, and understand that you are doing me a favour by staying."

"It is very handsome of you, Larkom, to put it in that way," said Walker, a little huskily. "Of course, I understand the position and I

44

accept your offer gratefully. But we must put the arrangement on a business footing. I'm not going to sponge on you. I must pay my share of the expenses, and if I can give you any help in working the factory – "

"Don't you be afraid, old chappie," interrupted Larkom. "I'll keep your nose on the grindstone, and as to sharing up, we can see to that later when we cast up the accounts. As soon as we have lapped up our tea, we will go out to the store and I will show you the ropes. They aren't very complicated, though they are in a bit of a tangle just now. But that is where you will come in, dear boy."

Larkom's statement as to the "tangle" was certainly no exaggeration. The spectacle of muddle and disorder that the store presented filled Walker at once with joy and exasperation. After a brief tour of the premises, during which he listened in grim silence to Larkom's explanations, he deliberately peeled off his jacket – which he folded up neatly and put in a place of safety – and fell to work on the shelves and lockers with a concentrated energy that reduced the native helper to gibbering astonishment and Larkom to indulgent sniggers.

"Don't overdo it, old chap," the latter admonished. "Remember the climate. And there's no hurry. Plenty of spare time in these parts. Leave yourself a bit for to-morrow." To all of which advice Walker paid no attention whatever, but slogged away at the confused raffle of stock-in-trade without a pause until close upon noon, when the cook came out to announce that "Chop live for table." And even this was but a temporary pause, for soon after breakfast – or tiffin, as the Anglo-Indian calls it – when Larkom showed a tendency to doze in his chair with a tumbler of gin toddy, he stole away to renew his onslaught while the native assistant attended to the "trade".

During the next few days he was kept pretty fully occupied. Not that there was much business doing at the factory, but Larkom's hand having become of late so tremulous that writing was impossible, the posting of books and answering of letters had automatically ceased.

"You're a perfect godsend to me, old chappie," said Larkom, when, by dint of two days' continuous labour, the books had been brought up to date, and Walker attacked the arrears of correspondence. "The firm wouldn't have stood it much longer. They've complained of my handwriting already. If you hadn't come I should have got The Order of the Boot to a certainty. Now they'll think I've got a native clerk from somewhere at my own expense."

"How about the signature?" Walker asked. "Can you manage that?"

"That's all right, dear boy," said Larkom cheerfully. "You sign slowly while I kick the table. They'll never twig the difference."

By means of this novel aid to calligraphy the letter was completed and duly dispatched by a messenger to catch the land post at Quittah. Then Walker had leisure to look about him and study the methods of West Coast trade and the manners and customs of his host. Larkom sober was not very different from Larkom drunk – amiable, easy-going, irresponsible, and only a little less cheerful. Perhaps he was better drunk. At any rate, that was his own opinion, and he acted up to it consistently. What would have happened had there had been any appreciable trade at Adaffia it is impossible to guess. As it was, the traffic was never beyond the capacity of Larkom even at his drunkest. Once or twice during the day a party of bush natives would stroll into the compound with a demijohn of palm oil or a calabash full of kernels, or a man from a neighbouring village would bring in a bushel or so of copra, and then the premises would hum with business. The demijohn would be emptied into a puncheon or the kernels stowed in bags ready for shipment, and the vendors would receive their little dole of threepenny pieces – the ordinary currency of the coast. Then the vendors would change into purchasers. A length of baft or calico, a long flint-lock gun with red-painted stock, a keg of powder, or a case of gin would replace the produce they had brought, the threepenny pieces would drift back into the chest whence they had come, and the deal would be completed.

At these functions Walker, owing to his ignorance of the language, appeared chiefly in the role of onlooker, though he took a hand at the scales, when he was about, and helped to fill the canvas bags with kernels. But he found plenty of time to wander about the village and acknowledge the appreciative grins of the men whom he had hammered on the night of his arrival or the courteous salutations of the women. Frequently in the afternoons he would stroll out to sit on the dry sand at high-water mark and, as the feathery leaves of the sea-washed palms pattered above him in the breeze, would gaze wistfully across the blue and empty ocean. One day a homeward-bound steamer came into the bay to anchor in Quittah roads, and then his gaze grew more wistful and the stern face softened into sadness.

Presently Larkom hove in sight under the palms, carolling huskily and filling a gaudy trade pipe. He came and sat down by Walker and, having struck some two dozen Swedish matches without producing a single spark, gazed solemnly at the steamer.

"Yellow funnel boat," he observed. "That'll be the *Niger*, old Rattray's boat. She's going home, dear boy, home to England, where hansom cabs and green peas and fair ladies and lamb chops –"

"Oh, shut up, Larkom!" exclaimed the other, gruffly.

"Right, dear boy. Mum's the word," was the bland reply, as Larkom resumed his fruitless attack on the matches. "But there's one thing I've been going to say to you," he continued after a pause, "and it's this – confound these damstinkers, I've used up a whole box for nothing – I was going to say that you'd better not show yourself out on the beach unnecessarily. I don't know what your little affair amounts to, but I should say that, if it was worth your while to cut away from home, it's worth your while to stop away."

"What do you mean?"

"I mean that you are still within the jurisdiction of the English courts, and if you should have been traced to the ship and you let yourself be seen, say, by any of the Germans who pass up and down from Quittah to Lomé or Bagidá, why, some fine day you may see an officer of the Gold Coast bearing down on you with a file of Hausas, and then it would be Ho! For England, home, and beauty. You sabby?"

"I must take that risk," growled Walker. "I can't stay skulking in the house, and I'm not going to."

"As you please, dear boy," said Larkom. "I only mentioned the matter. Verbum sap. No offence, I hope."

"Of course not," replied Walker.

"I don't think you are in any immediate danger," pursued Larkom. "Old chief Akolatchi looked in on me just now and he tells me that there are no white officers at Quittah. The doctor died of blackwater fever two days ago, and the commissioner is sick and is off to Madeira by this steamer. Still, you had better keep your weather eyelid lifting."

"I mean to," said Walker and, knocking out his pipe on the heel of his shoe, he rose and shook the sand from his clothes.

"If you'll excuse my harping on a disagreeable topic, old chappie," said Larkom, as they strolled homewards along the beach, "I think you would be wise to take some elementary precautions."

"What sort?" asked Walker.

"Well, supposing you were traced to that barque, the *Sappho*, it would be easy to communicate with her skipper when she comes to her station at Half-Jack. Then they might ascertain that a gent named Johnny Walker with a golden beard and a Wellington nose had been put ashore at Adaffia. You're a fairly easy chappie to describe, with that Romanesque boko, and fairly easy to recognize from a description."

"But, damn it, Larkom! You're not suggesting that I should cut off my nose, are you?"

"God forbid, dear boy! But you might cut off your beard and drop Johnny Walker. A clean shave and a new name would make a world of difference. No native would recognize you without your beard."

47

"Perhaps not. But a white police officer would spot me all right. A clean shave and a different name wouldn't deceive him."

"Not if he really meant business. But the local officials here will be pretty willing to turn a blind eye. They are not keen on arresting a someone with a parcel of witnesses looking on. If a constabulary officer came down here to arrest a bearded man named Walker and found only a clean-shaved covey of the name of Cook, he'd probably say that there was no one here answering the description and go back perfectly satisfied with his tongue in his cheek."

"Do you think he really would?"

"I do. At any rate, you may as well give the authorities a chance, meet 'em half-way. Don't you think so?"

"I suppose it is the reasonable thing to do. Very well, Larkom, I will take your advice and turn myself into a bald-faced stag – I noticed that you have some razors in the store. And as to the name – well, I will adopt your suggestion in that, too. 'Cook' will do as well as any other."

"Better, old chap. Distinguished name. Great man, James Cook. Circumnavigator, all round my hat."

"All the same," said Walker, alias Cook, "I fancy you are a trifle over-optimistic. If an officer were sent down here with a warrant, I think he would have to execute it if he could. He would be running a biggish risk if he let himself be bamboozled."

"Well, dear boy," replied Larkom, "you do the transformation trick and trust in Providence. It's quite likely that the local authorities will make no move, and if a G.C.C. Officer should turn up and insist on mistaking James Cook for Johnny Walker, I daresay we could find some way of dealing with him."

The other man smiled grimly. "Yes," he agreed. "I don't think he'd mistake James Cook for Mary's little lamb."

As they entered the compound a quarter-of-an-hour later, a native rose from the kernel bag on which he had been seated, and disengaging from the folds of his cloth a soiled and crumpled letter, held it out to Larkom. The latter opened it with tremulous haste and, having glanced through it quickly, emitted a long, low whistle.

"Sacked, by jiggers!" he exclaimed, and handed the letter to his guest. It was a brief document and came to the point without circumlocution. The Adaffia factory was a financial failure, *"whatever it might have been under other management"*, and the firm hereby dispensed with Mr. Larkom's services. "But," the letter concluded, "as we are unwilling to leave a white man stranded on the Coast, we hereby make over to you, in lieu of notice, the factory and such stock as remains in it, the same to be your own property, and we hope that you will be able to carry on the trade to more advantage for yourself than you have for us."

"Devilish liberal of them," groaned Larkom, "for I've been a rotten bad servant to the firm. But I shall never make anything of it. I'm a regular waster, old chappie, and the sooner the land-crabs have me, the better it will be for everyone." He lifted the lid of a gin-case and dejectedly hoisted out a high-shouldered, square-faced Dutch bottle.

"Stop this boozing, Larkom," said Cook, late Walker. "Pull yourself together, man, and let us see if we can't make a do of it." He spoke gently enough, with his hand on the other man's shoulder, for the thought of his own wrecked life had helped him to understand. It was not the mere loss of employment that had hit Larkom so hard. It was the realization, sudden and complete, of his utter futility, of his final irrevocable failure in the battle of life.

"It's awfully good of you, old chap," he said dismally, "but I tell you, I'm beyond redemption." He paused irresolutely and then added, "However, we'll stow the lush for the present and talk things over," and he let the bottle slip back into its compartment and, shut down the lid.

But he was in no mood for talking things over, at present. The sense of utter failure appeared to have overwhelmed him completely, and, though he made no further attempt upon the gin-case that evening, his spirits seemed to sink lower and lower until, about ten o'clock, he rose from his chair and silently tottered off to bed, looking pitiably frail and broken.

It was about two o'clock in the morning when Cook awoke to the consciousness of a very singular noise. He sat up in bed to listen. A strange, quick rattle, like the chatter of a jigsaw, came from the rickety bed on which Larkom slept, and with it was mingled a confused puffing that came and went in quick gusts.

"Anything the matter, Larkom?" he asked anxiously, and then, as a broken mumble and a loud chattering of teeth came in reply, he sprang from the bed and struck a match. A single glance made everything clear. The huddled body, shaking from head to foot, the white, pinched face, the bloodless hands with blue finger-nails, clutching the scanty bed-coverings to the trembling chin, presented a picture of African fever that even a newcomer could recognize. Hastily he lit a candle and, gathering up every rag that he could lay hands on, from his own travelling-rug to the sitting room table-cloth, piled them on to his shivering comrade until the sick man looked like a gigantic caddis worm.

After an hour or so the violence of the shivering fit abated, gradually the colour returned to the white face until its late pallor gave place to a deep flush. The heaped coverings were thrown on the floor, the sufferer fidgeted restlessly about the bed, his breathing became hurried, and presently he began to babble at intervals, This state of affairs lasted for upwards of an hour. Then a few beads of perspiration appeared on the sick man's forehead, the chatterings and mumblings and broken snatches of song died away, and, as the parched skin broke out into dewy moisture, a look of intelligence came back to the vacant face.

"Cover me up, old chappie," said Larkom, turning over with a deep sigh. "Air strikes chilly. Thanks, old fellow. Let's have the table-cloth, too. That's ripping. Now you turn in and get a bit of sleep. Sorry to have routed you up like this." He closed his eyes and at once began to doze, and Cook, creeping back to bed, lay and watched him by the light of the flickering candle. Then he, too, fell asleep.

When he awoke it was broad daylight, and through the open door he could see Larkom standing by the table in the sitting room, wrapped in the rug. The Fanti cook was seated at the table and the solitary Kroo boy, who formed the staff of the factory, stood by his supplementary chair, his eyes a-goggle with curiosity.

"Now, Kwaku," Larkom was saying, "you see that pencil mark. Well, you take this pen and make a mark on top of it – so." He handed the pen to the cook, who evidently followed the instructions, for his tongue protruded several inches, and he presently rose, wiping his brow. The Kroo boy took his place and the ceremony was repeated, after which the two natives retired grinning with pride.

"Gad, Larkom," exclaimed Cook, when he came out and joined his host, "that dose of fever has taken the starch out of you. You oughtn't to be up, surely?" He looked earnestly at his comrade, shocked at the aspect of the pitiful wreck before him and a little alarmed at the strange, greenish-yellow tint that showed through the waxen pallor of the face.

"Shan't be up long, dear boy," said Larkom. "Just setting things straight before I turn in for good. Now, just cast your eye over this document – devil of a scrawl, but I expect you can make it out." He took up a sheet of paper and handed it to Cook. The writing was so tremulous as to be almost illegible, but with difficulty Cook deciphered it, and its purport filled him with astonishment. It read thus:

> *This is the last will and testament of me John Larkom of Adaffia in the Gold Coast Colony, West Africa. I give and devise all my estate and effects, real and personal, which I may die possessed of or be entitled to, unto James Cook absolutely, and I appoint him the executor of this my will.*

Dated this Thirteenth day of November, One-thousand eight-hundred-and-ninety-seven.

Signed by the testator in the presence of us, who thereupon made our marks in his and each other's presence.

John Larkom

Kwaku Mensah of Cape Coast. His + mark

Pea Soup of Half-Jack. His + mark

"I've given you your new name, you see," Larkom explained. "Take charge of this precious document and keep that letter from the firm. Burn all other papers."

"But," exclaimed Cook, "why are you talking as if you expected to snuff out? You've had fever before, I suppose?"

"Rather," said Larkom. "But you're a new-comer, you don't sabby. I'm an old coaster, and I sabby proper. Look at that, dear boy. Do you know what that means?" He held out a shaking, lemon-coloured hand, and as his companion regarded it silently, he continued, "That means blackwater fever, and when a Johnny like me goes in for that luxury, it's a job for the gardener. And talking of that, you'd better plant me in the far corner of the compound where the empty casks are kept, by the prickly-pear hedge, I shall be out of the way of traffic there, though graves are a damned nuisance in business premises, anyhow."

"Oh, dry up, Larkom, and get to bed," growled Cook, "and, I say, aren't there any doctors in this accursed place?"

Larkom grinned. "In the fossil state, dear boy, they are quite numerous. Otherwise scarce. The medico up at Quittah died three days ago, as I told you, and there are no others on tap just now. No good to me if they were. Remember what I've told you. Burn all papers and, when you've planted me, take over the factory and make things hum. There's a living to be made here and you'll make it. Leave the swizzle-stick alone, old chappie, and if ever you should chance to meet Hepburn again, give him my love and kick him – kick him hard. Now I'm going to turn in."

Larkom's forecast of the probable course of his illness bid fair to turn out correct. In the intervals of business – which, perversely enough, was unusually brisk on this day – Cook looked in on the invalid and at each visit found him visibly changed for the worse. The pale-lemon tint of his skin gave place to a horrible dusky yellow, his voice grew weaker and his mind more clouded, until at last he sank into a partial stupor from

51

which it was almost impossible to rouse him. He wanted nothing, save an occasional sip of water, and nothing could be done to stay the march of the fell disease.

So the day passed on, a day of miserable suspense for Cook, the little caravans filed into the compound, the kernels and copra and knobs of rubber rolled out of the calabashes on to the ground, the oil gurgled softly into the puncheon, the bush people chattered vivaciously in the store and presently departed gleefully with their purchases, and still Larkom lay silent and apathetic and ever drawing nearer to the frontier between the known and the unknown. The evening fell, the store was locked up, the compound gate was shut, and Cook betook himself with a shaded lamp to sit by the sick man's bed.

But presently the sight of that yellow face, grown suddenly so strangely small and pinched, the sharpened nose, and the sunken eyes with the yellow gleam of the half-seen eyeballs between the lids, was more than he could bear, and he stole softly through into the sitting room, there to continue his vigil. So hour after weary hour passed. The village sank to rest (for it was a moonless night) and the sounds that came in through the open window were those of beast and bird and insect. Bats whistled out in the darkness, cicadas and crickets chirred and chirruped, the bark of the genet and the snuffling mutter of prowling civets came from without the compound, while far away the long-drawn, melancholy cry of a hyena could be heard in the intervals of the booming surf.

And all the while the sick man slowly drew nearer to the dread frontier.

It wanted but an hour to dawn when a change came. The feeble babblings and mumblings, the little snatches of forgotten songs chanted in a weak, quavering treble, had ceased for some time, and now through the open door came a new sound – the sound of slow breathing mingled with a soft, moist rattling. The watcher rose from his chair and once again crept, lamp in hand, into the dimly-lighted room, there to stand looking down gloomily at the one friend that Fate had left him. Larkom was now unconscious and lay quite still, save the heaving chest and the rise and fall of the chin with each breath.

Cook took put down the lamp, and, sitting down, gently took the damp and chilly hand in his, while he listened, in agony at his own helplessness, to the monotonous, rattling murmur that went on and on, to and fro, like the escapement of some horrible clock.

By and by it stopped, and Cook fumbled at the tepid wrist, then, after a pause, it began again with an altered rhythm and presently paused again, and again went on, and so the weary, harrowing minutes passed, the pauses growing ever longer and the rattling murmur more and more shallow. At last there came a pause so long that Cook leaned over the bed to listen. A little whispering sigh was borne to his ear, then all was still, and when, after waiting yet several minutes more, he had reverently drawn the gaudy table-cloth over the silent figure, he went back to his chair in the sitting room, there to wait, with grim face and lonely heart, for the coming of the day.

The late afternoon sun was slanting eagerly over the palm-tops as he took his way to the far corner of the compound that faced towards the western beach. The empty barrels had been rolled away and, in the clear space, close to the low prickly-pear hedge, a smooth mound of yellow sand and a rough wooden cross marked the spot where Larkom, stitched up in sacking in lieu of a coffin, had been laid to rest. The cross had occupied most of Cook's scanty leisure since the hurried burial in the morning (for trade was still perversely brisk, despite the ragged house-flag half-mast on the little flag-pole), and he was now going to put the finishing touches to it.

It was a rude enough memorial, the upright from a board from one of the long gun-crates, and the cross-piece formed by a new barrel stave cut to the requisite length, and the lack of paint left it naked and staring.

Cook laid down on the sand a box containing his materials – a set of zinc stencil plates, used for marking barrels and cases, a stencil brush, and a pot of thin black paint – and sketched out lightly in pencil the words of the inscription:

JOHN LARKOM 14th November 1897

Then he picked out a *J* from the set of stencil plates, dipped the brush in the pot, and made the first letter, following it in order with *O*, *H*, and *N*. Something in the look of the familiar name – his own name as well as Larkom's – made him pause and gaze at it thoughtfully, and his air was still meditative and abstracted as he stooped and picked up the *L* to commence the following word. Rising with the fresh plate in his hand, he happened to glance over the low hedge along the stretch of beach that meandered away to a distant, palm-clad headland, and then he noticed for the first time a little group of figures that stood out sharply against the yellow background. They were about half-a-mile distant and were evidently coming towards the village, and there was something in their appearance that caused him to examine them narrowly. Four of the figures walked together and carried some large object that he guessed to be a travelling hammock, four others straggled some little distance behind, and yet three more, who walked ahead of the hammock, seemed to carry guns or rifles on their shoulders.

Still holding the plate and brush, Cook stood motionless, watching with grim attention the approach of the little procession. On it came, at a rapid pace, each step bringing it more clearly into view. The hammock was now quite distinct and the passenger could be seen lying in the sagging cloth, eight of the figures were evidently ordinary natives while the other three were plainly black men dressed in a blue uniform, wearing red caps and carrying rifles and bayonets.

Cook stooped and dropped the plate back into the box, picking out, in place of it, a plate pierced with the letter O. Dipping his brush into the paint, he laid the plate over the pencilled L on the cross and brushed in the letter. Quietly and without hurry, he followed the O with an S, M, O, N, and D, and he had just finished the last letter when an English voice hailed him from over the hedge.

He turned and saw, a little distance away, a fresh-laced Englishman in a quiet undress uniform and a cheese-cutter cap, peering at him curiously from the top a sand-hill, at the base of which stood the group of hammockmen and the three Hausas.

"There's a gate farther down," said Cook, and, as the officer turned away, he dropped the plate that he was holding back into the box, laid down the brush, and took up a camel's-hair pencil. Dipping this into the paint-pot, he proceeded deliberately and with no little skill to write the date in small letters under the name. Presently the sound of footsteps was audible from behind. Cook continued his writing with deliberate care and the footsteps drew nearer, slowing as they approached. Close behind him they halted, and a cheery voice exclaimed, "Good Lord! What a let-off!" and then added, "Poor beggar! When did he die?"

"This morning, just before dawn," replied Cook.

"Phew!" whistled the officer. "He wasn't long getting his ticket. But, I say, how did you know his name? I thought he called himself Walker."

"So he did. But he wished his name to be put on his grave."

"Naturally," said the officer. "It's no use giving an alias at the last muster. Well, poor devil! He's had rough luck, but perhaps it's best, after all. It's certainly best for me."

"Why for you?" asked Cook.

"Because I've got a warrant in my pocket to arrest him for some trouble at home – signed the wrong cheque or something of that kind – and I wasn't very sweet on the job, as you may guess. Blood's thicker than water, you know, and the poor chap was an English gentleman after all. However, those black devils of mine don't know what I have come for, so now nothing need be said."

"No." He looked round into the bluff, rosy face and clear blue eyes of the officer and asked, "How did you manage to run him to earth?"

"He was traced to Bristol and to the barque *Sappho* after she had sailed. Then the *Sappho* was seen from Quittah to bring up here, right off her station – she trades to Half-Jack – and, as we were on the look-out, we made inquiries and found that a white man had come ashore here. Good thing we didn't find out sooner. Well, I'll be getting back to Quittah. I've just come down with a new doctor to take over there. My name's Cockeram, Assistant Inspector G.C.C. You're Mr. Larkom, I suppose?"

"Won't you stop and have a cocktail?" asked Cook, ignoring the question.

"No, thanks. Don't take 'em. H-two-O is the drink for this country."

He touched his cap and sauntered to the gate, and Cook saw him walk slowly up and down behind the hedge, apparently gathering something. Presently he sauntered back into the compound looking a little sheepish, and, as he came, twisting some blossoming twigs of wild cotton into a kind of grommet and shelling the little 'prayer-beads' out of some Jequirity pods that he had gathered. He walked up the sandy mound and, sprinkling the scarlet seeds in the form of a cross, laid the loop of cotton-blossoms above it.

"It's a scurvy wreath," he said, gruffly, without looking at Cook, "but it's a scurvy country. So long." He walked briskly out of the compound and, flinging himself into the hammock, gave the word to march.

The other looked after him with an unwonted softening of the grim face – yet grimmer and more lean now that the beard was gone – only resuming his writing when the little procession was growing small in the distance. The date was completed now, but, dipping his brush afresh, he wrote below in still smaller letters: "*Now shall I sleep in the dust, and thou shalt seek me in the morning, but I shall not be.*"

Then he picked up the box and went back into the house.

Chapter III
The Mutiny on the *Speedwell*

For a man in search of quiet and retirement, the village of Adaffia would seem to be an ideally eligible spot, especially if the man in question should happen be under a rather heavy cloud. Situated in a little known part of the Slave Coast, many miles distant from any town or settlement where white men had their abodes, it offered a haven of security to the Ishmaelite if it offered little else.

Thus reflected John Osmond, late John Walker, and now "Mr. James Cook", if the need for a surname should arise. But hitherto it had not arisen, for, to the natives, he was simply "the white man", and no other European had passed along the coast since the day on which he had buried Larkom – and his own identity – and entered into his inheritance.

He reviewed the short interval with its tale of eventless and monotonous days as he sat smoking a thoughtful pipe in the shady coconut grove that encompassed the hamlet, letting his thoughts travel back anon to a more distant and eventful past, and all the while keeping an attentive eye on a shabby-looking brigantine that was creeping up from the south. It was not, perhaps, a very thrilling spectacle, but yet Osmond watched the approaching vessel with lively interest. For though, on that deserted coast, ships may be seen to pass up and down on the rim of the horizon, two or three, perhaps, in a month, this was the first vessel that had headed for the land since the day on which he had become the owner of the factory and the sole representative of European civilization in Adaffia. It was natural, then, that he should watch her with interest and curiosity, not only as a visitor from the world which he had left, but as one with which he was personally concerned, for if her people had business ashore, that business was pretty certainly with him.

At a distance of about a mile-and-a-half from the shore the brigantine luffed up, fired a gun, hoisted a dirty red ensign, let go her anchor, scandalized her mainsail, lowered her head-sails, and roughly dewed up the square-sails. A fishing canoe, which had paddled out to meet her, ran alongside and presently returned shoreward with a couple of white men on board. And still Osmond made no move. Business considerations should have led him to go down to the beach and meet the white men, since they were almost certainly bound for his factory, but other considerations restrained him. The fewer white men that he met, the safer he would be, for, to the Ishmaelite, every stranger is a possible

56

enemy or, worse still, a possible acquaintance. And then, although he felt no distaste for the ordinary trade with the natives, he did not much fancy himself standing behind a counter selling gin and tobacco to a party of British shell-backs. So he loitered under the coconuts and determined to leave the business transactions to his native assistant, Kwaku Mensah.

The canoe landed safely through the surf, the two white men stepped ashore, and disappeared towards the village. Osmond refilled his pipe and walked a little farther away. Presently a file of natives appeared moving towards the shore, each carrying on his head a green-painted gin-case. Osmond counted them – there were six in all – and watched them stow the cases in the canoe. Then, suddenly, the two white men appeared, running furiously. They made straight for the canoe and jumped in, the canoe men pushed off, and the little craft began to wriggle its way cautiously through the surf. And at this moment another figure made its appearance on the beach and began to make unmistakable demonstrations of hostility to the receding canoe.

Now, a man who wears a scarlet flannelette coat, green cotton trousers, yellow carpet slippers, and a gold-laced smoking-cap is not difficult to identify even at some little distance. Osmond instantly recognized his assistant and strode away to make inquiries.

There was no need to ask what was the matter. As Osmond crossed the stretch of blown sand that lay between the palm-grove and the beach, his retainer came running towards him, flourishing his arms wildly and fairly gibbering with excitement.

"Dem sailor man, sir!" he gasped, when he had come within earshot. "He damn t'ief, sir! He t'ief six case gin!"

"Do you mean that those fellows didn't pay for that gin?" Osmond demanded.

"No, sir. No pay nutting. They send the case down for beach and they tell me find some country cloth. I go into store to look at the cloth – then they run away for their canoe. They no pay nothing."

"Very well, Mensah. We'll go on board and collect the money or bring back the gin. Can you get a canoe?"

"All canoe go out fishing excepting that one," said Mensah.

"Then we must wait for that one to come back," was the reply, and Osmond seated himself on the edge of dry sand that overhung the beach and fixed a steady gaze on the dwindling canoe. Mensah sat down likewise and glanced dubiously at his grim-faced employer, but whatever doubts he had as to the wisdom of the proposed expedition, he kept them to himself. For John Osmond – like Father O'Flynn – had a "wonderful way with him", a way that induced unruly intruders to leave the compound hurriedly and rub themselves a good deal when they got outside. So Mensah kept his own counsel.

The canoe ran alongside the brigantine and, having discharged its passengers and freight, put off for its return shorewards. Then a new phase in the proceedings began. The brigantine's head-sails, which lay loose on the jib-boom, began to slide up the stays, the untidy bunches of canvas aloft began to flatten out to the pull of the sheets. The brigantine, in fact, was preparing to get under way. But it was all done in a very leisurely fashion, so deliberately that the last of the square-sails was barely sheeted home when the canoe grounded on the beach.

Osmond wasted no time. While Mensah was giving the necessary explanations, he set his shoulder to the peak of the canoe and shoved her round head to sea, regardless of the cloud of spray that burst over him.

The canoe-men were nothing loath, for the African is keenly appreciative of a humorous situation. Moreover, they had some experience of the white man's peculiar methods of persuasion and felt a natural desire to see them exercised on persons of his own colour – especially as those persons had been none too civil. Accordingly they pushed off gleefully and plunged once more into the breakers, digging their massive, trident-shaped paddles into the water to the accompaniment of those uncanny hisses, groans, and snatches of song with which the African canoe-man sweetens his labour.

Meanwhile their passenger sat in the bow of the canoe, wiping the sea water from his face and fixing a baleful glance on the brigantine, as she wallowed drunkenly on the heavy swell. Slowly the tack of the mainsail descended, and then, to a series of squeaks from the halyard-blocks, the peak of the sail rose by stow jerks. The canoe bounded forward over the great rollers, the hull of the vessel rose and began to loom large above the waters, and Osmond had just read the name "*Speedwell, Bristol*" on her broad counter, when his ear caught a new sound – the "clink, clink" of the windlass-pawl. The anchor was being hove up.

But the canoe-men had heard the sound, too, and, with a loud groan, dug their paddles into the water with furious energy. The canoe shot forward under the swaying counter and swept alongside, the brigantine rolled over as if she would annihilate the little craft, and Osmond, grasping a chain-plate, swung himself up into the channel, whence he climbed to the bulwark rail and dropped down on the deck.

The windlass was manned by six of the crew, who bobbed up and down slowly at the ends of the long levers. A seventh man was seated on the deck, with one of the gin cases open before him, in the act of uncorking a bottle. The other five cases were ranged along by the bulwark.

"Good afternoon," said Osmond, whose arrival had been unnoticed by the preoccupied crew. "You forgot to pay for that gin."

The seated man looked up with a start, first at Osmond and then at Mensah, who now sat astride the rail in a strategic position that admitted of advance or retreat as circumstances might suggest. The clink of the windlass ceased, and the six men came sauntering aft with expectant grins.

"What are you doin' aboard this ship?" demanded the first man.

"I've come to collect my dues," replied Osmond.

"Have yer?" said the sailor. "You'll be the factory bug, I reckon?"

"I'm the owner of that gin."

"Now that's where you make a mistake, young feller. I'm the owner of this here gin."

"Then you've got to pay me one pound four."

The sailor set the bottle down on the deck and rose to his feet.

"Look here, young feller," said he, "I'm goin' to give you a valuable tip – gratis. You git overboard. Sharp. D'ye hear?"

"I want one pound four," said Osmond, in a misleadingly quiet tone.

"Pitch 'im overboard, Dhoody," one of the other sailors counselled. "Send 'im for a swim, mate."

"I'm a-goin' to," said Dhoody, "if he don't clear out," and he began to advance, crabwise, across the deck in the manner of a wrestler attacking.

Osmond stood motionless in a characteristic attitude, with his long legs wide apart, his hands clasped behind him, his gaunt shoulders hunched up, and his chin thrust forward, swaying regularly to the heave of the deck, and with his grim, hatchet face turned impassively towards his adversary, presented a decidedly uninviting aspect. Perhaps Dhoody appreciated this fact. At any rate, he advanced with an ostentatious show of strategy and much intimidating air-clawing. But he made a bad choice of the moment for the actual attack, for he elected to rush in just as the farther side of the deck was rising. In an instant Osmond's statuesque immobility changed to bewilderingly rapid movement. There was a resounding "Smack, smack". Dhoody flew backwards, capsizing two men behind him, staggered down the sloping deck, closely followed by Osmond (executing a continuous series of "postman's knocks" on the Dhoodian countenance), and finally fell sprawling in the scuppers, with his head jammed against a stanchion. The two capsized men scrambled to their feet, and, with their four comrades, closed in on Osmond with evidently hostile intentions. But the latter did not wait to be attacked.

59

Acting on the advice of the Duke of Wellington – whom, by the way, he somewhat resembled in appearance – to "hit first and keep on hitting", he charged the group of seamen like an extremely self-possessed bull, hammering right and left, regardless of the unskilful thumps that he got in return, and gradually drove them, bewildered by his extraordinary quickness and the weight of his well-directed blows, through the space between the foremast and the bulwark. Slowly they backed away before his continuous battering, hitting out at him ineffectively, hampered by their numbers and the confined space, until one man, who had had the bad luck to catch two upper cuts in succession, uttered a howl of rage and whipped out his sheath-knife. Osmond's quick eye caught the dull glint of the steel just as he was passing the fife-rail. Instantly he whisked out an unoccupied iron belaying-pin, whirled it over and brought it down on the man's head. The fellow dropped like a pole-axed ox, and as the belaying-pin rose aloft once more, the other five men sprang back out of range.

How the combat might have ended under other circumstances it is impossible to say. Dhoody had disappeared – with a bloody scalp and an obliterated eye, the man with the knife lay unconscious on the deck with a little red pool collecting by his head, the other five men had scattered and were hastily searching for weapons and missiles, so far as was possible with this bloodthirsty Bedlamite of a "factory bug" flying up and down the deck flourishing a belaying-pin. Their principal occupation, in fact, was in keeping out of reach, and they did not always succeed.

Suddenly a shot rang out. A little cloud of splinters flew from the side of the mainmast, and the five seamen ducked simultaneously. Glancing quickly forward, Osmond beheld his late antagonist, Dhoody, emerging from the forecastle hatch and taking aim at him with a still smoking revolver. Now, the "factory bug" was a pugnacious man and perhaps over-confident, too. But he had some idea of his limitations. You can't walk up twenty yards of deck to punch the head of a man who is covering you with a revolver. At the moment, Osmond was abreast of the uncovered main hatch. A passing glance had shown him a tier of kernel bags covering the floor of the hold. Without a moment's hesitation he stooped with his hands on the coaming, and, vaulting over, dropped plump on the bags, and then, picking himself up, scrambled forward under the shelter of the deck.

The hold of the *Speedwell*, like that of most vessels of her class, was a simple cavity, extending from the forecastle bulkhead to that of the after-cabin. Of this the forward part still contained a portion of the outward cargo, while the homeward lading was stowed abaft the main

60

hatch. But the hold was two-thirds empty and afforded plenty of room to move about.

Osmond took up a position behind some bales of Manchester goods and waited for the next move on the part of the enemy. He had not long to wait. Voices from above told him that the crew had gathered round the hatch. Indeed, from his retreat, he could see some of them craning over the coamings, peering into the dark recesses of the hold.

"What are yer goin' to do, Dhoody?" one of the men asked.

"I'm goin' below to finish the beggar off," was the reply in a tone of savage determination.

The place of a ladder was supplied by wooden footholds nailed to the massive stanchion that supported the deck and rested on the kelson. Osmond kept a sharp eye on the top foothold, clambering quickly on the closely packed bales to get within reach, and as a booted foot appeared below the beam and settled on the projection, he brought down his belaying-pin on the toe with a rap that elicited a yell of agony and caused the hasty withdrawal of the foot. For a minute or more the air was thick with execrations and, as Osmond crept back into shelter, an irregular stamping on the deck above suggested some person hopping actively on one leg.

But the retreat was not premature. Hardly had Osmond squeezed himself behind the stack of bales when a succession of shots rang out from above, and bullet after bullet embedded itself in the rolls of cotton cloth. Osmond counted five shots and when there came an interval – presumably to reload – he ventured to peer between the bales, and was able to see Dhoody frantically emptying the discharged chambers of the revolver and ramming in fresh cartridges, while the five sailors stared curiously into the hold.

"Now then," said Dhoody, when he had re-loaded, "you just nip down, Sam Winter, and see if I've hit him, and I'll stand by here to shoot if he goes for yer."

"Not me," replied Sam. "You 'and me the gun and just pop down yerself. I'll see as he don't hurt yer."

"How can I?" roared Dhoody, "with me fut hammered into a jelly?"

"Well," retorted Sam, "what about my feet? D'ye think I can fly?"

"Oh," said Dhoody, contemptuously, "if you funk the job, I won't press yer. Bob Simmons ain't afraid, I know. He'll go."

"Will he?" said Simmons. "I'm jiggered if he will! That bloke's too handy with that pin for my taste. But I'll hold the gun while you go, Dhoody."

Dhoody cursed the whole ship's company collectively and individually for a pack of chicken-livered curs. But not one of them

61

would budge. Each was quite willing, and even eager, to do the shooting from above, but no one was disposed to go below and "draw the badger". The proceedings seemed to have come to a deadlock when one of the sailors was inspired with a new idea.

"Look 'ere, mates," he said, oracularly, "'Tis like this 'ere: 'Ere's this 'ere bloomin' ship with a nomicidal maniac in 'er 'old. Now, none of us ain't a-goin' down there for to fetch 'im out. We don't want our 'eds broke same as what 'e's broke Jim Darker's 'ed. Contrarywise, so long as 'e's loose on this ship, no man's life ain't worth a brass farden. Wherefore I says, bottle 'im up, I says, clap on the hatch-covers and batten down. Then we've got 'im, and then we can sleep in our bunks in peace."

"That's right enough, Bill," another voice broke in, "but you're forgettin' that we've got a little job to do down below there."

"Not yet, we ain't," the other rejoined, "not afore we gets down Ambriz way, and he'll be quiet enough by then."

This seemed to satisfy all parties, including even the ferocious Dhoody, and a general movement warned Osmond that his incarceration was imminent, For one moment he was disposed to make a last, desperate sortie, but the certainty that he would be a dead man before he reached the deck decided him to lie low. Many things might happen before the brigantine reached Ambriz.

As the hatchcovers grated over the coaming and dropped into their beds, the prisoner took a rapid survey of his surroundings before the last glimmer of daylight should be shut out. But he had scarcely time to memorize the geographical features of the hold before the last of the hatch-covers was dropped into its place. Then he heard the tarpaulin drag over the hatch, shutting out the last gleams of light that had filtered through the joints of the covers, the battens were dropped into their catches, the wedges driven home, and he sat, in a darkness like that of the tomb.

The hold was intolerably hot and close. The roasting deck above was like the roof of an oven. A greasy reek arose from the bags of kernels, a strange, mixed effluvium from the bales of cotton cloth. And the place was full of strange noises. At every roll of the ship, as the strain of the rigging changed sides, a universal groan arose, bulkheads squeaked, timbers grated, the masts creaked noisily in their housings, and unctuous gurgles issued from the tier of oil puncheons. It was clear to Osmond that this was no place for a prolonged residence. The sweat that already trickled down his face meant thirst in the near future, and death if he failed to discover the tank or water-casks. A diet of palm kernels did not commend itself, and, now that the hatch was covered, the water in the bilge made its peculiar properties manifest. The obvious necessity was to get out, but the method of escape was not obvious at all.

From his own position, Osmond's thoughts turned to the state of the vessel. From the first, it had been evident to him that there was something very abnormal about this ship. Apart from the lawless behaviour of the crew, there was the fact that since he had come on board he had seen no vestige of an officer. Dhoody had seemed to have some sort of authority, but the manner in which the men addressed him showed that he had no superior status. Then, where was the "afterguard"? They had not gone ashore. And there had been enough uproar to bring them on deck if they had been on board. There was only one reasonable conclusion from these facts, and it was confirmed by Dhoody's proprietary air and by a certain brown stain that Osmond had noticed on the deck. There had been a mutiny on the *Speedwell*.

The inveterate smoker invokes the aid of tobacco in all cases where concentrated thought is required. Osmond made shift to fill his pipe in the dark and, noting that his tobacco was low, struck a match. The flame lighted up the corner into which he had crept and rendered visible some objects that he had not noticed before, and, at the first glance, any lingering uncertainty as to the state of affairs on the *Speedwell* vanished in an instant. For the objects that he had seen comprised a shipwright's auger, a caulking mallet, and a dozen or more large wooden pegs cut to a taper at one end.

The purpose of these appliances was unmistakable, and very clearly explained the nature of the "little job" that the sailors had to do down below. Those rascals intended to scuttle the ship. Holes were to be bored in the bottom with the auger and the plugs driven into them. Then, when the mutineers were ready to leave, the plugs would be pulled out, and the ship abandoned with the water pouring into her hold. It was a pretty scheme, if not a novel one, and it again suggested the question: Where were the officers?

Turning over this question, Osmond remembered that Dhoody had gone to the forecastle to fetch his revolver. Then the crew would appear to be still occupying their own quarters, whence it followed that, if the officers were on board, they were probably secured in their berths aft.

This consideration suggested a new idea. Osmond lit another match and explored the immediate neighbourhood in the hope of finding more tools, but there were only the auger and the mallet, the pegs having probably been tapered with a sheath-knife. As the match went out, Osmond quenched the glowing tip, and, picking up the auger and mallet, though for the latter he had no present use, began to grope his way aft. The part of the hold abaft the main hatch had a ground tier of oil-

63

puncheons, above which was stowed a quantity of produce, principally copra and kernels in bags. Climbing on top of this, Osmond crawled aft until he brought up against the bulkhead that separated the cabin from the hold. Here he commenced operations without delay. Rapping with his knuckles to make sure of the absence of obstructing stanchions, he set the point of the auger against the bulkhead, and, grasping the cross lever, fell to work vigorously. It was a big tool, boring an inch and a half hole, and correspondingly heavy to turn, but Osmond drove it with a will, and was soon rewarded by feeling it give with a jerk, and when he withdrew it, there was a circular hole through which streamed the welcome daylight.

He applied his eye to the hole (which, in spite of the thickness of the planking, afforded a fairly wide view) and looked into what was evidently the cuddy or cabin. He could see a small, nearly triangular table fitted with "fiddles", or safety rims, between which a big water-bottle slid backwards and forwards as the ship rolled, pursued by a dozen or more green limes and an empty tumbler – a sight which made his mouth water. Opposite was the companion-ladder and at each side of it a door – probably those of the captain's and mate's cabins. Above the table would be the sky light, though he could not see it, but he could make out some pieces of broken glass on the floor and one or two on the table, and he now recalled that he had noticed, when on deck, that the skylight glass was smashed.

Having made this survey, he returned to his task. Above the hole that he had bored, he proceeded to bore another, slightly intersecting it, and above this another, and so on, tracing a continuous curved row of holes, each hole encroaching a little on the next, and the entire series looking, from the dark hold, like a luminous silhouette of a string of beads. It was arduous work, and monotonous, but Osmond kept at it with only an occasional pause to wipe his streaming face and steal a wistful look at the water-bottle on the cabin table. No sign did he perceive there of either officers or crew. Indeed, the latter were busy on deck, for he had heard the clink of the windlass, and when that had ceased, the rattle of running gear as the sails were trimmed. And meanwhile the curved line of holes extended along the bulkhead and began to define an ellipse some eighteen inches by twelve.

By the time he had made the twenty-fourth hole, a sudden weakening of the light that came through informed him that the sun was setting. He took a last peep into the cabin before the brief tropic twilight should have faded, and was surprised to note that the tumbler seemed to have vanished and that there appeared to be less water in the bottle. Speculating vaguely on the possible explanation of this, he fell to work

64

again, adding hole after hole to the series, guiding himself by the sense of touch when the light failed completely.

The thirty-eighth hole nearly completed the ellipse, and was within an inch of the first one bored. Standing back from the bulkhead, Osmond gave a vigorous kick on the space enclosed by the line of holes, and sent the oval piece of planking flying through into the cabin. Passing his head through the opening, he listened awhile. Sounds of revelry from the deck, now plainly audible, told him that the gin was doing its work and that the crew were fully occupied. He slipped easily through the opening, and, groping his way to the table, found the water-bottle and refreshed himself with a long and delicious draught. Then, feeling his way to the companion-ladders he knocked with his knuckles on the door at its port side.

No one answered, and yet he had a feeling of some soft and stealthy movement within. Accordingly he knocked again, a little more sharply, and as there was still no answer, he turned the handle and pushed gently at the door, which was, however, bolted or locked. But the effort was not in vain, for as he gave a second, harder push, a woman's voice – which sounded quite near, as if the speaker were close to the door – demanded, "Who is there?"

Considerably taken aback by the discovery of this unexpected denizen of the mutiny-ridden ship, Osmond was for a few moments at a loss for a reply. At length, putting his mouth near to the keyhole (for the skylight was open and the steersman, at least, not far away), he answered softly, "A friend."

The reply did not appear to have the desired effect, for the woman – also speaking into the keyhole – demanded sharply, "But who are you? And what do you want?"

These were difficult questions. Addressing himself to the first, and boggling awkwardly at the unaccustomed lie, Osmond stammered, "My name is – er – is Cook, but you don't know me. I am not one of the crew. If you wouldn't mind opening the door, I could explain matters."

"I shall do nothing of the kind," was the reply.

"There's really no occasion for you to be afraid," Osmond urged.

"Isn't there?" she retorted. "And who said I was afraid? Let me tell you that I've got a pistol, and I shall shoot if I have any of your nonsense. So you'd better be off."

Osmond grinned appreciatively but decided to abandon the parley.

"Is there anyone aft here besides you?" he asked.

"Never you mind," was the tart reply. "You had better go back where you came from."

Osmond rose with a grim smile and began cautiously to feel his way towards the companion-steps and past them to the other door that he had seen. Having found it and located the handle, he rapped sharply but not too loudly.

"Well?" demanded a gruff voice from within.

Osmond turned the handle, and, as a stream of light issued from the opening door, he entered hastily and closed it behind him. He found himself in a small cabin lighted by a candle-lamp that swung in gimballs from the bulkhead. One side was occupied by a bunk in which reclined a small, elderly man, who appeared to have been reading, for he held an open volume, which Osmond observed with some surprise to be Applin's *Commentary On the Book of Job*. His head was roughly bandaged and he wore his left arm in a primitive sling.

"Well," he repeated, taking off his spectacles to look at Osmond.

"You are the captain, I presume?" said Osmond.

"Yes. Name of Hartup. Who are you?"

Osmond briefly explained the circumstances of his arrival on board.

"Ah!" said the captain. "I wondered who was boring those holes when I went into the cabin just now. Well, you've put your head into a hornet's nest, young man."

"Yes," said Osmond "and I'm going to keep it there until I'm paid to take it out."

The captain smiled sourly. "You are like my mate, Will Redford – very like him you are to look at, and the same quarrelsome disposition, apparently."

"Where is the mate now?"

"Overboard," replied the captain. "He got flourishing a revolver and the second mate stabbed him."

"Is the second mate's name Dhoody?"

"Yes. But he's only a substitute. The proper second mate died up at Sherbro, so I promoted Dhoody from before the mast."

"I take it that your crew have mutinied?"

"Yes," said the captain, placidly. "There is over a ton of ivory on board and two-hundred ounces of gold dust in that chest that you are sitting on. It was a great temptation. Dhoody began it and Redford made it worse by bullying."

"Dhoody seems to be a tough customer."

"Very," said the captain. "A violent man. A man of wrath. I am surprised that he didn't make an end of you."

"So is he, I expect," Osmond replied with a grin, "and I hope to give him one or two more surprises before we part. What are you going to do?"

The captain sighed. "We are in the hands of Providence," said he.

"You'll be in the hands of Davy Jones if you don't look out," said Osmond. "They are going to scuttle the ship when they get to Ambriz. Can I get anything to eat?"

"There is corned pork and biscuit in that locker," said the captain "and water and limes on the cabin table. No intoxicants. This is a temperance ship."

Osmond smiled grimly as a wild chorus from above burst out as if in commentary on the captain's statement. But he made no remark. Corned pork was better than discussion just now.

"You seem to have been in the wars," he remarked, glancing at the skipper's bandaged head and arm.

"Yes. Fell down the companion, at least, Dhoody shoved me down. I'll get you to fix a new dressing on my arm when you've finished eating. You'll find some lint and rubber plaster in the medicine chest there."

"By the way," said Osmond, as he cracked a biscuit on his knee, "there's a woman in the next berth. Sounded like quite a ladylike person, too. Who is she?"

The captain shook his head. "Yes," he groaned, "there's another complication. She is a Miss Burleigh, daughter of Sir Hector Burleigh, the Administrator or Acting Governor, or something of the sort, of the Gold Coast."

"But what the deuce is she doing on an old rattle trap of a windjammer like this?"

The captain sat up with a jerk. "I'll trouble you, young man," he said, severely, "to express yourself with more decorum. I am the owner of this vessel, and if she is good enough for me she will have to be good enough for you. Nobody asked you to come aboard, you know."

"I beg your pardon," said Osmond. "Didn't mean to give offence. But you'll admit that she isn't cut out for the high-class passenger trade."

"She is not," Captain Hartup agreed, "and that is what I pointed out to the young woman when she asked for a passage from Axim to Accra. I told her we had no accommodation for females, but she just giggled and said that didn't matter. She is a very self-willed young woman."

"But why didn't she take a passage on a steamer?"

"There was no steamer due for the Leeward Coast. Her father, Sir Hector, tried to put her off, but she would have her own way. Said it would be a bit of an adventure, travelling on a sailing ship."

"Gad! She was right there," remarked Osmond.

"She was, indeed. Well, she came aboard and Redford gave her his berth, he moving into the second mate's berth, as Dhoody remained in the forecastle. And there she is, and I wish she was at Jericho."

"I expect she does, too. What happened to her when the mutiny broke out?"

"I told her to go to her berth and lock herself in. But no one attempted to molest her."

"I am glad to hear that," said Osmond, and as he broke another biscuit, he asked, "Did you secure the companion-hatch?"

"Miss Burleigh did. She fixed the bar across the inside of the doors. But it wasn't necessary, for they had barricaded the doors outside. They didn't want to come down to us, they only wanted to prevent us from going up on deck."

"She was wise to bolt the doors, all the same," said Osmond, and for a time there was silence in the cabin, broken only by the vigorous mastication of stony biscuit.

Chapter IV
The Phantom Mate

W hen he had finished his rough and hasty meal, Osmond attended to his host's injuries, securing a pad of lint on the lacerated arm with strips cut from a broad roll of the sticky rubber plaster. Then he went out into the cabin to reconnoitre and take a drink of water, closing the door of the captain's berth so that the light should not be seen from above.

The hubbub on deck had now subsided into occasional snatches of indistinct melody. The men had had a pretty long bout and were – to judge by the tone of the songs – getting drowsy. Osmond climbed on to the table and began carefully to pick the remainder of the glass out of the skylight frame. The skylight had a fixed top – there being a separate ventilator for the cabin – and, instead of the usual guard-bars, had loose wood shutters for use in bad weather. Hence the present catastrophe, and hence, when Osmond had picked away the remains of the glass, there was a clear opening through which he could, by hoisting himself up, thrust out his head and shoulders. To avoid this fatiguing position, however, he descended and placed on the table a case that he had noticed by daylight on a side-locker, then, mounting, he was able, by standing on this, to look out at his ease, and yet pop down out of sight if necessary.

When he cautiously thrust out his head to look up and down the deck, he was able at first to see very little, though there was now a moderate starlight. Forward, whence drowsy mumblings mingled with snores came from the neighbourhood of the caboose, he could see only a projecting pair of feet, and aft, where a single voice carolled huskily intervals, his view was cut off by the boat – which lay at the side of the deck – and by the hood of the companion-hatch. He craned out farther, and now he could catch a glimpse of the man at the wheel. The fellow was not taking his duties very seriously, for he was seated on the grating unhandily filling his pipe and letting the ship steer herself, which she did well enough, if direction was of no consequence, the light breeze being a couple of points free and the main-sheet well slacked out. Osmond watched the man light his pipe, recognizing then the flat, shaven face – which he had punched earlier in the day – and as he watched he rapidly reviewed the strategic position and considered its possibilities. The flat, shaven face, with its wide mouth, offered a vague suggestion. He considered, looked out again, listened awhile, and then descended with a distinctly purposeful air. First he crept silently up the steps of the

69

companion and softly removed the bar from the inside of the doors. Then he made his way to the skipper's cabin.

As he entered, the "old man" looked up from his book inquiringly.

"I've come down for a bit of rubber plaster," said Osmond.

The skipper nodded towards the medicine-chest and resumed his studies, while Osmond cut off a strip of plaster some seven inches by four.

"You haven't got any thin rope or small-stuff in here, I suppose?" said Osmond.

"There's a coil of rope-yarn on the peg under those oilskins – those smart yellow ones. Those were poor Redford's. He was too much of a dandy to wear common black oilies like the rest of us. What do you want the stuff for?"

"I want to try a little experiment," replied Osmond. "But I'll tell you about it afterwards." And he took down the oilskins and the coil of line, the latter of which he carried away with him to the main cabin, together with the roll of plaster and the scissors. Here, by the faint starlight that now mitigated the darkness, he cut off a couple of lengths of the line and, having pocketed one and made a bowline-knot or fixed loop in the end of the other, ascended the table and once more looked out on deck. Save for some resonant snoring from forward, all was quiet and the ship seemed to have settled down for the night. The helmsman, however, was still awake, for Osmond heard him yawn wearily, but he had left the wheel with a rope hitched round one of the spokes, and was now leaning over the quarter-rail, apparently contemplating the passing water.

It was an ideal opportunity. Grasping the frame of the skylight, Osmond gave a light spring and came through the opening like a very stealthy harlequin. Then, creeping along the deck in the shelter of the boat and that of the companion-hood, he rose and stole noiselessly on the toes of his rubber-soled shoes towards the preoccupied seaman. Nearer and nearer he crept, grasping an end of the line between the fingers of either hand, and holding the strip of plaster spread out on the palm of the left, until he stood close behind his quarry. Then, as the sailor removed his pipe to emit another enormous yawn, he slipped his left hand round, clapped the plaster over the open mouth, and instantly pinioned the man's arms by clasping him tightly round the chest. The fellow struggled furiously and would have shouted, but was only able to utter muffled grunts and snorts through his nose. His arms were gripped to his sides as if in a vice and his efforts to kick were all foreseen and adroitly frustrated. He had been taken by surprise by a man who was his superior in mere strength and who was an expert wrestler into the bargain, and he was further handicapped by superstitious terror and lack of breath.

70

The struggle went on with surprisingly little noise – since the sailor could not cry out – and meanwhile Osmond contrived to pass the end of the line through the loop of the bowline and draw it inch by inch until it was ready for the final pull. Then, with a skilful throw, he let the man down softly, face downwards, on the deck, jerked the line tight and sat on his prisoner's legs. He was now master of the situation. Taking another turn with the line round the man's body, he secured it with a knot in the middle of the back, and with the other length of line, which he had in his pocket, he lashed his captive's ankles together.

The almost noiseless struggle had passed unnoticed by the sleepers forward. No watch or look-out had been set, and it had apparently been left to the helmsman to rouse up his relief when he guessed his "trick" at the wheel to have expired. Osmond listened for a few moments, and then, removing the batten with which the doors of the companion had been secured on the outside, opened the hatch, slid his helpless prisoner down the ladder, closed the doors again, replaced the batten, and, creeping through the opening of the sky light, let himself down into the cabin. Here he seized his writhing captive, and, dragging him across the cabin, thrust him head-first through the hole in the bulkhead and followed him into the hold, where he finally deposited him as comfortably as possible on the kernel bags under the main hatch.

"Now, listen," he said, sternly. "I'm going to take that plaster off your mouth, but if you utter a sound, I shall stick it on again and fix it with a lashing." He peeled the plaster off, and, as the man drew a long breath, he demanded, "Do you hear what I say?

"Yes," was the reply, "I hear. You've got me, governor, fair on the hop, you have. You won't hear no more of me. And if you can cop that there Dhoody the same way, there won't be no more trouble on this ship."

"I'll see what can be done," said Osmond, and with this he returned into the cabin and, cutting off two fresh lengths of rope-yarn and another piece of plaster, prepared for a fresh capture.

But, at present, there was no one to capture. The wheel jerked to and fro in its lashing, the brigantine walloped along quietly before the soft breeze, the crew slumbered peacefully forward, and Osmond looked out of the skylight on an empty deck, listening impatiently to the chorus of snores and wondering if he would get another chance.

It is impossible to say how long this state of affairs would have lasted if nothing had happened to disturb it. As it was, a sudden accident dispelled the universal repose. The unsteered vessel, yawing from side to side, lifted her stern to a following sea and yawed so far that her mainsail got by the lee. The long boom swung inboard and the big sail jibed over

71

with a slam that shook the entire fabric. The vessel immediately broached to with all her square-sails aback, and heeled over until the water bubbled up through her scupper holes.

The noise and the jar roused some of the sleepers forward and a hoarse voice bawled out angrily, "Now you, Sam! What the devil are you up to? You'll have the masts overboard if you don't look out."

Immediately after, Dhoody came staggering aft along the sloping deck, followed by one or two bewildered sailors. The group stood gazing in muddled surprise at the untended wheel, and Dhoody exclaimed, "Where's the beggar gone to? Here, you Sam! Where are you?"

"P'raps he's gone down to the cabin," one of the men suggested.

"No, he ain't," said Dhoody. "The companion's fastened up."

"So it is, mate," agreed the other with a glance at the battened doors, and the party rambled slowly round the poop, peering out into the darkness astern and speculating vaguely on the strange disappearance.

"He's gone overboard," said Dhoody, "that's what he's done. So you'd better take the wheel now, Bob Simmons, and you just mind yer helm, or you'll be goin' overboard, too, with all that lush in yer 'ed."

Accordingly Simmons, protesting sleepily that it "wasn't his trick yet", took his place at the wheel. The vessel was put once more on her course, and the men, with the exception of Dhoody, crawled forward to the shelter of the caboose. The second mate remained awhile, yawning drearily and impressing on the somnolent Simmons the responsibilities of his position. Then, at last, he too went forward, and the ship settled down to its former quiet.

Osmond waited for some time in case Dhoody should return to see that the new helmsman was attending to his instructions, but as he made no reappearance and was now probably asleep, it seemed safe to resume operations. Osmond thrust his head and shoulders out through the opening, but, though he could see that the wheel was already deserted, the unfaithful Simmons was invisible. Presently, however, a soft snore from somewhere close by invited him to further investigation, and as he crept out on deck, the enormity of Simmons's conduct was revealed. He had not sunk overpowered at his post, but had deliberately seated himself on the deck in a comfortable position with his back against the doors of the companion, where he now reclined at his ease, wrapped in alcoholic slumber. If only Dhoody would keep out of the way, the capture was as good as made.

Osmond stole up to the sleeping seaman and softly encircled his arms with the noose, leaving it slack with the end handy for the final pull. Then he put the man's feet together, and passing the lashing round the ankles, secured it firmly. This aroused the sleeper, who began to

72

mumble protests. Instantly, Osmond slapped the plaster on his mouth, jerked the arm-lashing tight and secured it with a knot, unbattened the doors, and, opening them, slid the wriggling captive down the ladder on to the cabin floor. Then he came up, closed and re-battened the doors, slipped down through the skylight, and, dragging his prisoner to the bulkhead, bundled him neck and crop through the opening and finally deposited him on the kernel-bags beside the other man, who was now slumbering peacefully. Having removed the plaster, he remained awhile, for Simmons was in no condition to give promises of good behaviour, but in a few minutes he gave what was more reassuring, a good healthy snore, on which Osmond departed, leaving him to sleep the sleep of the drunk.

The capture had been made none too soon. As Osmond came through into the cabin, he was aware of voices on deck, and, climbing on to the table, put his head up to listen, but keeping carefully out of sight.

"It's a damn rum go," a hoarse voice exclaimed. "Seems as if there was somethink queer about this bloomin' ship. First of all this factory devil comes aboard like a roarin' lion seekin' who he can bash on the 'ed, then Sam goes overboard, then Bob Simmons goes overboard. 'Tain't nateral, I tell yer. There's somethink queer, and it's my belief as it's all along o' this mutiny."

"Oh, shut up, Bill," growled Dhoody.

"Bill's right, though," said another voice. "We ain't 'ad no luck since we broke out. I'm for chuckin' this Ambriz job and lettin' the old man out."

"And what about Redford?" demanded Dhoody.

"Redford ain't no affair of mine," was the sulky reply, to which Dhoody rejoined in terms that cannot, in the interests of public morality, be literally recorded, concluding with the remark that "if he'd got to swing, it wouldn't be for Redford only".

"Then," said the first speaker, "you'd better take the wheel yerself. I ain't goin' to."

"More ain't I," said another. "I don't want to go overboard."

A prolonged wrangle ensued, the upshot of which was that the men drifted away forward, leaving Dhoody to steer the ship.

Osmond quietly renewed his preparations, though he realized that a considerably tougher encounter loomed ahead. Dhoody was not only less drunk than the others, he was a good deal more alert and intelligent and he probably had a revolver in his pocket. And the other men would now be more easily roused after this second catastrophe. He peeped out from time to time, always finding Dhoody wide awake at his post, and sensible of drowsy conversation from the sailors forward.

73

It was fully an hour before a chance seemed to present itself, and Osmond was too wary to attack blindly without a chance. By that time the mumblings from forward had subsided into snores and the ship was once more wrapped in repose. Looking out at that moment, he saw Dhoody staring critically aloft, as if dissatisfied with the trim of the sails. Presently the second mate stepped away from the wheel, and, casting off one of the lee braces, took a long pull at the rope. Now was the time for action. Slipping out through the skylight, Osmond stole quickly along in the shelter of the boat, and, emerging behind Dhoody, stood up just as the latter stooped to belay the rope. He waited until his quarry had set a half-hitch on the last turn and rose to go back to the wheel, then he sprang at him, clapped the plaster on his mouth, and encircled him with his arms.

But Dhoody was a tough adversary. He was stronger, more sober, and less nervous than the others. And he had a moustache, which interfered with the set of the plaster, so that his breathing was less hampered. In fact, Osmond had to clap his hand on it to prevent the man from calling out, and thus it was that the catastrophe befell. For as Osmond relaxed his bear-hug with one arm, Dhoody wriggled himself partly free. In a moment his hand flew to his pocket, and Osmond grabbed his wrist only just in time to prevent him from pointing the revolver. Then followed a struggle at the utmost tension of two strong men, a struggle, on Osmond's side, at least, for dear life. Gripping the other man's wrists, he watched the revolver, all his strength concentrated on the effort to prevent its muzzle from being turned on him. And so the two men stood for a space, nearly motionless, quite silent, trembling with the intensity of muscular strain.

Suddenly Dhoody took a quick step backwards. A fatal step, for the manoeuvre failed, and Osmond followed him up, pressing him farther backward. The bulwark on the poop was comparatively low. As Dhoody staggered against it with accumulated momentum, his body swung outboard and his feet rose from the deck. It was impossible to save him without releasing the pistol hand. He remained poised for an instant on the rail and then toppled over, and as he slithered down the side and his wrist slipped from Osmond's grasp, the revolver discharged, blowing a ragged hole in the bulwark and waking the echoes in the sails with the din of the explosion.

Osmond sprang back to the companion-hatch and crouched behind the hood. There was no time for him to get back to the skylight. Indeed, he hardly had time to unfasten the doors and drop on to the ladder before the men came shambling aft, muttering and rubbing their eyes. Quietly closing the doors, he descended to the cabin and took up his old post of observation on the table.

"He's gone, right enough," said an awe-stricken voice, "and I reckon it'll be our turn next. This is a bad look-out, mates."

There was a brief and dismal silence, then a distant report was heard, followed quickly by two more.

"That's Dhoody," exclaimed another voice. "He's a-swimmin' and makin' signals. What's to be done? We can't let 'im drownd without doin' nothin '."

"No," agreed the first man, "we must have a try at pickin' 'im up. You and me, Tom, will put off in the dinghy, while Joe keeps the ship hove-to."

"What!" protested Joe. "Am I to be left alone on the ship with no one but Jim Darker, and him below in his bunk?"

"Well, yer can't let a shipmate drownd, can yer?" demanded the other. "And look here, Joe Bradley, as soon as you've got the ship hove-to, you just fetch up the fo'c'sle lamp and show us a glim, or we shall be goners, too. Now hard down with the helm, mate!"

Very soon the loud flapping of canvas announced that the ship had come up into the wind, and immediately after the squeal of tackle-blocks was heard. The *Speedwell* carried a dinghy, slung from davits at the taffrail, in addition to the larger boat on deck, and it was in this that the two men were putting out on their rather hopeless quest.

Osmond rapidly reviewed the situation. Of the original seven men one was overboard, two were in the hold, one was below in his bunk, and two were away in the boat. There remained only Joe Bradley. It would be pretty easy to overpower him and stow him in the hold, but a yet easier plan suggested itself. Joe was evidently in a state of extreme superstitious funk and the other two were in little better case. He recalled the captain's remark as to his resemblance to the dead mate and also the fact that Redford's oilskins were different from any others on board. These circumstances seemed to group themselves naturally and indicate a course of action.

He made his way to the captain's berth and, knocking softly and receiving no answer, entered. The skipper had fallen asleep over his book and lay in his bunk, a living commentary on the Book of Job. Osmond took the oilskins from the peg, and, stealing back silently to the cabin, invested himself in the borrowed raiment. Presently a passing gleam of light from above told him that Joe was carrying the forecastle lamp aft to "show a glim" from the taffrail. Remembering that he had left the companion hatch unfastened, he ascended the ladder, and, softly opening one door, looked out. At the moment, Joe was engaged in hanging the

75

lamp from a fair-lead over the stern, and, as his back was towards the deck, Osmond stepped out of the hatch and silently approached him.

Having secured the lamp, Joe took a long look over the dark sea and then turned towards the deck, and as his eyes fell on the tall, oilskinned figure, obscurely visible in the gloom – for the lamp was below the bulwark – he uttered a gasp of horror and began rapidly to shuffle away backwards. Osmond stood motionless, watching him from under the deep shade of his sou'wester as he continued to edge away backwards. Suddenly his heel caught on a ring-bolt and he staggered and fell on the deck with a howl of terror, but in another instant he had scrambled to his feet and raced away forward, whence the slam of the forecastle scuttle announced his retirement to the sanctuary of his berth.

More than a quarter-of-an-hour elapsed before a hoarse hail from the sea heralded the return of the boat.

"Joe ahoy! It's no go, mate. He's gone." There was a pause. Then came the splash of oars, a bump under the counter, the sound of the hooking on of tackles, and another hail.

"Joe ahoy! Is all well aboard?"

Osmond stepped away into the shadow of the main sail, whence he watched the taffrail. Soon the two men came actively up the tackle-ropes, their heads appeared above the rail, and they swung themselves on board simultaneously.

"Joe ahoy!" one of them sang out huskily, as he looked blankly round the deck. "Where are yer, Joe?" There was a brief silence, then, in an awe-stricken voice, he exclaimed, "Gawd-amighty, Tom! If he ain't gone overboard, too!"

At this moment the other man caught sight of Osmond, and, silently touching his companion on the shoulder, pointed to the motionless figure. Osmond moved a little out of the shadow and began to pace aft, treading without a sound. For one instant the two men watched as if petrified, then, with one accord, they stampeded forward, and once more the forecastle scuttle slammed. Osmond followed, and quietly thrusting a belaying-pin through the staple of the scuttle, secured them in their retreat.

Chapter V
The New Afterguard

When Captain Hartup, brusquely aroused from his slumbers, opened his eyes and beheld a tall, yellow oilskinned figure in his berth, the Book of Job faded instantly from his memory and he scrambled from his bunk with a yell of terror. Then, when Osmond took off his sou'wester, he recognized his visitor and became distinctly uncivil.

"What the devil do you mean by masquerading in this idiotic fashion?" he demanded angrily. "I don't want any of your silly schoolboy jokes on this ship, so you please understand that."

"I came down," said Osmond, smothering a grin and ignoring the reproaches, "to report progress. I have hove the ship to, but there is no one at the wheel and no look-out."

The skipper stared at him in bewilderment as he crawled back into his bunk. "What do you mean?" he asked. "You've hove the ship to? Isn't there anybody on deck?"

"No. The ship is taking care of herself at the moment."

"Queer," said the skipper. "I wonder what Dhoody's up to."

"Dhoody is overboard," said Osmond.

"Overboard!" exclaimed the skipper, staring harder than ever at Osmond. Then, after an interval of silent astonishment, he said severely, "You are talking in riddles, young man. Just try to explain yourself a little more clearly. Do I understand that you have hove my second mate overboard?"

"No," replied Osmond. "He went overboard by accident. But it was all for the best." And hereupon he proceeded to give the skipper a somewhat sketchy account of the stirring events of the last few hours, to which the latter listened with sour disapproval.

"I don't hold with deeds of violence," he said when the story was finished, "but what you have done is on your own head. Where do you say the crew are?"

"Two are in the hold and the other four in the fo'c'sle, bolted in. They are all pretty drunk, but you'll find them as quiet as lambs when they've slept off their tipple. But the question is, what is to be done now. The men won't be any good for an hour or two, but there ought to be someone at the wheel and some sort of watch on deck. And I can't take it on until I have had a sleep. I've been hard at it ever since I came on board yesterday."

77

"Yes," Captain Hartup agreed, sarcastically, "I daresay you found it fatiguing, chucking your fellow-creatures overboard and breaking their heads. Well, you had better take the second mate's berth – the one Redford had – and I will go on deck and keep a look out. But I can't do much with my arm in a sling."

"What about the lady?" asked Osmond. "Couldn't she hold on to the wheel if you stood by and told her what to do?"

"Ha!" exclaimed the skipper. "I had forgotten her. Yes, she knows how to steer – in a fashion. She used to wheedle Redford into letting her take a trick in his watch while he stood by and instructed her, a parcel of silly philandering, really, but it wasn't any affair of mine. I'd better go and rouse her up."

"Wait till I've turned in," said Osmond. "I am not fit to meet a lady until I have had a sleep and a wash. If you will show me my berth, I will go and cast the lashings off those two beggars in the hold and then turn in for an hour or two."

The captain smiled sardonically but made no comment, and when Osmond, furnished with a lantern, had visited the hold and removed the lashings from the still slumbering seamen, he entered the tiny berth that the skipper pointed out to him, closed the door and, having taken off his jacket and folded it carefully, and wound his watch, blew out the candle in the lantern, stretched himself in the bunk, and instantly fell asleep.

When he awoke, the gleam from the deck-light over his head – the berth had no port-hole – informed him that it was day. Reference to his watch showed the hour to be about half-past eight, and the clink of crockery and a murmur of voices – one very distinctly feminine – suggested that breakfast was in progress.

Which, again, suggested that the conditions of life on board had returned to the more-or-less normal.

Osmond sprang out of the bunk and, impelled by hunger and curiosity, made a lightning toilet with the aid of Redford's razor, sponge, and brushes. There was, of course, no bath, but a 'dry' rub-down in the oven-like cabin was a fair substitute. In a surprisingly short time, with the imperfect means at hand, he had made himself almost incredibly presentable and after a final "look over" in Redford's minute shaving-glass, he opened the door and entered the cuddy.

The little table, roughly laid for breakfast, was occupied by Captain Hartup and a lady, and a flat-faced seaman with a black eye officiated as cabin steward. They all looked up as Osmond emerged from his door and the sailor grinned a little sheepishly.

"Had a short night, haven't you?" said the captain. "Didn't expect you to turn out yet. Let me present you to our passenger. Miss Burleigh, this is Mr. – Mr. – "

"Cook," said Osmond, ready for the question this time.

"Mr. Cook, the young man I was telling you about."

Miss Burleigh acknowledged Osmond's bow, gazing at him with devouring curiosity and marvelling at his cool, trim, well appearance.

"I think," she said, "we had a brief interview last night, if you can call it an interview when there was a locked door between us. I am afraid I wasn't very civil. But you must try to forgive me. I've been sorry since."

"There is no need to be," replied Osmond. "It was perfectly natural."

"Oh, but it isn't mere remorse. I am so mad with myself for having missed all the excitements. If I had only known! But, you see, I had happened to look out of my door in the evening, hearing a peculiar sort of noise, and then I saw somebody boring holes in the partition, and of course I thought it was those wretches trying to get into the cabin. Then, when I heard your voice, I made sure it was Dhoody or one of those other ruffians, trying to entice me out. And so I missed all the fun."

"Just as well that you did," said the captain. "Females are out of place in scenes of violence and disorder. What are you going to have, Mr. Cook? There's corned pork and biscuit and I think there's some lobscouse or sea-pie in the galley, if the men haven't eaten it all."

Osmond turned suddenly to the sailor, who instantly came to "attention".

"You're Sam Winter, aren't you?"

"Aye, sir," the man replied, considerably taken aback by the 'factory bug's' uncanny omniscience. "Sam Winter it is, sir."

"How is Jim Darker?"

"He's a-doin' nicely, sir," replied Sam, regarding Osmond with secret awe. "Eat a rare breakfast of lobscouse, he did."

"Is there any left?"

"I think there is, sir."

"Then I'll have some," and, as the man saluted and bustled away up the companion-steps, he seated himself on the fixed bench by the table.

Captain Hartup smiled sourly, while Miss Burleigh regarded Osmond with delighted amusement.

"Seem quite intimate with 'em all," the former remarked. "Regular friend of the family. I suppose it was you who gave Winter that black eye?"

"I expect so," replied Osmond. "He probably caught it in the scrum when I first came on board. Did you have any trouble in getting the men to go back to duty?"

"The men in the fo'c'sle wouldn't come out till daylight, and the two men in the hold took a lot of rousing from their drunken sleep. Of course, I couldn't get through that hole with my arm in this sling, so I had to prod them with a boat-hook. It's a pity you made that hole. Lets the smell of the cargo and the bilge through into the cabin."

He looked distastefully at the dark aperture in the bulkhead and sniffed – quite unnecessarily, for the air of the cuddy was charged with the mingled aroma of bilge and kernels.

"Well, it had to be," said Osmond, "and it will be easy to cover it up. After all, a smell in the cuddy is better than sea-water."

Here Sam Winter was seen unsteadily descending the companion-steps with a large enamelled-iron plate in his hands, which plate, being deferentially placed on the table before Osmond, was seen to be loaded with a repulsive-looking mixture of "salt horse", shreds of fat pork, and soaked biscuit floating in a greasy brown liquid.

"That's all there was left, sir," said he, transferring a small surplus from his hands to the dorsal aspect of his trousers.

Osmond made no comment on this statement but fell-to on the unsavoury mess with wolfish voracity, while the captain filled a mug with alleged coffee and passed it to him.

"Who is at the wheel, Winter?" the captain asked.

"Simmons, sir," was the reply. "I woke him up again as I come aft."

"Well, you'd better go up and take it from him. Carry on till I come up."

As Winter disappeared up the companionway Miss Burleigh uttered a little gurgle of enjoyment. "Aren't they funny?" she exclaimed. "Fancy waking up the man at the wheel! It's like a comic opera."

The captain looked at her sourly as he tapped the table with a piece of biscuit for the purpose of evicting a couple of fat weevils, but he made no comment, and for a time the meal proceeded in silence. The skipper was fully occupied with cutting up his corned pork with one hand and in breaking the hard biscuit and knocking out the weevils, while Osmond doggedly worked his way through the lobscouse with the silent concentration of a famished man, all unconscious of the interest and curiosity with which he was being observed by the girl opposite him.

However, the lobscouse came to an end – all too soon – and as he reached out to the bread-barge for a handful of biscuit he met her eyes, and fine, clear, bright blue eyes they were, sparkling with vivacity and humour. She greeted his glance with an affable smile and hoped that he was feeling revived.

"That looked rather awful stuff," she added.

"It was all right," said he, "only there wasn't enough of it. But I hope you had something more suitable."

"She has had what the ship's stores provide, like the rest of us," snapped the captain. "This is not a floating hotel."

"No, it isn't," Osmond agreed, "and that's a fact. But it is something that she still floats, and it would be just as well to keep her floating."

"What do you mean?" demanded the skipper.

Osmond thoughtfully extracted a weevil with the prong of his fork as he replied, "You've got a crew of six, three to a watch, and one of them has got to do the cooking. But you have got no officers."

"Well, I know that," said the captain. "What about it?"

"You can't carry on without officers."

"I can and I shall. I shall appoint one of the men to be mate and take the other watch myself."

"That won't answer," said Osmond. "There isn't a man among them who could be trusted or who is up to the job, and you are not in a fit state to stand regular watches."

Captain Hartup snorted. "Don't you lay down the law to me, young man. I am the master of this ship." And then he added, a little inconsistently "Perhaps you can tell me how I am to get a couple of officers."

"I can," replied Osmond. "There will have to be some responsible person on deck with each watch."

"Well?

"Well, there are two responsible persons sitting at this table with you."

For a few moments the captain stared at Osmond in speechless astonishment (while Miss Burleigh murmured "Hear, hear!" and rapped the table with the handle of her knife). At length he burst out, "What! Do I understand you to suggest that I should navigate this vessel with a landsman and a female as my mates?"

"I am not exactly a landsman," Osmond replied. "I am an experienced yachtsman and I have made a voyage in a sailing ship."

"Pah!" exclaimed the skipper. "Fresh-water sailor and a passenger! Don't talk nonsense. And a female, too!"

"What I am suggesting," Osmond persisted calmly, "is that you should be about as much as is possible in your condition and that Miss Burleigh and I should keep an eye on the men when you are below. I

81

could take all the night watches and Miss Burleigh could be on deck during the day."

"That's just rank foolishness," said the skipper. "Talk of a comic opera! Why, you are wanting to turn the ship into a Punch and Judy show! I've no patience to listen to you." And the captain rose in dudgeon and crawled – not without difficulty – up the companion-steps. Miss Burleigh watched him with a mischievous smile, and as his stumbling feet disappeared she turned to Osmond.

"What a lark it would be!" she exclaimed, gleefully. "Do you think you will be able to persuade him? He is rather an obstinate little man."

"The best way with obstinate people," replied Osmond, "is to assume that they have agreed, and carry on. Can you steer – not that you need, being an officer. But you ought to know how to."

"I can steer by the compass. But I don't know much about the sails excepting that you have to keep the wind on the right side of them."

"Yes, that is important with a square vessel. But you will soon learn the essentials – enough to enable you to keep the crew out of mischief. We will go on deck presently and then I will show you the ropes and explain how the gear works."

"That will be jolly," said she. "But there's another thing that I want you to explain: About this mutiny, you know. Captain Hartup was awfully muddled about it. I want to know all that happened while I was locked in my berth."

"I expect you know all about it now," Osmond replied evasively. "There was a bit of a rumpus, of course, but as soon as Dhoody was overboard it was all plain sailing."

"Now, you are not going to put me off like that," she said, in a resolute tone. "I want the whole story in detail, if you please, sir. Does a second mate say 'sir' when he, or she, addresses the first mate?"

"Not as a rule," Osmond replied, with a grin.

"Then I won't. But I want the story. Now." Osmond looked uneasily into the delicately fair, slightly freckled face and thought it, with its crown of red-gold hair, the prettiest face that he had ever seen. But it was an uncommonly determined little face, all the same.

"There really isn't any story," he began.

But she interrupted sharply, "Now listen to me. Yesterday there were seven ferocious men going about this ship like roaring and swearing lions. To-day there are six meek and rather sleepy lambs – I saw them just before breakfast. It is you who have produced this miraculous change, and I want to know how you did it. No sketchy evasions, you know. I want a clear, intelligible narrative."

"It isn't a very suitable occasion for a long yarn," he objected. "Don't you think we ought to go on deck and keep an eye on the old man?"

"Perhaps we ought," she agreed. "But I'm not going to let you off the story, you know. That is understood, isn't it?"

He gave a reluctant assent, and when she had fetched her pith helmet from her cabin and he had borrowed a Panama hat of Redford's, they ascended together to the deck.

The scene was reminiscent of "The Ancient Mariner". The blazing sun shone down on a sea that seemed to be composed of oil, so smooth and unruffled was its surface. The air was absolutely still, and the old brigantine wallowed foolishly as the great, glassy rollers swept under her, her sails alternately filling and backing with loud, explosive flaps as the masts swung from side to side, and her long main-boom banging across with a heavy jar at each roll. Sam Winter stood at the wheel in a posture of easy negligence (but he straightened up with a jerk as Osmond's head rose out of the companion-hood). The rest of the crew, excepting Jim Darker, lounged about drowsily forward, and the skipper appeared to be doing sentry-go before a row of green gin-cases that were ranged along the side of the caboose. He looked round as the new-comers arrived on deck, and pointing to the cases, addressed Osmond.

"These boxes of poison belong to you, I understand. I can't have them lying about here."

"Better stow them in the lazarette when I've checked the contents," replied Osmond.

"I can't have intoxicating liquors in my lazarette. This is a temperance ship. I've a good mind to chuck 'em overboard."

"All right," said Osmond. "You pay me one pound four, and then you can do what you like with them."

"Pay!" shrieked the captain. "I pay for this devil's elixir! I traffic in strong drink that steals away men's reason and turns them into fiends! Never! Not a farthing!"

"Very well," said Osmond, "then they had better go below. Here, you, Simmons and Bradley, bear a hand with those cases. Will you see them stowed away in the lazarette, Miss Burleigh?"

"Aye, aye, sir," the latter replied, touching her helmet smartly, whereupon the two men, with delighted grins, pounced upon two of the cases, while Miss Burleigh edged up close to Osmond.

"What on earth is the lazarette?" she whispered, "and where shall I find it?"

"Under the cuddy floor," he whispered in reply. "The trap is under the table."

83

As the two seamen picked up their respective loads and went off beaming, followed by Miss Burleigh, the captain stood gazing open-mouthed. "Well, I'm – I'm – sure!" he exclaimed, at length. "What do you mean by giving orders to my crew? And I said I wouldn't have that gin in my lazarette."

"Can't leave it about for the men to pinch. You'll have them all drunk again. And what about the watches? We can't have the regular port and starboard watches until you are fit again. Better do as I suggested. Let me keep on deck during the night, and you take charge during the day. Miss Burleigh can relieve you if you want to go below."

"I'll have no women playing the fool on my ship," snapped the skipper, "but as to you, I don't mind your staying on deck at night if you undertake to call me up when you get into a mess – as you certainly will."

"Very well," said Osmond, "we'll leave it at that. And now you'd better come below and let me attend to your bandages. There's nothing to do on deck while this calm lasts."

The skipper complied, not unwillingly, and when Osmond had very gently and skilfully renewed the dressings and rebandaged the injured arm and head – the captain reclining in his bunk for the purpose – he retired, leaving his patient to rest awhile with the aid of the *Commentary on The Book of Job*.

As soon as he arrived on deck, he proceeded definitely to take charge. The stowage of the gin was now completed and the crew were once more collected forward, gossiping idly but evidently watchful and expectant of further developments from the "after-guard". Osmond hailed them in a masterful tone. "Here, you men, get a pull on the main-sheet and stop the boom from slamming. Haul her in as taut as she'll go."

The men came aft with ready cheerfulness, and as Osmond cast off the fall of the rope and gave them a lead, they tailed on and hauled with a will until the sheet-blocks were as close as they could be brought. Then, when the rope had been belayed, Osmond turned to the crew and briefly explained the arrangements for working the ship in her present, short-handed state.

"So you understand," he concluded, "I am the mate for the time being, and Miss Burleigh is taking the duties of the second mate. Is that clear?"

"Aye, aye, sir," was the reply, accompanied by the broadest of grins. "We understands, sir."

"Who is the cook?" inquired Osmond.

"Bill Foat 'as been a-doin' the cookin', sir," Simmons explained.

"Then he'd better get on with it. Whose watch on deck is it?"

"Starboard watch, sir," replied Simmons, "that's me and Winter and Darker."

"I must have a look at Darker," said Osmond. "Meanwhile you take the wheel, and you, Winter, keep a look-out forward. I haven't heard the ship's bell sounded this morning."

"No, sir," Winter explained. "The clock in the companion has stopped and none of us haven't got the time."

"Very well," said Osmond. "I'll wind it up and start it when I make eight bells."

The routine of the duties being thus set going, Osmond went forward and paid a visit to the invalid in the forecastle, with the result that Jim Darker presently appeared on deck with a clean bandage and a somewhat sheepish grin. Then the chief officer turned his attention to the education of his subordinate, observed intently by six pairs of inquisitive eyes.

"I think, Miss Burleigh," he said, "you had better begin by learning how to take an observation. Then you will be able to do something that the men can't, as an officer should. Do you know anything about mathematics?"

"As much as is necessary, I expect. I took second class honours in maths. Will that do?"

"Of course it will. By the way, where did you take your degree?"

"Oxford – Somerville, you know."

"Oh," said Osmond, rather taken aback. "When were you up at Oxford?"

She regarded him with a mischievous smile as she replied, "After your time, I should say. I only came down a year ago."

It was, of course, but a chance shot. Nevertheless, Osmond hastily reverted to the subject of observations. "It is quite a simple matter to take the altitude of the sun, and you work out your results almost entirely from tables. You will do it easily the first time. I'll go and get Redford's sextant – or better still, we might go below and I can show you how to use a sextant and how to work out your latitude."

"Yes," she agreed eagerly, "I would sooner have my first lesson below. Our friends here are so very interested in us."

She bustled away down to the cabin, and Osmond, following, went into his berth, whence he presently emerged with two mahogany cases and a portly volume, inscribed *Norie's Navigation*.

"I've found the second mate's sextant as well as Redford's, so we can have one each," he said, laying them on the table with the volume. "And now let us get to work. We mustn't stay here too long or we shall miss the transit."

The two mates seated themselves side by side at the table, and Osmond, taking one of the sextants out of its case, explained its construction and demonstrated its use. Then the volume was opened, the tables explained, the mysteries of "dip" refraction and "parallax" expounded, and finally an imaginary observation was worked out on the back of an envelope.

"I had no idea," said Miss Burleigh, as she triumphantly finished the calculation, "that the science of navigation was so simple."

"It isn't," replied Osmond. "Latitude by the meridian altitude of the sun is the A B C of navigation. Some of it, such as longitude by lunar distance, is fairly tough. But it is time we got on deck. It is past eleven by my watch and the Lord knows what the time actually is. The chronometer has stopped. The skipper bumped against it when he staggered into his berth on the day when the mutiny broke out."

"Then how shall we get the longitude?" Miss Burleigh asked.

"We shan't. But it doesn't matter much. We must keep on a westerly course. There is nothing, in that direction, between us and America."

The appearance on deck of the two officers, each armed with a sextant, created a profound impression. It is true that, so far as the "second mate" was concerned, the attitude of the crew was merely that of respectful amusement. But the effect, in the case of Osmond, was very different. The evidence that he was able to "shoot the sun" established him in their eyes as a pukka navigator, and added to the awe with which they regarded this uncannily capable "factory bug". And there was plenty of time for the impression to soak in, for the first glance through the sextant showed that the sun was still rising fairly fast, that there was yet some considerable time to run before noon. In fact, more than half-an-hour passed before the retardation of the sun's motion heralded the critical phase. And at this moment the skipper's head rose slowly above the hood of the companion-hatch.

At first his back was towards the observers, but when he emerged and, turning forward, became aware of them, he stopped short as if petrified. The men ceased their gossip to watch him with ecstatic grins, and Sam Winter edged stealthily towards the ship's bell.

"What is the meaning of this play-acting and tom foolery?" the skipper demanded, sourly. "Women and landsmen monkeying about with nautical instruments."

Osmond held up an admonitory hand, keeping his eye glued to the eyepiece of the sextant.

"I'm asking you a question," the captain persisted.

There was another brief silence. Then, suddenly, Osmond sang out "Eight bells!" and looked at his watch. Winter, seizing the lanyard that hung from the clapper of the bell, struck the eight strokes, and the second mate – prompted in a hoarse whisper – called out, "Port watch, there! Bradley will take the first trick at the wheel."

"Aye, aye, sir – Miss, I mean," responded Bradley, and proceeded purple-faced and chuckling aloud, to relieve the gratified Simmons.

At these proceedings the captain looked on in helpless bewilderment. He watched Osmond wind and set the clock in the companion and saw him disappear below, followed by his accomplice, to work out the reckoning, and shook his head with mute disapproval. But yet to him, as to the rest of the ship's company, there came a certain sense of relief. Osmond's brisk, confident voice, the cheerful sound of the ship's bell, and the orderly setting of the watch, seemed definitely to mark the end of the mutiny and the return to a reign of law and order.

Chapter VI
Betty Makes a Discovery

For reasons best known to herself, Miss Burleigh made no further attempt that day to satisfy her curiosity as to the quelling of the mutiny. There was, in fact, little opportunity. For shortly after the mid-day meal – sea-pie and corned pork with biscuit – Osmond turned in regardless of the heat, to get a few hours' sleep before beginning his long night vigil. But on the following day the captain was so far recovered as to be able to take the alternate watches – relieved to some extent in the daytime by the second mate – and this left ample time for Osmond to continue the education of his junior, which now extended from theoretical navigation to practical seamanship.

It was during the afternoon watch, when the two mates were seated on a couple of spare cases in the shadow of the main-sail, practising the working of splices on some oddments of rope, that the "examination-in-chief" began, and Osmond, recognizing the hopelessness of further evasion, was fain to tell the story of his adventure – dryly enough, indeed, but in fairly satisfying detail. And as he narrated, in jerky, colourless sentences, with his eyes riveted on the splice that he was working, his spellbound listener let her rope's-end and marlinspike lie idle on her lap while she watched his impassive face with something more than mere attention.

"I wonder," she said when the tale was told, "whether the men realize who the spectre mate really was."

"I don't think they can quite make out what happened. But I fancy they look upon me as something rather uncanny, which is all for the best, seeing how short we are and what a helpless worm the skipper is."

"Yes, they certainly have a holy fear of you," she agreed, smiling at the grim, preoccupied face. She reflected awhile and then continued, "But I don't quite understand what brought you on board. You say that Dhoody had stolen those cases of gin. But what business was that of yours?"

"It was my gin."

"Your gin? But you don't drink gin."

"No, I sell it. I am a trader. I run a store, or factory, as they call it out here."

As Osmond made this statement, her look of undisguised admiration changed to one of amazement. She smothered an exclamation and managed to convert it at short notice into an unconcerned, "I see", but her astonishment extinguished her powers of conversation for the time being. She could only gaze at him and marvel at the incongruity of his personality with his vocation. She had encountered a good many traders, and though she had realized that the "palm-oil ruffian" was largely the invention of the missionary and the official snob and that West African traders are a singularly heterogeneous body, still that body did not ordinarily include men of Osmond's class. And her sly suggestion of his connection with Oxford had been something more than a mere random shot. There are certain little tricks of speech and manner by which members of the ancient universities can usually be recognized, especially by their contemporaries and though Osmond was entirely free from the deliberate affectations of a certain type of "varsity" man, her quick ear had detected one or two turns of phrase that seemed familiar. And he had not repudiated the suggestion.

"I wonder," she said, after an interval of somewhat uncomfortable silence, "what made you take to trading. The *métier* doesn't seem to fit you very well."

"No," he admitted with a grim smile, "I am a bit of a mug at a business deal."

"I didn't mean that," she rejoined hastily. "But there are such a lot of things that would suit you better. It is a sin for a man of your class and attainments to be keeping a shop – for that is what it amounts to."

"That is what it actually is," said he.

"Yes. But why on earth do you do it?"

"Must do something, you know," he replied, lamely.

"Of course you must, but it should be something suitable, and selling gin is not a suitable occupation for a gentleman. And it isn't as if you were a 'lost dog'. You are really extremely capable."

"Yes," he admitted with a grin, "I'm pretty handy in a scrum."

"Don't be silly," she admonished, severely. "I don't undervalue your courage and strength – I shouldn't be a natural woman if I did – but I am thinking of your resourcefulness and ingenuity. It wasn't by mere thumping that you got your ascendancy over the men. You beat them by sheer brains."

"Jim Darker thinks it was an iron belaying-pin."

"Now don't quibble and prevaricate. You know as well as I do that, if it had been a matter of mere strength and courage, you would never have got out of the hold, and we should have been at the bottom of the sea by now. It was your mental alertness that saved us all."

"I'm glad to hear it," said Osmond. "But you aren't getting on very fast with that splice. Have you been watching me?"

89

"Oh! Bother the splices!" she exclaimed, impatiently. "I want you to tell me why you are throwing yourself away on this ridiculous factory."

"It isn't a bad sort of life," he protested. "I don't think I mind it."

"Then you ought to," she retorted. "You ought to have some ambition. Think of all the things that you might have done – that you still might do with – your abilities and initiative."

She looked at him earnestly as she spoke, and something that she saw in his face as she uttered those last words gave her pause. Suddenly it was borne in on her that she had met other men who seemed to be out of their element, men who, report whispered, had been driven by social misadventure – by debt, entanglements, or drink – to seek sanctuary on the remote West Coast. Was it possible that he might be one of these refugees? He was obviously not a drinker, and he did not look like a wastrel of any kind. Still, there might be a skeleton in his cupboard. At any rate, he was extraordinarily reticent about himself.

She changed the subject rather abruptly. "Is your factory in the British Protectorate?"

"Yes. At Adaffia, a little, out-of-the-way place about a dozen miles east of Quittah."

"I know it – at least I have heard of it. Isn't it the place where that poor fellow Osmond died?"

"Yes," he replied, a little startled by the question.

"What was he like? I suppose you saw him?"

"Yes. A biggish man. Short moustache and Vandyke beard."

"Quite a gentlemanly man, wasn't he?"

"He seemed to be. But he didn't have a great deal to say to anybody."

"It was rather pathetic, his dying in that way, like a hunted ox that has run into a trap."

"Well," said Osmond, "there wasn't much to choose. If the climate hadn't had him, the police would."

"I am not so sure," she replied. "We all hoped he would get away, especially the officer who was detailed to arrest him. I think he meant to make a fussy search of all the wrong houses in the village by way of giving notice that he was there and scaring the fugitive away. Still, I think he was rather relieved when he found that trader man – what was his name? – Larkin or Larkom? – painting the poor fellow's name on the cross above his grave. You heard about that, I suppose?"

"Yes. Queer coincidence, wasn't it?"

"Don't be so callous. I think it was a most pathetic incident."

"I suppose it was," Osmond agreed. "And now, don't you think you had better have another try at that splice?"

90

With a little grimace she took up the piece of rope and began obediently to unlay its ends and the interrupted course of practical seamanship was resumed, with intervals of desultory conversation, until eight bells, when the teapot was brought forth from the galley and conveyed below to the cabin. After tea, through what was left of the first dog-watch, there was another spell of knots and splices, and then, when the sun set and darkness fell on the sea, more desultory talk, in which Osmond mostly played the role of listener, which – with an interval for dinner – lasted until it was time for the second mate to turn in.

So life went on aboard the *Speedwell* day after day.

The calm persisted as calms are apt to do in the Doldrums, with nothing to suggest any promise of a change. Now and again, at long intervals, the oily surface of the sea would be dimmed by a little draught of air – just enough to 'put the sails asleep' and give momentary life to the steering-wheel. But in a few minutes it would die away, leaving the sails to back and fill as the vessel rolled inertly on the glassy swell. The first observation had shown the ship's position to be about four degrees north of the equator, with the coast of the Bight of Benin some eighty miles away to the north, and subsequent observations revealed a slow southerly drift. It was pretty certain that she had a more rapid easterly drift on the Guinea current, but as the chronometer was out of action, there was no means of ascertaining this or of determining her longitude. Sooner or later, if the calm continued, she would drift into the Bight of Biafra, where she might pick up the land and sea breezes or find an anchorage where she could bring up and get the chronometer rated.

To a seaman there is nothing more exasperating than a prolonged calm. The crew of the *Speedwell* were not sailors of a strenuous type, but the inaction and monotony that prevailed on the idly ship bored them – if not to tears, at least to bad language and chronic grumbling. They lounged about with sulky looks and yawned over the odd jobs that Osmond found for them, whistling vainly for a breeze and crawling up the rigging from time to time to see if anything – land or another ship – was in sight. As to the captain, he grew daily more sour and taciturn as he saw his stores of provisions dwindling with nothing to show for the expenditure.

But by two of the ship's company the calm was accepted with something more than resignation. The two mates had no complaint whatever to make. They were, indeed, cut off from all the world, marooned on a stationary ship in an unfrequented sea. But they had one another and asked for nothing better, and the longer the calm lasted the more secure were they of the continuance of this happy condition. For the inevitable thing had happened. They had fallen in love.

It was very natural. Both were more than commonly attractive, and circumstances had thrown them together in the closest and most intimate companionship through every hour of the long days. They had worked together, though the work was more than half play, they had a common interest which kept them apart from the others. Together they had sat, talking endlessly, in little patches of shadow when the sun was high in the heavens, or leaned upon the bulwark rail and watched the porpoises playing round the idle ship or the Portuguese men-of-war gliding imperceptibly past on their rainbow-tinted floats. They had paced the heaving deck together when the daylight was gone and earnestly studied the constellations "that blazed in the velvet blue", or peered down into the dark water alongside where the Nautilus shone like submarine stars and shoals of fish darted away before the pursuing dolphin with lurid flashes of phosphorescent light. No more perfect setting for a romance could be imagined.

And then the personality of each was such as to make a special appeal to the other. In the eyes of the girl, Osmond was a hero, a paladin. His commanding stature, his strength, his mastery of other men, and above all his indomitable courage, had captured her imagination from the first. And in his rugged way he was a handsome man, and if he could be a little brutal on occasion, he had always been, to her, the soul of courtesy and chivalry. As to the "past" of which she had a strong suspicion, that was no concern of hers. Perhaps it even invested him with an added interest.

As to Osmond, he had been captivated at once and, to do him justice, he had instantly perceived the danger that loomed ahead. But he could do nothing to avoid it. Flight was impossible from this little self-contained world, so pleasantly cut off from the unfriendly world without. Nor could he, even if he had tried, help being thrown constantly into the society of this fascinating little lady. And if, during the long, solitary night-watches, or in his stifling berth, he gnashed his teeth over the perverseness of Fate and thought bitterly of what might have been, that did not prevent him from succumbing during the day to the charm of her frank, unconcealed friendliness.

It was in the forenoon of the eighth day of the calm that the two cronies were leaning on the rail, each holding a stout line. The previous day, Osmond had discovered a quantity of fishing tackle among Redford's effects, and a trial cast had provided not only excellent sport, but a very welcome addition to the ship's meagre diet. Thereupon an epidemic of sea-angling had broken out on board, and Bill Foat, the cook, had been kept busy with the preparation of snappers, horse, and other deep-sea fish.

"I wonder," the girl mused as she peered over the side, "how much longer this calm is going to last."

"It may last for weeks," Osmond replied. "I hope it won't for your sake. You must be getting frightfully bored."

"Indeed, I'm not," she rejoined. "It is the jolliest holiday I have ever had. The only fly in the ointment is the fear that my father may be a little anxious about me. But I don't suppose he is really worrying. He is like me – not much given to fussing and he knows that I am fairly well able to take care of myself, though he doesn't know that I have got a Captain James Cook to stand by me. But I expect you are getting pretty sick of this monotonous life, aren't you, Captain J.?"

Osmond shook his head. "Not a bit," he replied. "It has been a delightful interlude for me. I should be perfectly satisfied for it to go on for the rest of my life."

She looked at him thoughtfully, speculating on the inward meaning of this statement and noting a certain grave wistfulness that softened the grim face.

"That sounds rather as if Adaffia were not a perfect Paradise, for it has been a dull life for you since the mutiny collapsed and the calm set in, with no one to talk to but me."

"Adaffia would be all right under the same conditions," said he.

"What do you mean by the same conditions?" she asked, flushing slightly, and as he did not immediately answer, she continued, "Do you mean that life would be more pleasant there if you had your second mate to gossip with?"

"Yes," he answered, reluctantly, almost gruffly. "Of course that is what I mean."

"It is very nice of you, Jim, to say that, but you needn't have spoiled it by speaking in that crabby tone. It is nothing to be ashamed of. I don't mind admitting that I shall miss you most awfully if we have to separate when this voyage is over. You have been the best of chums to me."

She flushed again as she said this and then looked at him a little shyly. For nearly a minute he made no response, but continued to gaze intently and rather gloomily at the water below. At length he said, gravely, still looking steadily at the water, "There is something, Miss Burleigh, that I feel I ought to tell you, that I wouldn't tell any one else in the world."

"Thank you, Jim," she said. "But please don't call me Miss Burleigh. It is so ridiculously stiff between old chums like us. And, Jim, you are not to tell me anything that it might be better for you that I should not know. I am not in the least inquisitive about your affairs."

93

"I know that," he replied. "But this is a thing that I feel you ought to know. It has been on my mind to tell you for some days past." He paused for a few seconds and then continued, "You remember, Betty, that man Osmond that you spoke about?"

"Yes, but don't call him 'that man Osmond.' Poor fellow! I don't suppose he had done anything very dreadful, and at any rate we can afford to speak kindly of him now that he is dead."

"Yes, but that is just the point. He isn't dead."

"Isn't dead?" she repeated. "But Captain Cockcram saw that other man, Larkom, painting the name on his grave. Was it a dummy grave?"

"No. But it was Larkom who died. The man Cockeram saw was Osmond."

"Are you sure? But of course you would be. Oh, Jim! You won't tell anybody else, will you?"

"I am not very likely to," he replied with a grim smile, "as I happen to be the said John Osmond."

"Jim!" she gasped, gazing at him with wide eyes and parted lips. "I am astounded! I can't believe it."

"I expect it is a bit of a shock," he said bitterly, "to find that you have been socialising for more than a week with a man who is wanted by the police."

"I didn't mean that," she exclaimed, turning scarlet. "You know I didn't. But it is so astonishing. I can't understand how it happened. It seems so extraordinary, and so – so opportune."

Osmond chuckled grimly. "It does," he agreed. "Remarkably opportune. Almost as if I had polished Larkom off *ad hoc*. Well, I didn't."

"Of course you didn't. Who supposed for a moment that you did? But do tell me exactly how it happened."

"Well, it was quite simple. Poor old Larkom died of blackwater fever. He was a good fellow. One of the very best, and the only friend I had. He knew all about me – or nearly all – and he did everything he could to help me. It was an awful blow to me when he died. But he never had a chance when once the fever took hold of him. He was an absolute wreck and he went out like the snuff of a candle, though he managed to make a will before he died, leaving the factory and all his effects to his friend James Cook. It was he who invented that name for me.

"Well, of course, when he was dead, I had to bury him and stick up a cross over his grave. And – then I just painted the wrong name on it. That's all."

She nodded without looking at him and a shadow seemed to fall on her face. "I see," she said, a little coldly. "It was a tempting opportunity, and events have justified you in taking it."

Something in her tone arrested his attention. He looked at her sharply and with a somewhat puzzled expression. Suddenly he burst out, "Good Lord, Betty! You don't think I did this thing in cold blood, do you?"

"Didn't you?" she asked. "Then how did you come to do it?"

"I'll tell you. Poor old Larkom's name was John, like mine. I had painted in the 'John' and was just going to begin the 'Larkom' when I happened to look along the beach. And there I saw Cockeram with his armed party bearing down on Adaffia. Of course, I guessed instantly what his business was, and I saw that there was only one thing to be done. There was the blank space on the cross. I had only to fill it in with my own name and the situation would be saved. So I did."

Her face cleared at this explanation. "I am glad," she said, "that it was only done on the spur of the moment. It did seem a little callous."

"I should think so," he agreed, "if you thought of me sitting by the poor old fellow's bedside and calmly planning to use his corpse to cover my retreat. As it was, I hated doing it, but necessity knows no law. I have thought more than once of making a dummy grave for myself and shifting the cross to it and of setting up a proper memorial to Larkom. And I will do it when I get back."

She made no comment on this, and as, at the moment her line tightened, she hauled it in, and impassively detaching a big red snapper from the hook, re-baited, and cast the line overboard with a curiously detached, preoccupied air. Apparently, she was reflecting profoundly on what she had just learned, and Osmond, glancing at her furtively from time to time, abstained from interrupting her meditations. After a considerable interval, she turned towards him and said in a low, earnest tone: "There is one thing that I want to ask you. Just now you said that you felt you ought to tell me this, that I ought to know. I don't quite see why."

"There was a very good reason," he replied, "and I may as well make a clean breast of it. To put it bluntly, I fell in love with you almost as soon as I saw you, and naturally, I have grown to love you more with every day that has passed."

She flushed deeply, and glancing at him for an instant, turned her eyes once more on her line.

"Still," she said in a low voice, "I don't see why you thought I ought to know."

"Don't you?" he rejoined. "But surely it is obvious. You accepted me as your chum and you seemed to like me well enough. But you had no inkling as to who or what I was. It was my clear duty to tell you."

"You mean that there was the possibility that I might come to care for you and that you felt it your duty to warn me off?"

"Yes. It wasn't very likely that there would be anything more than friendship on your side, but still it was not impossible. Women fall in love with the most unlikely men."

At this she smiled and looked him squarely in the face, "I thought you meant that," she said, softly, "and, of course, you were quite right. But if your intention was to put me on my guard and prevent me from caring for you, your warning has come too late. You would have had to tell me before I had seen you – and I don't believe it would have made a scrap of difference even then. At any rate, I don't care a fig what you have done – I know it was nothing mean. But all the same, I am glad you told me. I should have hated to find it out afterwards by myself."

He gazed at her in dismay. "But, Betty," he protested, "you don't seem to grasp the position. There is a warrant out for my arrest."

"Who cares?" she responded. "Besides, there isn't. John Osmond is dead and there is no warrant out for Captain James Cook. It is you who don't grasp the position."

"But," he expostulated, "don't you realize that I can never go home? That I can't even show my face in Europe?"

"Very well," said she. "So much the worse for Europe. But there are plenty of other places, and what is good enough for you is good enough for me. Now, Jim, dear," she added, coaxingly, "don't create difficulties. You have said that you love me – I think I knew it before you told me – and that is all that matters to me. Everything else is trivial. You are the man to whom I have given my heart, and I am not going to have you crying off."

"Good God, Betty!" he groaned, "don't talk about 'crying off'. If you only know what it means to me to look into Paradise and be forced to turn away! But, my dearest love, it has to be. I would give my life for you gladly, joyfully. I am giving more than my life in refusing the sacrifice that you, in the nobleness of your heart, are willing to make. But I could never accept it. I could never stoop to the mean selfishness of spoiling the life of the woman who is more to me than all the world."

"I am offering no sacrifice," she said. "I am only asking to share the life of the man I love. What more does a woman want?"

"Not to share such a life as mine," he replied, bitterly. "Think of it, Betty, darling! For the rest of my days I must sneak about the world under a false name, hiding in obscure places, scanning the face of every stranger with fear and suspicion lest he should discover my secret and drag me from my sham grave. I am an outcast, an Ishmaelite. Every man's hand is against me. Could I allow a woman – a beautiful girl, a lady of position – to share such a sordid existence as mine? I should be a poor lover if I could think of such contemptible selfishness."

"It isn't so bad as that, Jim, dear," she pleaded. "We could go abroad – to America – and make a fresh start. You would be sure to do well there with your abilities, and we could just shake off the old world and forget it."

He shook his head, sadly. "It is no use, darling, to delude ourselves. We must face realities. Mine is a wrecked life. It would be a crime, even if it were possible, for me to take you from the surroundings of an English lady and involve you in the wreckage. It was a misfortune, at least for you, that we ever met, and there is only one remedy. When we separate, we must try to forget one another."

"We shan't, Jim," she exclaimed, passionately. "You know we shan't. We aren't, either of us, of the kind that forgets. And we could be so happy together! Don't let us lose everything for a mere scruple."

At this moment all on deck were startled by a loud hail from aloft. One of the men had climbed up into the swaying foretop and stood there holding on to the topmast shrouds and with his free hand pointing to the north. Osmond stepped forward and hailed him.

"Foretop there! What is it?"

"A steamer, sir. Seems to be headin' straight on to us."

Osmond ran below, and having fetched Redford's binocular from the berth, climbed the main rigging to just below the cross-tree. There, securing himself with one arm passed round a shroud, he scanned the northern horizon intently for a minute or two and then descended slowly with a grave, set face. From his loftier station he had been able to make out the vessel's hull, and the character of the approaching ship had left him in little doubt as to her mission. His comrade met him with an anxious, inquiring face as he jumped down from the rail.

"Small man-o'-war," he reported in response to the unspoken question, "barquentine-rigged, buff funnel, white hull. Looks like a gun-boat."

"Ha!" she exclaimed. "That will be the *Widgeon*. She was lying off Accra."

The two looked at one another in silence for a while as they look who have heard bad tidings. At length Osmond said, grimly, "Well, this is the end of it, Betty. She has been sent out to search for you. It will be 'Good-bye' in less than an hour."

"Not 'Good-bye', Jim," she urged. "You will come, too, won't you?"

"No," he replied, "I can't leave the old man in this muddle."

"But you'll have to leave him sooner or later."

"Yes, but I must give him the chance to get another mate, or at least to ship one or two native hands."

"Oh, let him muddle on as he did before. My father will be wild to see you when he hears of all that has happened. Don't forget, Jim, that you saved my life."

"I saved my own," said he, "and you chanced to benefit. But I couldn't come with you in any case, Betty. You are forgetting that I have to keep out of sight. There may be men up at headquarters who know me. There may be even on this gun-boat."

She gazed at him despairingly and her eyes filled. "Oh, Jim," she moaned, "how dreadful it is. Of course I must go. But I feel that we shall never see one another again."

"It will be better if we don't," said he.

"Oh, don't say that!" she pleaded. "Think of what we have been to one another and what we could still be forever and ever if only you could forget what is past and done with. Think of what perfect chums we have been and how fond we are of one another. For we are, Jim. I love you with my whole heart and I know that you are just as devoted to me. It is a tragedy that we should have to part."

"It is," he agreed, gloomily, "and the tragedy is of my making."

"It isn't," she dissented, indignantly, and then, softly and coaxingly, she continued, "But we won't lose sight of each other altogether, Jim, will we? You will write to me as soon as you get ashore. Promise me that you will."

"Much better not," he replied, but with so little decision that she persisted until, in the end, and much against his judgment, he yielded and gave the required promise.

"That makes it a little easier," she said, with a sigh. "It leaves me something to look forward to."

She took the glasses from him and searched the rim of the horizon, over which the masts of the approaching ship had begun to appear.

"I suppose I ought to report to the old man," said Osmond, and he was just turning towards the companion when Captain Hartup's head emerged slowly and was in due course followed by the remainder of his person. His left arm was now emancipated from the sling and in his right hand he carried a sextant.

"Gun-boat in sight, sir," said Osmond. "Seems to be coming our way."

The captain nodded, and stepping to the taffrail, applied his eye to the eyepiece of the sextant.

"It has gone seven bells," said he. "Isn't it about time you got ready to take the latitude – you and the other officer?" he added, with a sour grin.

In the agitating circumstances, Osmond had nearly forgotten the daily ceremony – a source of perennial joy to the crew. He now ran below and presently returned with the two sextants, one of which he handed to "the other officer".

"For the last time, little comrade," he whispered.

"And we'll work the reckoning together. Norie's *Navigation* will be a sacred book to me after this."

She took the instrument from him and advanced with him to the bulwark. But if the truth must be told, her observation was a mere matter of form, and twice before the skipper called "eight bells" she had furtively to wipe a tear from the eyepiece. But she went below to the cuddy and resolutely worked out the latitude (from the reading on Osmond's sextant), and when the brief calculation was finished, she silently picked up the scrap of paper on which Osmond had worked out the reckoning and laid hers in its place. He took it up without a word and slipped it into his pocket.

"They are queer keepsakes," she said in a half-whisper as the door of the captain's cabin opened, "but they will tell us exactly when and where we parted. Who knows when and where we shall meet again – if we ever do?"

"If we ever do," he repeated in the same tone, and then, as the captain came out and looked at them inquiringly, he reported the latitude that they had found, and followed him up the companion-steps.

When they arrived on deck, they found the crew ranged along the bulwark watching the gun-boat, which was now fully in view, end-on to the brigantine, and approaching rapidly, her bare masts swinging like pendulums as she rolled along over the big swell.

"I suppose we shall make our number, sir," said Osmond, and as the skipper vouchsafed no reply beyond an unintelligible grunt, he added, "The flag locker is in your cabin, isn't it?

"Never you mind about the flag locker," was the sour reply. "Our name is painted legibly on the bows and the counter, and I suppose they've got glasses if they want to know who we are." He took the binocular from Osmond, and after a leisurely inspection of the gun-boat, continued, "Looks like the *Widgeon*. Coming to pick up a passenger, I reckon. About time, too. I suppose you are both going – if they'll take you?"

"I am not," said Osmond. "I am going to stay and see you into port."

The skipper nodded and emitted an ambiguous grunt, which he amplified with the addition, "Well, you can please yourself," and resumed his inspection of the approaching stranger.

His forecast turned out to be correct, for the gunboat made no signal, but, sweeping past the *Speedwell*'s stern at a distance of less than a quarter-of-a-mile, slowed down and brought-to on the port side, when she proceeded to lower a boat, whereupon Captain Hartup ordered a rope ladder to be dropped over the port quarter. These preparations Miss Burleigh watched anxiously and with an assumption of cheerful interest, and when the boat ran alongside, she joined the skipper at the head of the ladder, while Osmond, lurking discreetly in the background, kept a watchful eye on the officer who sat in the stern-sheets until the lessening distance rendered him distinguishable as an undoubted stranger, when he also joined the skipper.

As the new-comer – a pleasant-faced, clean-shaved man in a lieutenant's uniform – reached the top of the ladder, he exchanged salutes with the skipper and the lady, who advanced and held out her hand.

"Well, Miss Burleigh," said the lieutenant as he shook her hand, heartily, "this is a relief to find you safe and sound and looking in the very pink of health. But you have given us all a rare fright. We were afraid the ship had been lost."

"So she was," replied Betty. "Lost and found. I think I have earned a fatted calf, don't you, Captain Darley?"

"I don't know," rejoined the lieutenant. (The honorary rank was in acknowledgment of his position as commander of the gun-boat.) "We must leave that to His Excellency. But it doesn't sound very complimentary to your shipmates or to your recent diet. I needn't ask if you are coming back with us. My cabin has been made ready for you."

"But how kind of you, Captain Darley. Yes, I suppose I must come with you, though I have been having quite a good time here – mutinies, fishing, and all sorts of entertainments."

"Mutinies, hey!" exclaimed Darley, with a quick glance at the captain. "Well, I am sorry to tear you away from these entertainments, but orders are orders. Perhaps you will get your traps packed up while I have a few words with the captain. I shall have to make a report of what has happened."

On this there was a general move towards the companion. Betty retired – somewhat precipitately – to her berth and the lieutenant followed Captain Hartup to his cabin.

Both parties were absent for some time. The first to reappear was Betty, slightly red about the eyes and carrying a small hand-bag. Having dispatched Sam Winter below to fetch up her portmanteau, she drew Osmond away to the starboard side.

"Jack," she said, in a low, earnest tone – "I may call you by your own name just for once, mayn't I? – you have made me a promise. You won't go back on it, will you, Jack?"

"Of course I shan't, Betty," he replied.

"I want you to have my cabin when I've gone," she continued. "It is a better one than yours and it has a tiny port-hole. And if you open the locker, you will find a little note for you. That is all. Here they come. Good-bye, Jack, darling!"

She turned away abruptly as he murmured a husky farewell, and having shaken hands with Captain Hartup and thanked him for his hospitality, was stepping on to the ladder when she paused suddenly and turned back.

"I had nearly forgotten," said she. "I haven't paid my passage."

"There is no passage-money to pay," the skipper said, gruffly. "My contract was to deliver you at Accra, and I haven't done it. Besides," he added, with a sour grin, "you've worked your passage."

"Worked her passage!" exclaimed the lieutenant. "What do you mean?"

"She has been taking the second mate's duties," the skipper explained.

Darley stared open-mouthed from the skipper to the lady. Then, with a fine, hearty British guffaw, he assisted the latter down to the boat.

Chapter VII
The Mate Takes His Discharge

As an instance of the malicious perversity which the forces of nature often appear to display, the calm which had for so many days cut off Miss Betty from any communication with the world at large seemed unable to survive her departure. Before the gun-boat was fairly hull down on the horizon, a dark line on the glassy sea announced the approach of a breeze, and a few minutes later the brigantine's sails filled, her wallowings subsided, and a visible wake began to stream out astern.

The change in the vessel's motion brought the captain promptly on deck, and Osmond listened somewhat anxiously for the orders as to the course which was to be set. But he knew his commander too well to make any suggestions.

"Breeze seems to be about sou'-sou'west," the skipper remarked with one eye on the compass-dial and the other on the upper sails. "Looks as if it was going to hold, too. Put her head west-nor'west."

"Did the lieutenant give you our position?" Osmond inquired.

"No, he didn't," the skipper snapped. "He wasn't asked. I don't want any of your brass-bound dandies teaching me my business. The continent of Africa is big enough for me to find without their help."

Osmond smothered a grin as he thought of the chronometer, re-started and ticking away aimlessly in the captain's cabin, its error and rate alike unknown. But again he made no comment, and presently the skipper resumed, "I suppose you will be wanting to get back to Adaffia?"

"I'm not going to leave you in the lurch."

"Well, you can't stay with me for good excepting as a seaman, as you haven't got a ticket – at least, I suppose you haven't."

"No. I hold a master's certificate entitling me to navigate my own yacht, but, of course, that is no use on a merchant vessel, excepting in an emergency. But I don't quite see what you are going to do."

"It is a bit of a problem," the skipper admitted. "I shall take on one or two native hands to help while we are on the Coast, and appoint Winter and Simmons to act as mates. Then perhaps I shall he able to pick up an officer from one of the steamers for the homeward trip."

"I will stay with you until you are fixed up, if you like," said Osmond, but the captain shook his head.

"No," he replied. "I shall put you ashore at Adaffia. I can manage all right on the Coast, and I must have a regular mate for the homeward voyage."

Thus the programme was settled, and, on the whole, satisfactorily to Osmond. It is true that, if there had been no such person as Elizabeth Burleigh, he would have held on to his position, even with the rating of ordinary seaman, for the homeward voyage, on the chance of transferring later to some ship bound for South America or the Pacific Islands. But although he had renounced all claim to her and all hope of any future connected with her, he still clung to the ill omened land that was made glorious to him by her beloved presence.

The captain's forecast was justified by the event. The breeze held steadily and seemed inclined to freshen rather than to fail. The old brigantine heeled over gently and forged ahead with a pleasant murmur in her sails and quite a fine wake trailing astern. It was a great relief to everybody after the long calm, with its monotony and inaction and the incessant rolling of the ship and flapping of the sails. The captain was almost pleasant and the crew were cheerful and contented, though they had little to do, for when once the course was set there was no need to touch sheet or brace, and the trick at the wheel was the only active duty apart from the cook's activities.

To Osmond alone the change brought no obvious satisfaction. All that had recently happened had been, as he could not but recognize, for the best. The parting had to come, and every day that it was delayed forged his fetters only the more firmly. But this reflection offered little consolation. He loved this sweet, frank, open-hearted girl with an intensity possible only to a man of his strength of will and constancy of purpose. And now she was gone, gone out of his life forever. It was a final parting. There was no future to look forward to, not even the most distant and shadowy. The vision of a great happiness had floated before him and had passed, leaving him to take up again the burden of his joyless life, haunted for ever by the ghost of the might-have-been.

Nevertheless, he went about his duties briskly enough, finding jobs for the men and for himself, overhauling the cordage, doing small repairs on the rigging, and even, with his own hands, putting a patch on a weak spot on the bottom of the long-boat and lining it inside and out with scraps of sheet copper. And if he was a little grimmer and more silent than before, the men understood and in their rough way sympathized, merely remarking that "Pore old Cook do seem cut up along o' losin' his Judy."

At dawn on the third day the land was in sight – that is to say to the north there was an appearance as if a number of small entomological pins

103

had been stuck into the sea-horizon in irregular groups. Viewed from the fore-top, however, through Redford's glasses, this phenomenon resolved itself into a narrow band of low-lying shore, dotted with coconut palms, the characteristic aspect of the Bight of Benin.

As the day wore on, the brigantine gradually closed in with the land. Before noon, the captain was able, through his telescope, to identify a group of white buildings as the German factories at the village of Bagidá. Then the neighbouring village of Lomé came in sight and slowly crept past, and as the *Speedwell* drew yet nearer to the land, Osmond was able to recognize, among a large grove of coconuts, the white-washed bungalow at Denu, and, a few miles ahead, the dark mass of palms that he knew to be Adaffia.

"Well, Mr. Cook," said the captain, "you'll soon be back by your own fireside. If the breeze holds, we ought to be in Adaffia roads by four at the latest. I suppose you have got all your portmanteaux packed?"

"I'm all ready to go ashore, if you are still of the same mind."

"I never change my mind," replied the skipper, and Osmond believed him.

"Are you making any stay at Adaffia?" he asked.

"I am going to put you ashore," the captain answered. "What I shall do after that is my business."

"I asked," said Osmond, "because I thought I might be able to get you one or two native hands. However, you can let me know about that later. Now, as it is your watch on deck, I will go below and take a bit of a rest."

He went down to the berth, into which he had moved when Betty departed, and, shutting the door, looked thoughtfully round the little apartment. Nothing had been altered since she left. All the little feminine tidinesses had been piously preserved. It was still, to the eye, a woman's cabin, and everything in its aspect spoke to him of the late tenant. Presently he lay down on the bunk – the bunk in which she had slept – and for the hundredth time drew from his pocket the letter which she had left in the locker. It was quite short – just a little note hastily written at the last moment when the boat was waiting. But to him it was inexhaustible, and though by now he knew it by heart, he read it again as eagerly as when he had first opened it.

My Dearest Jim, (it ran)

I am writing you a few words of farewell (since we must say "Good-bye" in public) to tell you that when you read them I shall be thinking of you. I shall think of you, best and dearest

104

comrade, every day of my life, and I shall go on hoping that somehow we shall meet again and be as we have been on this dear old ship. And Jim, dearest, I want you to understand that I am always yours. Whenever you want me — no, I don't mean that, I know you want me now — but whenever you can cast away things that ought to be forgotten, remember that I am waiting for you. Try, dear, to forget everything but your love and mine.

Au revoir!

Your faithful and loving
Betty

It was a sweet letter, written in all sincerity, and even though Osmond never wavered in the renunciation that honour demanded, still it told him in convincing terms that the door was not shut. The gate of Paradise was still ajar. If he could forget all justice and generosity, if he, who had nothing to give, could bring himself to accept the gift so generously held out to him, he still had the option to enter. He realized that — and never, for an instant, entertained the thought. Perhaps there were other ways out. But if there were, he dismissed them, too. Like Captain Hartup, he was not given to altering his mind. Free as he was from the captain's petty obstinacy, he was a man of inflexible purpose, even though the purpose might have been ill-considered.

His long reverie was at length interrupted by a voice which came in through the little port-hole. "No soundings!"

He glanced up at the tell-tale compass which formed a rather unusual fitting to the mate's bunk and noted that the ship's course had been altered three points to the north. She was now heading almost directly for the land and was presumably nearly opposite Adaffia. He re-folded the letter and put it away, but his thoughts went back to its message and to the beloved writer. Presently the voice of the man in the channel who was heaving the lead was heard again, and this time it told of a nearer approach to that dreary shore.

"By the deep, eighteen!"

He noted the depth with faint interest and began to think of the immediate future. As soon as he got ashore he must write to her. It was quite wrong, but he had promised, and he could not but be glad that she had exacted the promise. It would be a joy to write to her, and yet he could feel that he was doing it under compulsion. But it must be a careful letter. There must be in it no sign of weakening or wavering that might mislead her. She must be free and she must fully realize it, must realize that he belonged to her past and had no part in her future. It would be a difficult letter to write, and here he set himself to consider what he should say. And meanwhile the leads-man's voice came in from time to time, recording the gradual approach to the land.

"By the deep, ele-vern!"

"By the mark, ten!"

"By the deep, eight!"

At this point he was aware of sounds in the cuddy as if some heavy objects were being moved, and he surmised that the gin-cases were being disinterred from the lazarette. Then he heard the trap fall and heavy footsteps stumbled up the companion-stairs. A moment later the leadsman sang out, "By the mark, sev-ern!" and as Osmond rose from the bunk there came a thumping at his door and a voice sang out, "The captain wants you on deck, sir, and there's a canoe a-comin' alongside."

Osmond cast a farewell glance round the little cabin and followed the man up on deck, where he found the captain waiting on the poop, standing guard, apparently, over two leathern bags and one of canvas. Looking forward, he saw the crew gathered at the open gangway, regarding with sheepish grins four unopened gin-cases, while a canoe, bearing a scarlet-coated grandee, was just running alongside. As he stepped out of the companion, the captain picked up the three bags, and walking with him slowly towards the gangway, addressed him in a gruff tone and a somewhat aggressive manner.

"According to law," said he, "I believe you are entitled to a third of the ship's value for salvage services. There are nearly two-hundred ounces of gold-dust in these two leather bags – that is, roughly, eight-hundred pounds – and there is forty-eight pounds ten in sovereigns and half-sovereigns, in the canvas bag. Will that satisfy you?"

"Rubbish," said Osmond. "I want eight shillings for two cases of gin broached by your men."

"You won't get it from me," snapped the skipper. "I'll have nothing to do with intoxicating liquor."

"If you don't pay, I'll sue you," said Osmond.

"I haven't had the gin," retorted the skipper. "It was brought on board without my authority. You must recover from the men who had it. But what do you say about the question of salvage?"

"Hang the salvage!" replied Osmond. "I want to be paid for my gin."

"You won't get a ha'penny from me for your confounded poison," exclaimed the skipper, hotly. "I hold very strict views on the liquor traffic. There are the men who drank the stuff. Make them pay. It's no concern of mine. But about this salvage question: Are you satisfied with what I offer?"

Osmond glanced through the gangway. The gin-cases were all stowed in the canoe, Mensah was beaming up at him with an expectant grin, and the canoe-men grasped their paddles. He felt in his pocket, and then, taking the canvas bag from the skipper, thrust his hand in and brought out a handful of coins. From these he selected a half-sovereign, and returning the others, dropped in a couple of shillings from his pocket.

"Two shillings change," he remarked. He threw the bag down on the deck, and pocketing the half sovereign, dropped down into the canoe. But he had hardly taken his seat on the tie-tie thwart when two heavy thumps on the floor of the canoe, followed by a jingling impact, announced the arrival of the two bags of gold-dust and the bag of specie.

Osmond stood up in the dancing canoe with a leather bag in each hand.

"Now, Mensah," he sang out, "tell the boys to get away one time."

The paddles dug into the blue water, the canoe bounded forward. Aiming skilfully at the open gang way, Osmond sent the heavy leathern bags, one after the other, skimming along the deck, and the little bag of specie after them. The skipper grabbed them up and rushed to the gangway. But he was too late. The canoe was twenty yards away and leaping forward to the thud of the paddles. Looking back at the brigantine with a satisfied smile, Osmond saw a row of six grinning faces at the rail, and at the gangway a small figure that shook its fist at the receding canoe with valedictory fury.

His homecoming was the occasion of a pleasant surprise. At intervals during his absence he had given a passing thought to his factory and the little solitary house by the beach and had wondered how they would fare while their master was away. Now he found that in Kwaku Mensah he had a really faithful steward, and not only faithful but strangely competent in his simple way. The house was in apple-pie order and the store was neatly kept and evidently a going concern, for when he arrived, Mensah's pretty Fanti wife was behind the counter, chaffering persuasively with a party of "bush" people from Agotimé, and a glance into the compound showed a good pile of produce, awaiting removal to the produce store. Accounts, of course, there were none, since Mensah "no sabby book", but nevertheless that artless merchantman had kept an exact record of all the transactions with that uncanny precision of memory that one often observes in the intelligent illiterate.

So Osmond settled down at once, with a satisfaction that rather surprised him, into the old surroundings, and as he sat that evening at the table, consuming with uncommon relish a dinner of okro soup, "chickum cotrecks", and "banana flitters", the product of Mrs. Mensah's skill (her name was Ekua Bochwi, from which one learned that she had been born on Wednesday and was the eighth child of her parents), he was inclined to congratulate himself on Captain Hartup's refusal to retain him as the provisional mate of the *Speedwell*.

But in spite of the triumphant way in which he had out-manoeuvred the skipper, Osmond had a suspicion that he had not seen the last of his late commander. For the brigantine, which he had left hove-to and apparently ready to proceed on her voyage, had presently let go her anchor and stowed her sails as if the captain contemplated a stay at Adaffia. And the event justified his suspicions. On the following morning, while he was seated at the breakfast-table, with a fair copy of his letter to Betty before him, he became aware of shod feet on the gravelled compound, and a few moments later the doorway framed the figure of Captain Hartup, while in the background lurked Sam Winter, grinning joy and carrying two leathern bags.

The captain entered, and regarding his quondam mate with an expression that almost approached geniality, wished him "Good morning" and even held out his hand. Osmond grasped it cordially, and drawing up a second chair, pressed his visitor to join him.

"A little fresh food," he remarked, untactfully, with his eye on the leathern bags, "and a cup of real coffee will do you good."

"I don't know what you mean by that," snorted the skipper. "I'm not starving, and neither are you. The ship's grub hasn't killed you. Still," he added, "as I see you are breakfasting like a Christian and not in the beastly Coast fashion, I don't mind if I do try a bit of shore tack with you. And you needn't look at those bags like that. I am not going to force anything on you. I am not an obstinate man," (which was a most outrageous untruth).

"What have you brought them here for?" Osmond demanded stolidly.

"I'll tell you presently," replied the skipper. "Bring 'em in, Winter, and dump 'em on that sideboard."

Winter deposited the two bags on the stack of empty cases thus politely designated and then backed to the doorway, where he was encountered by Kwaku, who was directed to take him to the store and feed him.

"I've come ashore," the captain explained when they were alone, "to see if I can make one or two little arrangements with you."

Osmond nodded as he helped his guest to stuffed okros and fried eggs (eggs are usually served, on the Coast, fried or poached or in some other overt form, as a precaution against embryological surprises).

108

"To begin with," continued the skipper, "I want about half-a-dozen men – a cook, a cabin-boy, and a few hands to do the rough work. Do you think you can manage that for me?"

"I've no doubt I can," was the reply.

"Good. Well, then, there is this gold-dust. If you care to change your mind, say so, and the stuff is yours."

Osmond shook his head. "I came on board for my own purposes," said he, "and I am not going to take any payment for looking after my own business."

"Very well," the skipper rejoined. "Then if you won't have it, I may as well keep it, and I shan't if it remains on board. It was that gold-dust that tempted Dhoody and the others. Now I understood from you that you have got a safe. Is it a pretty strong one?"

"It's strong enough. There are no skilled burglars out here."

"Then I'm going to ask you to take charge of this stuff for me. You see that both bags are sealed up, and there is a paper inside each giving particulars of the contents and full directions as to how they are to be disposed of if anything should happen to me. Will you do this for me – as a matter of business, of course?"

"Not as a matter of business," replied Osmond. "That would make me responsible for the safe custody of the bags, which I can't be, as I may have to be absent from Adaffia and leave my man, Mensah, in charge of the factory. I will put the stuff in my safe with pleasure, and I think it will be perfectly secure there, but I won't take any payment or accept any responsibility beyond exercising reasonable care. Will that do?"

"Yes," replied the captain, "that will do. What is good enough for your own property is good enough for mine. So I will ask you to lock the stuff up for me and keep it till I ask for it, but if you should hear that anything has happened to me – that I am dead, in fact – then you will open the bags and read the papers inside and dispose of the property according to the directions written in those papers. Will you do that? It will be a weight off my mind if you will."

"Certainly I will," said Osmond. "But have you any reason to expect that anything will happen to you?"

"Nothing immediate," the captain replied. "But, you see, I am not as young as I was, and I am not what you would call a very sound man. I am subject to occasional attacks of giddiness and faintness. I don't know how much they mean, but my doctor at Bristol warned me not to treat them too lightly. He gave me a supply of medicine, which I keep in the chest, and when I feel an attack coming on, I turn in and take some. But still, 'in the midst of life we are in death', you know, and I'm ready to answer to my name when the call comes."

"Well," said Osmond, "let us hope it won't come until you have got your goods safely home to Bristol. But in any case, you can depend on me to carry out your instructions."

"Thank you, Mr. Cook," said the captain. "I am glad to get that little matter settled. The only anxiety that is left now is the ivory. I had thought of asking you to take charge of that, too, but it would be awkward for you to store. And, after all, it's fairly safe in the hold. A man can't nip off with a dozen eighty-pound tusks in his pocket. So I think we will leave that where it is, ready stowed for the homeward voyage. By the way, have you got any produce that you want to dispose of?"

"Yes, I have a ton or two of copra and a couple of puncheons of oil, and I can let you have some kernels and rubber. Perhaps you would like to take some of the produce in exchange for trade goods."

The arrangement suited Captain Hartup exactly, and accordingly, when they had finished breakfast and stowed the gold-dust in the safe, they adjourned to the produce store to settle the details of the exchange. Then half-a-dozen canoes were chartered, the new hands mustered by Kwaku, and for the rest of the day the little factory compound and the usually quiet beach were scenes of unwonted bustle and activity. Sam Winter (secretly fortified with a substantial "tot" of gin) was sent on board to superintend the stowage and breaking-out of cargo, while the skipper remained ashore to check off the goods landed and embarked.

The sun was getting low when the two white men set forth to follow the last consignment down to the beach. When they had seen it loaded into the canoes and watched its passage through the surf, Captain Hartup turned to Osmond, and having shaken his hand with almost unnatural cordiality, said, gruffly but not without emotion, "Well, good-bye, Mr. Cook. I've a good deal to thank you for, and I don't forget it. Providence brought us together when I badly needed a friend, and He will bring us together again, no doubt, in His own good time. But how or when, no one can foresee."

He shook Osmond's hand again and, stepping into the waiting canoe, took his seat on a parcel of rubber. The incoming breaker surged up and spent its last energy in a burst of spray on the canoe's beak. The little craft lifted and, impelled by a hearty shove from the canoe-men, slid down the beach on the backwash and charged into the surf. For a few minutes Osmond stood at the brink of the sea watching the canoe as it hovered amidst clouds of spray, dodging the great combers and waiting for its chance to slip through the "shouting seas" to the quiet rollers

110

outside. At length the periodical "lull" came, the paddles drummed furiously on the green-blue water, the canoe leaped at the following wave, disappeared in a burst of snowy froth, and reappeared prancing wildly but safely outside the line of surf. A little figure in the canoe turned and waved its hand, and Osmond, after a responsive flourish of his hat and a glance at the anchored brigantine, turned away from the beach with an odd feeling of regret and walked slowly back to the factory, pondering on the captain's curious and rather cryptic farewell.

Chapter VIII
The Last of the *Speedwell*

For a couple of months Osmond's life at Adaffia drifted on monotonously enough, yet not at all drearily to a man of his somewhat solitary habits and self-contained nature. The factory prospered in a modest way with very little attention on his part, causing him often to reflect regretfully on poor Larkom's melancholy and unnecessary failure. That kindly wastrel was now secured – for a time – from oblivion by a neatly-made wooden cross, painted white and inscribed with his name, a date, and a few appreciative words, which had been set above his grave when the other cross had been removed to grace an elongated heap of sand which represented the resting-place of the late John Osmond.

Moreover, there were breaks in the monotony which had not existed before the adventure of the *Speedwell*. His letter to Betty (in which, among other matters, he had related with naive satisfaction the incident of the leathern bags and the defeat of Captain Hartup) had evoked a lengthy reply with a demand for a further letter, and so, much against his judgment, he had been drawn into a regular correspondence which was the occasion of alternate and conflicting emotions. Every letter that he wrote racked his conscience and filled him with self-contempt. But the arrival of the inevitable and always prompt reply was a delight which he accepted and enjoyed without a qualm. It was very inconsistent. To the half-naked native who acted as the semi-official postman, he would hand his letter shamefacedly, with a growl of disapproval, admonishing himself that "this sort of thing has got to stop". And then, on the day when the reply was expected, he would take a telescope out on the sand-hills and remain for hours watching the beach for the appearance in the remote distance of that same native postman.

These letters, mostly written from headquarters, kept him informed respecting events of local interest and, what was much more to the point, of Betty's own doings and movements. He learned, for instance, that there were rumours of a native rising in Anglóh (officially spelt Awuna), the region at the back of Adaffia, and that – regardless of this fact – Betty was trying to get her father's permission for a little journey of exploration into this very district.

This latter item of news set his emotional see-saw going at double speed. His judgment denounced the project violently. First, there was the danger – obvious, though not so very great, for the African is essentially a gentlemanly fighter, if rather heavy-handed, and would avoid injuring a white woman. But he is a shockingly bad marksman and uses slugs and gravel for ammunition, so that accidents are very liable to happen. But apart from the danger, this expedition was highly undesirable, for it would bring Betty into his neighbourhood, and of course they would meet – she would see to that. And that meeting ought not to take place. It would only prolong a state of affairs that was disturbing to him and ruinous to her future prospects. He felt this very sincerely, and was foolish enough to say so in his reply to her letter.

From time to time his thoughts wandered to Captain Hartup, and always with a tendency to speculate on the meaning – if there were any – of the note of foreboding which he thought he had detected in the captain's last words as they said "Good-bye" on the beach. Those words – together with something final and testamentary in his manner when he had deposited the bags of gold-dust in the safe – seemed to hint at an uncertainty of life and distrust of the future on the captain's part, on which Osmond reflected uneasily. And at last, there came a day on which the skipper's meaning was made clear.

One morning, in the short interval between the night and the dawn, he awoke suddenly and became aware of a dusky figure between his bed and the window.

"Look!" the voice of Mensah exclaimed, excitedly. "The ship, *Speedwell*! I looked. He fit for to come on the beach."

Osmond lifted the mosquito-curtain and, springing out of bed, dropped into his slippers, snatched up the telescope, and followed Mensah out to the end of the compound whence there was a clear view of the sea. And there she was looming up sharp and clear against the grey dawn, and the first glance of a nautical eye read tragedy and disaster in every detail of her aspect. No telescope was needed. She was close in shore, within a couple of cable-lengths of the surf, with her square-sails aback and head-sails shivering, drifting slowly but surely to the destruction that roared under her lee. Obviously, there was no one at the wheel, nor was there any sign of life on board. She was a perfect picture of a derelict.

For a few moments Osmond stared at her in horrified amazement. Then, with a sharp command to Mensah to "get canoe one time", he ran out of the compound and made his way to the beach.

But his order had been anticipated. As he and Mensah came out on the shore, they found a group of excited fishermen dragging a canoe down to the water's edge, while another party were already afloat and paddling out through the surf towards the derelict brigantine. Osmond and his henchman at once joined the fishermen, and though the latter

113

looked askance at the white man – for the accommodation of the little craft was rather limited – they made no demur, experience having taught them that he would have his own way – and pay for it. Accordingly they hauled and shoved with a will, and in a very few moments got the canoe down to the water's edge. Osmond and Mensah stepped in and took their seats, the fishermen grasped the gunwales, and when a big wave swept in and lifted the canoe, they shoved off and went sliding down on the backwash and charged into the surf.

Meanwhile the brigantine continued to drift by the wind and current nearly parallel to the shore, but slowly approached the latter. At the moment she was turning sluggishly and beginning to "pay off" on the starboard tack. Her sails filled and she began to move ahead. If anyone had been on board she might even now have been saved, for there was still room for her to "claw off" the lee shore. Osmond gazed at her with his heart in his mouth and urged the canoe-men to greater efforts, though they wanted little urging, seeing that their friends in the other canoe were now quite near to the receding ship. Moment by moment his hopes rose as the brigantine gathered way, though she was now less easy to overtake. Breathlessly he watched the leading canoe approach her nearer and nearer until at last the fishermen were able to lay hold of the vacant tackles that hung down from the stern davits and swarm up them to the poop. And even as they disappeared over the taffrail, the flicker of life that the old brigantine had displayed faded out. Under the pressure of the mainsail she began slowly to turn to windward. The head-sails shivered, the square-sails blew back against the mast, she ceased to move ahead, and then began once more to drift stern-foremost towards the white line of surf.

As Osmond's canoe ran alongside, where the other canoe was now towing, the first arrivals came tumbling over the side in a state of wild excitement. Mensah proceeded hastily to interpret.

"Dose fishermen say dis ship no good. Dead man live inside him."

Osmond acknowledged the information with an in articulate growl and, grasping a chain-plate, hauled himself up into the channel, whence he climbed over the rail and dropped on deck.

His first act was to run to the wheel, jam it hard over to port and fix it with a lashing. Then he ran forward to look at the anchors, but both of them were stowed securely and – for the present purposes – useless. He looked up despairingly at the sails, and for a moment thought of trying to swing the yards, but a glance over the stern at the snowy line of surf showed him that the time for manoeuvring was past. For an instant he stood scanning the deck, noting the absence of both boats and the

114

yawning main hatch. Then he ran aft and scrambled down the companion-steps.

The door of the captain's cabin was open – had been left open by the fishermen – and was swinging idly as the ship rolled. But though the whereabouts of the dead man was evident enough before he reached it, he entered without hesitation, intent only on learning exactly what had happened on that ill-omened ship.

The little cabin was just as he had last seen it – with certain differences. And in the bunk lay something that had once been Captain Hartup. It was a dreadful thing to look upon, for the Tropics deal not kindly with the unsepulchred dead. But as Osmond stood looking down on the bunk, mere physical repulsion was swallowed up in a profound feeling of pity for the poor, cross-grained, honest-hearted little shipmaster. There he lay – all that was left of him. There, in the bunk, still lightly held by the blackened, puffy hand, was the inexhaustible Commentary, and on the deck, by the bunk-side, an open box containing a tumbler and a large medicine-bottle, the label of which bore written directions and a Bristol address.

Osmond picked up the bottle and read the minute directions with a sense of profound relief. Its presence suggested what his inspection of the dead man confirmed, that at least death had come to Captain Hartup peaceably and decently. The traces of a murderous attack which he had feared to find were not there. Everything tended to show that the captain had died, as he had seemed to expect, from the effects of some long-standing malady.

From the dead man Osmond turned a swift attention to the cabin. He had noticed, when he entered, that the chronometer was not in its place on the little chart-table. He now observed that other things had disappeared – the telescope, the marine glasses, the sextant, and the mathematical instrument case In short, as he looked round, he perceived that the little cabin had been gutted. Every portable thing of value had been taken away.

His observations were interrupted by the voice of Mensah calling to him urgently to come away "one time", and at the same moment he felt the ship give a heavy lurch followed by a quick recovery. He backed out of the cabin and was about to run up the companion-steps when his glance fell on the door of the adjoining berth, which had been his own and Betty's, and he was moved irresistibly to take a last, farewell look at the little hutch which held so many and so dearly prized memories. He thrust the door open and looked in, and even as he looked, a flash of dazzling white came through the tiny porthole, and a moment later a

115

thunderous crash resounded and the ship trembled as if struck by a thousand monstrous hammers.

He waited no more, but, springing up the steps, thrust his head cautiously out of the companion-hatch. Glancing seaward, he saw a great, sparkling green mass sweeping down on the ship. In another instant, its sharp, tremulous crest whitened, a hissing sound was borne to his ears and quickly rose to a hoarse roar which ended in a crash that nearly shook him off his feet. Then sea and sky, masts and deck, were swallowed up in a cloud of blinding white, there was another roar, and the snowy cataract descended, filling the deck with a seething torrent of foaming water.

Osmond sprang out of the hatch and took a quick glance round. The two canoes were hovering on the outside edge of the surf and obviously unable to approach the ship. Towards the land, the sea was an unbroken expanse of white, while to seaward the long ranks of sharp-crested waves were turning over and breaking as they approached. Warned by a hissing roar from the nearest wave, he stepped back into the shelter of the companion. Again the ship staggered to the crashing impact. Again the visible world was blotted out by the white cloud of spray and foam, and then, as the deluge fell, came a sickening jar with loud cracking noises as the ship struck heavily on the ground. Twice she lifted and struck again, but the third time, rending sounds from below told that her timbers had given way and she lifted no more. Then, under the hammering of the surf, which filled her lower sails with green water, she heeled over towards the shore until the deck was at an angle of nearly forty-five.

Osmond looked out from his shelter and rapidly considered what he should do. There was not much time to consider, for the ship would soon begin to break up. He thought of dropping overboard on the land side and swimming ashore, but it was not a very safe plan, for at any moment the masts might go over the side, and it would not do for him to be underneath when they fell.

Still, he had to act quickly if he were to escape from the impending collapse of the whole fabric, and he looked about eagerly to find the least perilous method. Suddenly his glance fell upon a large cork fender which was washing about in the lee scuppers. The way in which it floated showed that it was dry and buoyant, and it appeared to him that with its aid he might venture into the surf beyond the shelter of the ship and wash safely ashore.

He watched for an opportunity to secure it. Waiting for the brief interval between the descent of the deluge and the bursting of the next wave, he slipped out and, grasping the end of the main sheet, which had washed partly loose from the cleat, ran down to the scupper, seized the fender, and hauling himself up again, crept into his shelter just in time to escape the next wave. When this had burst on the ship and the cataract had fallen, he kicked off his slippers, darted out, and clawing his way past the wheel, reached the taffrail. Holding on firmly to the fender with one hand, with the other he grasped the lee davit-tackle, and springing out, let the tackle slip through his hand.

Just as he reached the water, the next wave burst on the ship, and for the next few moments he was conscious of nothing but a roaring in his ears, a sudden plunge into darkness, and a sense of violent movement. But he still clung tenaciously to the fender, and presently his head rose above the seething water. He took a deep breath, shook the water from his eyes, and began to strike out with his feet, waiting anxiously for the next wave and wondering how much submersion he could stand without drowning. But when the next wave came, its behaviour rather surprised him. The advancing wall of hissing foam seemed simply to take hold of the fender and bear it away swiftly shoreward, leaving him to hold on and follow with his head comfortably above the surface.

In this way, amidst a roar like that of steam from an engine's escape-valve, he was borne steadily and swiftly for about a quarter-of-a-mile. Then the spent wave left him and he could see it travelling away towards the shore. But the following wave overtook him after a very short interval and carried him forward another stage. And so he was borne along with surprising ease and speed until he was at last flung roughly on the beach and forthwith smothered in foaming water. He clawed frantically at the wet sand and strove to rise. But the beach was steep and the undertow would have dragged him back but for the help of a couple of fishermen who, holding on to a grass rope that was held by their companions, waded into the surf, and grabbing him by the arms, dragged him up on to the dry sand beyond the reach of the waves.

As he rose to his feet, he turned to look at the ship. But she was a ship no longer. The short time occupied by his passage ashore had turned her into a mere wreck. Her masts lay flat on the water and her deck had been burst through from below, and through the yawning spaces where the planks had been driven out, daylight could be seen in several places where her side was stove in. The two canoes had already come ashore, and their crews stood at the water's edge, watching the flotsam that was even now beginning to drift shoreward on the surf.

Osmond, too, watched it with interest, for he now recalled that the instantaneous glance that he had cast through the open main hatch had shown an unexpectedly empty condition of the hold. And this impression was confirmed when Mensah joined him (apparently quite unmoved by the proceedings of his eccentric employer) and remarked, "Dose fishermen say only small-small cargo live in side that ship. They say the sailor-man t'ief the cargo and go away in the boats."

Osmond made no comment on this. Obviously the cargo could not have been taken away in two small boats. But equally obviously it was not there, nor were the boats. It was clear that the ship had been abandoned – probably after the skipper's death – and she had been abandoned at sea. The suggestion was that the crew had transhipped on to some passing vessel and that the cargo had been transferred with them. It might be a perfectly legitimate transaction. But the presence in the cabin of the unburied body of the captain, and the open main hatch, hinted at hurried proceedings of not very scrupulous agents. A responsible shipmaster would certainly have buried the dead captain. Altogether it was a mysterious affair, on which it was possible only to speculate.

The spot where the brigantine had come ashore was about halfway between Adaffia and the adjoining village of Denu. Osmond decided to walk the three or four miles into Adaffia, and when he had washed, dressed, and breakfasted, to return and examine the wreckage. Meanwhile, he left Mensah on guard to see that nothing was taken away – or at any rate, to keep account of anything that was removed by the natives, who were now beginning to flock in from the two villages. Accordingly, having borrowed from the fishermen a large, shallow calabash to put over his head – for the sun was now well up and making itself felt – he strode away westward along the beach, walking as far as was possible on the wet sand to avoid delivering his bare feet to the attacks of the chiggers – sand-fleas – which infested the "Aeolian sands" above the tide-marks.

When he returned some three hours later, all that was left of the *Speedwell* was a litter of wreckage and flotsam strewn along the margin of the sea or on the blown sand, to which some of the more valuable portions had been carried. The vessel's keel, with the stem and stern-posts and a few of the main timbers still attached, lay some distance out, but even this melancholy skeleton was gradually creeping shoreward under the incessant pounding of the surf. The masts, spars, and sails were still in the water, but they, too, were slowly creeping up the beach as the spent waves struck them every few seconds. As to the rest, the ship seemed almost to have decomposed into her constituent planks and beams. There is no ship-breaker like an Atlantic surf.

Osmond cast a pensive glance over the disorderly frame that had once been a stout little ship, and as Mensah observed him and approached, he asked, "How much cargo has come ashore, Kwaku?"

Mensah flung out his hands and pointed to the litter on the shore. "Small, small cargo come," said he. "One, two puncheons of oil, two or tree dozen bags kernels, some bags copra, two, tree bales Manchester goods – finish."

"I don't see any Manchester goods," said Osmond.

"No, sir. They country people. They damn t'ief. They take everyt'ing. They no leave nutting", and in confirmation he pointed to sundry little caravans of men, women, and children, all heavily laden and all hurrying homeward, which were visible, mostly in the distance. Indeed, Osmond had met several of them on his way.

"You have not seen any ivory?"

"No, sir. I look for him proper but I no see him."

"Nor any big crates or cases?"

"No, sir. Only the bales and crates of Manchester goods, and the country people break d'em up."

"Has the captain – the dead man – come ashore?"

"Yes, sir. He live for that place," and Mensah pointed to a spot at the eastern end of the beach where a clump of coconut palms grew almost at high-water mark. Thither Osmond proceeded with Mensah, and there, at the spot indicated, he found the uncomely corpse of the little skipper lying amidst a litter of loose planks and small flotsam, on the wet sand in the wash of the sea, and seeming to wince as the spent waves alternately pushed it forward and drew it back.

"Mensah," said Osmond, looking down gravely at the body, "this man my countryman, my friend. You sabby?"

"Yes, sir. I sabby he be your brother."

"Well, I am going to bury him in the compound with Mr. Larkom and Mr. Osmond."

"Yas, sir," said Mensah, with a somewhat puzzled expression. That second grave was a mystery that had caused him much secret cogitation. But discretion had restrained him from asking questions.

"You think," pursued Osmond, "these people fit for bring the dead man to Adaffia?"

"They fit," replied Mensah. "S'pose you dash it plenty money."

"Very well," said Osmond, with characteristic incaution. "See that he is brought in and I will pay them what they ask."

"I go look them people one time," said Mensah, who had instantly decided that, on these advantageous terms, he would undertake the contract himself.

Before starting to walk back, Osmond took another glance at the wreckage and at the crowd of natives who were, even now, carrying it away piecemeal. For a moment he had a thought of constituting himself

119

Lloyd's agent and taking possession of what was left. But he had no authority, and as the mere wreckage was of no realizable value, and as the little cargo there had been was already carried away, he dismissed the idea and set out homeward, leaving the delighted natives in undisputed possession.

His first proceeding on arriving home was to unlock the safe and break open the leathern bags to see what directions Captain Hartup had given as to the disposal of his property. He was not entirely unprepared to find that the captain had formally transferred the gold-dust to him. But he was totally unprepared for the contents of the bulky paper which he drew out of the second bag, and as he opened and read it he could hardly believe the evidence of his eyesight. The paper was a regularly-drawn will, witnessed by Winter and Simmons, which made "*My friend and temporary mate, Mr. James Cook*", sole executor and legatee.

It began with a preamble, setting forth that "*I, Nicholas Hartup, being a widower without offspring, dependants, or near relations, give and bequeath my worldly possessions to the man who has dealt with me honestly, faithfully, and without thought of material profit or reward,*" and then went on to make the specific bequests, describing each of the items clearly and in detail. These included the gold-dust, giving the exact weight, a consignment of ivory consisting of "*thirty-nine large tusks in three large crates, at present in the hold of the brigantine Speedwell, and fifty-one scribellos in a large canvas bag wired up and sealed, also in the hold,*" also the vessel herself, and, most astonishing of all, "*my freehold house in Bristol, known as Number Sixty-five Garlic Street,*" and a sum of about three-thousand pounds, a part invested in certain named securities and the remainder lying on deposit at a specified bank in Bristol. It was an amazing document. As Osmond read and re-read it he found himself wondering at the perverseness of the little shipmaster in hiding his kindly, appreciative feelings under so forbidding an exterior. But, to judge by the wording of the preamble, his experience of men would seem not to have been happy. Osmond, having put back the will in the bag, tied up that and the other and replaced them in the safe. As he locked the door and pocketed the key, he reflected on the irony of his present position. In all the years during which he had lived amidst his friends and relatives, no one had ever bequeathed to him a single penny. Yet in the course of a few months, in this unfrequented and forgotten corner of the world, he had twice been made the sole legatee of almost complete strangers. And now he had be come a man of modest substance, an owner of landed property, and that in a country which prudence insisted that he must never revisit.

Chapter IX
Arms and the Man

Speaking in general terms, Welshmen cannot be fairly described as excessively rare creatures, in fact, there are some parts of the world – Wales, for instance – in which they are quite common. But circumstances alter cases. When Jack Osmond, busily engaged in posting up his account-books, lifted his eyes and beheld a specimen of this well-known type of mammal, he was quite startled, not merely because he had never before heard anyone say "Good morning" with an accent on the "ning" – which the present example did, although it was actually three in the afternoon – but because no ship had called in the neighbourhood quite lately and he had not known of the presence of any European in the village.

The stranger introduced himself by the name of Jones, which being not entirely without precedent was accepted without difficulty. He had an additional name, but as Osmond failed to assimilate it, and it could be expressed in writing only by an extravagant expenditure of *l*'s and double *d*'s, it is omitted from this merely Saxon chronicle. He shook Osmond's hand exuberantly and smiled until his face – particularly the left side – was as full of lines as a ground-plan of Willesden Junction.

"I come to you, Mr. Larkom," said the visitor, retaining Osmond's unwilling hand and apparently adopting the name that remained unaltered over the door of the factory, "as a fellow-countryman in distress, craving a charitable judgment and a helping hand."

He would have been well advised to leave it at that, for Osmond's natural generosity needed no spur, and the memory of his own misfortunes was enough to ensure his charity to others. But Mr. Jones continued, smiling harder than ever, "I come to you confidently for this help because of the many instances of your kindness and generosity and good-fellowship that I have heard – "

"From whom?" interrupted Osmond.

"From – er – from – well, I may say, from everyone on the Coast who knows you."

"Oh," said Osmond, and his face relaxed into a grim smile. Jones saw that he had made a mistake and wondered what the deuce it was.

"Come into my room," said Osmond, "and tell me what you want me to do. Have a cocktail?"

121

Mr. Jones would have a cocktail, thank you, and while Osmond twirled the swizzle-stick and raised a pink froth in the tumbler, he cautiously opened his business.

"I am taking some risk in telling you of my little affair, but I am sure I can trust you not to give me away."

"Certainly you can," Osmond replied, incautiously.

"You promise on your honour as a gentleman not to give me away?"

"I have," said Osmond, handing him the cocktail.

Jones still hesitated somewhat, as if desirous of further formalities, but at length plunged into the matter in a persuasive whisper, with much gesticulation and a craftily watchful eye on Osmond's face.

It was not an encouraging face. A portrait of the "Iron Duke" at the age of thirty, executed in very hard wood by a heavy-handed artist with a large chisel and mallet, would give you the kind of face that Mr. Jones looked upon, and as the "little affair" unfolded itself, that face grew more and more wooden. For Osmond's charity in respect of errors of conduct did not extend to those that were merely in contemplation.

It transpired gradually that Mr. Jones's sufferings and distress were occasioned by a little cargo that he had been unable to land, which cargo happened to include – er – in fact, to be quite candid, consisted largely of Mauser rifles, together with some miscellaneous knick-knacks – such as Mauser cartridges, for instance – all of which were at present rolling in the hold of a privately-chartered vessel (name not mentioned). It also appeared that the Colonial Government had most unreasonably prohibited the importation of arms and ammunition on account of the silly little insurrection that had broken out inland, which very circumstance created an exceptional opportunity – Don't you understand? – for disposing of munitions of war on profitable terms. It appeared, finally, that Mr. Larkom's factory was an ideal place in which to conceal the goods and from which to distribute them among local sportsmen interested in target-practice or partridge-shooting.

"To put it in a nutshell," said Osmond, "you're doing a bit of gun-running and you want to use me as a cat's paw, and to put it in another nutshell, I'll see you damned first."

"But," protested Jones, "you sell arms yourself, don't you?"

"Not while this row is on. Besides, the natives don't buy my gas-pipes for war-palaver. My customers are mostly hunters from the bush."

Mr. Jones lingered a while to ply the arts of persuasion and consume two more cocktails, and when at last he departed, more in sorrow than in anger, he paused on the threshold to remark, "You have promised, on your honour, not to give me away."

122

"I know I have, like a fool," replied Osmond "Wish I hadn't. Know better next time. Good day." And he followed his departing guest to the compound gate and shut it after him.

From that moment Mr. Jones seemed to vanish into thin air. He was seen no more in the village, and no whispers as to his movements came from outside. But a few nights later Osmond had a rather curious experience that somehow recalled his absent acquaintance. He had gone out, according to his common custom, to take a quiet stroll on the beach before turning in, and think of his future movements and of the everlasting might-have-been. Half-a-mile west of the village he came on a fishing canoe, drawn up above tide-marks, and as he had just filled his pipe he crept under the lee of the canoe to light it – for one learns to husband one's matches in West Africa. Having lighted his pipe, he sat down to think over a trading expedition that he had projected but, finding himself annoyed by the crabs, which at nightfall pour out of their burrows in myriads, he shifted to the interior of the canoe. Here he sat, looking over the spectral breakers out into the dark void which was the sea, and immersed in his thoughts until he was startled by the sudden appearance of a light. He watched it curiously and not without suspicion. It was not a ship's anchor-light, nor was it a flare-lamp in a fishing-canoe. By the constant variation in its brightness Osmond judged it to be a bull's-eye lantern which was being flashed to-and-fro along the coast from some vessel in the offing to signal to someone ashore.

He looked up and down the dark beach for the answering signal, and presently caught a dull glimmer, as of a bull's-eye lantern seen from one side, proceeding from the beach a short distance farther west. Watching this spot, he soon made out a patch of deeper darkness which grew in extent, indicating that a crowd of natives had gathered at the water's edge and, after a considerable interval a momentary flash of the lantern fell on a boat dashing towards the beach in a smother of spray.

Soon after this a number of dark shapes began to separate themselves from the mass and move in single file across the low sand-dunes, passing within a few dozen yards of the canoe. Osmond could see them distinctly, though himself unseen, a long procession of carriers, each bearing a load on his head, and whereas some of these loads were of an oblong shape, like small gun-crates – about the length of a Mauser rifle – the others were more nearly cubical and quite small, though obviously heavy. Osmond watched the file of carriers and counted upwards of forty loads. Perhaps it was none of his business. But as those parcels of death and destruction were borne silently away into the darkness to swell the tale of slaughter in the inland villages, he cursed Mr. Jones and his own folly in giving that unconsidered promise.

123

The last of the carriers had vanished and he had just risen from the canoe to return up the now deserted beach when a new phenomenon presented itself. The clouds, which had hidden the rising moon, thinned for a few moments, leaving a patch of coppery light in the eastern sky, and against this, sharp and distinct as if cut out of black paper, stood the shape of a schooner. But not an ordinary trading schooner. Brief as was the gleam that rendered her visible, her character was perfectly obvious to a yachtsman's eye. She was a large yacht of the type that was fashionable when the America Cup was new, when spoon bows and bulb keels were things as yet undreamed of. Osmond stared at her in astonishment, and even as he looked, the clouds closed up, the sky drew dark, and she was lost in the blackness of the night.

He was up betimes on the following morning and out on the beach in the grey dawn to see if any confirmatory traces of these mysterious proceedings were visible. But his questioning eye ranged over the grey sea in vain. The schooner had vanished as if she had never been. There were, however, multitudinous tracks of bare feet leading up from the shore to the sand-hills, where they were lost, deep footprints such as would be made by heavily-laden men. And there was something else, even more significant. Just at high-water mark, hardly clear of the wash of the sea, was a ship's boat, badly battered, broken-backed, and with one bilge stove in. Some fool, who knew not the West Coast surf, had evidently landed a heavy lading in her with this inevitable result.

But it was not her condition alone that caused Osmond to stride so eagerly towards her. There was something in her size and build that he seemed to recognize. As he reached her, he walked round to examine her stern. There had, of course, been a name painted on her transom, but it had been scraped out and the stern re-painted. Then Osmond stepped in and lifted one of the bottom-boards, and there, on the starboard side close to the keel, was a patch covered with sheet-copper, while inspection from without showed an external covering of copper. There was no mistaking that patch. It was his own handiwork. This poor battered wreck was the *Speedwell*'s long-boat, and as he realized this, he realized, too, what had become of the *Speedwell*'s cargo.

The discovery gave Osmond considerable food for thought for the remainder of the morning. But about mid-day an unlooked-for letter from Betty arrived and for the time being occupied his attention to the exclusion of all other matters. And not entirely without reason. For it conveyed tidings of a somewhat disturbing kind. The message was, indeed, smuggled in inconsequently, as important messages often are in ladies' letters, at the end. But there it was, and Osmond read it with deep disapproval and no small uneasiness.

You will probably not hear from me again for a week or two as I am going for a little trip inland and may not have a chance to send a letter. I shall let you know directly I get back, and until you hear from me you had better not write – or, at least, you can write, and make it a nice long letter, but don't send it until you get mine.

That was the message. She did not give a hint as to the region into which the "little trip" would take her. But Osmond had a strong and uncomfortable suspicion that her route would take her into the country at the back of the great lagoon and would bring her finally to Adaffia.

He pondered the situation at length. As to the danger of such a journey, it was probably negligible – if the reports were correct. The disturbed area was far away to the north, on the borders of Krepi. The country at the back of the lagoon was believed to be quite peaceful and safe. But one never knew. These Efé peoples were naturally warlike and turbulent. At any moment they might break out in support of their inland relatives. Even now they might have provided themselves with some of Mr. Jones's knick-knacks and be preparing for "war-palaver".

The result of his cogitations was somewhat curious and not very easy to understand. For some time past he had been turning over in his mind a project which had really been held up by the regular arrival of Betty's letters. That project was concerned with a trading expedition to the interior – to the country at the back of the lagoon. But that "little trip" would have taken him out of the region in which the receipt of letters was possible, and he had accordingly put it off to some more opportune time. Now that more opportune time seemed to have arrived. There would be no more letters for a week or two, so there was nothing to prevent him from starting. That was how he put it to himself, What was actually in his mind it is impossible to guess. Whether his purpose was to be absent from Adaffia when Betty should make her inevitable visit, to avoid the meeting for which he had yearned but which he felt to be so undesirable, or whether he had some vague hopes of a possible encounter on the road – who can say? Certainly not the present chronicler, and probably not Osmond himself. At any rate, the upshot of it was that he decided on the journey, and with characteristic promptitude set about his preparations forthwith, and as they were far from elaborate and had been well considered before hand, a single day's work saw everything ready for the start.

On the following morning he set forth, leaving the faithful Mensah in charge of the factory. A dozen carriers bore the loads of goods for the trading venture, and his recently engaged servant, Koffi Kuma, carried his simple necessaries in a light box. In spite of his anxieties and haunting regrets, he was in high spirits at the promised change from the monotony of Adaffia, which, but for the infinitely precious letters, would have been intolerably wearisome. The universal sand, varied only by the black lagoon mud, the everlasting coconut palms chattering incessantly in the breeze, and the bald horizon of the unpeopled sea, had begotten in him an intense yearning for a change of scene, for the sight of veritable trees with leaves, growing in actual earth, and of living things other than the sea-birds and the amphibious denizens of the beach.

A couple of hours' steady marching carried him and his little party across the bare plain of dry mud that had once been part of the great lagoon and brought him to the mainland and the little nine-inch trail that did duty as a road. Gleefully he strode along in the rear of his little caravan, refreshing his eyes and ears with the novel sights and sounds. The tiresome boom of the surf had faded into a distant murmur that mingled with the stirring of leaves, strange birds, unseen in the bush, piped queer little Gregorian chants, while others, silent, but gorgeous of plumage – scarlet cardinals and rainbow-hued sun-birds – disported themselves visibly among the foliage. Little striped Barbary mice gambolled beside the track, and great, blue-bodied lizards with scarlet heads and tails perched on the tall ant-hills that rose on all sides like pink monuments, and nodded their heads defiantly at the passing strangers. It was a new world to Osmond. The bright pink soil, the crowded bush, the buttressed forest trees, the uncouth baobabs, with their colossal trunks and absurdly dwarfed branches – all were new and delightful after the monotony of the beach village, and so fully occupied his attention that when they entered a hamlet of pink-walled houses, he was content to leave the trading to Koffi, while he watched a troop of dog-faced monkeys who seemed to have established a sort of *modus vivendi* with the villagers.

Thus, with occasional halts for rest or barter, the caravan worked its way through the bush until about four o'clock in the afternoon, when Osmond, who had lagged behind to avoid the chatter of his carriers, rounded a sharp turn in the road and found himself entering the main street of a village. But he was not the only visitor. An instantaneous glance showed him a couple of stands of piled arms, by the side of which some half-dozen bare-footed native soldiers were seated on the ground eating from a large calabash, a fierce and sullen looking native, secured with manacles and a leading-rope and guarded by two more of the Hausa soldiers as he was fed by some of the villagers, and two white officers, seated under the village shade tree and engaged at the moment in conversation with Koffi, who seemed to have been captured by a Hausa sergeant.

As Osmond came in sight the two officers looked at one another and rose with a rather stiff salutation.

"You are Mr. Cook of Adaffia, I understand?" one of them said.

"Yes," Osmond replied, and as the two officers again looked at one another with an air of some embarrassment, he continued, bluntly, "I suppose you want to know if I have got any contraband of war?"

"Well, you know," was the half-apologetic reply, "someone has been selling rifles and ammunition to the natives, so we have to make inquiries."

"Of course you do," said Osmond, "and you'd better have a look at my goods. Koffi, tell the carriers to bring their loads here and open them."

A very perfunctory inspection was enough to satisfy the constabulary officers of the harmless character of the trade goods, and having made it, they introduced themselves by the respective names of Stockbridge and Westall and invited Osmond to join them in their interrupted tea under the shade tree.

"Troublesome affair, this rising," said Westall, as he handed Osmond a mug of tea. "There'll be wigs on the green before it's over. Now that the beggars have got rifles, they are ready to stand up to the constabulary. Think they're as good as we are, and they're not so far wrong, either."

"Where are you bound for now?" Osmond asked.

"We are going back to Quittah with some prisoners from Agotimé." Westall nodded at the manacled native and added, "That's one of the ring-leaders – a rascal named Zippah, a devil of a fellow, vicious as a bush-cat and plucky, too. Stockbridge and I are keeping him with us, in case of a rescue, but there are over a dozen other prisoners with the main body of Hausas. They marched out of the village just before you turned up."

"And we'd better be marching out, too," said Stockbridge, "or we shan't catch them up. Will you have any more tea, Cook? If not, we'd better get on the road. There's only a native sergeant-major with those men ahead. Are you coming our way?"

"Yes," replied Osmond, "I'll come with you as far as Affieringba, and then work my way home along the north shore of the lagoon."

The three Englishman rose and, as Westall's servant repacked the tea apparatus, the little procession formed up. The six Hausas led with fixed bayonets. Then came Westall, followed by the prisoner, Zippah, and his guard. Next came half-a-dozen carriers loaded with bundles of

127

confiscated muskets and powder. Then Osmond and Stockbridge, and the rear was brought up by Osmond's carriers and the three servants.

The road, or path, after leaving the village, passed through a number of yam and cassava plantations and then entered a forest of fan-palms, a dim and ghostly place now that the sun was getting low, pervaded by a universal rustling from the broad, ragged leaves above and a noisy crackling from the dry branches underfoot. For nearly an hour the party threaded its way through the gloomy aisles. Then the palms gradually thinned out, giving place to ordinary forest trees and bush.

"Quite pleasant to get a look at the sky again," Osmond remarked as they came out into the thin forest.

"Yes," said Stockbridge, "but you won't see it for long. There's a bamboo thicket just ahead."

Even as he spoke there loomed up before them an immense, cloudy mass of soft, blue-green foliage, then appeared a triangular black hole like the entrance to a tunnel, into which the Hausas, the prisoners, and the carriers successively vanished. A moment later and Osmond himself had entered through that strange portal and was groping his way in almost total darkness through a narrow passage, enclosed and roofed in by solid masses of bamboo stalks. Ahead, he could dimly make out the vague shapes of the carriers, while all around the huge clusters of bamboos rose like enormous piers, widening out until they met overhead to form a kind of groined roof. It was an uncanny place, a place in which voices echoed weirdly, mingling with strange, unexplained noises and with the unceasing, distant murmur of the soft foliage far away overhead.

Osmond stumbled on over the crackling canes that formed the floor, gradually growing accustomed to the darkness until there appeared ahead a triangular spot of light that grew slowly larger, framing the figures of the Hausas and carriers, and then, quite suddenly, he emerged, blinking, into broad daylight on the margin of a smallish but deep and rapid river, which at this spot was spanned by a primitive bridge.

Now a native bridge is an excellent contrivance – for natives – for the booted European it is much less suitable. The present one was formed of the slender trunk of a young silk-cotton tree, barkless and polished by years of wear, and Osmond watched enviously as the Hausas strolled across, grasping the cylindrical surface handily with their bare feet, and wondered if he had not better take off his boots. However, Westall had no false pride. Recognizing the disabilities involved by boots, he stooped and, getting astride the slender log, crossed the river with ease and safety, if without much dignity, and the other two white men were not too proud to follow his example.

128

Beyond the river the path, after crossing a narrow belt of forest, entered a valley bordered by hills covered with dense bush, which rose steeply on either side. Osmond looked at the little party ahead, straggling in single file along the bottom of the valley, and inwardly wondered where Westall had picked up his strategy.

"It's to be hoped, Stockbridge," he remarked, "that there are none of Mr. Zippah's friends hanging about here. You couldn't want a prettier spot for an ambush."

He had hardly spoken when a tall man, wearing a hunter's lionskin cap and carrying a musket, stepped quietly out of the bush on to the track just in front of Westall. The prisoner, Zippah, uttered a yell of recognition and held up his manacled hands. The deep, cannon-like report of the musket rang out and the narrow gorge was filled with a dense cloud of smoke.

There was an instant's silence. Then a scattering volley was heard from the Hausas ahead, the panic-stricken carriers came flying back along the trail, shouting with terror, and the two white men plunged forward into the stinking smoke. Leaping over the prostrate Zippah, who was being held down by two Hausas, they came upon Westall, lying across the path, limp and motionless. A great ragged patch on his breast, all scorched and bloody, told the tale that his pinched, grey face and glazing eyes confirmed. Indeed, even as they stooped over him, heedless of the bellowing muskets and the slugs that shrieked past, he drew one shallow breath and was gone.

There was no time for sentiment. With set faces the two men turned from the dead officer and ran forward to where the shadowy forms of the Hausas appeared through the smoke, holding their ground doggedly and firing right and left into the bush. But a single glance showed the hopelessness of the position. Two of the Hausas were down, and of the remaining four, three – including the sergeant – were more-or-less wounded. Not a man of the enemy was to be seen, but from the wooded slope on either hand came jets of flame and smoke, accompanied by the thunderous reports of the muskets and the whistle of flying slugs, while a thick cloud of smoke rolled down the hillsides and filled the bottom of the valley as with a dense fog.

Osmond snatched up the rifle of one of the fallen Hausas and, clearing out the man's cartridge-pouch, began firing into likely spots in the bush when Stockbridge interposed. "It's no go, Cook. We must fall back across the bridge. You clear out while you've got a whole skin. Hallo! Did you hear that? Those weren't trade guns."

129

As he spoke there were heard, mingling with the noisy explosions of the muskets, a succession of sharp, woody reports, each followed by the musical hum of a high-speed bullet.

"Back you go, Cook," he urged. "This is no place for – "

He stopped short, staggered back a few paces, and fell, cursing volubly, with a bloody hand clasped on his leg just below the knee.

Osmond stooped over him, and, finding that the bone was not broken, quickly tied his handkerchief over the wound to restrain the bleeding. "That will do for the present," said he. "Now you tell the men to fall back, and I'll bring the prisoner."

"Never mind the prisoner," said Stockbridge. "Get the wounded back and get back yourself."

"Not at all," said Osmond. "The prisoner is going to cover our retreat. Put your arm round the sergeant's neck and hop along on your sound leg."

In spite of the galling fire, the retreat was carried out quickly and in good order. Stockbridge was hustled away by the sergeant – who was only disabled in one arm – and the two helpless men and the dead officer were borne off by the three native servants. Meanwhile Osmond took possession of the prisoner – just as one of his guards was preparing to cut his throat with a large and very unofficial-looking knife – and, rapidly pinioning his arms with the leading-rope, held him up with his face towards the enemy, in which position he served as excellent cover, not only for Osmond but also for the two Hausas, who were able to keep up a brisk fire over his shoulders.

In this fashion Osmond and his two supporters slowly backed after the retreating party. The firing from the bush practically ceased, since the enemy had now no mark to fire at but their own chief, and though they continued to follow up, as the moving bushes showed, their wholesome respect for the Snider rifle – with which the Hausas were armed – prevented them from coming out of cover or approaching dangerously near.

In less than a quarter-of-an-hour, the open space by the river was reached, and here Osmond's retreat was covered by the rest of the party, who had crossed the river and had taken up a safe position in the bamboo thicket, whence they could, without exposing themselves, command the approaches to the bridge. The two Hausas were turning to run across the log when Osmond noticed a large basket of produce – containing among other things, a number of balls of shea butter – which one of his carriers had dropped in retreat.

130

"Hi!" he sang out. "Pick up that basket and take him across." And then, as a new idea suggested itself: "Put those balls of *shea tulu* in my pocket."

The astonished Hausa hesitated, especially as a Mauser bullet had just hummed past his head, but when Osmond repeated the order impatiently he hurriedly grabbed up the unsavoury-looking balls of grease and emptied them into Osmond's pocket. Then he turned and ran across the bridge.

Osmond continued to back towards the river, still holding the struggling Zippah close before him as a shield. Arriving at the end of the bridge, he cautiously sat down and got astride the log, pulling his captive, with some difficulty, into the same position, and began to wriggle across. Once started, Zippah was docile enough, for, with his pinioned arms, he could not afford to fall into the swirling water. He even assisted his captor so far as he was able, being evidently anxious to get the perilous passage over as quickly as possible. When they had crept about a third of the way across, Osmond took one of the balls of shea butter from his pocket and, reaching past his prisoner, smeared the mass thickly on the smooth surface of the log, and this proceeding he repeated at intervals as he retired, leaving a thick trail of the solid grease behind him. Zippah was at first profoundly mystified by the white man's manoeuvres, which he probably regarded as some kind of fetish ceremonial or magic, but when its purpose suddenly dawned on him, his sullen face relaxed into a broad and appreciative grin, and as he was at length dragged backwards from the head of the bridge, through the opening into the dark bamboo thicket, he astonished the besieged party (and no doubt the besiegers also) by letting off a peal of honest African guffaws.

131

Chapter X
Betty's Appeal

As the prisoner was withdrawn by his guard into the dark opening of the thicket, Osmond halted for a moment to look back across the river. Not a sign of the enemy was to be seen excepting the pall of smoke that hung over the wooded shore. But the reports of unseen muskets and rifles and the hum of slugs and bullets warned him of the danger of exposing himself – though he, too, was probably hidden from the enemy by the dense smoke of the black powder. Accordingly he turned quickly and, plunging into the dark tunnel-like passage, groped his way forward, unable, at first, to distinguish anything in the all-pervading gloom. Presently he perceived a little distance ahead a cluster of the great bamboo stalks faintly lighted as if by a hidden fire or torch, and a moment later, a turn of the passage brought him in view of the light itself, which seemed to be a rough shea-butter candle or lamp, set on the ground and lighting up dimly the forlorn little band whose retreat he had covered.

This much he took in at the first glance. But suddenly he became aware of a new presence at the sight of which he stopped short with a smothered exclamation. Stockbridge, sitting beside his dead comrade, had uncovered his wounded leg, and kneeling by him as she applied a dressing to the wound was a woman. He could not see her face, which was partly turned away from him and concealed by a wide pith helmet, but the figure was – to him – unmistakable, as were the little, dainty, capable hands on which the flickering light shone. He approached slowly, and as Stockbridge greeted him with a wry grin, she turned her head quickly and looked up at him. "Good evening, Mr. Cook," she said, quietly. "What a fortunate chance it is that you should be here."

"Yes, by Jove," agreed Stockbridge, "at least a fortunate chance for us. He is a born tactician."

Osmond briefly acknowledged the greeting, and in the ensuing silence, as Betty methodically applied the bandage, he looked about him and rapidly assessed the situation. Stockbridge looked weak and spent and was evidently in considerable pain, though he uttered no complaint. The wounded Hausas lay hard by, patiently awaiting their turn to have their injuries attended to, and the carriers crouched disconsolately in gloomy corners out of the way of chance missiles. A continuous firing was being kept up from the other side of the river, and slugs and Mauser bullets ploughed noisily through the bamboo, though none came near the fugitives. The position of the latter, indeed, was one of great natural strength, for the river made a horse-shoe bend at this spot and the little peninsula enclosed by it was entirely occupied by the bamboo. An attack was possible in only two directions, by the bridge, or by the path that entered the thicket at the other end.

"Well," said Osmond, as Betty, having finished the dressing, transferred her attention to one of the wounded Hausas, "here we are, safe for the moment. They can't get at us in here."

"No," agreed Stockbridge. "It's a strong position, if we could stay here, though they will probably try to rush the bridge when it's dark."

Osmond shook his head with a grim smile. "They won't do that," said he. "I've taken the precaution to grease the log, so they'll have to crawl across carefully, which they won't care to do with the Hausas potting at them from shelter. But we can't stay here. We'd better clear out as soon as it is dark, and the question is, which way?"

"We must follow the river, I suppose," said Stockbridge, in a faint voice. "But you'd better arrange with the sergeant. I'm no good now. Tell him he's to take your orders. Our carriers know the country."

The sergeant, who had witnessed Osmond's masterly retreat, accepted the new command without demur. A guard was posted to watch the bridge from safe cover, and the carriers were assembled to discuss the route.

"Now," said Osmond, "where is the next bridge?" There was apparently no other bridge, but there was a ford some miles farther up, and a couple of miles below there was a village which possessed one or two of the large, punt-shaped canoes that were used for trading across the lagoon.

"S'pose they no fit to pass the bridge," said the head carrier. "They go and fetch canoe for carry 'em across the river."

"I see," said Osmond. "Then they'd attack us from the rear and we should be bottled up from both sides. That won't do. You must get ready to march out as soon as it is dark, Sergeant. Your carriers can take Mr. Westall's body and some of the wounded and the sound men must carry the rest. And send my carriers back the way they came. There are too many of us as it is."

"And them muskets and powder, that we bring in from the villages?" said the sergeant. "What we do with them?"

"We must leave them here or throw them in the river. Anyhow, you get off as quickly as you can."

The sergeant set about his preparations without delay and Osmond's carriers departed gleefully towards the safe part of the country.

Meanwhile Osmond considered the situation. If the enemy obtained canoes from the lower river, they would probably ferry a party across and attack the bamboo fortress from front and rear simultaneously. Then they would find the nest empty, and naturally would start in pursuit, which would be unpleasant for the helpless fugitives, crawling painfully along the river bank. He turned the position over again and again with deep dissatisfaction, while Stockbridge watched him anxiously and Betty silently continued her operations on the wounded. If they were pursued, they were lost. In their helpless condition they could make no sort of stand against a large body attacking from the cover of the bush. And the pursuit would probably commence before they had travelled a couple of miles towards safety.

Suddenly his eye fell on the heap of captured muskets and powder-kegs that, were to be left behind or destroyed. He looked at them meditatively, and, as he looked, there began to shape itself in his mind a plan by which the fugitives might at least increase their start by a mile or so. A fantastic scheme, perhaps, but yet, in the absence of any better, worth trying.

With characteristic energy, he set to work at once, while the carriers hastily fashioned rough litters of bamboo for the dead and wounded. Broaching one of the powder-kegs, he proceeded to load all but two of the muskets – of which there were twenty-three in all – cramming the barrels with powder and filling up each with a heavy charge of gravel. Six of the loaded and primed muskets he laid on the ground about fifty yards from the bridge end of the long passage, with their muzzles pointing towards the bridge, the remaining fifteen he laid in batches of five about the same distance from the opposite entrance, towards which their muzzles pointed. Then, taking a length of the plaited cord with which the muskets had been lashed into bundles, he tied one end to the stock of one of the unloaded guns and the other to the trigger of one of the wounded Hausas' rifles. Fixing the rifle upright against the bamboo with its muzzle stuck in the half-empty powder-keg, of which he broke out two or three staves, he carried the cord – well-greased with shea butter – through a loop tied to one of the slanting bamboos. Then he propped the musket in a standing position on two bamboo sticks, to one of which he attached another length of cord. It was the mechanism of the common sieve bird-trap. When the cord was pulled, the stick would be dislodged, the musket would fall, and in falling jerk the other cord and fire the rifle.

Broaching another keg, he carried a large train of powder from the first keg to the row of loaded muskets, over the pans of which he poured a considerable heap. Leaving the tripping-cord loose, he next proceeded

134

to the opposite end of the thicket and set up a similar trap near the landward entrance, connecting it by a large powder train with the three batches of loaded muskets.

"You seemed to be deuced busy, Cook," Stockbridge remarked as Osmond passed the hammock in which he was now reclining.

"Yes," Osmond replied, "I am arranging a little entertainment to keep our friends amused while we are getting a start. Now, sergeant, if you are ready, you had better gag the prisoner and move outside the bamboos. It will be dark in a few minutes. And give me Mr. Westall's revolver and pouch."

At this moment, Betty, having applied such "first aid" as was possible to the wounded Hausas, came to him and said in a low voice, "Jim, dear, you will let me help you, if I can, won't you?"

"Certainly I will, dearest," he replied, "though I wish to God you weren't here."

"I don't," said she. "If it comes to the worst, we shall go out together. But it won't. I am not a bit frightened now you are with me."

"I see you have given Stockbridge your hammock," said he. "How far do you think you can walk?"

"Twenty miles, easily, or more at night. Now, Jim, don't worry about me. Just tell me what I am to do and forget me. You have plenty to think about."

"Well, then, I want you and Stockbridge to keep in the middle of the column. The carrier who knows the way will lead, and the sergeant and I will march at the rear to look out for the pursuers. And you must get along as fast as you can."

"Aye, aye, sir," she replied, smiling in his face and raising her hand smartly to the peak of her helmet, and without another word she turned away to take her place in the retiring column.

As the little procession moved towards the opening, Osmond ran back to the bridge end of the track to clear out the guard before he set his traps. A brisk fusillade was proceeding from the concealed enemy when he arrived, to which the guards were replying from their cover.

"I think they fit for come across the bridge," one of the Hausas remarked as Osmond gave them the orders to retire.

"Very well," he replied, "you be off one time. I stop to send them back."

The two Hausas accordingly retired, reluctant and protesting, and Osmond took their place behind the screen of bamboo, from which he looked out across the river. It was evident by the constant stirring of the bush and the occasional appearance of men in the openings that some sort of move was in progress, and in fact the footsteps of the two Hausas

135

had hardly died away when it took definite shape. The attack opened with a thundering volley which sent the leaves and splinters of bamboo flying in all directions. Then, out of the bush, a compact body of warriors each armed with a Mauser rifle, emerged in single file and advanced towards the bridge at a smart trot. Osmond watched them with a grim smile. Down the narrow track they came in perfect order and on to the foot of the bridge, stepping along the smooth log with perfect security they reached the greased portion. Then came the catastrophe. As the leading warrior stepped on the greasy surface, his feet flew from under him and down he slithered, grabbing frantically at the legs of the next man, who instantly clawed hold of his neighbour and thus passed on the disturbance. In a moment the whole file was capsized like a row of ninepins, and as each man's rifle exploded as he fell and the whole body broke out into simultaneous yells of rage and terror, the orderly dignity of the attack was destroyed utterly.

The cause of the disaster was not immediately perceived, and as soon as the struggling warriors had been rescued from the river or had drifted down stream, the attack was renewed, to end in another wholesale capsize. After the third attempt, however, it apparently began to dawn on the warriors that there was something unnatural about the bridge. A noisy consultation followed, and when Osmond opened a smart fire with his revolver, the entire body retreated hastily into the bush.

As it was pretty certain that there would be no further attempt to rush the bridge at present, and as the darkness was fast closing in, Osmond proceeded to finish his arrangements before evacuating the fortress. Having set the tripping-cord across the path about six inches from the ground, he loaded and cocked the rifle. The trap was now set. If the warriors should presently manage to crawl across the bridge and enter the thicket, the first comer would certainly strike the cord, and the musket volley and the flying gravel, though they would probably do little harm, would send the attacking party back to the cover of the bush.

Having set the trap, Osmond knocked in the heads of the remaining powder-kegs and spread the powder about among the dry dead bamboo stalks that covered the ground. Then he retired to the landward end of the thicket and, having set the second trap, started in pursuit of his friends.

The fugitives had evidently travelled at a good pace despite their encumbrances, for he had walked nearly a mile along the riverside track before he overtook them. As he turned a sharp bend he came on them quite suddenly, crouching down in the undergrowth as if in hiding, and, as he appeared, the two Hausas who formed the rear-guard motioned to him to crouch down too.

"What is it?" he whispered, kneeling beside the last Hausa.

"S't! Someone live for river. You no hear 'em, sir?"

Osmond listened attentively. From somewhere down the river came a sound of muffled voices and the rhythmical swish of something moving through water. He crept nearer to the brink and cautiously peered through the bushes across the dark river. The sounds drew nearer, and soon he could dimly make out the shapes of two long canoes poling upstream in the shallows on the other side. Each canoe held only three or four men, just enough to drive it swiftly against the stream, but in spite of this, there could be little doubt as to the business on which these stealthily-moving craft were bent. As they faded into the darkness, Osmond touched the Hausa on the shoulder, and, whispering to him to follow, began softly to retrace his steps. His experience of the happy-go-lucky native had inspired him with a new hope.

Attended by the puzzled but obedient Hausa, he followed the sound of the retreating canoes until it suddenly ceased. Then he crept forward still more cautiously and presently caught sight of the two craft, brought up under the opposite bank and filling rapidly with men. He crouched down among the bushes and watched. Very soon the canoes, now crowded with men, put out, one after the other, and swiftly crossing the river, grounded on a small beach or hard under the high bank, when the men, each of whom, as Osmond could now see, carried a gun or rifle, landed and crept up a sloping path. The canoe immediately put off and returned to the other side, whence, having taken up a fresh batch of passengers they crossed to the hard. This manoeuvre was repeated six times, and, as each canoe carried over a dozen men, there were now assembled on the near bank about a hundred-and-fifty warriors who remained in a mass, talking in hoarse undertones and waiting for the word to advance.

The last load apparently completed the contingent, for, this time, all the passengers landed and crept up the path, leaving the two canoes drawn up on the hard. This was what Osmond had hoped for and half expected. Feverishly he watched the mob of warriors form up and move off in orderly single file, each shouldering his musket or rifle and no one making a sound. As the silent procession vanished towards the lately evacuated fortress, he craned forward to see if any guards had been posted. But not a soul was in sight. Then he stole along the track until he was above the hard, when he turned to the Hausa.

"Wait," he whispered, "until I get the canoes. Then go back quickly and tell the sergeant I come."

He crept down the path to the hard and, stepping into one of the canoes, walked to the stern, holding on to the second canoe. As his weight depressed the stern, the bow lifted from the ground and he was able to push off, walking slowly forward as the craft went astern. Then, from the bow, he threw his weight on the stern of the second canoe, which lifted free of the ground in the same manner, and the two craft began silently to drift away downstream on the swift current.

Osmond waved his free hand to the Hausa, and, when he had seen the man steal away to carry the good tidings to the fugitives, he set himself to secure the two canoes together. Each had a primitive painter of grass rope rove through a hole in the bluff bow and a small thwart or cross-band of the same material close to the stern to strengthen the long sides. By making fast the painter of the second canoe to the stern thwart of the one he was in, he secured them together and left himself free to ply the pole, which he began to do as noiselessly as possible, when he had drifted down about a quarter-of-a-mile from the hard, steering the canoes close along the side on which his friends would be waiting. Presently there came a soft hail from the bank, on which, checking their way with the pole, he brought the two canoes up on a spit of sandy mud close underneath.

As he stepped ashore, holding on to the painter of the leading canoe, a little, white-skirted figure came scrambling down the bank, and running to him, seized both his hands.

"Jim!" she whispered, "you are a wonder! You have saved us all! Of course you have! I knew you would!" She gave his hands a final squeeze and then abruptly returned to business. "I will see to the wounded if you tell me where they are to go."

Osmond indicated the larger of the two canoes, and she at once climbed up the bank to arrange the embarkation, while Osmond, having drawn both canoes up on the spit, called to two of the Hausas to take charge of the painters so that the craft should not get adrift while loading. Then he went up to superintend. The first problem, that of canoe-men, was easily solved, for the carriers, who were natives of the lagoon country, all had some skill in the use of the pole and cheerfully volunteered for duty.

But it was not without some difficulty that the three rough litters – one of them containing the body of poor Westall – were lowered down the steep bank and the wounded men helped down to the spit, but when once they were there, the roomy, punt-like canoes afforded ample and comfortable accommodation for the whole party. The sound men, with three canoe-men and the prisoner, were packed into the smaller canoe, leaving plenty of space in the other for the wounded to lie at their ease. Stockbridge's hammock was stowed in the bows, so that he should not be disturbed by the movements of the canoe-men, the body of Westall came next, decently covered with a country cloth, and then the rest of the

138

wounded. When all was ready, Betty and Osmond stepped on board and took their places side by side in the stern.

As they pushed off into the river Stockbridge settled himself comfortably on his pillow with a sigh of relief at exchanging the jolting of the bush road for the easy motion of the canoe.

"By Jove, Cook!" he exclaimed, "it was a stroke of luck for us that you happened to overtake us. But for your wits they would have made a clean sweep of us. Hallo! What the deuce is that?"

From up the river came three thunderous volleys in quick succession, followed by a confused noise of shouting and the reports of muskets and rifles, then the sound of another volley, more shouts and rattling reports, and as they looked back, the sky was lighted for a few moments by a red glare. Osmond briefly explained the nature of his "little arrangements", while the alarmed carriers poled along the shallows for dear life.

"But," said Stockbridge, after listening awhile, "what are the beggars going on firing for? Just hark at them! They're blazing away like billy-oh!"

"I take it," replied Osmond, "that they have gorged the bait. Apparently, a party has managed to crawl across the bridge to attack the bamboo thicket from the front while the other force, which ferried across the river, attacked from the rear, and that each party is mistaking the other for us. The trifling error ought to keep them amused for quite a long time – in fact until we are beyond reach of pursuit."

Stockbridge chuckled softly. "You are an ingenious beggar, Cook," he declared with conviction. "And how you managed to keep your wits about you in that hurly-burly, I can't imagine. However, I think we are safe enough now." With this comfortable conclusion, he snuggled down into his hammock and settled himself for a night's rest.

"Oh, Jim, dear," whispered Betty, "how like you! To think out your plans calmly with the bullets flying around and everybody else in a hopeless twitter. It reminds me of the 'phantom mate' on the dear old *Speedwell*. By the way, how did you happen to be there in that miraculously opportune fashion?"

Osmond chuckled. "Well," he exclaimed, "you are a pretty cool little fish, Betty. You drop down from the clouds and then inquire how *I* happened to be there. How did *you* happen to be there?"

"Oh, that is quite simple," she replied. "I got Daddy's permission to take a trip from Accra across the Akwapim Mountains to Akuse, and when I got there I thought I should like to have a look at the Country where the bobbery was going on. So I crossed the river and was starting off gaily towards the Krepi border when an interfering though well-

139

meaning old chief stopped me and said I mustn't go any farther because of war-palaver. I wanted to go on, but my carriers wouldn't budge, so back I came, taking the road for Quittah, and by good luck dropped into a little war-palaver after all."

"Why were you going to Quittah?"

"Now, Jim, don't ask silly questions. You know perfectly well. Of course I was going to run over to Adaffia to call on my friend Captain J., and by the same token, I shouldn't have found him there. Now tell me how you came to be in the bush at this particular time."

Osmond stated baldly the ostensible purpose of his expedition, to which Betty listened without comment. She had her suspicions as to the ultimate motive, but she asked no questions. The less said on that subject, the better.

This was evidently Osmond's view, for he at once plunged into an account of the loss of the *Speedwell* and of Captain Hartup's testamentary arrangements. Betty was deeply affected, both by the loss of the ship and the death of the worthy but cross-grained little skipper.

"How awfully sad!" she exclaimed, almost in tears. "The dear old ship, where I spent the happiest days of my life! And poor Captain Hartup! I always liked him, really. He was quite nice to me, in spite of his gruff manner. I used to feel that he was just a little human porcupine with India-rubber quills. And now I love him because, in his perverse little heart, he understood and appreciated my Captain Jim. May I come, one day, and put a wreath on his grave?"

"Yes, do, Betty," he replied. "I buried him next to Osmond's new grave, and I put up an oaken cross which I made out of some of the planking of the old *Speedwell*. He was very fond of his ship. And I have kept a couple of her beams – thought you might like to have something made out of one of them."

"How sweet of you, Jim, to think of it!" she exclaimed, nestling close to him and slipping her hand round his arm, "and to know exactly what I should like! But we do understand each other, don't we, Jim, dear?

"I think we do, Betty, darling," he replied, pressing the little hand that had stolen into his own.

For a long time nothing more was said. After the turmoil and the alarms of the escape, it was very peaceful to sit in the gently-swaying canoe and listen to the voices of the night, the continuous "chirr" of countless cicadas, punctuated by the soft swish of the canoe-poles as they were drawn forward for another stroke, the deep-toned, hollow whistle of the great fox-bats, flapping slowly across the river, the long drawn cry, or staccato titter, of far-away hyenas, and now and again, the startling

140

shriek of a potto in one of the lofty trees by the river-bank. It was more soothing than absolute silence. The sounds seemed so remote and unreal, so eloquent of utter solitude, of a vast, unseen wilderness with its mysterious population of bird and beast, living on its strange, primeval life unchanged from the days when the world was young.

After a long interval, Betty spoke again. "It seems," she said, reflectively, "dreadfully callous to be so perfectly happy. I wonder if it is."

"Why should it be?" her companion asked.

"I mean," she explained, "with poor Mr. Westall lying there dead, only a few feet away."

Osmond felt inwardly that Westall had not only thrown away his own life but jeopardized the lives of the others which were in his custody. But he forbore to express what he felt and answered, simply, "I don't suppose the poor chap would grudge us our happiness. It won't last very long."

"Why shouldn't it, Jim?" she exclaimed. "Why should we part again and be miserable for the want of one another? Oh, Jim, darling, my own mate, won't you try to put away your scruples – your needless scruples, though I love and respect you for having them? But don't let them spoil our lives. Forget John Osmond. He is dead and buried. Let him rest. I am yours, Jim, and you know it, and you are mine, and I know it. Those are the realities, which we could never change if we should live for a century. Let us accept them and forget what is past and done with. Life is short enough, dear, and our youth is slipping away. If we make a false move, we shall never get another chance. Oh, say it, Jim. Say you will put away the little things that don't matter and hold fast to the reality of our great love and the happiness that is within our reach. Won't you, Jim?"

He was silent for a while. This was what he had dreaded. To have freely offered, yet again, the gift beside which all the treasures of the earth were to him as nothing, and, even worse, to be made to feel that he, himself, had something to give which he must yet withhold, it was an agony. The temptation to yield – to shut his eyes to the future and snatch at the golden present – was almost irresistible. He knew that Betty was absolutely sincere. He knew quite well that whatever might befall in the future, she would hold him blameless and accept all mischances as the consequences of her own considered choice. His confidence in her generosity was absolute, nor did he undervalue her judgment. He even admitted that she was probably right. John Osmond was dead. The pursuit was at an end and the danger of discovery negligible. In a new country and in a new character he was sure that he could make her life all that she hoped. Then why not forget the past and say "Yes"?

It was a great temptation. One little word, and they would possess all that they wished for, all that mattered to either of them. And yet – "Betty," he said at length, in a tone of the deepest gravity, "you have said that we understand one another. We do, perfectly, absolutely. There is no need for me to tell you that I love you, or that if there were any sacrifice that I could make for you, I would make it joyfully and think it an honour and a privilege. You know that as well as I do. But there is one thing that I cannot do. Whatever I may be or may have done, I cannot behave like a cad to the woman I love. And that is what I should do if I married you. I should accept your sterling gold and give you base metal in exchange. You would be the wife of an outlaw. You would live under the continual menace of scandal and disaster. Your children would be the children of a nameless man and would grow up to the inheritance of an ancestry that could not be spoken of.

"Those are the realities, Betty. I realize, and I reverence, your great and noble love for me, unworthy as I am. But I should be a selfish brute if I accepted what you offer to me with such incredible generosity. I can't do it, Betty. It was a disaster that you ever met me, but that we cannot help. We can only limit its effects."

She listened silently while he pronounced the doom of her newly-born hopes, holding his hand tightly grasped in hers and scarcely seeming to breathe. She did not reply immediately when he ceased speaking, but sat a while, her head resting against his shoulder and her hand still clasped in his. Once she smothered a little sob and furtively wiped her eyes. But she was very quiet, and, at length, in a composed, steady voice, though sadly enough, she rejoined, "Very well, Jim, dear. It must be as you think best, and I won't tease you with any more appeals. At any rate, we can go on loving each other, and that will be something. The gift of real love doesn't come to everyone."

For a long time they sat without further speech, thinking each their own thoughts. To Betty the position was a little puzzling. She understood Osmond's point of view and respected it, for she knew that the sacrifice was as great to him as to her. And though, woman-like, she felt their mutual devotion to be a full answer to all his objections, yet – again, woman-like – she approved, though reluctantly, of his rigid adherence to a masculine standard of conduct.

But here came another puzzle. What was it that he had done? What could it possibly be that a man like this should have done? He had said plainly – and she knew that it was true – that there had been a warrant for his arrest. He had been, and in a sense still was, a fugitive from justice.

142

Yet his standard of honour was of the most scrupulous delicacy. It had compelled him quite unnecessarily to disclose his identity. It compelled him now to put away what she knew was his dearest wish. Nothing could be more unlike a criminal, who, surely, is above all things self-indulgent. Yet he was an offender against the law. Now, what, in the name of Heaven, is the kind of offence against the law of which a man of this type could be guilty? He had never given a hint upon the subject, and of course she had never sought to find out. She was not in the least inquisitive now. But the incongruity, the discrepancy between his character and his circumstances, perplexed her profoundly.

Finally, she gave up the puzzle and began to talk to him about Captain Hartup and the pleasant old times on board the *Speedwell*. He responded with evident relief at having passed the dreaded crisis, and so, by degrees, they got back to cheerful talk and frank enjoyment of one another's society, letting the past, the future, and the might-have-been sink into temporary oblivion.

Chapter XI
The Order of Release

It was a long journey down the winding river and across the great lagoon. How long Osmond never knew, for, as hour after hour passed and the canoe sped on noiselessly through the encompassing darkness, the fatigues of the day began to take effect, not only on him, but on his companion too. Gradually the conversation slackened, the intervals of silence grew longer and longer, merging into periods of restful unconsciousness and punctuated by little smothered yawns on the part of Betty, until, at length, silence fell upon the canoe, unbroken save by the sounds of sleeping men and the rhythmical "swish" of the poles.

At the sound of a distant bugle, Osmond opened his eyes and became aware that the day was breaking and that the journey was nearly at an end. Also that his head was very comfortably pillowed on the shoulder of his companion, who now slumbered peacefully at his side. Very softly he raised himself and looked down at the sleeping girl, almost holding his breath lest he should disturb her. How dainty and frail she looked, this brave, hardy little maid! How delicate, almost childlike, she seemed as she lay, breathing softly, in the easy posture of graceful youth! And how lovely she was! He gazed adoringly at the sweet face, so charmingly wreathed with its golden aureole, at the peacefully-closed eyes with their fringes of long, dark lashes, and thought half-bitterly, half-proudly, that she was his own for the asking, and even as he looked, she opened her eyes and greeted him with a smile.

"What are you looking so solemn about, Jim?" she asked, as she sat up and reached for her helmet.

"Was I looking solemn? I expect it was only foolishness. Most fools are solemn animals."

"Don't be a guffin, Jim," she commanded, reprovingly.

"What is a guffin?" he asked.

"It is a thing with a big, Roman nose and most abnormal amount of obstinacy, which makes disparaging comments on my Captain Jim."

"A horrid sort of beast it must be. Well, I won't, then. Is that Quittah, where all those canoes are?"

"I suppose it is, but I've never been there. Yes, it must be. I can see Fort Firminger – that thing like a Martello tower out in the lagoon opposite the landing-place. Mr. Cockeram says it is an awfully strong fort. You couldn't knock it down with a croquet mallet."

Osmond looked about him with the interest of a traveller arriving at a place which he has heard of but never seen. Behind and on both sides, the waste of water extended as far as the eye could see. Before them was a line of low land with occasional clumps of coconut palms that marked the position of beach villages. Ahead was a larger mass of palms, before which was a wide "hard", or landing-place, already thronged with market people, towards which numbers of trading canoes were converging from all parts of the lagoon.

As they drew nearer, an opening in the palms revealed a whitewashed fort above which a flag was just being hoisted, and now, over the sandy shore, the masts of two vessels came into view.

"There is the *Widgeon*," said Betty, pointing to the masts of a barquentine, "and there is another vessel, a schooner. I wonder who she is."

Osmond had observed and was also wondering who she was, for he had a suspicion that he had seen her before. Something in the appearance of the tall, slim masts seemed to recall the mysterious yacht-like craft that he had seen one night at Adaffia revealed for a moment in "the glimpses of the moon".

They were now rapidly approaching the landing-place. The other canoe had already arrived, and its disembarked crew could be seen on the hard surrounded by a crowd of natives.

"That looks like a naval officer waiting on the beach," said Osmond, looking at a white-clad figure which had separated itself from the crowd and appeared to be awaiting their arrival.

"It is," replied Betty. "I believe it is Captain Darley. And there is a constabulary officer coming down, too. I expect they have heard the news. You'll get a great reception when they hear Mr. Stockbridge's story – and mine. But they will be awfully upset about poor Mr. Westall. You are coming up to the fort with me, of course?"

Osmond had intended to go straight on to Adaffia, but he now saw that this would be impossible. Besides, there was the schooner. "Yes," he replied, "I will see you to your destination."

"It isn't my destination," said she. "I shall rest here for a day – the German deaconesses will give me a bed, I expect – and then I am coming on with you to Adaffia to put a wreath on Captain Hartup's grave. You can put up either at the fort or with one of the German traders or missionaries. There are no English people here excepting the two officers at the fort."

Osmond made no comment on this, for they were now close inshore. The canoe slid into the shallows and in a few moments more was hauled up by a crowd of willing natives until her bows were high and dry on the hard.

The officer who had joined Darley turned out to be the doctor, under whose superintendence Stockbridge's hammock was carefully landed and the rest of the wounded brought ashore. Then the litter containing the body of the dead officer was lifted out and slowly borne away, while Darley and the native soldiers stood at the salute, and the doctor, having mustered the wounded, led the way towards the little hospital. As the melancholy procession moved off, Darley turned to greet Betty and Osmond, who had stepped ashore last.

"How do you do, Miss Burleigh? None the worse for your adventures, I hope. Been having rather a strenuous time, haven't you?"

"We have rather," she replied. "Isn't it a dreadful thing to have lost poor Mr. Westall?"

"Yes," he replied, as they turned away from the lagoon and began to walk towards the fort. "Shocking affair. Still, fortune of war, you know. Can't make omelettes without breaking eggs. And here is Mr. Cook, in the thick of the bobbery, as usual. What a fellow you are, Cook! Always in hot water."

As he shook Osmond's hand heartily, the latter replied, "Well, the bobbery wasn't of my making, this time. I found it ready-made and just bore a hand. By the way, what schooner is that out in the roads?"

"That," replied Darley, "is an ancient yacht named the *Primula* – a lovely old craft – sails like a witch. But she has come down in the world now. We met her coming up from the leeward coast and brought her in here."

"Brought her in? Is she in custody, then?"

"Well, we brought her in to overhaul her and make some inquiries. There is just a suspicion that she has been concerned in the gun-running that has been going on. But we haven't found anything up to the present. She seems to be full up with ordinary, legitimate cargo."

"Ha!" exclaimed Osmond.

"Why 'ha'?" demanded Darley with a quick look at Osmond. "Do you know anything about her?"

"Let us hear some more," said Osmond. "Is there a Welshman named Jones on board?"

"There is. He's the skipper, purser, and super-cargo all combined."

"Have you looked through her manifest?"

"I have, and I've jotted down some notes of the items of her lading."

"Is there any ivory on board?"

"Yes," replied Darley, with growing excitement.

"Three large crates and a big canvas bag?"

146

"Yes!"

"Containing in all, thirty-nine large tusks and fifty-one scribellos?"

Darley dragged a pocket-book out of his pocket and feverishly turned over the leaves. "Yes, by Jove!" he fairly shouted. "The very numbers. Now, what have you got to tell us?"

"I think you can take it that the ivory and probably the rest of the lading, too, is stolen property."

"Why," exclaimed Betty, "that must be your ivory, Jim."

Darley flashed an astonished glance at her and then looked inquiringly at Osmond. "Is that so?" he asked.

"I have no doubt that it is," the latter replied. "But if it should happen that there is a man on board named Sam Winter – "

"There is," interrupted Darley.

"And another named Simmons and others named Foat, Bradley, and Darker – I think, if you introduce me to them, that we shall get the whole story. And as to the gun-running, I can't make a voluntary statement, but if you were to put me in the witness-box, I should have to tell you all that I know, and I may say that I know a good deal. Will that do, for the present?"

Darley smiled complacently. "It seems like a pretty straight tip," said he. "I will just skip on board now and take possession of the manifest, and if you will give me that list of names again, I will see if those men are on board, and bring them ashore, if they are. You will be staying at the fort, I suppose? There are only Cockeram and the doctor there."

"Yes," said Betty, "I shall ask Mr. Cockeram to put him up, for to-night, at any rate."

"Very well," said Darley, "then I shall see you again later. And now I will be off and lay the train."

He touched his cap, and as they emerged into an open space before the gateway of the fort, he turned and walked away briskly down a long, shady avenue of wild fig-trees that led towards the shore.

Quittah Fort was a shabby-looking, antique structure adapted to the conditions of primitive warfare. It was entered by an arched gateway graced by two ancient cannon set up as posts and guarded by a Hausa sentry in a blue serge uniform and a scarlet fez. Towards the gateway Osmond and Betty directed their steps, and as they approached, the sentry sprang smartly to attention and presented arms, whereupon Betty marched in with impressive dignity and two tiny fingers raised to the peak of her helmet.

"This seems to be the way up," she said, turning towards a mouldering wooden staircase, as a supercilious-looking pelican waddled towards them and a fish-eagle on a perch in a corner uttered a loud yell. "What a queer place it is! It looks like a menagerie. I wonder if there is anyone at home."

She tripped up the stairs, followed by Osmond and watched suspiciously by an assemblage of storks, coots, rails, and other birds which were strolling about at large in the quadrangle, and came out on an open space at the top of a corner bastion. Just as they reached this spot, a man came hurrying out of a shabby building which occupied one side of the square, and at the first glance Osmond recognized him as the officer who had come to Adaffia to execute the warrant on the day when he had buried poor Larkom. The recognition was mutual, for as soon as he had saluted Betty, the officer turned to him and held out his hand.

"Larkom, by Jove!" said he.

"My name is Cook," Osmond corrected.

"Oh," said the other, "glad you set me right, because I have been going to send you a note. You remember me – Cockeram. I came down to Adaffia, you know, about that poor chap, Osmond."

"I remember. You said you had been going to write to me."

"Yes. I was going to send you something that I thought would interest you. I may as well give it to you now." He began to rummage in his pockets and eventually brought forth a bulging letter-case, the very miscellaneous contents of which he proceeded to sort out. "It's about poor Osmond," he continued, disjointedly, and still turning over a litter of papers. "I felt that you would like to see it. Poor chap! It was such awfully rough luck."

"What was?" asked Osmond.

"Why, you remember," replied Cockeram, suspending his search to look up, "that I had a warrant to arrest him. It seemed that he was wanted for some sort of jewel robbery and there had been a regular hue-and-cry after him. Then he managed to slip away to sea and had just contrived to get into hiding at Adaffia when the fever got him. Frightful hard lines!"

"Why hard lines?" demanded Osmond.

"Why? Because he was innocent."

"Innocent!" exclaimed Osmond, staring at the officer in amazement.

"Yes, innocent. Had nothing whatever to do with the robbery. No one can make out why on earth he scooted."

As Cockeram made his astounding statement, Betty turned deathly pale. "Is it quite certain that he was innocent?" she asked in a low, eager tone.

"Perfectly," he replied, turning an astonished blue eye on the white-faced girl and then hastily averting it. "Where is that confounded paper – newspaper cutting? I cut it out to send to Lark – Cook. There is no doubt

148

whatever. It seems that they employed a criminal lawyer chap – a certain Dr. Thorndyke – to work up the case against Osmond. So this lawyer fellow got to work. And the upshot of it was that he proved conclusively that Osmond couldn't possibly be the guilty party."

"How did he prove that?" Osmond demanded.

"In the simplest and most satisfactory way possible," replied Cockeram. "He followed up the tracks until he had spotted the actual robber and held all the clues in his hand. Then he gave the police the tip, and they swooped down on my nabs – caught him fairly on the hop with all the stolen property in his possession. There isn't the shadow of a doubt about it."

"What was the name of the man who stole the gems?" Osmond asked anxiously.

"I don't remember," Cockeram replied. "What interested me was the name of the man who *didn't* steal them."

Betty, still white-faced and trembling, stood gazing rather wildly at Osmond, for his face bore a very singular expression – an expression that made her feel sick at heart. He did not look relieved or joyful. Surprised he certainly was. But it was not joyous surprise. Rather was it suggestive of alarm and dismay. And meanwhile Cockeram continued to turn over the accumulations in his letter-case. Suddenly he drew forth a crumpled and much-worn envelope from which he triumphantly extracted a long newspaper cutting.

"Ah!" he exclaimed, as he handed it to Osmond, "here we are. You will find full particulars in this. You needn't send it back to me. I have done with it. And now I must hook off to the court-house. You will take possession of the mess-room, Miss Burleigh, won't you? And order whatever you want. Of course, Mr. Cook is my guest." With a formal salute he turned, ran down the rickety stairs and out at the gate, pursued closely as far as the wicket by the pelican.

But Betty's whole attention was focussed on Osmond, and as he fastened hungrily on the newspaper cutting, she took his arm and drew him gently through a ramshackle lattice porch into the shabby little white washed mess-room, where she stood watching with mingled hope and terror the strange, enigmatical expression on his face as he devoured the printed lines.

Suddenly – in the twinkling of an eye – that expression changed. Anxiety, even consternation, gave place to the wildest astonishment, his jaw fell, and the hand which held the newspaper cutting dropped to his side. And then he laughed aloud, a weird, sardonic laugh that made poor Betty's flesh creep.

"What is it, Jim, dear?" she asked nervously.

He looked in her face and laughed again.

"My name," said he, "is not Jim. It is John. John Osmond."

"Very well, John," she replied, meekly. "But why did you laugh?"

He placed his hands on her shoulders and looked down at her with a smile.

"Betty, darling," said he, "do I understand that you are willing to marry me?"

"Willing indeed!" she exclaimed. "I am going to marry you."

"Then, my darling," said he, "you are going to marry a fool."

Book II – The Investigator

Chapter XII
The Indictment

Mr. Joseph Penfield sat behind his writing-table in a posture of calm attention, allowing his keen grey eyes to travel back and forth from the silver snuff box which lay on the note-pad before him to the two visitors who confronted him from their respective chairs. One of these, an elderly hard-faced man, square of jaw and truculent of eye, was delivering some sort of statement, while the other, a considerably younger man, listened critically, with his eyes cast down, but stealing, from time to time, a quick, furtive glance either at the speaker or at Mr. Penfield. He was evidently following the statement closely, and to an observer there might have appeared in his concentrated attention something more than mere interest – something inscrutable, with, perhaps, the faintest suggestion of irony.

As the speaker came, somewhat abruptly, to an end, Mr. Penfield opened his snuff-box and took a pinch delicately between finger and thumb.

"It is not quite clear to me, Mr. Woodstock," said he, "why you are consulting me in this matter. You are an experienced practitioner, and the issue is a fairly simple one. What is there against your dealing with the case according to your own judgment?"

"A good deal," Mr. Woodstock replied. "In the first place, I am one of the interested parties – the principal one, in fact. In the second, I practise in a country town, whereas you are here in the very heart of the legal world, and in the third, I have no experience whatever of criminal practice, I am a conveyancer pure and simple."

"But," objected Mr. Penfield, "this is not a matter of criminal practice. It is just a question of your liability as a bailee."

"Yes, true. But that question is closely connected with the robbery. Since no charge was made for depositing this property in my strong-room, obviously, I am not liable unless it can be shown that the loss was due to negligence. But the question of negligence turns on the robbery."

"Which I understand was committed by one of your own staff?"

"Yes, the man Osmond, whom I mentioned, one of my confidential clerks – Hepburn, here, is the other – who had access to the strong-room and who absconded as soon as the robbery was discovered."

"When you say he had access," said Mr. Penfield. "You mean – "

"That he had access to the key during office hours. As a matter of fact, it hangs on the wall beside my desk, and when I am there the strong-room is usually kept open – the door is in my private office and opposite to my desk. Of course, when I leave at the end of the day, I lock up the strong-room and take the key away with me."

"Yes. But in the interval – hmm? It almost looks as if a claim might be – hmm? But you have given me only an outline of the affair. Perhaps a more detailed account might enable us better to form an opinion on the position. Would it be troubling you too much?"

"Not at all," replied Mr. Woodstock, "but it is rather a long story. However, I will cut it as short as I can. We will take the events in the order in which they occurred, and you must pull me up, Hepburn, if I overlook anything.

"The missing valuables are the property of a client of mine named Hollis, a retired soap manufacturer, as rich as Croesus, and like most of these over-rich men, having made a fortune was at his wit's end what to do with it. Eventually, he adopted the usual plan. He became a collector. And having decided to burden himself with a lot of things that he didn't want, he put the lid on it by specializing in goldsmith's work, jewellery, and precious stones. Wanted a valuable collection, he said, that could be kept in an ordinary dwelling-house.

"Well, of course, the acquisitive mania, once started, grew by what it fed on. The desire to possess this stuff became an obsession. He was constantly planning expeditions in search of new rarities, scouring the Continent for fresh loot, flitting from town to town and from dealer to dealer like an idiotic bee. And whenever he went off on one of these expeditions he would bring the pick of his confounded collection to me to have it deposited in my strong-room. I urged him to take it to the bank, but he doesn't keep an account with any of the local branches and didn't want to take the stuff to London. Moreover, he had inspected my strong-room and was a good deal impressed by it."

"It is really strong, is it?" asked Mr. Penfield.

"Very. Thick reinforced concrete lined with steel. Very large, too. Not that the strength is material, as it was not broken into. Well, eventually I agreed to deposit the things in the strong-room – couldn't refuse an important client – but I resolutely declined to make any charge or accept any sort of consideration for the service. I wasn't going to make myself responsible for the safety of things of that value. And I

152

explained my position to Hollis, but he said that a strong-room that was good enough for my valuable documents was good enough for his jewels. Which was talking like a fool. Burglars don't break into safes to steal leases.

"Well, this business began about six years ago, and – so far as I can tell – nothing amiss occurred until quite lately. I say so far as I can tell, for of course we can't date the robbery. We only know when it was discovered. But I assume that the theft was committed pretty recently, or it would surely have been discovered sooner."

"And when was it first ascertained that a robbery had been committed?" asked Mr. Penfield, dipping a quill into the ink.

"On the fourth of October," replied Mr. Woodstock, and having paused while Mr. Penfield noted the date, he continued, "On that day Hollis took a great ruby up to South Kensington, where it had been accepted for a loan exhibition. He delivered it himself to the keeper of the precious stones, and was a little taken aback when that gentleman, after a preliminary inspection, began to pore over it with a magnifying-glass and then sent for one of his colleagues. The second expert raised his eyebrows when he had looked at the gem, and he, too, made a careful scrutiny with the lens. Finally, they sent for a third official, and the upshot of it was that the three experts agreed that the stone was not a ruby at all but only a first-class imitation.

"Of course Hollis didn't believe them, and said so. He had bought the stone for four-thousand pounds from a well-known dealer and had shown it to a number of connoisseurs who had all been enthusiastic about the colour and lustre of the gem. There had never been any question that it was not merely a genuine ruby, but a ruby of the highest class. However, when he had heard the verdict of the experts, he pocketed his treasure and went straight off to Cawley's in Piccadilly. But when Mr. Cawley shook his head over the gem and pronounced it an unquestionable counterfeit, he became alarmed and danced off in a deuce of a twitter to the dealer from whom he had bought it.

"That interview settled the matter. The dealer remembered the transaction quite well and knew all about the stone, for he had full records of the circumstances under which he had acquired it. Moreover, he recognized the setting – a pendant with a surround of small diamonds – but he was quite clear that the stone in it was not the stone that he had sold to Hollis. In fact it was not a stone at all, it was just a good-class paste ruby. The original had been picked out of the setting and the counterfeit put in its place, and the person who had done the job was apparently not a skilled jeweller, for there were traces on the setting of some rather amateurish work."

153

"There is no doubt, I suppose," said Mr. Penfield, "of the bona-fides of the dealer?"

"Not the slightest," was the reply. "He is a man of the highest reputation, and as a matter of fact, no regular dealer would palm off a counterfeit. It wouldn't be business. But the question doesn't really arise, as you will see when I proceed with the story.

"As soon as Hollis was convinced that a substitution had been effected, he commissioned an independent expert to come down and make a critical survey of his collection, and it was then ascertained that practically every important gem in his cabinets was a counterfeit. And in every case in which the stone was a false one, the same traces of clumsy workmanship were discoverable by an expert eye.

"The conclusion was obvious. Since the original gems had come from all sorts of different sources, there could he no question of fraud on the part of the various vendors, to say nothing of the fact that Hollis – who has practically no knowledge of stones himself – always obtained an expert opinion before concluding a deal. It was obvious that a systematic robbery had been carried out, and the question that arose was, who could the robber be?

"But that question involved certain others – as, for instance, when had the robbery been committed? Where were the jewels at that time? And who had access to the place in which they were?

"These were difficult questions. At first it seemed as if they were unanswerable, and perhaps some of them would have been if the robber had not lost his nerve. But I am anticipating. Let us take the questions in their order.

"First as to the date of the robbery. It happens that a little less than two years ago Professor Eccles came down by invitation and made a careful inspection of Hollis's collection with a view to a proposed bequest to the nation, and marked off what he considered to be the most valuable specimens. Now, I need not say that if Professor Eccles detected no counterfeit stones, we may take it that no counterfeits were there. Consequently, the collection was then intact and the robbery must have been committed since that date. But it happens that that date coincides almost exactly with the arrival of Osmond at my office. Just two years ago Hepburn introduced him to me, and as he is Hepburn's brother-in-law, I accepted him with perfect confidence.

"The other questions seemed more difficult. As to Hollis's own premises, the jewel-room had a Chubb detector lock on its only door, the cabinets have similar locks, the windows are always kept securely fastened, and no attempt has ever been made to break into the place. Besides, burglars would simply have taken the jewels away. They would not have left substitutes. The personnel of his household – a lady secretary, a housekeeper, and two maids – appear beyond suspicion. Moreover, they had all been with him many years before the robbery occurred. In short, I think we may consider Hollis's premises as outside the field of inquiry."

"Do you really?" said Mr. Penfield, in a tone which clearly indicated that he did not.

"Certainly, and so will you when you have heard the rest of the story. We now come to the various occasions on which the more valuable parts of this collection were deposited in my strong-room. Let me describe the procedure. In the first place, Hollis himself packed the jewels in a number of wooden boxes which he had had made specially for the purpose, each about fourteen inches by nine by about five inches deep. Every box had a good lock with a sunk disc on each side of the keyhole for the seals. When the boxes were packed they were locked and a strip of tape put across the keyhole and secured at each end with a seal. They were then wrapped in strong paper and sealed at all the joints with Hollis's seal – an antique Greek seal set in a ring which he always wears on his finger. On the outside of the cover was written a list of the contents in Hollis's own handwriting and signed by him, and each box bore in addition a number. The boxes were brought to my office by Hollis and by him delivered personally to me, and I gave him a receipt, roughly describing and enumerating the boxes, but, of course, not committing myself in respect of the contents. I then carried them myself into the strong-room and placed them on an upper shelf which I reserved for them, and there they remained until Hollis fetched them away, when he used to give me a receipt in the same terms as my own. That concluded the particular transaction.

"Now, it happened that at the time when the robbery was discovered, several of the boxes which Hollis had taken back from me about a month previously still remained packed and in their paper wrappings. And it further happened that one of these – there were eight in all – contained an emerald which Hollis had bought only a few days before he packed it. There was no question as to the genuineness of this stone, and when the box was opened, there was no question as to the fact that it had been replaced by a counterfeit. Even Hollis was able to spot the change. So that seemed to fix the date of the robbery to the period during which the box had been in my strong-room."

"Apparently," Mr. Penfield agreed. "But you speak of the box as being still in its paper wrapping. What of the seals?"

"Ah!" exclaimed Woodstock, "that is the most mysterious feature of the affair. The seals were unbroken and, so far as Hollis could see, the package was absolutely intact, just as it had been handed to me."

Mr. Penfield pursed up his lips and took snuff to the verge of intemperance.

"If the seals were unbroken," said he, "and the package was in all other respects intact, that would seem to be incontestable proof that it had never been opened since it was closed and sealed."

"That was what I pointed out," interposed Hepburn, "when Mr. Woodstock talked the matter over with Osmond and me. The unbroken seals seemed a conclusive answer to any suggestion that the robbery took place in our office."

"So they did," Woodstock agreed, "and so they would still if Osmond had kept his head. But he didn't. He had evidently reckoned on the question of a robbery from our strong-room never being raised, and I imagine that it was that emerald that upset his nerve. At any rate, within a week of our discussion he bolted, and then, of course, the murder was out."

Mr. Penfield nodded gravely and asked, after a short pause, "And how is Mr. Hollis taking it? Is he putting any pressure on you?"

"Oh, not at all – up to the present. He has not suggested any claim against me. He merely wants to lay his hand on the robber and, if possible, get his jewels back. He entirely approves of what I have done."

"What have you done?" Mr. Penfield asked.

"I have done the obvious thing," was the reply, delivered in a slightly truculent tone. "As soon as it was clear that Osmond had absconded, I communicated with the police. I laid an information and gave them the leading facts."

"And do they propose to take any action?"

"Most undoubtedly. In fact I may say that they have been most commendably prompt. They have already traced Osmond to Bristol, and I have every hope that in due course they will run him to earth and arrest him."

"That is quite probable," said Mr. Penfield. "And when they have arrested him – ?"

"He will be brought back and charged before a magistrate, when we may take it that he will be committed for trial."

"It is possible," Mr. Penfield assented, doubtfully. "And then – "

"Then," replied Woodstock, reddening and raising his voice, "he will be put on his trial and, I make no doubt, sent to penal servitude."

156

Mr. Penfield took snuff deprecatingly and shook his head. "I think not," said he. "But perhaps there is some item of evidence which you have omitted to mention?"

"Evidence!" Woodstock repeated impatiently. "What evidence do you want? The property has been stolen and the man who had an opportunity to steal it has absconded. What more do you want?"

Mr. Penfield looked at his brother solicitor with mild surprise.

"The judge," he replied, "and I should think the magistrate, too, would want some positive evidence that the accused stole the jewels. There appears to be no such evidence. The unexplained disappearance of this man is a suspicious circumstance, but it is useless to take suspicions into court. You have got to make out a case, and at present you have no case. If the charge were not dismissed by the magistrate, the bill would certainly be thrown out by the Grand Jury."

Mr. Woodstock glowered sullenly at the old lawyer, but he made no reply, while Hepburn sat with down cast eyes and the faintest trace of an ironical smile.

"Consider," Mr. Penfield resumed, "what would be the inevitable answer of the defence. They would point out that there is not a particle of evidence that the robbery – if there has really been a robbery – occurred in your office at all, and that there are excellent reasons for believing that it did not."

"What reasons are there?"

"There are the unbroken seals. Until you can show how the jewels could have been abstracted without breaking the seals, you have not even a *prima facie* case. Then there is the method of the alleged robbery. It would have required not merely access but undisturbed possession for a considerable time. It was not just a matter of picking out the stones. They were replaced by plausible counterfeits which had to be made or procured. Take the case of the ruby that you mentioned. It deceived Hollis completely. Then it must have been very like the original in size, form, and colour. It could not have been picked up casually at a theatrical property dealer's, it must have been made *ad hoc* by careful comparison with the original. But all this and the subsequent setting and finishing would take time. It would be quite possible while the jewels were lying quietly in Hollis's cabinets, but it would seem utterly impossible under the alleged circumstances. In short," Mr. Penfield concluded, "I am astounded that you ever admitted the possibility of the robbery having occurred on your premises. What do you say, Mr. Hepburn?"

"I agree with you entirely," the latter replied. "My position would have been that we had received certain sealed packages and that we had handed them back in the same condition as we received them. I should have left Hollis to prove the contrary."

"And I think he could have done it," said Woodstock doggedly. "You seem to be forgetting that emerald. But in any case, I have accepted the suggestion and I am not going to draw back, especially as my confidential clerk has absconded and virtually admitted the theft. The question is, what is to be done? Hollis is mad to get hold of the robber and recover his gems, and he is prepared to stand the racket financially."

"In that case," said Mr. Penfield, taking a final pinch and pocketing his snuff-box, "I will venture to make a suggestion. This case is out of your depth and out of mine. I suggest that you allow me to take counsel's opinion, and the counsel I should select would be Dr. John Thorndyke."

"Thorndyke – hmm!" grunted Woodstock. "Isn't he an irregular practitioner of some sort?"

"Not at all," Mr. Penfield dissented warmly. "He is a scientific expert with an unrivalled knowledge and experience of criminal practice. If it is possible for anyone to unravel this tangle, I am confident that he is the man, and I know of no other."

"Then," exclaimed Woodstock, "for God's sake get hold of him, and let me know what he says, so that I can report to Hollis. And let him know that there will be no trouble about costs."

With this Mr. Woodstock rose and, after an unemotional leave-taking, made his way out of the office, followed by Hepburn.

Chapter XIII
Thorndyke Takes Up the Inquiry

Mr. Penfield's visit to Dr. Thorndyke's chambers in King's Bench Walk, Inner Temple, was productive of some little surprise, as such visits were rather apt to be. For the old solicitor had definitely made up his mind that Woodstock's theory of the robbery was untenable and that the burden of proof ought to be cast on Hollis, and he was therefore not a little disconcerted to find Thorndyke tending to favour the view that the probabilities pointed to the strong-room as the scene of the robbery.

"After all," the latter said, "we must not ignore the obvious. It is undeniable that Osmond's disappearance – which has the strongest suggestion of flight – is a very suspicious circumstance. It occurred almost immediately after the discovery of the thefts and the suggestion that the gems had been stolen from the strong-room. Osmond had access to the strong-room – though I admit that a good many other persons had, too. Then there is the striking fact that the period of the robberies coincides exactly with the period of Osmond's presence at the office. During the four years which preceded his arrival no robbery appears to have occurred, although all the other conditions seem to have been the same. So far as we can see, the robberies must have commenced very shortly after his arrival. These are significant facts which, as I have said, we cannot ignore."

"I am entirely with you," Mr. Penfield replied, "when you say that we must not ignore the obvious. But are you not doing so? These packages were most carefully and elaborately sealed, and it is admitted that they were returned to the owner with the seals unbroken. Now, it seems to me obvious that if the seals were unbroken, the packages could not have been opened. But apparently you think otherwise. Possibly you attach less importance to seals than I do?"

"Probably," Thorndyke admitted. "It is easy to exaggerate their significance. For what is a seal, when all is said? It is an artificial thing which some artist or workman has made and which another artist or workman could copy if necessary. There is no magic in seals."

"Dear, dear!" Mr. Penfield exclaimed with a wry smile. "Another illusion shattered! But I think a Court of Law would share my erroneous view of the matter. However, we will let that pass. I understand that you look upon Osmond as the probable delinquent?"

159

"The balance of probabilities is in favour of that view. But I am keeping an open mind. There are other possibilities, and they will have to be explored. We must take nothing for granted."

Mr. Penfield nodded approvingly. "And suppose," he asked, "the police should arrest Osmond?"

"Then," replied Thorndyke, "Mr. Woodstock would be in difficulties, and so would the police – who have shown less than their usual discretion – unless the prisoner should get in a panic and plead 'guilty'. There is not even a *prima facie* case. They can't call upon Osmond to prove that he did not steal the gems."

"Exactly," Mr. Penfield agreed. "That is what I tried to impress on Woodstock – who is really a most extraordinarily unlegal lawyer. But have you any suggestion to offer?"

"I can only suggest that, as we are practically without data, we should endeavour to obtain some. The only fact that we have is that the stones have been removed from their settings and replaced by imitations. There seems to be no doubt about that. As to how they came to be removed, there are evidently four possibilities. First, they may have been taken from Hollis's cabinets by some person unknown. Second, the substitution may have been effected by Hollis himself, for reasons unknown to us and by no means easy to imagine. Third, they may have been stolen from the strong-room by some person other than Osmond. Fourth, they may have been stolen from the strong-room by Osmond. The last is, I think, the most probable. But all of the four hypotheses must be impartially considered. Do I understand that Hollis is prepared to offer facilities?"

"He agrees to give every assistance, financial or other."

"Then," said Thorndyke, "I suggest that we make a beginning by inspecting the boxes. I understand that there are still some unopened."

"Yes, six. Hollis reserved them to be opened in the presence of witnesses."

"Let Hollis bring those six boxes together with those that have been opened, with their packings and wrappings, if he has them. If we can fix a day, I will arrange for an expert to be present to witness the opening of the six boxes and give an opinion on the stones in them. If it appears that any robbery has been committed, I shall ask Hollis to leave the boxes and the counterfeit jewels that I may examine them at my leisure."

Mr. Penfield chuckled softly and helped himself to a pinch of snuff.

"Your methods, Dr. Thorndyke," said be, "are a perennial source of wonder to me. May I ask what kind of information you expect to extract from the empty boxes?"

160

"I have no specific expectations at all," was the reply, "but it will be strange indeed if we learn nothing from them. They will probably have little enough to tell us but, seeing that we have, at present, hardly a single fact beyond that of the substitution – and that is not of our own observing – a very small addition to our knowledge would be all to the good."

"Very true, very true," agreed Mr. Penfield. "A single definite fact might enable us to decide which of those four possibilities is to be adopted and pursued, though how you propose to extract such a fact from an empty box, or even a full one, I am unable to imagine. However, I leave that problem in your hands. As soon as you have secured your expert, perhaps you will kindly advise me and I will then make the necessary arrangements with Mr. Hollis."

With this Mr. Penfield rose and took his departure, leaving Thorndyke to read over and amplify the notes that he had taken during the consultation.

As matters turned out, he was able to advise Mr. Penfield within twenty-four hours that he had secured the services of an expert who was probably the greatest living authority on gem stones, with the result that a telegram arrived from Mr. Hollis accepting the appointment for the following day at eleven in the forenoon, that time having been mentioned by the expert as the most suitable on account of the light.

It wanted several minutes to the appointed hour when the first visitor arrived, for the Treasury clock had hardly struck the third quarter when, in response to a smart rat-tat on the little brass knocker, Thorndyke opened the door and admitted Professor Eccles.

"I am a little before my time," the latter remarked as he shook hands, "but I wanted to have a few words with you before Mr. Hollis arrived. I understand that you want me to give an opinion on some doubtful stones of his. Are they new ones? Because I may say that I looked over his collection very carefully less than two years ago and I can state confidently that it contained no gems that were not unquestionably genuine. But I have heard some rumours of a robbery – unfounded, I hope, seeing that Hollis proposes to bequeath his treasures to the national collection."

"I am afraid," replied Thorndyke, "that the rumours are correct, but that is what you are going to help us to decide. It is not a case of simple robbery. The stolen stones seem to have been replaced by imitations, and as you examined the collection when it was undoubtedly intact, you will see at once if there has been any substitution."

He proceeded to give the professor a brief account of the case and the curious problem that it presented, and he had barely finished when a cab was heard to draw up below. A minute later, as the two men stood at

161

the open door, the visitor made his appearance, followed by the cabman, each carrying a bulky but apparently light wooden case.

Mr. Hollis was a typical business man – dry, brisk, and shrewd-looking. Having shaken hands with the professor and introduced himself to Thorndyke, he dismissed the cabman and came to the point without preamble.

"This case, marked *A*, contains the full boxes. The other, marked *B*, contains the empties. I will leave you to deal with that at your convenience. My concern and Professor Eccles's is with the other, which I will open at once and then we can get to work."

He thrust the despised case *B* into a corner, and hoisting the other on to the table, unbuckled the straps, unlocked it, threw open the lid, and took out six sealed packages, which he placed side by side on the table.

"Shall I open them?" he asked, producing a pocket knife, "or will you?

"Before we disturb them," said Thorndyke, "we had better examine the exteriors very carefully."

"I've done that," said Hollis. "I've been over each one most thoroughly and, so far as I can see, they are in exactly the same condition as they were when I handed them to Woodstock. The writing on them is certainly my writing and the seals are impressions of my seal, which, as you see, I carry on my finger in this ring."

"In that case," said Thorndyke, "we may as well open them forthwith. Perhaps I had better take off the wrappings, as I should like to preserve them and the seals intact."

He took up the first package and turned it over in his hands, examining each surface closely. And as he did so, his two visitors watched him – the professor with slightly amused curiosity, the other with a dry, rather impatient manner not without a trace of scepticism. The package was about fourteen inches in length by nine wide and five inches deep. It was very neatly covered with a strong, smooth white paper bearing a number – thirteen – and a written and signed list of the contents, and sealed at each end in the middle. The paper was further secured by a string, tied tightly and skilfully, of which the knot was embedded in a mass of wax on which was an excellent impression of the seal.

"You see," Hollis pointed out, "that the parcel has been made as secure as human care could make it. I should have said that it was perfectly impossible to open it without breaking the seals."

"But surely," exclaimed the professor, "it would be an absolute impossibility! Don't you agree, Dr. Thorndyke?"

162

"We shall be better able to judge when we have seen the inside," the latter replied. With a small pair of scissors he cut the string, which he placed on one side, and then, with great care, cut round each of the seals, removing them with the portions of paper on which they were fixed and putting them aside with the string. The rest of the paper was now taken off, disclosing a plain, white-wood box, the keyhole of which was covered by a strip of tape secured at each end by a seal seated in a small circular pit. Thorndyke cut the tape and held the box towards Hollis, who already held the key in readiness. This having been inserted and turned, Thorndyke raised the lid and laid the box on the table.

"There, Professor," said he, "you can now answer your own question. The list of contents is on the cover. It is for you to say whether that list correctly describes the things which are inside."

Professor Eccles drew a chair up to the table and, lifting from the inside of the box a thick pad of tissue paper (which Thorndyke took from him and placed with the string and the seals), ran his eye quickly over the neatly-arranged assemblage of jewels that reposed on a second layer of tissue. Very soon a slight frown began to wrinkle his forehead. He bent more closely over the box, looked narrowly first at one gem, then at another, and at length picked out a small, plain pendant set with a single oval green stone about half-an-inch in diameter.

"'*Leaf-green jargoon*'," said he, reading from the list as he produced a Coddington lens from his pocket. "That is the one, isn't it?"

Hollis grunted an assent as he watched the professor inspecting the gem through his lens.

"I remember the stone," said the professor. "It was one of the finest of the kind that I have ever seen. Well, this isn't it. This is not a jargoon at all. It is just a lump of green glass – flint glass, in fact. But it is quite well cut. The lapidary knew his job better than the jeweller. There has been some very rough work on the setting."

"How much was the stone worth?" Thorndyke asked.

"The original? Not more than thirty pounds, I should say. It was a beautiful and interesting stone, but rather a collector's specimen than a jeweller's piece. The public won't give big prices for out-of-the-way stones. They like diamonds, rubies, sapphires, and emeralds."

"Is this counterfeit a true facsimile of the original? I mean as to size and style of cutting?"

Professor Eccles took from his pocket a small leather case, from which he extracted a calliper gauge. Applying this delicately to the exposed edges of the "girdle" between the claws, he read the vernier and then reapplied it in the other diameter.

"Seven-twelfths by three-quarters of an inch, brilliant cut," he announced. "Do you happen to remember the dimensions, Mr. Hollis? These can't be far out, as the stone fits the setting."

"I've brought my catalogue," said Hollis, producing a small, fat volume from his pocket. "Thought we might want it. What's the number? Three-sixty-three. Here we are. '*Jargoon. Full leaf-green. Brilliant cut. Seven-twelfths by three-quarters*'."

"Then," said the professor, "this would seem to be a perfect replica. Queer, isn't it? I see your point, Doctor. This fellow has been to endless pains and some expense in lapidary's charges – unless he is a lapidary himself – to say nothing of the risk, and all to get possession of a stone worth only about thirty pounds, and not easily marketable at that."

"Some of the other stones are worth more, though," remarked Hollis.

"True, true," agreed the professor. "Let us look at some of the others. Ha! Here is one that looks a little suspicious, if my memory serves."

He picked out a gold ornament set with a large cat's-eye bordered with small diamonds and exhibited it to Hollis, who bent down to inspect it.

"Cat's-eye," he commented, after a long and anxious inspection. "Well, it looks all right to me. What's the matter with it?"

"Oh, it is a cat's-eye, sure enough, but not the right kind, I think. What does the catalogue say?"

Hollis turned over a page and read out, "'*Chrysoberyl. Cymophane or cat's-eye. Brown, oval, cut en cabochon. Five-eighths by half-an-inch. Bordered by twelve diamonds*'."

"I thought so," said the professor. "This is a cat's-eye, but not a chrysoberyl. It is a quartz cat's-eye. But I should hardly have thought it would have been worth the trouble and expense of making the exchange. You see," he added, taking the dimensions with his gauge, "this stone is apparently a facsimile of the missing one in size and shape and not a bad match in colour. The diamonds don't appear to have been tampered with."

"What about that emerald?" Hollis asked anxiously, indicating a massive ring set with a large, square stone bordered with diamonds. Professor Eccles picked up the ring, and at the first glance he pursed up his lips, dubiously. But he examined it carefully through his lens, nevertheless.

"Well?" demanded Hollis.

The professor shook his head sadly. "Paste," he replied. "A good imitation as such things go, but unmistakable glass. Will you read out the description?"

Hollis did so, and once again the correspondence in dimensions and cutting showed the forgery to be a carefully-executed facsimile.

"This fellow was a conscientious rascal," said the professor. "He did the thing thoroughly – excepting the settings."

"Yes, damn him!" Hollis agreed, savagely. "That ring cost me close on twelve-hundred pounds. It came from Lord Pycroft's collection."

Professor Eccles was deeply concerned, naturally enough, for any robbery of precious things involves a wicked waste. And then there was the depressing fact that the valuable "Hollis bequest" was melting away before his eyes. Gloomily, he picked out one after another of the inmates of the box and regretfully added them to the growing heap of the rejected.

When the first box had been emptied, the second was attacked with similar procedure, and so on with the remainder, until the last box had been probed to the bottom, when the professor sat back in his chair and drew a deep breath. "Well," he exclaimed, "it is a terrible disaster and profoundly mysterious. In effect, the collection has been skimmed of everything of real value. Even the moonstones have been exchanged for cheap specimens with the rough native cutting untouched. I have never heard of anything like it. But I don't understand why the fellow took all this trouble. He couldn't have supposed that the robbery would pass undetected."

"It might easily have remained undetected long enough to confuse the issues," said Thorndyke. "If the jewels had been returned to the cabinets and lain there undisturbed for a few months, it would have been very difficult to determine exactly when, or where, or how the robbery had been carried out."

"Yes," growled Hollis. "The scoundrel must have known that I am no expert and reckoned on my not spotting the change. And I don't suppose I should, for that matter. However, the cat slipped out of the bag sooner than he expected and now the police are close on his heels. I'll have my pound of flesh out of him yet."

As he snapped out this expression of his benevolent intentions, Mr. Hollis gathered up the remnant of unrifled jewels and was about to deposit them in one of the empty boxes when Thorndyke interposed.

"May I lend you a deed-box with some fresh packing? I think we agreed that the empty boxes and the packing should be left with me, that I might examine them thoroughly before returning them."

"Very well," said Hollis, "though it seems a pretty futile thing to do. But I suppose you know your own business. What about those sham stones?"

"I should like to examine them too, as they are facsimile imitations, and we may possibly learn some thing from the settings."

"What do you expect to learn?" Hollis inquired in a tone which pretty plainly conveyed his expectations.

"Very little," Thorndyke replied (on which Hollis nodded a somewhat emphatic agreement). "But," he continued, "this case will depend on circumstantial evidence – unless the robber confesses – and that evidence has yet to be discovered. We can do no more than use our eyes to the best advantage in the hope that we may light on some trace that may give us a lead."

Hollis nodded again. "Sounds pretty hopeless," said he. "However, Mr. Penfield advised me to put the affair in your hands, so I have done so. If you should discover anything that will help us with the prosecution, I suppose you will let me know."

"I shall keep Mr. Penfield informed as to what evidence, if any, is available, and he will, no doubt, communicate with you."

With this rather vague promise Mr. Hollis appeared to be satisfied, for he pursued the subject no farther, but, having packed the poor remainder of his treasures in the deed-box, prepared to depart.

"Before you go," said Thorndyke, "I should like to take a trial impression of your seal, if you would allow me."

Hollis stared at him in amazement. "My seal!" he exclaimed. "Why, good God, sir, you have already got some seventy impressions – six from each of these boxes and all those from the empties!"

"The seals that I have," Thorndyke replied, "are the questioned seals. I should like to have what scientists call a 'control'."

"I don't know what you mean by 'questioned seals'," Hollis retorted. "I haven't questioned them, I have acknowledged them as my own seals."

"I think," Thorndyke rejoined with a faint smile, "that Mr. Penfield would advise you to acknowledge nothing. But, furthermore, none of these seals is a really perfect impression such as one would require for purposes of comparison."

"Comparison!" exclaimed Hollis. "Comparison with what? But there," he concluded with a sour smile, "it's no use arguing. Have it your own way. I suppose you know what you are about."

With this, he drew off the ring and, laying it on the table, bestowed a glance of defiance on Thorndyke. The latter had, apparently, made his preparations, for he promptly produced from a drawer a small box, the

166

opening of which revealed a supply of sealing-wax, a spirit-lamp, a metal plate, a little crucible or melting-ladle with a wooden handle, a bottle of oil, a camel's-hair brush, and a number of small squares of white paper. While he was setting out this apparatus the professor examined the seal through his lens.

"A fine example," he pronounced. "Syracusan, I should say, fourth or fifth century B.C. Not unlike the decadrachm of that period – the racing Quadriga with the winged Victory above and the panoply of armour below seem to recall that coin. The stone seems to be green chalcedony. It is a beautiful work. Seems almost a pity to employ it in common use."

He surrendered it regretfully to Thorndyke who, having taken an infinitesimal drop of oil on the point of the brush and wiped it off on the palm of his hand, delicately brushed the surface of the seal. Then he laid a square of paper on the metal plate, broke off a piece from one of the sticks of sealing-wax and melted it in the crucible over the lamp. When it was completely liquefied, he poured it slowly on the centre of the square of paper, where it formed a circular, convex pool. Having given this a few seconds to cool, he took the ring and pressed it steadily on the soft wax. When he raised it – which he did with extreme care, steadying the paper with his fingers – the wax bore an exquisitely perfect impression of the seal.

Hollis was visibly impressed by the careful manipulation and the fine result, and when Thorndyke had repeated the procedure, he requested that a third impression might be made for his own use. This having been made and bestowed in the deed-box, he replaced the ring on his finger, bade the professor and Thorndyke a curt farewell, and made his way down to the waiting cab.

As the door closed behind him, the professor turned to Thorndyke with a somewhat odd expression on his face.

"This is a very mysterious affair, Doctor," said he.

The curiously significant tone caused Thorndyke to cast a quick, inquiring glance at the speaker. But he merely repeated the latter's remark.

"A very mysterious affair, indeed."

"As I understand it," the professor continued, "Hollis claims that these gems were stolen from the boxes while they were in the solicitor's strong-room, and that they were taken without breaking the seals. But that sounds like sheer nonsense. And yet the solicitor appears to accept the suggestion."

"Yes. Hollis claims that the gems that were put into the boxes were the real gems, and both he and the solicitor, Woodstock, base their beliefs on the fact that Woodstock's confidential clerk appears to have absconded immediately after the discovery of the robbery."

"Hmm!" grunted the professor. "Is it quite clear that the clerk has really absconded?"

"He has disappeared for no known reason."

"Hmm. Not quite the same thing, is it? But has it been established that the real stones were actually in the boxes when they were handed to the solicitor?"

"I wouldn't use the word 'established'," Thorndyke admitted. "There is evidence that one stone, at least, was intact a day or two before the boxes were deposited, and that stone – a large emerald – was found to have been changed when the box was opened."

The professor grunted dubiously and reflected awhile. Then he looked hard at Thorndyke and appeared to be about to make some observation, and then he seemed to alter his mind, for he concluded with the somewhat colourless remark, "Well, I daresay you are quite alive to all the possibilities." And with this he prepared to take his departure.

"Do you happen," asked Thorndyke, "to know the addresses of any lapidaries who specialize in imitation stones?"

Professor Eccles reflected. "Imitations are rather out of my province," he replied. "Of course any lapidary could cut a paste gem or make a doublet or triplet, and would if paid for the job. I will write down the addresses of one or two men who have worked for me and they will probably be able to give you any further information." He wrote down two or three addresses, and as he put away his pencil, he asked, "How is your colleague, Jervis? He is still with you, I suppose?

"Jervis," was the reply, "is at present an independent practitioner. He accepted, on my advice, a whole-time appointment at the Griffin Life Assurance Office. But he drops in from time to time to lend me a hand. I will tell him you asked after him. And let me tender you my very warmest thanks for your invaluable help to-day."

"Tut, tut," said the professor, "you need not thank me. I am an interested party. If Hollis doesn't recover his gems, the national collection is going to lose a valuable bequest. Bear that in mind as an additional spur to your endeavours. Good-bye, and good luck!"

With a hearty handshake and a valedictory smile, Professor Eccles let himself out and went his way, apparently in a deeply thoughtful frame of mind, as Thorndyke judged by observing his receding figure from the window.

Chapter XIV
Thorndyke Makes a Beginning

The profound cogitations of Professor Eccles set up in the mind of Thorndyke a sort of induced psychic current. As he turned from the window and began to occupy himself in sorting his material preparatory to examining it, his thoughts were busy with his late visitor. The professor had been about to say something and had suddenly thought better of it. Now, what could it have been that he was about to say? And why had he not said it? And what was the meaning of that strangely intent look that he had bestowed on Thorndyke, and that rather odd expression that his face had borne? And, finally, what were those "possibilities" at which he had hinted?

These were the questions that Thorndyke asked himself as he carried out, quietly and methodically, the preliminaries to his later investigations, with the further questions: Did the professor know anything that bore on the mystery? And if so, what was it that he knew? He evidently had no knowledge either of Woodstock or of Osmond, but he was fairly well acquainted with Hollis. It was manifest that he rejected utterly the alleged robbery from the strong-room, which implied a conviction that the exchange of stones had been made either before the boxes were handed to Woodstock or after they had been received back from him.

It was a perfectly natural and reasonable belief. Mr. Penfield had been of the same opinion. But Mr. Penfield had no special knowledge of the matter. His opinion had been based exclusively on the integrity of the seals. Was this the professor's case, too? Or was he in possession of some significant facts which he had not disclosed? His manner rather suggested that he was. Perhaps it might be expedient, later, to sound him cautiously. But this would depend on the amount and kind of information that was yielded by other sources.

By the time he reached this conclusion the sorting process was completed. The six boxes with their contents replaced were set out in order, the empties put together as well as was possible, and the seals from the wrapping of each box put into a separate envelope on which the number and description was written. A supply of white paper was laid on the table together with a number of new paper bags, and a little simple microscope which consisted of a watchmaker's compound eye-glass mounted on a small wooden stand. Thorndyke ran his eye over the collection to see that everything was in order, then, dismissing the professor from his mind, he drew a chair up to the table and fell to work.

He began with the seals. Opening one of the envelopes, he took out the four seals – including that on the knot, which he had cut off – and laying them out on the table, examined them quickly, one after the other. Then he picked up one of them, laid it on a card, and placed the card on the stage of the magnifier, through which he made a more prolonged examination, turning the card from time to time to alter the incidence of the light, and jotting down on a note-block a few brief memoranda. The same procedure was followed with the other three seals, and when they had all been examined they were returned to their envelope, the top sheet of the note-block was detached and put in with them, the envelope was put aside and a fresh one opened. Finally he came to the envelope which contained the two impressions that he had, himself, taken from Hollis's seal, but these were not subjected to the minute scrutiny that the others had received. They were merely laid on the card, slipped under the magnifier, and after a single, brief glance, returned to their envelope and put aside. Next, the seals in the recesses by the keyholes of the boxes were scrutinized, the eyeglass being swung clear of its stand for the purpose, and when this had been done, the fresh set of notes was detached and slipped into one of the envelopes.

But this did not conclude the examination. Apparently there was some further point to be elucidated. Rising from his chair, Thorndyke fetched from a cabinet a microscope of the kind used for examining documents – a heavy-based instrument with a long, pivoted arm and a bull's-eye condenser. With this he re-examined the seals in succession, beginning with the two impressions that he had, himself, taken, and it might have been noticed that this examination concerned itself exclusively with a particular spot on the seal – a portion of the background just in front of the chariot and above the back of the near horse.

He had just finished and was replacing the microscope in the cabinet when the door opened silently and a small, clerical-looking man entered the room and regarded him benevolently.

"I have laid a cold lunch, sir, in the small room upstairs," he announced, "and I have put everything ready in your laboratory. Can I help you to carry anything up?" As he spoke, he ran an obviously inquisitive eye over the row of boxes and the numbered envelopes.

"Thank you, Polton," Thorndyke replied. "I think we will take these things up out of harm's way and I will just look them over before lunch. But meanwhile there is a small job that you might get on with. I have here a collection of seals of which I want enlarged photographs made –

four diameters magnification and each set on a separate negative and numbered similarly to the envelopes."

He exhibited the collection to his trusty coadjutor with a few words of explanation, when Polton tenderly gathered together the seven envelopes, and master and man betook themselves to the upper regions, each laden with a consignment of Mr. Hollis's boxes, full and empty.

The laboratory of which Polton had spoken was a smallish room which Thorndyke reserved for his own use, and which was on the same floor as the large laboratory and the workshop over which Polton presided. Its principal features were a long work-bench, covered with polished linoleum and at present occupied by a microscope and a tray of slides, needles, forceps, and other accessories, a side-table, a cupboard, and several sets of shelves.

"Is there anything more, sir?" Polton asked when the boxes had been stacked on the side-table. He looked at them wistfully as he spoke, but accepted with resignation the polite negative and stole out, shutting the door silently behind him. As soon as he had gone, Thorndyke fell to work with a rapid but unhurried method suggestive of a fixed purpose and a considered plan. He began by putting on a pair of thin rubber gloves. Then, spreading on the bench a sheet of white demy paper such as chemists use for wrapping bottles, he took one of the boxes, detached its wrapping paper, opened the box, and taking out the jewels and the pads of tissue paper, deposited the former at one end of the bench and the latter at the other, together with the empty box. First he dealt with the pads of tissue paper, one of which he placed on the sheet of white paper, and having opened it out and smoothed it with an ivory paper-knife, examined it closely on both sides with the aid of a reading glass. Then he took from a drawer a large tuning-fork, and holding the packing paper vertically over the middle of the sheet on the bench, he struck the tuning-fork sharply, and while it was vibrating, lightly applied its tip to the centre of the suspended paper, causing it to hum like a gigantic bumble-bee and to vibrate visibly at its edges. Having repeated this proceeding two or three times, he laid the paper aside and with the reading glass inspected the sheet of demy, on which a quite considerable number of minute specks of dust were now to be seen. This procedure he repeated with the other pads of tissue paper from the box, and as he worked, the sheet of white paper on the bench became more and more conspicuously sprinkled with particles of dust until, by the time all the pads had been treated, a quite appreciable quantity of dust had accumulated. Finally, Thorndyke took the box itself and, having opened it, placed its bottom on the sheet of paper and with a small mallet tapped it lightly but sharply all over the bottom and sides. When he lifted it from the paper, the further contribution of dust could be plainly seen in a speckling of the surface corresponding to the shape of the box.

For some moments Thorndyke stood by the bench looking down on this powdering of grey that occupied the middle of the sheet of white paper. Some of the particles, such as vegetable fibres, were easily recognizable by the unaided eye, and there were two hairs, evidently moustache hairs, both quite short and of a tawny brown colour. But he made no detailed examination of the deposit. Taking from the cupboard a largish flat pill-box, he wrote on its lid the number of the box, and then, having lightly folded the sheet of paper, carefully assembled the dust into a tiny heap in the middle and transferred it to the pill-box, applying the tuning-fork to the sheet to propel the last few grains to their destination. Then, having put the box aside and deposited the sheets of tissue paper – neatly folded – in a numbered envelope, he spread a fresh sheet of demy on the bench, and taking up another box from the side-table, subjected it to similar treatment, and so, carefully and methodically, he dealt with the entire collection of boxes, never pausing for more than a rapid glance at the sprinkling of dust that each one yielded.

He was just shooting the "catch" from the last package into the pill-box when a quick step was audible on the stairs, and after a short interval Polton let himself in silently.

"Here's Dr. Jervis, sir," said he, "and he says he hasn't had lunch yet. It is past three o'clock, sir."

"A very delicate hint, Polton," said Thorndyke. "I will join him immediately – but here he is, guided by instinct at the very psychological moment."

As he spoke, Dr. Jervis entered the room and looked about him inquisitively. From the row of pill-boxes his glance travelled to the little heaps of jewellery, each on a numbered sheet of paper.

"This is a quaint collection, Thorndyke," said he, stooping to inspect the jewels. "What is the meaning of it? I trust that my learned senior has not, at last, succumbed to temptation, but it is a suspicious looking lot."

"It does look a little like a fence's stock-in-trade or the product of a super-burglary," Thorndyke admitted. "However, I think Polton will be able to reassure you, when he has looked over the swag. But let us go and feed, and I will give you an outline sketch of the case in the intervals of mastication. It is quite a curious problem."

"And I take it," said Jervis, "that those pill-boxes contain the solution. There is a necromantic look about them that I seem to recognize. You must tell me about them when you have propounded the problem."

172

He followed Thorndyke into the little breakfast room, and when they had taken their seats at the table and fairly embarked on their immediate business, the story of the gem robbery was allowed to transpire gradually. Jervis followed the narrative with close attention and an occasional chuckle of amusement.

"It is an odd problem," he commented when the whole story had been told. "There doesn't seem to be any doubt as to who committed the robbery, and yet if you were to put this man Osmond into the dock, although the jury would be convinced to a man of his guilt, they would have to acquit him. I wonder what the deuce made him bolt."

"Yes," said Thorndyke, "that is what I have been asking myself. He may be a nervous, panicky man, but that does not look like the explanation. The suggestion is rather that he knew of some highly incriminating fact which he expected to come to light, but which has not come to light. As it is, the only incriminating fact is his own disappearance, which is evidentially worthless by itself."

"Perfectly. And you are now searching for corroborative facts in the dust from those boxes. It doesn't look a very hopeful quest."

"It doesn't," Thorndyke agreed. "But still, circumstantial evidence gains weight very rapidly. A grain of positive evidence would give quite a new importance to the disappearance. For instance, no less than seven of those boxes have yielded moustache hairs, all apparently from the same person – a fair man with a rather closely cropped moustache of a tawny colour. Now, if it should turn out that Osmond has a moustache of that kind and that no other person connected with those boxes has a moustache of precisely that character, this would be a really important item of evidence, especially coupled with the disappearance."

"It would, indeed, and even the number might be illuminating. I mean that, although moustache hairs are shed pretty freely, one would not have expected to find so many. But if the man had the not uncommon habit of stroking or rubbing his moustache, that would account for the number that had got detached."

Thorndyke nodded approvingly. "Quite a good point, Jervis. I will make a note of it for verification. And now, as we seem to have finished, shall we take a look at one or two of the samples."

"Exactly what I was going to propose," replied Jervis, and as they rose and repaired to the small laboratory, he added, "It's quite like old times to be pursuing a mysterious unknown quantity with you. I sometimes feel like chucking the insurance job and coming back."

"It is better to come back occasionally and keep the insurance job," Thorndyke rejoined as he placed two microscopes on the bench facing the window and drew up a couple of chairs. "You had better note the number of each box that you examine, though it is probably of no consequence."

He took up the collection of pill-boxes and, having placed them between the two microscopes, sat down, and the two friends then fell to work, each carefully tipping the contents of a box on to a large glass slip and laying the latter on the stage of the microscope.

For some time they worked on in silence, each jotting down on a note-block brief comments on the specimens examined. When about half of the boxes had been dealt with – and their contents very carefully returned to them – Jervis leaned back in his chair and looked thoughtfully at his colleague.

"This is very commonplace, uncharacteristic dust in most respects," said he, "but there is one queer feature in it that I don't quite make out. I have found in every specimen a number of irregularly oval bodies, some of them with pointed ends. They are about a hundredth-of-an-inch long by a little more than a two-hundredth wide, a dull pink in colour and apparently of a granular homogeneous substance. I took them at first for insect eggs, but they are evidently not, as they have no skin or shell. I don't remember having seen anything exactly like them before. Have you found any of them?"

"Yes. Like you, I have found some in every box."

"And what do you make of them? Do you recognize them?"

"Yes," replied Thorndyke. "They are the castings of a wood-boring beetle, particles of that fine dust that you see in the worm-holes of worm-eaten wood. Quite an interesting find."

"Quite, unless they come from the boxes that the jewels were packed in."

"I don't think they do. Those boxes are white wood, whereas these castings are from a red wood. But we may as well make sure."

He rose and took up the empty boxes one by one, turning each one over and examining it closely on all sides.

"You see, Jervis," he said as he laid down the last of them, "there is not a trace of a worm-hole in any of them. No, that worm-dust came from an outside source."

"But," exclaimed Jervis, "it is very extraordinary. Don't you think so? I mean," he continued in response to an inquiring glance from his colleague, "that the quantity is so astonishing. Just think of it. In every one of these boxes we have found an appreciable number of these castings – quite a large quantity in the aggregate. But the amount of dust that will fall from a piece of worm-eaten furniture must be infinitesimal."

"I would hardly agree to that, Jervis. A really badly wormed piece – say an old walnut chair or armoire – may, in the course of time, shed a

174

surprisingly large amount of dust. But, nevertheless, my learned friend has, with his usual perspicacity, laid his finger on the point that is of real evidential importance – the remarkable quantity of this dust and its more or less even distribution among all these boxes. And now you realize the truth of what I was saying just now as to the cumulative quality of circumstantial evidence. Here we have a number of boxes which have undoubtedly been tampered with by some person. That person is believed to be the man Osmond on the ground that he has absconded. But his disappearance, by itself, furnishes no evidence of his guilt. It merely offers a suggestion. He may have gone away for some entirely different reason.

"Then we find in these boxes certain moustache hairs. If it should turn out that Osmond has a moustache composed of similar hairs, that fact alone would not implicate him, since there are thousands of other men with similar moustaches. But taken in conjunction with the disappearance, the similarity of the hairs would constitute an item of positive evidence.

"Then we find some dust derived from worm-eaten wood. Its presence in these boxes, its character, and its abundance offer certain suggestions as to the kind of wood, the nature of the wooden object, and the circumstances attending its deposition in the boxes. Now, if it should be possible to ascertain the existence of a wooden object of the kind suggested and associated with the suggested circumstances, and if that object were the property of, or definitely associated with, the man Osmond, that fact, together with the hairs and the disappearance, would form a really weighty mass of evidence against him."

"Yes, I see that," said Jervis, "but what I don't see is how you arrive at your inferences as to the object from which the dust was derived."

"It is a question of probabilities," replied Thorndyke. "First, as to the kind of wood. It is a red wood. It is pretty certainly not mahogany, as it is too light in colour and mahogany is very little liable to 'the worm'. But the abundance of dust suggests one of those woods which are specially liable to be worm eaten. Of these the fruit woods – walnut, cherry, apple, and pear – are the most extreme cases, cherry being, perhaps, the worst of all and therefore usually avoided by the cabinet-maker. But this dust is obviously not walnut. It is the wrong colour. But it might be either cherry, apple, or pear, and the probabilities are rather in favour of cherry, though, of course, it might be some other relatively soft and sappy red wood."

"But how do you infer the nature of the object?"

"Again, by the presence of the dust in these boxes, by the properties of that dust and the large quantity of it. Consider the case of ordinary room dust. You find it on all sorts of surfaces, even high up on the walls or on the ceiling. There is no mystery as to how it gets there. It consists of minute particles, mostly of fibres from textiles, so small and light that they float freely in the air. But this wood consists of relatively large and heavy bodies – over a hundredth-of-an-inch long. From the worm-holes it will fall to the floor, and there it will remain even when the floor is being swept. It cannot rise in the air and become deposited like ordinary dust, and it must therefore have made its way into these boxes in some other manner."

"Yes, I realize that, but still I don't see how that fact throws any light on the nature of the wooden object."

"It is merely a suggestion," replied Thorndyke, "and the inference may be quite wrong. But it is a perfectly obvious one. Come now, Jervis, don't let your intellectual joints get stiff. Keep them lissom by exercise. Consider the problem of this dust. How did it get into these boxes and why is there so much of it? If you reason out the probabilities, you must inevitably reach a conclusion as to the nature of the wooden object. That conclusion may turn out to be wrong, but it will be logically justifiable."

"Well, that is all that matters," Jervis retorted with a sour smile, as he rose and glanced at his watch. "The mere fact of its being wrong we should ignore as an irrelevant triviality, just as the French surgeon, undisturbed by the death of the patient, proceeded with his operation and finally brought it to a brilliantly successful conclusion. I will practise your logical dumbbell exercise, and if I reach no conclusion after all I shall still be comforted by the mental vision of my learned senior scouring the country in search of a hypothetical worm-eaten chest of drawers."

Thorndyke chuckled softly. "My learned friend is pleased to be ironical. But nevertheless his unerring judgement leads him to a perfectly correct forecast of my proceedings. The next stage of the inquiry will consist in tracing this dust to its sources, and the goal of my endeavours will be the discovery and identification of this wooden object. If I succeed in that, there will be, I imagine, very little more left to discover."

"No," Jervis agreed, "especially if the owner of the antique should happen to be the elusive Mr. Osmond. So I wish you success in your quest, and only hope it may not resemble too closely that of the legendary blind man, searching in a dark room for a black hat – that isn't there."

With this parting shot and a defiant grin, Jervis took his departure, leaving Thorndyke to complete the examination of the remaining material.

Chapter XV
Mr. Wampole is Highly Amused

On a certain Saturday afternoon at a few minutes to three the door of Mr. Woodstock's office in High Street, Burchester, opened somewhat abruptly and disclosed the figures of the solicitor himself and his chief clerk.

"Confounded nuisance all this fuss and foolery," growled the former, pulling out his watch and casting an impatient glance up the street. "I hope he is not going to keep us waiting."

"He is not due till three," Hepburn remarked, soothingly, and then, stepping out and peering up the nearly empty street, he added, "Perhaps that may be he – that tall man with the little clerical-looking person."

"If it is, he seems to be bringing his luggage with him," said Mr. Woodstock, regarding the pair, and especially the suit-cases that they carried, with evident disfavour, "but you are right. They are coming here."

He put away his watch and, as the two men crossed the road, he assumed an expression of polite hostility.

"Dr. Thorndyke?" he inquired as the newcomers halted opposite the doorway, and having received confirmation of his surmise, he continued, "I am Mr. Woodstock, and this is my colleague, Mr. Hepburn. May I take it that this gentleman is concerned in our present business?" As he spoke he fixed a truculent blue eye on Thorndyke's companion, who crinkled apologetically.

"This is Mr. Polton, my laboratory assistant," Thorndyke explained, "who has come with me to give me any help that I may need."

"Indeed," said Woodstock, glaring inquisitively at the large suit-case which Polton carried. "Help? I gathered from Mr. Penfield's letter that you wished to inspect the office, and I must confess that I found myself utterly unable to imagine why. May I ask what you expect to learn from an inspection of the premises?"

"That," replied Thorndyke, "is a rather difficult question to answer. But as all my information as to what has occurred here is second-or third-hand, I thought it best to see the place myself and make a few inquiries on the spot. That is my routine practice."

"Ah, I see," said Woodstock. "Your visit is just a matter of form, a demonstration of activity. Well, I am sorry I can't be present at the ceremony. My colleague and I have an engagement elsewhere, but my office-keeper, Mr. Wampole, will be able to tell you anything that you may wish to know and show you all there is to see excepting the strong-room. If you want to see that, as I suppose you do, I had better show it to you now, as I must take the key away with me."

He led the way along the narrow hall, halfway down which he opened a door inscribed "*Clerks' Office*", and entered a large room, now unoccupied save by an elderly man who sat at a table with the parts of a dismembered electric bell spread out before him. Through this Mr. Woodstock passed into a somewhat smaller room furnished with a large writing-table, one or two nests of deed-boxes, and a set of bookshelves. Nearly opposite the table was the massive door of the strong-room, standing wide open with the key in the lock.

"This is my private office," said Mr. Woodstock, "and here is the strong-room. Perhaps you would like to step inside. I am rather proud of this room. You don't often see one of this size. And it is absolutely fire-proof, thick steel lining, concrete outside that, and then brick. It is practically indestructible. Those confounded boxes occupied that long upper shelf."

Thorndyke did not appear to be specially interested in the strong-room. He walked in, looked round at the steel walls with their ranks of steel shelves, loaded with bundles of documents, and then walked out.

"Yes," he said, "it is a fine room, as strong and secure as one could wish – though, of course, its security has no bearing on our case, since it must have been entered either with its own key or a duplicate. May I look at the key?"

Mr. Woodstock withdrew it from the lock and handed it to him without comment, watching him with undisguised impatience as he turned it over and examined its blade.

"Not a difficult type of key to duplicate," he remarked as he handed it back, "though these wardless pin-keys are more subtle than they look."

"I suppose they are," Woodstock assented indifferently. "But really, these investigations appear to me rather pointless, seeing that the identity of the thief is known. And now I must be off, but first let me introduce you to my deputy, Mr. Wampole."

He led the way back to the clerks' office, where his subordinate was busily engaged in assembling the parts of the bell.

"This is Dr. Thorndyke, Wampole, who has come with his assistant, Mr. – er – Bolton, to inspect the premises and make a few inquiries. You can show him anything that he wants to see and give him all the assistance that you can in the way of answering questions. And," concluded Mr. Woodstock, shaking hands stiffly with Thorndyke, "I wish you a successful issue to your labours."

As Mr. Woodstock and his colleague departed, closing the outer door after them, Mr. Wampole laid down his screw-driver and looked at Thorndyke with a slightly puzzled expression.

"I don't quite understand, sir, what you want to do," said he, "or what sort of inspection you want to make, but I am entirely at your service, if you will kindly instruct me. What would you like me to show you first?"

"I don't think we need interrupt your work just at present, Mr. Wampole. The first thing to be done is to make a rough plan of the premises, and while my assistant is doing that, perhaps I might ask you a few questions, if it will not distract you too much."

"It will not distract me at all," Mr. Wampole replied, picking up his screw-driver. "I am accustomed to doing odd jobs about the office – I am the handy man of the establishment – and I am not easily put out of my stride."

Evidently he was not, for even as he was speaking his fingers were busy in a neat, purposive way that showed clearly that his attention was not wandering from his task. Thorndyke watched him curiously, not quite able to "place" him. His hands were the skilful, capable hands of a mechanic, and this agreed with Woodstock's description of him and his own. But his speech was that of a passably educated man and his manner was quite dignified and self-possessed.

"By the way," said Thorndyke, "Mr. Woodstock referred to you as the office-keeper. Does that mean that you are the custodian of the premises?"

"Nominally," replied Wampole. "I am a law-writer by profession, but when I first came here, some twenty years ago, I came as a caretaker and used to live upstairs. But for many years past, the upstairs rooms have been used for storage – obsolete books, documents, and all sorts of accumulations. Nobody lives in the house now. We lock the place up when we go away at night. As for me, I am, as I said, the handyman of the establishment. I do whatever comes along – copy letters, engross leases, keep an eye on the state of the premises, and so on."

"I see. Then you probably know as much of the affairs of this office as anybody."

"Probably, sir. I am the oldest member of the staff, and I am usually the first to arrive in the morning and the last to leave at night. I expect I can tell you anything that you want to know."

"Then I will ask you one or two questions, if I may. You probably know that my visit here is connected with the robbery of Mr. Hollis's gems?"

179

"The alleged robbery," Mr. Wampole corrected. "Yes, sir. Mr. Woodstock told me that."

"You appear to be somewhat doubtful about the robbery."

"I am not doubtful at all," Wampole replied in a tone of great decision. "I am convinced that the whole thing is a mare's nest. The gems may have been stolen. I suppose they were as Mr. Hollis says they were. But they weren't stolen from here."

"You put complete trust in the strong-room?"

"Oh no, I don't, sir. This is a solicitor's strong-room, not a banker's. It is secure against fire, not against robbery. It was designed for the custody of things such as documents, of great value to their owners but of no value to a thief. It was no proper receptacle for jewels. They should have gone to a bank."

"Do I understand, then, that unauthorized persons might have obtained access to the strong-room?"

"They might, during business hours. Mr. Woodstock unlocks it when he arrives and it is usually open all day, or if it is shut, the key is left hanging on the wall. But it has never been taken seriously as a bank strong-room is. Mr. Hepburn and Mr. Osmond kept their cricket-bags and other things in it, and we have all been in the habit of putting things in there if we were leaving them here over-night."

"Then, really, any member of the staff had the opportunity to make away with Mr. Hollis's property?"

"I wouldn't put it as strongly as that," replied Wampole, with somewhat belated caution. "Any of us could have gone into the strong-room, but not without being seen by some of the others. Still, one must admit that a robbery might have been possible, the point is that it didn't happen. I checked those boxes when I helped to put them in, and I checked them when we took them out. They were all there in their original wrappings with Mr. Hollis's handwriting on them and all the seals intact. It is nonsense to talk of a robbery in the face of those facts."

"And you attach no significance to Mr. Osmond's disappearance?"

"No, sir. He was a bachelor and could go when and where he pleased. It was odd of him, I admit, but he sometimes did odd things – a hasty, impulsive gentleman, quick to jump at conclusions and make decisions and quick to act. Not a discreet gentleman at all. Rather an unreasonable gentleman, perhaps, but I should say highly scrupulous. I can't imagine him committing a theft."

"Should you describe him as a nervous or timid man?"

Mr. Wampole emitted a sound as if he had clock work in his inside and was about to strike. "I never met a less nervous man," he replied with emphasis. "No, sir. Bold to rashness would be my description of

180

Mr. John Osmond. A buccaneering type of man. A yachtsman, a boxer, a wrestler, a footballer, and a cricketer. A regular hard nut, sir. He should never have been in an office. He ought to have been a sailor, an explorer, or a big-game hunter."

"What was he like to look at?"

"Just what you would expect – a big, lean, square-built man, hatchet-faced, Roman-nosed, with blue eyes, light-brown hair, and a close-cropped beard and moustache. Looked like a naval officer."

"Do you happen to know if his residence has been examined?"

"Mr. Woodstock and the Chief Constable searched his rooms, but of course they didn't find anything. He had only two small rooms, as he took his meals and spent a good deal of his time with Mr. Hepburn, his brother-in-law. He seemed very fond of his sister and her two little boys."

"Would it be possible for me to see those rooms?"

"I don't see why not, sir. They are locked up now, but the keys are here and the rooms are only a few doors down the street."

Here occurred a slight interruption, for Mr. Wampole, having completed his operations on the bell, now connected it with the battery – which had also been under repair – when it emitted a loud and cheerful peal. At the same moment, as if summoned by the sound, Polton entered holding a small drawing-board on which was a neatly executed plan of the premises.

"Dear me, sir!" exclaimed Mr. Wampole, casting an astonished glance at the plan. "You are very thorough in your methods. I see you have even put in the furniture."

"Yes," Thorndyke agreed, with a faint smile, "we must needs be thorough even if we reach no result."

Mr. Wampole regarded him with a sly smile. "Very true, sir," he chuckled – "very true, indeed. A bill of costs needs something to explain the total. But, God bless us! What is this?"

"This" was, in effect, a diminutive vacuum cleaner, fitted with a little revolving brush and driven by means of a large dry battery, which Polton was at the moment disinterring from his suit-case. Thorndyke briefly explained the nature of the apparatus while Mr. Wampole stared at it with an expression of stupefaction.

"But why have you brought it here, sir?" he exclaimed. "The premises would certainly be the better for a thorough cleaning, but surely – "

"Oh, we are not going to 'vacuum clean' you," Thorndyke reassured him. "We are going to take samples of dust from the different parts of the premises."

"Are you, indeed, sir? And, if I may take the liberty of asking, what do you propose to do with them?"

"I shall examine them carefully when I get home," Thorndyke replied, "and I may then possibly be able to judge whether the robbery took place here or elsewhere."

As Thorndyke furnished this explanation, Mr. Wampole stood gazing at him as if petrified. Once he opened his mouth, but shut it again tightly as if not trusting himself to speak. At length he rejoined, "Wonderful! Wonderful!" and then, after an interval, he continued meditatively, "I seem to have read somewhere of a wise woman of the East who was able, by merely examining a hair from the beard of a man who had fallen downstairs, to tell exactly how many stairs he had fallen down. But I never imagined that it was actually possible."

"It does sound incredible," Thorndyke admitted, gravely. "She must have had remarkable powers of deduction. And now, if Mr. Polton is ready, we will begin our perambulation. Which was Mr. Osmond's office?"

"I will show you," replied Mr. Wampole, recovering from his trance of astonishment. He led the way out into the hall and thence into a smallish room in which were a writing-table and a large, old-fashioned, flap-top desk.

"This table," he explained, "is Mr. Hepburn's. The desk was used by Mr. Osmond and his belongings are still in it. That second door opens into Mr. Woodstock's office."

"Is it usually kept open or closed?" Thorndyke asked.

"It is nearly always open, and as it is, as you see – " Here he threw it open. " – exactly opposite the door of the strong-room, no one could go in there unobserved unless Mr. Woodstock, Mr. Hepburn, and Mr. Osmond had all been out at the same time."

Thorndyke made a note of this statement and then asked, "Would it be permissible to look inside Mr. Osmond's desk? Or is it locked?"

"I don't think it is locked. No, it is not," he added, demonstrating the fact by raising the lid, "and, as you see, there is nothing very secret inside."

The contents, in fact, consisted of a tobacco-tin, a couple of briar pipes, a ball of string, a pair of gloves, a clothes-brush, a pair of much-worn hair-brushes, and a number of loose letters and bills. These last Thorndyke gathered together and laid aside without examination, and then proceeded methodically to inspect each of the other objects in turn, while Mr. Wampole watched him with the faintest shadow of a smile.

"He seems to have had a pretty good set of teeth and a fairly strong jaw," Thorndyke remarked, balancing a massive pipe in his fingers and glancing at the deep tooth-marks on the mouth-piece, "which supports your statement as to his physique."

He peered into the tobacco-tin, smelt the tobacco, inspected the gloves closely, especially at their palmar surfaces, and tried them on, examined the clothes brush, first with the naked eye and then with the aid of his pocket-lens, and, holding it inside the desk, stroked its hair backwards and forwards, looking closely to see if any dust fell from it. Finally, he took up the hair-brushes one at a time and, having examined them in the same minute fashion, produced from his pocket a pair of fine forceps and a seed-envelope. With the forceps he daintily picked out from the brushes a number of hairs which he laid on a sheet of paper, eventually transferring the collection to the little envelope, on which he wrote: "*Hairs from John Osmond's hair-brushes*".

"You don't take anything for granted, sir," remarked Mr. Wampole, who had been watching this proceeding with concentrated interest. (Perhaps he was again reminded of the wise woman of the East.)

"No," Thorndyke agreed. "Your description was hearsay testimony, whereas these hairs could be produced in Court and sworn to by me."

"So they could, sir, though, as it is not disputed that Mr. Osmond has been in this office, I don't quite see what they could prove."

"Neither do I," rejoined Thorndyke. "I was merely laying down the principle."

Meanwhile, Polton had been silently carrying out his part of the programme, not unobserved by Mr. Wampole, and a pale patch about a foot square, between Mr. Hepburn's chair and the front of the table, where the pattern of the grimy carpet had miraculously reappeared, marked the site of his operations. Tenderly removing the little silken bag, now bulging with its load of dust, he slipped it into a numbered envelope and wrote the number on the spot on the plan to which it corresponded.

Presently a similar patch appeared on the carpet in front of Osmond's desk, and when the sample had been disposed of and the spot on the plan marked, Polton cast a wistful glance at the open desk.

"Wouldn't it be as well, sir, to take a specimen from the inside?" he asked.

"Perhaps it would," Thorndyke replied. "It should give us what we may call a 'pure culture'." He rapidly emptied the desk of its contents, when Polton introduced the nozzle of his apparatus and drew it slowly over every part of the interior. When this operation was completed, including the disposal of the specimen and the marking of the plan, the party moved into Mr. Woodstock's office, and from thence back into the clerks' office.

183

"I find this investigation intensely interesting," said Mr. Wampole, rubbing his hands gleefully. "It seems to combine the attractions of a religious ceremony and a parlour game. I am enjoying it exceedingly. You will like to have the names of the clerks who sit at those desks, I presume."

"If you please," replied Thorndyke.

"And, of course, you will wish to take samples from the insides of the desks. You certainly ought to. The informal lunches which the occupants consume during the forenoon will have left traces which should be most illuminating. And the desks are not locked, as there are no keys."

Mr. Wampole's advice produced on Polton's countenance a smile of most extraordinary crinkliness, but Thorndyke accepted it with unmoved gravity and it was duly acted upon. Each of the desks was opened and emptied of its contents – instructive enough as to the character and personal habits of the tenant – and cleared of its accumulation of crumbs, tobacco-ash, and miscellaneous dirt, the "catch" forming a specimen supplementary to those obtained from the floor. At length, when they had made the round of the office, leaving in their wake a succession of clean squares on the matting which covered the floor, Mr. Wampole halted before an old-fashioned high desk which stood in a corner in company with a high office-stool.

"This is my desk," said he. "I presume that you are going to take a little souvenir from it?"

"Well," replied Thorndyke, "we may as well complete the series. We operated on Mr. Hollis's premises this morning."

"Did you indeed, sir! You went there first, and very proper too. I am sure Mr. Hollis was very gratified."

"If he was," Thorndyke replied with a smile, "he didn't make it obtrusively apparent. May I compliment you on your desk? You keep it in apple-pie order."

"I try to show the juniors an example," replied Mr. Wampole, throwing back the lid of the desk and looking complacently at the neatly stowed contents. "It is a miscellaneous collection," he added as he proceeded to transfer his treasures from the desk to a cleared space on the table.

It certainly was. There were a few tools – pliers, hack-saw, hammer, screw-driver, and a couple of gimlets – a loosely folded linen apron, one or two battery terminals and a coil of insulated wire, a stamp-album, a cardboard tray full of military buttons, cap-badges, and old civilian coat buttons, and a smaller tray containing one or two old copper and silver coins.

184

"I see you are a stamp collector," remarked Thorndyke, opening the album and casting a glance of lukewarm interest over its variegated pages.

"Yes," was the reply, "in a small way. It is a poor man's hobby, unless one seeks to acquire costly rarities, which I do not. As a matter of fact, I seldom buy specimens at all. This album has been filled principally from our foreign correspondence. And the same is true of the coins. I don't regularly collect them, I just keep any odd specimens that come my way."

"And the buttons? You have a better opportunity there, for you have practically no competitors. And yet it seems to me that they are of more interest than the things that the conventional collectors seek so eagerly."

"I entirely agree with you, sir," Mr. Wampole replied, warmly. "It is the common things that are best worth collecting – the things that are common now and will be rare in a few years' time. But the collector who has no imagination neglects things until they have become rare and precious. Then he buys at a high price what he could have got a few years previously for nothing. Look at these old gilt coat-buttons. I got them from an old-established tailor who was clearing out his obsolete stock. Unfortunately, he had thrown away most of them and nearly all the steel button-dies. I just managed to rescue these few and one or two dies, which I have at home. They are of no value now, but when the collectors discover the interest of old buttons, they will be worth their weight in gold. I am collecting all the buttons I can get hold of."

"I think you are wise, from a collector's point of view. By the way, did you ever meet with any of those leather-bound sample wallets that the old button-makers used to supply to tailors?"

"Never," replied Mr. Wampole. "I have never even heard of them."

"I have seen one or two," said Thorndyke, "and each was a collection in itself, for it contained some two or three-hundred buttons, fixed in sheets of mill-board, forming a sort of album, and, of course, every button was different from every other."

Mr. Wampole's eyes sparkled. "What an opportunity you had, sir!" he exclaimed. "But probably you are not a collector. It was a pity, though, for, as you say, one of those wallets was a museum in itself. If you should ever chance to meet with another, would it be too great a liberty for me to beg you to secure an option for me, at a price within my slender means?"

"It is no liberty at all," Thorndyke replied. "It is not likely that I shall ever come across one again, but if I should, I will certainly secure it for you."

"That is most kind of you, sir," exclaimed Mr. Wampole. "And now, as Mr. Polton seems to have completed the cleansing of my desk – the first that it has had, I am afraid, for a year or two – we may continue our exploration. Did you wish to examine the waiting room?"

"I think not. I have just looked into it, but its associations are too ambiguous for the dust to be of any interest. But I should like to glance at the rooms upstairs."

To the upstairs rooms they accordingly proceeded, but the inspection was little more than a formality. They walked slowly through each room, awakening the echoes as they trod the bare floors, and as they went, Thorndyke's eye travelled searchingly over the shelves and rough tables, stacked with documents and obsolete account-books, and the few rickety Windsor chairs. There was certainly an abundance of dust, as Mr. Wampole pointed out, but it did not appear to be of the brand in which Thorndyke was interested.

"Well," said Mr. Wampole, as they descended to the ground floor, "you have now seen the whole of our premises. I think you said that you would like to inspect Mr. Osmond's rooms. If you will wait a few moments, I will get the keys."

He disappeared into the principal's office, and meanwhile Polton rapidly packed his apparatus in the suit case, so that by the time Mr. Wampole reappeared, he was ready to start.

"Mr. Osmond's rooms," said Mr. Wampole, as they set forth, "are over a bookseller's shop. This is the place. If you will wait for a moment at the private door, I will notify the landlord of our visit." He entered the shop and after a short interval emerged briskly and stepped round to the side-door, into which he inserted a latch-key. He led the way along the narrow hall, past a partially open door, in the opening of which a portion of a human face was visible, to the staircase, up which the little procession advanced until the second-floor landing was reached. Here Mr. Wampole halted and, selecting a key from the small bunch, unlocked and opened a door, and preceded his visitors into the room.

"It is just as well that you came to-day," he remarked, "for I understand that Mrs. Hepburn is going to take charge of these rooms. A day or two later and she would have been beforehand with you in the matter of dust. As it is, you ought to get quite a good haul."

"Quite," Thorndyke agreed. "There is plenty of dust, but in spite of that, the place has a very neat, orderly appearance. Do you happen to know whether the rooms have been tidied up since Mr. Osmond left?"

"They are just as he left them," was the reply, "excepting that the Chief Constable and Mr. Woodstock came and looked over them. But I

186

don't think they disturbed them to any extent. There isn't much to disturb, as you see."

Mr. Wampole was right. The furnishing of the room did not go beyond the barest necessities, and when Thorndyke opened the door of communication and looked into the bedroom, it was seen to be characterized by a like austere simplicity. Whatever might be the moral short-comings of the vanished tenant, softness or effeminate luxuriousness did not appear to be among them.

As his assistant refixed the "extractor", Thorndyke stood thoughtfully surveying the room, trying to assess the personality of its late occupant by the light of his belongings. And those belongings and the room which held them were highly characteristic. The late tenant was clearly an active man, a man whose interests lay out-of-doors, an orderly man, too, with something of a sailor's tidiness. He had the sailor's knack of keeping the floor clear by slinging things aloft out of the way. Not only small articles such as rules, dividers, marlinspike, and sheath-knife, but a gun-case, fishing-rods, cricket-bats, and a bulky roll of charts were disposed of on the walls by means of picture-hooks and properly-made slings – the height of which gave a clue to the occupant's stature and length of arm. And the nautical flavour was accentuated by the contents of a set of rough shelves in a recess, which included a boat compass, a nautical almanack, a volume of sailing directions, and a manual of naval architecture. The only touch of ornament was given by a set of four photographs in silver frames, which occupied the mantelpiece in company with a pipe-rack, a tobacco-jar, an ash-bowl, and a box of matches.

Thorndyke stepped across to the fireplace to look at them more closely. They were portraits of five persons: A grave-looking, elderly clergyman, a woman of about the same age with a strong, alert, resolute face and markedly aquiline features, and a younger woman, recognizably like the clergyman, and two boys of about seven and eight, photographed together.

"Those," said Mr. Wampole, indicating the older persons, "are Mr. Osmond's parents – both, I regret to say, deceased. The younger lady is Mrs. Hepburn, Mr. Osmond's sister, and those little boys are her sons. Mr. Osmond was very devoted to them, as I believe they were to him."

Thorndyke nodded. "They are fine little fellows," he remarked. "Indeed, it is a good-looking family. I gather from your description that Mr. Osmond must have taken rather strongly after his mother."

"You are quite right, sir," replied Mr. Wampole. "From that portrait of his mother, you would recognize Mr. Osmond without the slightest difficulty. The likeness is quite remarkable."

Thorndyke nodded again as he considered long and earnestly the striking face that looked out of the frame so keenly under its bold, straight brows. Strength, courage, determination, were written in every line of it, and as he stood with his eyes bent upon those of the portrait and thought of this woman's son – of the mean, avaricious crime, so slyly and craftily carried out, of the hasty, pusillanimous flight, unjustified by any hint of danger – he was sensible of a discrepancy between personality and conduct to which his experience furnished no parallel. A vast amount of nonsense has been talked and believed on the subject of physiognomy, but within this body of error there lies a soul of truth. "Character reading" in the Lavater manner is largely pure quackery, but there is a certain general congruity between a man's essential character and his bodily "make-up", including his facial type. Here, however, was a profound incongruity. Thorndyke found it difficult to identify the sly, cowardly knave whom he was seeking with the actual man who appeared to be coming into view.

But his doubts did not affect his actions. He had come here to collect evidence, and that purpose he proceeded to execute with a perfectly open mind. He pointed out to Polton the most likely spots to work for characteristic dust, he examined minutely every piece of furniture and woodwork in both the rooms, he made careful notes of every fact observed by himself or communicated by Wampole that could throw any light on the habits or occupations of the absent man. Even the secretly-amused onlooker was impressed by the thoroughness of the investigation for, as Polton finally packed his apparatus, he remarked, "Well, sir, I have told you what I think – that you are following a will-o'-the-wisp. But if you fail to run him to earth, it certainly won't be for lack of painstaking effort. You deserve to succeed."

Thorndyke thanked him for the compliment and retired slowly down the stairs while the rooms were being locked up. They called in at the office to collect Thorndyke's green canvas-covered case and then made their *adieux*.

"I must thank you most warmly, Mr. Wampole," said Thorndyke, "for the kind interest that you have taken in our investigations. You have given us every possible help."

Mr. Wampole bowed. "It is very good of you to say so. But it has really been a great pleasure and a most novel and interesting experience." He held the door open for them to pass out, and as they were crossing the threshold he added, "You won't forget about that button-wallet, sir, if the opportunity should arrive."

"I certainly will not," was the reply. "I will secure an option – or better still, the wallet itself and send it to you. By the way, should it be sent here or to your private address?"

Mr. Wampole reflected for a few moments. Then he drew from his pocket a much-worn letter-case from which he extracted a printed visiting-card.

"I think, sir, it would be best to send it to my private address. One doesn't want it opened by the wrong hands. This is my address, and let me thank you in advance, even if only for the kind intention. Good evening, sir. Good evening, Mr. Polton. I trust that your little dusty souvenirs will prove highly illuminating."

He stood on the threshold and gravely watched his two visitors as they retired down the street. At length, when they turned a corner, he re-entered, shutting and locking the outer door. Then in an instant his gravity relaxed, and flinging himself into a chair, he roused the echoes with peal after peal of joyous laughter.

Chapter XVI
Which Treats of Law and Buttons

"This seems highly irregular," said Mr. Penfield, settling himself comfortably in the easy-chair and smilingly regarding a small table on which were a decanter and glasses. "I don't treat my professional visitors in this hospitable fashion. And you don't even ask what has brought me here."

"No," replied Thorndyke, as he filled a couple of glasses, "I accept the gifts of Fortune and ask no questions."

Mr. Penfield bowed. "You were good enough to say that I might call out of business hours, which is a great convenience, so here I am, with a twofold purpose: First, to seek information from you, and second to give you certain news of my own. Perhaps I may take them in that order and begin by asking one or two questions?"

"Do so, by all means," replied Thorndyke.

"I have heard," pursued Mr. Penfield, "from our friends Hollis and Woodstock, and perhaps you will not be surprised to learn that you have made yourself somewhat unpopular with them. They have even applied disrespectful epithets to you."

"Such as mountebank, impostor, quack, and so forth," suggested Thorndyke.

Mr. Penfield chuckled as he sipped his wine. "Your insight is remarkable," said he. "You have quoted the very words. They complain that, after making a serious appointment with them and occupying their time, you merely asked a number of foolish and irrelevant questions, and then proceeded to sweep the floor. Is that an exaggeration, or did you really sweep the floor?"

"I collected a few samples of dust from the floor and elsewhere."

Mr. Penfield consumed a luxurious pinch of snuff and regarded Thorndyke with delighted amusement.

"Did you indeed? Well, I am not surprised at their attitude. But a year or so ago it would have been my own. It must have looked like sheer wizardry. But tell me, have your investigations and floor-sweepings yielded any tangible facts?

"Yes," replied Thorndyke, "they have, and those facts I will lay before you on the strict understanding that you communicate them to nobody. As to certain further inferences of a more speculative character,

I should prefer to make no statement at present. They may be entirely erroneous."

"Exactly, exactly. Let us keep scrupulously to definite facts which are susceptible of proof. Now, what have you discovered?"

"My positive results amount to this: In the first place, I have ascertained beyond the possibility of any reasonable doubt that those boxes had been opened by some person other than Mr. Hollis. In the second place, it is virtually certain that the person who opened them was in some way connected with Mr. Woodstock's office."

"Do you say that the boxes were actually opened in his office?

"No. The evidence goes to prove that they were taken from the office and opened elsewhere."

"But surely they would have been missed from the strong-room?"

"That, I think, was provided for. I infer that only one box was taken at a time and that its place was filled by a dummy."

"Astonishing!" exclaimed Mr. Penfield. "It seems incredible that you should have been able to discover this – or, indeed, that it should be true. The seals seem to me to offer an insuperable difficulty."

"On the contrary," replied Thorndyke, "it was the seals that furnished the evidence. They were manifest forgeries."

"Were they really! The robber had actually had a counterfeit seal engraved?"

"No. The false seal was not engraved. It was an electrotype made from one of the wax impressions, a much simpler and easier proceeding, and one that the robber could carry out himself and so avoid the danger of employing a seal engraver."

"No doubt it would be the safer plan, and probably you are right in assuming that he adopted it, but – "

"I am not assuming," said Thorndyke. "There is direct evidence that the seal used to make the false impressions was an electrotype."

"Now, what would be the nature of that evidence – or is it, perhaps, too technical for an ignorant person like me to follow?"

"There is nothing very technical about it," replied Thorndyke. "You know how an electrotype is made? Well, to put it briefly, the process would be this: One of the wax impressions from a box would be carefully coated with black lead or some other conducting material and attached to one of the terminals of an electric battery, and to the other terminal a piece of copper would be attached. The black-leaded wax impression and the piece of copper would be suspended from the wires of the battery, close together but not touching, in a solution of sulphate of copper. Then, as the electric current passed, the copper would dissolve in the solution and a film of metallic copper would become deposited on the

191

black-leaded wax and would gradually thicken until it became a solid shell of copper. When this shell was picked off the wax it would be, in effect, a copper seal which would give impressions on wax just like the original seal. Is that clear?"

"Perfectly. But what is the evidence that this was actually done?"

"It is really very simple," replied Thorndyke. "Let us consider what would happen in the two alternative cases. Take first that of the seal engraver. He has handed to him one or more of the wax impressions from the boxes and is asked to engrave a seal which shall be an exact copy of the seal which made the impressions. What does he do? If the wax impression were absolutely perfect, he would simply copy it in *intaglio*. But a seal impression never is perfect unless it is made with quite extraordinary care. But the wax impressions on the boxes were just ordinary impressions, hastily made with no attempt at precision, and almost certainly not a perfect one among them. The engraver, then, would not rigorously copy a particular impression, but, eliminating its individual and accidental imperfections, he would aim at producing a seal which should be a faithful copy of the original seal, without any imperfections at all.

"Now take the case of the electrotype. This is a mechanical reproduction of a particular impression. Whatever accidental marks or imperfections there may be in that impression will be faithfully reproduced. In short, an engraved seal would be a copy of the original seal, an electrotype would be a copy of a particular impression of that seal."

Mr. Penfield nodded approvingly. "An excellent point and very clearly argued. But what is its bearing on the case?"

"It is this: Since an electrotype seal is a mechanical copy of a particular wax impression, including any accidental marks or imperfections in it, it follows that every impression made on wax with such a seal will exhibit the accidental marks or imperfections of the original wax impression, in addition to any defects of its own. So that, if a series of such impressions were examined, although each would probably have its own distinctive peculiarities, yet all of them would be found to agree in displaying the accidental marks or imperfections of the original impression."

"Yes, I see that," said Mr. Penfield with a slightly interrogative inflexion.

"Well, that is what I have found in the series of seal-impressions from Mr. Hollis's boxes. They are of all degrees of badness, but in every one of the series two particular defects occur, which, as the series

192

consists of over thirty impressions, is utterly outside the limits of probability."

"Might those imperfections not have been in the seal itself?

"No. I took, with the most elaborate care, two impressions from the original seal, and those impressions are, I think, as perfect as is possible. At any rate, they are free from these, or any other visible defects. I will show them to you."

He took from a drawer a portfolio and an envelope. From the latter he produced one of the two impressions that he had made with Mr. Hollis's seal and from the former a half-plate photograph.

"Here," he said, handing them to Mr. Penfield, "is one of the seal impressions taken by me, and here is a magnified photograph of it. You can see that every part of the design is perfectly clear and distinct and the background quite free from indentations. Keep that photograph for comparison with these others, which show a series of thirty-two impressions from the boxes, magnified four diameters. In every one of them you will find two defects. First the projecting fore-legs of the left-hand horse are blurred and faint, second, there is, just in front of the chariot and above the back of the near horse, a minute pit in the back ground. It is hardly visible to the naked eye in the wax impressions, but the photographs show it plainly. It was probably produced by a tiny bubble of air between the seal and the wax.

"Now, neither of these defects is to be seen in Mr. Hollis's seal. Either of them might have occurred accidentally in one or two impressions. But since they both occur in every case, whether the impressions are relatively good or bad, it is practically certain that they existed in the matrix or seal with which the impressions were made. And this conclusion is confirmed by the fact that, in some cases, the defect in the horse's fore legs is inconsistent with other defects in the same impression."

"How inconsistent?" Mr. Penfield demanded.

"I mean that the faint impression of the horse's legs is due to insufficient pressure of the left side of the seal, the seal has not been put down quite vertically. But here – in number 23, for instance – the impression of the chariot and driver on the right-hand side is quite faint and shallow. In that case, the left-hand side of the impression should have been deep and distinct. But both sides are faint, whereas the middle is deep."

"Might not the seal have been rocked from side to side?"

"No, that would not explain the appearances, for if the seal were rocked from side to side, both sides would be deep, though the middle might be shallow. It is impossible to imagine any kind of pressure which would give an impression shallow on both sides and deep in the middle. The only possible explanation is that the matrix, itself, was shallow on one side."

Mr. Penfield reflected, helping his cogitations with a pinch of snuff.

"Yes," he agreed. "Incredible as the thing appears, I think you have made out your case. But doesn't it strike you as rather odd that this ingenious rascal should not have taken more care to secure a good impression from which to make his false seal?"

"I imagine that he had no choice," replied Thorndyke. "On each box were six seals, three on the paper wrapping, two in the recesses by the keyhole, and one on the knot of the string. Now, as the paper had to be preserved, the seals could not be torn or cut from that. It would be impossible to get them out of the recesses. There remained only the seals on the knots. These were, of course, much the least perfect, though the string was little more than thread and the knots quite small. But they were the only ones that it was possible to remove, and our friend was lucky to have got as good an impression as he did."

Mr. Penfield nodded. "Yes," said he, "you have an answer to every objection. By the way, if the paper had to be preserved so carefully, how do you suppose he got the parcels open? He would have had to break the seals."

"I think not. I assume that he melted the seals by holding a hot iron close to them and then gently opened the packets while the wax was soft."

Mr. Penfield chuckled. "Yes," he admitted, "it is all very complete and consistent. And now to go on to the next point. You say that there is evidence that these boxes were opened by some person other than Hollis himself, a person connected in some way with Woodstock's office. Further that they were opened, not in the office itself, but in some other place to which they had been taken. I should like to hear that evidence, especially if it should happen to be connected with those mysterious floor-sweepings."

"As a matter of fact, it is," Thorndyke replied, with a smile. "But the floor-sweeping was not the first stage. The investigation began with Mr. Hollis's boxes, from which I extracted every particle of dust that I could obtain, and this dust I examined minutely and exhaustively. The results were unexpectedly illuminating. For instance, from every one of the untouched boxes I obtained one or more moustache hairs."

"Really! But isn't that very remarkable?"

"Perhaps it is. But moustache hairs are shed very freely. If you look at the dust from a desk used by a man with a moustache, you will usually see in it quite a number of moustache hairs."

"I have not noticed that," said Mr. Penfield, "having no moustache myself. And what else did you obtain by your curious researches?"

"The other result was really very remarkable indeed. From every one of the boxes I obtained particles – in some cases only one or two, in others quite a number – of the very characteristic dust which is shed by worm-eaten furniture."

"Dear me!" exclaimed Mr. Penfield. "And you were actually able to identify it! Astonishing! Now, I suppose – you must excuse me," he interpolated with an apologetic smile, "but I am walking in an enchanted land and am ready to expect and believe in any marvels – I suppose you were not able to infer the character of the piece of furniture?"

"Not with anything approaching certainty," replied Thorndyke. "I formed certain opinions, but they are necessarily speculative, and we are dealing with evidence."

"Quite so, quite so," said Mr. Penfield. "Let us avoid speculation. But I now begin to see the inwardness of the floor-sweeping. You were tracing this mysterious dust to its place of origin."

"Exactly. And, naturally, I began with Mr. Hollis's premises – though the forgery of the seals seemed to put him outside the field of inquiry."

"Yes, he would hardly have needed to forge his own seal."

"No. But I examined his premises thoroughly, with an entirely negative result. There was no one on them with a moustache of any kind, the dust from his floors showed not a particle of the wood-dust, and I could find no piece of furniture in his house which could have yielded such dust.

"I then proceeded to Woodstock's office, and there I obtained abundant samples both of hairs and wood-dust. I found Osmond's hair-brushes in his desk, and from them obtained a number of moustache hairs which, on careful comparison, appear to be identically similar to those found in the boxes."

"Ha!" exclaimed Mr. Penfield in what sounded like a tone of disapproval. "And as to the wood-dust?"

"I obtained traces of it from every part of the floor. But it was very unequally distributed, so unequally as to associate it quite distinctly with a particular individual. I obtained abundant traces of it from the floor round that individual's desk, and even more from the inside of the desk, whereas, from the interiors of the other desks I recovered hardly a particle."

"You refer to 'a particular individual.' Do you mean John Osmond?"

195

"No," replied Thorndyke. "Osmond's desk contained no wood-dust."

"Ha!" exclaimed Mr. Penfield in what sounded very like a tone of satisfaction.

"As to the individual referred to," said Thorndyke, "I think that, for the present, it might be better – "

"Certainly," Mr. Penfield interrupted emphatically, "certainly. It will be much better to mention no names. After all, it is but a coincidence, though undoubtedly a striking one. But we must keep an open mind."

"That is what I feel," said Thorndyke. "It is an impressive fact, but there is the possibility of some fallacy. Nevertheless it is the most promising clue that offers, and I shall endeavour to follow it up."

"Undoubtedly," Mr. Penfield agreed, warmly. "It indicates a new line of inquiry adapted to your peculiar gifts, though to me I must confess it only adds a new complication to this mystery. And I do really find this a most perplexing case. Perhaps you do not?"

"I do, indeed," replied Thorndyke. "It bristles with contradictions and inconsistencies. Take the case against Osmond. On the one hand it is in the highest degree convincing. The robberies coincide in time with his presence in the office. His disappearance coincides with the discovery of the robbery, and then in the rifled boxes we find a number of hairs from his moustache."

"Can you prove that they are actually his?" Mr. Penfield asked.

"No," Thorndyke replied. "But I have not the slightest doubt that they are, and I think they would be accepted by a jury – in conjunction with the other circumstances – as good evidence. These facts seem to point quite clearly to his guilt. On the other hand, the wood-dust is not connected with him at all. None was found in his desk or near it, and when I examined his rooms – which by a fortunate chance I was able to do – I not only found no trace whatever of wood-dust, but from the appearance of the place I was convinced that the boxes had not been opened there. And furthermore, so far as I could ascertain, the man's personality was singularly out of character with a subtle, cunning, avaricious crime of this type – not that I would lay great stress on that point."

"No," agreed Mr. Penfield, "the information is too scanty. But tell me – you inferred that the boxes were not opened in Woodstock's office, but were taken away and opened in some other place. How did you arrive at that?"

"By means of the wood-dust. The place in which those boxes were opened and refilled must have contained some worm-eaten wooden object which yielded that very distinctive dust, and yielded it in large quantities. But there was no such object on Woodstock's premises. I searched the house from top to bottom and could not find a single piece of worm-eaten wood work."

"And may I inquire – mind, I am not asking for details – but may I inquire whether you have any idea as to the whereabouts of that piece of furniture?"

"I have a suspicion," replied Thorndyke. "But there is my dilemma. I have a strong suspicion as to the place where it might be found, but, unfortunately, that place is not accessible for exploration. So, at present, I am unable either to confirm or disprove my theory."

"But supposing you were able to ascertain definitely that the piece of furniture is where you believe it to be? What then?"

"In that case," Thorndyke replied, "provided that this worm-eaten object turned out to be the kind of object that I believe it to be, I should be disposed to apply for a search-warrant."

"To search for what?" demanded Mr. Penfield.

"The stolen property – and certain other things."

"But surely the stolen property has been disposed of long ago."

"I think," replied Thorndyke, "that there are reasons for believing that it has not. But I would rather not go into that question at present."

"No," said Mr. Penfield. "We agreed to avoid speculative questions. And now, as I think I have exhausted your supply of information, it is my turn to contribute. I have a rather startling piece of news to communicate. John Osmond is dead."

Thorndyke regarded Mr. Penfield with raised eyebrows. "Have you heard any particulars?" he asked.

"Woodstock sent me a copy of the police report, of which I will send you a duplicate if you would like one. Briefly, it amounts to this: Osmond was traced to Bristol, and it was suspected that he had embarked on a ship which traded from that port to the west coast of Africa. That ship was seen, some weeks later, at anchor off the coast at a considerable distance from her usual trading-ground, and on her arrival at her station – a place called Half-Jack on the Grain Coast – was boarded by an inspector of constabulary who had been sent up from the Gold Coast to make inquiries. To him the captain admitted that he had landed a passenger from Bristol at a place called Adaffia in the Bight of Benin. The passenger was a man named Walker whose description agreed completely with that of Osmond. Thereupon, the inspector returned to Accra to report, and from thence was sent down to Adaffia with an armed party to find the man and arrest him.

"But he was too late. He arrived only in time to find a trader named Larkom setting up a wooden cross over the grave. Walker had died early that morning or the night before."

"Is it quite clear that this man was really John Osmond?"

"Quite," replied Mr. Penfield. "Larkom had just painted the name John Osmond on the cross. It appeared that Osmond, when he realized that he was dying, had disclosed his real name and asked to have it written above his grave – naturally enough. One doesn't want to be buried under an assumed name."

"No," Thorndyke agreed. "The grave is a sufficiently secure sanctuary. Does the report say what was the cause of death?"

"Yes, though it doesn't seem very material. He is stated to have died from blackwater fever – whatever that may be."

"It is a peculiarly malignant type of malaria," Thorndyke explained, and he added after a pause, "Well, 'the White Man's Grave' is a pestilential region, but poor Osmond certainly wasted no time in dying. How does his death affect our inquiry?"

Mr. Penfield took snuff viciously. "Woodstock's view is – I can hardly speak of it with patience – that as the thief is dead, the inquiry comes automatically to an end."

"And Hollis, I take it, does not agree?"

"Indeed he does not. He wants his property traced and recovered."

"And do I understand that you instruct me to proceed with my investigations?

"Most certainly, especially in view of what you have told me."

"I am glad of that," said Thorndyke. "I dislike exceedingly leaving an inquiry uncompleted. In fact, I should have completed the case for my own satisfaction and as a matter of public policy. For if Osmond stole these gems, the fact ought to be proved, lest any other person should be suspected, and if he did not, his character ought to be cleared as a matter of common justice."

"That is exactly my own feeling," said Mr. Penfield. "And then, of course, there is the property. That ought to be recovered if possible – especially if, as you seem to think, it is still intact. And now," he added, draining his glass and rising, "it is time for me to depart. I have to thank you for a most interesting and pleasant evening."

As Thorndyke stood on the landing looking down upon his retreating guest, he was dimly aware of a presence on the stair above, and when he turned to re-enter his chambers, the presence materialized into the form of Polton. With silent and stealthy tread the "familiar spirit" stole down the stairs and followed his principal into the room, where, having closed both doors with a secret and portentous air, he advanced to the table.

"What have you got under your arm, Polton?" Thorndyke asked.

By way of reply, Polton regarded his employer with a smile of the most extraordinary crinkliness and began very deliberately to untie the string of a small parcel. From the latter he at length disengaged a kind of leathern wallet marked in gold lettering with what appeared to be a tradesman's name and address. This he bore, slowly and ceremoniously, to the table, where with a sudden movement he unrolled it, displaying a glittering constellation of metal buttons.

"Well done, Polton!" Thorndyke exclaimed. "What a man you are! Now, where might you have unearthed this relic?"

"I discovered it, sir," replied Polton, blushing with pleasure like a dried apricot, "in a little, old-fashioned tailor's trimming-shop in one of the courts off Carnaby Street. It is quite a well preserved specimen, sir."

"Yes, it is in wonderful condition, considering its age. Mr. Wampole will be delighted with it. He will be set up with buttons for life. I think, Polton, it would add to his pleasure if you were to run down and make the presentation in person. Don't you?"

Polton's features crinkled to the point of obliteration. "I do, indeed, sir," he replied. "At his private residence, I think, sir."

"Certainly, at his private residence. And we shall have to find out at what time he usually returns from the office."

"We shall, sir," Polton agreed, and thereupon proceeded to crinkle to a perfectly alarming extent.

Chapter XVII
The Lapidary

In a small street hard by Clerkenwell Green is a small shop of antique and mouldy aspect, the modest window of which is so obscured by a coat of paint on the inside as to leave the unaided observer to speculate in vain as to the kind of wares concealed within. A clue to the mystery is, however, furnished by an inscription in faded gilt lettering on the fascia above, which sets forth that the tenant's name is Lambert and that his vocation is that of a lapidary and dealer in precious stones.

On a certain afternoon a few days after his interview with Mr. Penfield, Dr. John Thorndyke might have been seen to turn into the small street with a brisk, decisive air suggestive of familiarity with the neighbourhood and a definite purpose, and the latter suggestion would have been confirmed when, having arrived at the shop, he pushed open the door and entered. A faded, elderly man confronted him across the counter and inquired what might be his pleasure.

"I have called," said Thorndyke, "to make some inquiries concerning artificial stones."

"Did you want them for theatrical purposes?"

"No. Those are usually cast or moulded, aren't they?"

"Sometimes. Not as a rule. Can't get much sparkle out of moulded glass, you know. But what was the class of goods you were wanting?"

"I wanted a set of imitation gems made to given shapes and dimensions to form a collection such as might be suitable for purposes of instruction in a technical school."

"Would the shapes and dimensions have to be exact?"

"Yes, quite exact. They are intended to be copies of existing specimens and the settings are already made."

Thorndyke's answer seemed to occasion some surprise, for the man to whom he made it reflected profoundly for a few moments and then looked round at a younger man who was sorting samples from the stock at a side-bench.

"Odd, isn't it, Fred?" said the former.

"What is odd?" inquired Thorndyke.

"Why, you see, sir, we had someone come in only a few days ago making the very same inquiry. You remember him, Fred?"

"Yes, I remember him, Mr. Lambert. Crinkly-faced little blighter."

"That's the man," said Mr. Lambert. "I rather wondered at the time what his game was. Seemed to know a lot about the trade, too, but you have to mind what you are about making strass facsimiles."

"Of course you have," Thorndyke agreed, "especially when you are dealing with these crinkly-faced people."

"Exactly," said Mr. Lambert, "But, of course, sir, in your case, we know where we are."

"It is very good of you to say so," rejoined Thorndyke. "But I gather that you are not often asked to make sets of facsimile imitations."

"No, not sets. Occasionally we get an order from a jeweller to duplicate the stones of a diamond necklace or tiara to be used while the original is in pawn, or for safety in a crowd. But not a collection such as you are speaking of. In fact, during all the thirty-five years that I have been in business, I have only had one order of the kind. That was between four and five years ago. A gentleman named Scofield wanted a set to offer to some local museum, and he wanted them to be copies of stones in various public collections. He got the shapes and dimensions from the catalogues – so I understood."

"Did you execute the order?"

"Yes, and quite a big order it was."

"I wonder," said Thorndyke, "whether he happened to have selected any of the stones that are in my list. Mine are mostly from the Hollis collection. But I suppose you don't keep records of the work you do?"

"I expect all the particulars are in the order book. We can soon see."

He went over to a shelf on which was ranged a row of books of all ages, and running his hand along, presently drew out a leather volume which he laid on the counter and opened.

"Ah! Here we are," said he, after a brief search. "Mr. Scofield. Perhaps you would like to glance over his list. You see there are quite a lot of them."

He pushed the book across to Thorndyke, who had already produced a note-book from his pocket, the entries in which he now proceeded to compare with those in Mr. Scofield's list. Mr. Lambert watched him with close interest as he placed his finger on one after another of the entries in the book, and presently remarked, "You seem to be finding some duplicates of your own lot."

"It is most remarkable," said Thorndyke, "and yet perhaps it isn't – but his selection coincides with mine in over a dozen instances. May I tick them off with a pencil?"

"Do, by all means," said Lambert. "Then I can copy them out afterwards – that is, if you want me to get the duplicates cut."

"I do, certainly. I will mark off those that I want, and, when you have cut those, I will give you a further list. And I may add that I should like you to use the best-quality strass that you can get. I want them to be as much like real stones as possible."

"I should do that in any case for good cut work," said Lambert, and he added, "I suppose there is no special hurry for these stones?

"None at all," replied Thorndyke. "If you will send me a card to this address when they are ready, I will call for them. Or, perhaps, if I pay for them now you could send them to me."

The latter alternative was adopted, and while the prices were being reckoned up and the bill was being made out, Thorndyke occupied himself in making, in shorthand, a copy of the list in the order book. He had finished and put away his note-book by the time the account was ready, when, having laid a visiting-card on the counter, he paid his score and began to put on his gloves.

"By the way," said he, "your customer would not happen to be Mr. Scofield of the Middle Temple, I suppose?

"I really couldn't say, sir," replied Lambert. "He never gave any address. But I had an idea that he came up from the country. He used to give his orders and then he would call, at longish intervals, and take away as many of the stones as were ready. He was a middle-aged man, a bit on the shady side, tallish, clean-shaved, iron-grey hair, and not too much of it."

"Ah, then I don't think that would be the same Mr. Scofield. It is not a very uncommon name. Good-afternoon."

With this Thorndyke took up his stick and, emerging from the shop, set a course southward for the Temple, walking quickly, as was his wont, with a long, swinging stride, and turning over in his mind the bearings of what he had just learned. In reality he had not learned much. Still, he had added one or two small items to his stock of facts, and in circumstantial evidence every added fact gives additional weight to all the others. He sorted out his new acquirements and considered each in turn.

In the first place, it was clear that Mr. Scofield's collection was a facsimile of the missing part of Hollis's. The list in Lambert's book was identical with the one in his own pocket-book, which, in its turn, was a list of the forgeries. The discovery of the maker of the forgeries (a result of extensive preliminary scouting on the part of Polton) was of little importance at the moment, though it might be of great value in the future. For, since the forgeries existed, it was obvious that someone must have made them. Much more to the point was the identity of the person for whom they were made. Whoever "Mr. Scofield" might have been, he certainly was not John Osmond. And this set Thorndyke once more puzzling over the really perplexing feature of this curious case. Why had Osmond absconded? That he had really done so, Thorndyke had no doubt, though he would have challenged the use of the word by anyone else. But why? There had been nothing to implicate him in any way. Beyond the hairs in the boxes – of which he could not have known and which were not at all conclusive – there was nothing to implicate him now but his own flight. All the other evidence seemed to point away from him. Yet he had absconded.

Thorndyke put to himself the various possibilities and argued them one at a time. There were three imaginable hypotheses: First, that Osmond had committed the robbery alone and unassisted. Second, that he had been an accessory or worked with a confederate. Third, that he had had no connection with the robbery at all.

The first hypothesis could be excluded at once, for Mr. Scofield must have been, at least, an accessory, and Mr. Scofield was not John Osmond. The second was much more plausible. It not only agreed with the known facts, but might even furnish some sort of explanation of the flight. Thus, supposing Osmond to have planned and executed the robbery with the aid of a confederate in the expectation that, even if discovered, it would never be traced to the office, might it not have been that, when, unexpectedly, it was so traced, Osmond had decided to take the onus on himself, and by absconding, divert suspicion from his accomplice? The thing was quite conceivable. It was entirely in agreement with Osmond's character as pictured by Mr. Wampole, that of a rash, impulsive, rather unreasonable man. And if it were further assumed that there had been known to him some incriminating fact which he had expected to leak out, but which had *not* leaked out, then the whole set of facts, including the flight, would appear fairly consistent.

Nevertheless, consistent as the explanation might be, Thorndyke did not find it convincing. The aspect of Osmond's rooms, with their suggestion of hardy simplicity and a robust asceticism, still lingered in his memory. Nor had he forgotten the impressive face of the gentlewoman whose portrait he had looked on with such deep interest in those rooms. These were, perhaps, but mere impressions, of no evidential weight, but yet they refused to be lightly dismissed.

As to the third hypothesis, that Osmond had not been concerned in the robbery at all, it would have been quite acceptable but for the irreconcilable fact of the flight. That seemed, beyond any question, to connect him with the crime. Of course it was conceivable that he might have some other reason for his flight. But no such reason had been suggested, whereas the circumstances in which he had elected to disappear – at the exact moment when the crime had been traced to the office – made it idle to look for any other explanation. And so, once more, Thorndyke found himself involved in a tangle of contradictions from which he could see no means of escape.

The end of his train of thought coincided with his arrival at the entry to his chambers. Ascending the stairs, he became aware of a light above as from an open door, and a turn of the staircase showed him that door – his own – framing a small, restless figure.

"Why, Polton," he exclaimed, "you are early, aren't you? I didn't expect you for another hour or two."

"Yes, sir," replied Polton, "I got away early. But I've seen it, sir. And you were perfectly right – absolutely right. It is a sparrowhawk, stuck in a little log of cherry wood. Exactly as you said."

"I didn't say a sparrowhawk," Thorndyke objected.

"You said, sir, that it was a stake or a bec iron or some kind of small anvil, and a sparrowhawk is a kind of small anvil."

"Very well, Polton," Thorndyke conceded. "But tell me how you managed it and why you are home so early."

"Well, sir, you see," Polton explained, fidgeting about the room as if he were afflicted with St. Vitus's dance, "it came off much easier than I had expected. I got to his house a good hour too soon. His housekeeper opened the door and wanted me to call again. But I said I had come down from London and would like to wait. And then I told her about the buttons and explained how valuable they were and asked her if she would like to see them, and she said she would. So she took me upstairs to his sitting room and there I undid the parcel and showed her the buttons.

"Then I got talking to her about the rooms, remarked what a nice place Mr. Wampole had got and how beautifully it was kept."

"Really, Polton!" Thorndyke chuckled, "I had no idea you were such a humbug."

"No more had I, sir," replied Polton, with a complacent crinkle. "But, you see, it was a case of necessity, and besides, the room was wonderfully neat and tidy. Well, I got her talking about the house, and very proud she seemed to be of it. So I asked her all the questions I could think of – whether she had a good kitchen and whether there was pipe water or a pump in the scullery, and so on. And she got so interested and pleased with herself that presently she offered to let me see over the house if I liked, and of course, I said that there was nothing in the world that I should like better. So she took me down and showed me the kitchen and the scullery and her own little sitting room and a couple of big cupboards for linen and stores, and it was all as neat and clean as a new pin. Then we went upstairs again, and as we passed a door on the

204

landing she said, 'That's a little room that Mr. Wampole does his tinkering in.'

"'Ah!' says I. 'But I'll warrant that room isn't quite so neat and tidy. I do a bit of tinkering myself and I know what a workroom looks like.'

"'Oh, it isn't so bad,' says she. 'Mr. Wampole is a very orderly man. You shall see for yourself, if it isn't locked. He usually locks it when he has a job in hand.'

"Well, it wasn't locked, so she opened the door and in we went, and the very moment I put my head inside, I saw it – on the table that he used for a bench. It was set in a little upright log, such as you get from the trimmings of fruit trees. And, my word! It was fairly riddled. – like a sponge – and where it stood on the bench there was a regular ring of powder round it.

"'That's a rare old block that his anvil is set in,' says I, going across to look at it.

"'Not so old as you'd think,' says she. 'He got it about five years ago, when we had the cherry tree lopped. You can see the tree in the garden from this window.'

"She went over to the window and I followed her, and as I passed the bench I picked up a pinch of the dust between my finger and thumb and put my hand in my pocket, where I had a pill-box that I had brought in case I should get a chance to collect a sample. As we were looking out of the window, I managed to work the lid off the pill-box and drop the pinch of dust in and slip the lid on again. Then I was happy, and as I had done all that I came to do, I thought I would rather like to clear off."

"Why?" asked Thorndyke.

"Well, sir," said Polton in a slightly apologetic tone, "the fact is that I wasn't very anxious to meet Mr. Wampole. It wouldn't have been quite pleasant, under the circumstances, to present those buttons and have him thanking me and shaking my hand. I should have felt rather like Pontius Pilate."

"Why Pontius Pilate?" asked Thorndyke.

"Wasn't he the chap – or was it Judas Iscariot? At any rate, I had a sudden feeling that I didn't want to hand him those buttons. So I looked up my time table and discovered that I couldn't wait to see him. 'But, however,' I said, 'it doesn't matter. I can leave the buttons with you to give him, and I will leave my card, too, so that he can send me a line if he wants to.' So with that I gave her the roll of buttons and nipped off to the station, just in time to catch the earlier train to town. I hope I didn't do wrong, sir."

"Not at all," Thorndyke replied heartily. "I quite understand your feeling on the matter. In fact, I think I should have done the same. Shall we look at that pill-box? I didn't expect such good fortune as to get a specimen."

Polton produced the little box, and having opened it to make sure that the contents were intact, handed it to Thorndyke, who forthwith made a preliminary inspection of the dust with the aid of his lens.

"Yes," he reported, "it is evidently the same dust as was in the other samples, so that aspect of the case is complete. I must compliment you, Polton, on the masterly way in which you carried out your really difficult and delicate mission. You have made a brilliant success of it. And you have been equally successful in another direction. I have just come from Lambert's, where I had a very instructive interview. You were perfectly correct. It was Lambert who cut those dummy stones."

"I felt sure it must be," said Polton, "when I had been round to those other lapidaries. He seems to be the only one who specializes in cutting strass gems. But did you find out who the customer was, sir?"

"I found out who he was not," replied Thorndyke, "and that was as far as it seemed wise to go. The rest of the inquiry – the actual identification – will be better carried out by the police. I think, if we give Mr. Lambert's address, with certain other particulars, to Mr. Superintendent Miller, we can safely leave him to do what is necessary."

206

Chapter XVIII
The End of the Clue

It was nearing the hour of six in the evening when five men made their appearance on the stretch of pavement on which Mr. Woodstock's office door opened. They did not, however, arrive in a solid body, but in two groups – of two and three, respectively – which held no mutual communication, but kept within easy distance of one another. The larger group consisted of Dr. Thorndyke, Mr. Lambert, the lapidary, and a tall, powerful man of distinctly military appearance and bearing, the smaller group consisted of a uniformed inspector of the local police and Mr. Lambert's assistant "Fred".

"I hope our friends are punctual in coming out," Thorndyke remarked as he stood with his two companions ostensibly inspecting the stock in a bookseller's window. "If we have to wait about long, we are likely to attract notice. Even a bookseller's window won't explain our presence indefinitely."

"No," the tall man agreed. "But there is a good deal of traffic in this street to cover us up and prevent us from being too conspicuous. All I hope is that he will take things quietly – that is, if he is the right man. You are sure you would know him again, Mr. Lambert?"

"Perfectly sure, Superintendent," was the confident reply. "I remember him quite well. I have a good memory for faces, and so has my man, Fred. But I tell you frankly that neither of us relishes this job."

"I sympathize with you, Mr. Lambert," said Thorndyke. "I don't relish it myself. We are both martyrs to duty. Ah! Here is somebody coming out. That is Mr. Woodstock. I mustn't let him see me."

He turned to the shop-window, presenting his back to the street, and the solicitor walked quickly past without noticing him. A few moments later Mr. Hepburn emerged and walked away in the opposite direction, furtively observed by Fred, who, with his companion, occupied a position on the farther side of the office door. He was followed after a short interval by two young men, apparently clerks, who walked away together up the street and were narrowly inspected by Fred as they passed. Close on their heels came an older man, who emerged with an air of business and, turning towards the three watchers, approached at a brisk walk.

"That the man, Mr. Lambert?" the superintendent asked in a low, eager tone, as the new-comer drew near.

"No," was the reply. "Not a bit like him."

Two more men came out, at both of whom Mr. Lambert shook his head. Then came a youth of about eighteen, and after his emergence an interval of several minutes, during which no one else appeared.

"That can't be the lot," said the superintendent, with a glance of anxious inquiry at Thorndyke.

"It isn't unless some of them are absent," the latter replied. "That would be rather a disaster."

"It would, indeed," the superintendent replied. "What do you say, Doctor, to going in – that is, if the door isn't locked?

"Not yet, Miller," Thorndyke replied. "Of course we can't wait indefinitely, but, if possible – Ah! Here is someone else."

As he spoke, an elderly man came out and stood for a few moments looking up and down the street. Then he turned and very deliberately locked the door behind him.

"That's the man!" Lambert exclaimed. "That is Mr. Scofield."

"You are quite sure?" demanded Miller.

"Positive," was the reply. "I recognized him instantly." And in confirmation, Fred was signalling with a succession of emphatic nods.

Superintendent Miller cast an interrogative glance at Thorndyke. "Your man, too?" he asked.

"Yes," replied Thorndyke. "Mr. Wampole."

The unconscious subject of these observations, having locked the door, slowly pocketed the key and began to walk at a leisurely pace and with a thoughtful air towards the three observers, closely followed by Fred and the inspector. Suddenly he became aware of Thorndyke, and the beginnings of a smile of recognition had appeared on his face when he caught sight of Mr. Lambert. Instantly, the smile froze, and as Superintendent Miller bore down on him with evident purpose, he halted irresolutely and cast a quick glance behind him. At the sight of Fred – whom he evidently recognized at once – and the inspector, his bewilderment changed to sheer panic, and he darted out into the road close behind a large covered van that was drawn up at the kerb.

"Look out!" roared Miller, as Wampole passed the rear of the van, but the only effect of the warning was to cause the fugitive to cast a terrified glance backward over his shoulder as he ran. And then, in an instant, came the catastrophe. An empty lorry was coming up the street at a brisk trot, but its approach had been hidden from Wampole by the van. As the unfortunate man ran out from behind the latter, still looking back, he charged straight in front of the horses. The driver uttered a yell of dismay and tugged at the reins, but the affair was over in a moment. The pole of the lorry struck Wampole at the side of the neck with the force of a battering-ram and flung him violently down on the road, where he lay motionless as the ponderous vehicle swerved past within an inch of his head.

A number of bystanders immediately gathered round, and the carman, having pulled up the lorry, climbed down from his high perch and came hurrying, white-faced and breathless, across the road. Through the gathering crowd the inspector made his way and piloted Thorndyke to the fatal spot.

"Looks a pretty bad case, sir," said he, casting a perturbed eye down at the motionless form, which lay where it had fallen. "Will you just have a glance at him?"

Thorndyke stooped over the prostrate figure and made a brief – a very brief – inspection. Then he stood up and announced curtly, "He is dead. The blow dislocated his neck."

"Ha!" the inspector exclaimed, "I was afraid he was – though perhaps it is all for the best. At any rate, we've done with him now."

"I haven't," said Miller. "I've got a search warrant, and I shall want his keys. We will come along with you to the mortuary. Can't very well get them here."

At this moment the carman presented himself, wiping his pale face with a large red handkerchief.

"Shockin' affair, this, Inspector," he said, huskily. "Pore old chap. I couldn't do no more than what I done. You could see that for yourself. He was down almost as soon as I see 'im."

"Yes," the inspector agreed, "he ran straight at the pole. It was no fault of yours. At least, that's my opinion," he added with official caution. "Just help me and the constable here to lift the body on to your lorry and then he will show you the way to the mortuary. You understand, Borman," he continued, addressing the constable. "You are to take the body to the mortuary, and wait there with the lorry until I come. I shall be there in a minute or two."

The constable saluted, and the inspector, having made a note of the carman's name and address, stood by while the ghastly passenger was lifted up on to the rough floor. Then, as the lorry moved off, he turned to Miller and remarked, "Your friend Mr. Lambert looks rather poorly, Superintendent. It has been a bit of a shock for him. Hadn't you better take him somewhere and give him a little pick-me-up? We shall want him and his assistant at the mortuary, you know, for a regular identification."

"Yes," agreed Miller, glancing sympathetically at the white-faced, shaking lapidary, "he does look pretty bad, poor old chap. Thinks it's all his doing, I expect. Well, you show us the way to a suitable place."

"The Blue Lion Hotel is just round the corner," said the inspector, "and it is on our way."

To the Blue Lion he accordingly led the way, while Thorndyke followed, assisting and trying to comfort the shaken and self-reproachful Lambert. From the hotel they proceeded to the mortuary, where Lambert having, almost with tears, identified the body of "Mr. Scofield", and the dead man's keys having been handed to Superintendent Miller, the latter departed with Thorndyke, leaving the inspector to conduct the carman to the police-station.

"You seem to be pretty confident," said Miller as they set forth, guided by Polton's written directions, "that the stuff is still there."

"Not confident, Miller," was the reply, "but I think it is there. At any rate, it is worthwhile to make the search. There may be other things to see besides the stones."

"Ah!" Miller agreed doubtfully. "Well, I hope you are right."

They walked on for some five minutes when Thorndyke, having again referred to his notes, halted before a pleasant little house in a quiet street on the outskirts of the town and, entering the front garden, knocked at the door. It was opened by a motherly-looking, middle-aged woman to whom Miller briefly but courteously explained his business and exhibited his warrant.

"Good gracious!" she exclaimed. "What on earth makes you think the missing property is here?"

"I can't go into particulars," replied Miller. "Here is the search warrant."

"Yes, I see. But couldn't you wait until Mr. Wampole comes home? He is due now, and his tea is waiting for him in his sitting room."

Miller cleared his throat. Then, hesitatingly and with manifest discomfort, he broke the dreadful news.

The poor woman was thunderstruck. For a few moments she seemed unable to grasp the significance of what Miller was telling her, then, when the horrid reality burst upon her, she turned away quickly, flinging out her hand towards the staircase, ran into her room, and shut the door.

The two investigators ascended the stairs in silence with an unconsciously stealthy tread. On the landing they paused, and as he softly opened the three doors and peered into the respective apartments, Miller remarked in an undertone, "Rather gruesome, Doctor, isn't it? I feel like a tomb-robber. Which one shall we go in first?"

"This one on the left seems to be the workshop," replied Thorndyke. "Perhaps we had better take that first, though it isn't likely that the gems are in there."

They entered the workshop, and Thorndyke looked about it with keen interest. On a small table, fitted with a metal-worker's bench-vice, stood the "sparrow-hawk", like a diminutive smith's anvil, in its worm-eaten block, surrounded by a ring of pinkish-yellow dust. A Windsor chair, polished by years of use, was evidently the one on which the workman had been accustomed to sit at his bench, and close inspection showed a powdering of the pink dust on the rails and other protected parts. On the right-hand side of the room was a small woodworker's bench, and on the wall above it a rack filled with chisels and other small tools. There was a tool cabinet ingeniously made from grocer's boxes, and a set of shelves on which the glue-pot and various jars and small appliances were stowed out of the way.

"Seems to have been a pretty handy man," remarked Miller, pulling out one of the drawers of the cabinet and disclosing a set of files.

"Yes," Thorndyke agreed, "he appears to have been quite a good workman. It is all very neat and orderly. This is rather interesting," he added, reaching down from the shelf a box containing two earthen ware cells filled with a blue liquid, and a wide jar with similar contents.

"Electric battery, isn't it?" said Miller. "What is the point of interest about it?"

"It is a two-cell Daniell's battery," replied Thorndyke, "the form of battery most commonly used for making small electrotypes. And in evidence that it was used for that purpose, here is the jar filled with copper sulphate solution, forming the tank, with the copper electrode in position. Moreover, I see on the shelf what look like some gutta-percha moulds." He reached one down and examined it. "Yes," he continued, "this is a squeeze from a coin. Apparently he had been making electrotype copies of coins, probably some that had been lent to him."

"Well," said Miller, "what about it?"

"The point is that whoever stole those gems made an electrotype copy of Hollis's seal. We now have evidence that Wampole was able to make electrotypes and did actually make them."

"It would be more to the point if we could find the gems themselves," rejoined Miller.

"Yes, that is undoubtedly true," Thorndyke admitted, "and as we are not likely to find them here, perhaps we had better examine the sitting room. That is much the most probable place."

"I don't quite see why," said Miller. "But I expect you do." And with this he followed Thorndyke across the landing to the adjoining room.

"Good Lord!" he exclaimed, stopping to gaze at the neatly-arranged tea-service on the table. "Just look at this! Uncanny, isn't it? Teapot under the cosy – quite hot still. And what's under this cover? Crumpets, by gum! And him lying there in the mortuary! Fairly gives one the creeps. Don't you feel a bit like a ghoul, Doctor?"

"I might, perhaps," Thorndyke replied, dryly, "if there had been no such person as John Osmond."

"True," said Miller. "He did do the dirty on Osmond, and that's the fact – unless Osmond was in it, too. Looks rather as if he was, but you don't seem to think so."

"As a mere guess, I do not, but it is a puzzling case in some respects."

He stood for a while looking about the room, letting his eye travel slowly along the papered walls as if in search of a possible hiding-place. From the general survey he proceeded to the consideration of details, turning the door-key – which was on the inside and turned smoothly and silently – and examining and trying a solid-looking brass bolt.

"You notice, Miller," he said, "that he seems to have been in the habit of locking and bolting himself in, and that the bolt has been fixed on comparatively recently. That is somewhat significant."

"It seems to suggests that the swag was hidden here at one time, if it isn't here now. I suppose we may as well look through these cabinets, just as a matter of form, for he won't have hidden the stuff in them."

He produced the dead man's bunch of keys, and having unlocked the hinged batten which secured the drawers of one, pulled out the top drawer.

"Coins," he announced, "silver coins. No! By jingo, they're copper, plated, and no backs to them. Just look at that!"

"Yes," said Thorndyke, taking the specimen from him. "A silver-faced copper electro, taken, no doubt, from a borrowed coin. Not a bad way of forming a collection. Probably, if he had been skilful enough to join the two faces and make a complete coin, it would have been the original owner who would have had the electrotype, and Wampole would have kept the genuine coin. While you are going through the cabinets, I think I will explore those two cupboards. They seem to me to have possibilities."

The cupboards in question filled the recesses on either side of the fireplace. Each cupboard was built in two stages – a lower about three feet in height, and an upper extending nearly to the ceiling. Thorndyke began with the right-hand one, throwing open both its pairs of folding doors, after unlocking them with the keys, handed to him by Miller. Then he cleared the shelves of their contents – principally stamp albums and back numbers of *The Connoisseur* – until the cupboard was completely empty, when he proceeded to a systematic survey of the interior, rapping with his knuckles on every part of the back and sides and testing each shelf by a vigorous pull. Standing on a chair, he inspected the top and ascertained, by feeling it simultaneously from above and below, that it consisted of only a single board.

Having thoroughly explored the upper stage with no result, he next attacked the lower story, rapping at the back, sides, and floor and pulling at the solitary shelf, which was as immovable as the others. Then he tested the ceiling or top by feeling it with one hand while the other was placed on the floor of the upper story.

Meanwhile, Miller, who had been systematically examining the row of home-made cabinets, shut the last of the multitudinous drawers and stood up.

"Well," he announced, "I've been right through the lot, Doctor, and there's nothing in any of them – nothing, I mean, but trash. This last one is full of buttons – brass buttons, if you'll believe it. How are you getting on? Had any luck?"

"Nothing definite, so far," replied Thorndyke, who was, at the moment, taking a measurement of the height of the lower story with a tape-measure, "but there is something here that wants explaining. The internal height of the lower part of this cupboard is two-feet-ten-inches, but the height from the floor of the lower part to the floor of the top part is three-feet-one-inch. So there seems to be a space of three inches, less the thickness of two boards, between the ceiling of the lower part and the floor of the top part. That is not a normal state of affairs."

"No, by jingo!" exclaimed the superintendent. "Ordinarily, the floor of the top part would be the ceiling of the bottom part. Carpenters don't waste wood like that. Either the floor or the ceiling is false. Let us see if we can get a move on the floor. That is the most likely, as it would be the lid of the space between the two."

He passed his hands over the board, feeling for a yielding spot, and craned in, searching for some indication of a joint, as he made heavy pressure on the edges and corners. But the floor showed no sign whatever of a tendency to move. He was about to transfer his attention to the ceiling underneath when Thorndyke stopped him.

"Wait," said he. "Here is another abnormal feature. This moulding along the front of the door is fastened on with three screws. They have been painted over with the rest of the moulding, but you can make out the slots quite plainly."

"Well?" queried Miller.

"Carpenters don't fix mouldings on with screws. They use nails and punch them in with a 'nail-set' and stop the holes with putty. Moreover, if you look closely at these screw-heads, you can see that they have been turned at some time since the moulding was painted."

As the superintendent stooped to verify this observation, Thorndyke produced from his pocket a small leather pouch of portable tools from which he took a screw-bit and the universal handle. Having fitted them together, he inserted the screwdriver into the slot of the middle screw and gave a turn.

"Ah!" said he. "This screw has been greased. Do you see how easily it turns?"

He rotated the tool rapidly, and as the screw emerged he picked it out and exhibited it to Miller.

"Not a trace of rust, you see, although the paint is some years old."

He laid it down and turned to the left-hand screw, which he extracted with similar ease. As he drew it out of its hole, the moulding became visibly loose, though still supported by the mitre, but when the last screw was extracted, the length of moulding came away in his hand, showing the free front edge of the floor, or bottom-board. This Thorndyke grasped with both hands and gave a steady pull, when the board slid forward easily, revealing a cavity about two inches deep.

"My eye!" exclaimed Miller, as Thorndyke drew the board right out. "This puts the lid on it – or rather takes the lid off."

He stood for a moment gazing ecstatically into the cavity, and especially at a collection of small, flat boxes that were neatly packed into it, then he grabbed up one of the boxes, and sliding back the hooked catch, raised the lid.

The expression of half-amused astonishment with which he viewed the open box was not entirely unjustified. As the receptacle for a robber's hoard, it was, to say the least, unconventional. The interior of the box was divided by partitions into a number of little square cells, and in each cell, reposing in a nest of black or white velvet according to its colour, was an unmounted gem.

The superintendent drew a deep breath. "Well," he exclaimed, "this knocks anything I've ever come across. Looks as if he never meant to sell the stuff at all. Just meant to keep it to gloat over. Is this what you had expected to find, Doctor? I believe it is, from what you said."

"Yes," Thorndyke replied. "This agrees exactly with my theory of the robbery. I never supposed that he had stolen the gems for the purpose of selling them."

"Didn't you?" said Miller. "Now, I wonder why."

"My dear Miller," Thorndyke answered, with a smile, "the answer is before you in those cabinets which you have just examined. The man was a human magpie. He had a passion for acquiring and accumulating.

He was the born, inveterate collector. Now, your half-baked collector will sell his treasures at a sufficient profit, but the real, thoroughbred collector, when once he has got hold, will never let go."

"Well," said Miller, who had been meanwhile lifting out the boxes and verifying their contents with a supercilious glance into each, "what is one man's meat is another man's poison. I can't see myself hoarding up expensive trash like this when I could swap it for good money."

"Nor I," said Thorndyke. "We both lack the acquisitive instinct. By the way, Miller, I think you will agree with me that all the circumstances point to Wampole's having done this single-handed?"

"Undoubtedly," was the reply. "This is a 'one-man show' if ever there was one."

"And, consequently, that this 'find' puts Osmond definitely out of the picture?"

"Yes," Miller agreed, "I think there is no denying that."

"Then you will also agree that, although we might wish it otherwise, the whole of the circumstances connected with this robbery must be made public. That is necessary as a measure of common justice to the memory of Osmond. He was publicly accused and he must be publicly exonerated."

"You are quite right, Doctor," Miller admitted, regretfully, "though it seems a pity, as the poor devil is dead and we've got the swag back. But, as you say, justice is justice. The innocent man ought to be cleared."

He took out the last remaining box, and having opened it and looked in, handed it to Thorndyke and cast a final glance into the cavity.

"Hallo!" he exclaimed, reaching into the back of the space, "here's something wrapped in paper – a key, by Jove!"

"Ah," said Thorndyke, taking it from him and inspecting it curiously, "the key of the strong-room. I recognize it. Quite a well-made key, too. I think we ought to hand that to Woodstock at once, and perhaps it would be as well to hand him the gems, too, and get his receipt for them. We don't want property of this value – something like a hundred-thousand pounds – on our hands any longer than we can help. What do you say?"

"I say let us get rid of them at once if we can. But we must seal the boxes before we hand them over. And we must seal up these rooms until the property has been checked by Hollis. Let us put the books back in the cupboard and then, perhaps, you might go and find Woodstock while I keep guard on the treasure-trove."

They fell to work repacking the cupboard with the albums and magazines which they had taken out, and had nearly finished when they became aware of voices below and then of hurried footsteps on the stairs.

215

A few moments later the door was flung open and Mr. Woodstock and Mr. Hepburn strode into the room.

"May I ask," the former demanded, glaring at Miller, "who the deuce you are and what is the meaning of this indecent invasion? The housekeeper tells me that you profess to have come here to search for missing property. What property are you searching for, and what is your authority?"

The superintendent quietly explained who he was and exhibited his warrant.

"Ha!" exclaimed Woodstock, with a withering glance at Thorndyke. "And I suppose you are making this ridiculous search at the suggestion of this gentleman?"

"You are quite correct, sir," replied Miller. "The warrant was issued on information supplied by Dr. Thorndyke."

"Ha!" was the contemptuous comment. "You obtained a warrant to search the private residence of a man of irreproachable character who has been in my employ for something like a score of years! Well, have you made your search? And if so, what have you found?"

"We have completed the search," replied Miller, "and we have found what we believe to be the whole of the stolen property, and this key, which I understand is the key of your strong-room."

As the superintendent made this statement, in studiously matter-of-fact tones, Mr. Woodstock's jaw fell and his eyes opened until he appeared the very picture of astonishment. Nor was his colleague, Mr. Hepburn, less amazed, and for a space of some seconds the two solicitors stood speechless looking from one another to the wooden-faced but secretly amused detective officer. Then Woodstock recovered somewhat and began to show signs of incredulity. But there was the key and there were the boxes, and it needed only a glance at the contents of the latter to put the matter beyond all question. Even Woodstock could not reject the evidence of his eyesight.

"But," he said with a puzzled air and with new born civility, "what I cannot understand is how you came to connect Wampole with the robbery. Where did you obtain the evidence of his guilt?"

"I obtained it," Thorndyke replied, "from the dust which I collected from your office floor."

Mr. Woodstock frowned impatiently and shook his head. "I am afraid," he said, coldly, "you are speaking a language that I don't understand. But no doubt you are right to keep your own counsel. What do you propose to do with this property?"

"We had proposed to hand it to you to hold pending the formal identification of the gems by Mr. Hollis."

"Very well," said Woodstock, "but I shall want you to seal the boxes before I put them in my strong-room. I can't accept any responsibility as to the nature of the contents."

"They shall be sealed with my seal and the superintendent's," Thorndyke replied, with a faint smile, "and we will hope that the seals will give more security than they did last time."

This understanding having been arrived at, the boxes were gathered up and distributed among the party for conveyance to the office, and after a short halt on the landing while Miller locked the doors and sealed the keyholes, they went down the stairs, at the foot of which the tearful housekeeper was waiting. To her Mr. Woodstock gave a brief and somewhat obscure explanation of the proceedings and the sealed doors, and then the party set forth for the office, the two solicitors leading and conversing in low tones as they went.

Arrived at their destination, the formalities were soon disposed of. Each box was tied up with red tape, sealed on the knot and on the opening of the lid. Then, when they had all been conveyed into the strong-room and locked in, Mr. Woodstock wrote out a receipt for "eight boxes, containing real or artificial precious stones, said to be the property of James Hollis, Esq., and sealed with the seals of Dr. Thorndyke and Superintendent Miller of the C.I.D.," and handed it to the latter officer.

"Of course," he said, "I shall communicate with Mr. Hollis at once and ask him to remove these things from my custody. Probably he will write to you concerning them, but, in any case, I shall wash my hands of them when I get his receipt – and I shall take very good care that nobody ever saddles me with portable property of this kind again."

"A very wise resolution," said Thorndyke. "Perhaps you might point out to Mr. Hollis that the boxes ought to be opened in the presence of witnesses – one of whom, at least, should be an expert judge of precious stones. I shall write to him to-night, before I leave the town, to the same effect. We all want the restitution to be definitely proved and acknowledged."

"That is perfectly true," Woodstock admitted, "and perhaps I had better make it a condition on which I allow him to take possession of the boxes."

The business being now concluded, Thorndyke and the superintendent prepared to take their departure. As they were turning away, Mr. Hepburn addressed Thorndyke for the first time.

"May I ask," he said, hesitatingly and with an air of some embarrassment, "whether the – er – the dust from our office floor or – er – any other observations of yours which led you to this surprising discovery seemed to suggest the existence of any confederate?"

"No," Thorndyke replied, decisively. "All the evidence goes to show, very conclusively, that Wampole carried out this robbery single-handed. Of that I, personally, have no doubt, and I think the superintendent agrees with me."

"Undoubtedly," Miller assented. "I, too, am perfectly convinced that our late lamented friend played a lone hand. You are thinking of John Osmond?"

"Yes," Hepburn admitted, with a frown of perplexity. "I am. I am wondering what on earth can have induced him to go off in that extraordinary manner and at that particular time."

"So am I," said Thorndyke.

"Well, I'm afraid we shall never learn now," said Woodstock.

"Apparently not," Thorndyke agreed, "and yet – who knows?"

Chapter XIX
Thorndyke Connects the Links

Early in the afternoon – at forty-minutes-past-twelve, to be exact – of a sunny day in late spring, a tall, hatchet-faced man, accompanied by a small, sprightly lady, strolled at a leisurely pace through Pump Court and presently emerged into the cloisters, where he and his companion halted and looked about them.

"What a lovely old place it is!" the latter exclaimed, letting her eyes travel appreciatively from the porch of the Temple Church to the façade of Lamb Buildings. "Wouldn't you like to live here, Jack?"

"I should," he replied. "It is delightful to look at whichever way you turn, and there is such a delicious atmosphere of peace and quiet."

She laughed merrily. "Peace and quiet!" she repeated. "Peace, perfect peace. That has always been the desire of your heart, hasn't it? Oh, you old humbug! Before you had been here a month you would be howling for the sea and someone to fight." Here her glance lighted on the little wig shop, tucked away in its shady corner, and she drew him eagerly towards it "Let us have a look at these wigs," said she. "I love wigs. It is a pity they have gone out of fashion for general use. They were such a let-off for bald-headed men. Which one do you like best, Jack? I rather fancy that big one – full-bottomed, I think, is its proper description. It would suit you to a *T*. It looks a little vacant with no face inside it, but it would have a grand appearance with your old nose sticking out in front. You'd look like the Great Sphinx before they knocked his nose off. Don't you think you'd look rather well in it?"

"I don't know that I am particularly keen on wigs," he replied.

"Unless they are on the green," she suggested with a roguish smile.

He smiled at her in return, with a surprising softening of the rather rugged face, and then glanced at his watch.

"We mustn't loiter here staring at these ridiculous wigs," said he, "or we shall be late. Come along, you little babbler."

"Aye, aye, sir," she responded, "come along, it is." And they resumed their leisurely progress eastward across the court.

"I wonder," he said, reflectively, "what sort of fellow Thorndyke is. Moderately human, I hope, because I want him to understand what I feel about all that he has done for us."

"I shall want to kiss him," said she.

219

"You had better not," he said, threateningly. "Still, short of that, I shall look to you to let him know how grateful, beyond all words, we are to him."

"You can trust me, Jack, darling," she replied, "to make it as clear as I can. When I think of it, I feel like crying. We owe him everything. He is our fairy-godmother."

"I don't think, Betty, dear," said Osmond with a faint grin, "that I should put it to him in exactly those words."

"I wasn't going to, you old guffin!" she exclaimed, indignantly. "But it is what I feel. He is a magician. A touch of his magic wand changed us in a moment from a pair of miserable, hopeless wretches into the pet children of Fortune, rich in everything we desired, and with the whole world of happiness at our feet. Oh, the wonder of it! Just think, darling! While you, with that ridiculous bee in your silly old bonnet, were doing everything that you could to make yourself – and me – miserable for life, here was this dry old lawyer, whose very existence we were unaware of, quietly, methodically working away to dig us out of our own entanglements. We can never even thank him properly."

"No. That's a fact," Osmond agreed. "And, in spite of Penfield's explanations, I can't in the least understand how he did it."

"Mr. Penfield admits that he has only a glimmering of an idea himself, but as he has promised to extract a full explanation to-day, we can afford to bottle up our curiosity a little longer. This seems to be the house, yes, here we are – '*1ˢᵗ Pair, Dr. John Thorndyke*'."

She tripped up the stairs, followed by Osmond, and on the landing was confronted by the open "oak" and a closed inner door, adorned by a small but brilliantly burnished brass knocker.

"What a dinkie little knocker!" she exclaimed, and forthwith executed upon it a most impressive flourish. Almost instantly the door was opened by a tall, dignified man who greeted the visitors with a smile of quiet geniality.

"I have no need to ask who you are," he said, as, having saluted the lady, he shook hands with Osmond. "Your resemblance to your mother is quite remarkable."

"Yes," replied Osmond, a little mystified, nevertheless. "I was always considered to be very like her. I should like to think that the likeness is not only a superficial one."

Here he became aware of Mr. Penfield, who had risen from an armchair and was advancing, snuff-box in hand, to greet them.

"It is very delightful to meet you both in these chambers," said he, with an old bow. "A most interesting and significant meeting. Your husband's name has often been spoken here, Mrs. Osmond, in the days when he was, to us, a mere abstraction of mystery."

"I've no doubt it has," said Betty, regarding the old lawyer with a mischievous smile, "and I don't suppose it was spoken of in very complimentary terms. But we are both absolutely bursting with gratitude and we don't know how to put our feelings into words."

"There is no occasion for gratitude." said Thorndyke. "It has been a mutual change of benefits. Your husband has provided us with a problem of the most thrilling interest, which we have had the satisfaction of solving, with the added pleasure of being of some service to you. We are really your debtors."

"Very kind of you to put it in that way," said Osmond, with a faint grin. "I seem to have played a sort of Falstaffian part. My deficiency of wit has been the occasion of wit in others."

"Well, Mr. Osmond," Thorndyke rejoined, with an appreciative side-glance at the smiling Betty, "you seem to have had wit enough to bring your affairs to a very happy conclusion. But let us draw up to the table. I understand that there are to be mutual explanations presently, so we had better fortify ourselves with nourishment."

He pressed an electric bell, and, as his guests took their places at the table, the door opened silently and Polton entered with demure gravity to post himself behind Thorndyke's chair and generally to supervise the proceedings.

Conversation was at first somewhat spasmodic and covered a good deal of mutual and curious inspection. Betty was frankly interested in her surroundings, in the homely simplicity of this queer bachelor household, in which everything seemed to be done so quietly, so smoothly, and so efficiently. But especially was she interested in her host. Of his great intellect and learning she had been readily enough convinced by Mr. Penfield's enthusiastic accounts of him, but his personality, his distinguished appearance, and his genial, pleasant manners were quite beyond her expectations. It was a pleasure to her to look at him and to reflect that the affectionate gratitude that she must have felt for him, whatever he had been like, had at least been worthily bestowed.

"My husband and I were speaking as we came along," she said, "of the revolution in our prospects that you created, in an instant, as it seemed, in the twinkling of an eye. One moment our affairs were at a perfectly hopeless deadlock – the next, all our difficulties were smoothed out, the tangle was unravelled, and an assured and happy future lay before us. It looked like nothing short of magic, for, you see, John had done everything that he possibly could to convince all the world that he was guilty."

221

"Yes," said Thorndyke, "that is how it appeared, and that is one of the mysteries which has to be cleared up presently."

"It shall be," Osmond promised, "if utterly idiotic, wrong-headed conduct can be made intelligible to reasonable men. But still, I agree with my wife. There is something quite uncanny in the way in which you unravelled this extraordinary tangle. I am a lawyer myself – a pretty poor lawyer, I admit – and I have heard Mr. Penfield's account of the investigation, but even that has not enlightened me."

"For a very good reason," said Mr. Penfield. "I am not enlightened myself. I am, I believe, in possession of most of the material facts. But I have not the special knowledge that is necessary to interpret them. I am still unable to trace the connection between the evidence and the conclusion. Dr. Thorndyke's methods are, to me, a source of endless wonder."

"And yet," said Thorndyke, "they are perfectly normal and simple. They differ from the methods of an orthodox lawyer merely in this: That whereas the issues that I have to try are usually legal issues, the means which I employ are those proper to scientific research."

"But surely," Betty interposed, "the purposes of legal and scientific research are essentially the same. Both aim at arrive at the truth."

"Certainly," he replied. "The purposes are identical. But the procedure is totally different. In legal practice the issues have to be decided by persons who have no first-hand knowledge of the facts – by the judge and jury. To them the facts are furnished by other persons – the witnesses – who have such first-hand knowledge and who are sworn to give it truly and completely. And on such sworn testimony the judges form their decision. The verdict has to be 'according to the evidence,' and its truth is necessarily subject to the truth of the testimony and the competence of the witnesses.

"But in scientific research there is no such division of function. The investigator is at once judge, jury, and witness. His knowledge is first-hand, and hence he knows the exact value of his evidence. He can hold a suspended judgment. He can form alternative opinions and act upon both alternatives. He can construct hypotheses and try them out. He is hampered by no rules but those of his own making. Above all, he is able to interrogate things as well as persons."

"Yes," agreed Mr. Penfield, "that is what has impressed me. You are independent of witnesses. Instead of having to seek somebody who can give evidence in respect of certain facts, you obtain the facts yourself and become your own witness. No doubt this will become evident in your exposition of this case, to which I – and our friends too, I am sure – are looking forward with eager interest."

"You are paying me a great compliment," said Thorndyke, "and as I hear Polton approaching with the coffee, I need not keep you waiting any longer. By the way, how much may I assume that our friends know?"

"They know all that I know," replied Mr. Penfield. "We have had a long talk and I have told them everything I have learned and that you have told me."

"Then I shall assume that they have all the main facts, and they must stop me if I assume too much." He paused while Polton poured out the coffee and partially disencumbered the table. Then as his familiar retired, he continued, "I think that the clearest and most interesting way for me to present the case will be by recounting the investigation as it actually occurred, giving the facts observed and the inferences from them in their actual order of occurrence."

"That will certainly be the easiest plan for us to follow," said Osmond, "if it will not be too wearisome for you."

"On the contrary," replied Thorndyke, "it will be quite interesting to me to reconstitute the case as a whole, and the best way will be to treat it in the successive stages into which the inquiry naturally fell. I will begin with the information which was given to me when the case was placed in my hands.

"A number of sealed boxes had been deposited by Mr. Hollis in the custody of Mr. Woodstock, who placed them in his strong-room. These boxes were stated by Hollis to contain a number of valuable gems, but the nature of the contents was actually known only to Hollis, who had packed the boxes himself. After an interval the boxes were returned to Hollis, and it was agreed by all the parties, including Hollis, that all the seals were then intact. Nevertheless, on opening the boxes, Hollis found that most of the gems had been abstracted and replaced by counterfeits. Thereupon he declared that a robbery had been committed while the boxes were reposing in the strong room, and this view was, strange to say, accepted by Mr. Woodstock.

"Now, it was perfectly obvious that these statements of alleged fact were mutually irreconcilable. They could not possibly be all true. The question was, Which of them was untrue? If the stones were in the boxes when they were handed to Woodstock and were not there when he returned them to Hollis, then the boxes must have been opened in the interval. But in that case the seals must have been broken. On the other hand, if the seals were really intact, the boxes could not have been opened while they were in Woodstock's custody. Woodstock's position – which was also that of Hollis – was a manifest absurdity. What they alleged to have happened was a physical impossibility.

"So far, however, the legal position was quite simple, if Woodstock had accepted it. The seals were admitted to be intact. Therefore no robbery could have occurred in Woodstock's office. But Woodstock accepted the impossible, and thereupon a certain Mr. John Osmond proceeded very deliberately to tip the fat into the fire."

"Yes, didn't he?" agreed Betty with a delighted gurgle. "You were an old guffin, Jack! Still, it was all for the best, wasn't it?"

"It was, indeed," assented Osmond. "Best stroke of work I ever did. You see, I knew that there is a Providence that watches over fools. But we mustn't interrupt the exposition."

"Well," continued Thorndyke, "the disappearance of Mr. Osmond settled the matter so far as Mr. Woodstock was concerned. He swore an information forthwith, and must have grossly misled the police, for they immediately obtained a warrant, which they certainly would not have done if they had known the real facts. Then Woodstock, distrusting his own abilities – very justly, but too late – consulted Mr. Penfield. But Mr. Penfield took the perfectly sound legal view of the case. The seals were admittedly unbroken. Therefore the boxes had been returned intact and there had been no robbery in the office. But if there had been no robbery, the disappearance of Osmond had no bearing on the case. Of course, neither Woodstock nor Hollis would agree to this view, and Mr. Penfield then recommended that the case should be put in my hands.

"Now it was obvious that the whole case turned on the seals. They had been accepted as intact – without any kind of inquiry or examination. But were they really intact? If they were, the case was against Hollis, and I could see that my friend Professor Eccles suspected him of having engineered a sham robbery to evade a bequest to the nation. But this seemed to me a wild and unfair suspicion, and for my own part I strongly suspected the seals. Accordingly, I examined a whole series of them, minutely and exhaustively, with the result that they proved to be impressions, not of the matrix in Mr. Hollis's ring, but of an electrotype matrix made from a wax impression.

"This new fact brought the inquiry to the next stage. It proved that the boxes had been opened and that they had been opened in Woodstock's office. For when they came there they were sealed with Hollis's seal, but when they left the office they were sealed with the forged seal. Things began to look rather black as regards Osmond, but, although I was retained ostensibly to work up a case against him, I kept an open mind and proceeded with the investigation as if he did not exist.

"The second stage, then, started with the establishment of these facts: A robbery had really occurred, it had occurred in Woodstock's office, and, since the boxes had been kept in the strong-room, it was from thence that they had been abstracted. The next question was: By whom had the robbery been committed? Now, since the property had been taken from the strong-room, and since the strong-room had not been broken into, it followed that the thief must have had, or obtained, access to it. Now, there were three persons who had easy access to it: Woodstock who possessed the key, Hepburn and Osmond, both of whom occasionally had the key in their custody. There might be others, but if so, they were at present unknown to me. But of the three who were known, one, Osmond, had apparently absconded as soon as the robbery was discovered and connected with the office. Moreover, the commencement of the robberies apparently coincided in time with the date on which he joined the staff.

"Evidently, then, everything that was known pointed to Osmond as the delinquent. But there was no positive case against him, and I decided to proceed as if nothing at all were known and seek for fresh data. And my first proceeding was to make an exhaustive examination of the boxes, the wrapping-paper, and the inside packing. As to the paper, I may say that I developed up a large number of finger-prints – on the outside surface only – I never examined, as the occasion did not arise. The investigation really concerned itself with the dust from the insides of the boxes and from the packing material. Of this I collected every particle that I could extract and put it aside in pill-boxes numbered in accordance with the boxes from which it was obtained. When I came to examine systematically the contents of the pill-boxes, I made two very curious discoveries.

"First, every pill-box – representing, you will remember, one of the gem-boxes – contained one or more hairs, usually one only and never more than three. They were all alike. Each was a hair from a moustache of a light-brown colour and cut quite short, and there could be no doubt that they were all from the same individual. Consequently they could not be chance hairs which had blown in accidentally. The gem-boxes had been packed at various times, and hence the uniformity of the hairs connected them definitely with the person who packed the boxes. In short, it seemed at first sight practically certain that they were the hairs of the actual robber, in which case we could say that the robber was a man with a short light-brown moustache.

"But when I came to reflect on the facts observed I was struck by their singularity. Moustache hairs are shed very freely, but they do not drop out at regular intervals. One, two, or more hairs in any one box would not have been surprising. A man who was in the habit of pulling at or stroking his moustache might dislodge two or three at once. The surprising thing was the regularity with which these hairs occurred – one, and usually one only, in each box, and no complete box in which there was none. It was totally opposed to the laws of probability.

"The point was highly significant. Anyone can recognize a hair. Most men can recognize a moustache hair. A detective certainly could. If these boxes had been opened by the police, as Hollis had originally intended, these hairs would almost certainly have been seen and eagerly fastened on as giving what would amount to a description of the thief. They would have been put in evidence at the trial and would have been perfectly convincing to the jury.

"The more I reflected on the matter the more did I suspect those hairs. If one assumed that they had been planted deliberately, say by a clean-shaved or dark-haired criminal, their regular occurrence in every box would be quite understandable. It would be a necessary precaution against their being overlooked. Otherwise it was unaccountable. Still, the fact of their presence had to be noted and the individual from whom they came identified, if possible.

"The second discovery that I made was, perhaps, even more odd. In every one of the boxes I found particles of the fine dust which falls out of the holes in worm-eaten wood, sometimes only a few grains, sometimes quite a large number of grains, and in the aggregate a really considerable quantity."

"But how astonishing," exclaimed Betty, "that you should be able to tell at once that these tiny grains came from worm-eaten wood."

"I make it my business," he replied, "to be able to recognize the microscopical appearances of the different forms of dust. But your remark indicates a very significant point. I imagine that there will be very few persons in the world who could identify these particles in a collection of miscellaneous dust. And therein lay the value of this discovery, for if the significance of the hairs was open to doubt, that of the wood certainly was not. There was no question of its having been purposely planted. It had certainly found its way into the boxes accidentally, and the person who had unconsciously introduced it was pretty certainly unaware of its presence. It was undoubtedly a genuine clue.

"The discovery of this characteristic dust raised several questions. In the first place, how came it into the boxes? Dust from worm-eaten furniture falls on the floor and remains there. It is too coarse and heavy to float in the air like the finer kinds of dust. In a room in which there is worm-eaten furniture, you will find the particles of dust all over the floor, but you will not find any on the tables or chair-rails or mantelpiece. But these boxes must have stood on a table or bench when they were being packed and when the dust got into them. Then the dust must have been on the table or bench. But how could it have got there? It was possible that the bench, itself, might have been worm-eaten. But that was not a probable explanation, for the dust tends to fall, not to rise. It would have fallen, for the most part, from the under surface onto the floor. The most likely explanation emerged from a consideration of the next question, which was, how could one account for the large quantity that was found?

"The quantity was extraordinarily large. From the whole set of boxes we collected something approaching a quarter-of-a-thimbleful, which seems an enormous amount if you consider that it must all have got into the boxes during the short time that they were open for packing. What could be the explanation?

"There were two factors which had to be considered: The nature of the wood and the nature of the object which had been fashioned from it, and both were important for purposes of identification. Let us consider the first factor – material. Now, these wood-boring insects do not bore through wood as the bookworm bores through paper, to get at something else. They actually feed upon the wood. Naturally, then, they tend to select the kind of wood which contains the most nourishment and which, incidentally, is usually the softest. But of all woods those of the fruit trees are richest in gum and sap and are most subject to the attacks of the worm. Walnut, pear, apple, plum, and cherry – all have this drawback, and of these cherry is so inveterately 'wormy' that it has usually been shunned by the cabinet-maker. Now, the quantity of the wood-dust pointed to some excessively worm-eaten object and suggested one of the fruit woods as the probable material, and the balance of probability was in favour of cherry, and this was supported by the pinkish colour of the dust. But, of course, this inference was purely hypothetical. It represented the general probabilities and nothing more.

"And now we come to the second factor. What was the nature of this wooden object? A piece of ordinary furniture we could dismiss for two reasons: First, the dust from such a piece will ordinarily fall upon the floor, from whence it could hardly have got into the boxes, and, second, no matter how badly wormed a piece of furniture may be, the quantity of dust which falls from it is relatively small and accumulates quite slowly, being practically confined to that which is pushed out of the holes by the movements of the insects within. This process would not account for the great quantity indicated by these samples of ours. My feeling was that this worm-eaten object was an appliance of some sort, subject to frequent and violent disturbance. Let us take an imaginary case as an illustration. Let us imagine a mallet with an excessively worm-eaten head. Whenever

227

that mallet is used, the shock of the impact will send a shower of wood-dust flying out on the bench, where it will rapidly accumulate.

"But, of course, this object of ours could not be a mallet for the reason that mallets are always made of hard wood, and jewellers' mallets are usually made of boxwood, *lignum vitae* or horn, none of which is subject to 'the worm'. Thinking over the various appliances used by jewellers – since it was with a jeweller we were dealing – I suddenly bethought me of one which seemed to fulfil the conditions exactly. Jewellers and goldsmiths, as you probably know, use a variety of miniature anvils, known as stakes, bec irons, sparrowhawks, etc. Now, these little anvils are usually stuck in a block of wood, just as a smith's anvil is planted on a tree-stump. These blocks are not usually hard wood. Indeed, soft wood is preferable as it absorbs the shock better. A favourite plan is to get a little log of wood and set the spike of the stake or sparrow-hawk in a hole bored in the end grain, and the most abundant source of these little logs – at least in the country – is the pile of trimmings from old fruit trees. Such a log would tend very soon to become worm-eaten, and if it did, every time it was used a ring of wood-dust would form around its base and would soon spread all over the bench, sticking to everything on it and straying on to the hands, arms, and clothing of the workman.

"This inference, you will observe, was, like the previous one, purely hypothetical. But it agreed perfectly with the observed facts and accounted for them in a reasonable way, and as I could think of no other that did, I adopted it with the necessary reservations. But, in fact, the correctness or incorrectness of this hypothesis was at present of no great importance. Apart from any question as to its exact origin, the wood-dust was an invaluable clue. We now knew that the unknown robber was a person whose clothing was more or less impregnated with wood-dust, that any places that he had frequented would yield traces of wood-dust from the floors, and that the place where the boxes had been packed abounded in wood-dust and contained a badly worm-eaten wooden object of some kind.

"The next proceeding was obvious. It was to find the places which had been frequented by that unknown person, to seek for the worm-eaten object, and, if possible, to identify the individual who appeared to be connected with it. The suspected places were two: Mr. Hollis's house and Mr. Woodstock's office. I did not, myself, suspect Hollis, but nevertheless I determined to examine his house as narrowly as the other. Accordingly I asked Mr. Penfield to obtain facilities for me to visit both places to make inquiries on the spot, which he did.

"Perhaps, before I describe that voyage of exploration, it may be as well to pause and consider what knowledge I now possessed and what I was going to look for. There was the wood-dust, of course. That was the visible trail that I hoped to pick up. But there were other matters. I knew that there was a man, in some way connected with the robbery, who had a short, fair moustache. I had to find out who he was. Also if there was any source from which some other person might collect specimen hairs from that moustache – a hair-brush, for instance – and if such source existed, who had access to it.

"Then there was the personality of the thief. One knew a good deal about him by this time. He was an ingenious man, a fairly good workman, at any rate, with metal-worker's tools, but not a skilled jeweller. He must have been able to make a key from a wax squeeze – unless he were Woodstock himself, which he pretty certainly was not, for none of the others had sufficiently free access to the strong-room to do what had been done. Then he must have had at least a simple working knowledge of electric batteries, since we could be fairly certain that he made the electrotypes himself, he would never have run the risk of putting the forgery out to the trade. He was clearly a secretive, self-contained man. The only fallacy that I had to guard against was the possibility of a confederate outside the office, who might have done the actual work, but this possibility seemed to be negatived by the whole character of the robbery and especially by one very odd feature in it, which was this: Professor Eccles had noticed with surprise that many of the stones which were taken were of quite trifling intrinsic value, so trifling that, if they had been sold, they would hardly have realized enough to pay the cost of replacing them with the specially-made counterfeits. Indeed, in one case, at least, the thief must have lost money on the transaction, for he had taken a fine moonstone and replaced it with an inferior one of the same dimensions. But the value of the original was only about ten shillings, and he must have spent more than that on the replacement. The professor was greatly puzzled by this, having assumed, of course, that the gems were stolen to sell. But to me, this rather anomalous feature of the robbery offered a very curious suggestion, which was that no sale of the booty had ever been contemplated. It looked like a collector's robbery, and if there had been a collector in any way connected with the parties, I should have given him my very close attention. But, so far as I knew, there was none. Nevertheless, this peculiarity of the robbery had to be borne in mind when I came to make my investigations on the spot.

"Let me now briefly describe those investigations. Their main object was to ascertain whether there were any traces of wood-dust in the premises of either Hollis or Woodstock, and the method was this: In each case, a rough ground-plan of the premises was made, then small areas of the floors were cleaned thoroughly with a specially constructed vacuum cleaner, and the dust from each area put into an envelope marked with a number, which number was also marked in the plan on the spot from which the dust had been collected. The collection was carried out by my laboratory assistant, Mr. Polton, whom you have seen, leaving me free to make inquiries and to inspect the premises. Of course, the samples of dust had to be brought home to be examined in the laboratory, so we were hampered by the circumstance that we did not know at the time whether any wood-dust had or had not been obtained. But this proved to be of no importance.

"We operated first at Mr. Hollis's house, regardless of his scornful protests. Then we went on to Mr. Woodstock's office, and there I had a rather remarkable experiences As I entered with Mr. Woodstock, I saw an elderly man engaged in repairing an electric bell, and a glance at his hands and the way in which he manipulated his tools showed the unmistakable facility and handiness of the skilled workman. It was a little startling, for here were two of the characteristics of the unknown person I was endeavouring to identify. This man had evident skill in the use of metal-worker's tools, and he clearly knew a good deal about electric batteries. And when I learned that this Mr. Wampole was the office-keeper and that he evidently had a key of the premises, I was still further impressed. I began to revise my opinion as to there being no confederate, for the fact remained that Osmond had absconded and that his disappearance – until it was otherwise explained – undeniably connected him with the robbery. I began to think it possible that there had been a partnership and that he had been used as a cat's paw. Meanwhile, I had to find out as much as I could about him, and to this end I sat down by Wampole, as he worked at refitting the batteries, and questioned him on the subject of Osmond's appearance, habits, temperament, and circumstances. It is only fair to him to say that he scouted the idea of Osmond's having committed the robbery and gave excellent reasons for rejecting it. On the other hand, his description of Osmond made it clear that the hairs which I had found in the boxes were Osmond's hairs, and when I expressed a wish to inspect Osmond's desk, he took me to it readily enough, and as it was unlocked, he threw up the lid and showed me the interior. The most interesting thing in it, from my point of view, was a pair of hair-brushes, from which I was able to extract several moustache hairs which appeared – and subsequently turned out to be – identically similar to those found in the boxes.

230

"The examination of Osmond's desk suggested a similar examination of all the other desks in the office, finishing up with that belonging to Mr. Wampole. And it was in examining that desk that I did really receive somewhat of a shock. For when we came to turn out its contents, I found that these included, in addition to a number of metal-worker's tools, a work man's linen apron and some battery terminals and insulated wire, a stamp-album, a tray of military buttons and badges and old civilian buttons, and another tray of old coins.

"The coincidence was too striking to be ignored. Here was a man who had free access to these premises night and day, and who corresponded in every particular with the unknown robber. We had already seen that he had the skill and special knowledge that were postulated – now this stamp-album, these buttons, badges, and coins, wrote him down an inveterate collector. If I had looked on Mr. Wampole with interest before, I now regarded him with very definite suspicion. Whatever significance the hairs had seemed to have was now entirely against him, for there were the brushes, easily available, and he knew it.

"I must confess that I was greatly puzzled. Every new fact that I observed seemed more and more to confuse the issues. With the exception of the hairs – which were, at least, doubtful evidence – I had found nothing whatever to incriminate Osmond, whereas Wampole presented a highly suspicious appearance. But Osmond had absconded, which seemed to put Wampole outside the inquiry, excepting as a confederate. And when I went with Wampole to Osmond's rooms, my inspection of them only left me more puzzled, for the personality that they reflected was the very opposite of that indicated by the nature and method of the robbery. Instead of the avarice and cunning that characterized the robber, the qualities suggested were those of a hardy, adventurous, open-air man, simple to austerity in his tastes and concerned with anything rather than wealth and worldly possessions. The very photographs on the mantelpiece proclaimed the incongruity, especially that of his mother, whom Wampole informed me he strongly resembled, which showed the face of a dignified, strong, resolute, courageous looking lady, whose son I found it hard to picture, first as a thief, and then as a panicky fugitive. Yet the fact remained that Osmond had absconded.

"However, when we got home and proceeded to question the samples of dust in the laboratory, they gave an answer that was unmistakable. The results were roughly thus: The samples from Hollis's house contained no wood-dust, those from Osmond's rooms contained none, that from the inside of his desk contained none, and that from his office floor barely a trace. Those from the floor of the clerks' office yielded a very small quantity, but that from the floor by Wampole's desk contained quite a large amount, while the dust extracted from the interior of his desk was full of the castings – derived, no doubt, to a large extent from the apron which he had kept in it. So the murder was out. The man who had packed those boxes was Mr. Wampole, and the hairs which I found in them had come from Osmond's brushes.

"One thing only remained to be done: The final verification. The wood-dust had to be traced to its ultimate source in Wampole's lair. This invaluable service was carried out by my assistant, Polton, who, with extraordinary tact and skill, contrived to get a glimpse into the workshop during Wampole's absence, and when he peeped in, the first object that met his eye was a sparrowhawk, planted in a little log of cherry-wood that was absolutely riddled by the worm. That concluded the inquiry so far as I was concerned, though some further work had to be done to enable the police to act. But no doubt Mr. Penfield has told you about the lapidary and the police raid which resulted in Wampole's death and the discovery of the gems in his possession."

"Yes," Osmond replied, "I think we have had full details of the final stages. Indeed, Mr. Penfield had given us most of the facts that you have mentioned, but neither he nor we were able to connect them completely. It seemed to us as if you had made one or two very fortunate guesses, but now that I have heard your reasoned exposition I can see that there was no element of guessing at all."

"Exactly," agreed Mr. Penfield. "Every stage of the argument rests securely on the preceding stages. I am beginning to suspect that we lawyers habitually underestimate the man of science."

"Yes," said Osmond, "I am afraid that is so. It is pretty certain that no lawyer could have solved this mystery."

"I have to remind you," Thorndyke remarked, "that the man of science was not able to solve it. He was able only to solve a part of it. The thief was identified and the stolen property traced to its hiding-place. But one question remained and still remains unanswered. Why did John Osmond disappear?"

Osmond and Betty both smiled, and the latter asked, "Did you never form any guess on the subject?"

"Oh, yes," replied Thorndyke, "I made plenty of guesses. But that was mere speculation which led to nothing. It occurred to me, for instance, that he was perhaps drawing a red-herring across the trail – that he was shielding the real criminal. But I could find no support for the idea. I could see no reason why he should shield Wampole – unless he was a confederate, which I did not believe. If the criminal had been Hepburn, it would have been at least imaginable. But there was never the

232

shadow of a suspicion in regard to Hepburn. No, I never had even a hypothesis, and I haven't now."

"I am not surprised," said Osmond, with a slightly sheepish grin. "It was beyond even your powers to conceive the possible actions of an impulsive fool who has mistaken the facts. However, as I have put you to the trouble of trying to account for my unaccountable conduct, it is only fair that I should make it clear, if I can, even though I know that when I have finished, your opinion of me will be like Bumble's opinion of the Law – that I am 'a ass and a idiot'."

"I hardly think that very likely," said Thorndyke, turning a twinkling eye on Betty. "As I said just now, you seem to have brought a most unpromising affair to an extraordinarily satisfactory conclusion which is not at all suggestive of 'a ass and a idiot'."

"But," objected Osmond, "the satisfactory conclusion which you are putting to my credit is entirely your own work. I set up the obstacles, you knocked them down. However, we need not argue the point in advance. I will tell you the story and you shall judge for yourself."

Chapter XX
Osmond's Motive

"In order to make my position clear," Osmond began, "it is necessary for me to say certain things to you, my best and kindest of friends, which I should not confide to any other human creature. I shall have to confess to thoughts and suspicions which were probably quite unjust and unreasonable and which are now uttered subject to the seal of the confession."

The two lawyers bowed gravely in acknowledgement, and Osmond continued. "I was introduced to Mr. Woodstock, as you know, by my brother-in-law, Mr. Hepburn, and I may say that I accepted the post chiefly that I might be near my sister. She and I had always been very devoted to one another, and from the time when I left Oxford up to the date of her marriage we had lived under one roof, and that was how she came to make the acquaintance of Hepburn.

"I did not encourage the intimacy, but neither could I hinder it. She was of a responsible age and she knew her own mind. The end of it was that, after an engagement lasting a few months, they were married, and there was nothing more to be said. But I was rather troubled about it. I had known Hepburn nearly all my life. We had been at school together and the greater part of our time at Oxford, where we belonged to the same college, Merton. Through all those years we were on the footing of intimate friends – rather oddly, for we were very different in temperament and tastes, and, indeed, had very little in common – and we knew one another extremely well. I don't know what Hepburn thought of me, but I must confess that I never had much of an opinion of him. He was a clever man – rather too clever, to my taste. An excellent manager, very much on the spot, and in fact decidedly cunning, fearfully keen on the main chance, fond of money and ambitious to be rich, and none too scrupulous in his ideas. At school he was one of those boys who contrive to increase their pocket-money by all sorts of mysterious little deals, and the same tendency showed up at Oxford. I didn't like his ways at all. I always had the feeling that, if he should ever be tempted by an opportunity to make a haul by illegitimate means, he might be led by his acquisitiveness to do something shady.

"However, his morals were not in my custody and were none of my business until he began to visit us at my rooms, where I was living with my sister. Then I gave her a few words of warning, but they took no

234

effect. He made himself acceptable to her, and, as I have said, they became engaged and eventually, when Hepburn took up his job with Woodstock, married. For a year or two I saw little of them – I was articled to a solicitor in London, but when I was fully qualified Hepburn, at my sister's suggestion, offered to speak to Woodstock on my behalf, and the result was that I entered the office, as you have heard.

"And now I come to the particular transaction. Woodstock's office was, as you know, conducted in a rather happy-go-lucky fashion, especially as regards the strong-room. The key hung on the wall practically all day. Usually, Woodstock took it away with him at night, but quite frequently, when Woodstock was away for a night, it would be left in Hepburn's charge. Occasionally it was left with me, and on one occasion, at least, Wampole had charge of it for a night. And each of us four, Woodstock, Hepburn, Wampole, and myself, had a key of the outer door and could enter the premises whenever we pleased. You will remember, too, that the house was empty, out of office hours. There was no caretaker.

"Now, one night when I had been out on the river and got home rather late, I found that I had run out of tobacco. The shops were all shut, but I remembered that there was a nearly full tin in my desk at the office, so I ran round there to fill my pouch. I am always rather quiet in my movements, and perhaps, as it was late, I may have moved, instinctively, more silently than usual. Moreover, I still wore my rubber-soled boating-shoes. Well, I let myself in with my key and entered the office, leaving the outer door ajar. As I came in through the clerks' office I could see through the open doorway that there was a light in Woodstock's office and that the door of the strong-room was open. A good deal surprised at this, I stopped and listened. There were sounds of someone moving about in the strong-room, and I was on the point of going in to see who it was when Hepburn came out with one of Hollis's boxes in his hand. And at that moment the outer door blew-to with a bang.

"At the sound of the closing door Hepburn started and whisked round to re-enter the strong-room. Then he saw me standing in the dark office, and I shall never forget his look of terror. He turned as white as a ghost and nearly dropped the box. Of course I sang out to let him know who I was and apologized for giving him such a start, but it was a minute or two before he recovered himself, and when he did he was decidedly huffy with me for creeping in so silently. His explanation of the affair was quite simple. He had been up to London with Woodstock, who had stayed in town for the night and had sent him down with a consignment of valuable securities which the firm were taking charge of. Not liking to have them in his personal possession, he had come on to the office to deposit them in the strong-room, and then, while he was there, he had taken the opportunity of checking Hollis's boxes, which he informed me he was in the habit of doing periodically, and usually after office hours.

"The explanation was, as I have said, quite simple, indeed, no explanation seemed to be called for. There was nothing in the least abnormal about the affair. When I had once more apologized for the fright that I had given him, I filled my pouch and we went away together, and I dismissed the matter from my mind.

"I don't suppose I should ever have given the incident another thought if nothing had occurred to remind me of it. The months went by and it seemed to have passed completely out of my memory. Then Hollis dropped his bomb-shell into the office. Someone among us, he declared, had secretly opened his boxes and stolen his gems, and until that somebody was identified, we were all more or less under suspicion.

"Of course, Hepburn scouted the idea of there having been any robbery at all, and so did Wampole. They both pointed to the unbroken seals and declared that the thing was a physical impossibility, and I should have been disposed to take the same view, in spite of the strong evidence of the missing emerald. But as soon as I heard the charge, that scene in the office came back to me in a flash, and now, somehow, it did not look by any means so natural and simple as it had at the time. I recalled Hepburn's terrified stare at me, his pale face and trembling hands. Of course, my sudden appearance must have been startling enough to upset anyone's nerves, but it now seemed to me that his fright had been out of all proportion to the cause.

"Then, when I came to think it over, the whole affair seemed very characteristic of Hepburn – of his greed for money, his slyness, his cunning, calculating ways. The property which had been stolen was of great value, and I did not doubt that Hepburn would have annexed it without a qualm if he could have done so with complete safety. But it had been done so skilfully that the risk had been almost entirely eliminated. It was a very clever robbery. But for the merest chance the things would have gone back to Hollis's cabinet unchallenged, and when they had been there a week or two the issues would have become hopelessly confused. It would have been impossible to say when or where the robbery had been committed. The whole affair had been most cunningly planned and neatly carried out. I felt that, if Hepburn had been the robber, that was just the way in which he would have done it.

"Moreover, the robbery – if there had really been one, as I had no doubt there had – seemed to lie between three, or at the most, four of us: Those who had easy access to the strong-room. But of these Woodstock was out of the question, Wampole had practically no access to the strong-room and was an old and trusted servant of irreproachable character, and as I was out of it, there remained only Hepburn. Whichever way I thought of the affair, everything seemed to point to him, and whenever I thought of it the vision came back to me of that scared figure standing by the the strong-room door with the box of gems in his hand.

"But I need not go into any further detail. The bald fact is that it appeared to me beyond a doubt that Hepburn was the thief, and the only question was, what was to be done. The fat was in the fire. The police would be called in. The stolen property would be traced, and the crime pretty certainly brought I home to Hepburn. That was how I forecast the probable course of events.

"Now, if Hepburn had been a single man it would have been no affair of mine. But he was my sister's husband and the father of my two little nephews, who had been to me like my own children. If Hepburn had been convicted of this crime, my sister's life would have been absolutely wrecked. It would have broken her heart, and as for the two little boys, their future would have been utterly and irrevocably damned. I couldn't bear to think of it. But was there any way out? It seemed to me that there was. I was a bachelor with no home-ties but my sister and the kiddies. I had always had a desire to travel and see the world. Well, now was the time. If I cleared off to some out-of-the-way region, the dangerous inquiries at the office would stop at once and the whole hue-and-cry would be transferred to me. So I decided to go. And the place that I selected as my destination was Adaffia, where I knew that an old friend of Hepburn's had settled as a trader.

"But I thought I would take Hepburn into my confidence and give him a chance of doing the same by me, only I am afraid I rather muddled the business. The fact is that, when it came to the point, I was a little shy of telling him exactly what was in my mind. It is a delicate business, telling a man that you have discovered him to be a thief. So I hummed and hawed and approached the subject gradually by remarking that it looked as if there would be wigs on the green presently. But that cat didn't jump. Hepburn declined to admit that any robbery had occurred in the office. However, I persisted that we should presently have the police buzzing about the office and that then the position would become mighty uncomfortable for some of us. Still, he professed to be – and, of course, was – quite unconcerned, but when I went on to suggest that if I took a little holiday the state of affairs at the office would be made more comfortable for everybody, he stared at me in astonishment, as well he might. Of course, I could think of nothing but what I had seen that night when I caught him coming out of the strong-room, and I took it for

237

granted that he realized what was in my mind, so that his astonishment didn't surprise me.

"'Wouldn't it look a bit queer if you went away just now?' he asked.

"'That is just the point,' I replied. 'I'll hop off, they will leave the office alone and there will be no more trouble.'

"He seemed a good deal puzzled, but he didn't raise any objections, and of course he did not make any confidences, which again did not very much surprise me. He was the very soul of caution and secretiveness.

"'Where did you think of going for your holiday?' he asked.

"I told him that I thought of running over to Adaffia to call on Larkom, the trader there, and suggested that he should send Larkom a letter introducing me. He didn't much like writing that letter, and he liked it less when I mentioned that I proposed to travel under the name of Walker. However, Larkom was an old friend whom he knew that he could trust, so, in the end, he agreed to write the letter. And that settled the affair. In due course I went off in the comfortable belief that he understood the position exactly, leaving him considerably surprised but quite confident that he knew all about the robbery. It was a very pretty comedy of errors, but it would have become a tragedy but for your wonderful insight and for the strange chance that the results of your investigations should have found their way into the newspapers. That is to say, if it was a chance."

"It was not a chance," said Mr. Penfield. "As a matter of fact, Dr. Thorndyke wrote out the account himself and broadcast it to all the papers, including those of the United States."

"Why did you do that?" Betty inquired, with a glance of intense curiosity at Thorndyke.

"For two reasons," the latter replied, "one obvious, the other less so. In the first place, Osmond had been publicly accused, and as there had been no trial, there had been no public withdrawal of the accusation. But he was a man of honourable antecedents and irreproachable character. Common justice demanded that his innocence should be proclaimed at least as widely as had been the presumption of his guilt. Even if he were dead, it was necessary that his memory should be cleared of all reproach. But, in the second place, it was not at all clear to me that he was dead."

"The deuce it wasn't!" exclaimed Osmond. "I thought I had settled that question beyond any possible doubt. But you were not satisfied?"

"No. The report which reached me was singularly unconvincing, and there were certain actual discrepancies. Take first the general appearance of the alleged occurrences: Here is a man, a fugitive from justice, whose purpose is to disappear. He lands at Adaffia and in the

238

course of a week or two is reported to have died. Now, West Africa is a very unhealthy place, but people don't usually drop down dead as soon as they arrive there. On the contrary. The mortality among new-comers is quite small. Death is most commonly due to the cumulative effects of repeated attacks of malaria and does not ordinarily occur during the first year of residence. Osmond's death under the circumstances alleged was not in agreement with ordinary probabilities.

"Then the fact of death was not certified or corroborated. The officer who reported it had not seen the body, he had only seen the grave. But to a man of my profession, the uncorroborated grave of a man who is admittedly trying to escape from the police is an object of deep suspicion. The possibility of a sham burial was obvious. This man, on leaving his home, had made a bee-line for Adaffia, an insignificant village on the African coast the existence of which was unknown to the immense majority of persons, including myself. How came he to know of Adaffia? And why did he select it as a hiding-place? The obvious answer suggested was that he had a friend there. But as there was only one white man in the place – who must have been that friend – a sham death and burial would have been perfectly easy and a most natural expedient.

"Then there was the discrepancy. Osmond was reported to have died of blackwater fever. Now, this was almost an impossibility. Blackwater fever is not a disease which attacks new-comers. It lies in wait for the broken-down coaster whose health has been sapped by long-standing chronic malaria. In the immense majority of cases it occurs during, or after, the third year of residence. I have found no record of a single case in which the patient was a new-comer to the coast. It was this discrepancy that immediately aroused my suspicions, and as soon as I came to consider the circumstances at large, the other improbabilities came into view. The conclusion that I arrived at was that there was a considerable probability that the trader, Larkom, had carried out a sham burial, or, if it it had really been a case of blackwater fever at Adaffia, the victim was Larkom himself, and that a false name had been put on the grave, in which case the man whom the officer saw must have been Osmond. You will note the suspicious fact that the name on the grave was 'John Osmond' – not 'Walker'. That impressed me very strongly. It met the necessities of the fugitive so very perfectly."

Osmond chuckled softly. "It seems to me, Dr. Thorndyke," said he, "that you and I represent the two opposite extremes. You take nothing for granted. You accept no statement at its face value. You weigh, measure, and verify every item of evidence put to you. Whereas I – well,

I wonder what you think of me. I shan't be hurt if you speak your mind bluntly."

"There is nothing in my mind," said Thorndyke, "by which you need be hurt. It would, of course, be insincere to pretend that you did not display very bad judgement in taking so momentous a course of action on a mere, unconfirmed suspicion. But perhaps there are qualities even more valuable than worldly wisdom, and certainly more endearing, such as chivalry, generosity, and self-forgetfulness. I can only say that what you have told us as to your motives has made my little service to you a great pleasure to me. It has turned a mere technical success into a source of abiding satisfaction – even though you did seek to defeat the ends of justice."

"It is nice of you to say that, Dr. Thorndyke," Betty exclaimed with brimming eyes. "After all, it is better to be generous than discreet – at least, I think so, and I don't mind admitting that I am proud to be the wife of a man who could cheerfully give up everything for the good of his kinsfolk."

"I think," said Mr. Penfield, tapping his snuff-box by way of emphasis, "you have very good reason to be proud of one another."

"Thank you, Mr. Penfield," she replied, smilingly. "And that brings me to what really was the object of our visit to-day. Only, here I am in rather a difficulty. I am commissioned to give thanks for all that has been done for us, and I really don't know how to express one-half of what we feel."

"Is there any need?" said Thorndyke. "Mr. Penfield and I already understand that you enormously overestimate your indebtedness to us. Isn't that enough?"

"Well, then," said Betty, "I will just say this. But for you, Jack and I could never have been married. It was really you who gave us to one another. We wish to say that we are extremely pleased with your gift and we are very much obliged."

The End

1928 Hodder & Stoughton, London Cover

Chapter I
The Invalid

Looking back on events by the light of experience, I perceive clearly that the thunder-cloud which burst on me and on those who were dear to me had not gathered unseen. It is true that it had rolled up swiftly, that the premonitory mutterings, now so distinct but then so faint and insignificant, gave but a brief warning. But that was of little consequence, since whatever warnings there were passed unheeded, as warnings commonly do, being susceptible of interpretation only by means of the subsequent events which they foreshadowed.

The opening scene of the tragedy – if I had but realized it – was the arrival of the Reverend Amos Monkhouse from his far-away Yorkshire parish at the house of his brother Harold. I happened to be there at the time, and though it was not my concern – since Harold had a secretary – I received the clergyman when he was announced. We knew one another well enough by name though we had never met, and it was with some interest and curiosity that I looked at the keen-faced, sturdy, energetic-looking parson and contrasted him with his physically frail and rather characterless brother. He looked at me, too, curiously and with a certain appearance of surprise, which did not diminish when I told him who I was.

"Ha!" said he. "Yes, Mr. Mayfield. I am glad to have the opportunity of making your acquaintance. I have heard a good deal about you from Harold and Barbara. Now I can fit you with a visible personality. By the way, the maid tells me that Barbara is not at home."

"No, she is away on her travels in Kent."

"In Kent!" he repeated, raising his eyebrows.

"Yes, on one of her political expeditions, organizing some sort of women's emancipation movement. I dare say you have heard about it."

He nodded a little impatiently. "Yes. Then I assume that Harold is not so ill as I had supposed?"

I was inclined to be evasive, for, to be quite candid, I had thought more than once that Barbara might properly have given a little less attention to her political hobbies and a little more to her sick husband. So I replied cautiously, "I really don't quite know what his condition is. You see, when a man has chronically bad health, one rather loses count. Harold has his ups and downs, but he always looks pretty poorly. Just now, I should say he is rather below his average."

"Ha! Well, perhaps I had better go up and have a look at him. The maid has told him that I am here. I wonder if you would be so kind as to show me the way to his room. I have not been in this house before."

I conducted him up to the door of the bedroom and then returned to the library to wait for him and hear what he thought of the invalid. And now that the question had been raised, I was not without a certain uneasiness. What I had said was true enough. When a man is always ailing one gets to take his ill-health for granted and to assume that it will go on without any significant change. One repeats the old saying of "the creaking gate" and perhaps makes unduly light of habitual illness. Might it be that Harold was being a little neglected? He had certainly looked bad enough when I had called on him that morning. Was it possible that he was really seriously ill? Perhaps in actual danger?

I had just asked myself this question when the door was opened abruptly and the clergyman strode into the room. Something in his expression – a mingling, as it seemed, of anger and alarm – rather startled me, nevertheless I asked him calmly enough how he found his brother. He stared at me, almost menacingly for a second or two, then slowly and with harsh emphasis he replied, "I am shocked at the change in him. I am horrified. Why, good God, sir! The man is dying!"

"I think that can hardly be," I objected. "The doctor saw him this morning and did not hint at anything of the sort. He thought he was not very well, but he made no suggestion as to there being any danger."

"How long has the doctor been attending him?"

"For something like twenty years, I believe, so by this time he ought to understand the patient's – "

"Tut-tut," the parson interrupted, impatiently, "what did you say yourself but a few minutes ago? One loses count of the chronic invalid. He exhausts our attention until, at last, we fail to observe the obvious. What is wanted is a fresh eye. Can you give me the doctor's address? Because if you can, I will call on him and arrange a consultation. I told Harold that I wanted a second opinion and he made no objection. In fact, he seemed rather relieved. If we get a really first-class physician, we may save him yet."

"I think you are taking an unduly gloomy view of Harold's condition," said I. "At any rate, I hope so. But I entirely agree with you as to the advisability of having further advice. I know where Dr. Dimsdale lives, so if you like I will walk round with you."

He accepted my offer gladly and we set forth at once, walking briskly along the streets, each of us wrapped in thought and neither speaking for some time. Presently I ventured to remark, "Strictly, I suppose, we ought to have consulted Barbara before seeking another opinion."

"I don't see why," he replied. "Harold is a responsible person and has given his free consent. If Barbara is so little concerned about him as to go away from home – and for such a trumpery reason, too – I don't see that we need consider her. Still, as a matter of common civility, I might as well send her a line. What is her present address?"

"Do you know," I said, shamefacedly, "I am afraid I can't tell you exactly where she is at the moment. Her permanent address, when she is away on these expeditions, is the headquarters of the Women's Friendship League at Maidstone."

He stopped for a moment and glowered at me with an expression of sheer amazement. "Do you mean to tell me," he exclaimed, "that she has gone away, leaving her husband in this condition, and that she is not even within reach of a telegram?"

"I have no doubt that a telegram or letter would be forwarded to her."

He emitted an angry snort and then demanded, "How long has she been away?"

"About a fortnight," I admitted, reluctantly.

"A fortnight!" he repeated in angry astonishment. "And all that time beyond reach of communication! Why, the man might have been dead and buried and she none the wiser!"

"He was much better when she went away," I said, anxious to make the best of what I felt to be a rather bad case. "In fact, he seemed to be getting on quite nicely. It is only during the last few days that he has got this set-back. Of course, Barbara is kept informed as to his condition. Madeline sends her a letter every few days."

"But, my dear Mr. Mayfield," he expostulated, "just consider the state of affairs in this amazing household. I came to see my brother, expecting – from the brief letter that I had from him – to find him seriously ill. And I do find him seriously ill, dangerously ill, I should say. And what sort of care is being taken of him? His wife is away from home, amusing herself with her platform fooleries, and has left no practicable address. His secretary, or whatever you call him, Wallingford, is not at home. Madeline is, of course, occupied in her work at the school. Actually, the only person in the house besides the servants is yourself – a friend of the family but not a member of the household at all. You must admit that it is a most astonishing and scandalous state of affairs."

I was saved from the necessity of answering this rather awkward question by our arrival at Dr. Dimsdale's house, and, as it fortunately

247

happened that the doctor was at home and disengaged, we were shown almost at once into his consulting room.

I knew Dr. Dimsdale quite well and rather liked him, though I was not deeply impressed by his abilities. However, his professional skill was really no concern of mine, and his social qualities were unexceptionable. In appearance and manner he had always seemed to me the very type of a high-class general practitioner, and so he impressed me once more as we were ushered into his sanctum. He shook hands with me genially, and as I introduced the Reverend Amos, he looked at him with a politely questioning expression. But the clergyman lost no time in making clear the purpose of his visit. In fact, he came to the point with almost brutal abruptness.

"I have just seen my brother for the first time for several months and I am profoundly shocked at his appearance. I expected to find him ill, but I did not understand that he was so ill as I find him."

"No," Dr. Dimsdale agreed, gravely, "I suppose not. You have caught him at a rather unfortunate time. He is certainly not so well today."

"Well!" exclaimed Amos. "To me he has the look of a dying man. May I ask what, exactly, is the matter with him?"

The doctor heaved a patient sigh and put his fingertips together.

"The word 'exactly'," he replied, with a faint smile, "makes your question a little difficult to answer. There are so many things the matter with him. For the last twenty years, on and off, I have attended him, and during the whole of that time his health has been unsatisfactory – most unsatisfactory. His digestion has always been defective, his circulation feeble, he has had functional trouble with his heart, and throughout the winter months, more-or-less continuous respiratory troubles – nasal and pulmonary catarrh and sometimes rather severe bronchitis."

The Reverend Amos nodded impatiently. "Quite so, quite so. But, to come from the past to the present, what is the matter with him *now*?"

"That," the doctor replied suavely, "is what I was coming to. I mentioned the antecedents to account for the consequents. The complaints from which your brother has suffered in the past have been what are called 'functional complaints'. But functional disease – if there really is such a thing – must, in the end, if it goes on long enough, develop into organic disease. Its effects are cumulative. Each slight illness leaves the bodily organs a little less fit."

"Yes?"

"Well, that is, I fear, what is happening in your brother's case. The functional illnesses of the past are tending to take on an organic character."

"Ha!" snorted the Reverend Amos. "But what is his actual condition now? To put it bluntly, supposing he were to die tonight, what would you write on die death certificate?"

"Dear me!" said the doctor. "That is putting it very bluntly. I hope the occasion will not arise."

"Still, I suppose you don't regard his death as an impossible contingency?"

"Oh, by no means. Chronic illness confers no immortality, as I have just been pointing out."

"Then, supposing his death to occur, what would you state to be the cause?"

Dr. Dimsdale's habitual suavity showed a trace of diminution as he replied, "You are asking a very unusual and hardly admissible question, Mr. Monkhouse. However, I may say that if your brother were to die tonight he would die from some definite cause, which would be duly set forth in the certificate. As he is suffering from chronic gastritis, chronic bronchial catarrh, functional disorder of the heart, and several other morbid conditions, these would be added as contributory causes. But may I ask what is the object of these very pointed questions?"

"My object," replied Amos, "was to ascertain whether the circumstances justified a consultation. It seems to me that they do. I am extremely disturbed about my brother. Would you have any objection to meeting a consultant?"

"But not in the least. On the contrary, I should be very glad to talk over this rather indefinite case with an experienced physician who would come to it with a fresh eye. Of course, the patient's consent would be necessary."

"He has consented, and he agreed to the consultant whom I proposed – Sir Robert Detling – if you concurred."

"I do certainly. I could suggest no better man. Shall I arrange with him or will you?"

"Perhaps I had better," the parson replied, "as I know him fairly well. We were of the same year at Cambridge. I shall go straight on to him now and will let you know at once what arrangement he proposes."

"Excellent," said the doctor, rising with all his suavity restored. "I shall keep tomorrow as free as I can until I hear from you, and I hope he will be able to manage it so soon. I shall be glad to hear what he thinks of our patient, and I trust that the consultation may be helpful in the way of treatment."

He shook our hands heartily and conducted us to the street door, whence he launched us safely into the street.

"That is a very suave gentleman," Amos remarked as we turned away. "Quite reasonable, too, but you see for yourself that he has no real knowledge of the case. He couldn't give the illness an intelligible name."

"It seemed to me that he gave it a good many names, and it may well be that it is no more than he seems to think, a sort of collective illness, the resultant of the various complaints that he mentioned. However, we shall know more when Sir Robert has seen him, and meanwhile, I wouldn't worry too much about the apparent neglect. Your brother, unlike most chronic invalids, doesn't hanker for attention. He has all he wants and he likes to be left alone with his books. Shall you see him again today?"

"Assuredly. As soon as I have arranged matters with Detling, I shall let Dr. Dimsdale know what we have settled and I shall then go back and spend the evening with my brother. Perhaps I shall see you tomorrow?"

"No. I have to run down to Bury St. Edmunds tomorrow morning and I shall probably be there three or four days. But I should very much like to hear what happens at the consultation. Could you send me a few lines? I shall be staying at the Angel."

"I will certainly," he replied, halting and raising his umbrella to signal an approaching omnibus. "Just a short note to let you know what Sir Robert has to tell us of poor Harold's condition."

He waved his hand and, stepping off the kerb, hopped on to the foot-board of the omnibus as it slowed down and vanished into the interior. I stood for a few moments watching the receding vehicle, half-inclined to go back and take another look at the sick man, but reflecting that his brother would be presently returning, I abandoned the idea and made my way instead to the Underground Railway station, and there took a ticket for the Temple.

There is something markedly infectious in states of mind. Hitherto I had given comparatively little attention to Harold Monkhouse. He was a more-or-less chronic invalid, suffering now from one complaint and now from another, and evidently a source of no particular anxiety either to his friends or to his doctor. He was always pallid and sickly-looking, and if, on this particular morning, he had seemed to look more haggard and ghastly than usual, I had merely noted that he was "not so well today".

But the appearance on the scene of the Reverend Amos had put a rather different complexion on the affair. His visit to his brother had resulted in a severe shock, which he had passed on to me, and I had to admit that our interview with Dr. Dimsdale had not been reassuring. For the fact which had emerged from it was that the doctor could not give the disease a name.

It was very disquieting. Supposing it should turn out that Harold was suffering from some grave, even some mortal disease, which ought to have been detected and dealt with months ago. How should we all feel? How, in particular, would Barbara feel about the easygoing way in which the illness had been allowed to drift on? It was an uncomfortable thought, and though Harold Monkhouse was really no concern of mine, excepting that he was Barbara's husband, it continued to haunt me as I sat in the rumbling train and as I walked up from the Temple station to my chambers in Fig Tree Court.

Chapter II
Barbara Monkhouse Comes Home

In the intervals of my business at Bury St. Edmunds, I gave more than a passing thought to the man who was lying sick in the house in the quiet square at Kensington. It was not that I had any very deep feeling for him as a friend, though I liked him well enough. But the idea had got into my mind that he had perhaps been treated with something less-than-ordinary solicitude, that his illness had been allowed to drift on when possibly some effective measures might have been taken for his relief. And as it had never occurred to me to make any suggestions on the matter or to interest myself particularly in his condition, I was now inclined to regard myself as a party to the neglect, if there had really been any culpable failure of attention. I therefore awaited with some anxiety the letter which Amos had promised to send.

It was not until the morning of my third day at Bury that it arrived, and when I had opened and read it I found myself even less reassured than I had expected.

Dear Mayfield, (it ran)

The consultation took place this afternoon and the result is, in my opinion, highly unsatisfactory. Sir Robert is, at present, unable to say definitely what is the matter with Harold. He states that he finds the case extremely obscure and reserves his opinion until the blood-films and other specimens which he took have been examined and reported on by an expert pathologist. But on one point he is perfectly clear: He regards Harold's condition as extremely grave – even critical – and he advised me to send a telegram to Barbara insisting on her immediate return home. Which I have done, and only hope it may reach her in the course of the day.

That is all I have to tell you and I think you will agree that it is not an encouraging report. Medical science must be in a very backward state if two qualified practitioners – one of them an eminent physician – cannot between them muster enough professional knowledge to say what is the matter with a desperately sick man. However, I hope that we shall have a diagnosis by the time you come back.

Yours sincerely,

Amos Monkhouse

I could not but agree, in the main, that my clerical friend's rather gloomy view was justified, though I thought that he was a trifle unfair to the doctors, especially to Sir Robert. Probably a less scientific practitioner, who would have given the condition some sort of name, would have been more satisfying to the parson. Meanwhile, I allowed myself to build on "the blood-films and other specimens" hopes of a definite discovery which might point the way to some effective treatment.

I despatched my business by the following evening and returned to London by the night train, arriving at my chambers shortly before midnight. With some eagerness I emptied the letter-cage in the hope of finding a note from Amos or Barbara, but there was none, although there were one or two letters from solicitors which required to be dealt with at once. I read these through and considered their contents while I was undressing, deciding to get up early and reply to them so that I might have the forenoon free, and this resolution I carried out so effectively that by ten o'clock in the morning I had breakfasted, answered and posted the letters, and was on my way westward in an Inner Circle train.

It was but a few minutes' walk from South Kensington Station to Hilborough Square, and I covered the short distance more quickly than usual. Turning into the square, I walked along the pavement on the garden side, according to my habit, until I was nearly opposite the house. Then I turned to cross the road and as I did so, looked up at the house. And at the first glance I stopped short and stared in dismay, for the blinds were lowered in all the windows. For a couple of seconds I stood and gazed at this ominous spectacle, then I hurried across the road and, instinctively avoiding the knocker, gave a gentle pull at the bell.

The door was opened by the housemaid, who looked at me somewhat strangely but admitted me without a word and shut the door softly behind me. I glanced at her set face and asked in a low voice, "Why are all the blinds down, Mabel?"

"Didn't you know, sir?" she replied, almost in a whisper. "It's the master – Mr. Monkhouse. He passed away in the night. I found him dead when I went in this morning to draw up the blinds and give him his early tea."

253

I gazed at the girl in consternation, and after a pause she continued. "It gave me an awful turn. sir, for I didn't see, at first, what had happened. He was lying just as he usually did, and looked as if he had gone to sleep, reading. He had a book in his hand, resting on the counterpane, and I could see that his candle-lamp had burned itself right out. I put his tea on the bedside table and spoke to him, and when he didn't answer I spoke again a little louder. And then I noticed that he was perfectly still and looked even paler and more yellow than usual and I began to feel nervous about him. So I touched his hand, and it was as cold as stone and as stiff as a wooden hand. Then I felt sure he must be dead and I ran away and told Miss Norris."

"Miss Norris!" I exclaimed.

"Yes, sir. Mrs. Monkhouse only got home about an hour ago. She was fearfully upset when she found she was too late. Miss Norris is with her now, but I expect she'll be awfully glad you've come. She was asking where you were. Shall I tell her you are here?"

"If you please, Mabel," I replied, and as the girl retired up the stairs with a stealthy, funereal tread, I backed into the open doorway of the dining room (avoiding the library, in case Wallingford should be there) where I remained until Mabel returned with a message asking me to go up.

I think I have seldom felt more uncomfortable than I did as I walked slowly and softly up the stairs. The worst had happened – at least, so I thought – and we all stood condemned, but Barbara most of all. I tried to prepare some comforting, condolent phrases, but could think of nothing but the unexplainable, inexcusable fact that Barbara had, of her own choice and for her own purposes, gone away leaving a sick husband and had come back to find him dead.

As I entered the pleasant little boudoir – now gloomy enough, with its lowered blinds – the two women rose from the settee on which they had been sitting together, and Barbara came forward to meet me, holding out both her hands.

"Rupert!" she exclaimed, "how good of you! But it is like you to be here just when we have need of you." She took both my hands and continued, looking rather wildly into my face, "Isn't it an awful thing? Poor, poor Harold! So patient and uncomplaining! And I so neglectful, so callous! I shall never, never forgive myself. I have been a selfish, egotistical brute."

"We are all to blame," I said, since I could not honestly dispute her self-accusations, "and Dr. Dimsdale not the least. Harold has been the victim of his own patience. Does Amos know?"

"Yes," answered Madeline, "I sent him a telegram at half-past-eight. I should have sent you one, too, but I didn't know that you had come back."

There followed a slightly awkward silence during which I reflected with some discomfort on the impending arrival of the dead man's brother, which might occur at any moment. It promised to be a somewhat unpleasant incident, for Amos alone had gauged the gravity of his brother's condition, and he was an outspoken man. I only hoped that he would not be too outspoken.

The almost embarrassing silence was broken by Barbara, who asked me in a low voice, "Will you go and see him, Rupert?" and added, "You know the way, and I expect you would rather go alone."

I said "Yes," as I judged that she did not wish to come with me and, walking out of the room, took my way along the corridor to the well-remembered door, at which I halted for a moment, with an unreasonable impulse to knock, and then entered. A solemn dimness pervaded the room, with its lowered blinds, and an unusual silence seemed to brood over it. But everything was clearly visible in the faint, diffused light – the furniture, the pictures on the walls, the bookshelves, and the ghostly shape upon the bed, half-revealed through the sheet which had been laid over it.

Softly, I drew back the sheet, and the vague shape became a man – or rather, as it seemed, a waxen effigy, with something in its aspect at once strange and familiar. The features were those of Harold Monkhouse, but yet the face was not quite the face that I had known. So it has always seemed to me with the dead. They have their own distinctive character which belongs to no living man – the physiognomy of death, impassive, expressionless, immovable – fixed forever, or at least, until the changes of the tomb shall obliterate even its semblance of humanity.

I stepped back a pace and looked thoughtfully at the dead man who had slipped so quietly out of the land of the living. There he lay, stretched out in an easy, restful posture, just as I had often seen him, the eyes half-closed and one long, thin arm lying on the counterpane, the waxen hand lightly grasping the open volume, looking – save for the stony immobility – as he might if he had fallen asleep over his book. It was not surprising that the housemaid had been deceived, for the surroundings all tended to support the illusion. The bedside table with its pathetic little provisions for a sick man's needs – the hooded candle-lamp, drawn to the table-edge and turned to light the book, the little decanter of brandy, the unused tumbler, the water-bottle, the watch, still ticking in its upright case, the candle-box, two or three spare volumes, and the hand-bell for night use – all spoke of illness and repose with never a hint of death.

There was nothing by which I could judge when he had died. I touched his arm and found it rigid as an iron bar. So Mabel had found it some hours earlier, whence I inferred that death had occurred not much past midnight. But the doctors would be able to form a better opinion, if it should seem necessary to form any opinion at all. More to the point than the exact time of death was the exact cause. I recalled the blunt question that Amos had put to Dr. Dimsdale and the almost indignant tone in which the latter had put it aside. That was less than a week ago, and now that question had to be answered in unequivocal terms. I found myself wondering what the politic and plausible Dimsdale would put on the death certificate and whether he would seek Sir Robert Detling's collaboration in the execution of that document.

I was about to replace the sheet when my ear caught the footsteps of someone approaching on tip-toe along the corridor. The next moment the door opened softly and Amos stole into the room. He passed me with a silent greeting and drew near the bed, beside which he halted with his hand laid on the dead hand and his eyes fixed gloomily on the yellowish-white, impassive face. He spoke no word, nor did I presume to disturb this solemn meeting and farewell, but silently slipped out into the corridor where I waited for him to come out.

Two or three minutes passed, during which I heard him, once or twice, moving softly about the room and judged that he was examining the surroundings amidst which his brother had passed the last few weeks of his life. Presently he came out, closing the door noiselessly behind him, and joined me opposite the window. I looked a little nervously into the stern, grief-stricken face, and as he did not speak, I said, lamely enough, "This is a grievous and terrible thing, Mr. Monkhouse."

He shook his head gravely. "Grievous indeed, and the more so if one suspects, as I do, that it need not have happened. However, he is gone and recriminations will not bring him back."

"No," I agreed, profoundly relieved and a little surprised at his tone, "whatever we may feel or think, reproaches and bitter words will bring no remedy. Have you seen Barbara?"

"No, and I think I won't – this morning. In a day or two, I hope I shall be able to meet and speak to her as a Christian man should. Today I am not sure of myself. You will let me know what arrangements are made about the funeral?"

I promised that I would, and walked with him to the head of the stairs, and when I had watched him descend and heard the street door close, I went back to Barbara's little sitting-room.

256

I found her alone, and when I entered she was standing before a miniature that hung on the wall. She looked round as I entered and I saw that she still looked rather dazed and strange. Her eyes were red, as if she had been weeping, but they were now tearless, and she seemed calmer than when I had first seen her. I went to her side, and for a few moments we stood silently regarding the smiling, girlish face that looked out at us from the miniature. It was that of Barbara's step-sister, a very sweet, loveable girl, little more than a child, who had died some four years previously, and who, I had sometimes thought, was the only human creature for whom Barbara had felt a really deep affection. The miniature had been painted from a photograph after her death and a narrow plait of her gorgeous, red-gold hair had been carried round inside the frame.

"Poor little Stella!" Barbara murmured, "I have been asking myself if I neglected her, too. I often left her for days at a time."

"You mustn't be morbid, Barbara," I said. "The poor child was very well looked after and as happy as she could be made. And nobody could have done any more for her. Rapid consumption is beyond the resources of medical science at present."

"Yes, unfortunately." She was silent for a while. Then she said, "I wonder if anything could have been done for Harold. Do you think it possible that he might have been saved?"

"I know of no reason for thinking so, and now that he is gone I see no use in raising the question."

She drew closer to me and slipped her hand into mine.

"You will be with us as much as you can, Rupert, won't you? We always look to you in trouble or difficulty, and you have never failed us. Even now you don't condemn me, whatever you may think."

"No, I blame myself for not being more alert, though it was really Dimsdale who misled us all. Has Madeline gone to the school?"

"Yes. She had to give a lecture or demonstration, but I hope she will manage to get a day or two off duty. I don't want to be left alone with poor Tony. It sounds unkind to say so, for no one could be more devoted to me than he is. But he is so terribly high-strung. Just now, he is in an almost hysterical state. I suppose you haven't seen him this morning?"

"No. I came straight up to you." I had, in fact, kept out of his way, for, to speak the truth, I did not much care for Anthony Wallingford. He was of a type that I dislike rather intensely – nervous, high-strung, emotional, and in an incessant state of purposeless bustle. I did not like his appearance, his manners, or his dress. I resented the abject fawning way in which he followed Barbara about, and I disapproved of his position in this house, which was nominally that of secretary to Barbara's husband, but actually that of tame cat and generally useless hanger-on. I think I was on the point of making some disparaging comments on him, but at that moment there came a gentle tap at the door and the subject of my thoughts entered.

I was rather sorry that Barbara was still holding my hand. Of course, the circumstances were very exceptional, but I have an Englishman's dislike of emotional demonstrations in the presence of third parties. Nevertheless, Wallingford's behaviour filled me with amazed resentment. He stopped short with a face black as thunder, and, after a brief, insolent stare, muttered that he was afraid he was "intruding" and walked out of the room, closing the door sharply after him.

Barbara flushed (and I daresay I did too), but made no outward sign of annoyance. "You see what I mean," she said. "The poor fellow is quite unstrung. He is an added anxiety instead of a help."

"I see that plainly enough," I replied, "but I don't see why he is unstrung, or why an unstrung man should behave like an ill-mannered child. At any rate, he will have to pull himself together. There is a good deal to be done and he will have to do some of it. I may assume, I suppose, that it will be his duty to carry out the instructions of the executors?"

"I suppose so. But you know more about such things than I do."

"Then I had better go down and explain the position to him and set him to work. Presently I must call on Mr. Brodribb, the other executor, and let him know what has happened. But meanwhile, there are certain things which have to be done at once. You understand?"

"Yes, indeed. You mean arrangements for the funeral. How horrible it sounds. I can't realize it yet. It is all so shocking and so sudden and unlooked-for. It seems like some dreadful dream."

"Well, Barbara," I said gently, "you shan't be troubled more than is unavoidable. I will see to all the domestic affairs and leave the legal business to Brodribb. But I shall want Wallingford's help, and I think I had better go down and see him now."

"Very well, Rupert," she replied with a sigh. "I shall lean on you now as I always have done in times of trouble and difficulty, and you must try to imagine how grateful I am since I can find no words to tell you."

She pressed my hand and released me, and I took my way down to the library with a strong distaste for my mission.

That distaste was not lessened when I opened the door and was met by a reek of cigarette smoke. Wallingford was sitting huddled up in an easy chair, but as I entered, he sprang to his feet and stood facing me with a sort of hostile apprehensiveness. The man was certainly unstrung – in fact, he was on wires. His pale, haggard face twitched, his hands

258

trembled visibly, and his limbs were in constant, fidgety movement. But, to me, there seemed to be no mystery about his condition. The deep yellow stains on his fingers, the reek in the air, and a pile of cigarette-ends in an ash-bowl were enough to account for a good deal of nervous derangement, even if there were nothing more – no drugs or drink.

I opened the business quietly, explaining what had to be done and what help I should require from him. At first he showed a tendency to dispute my authority and treat me as an outsider, but I soon made the position and powers of an executor clear to him. When I had brought him to heel, I gave him a set of written instructions, the following-out of which would keep him fairly busy for the rest of the day, and having set the dismal preparations going, I went forth from the house of mourning and took my way to New Square, Lincoln's Inn, where were the offices of Mr. Brodribb, the family solicitor and my co-executor.

Chapter III
A Shock for the Mourners

It was on the day of the funeral that the faint, unheeded mutterings of the approaching storm began to swell into audible and threatening rumblings, though, even then, the ominous signs failed to deliver their full significance.

How well do I recall the scene in the darkened dining room where we sat in our sable raiment, "ready to wenden on our pilgrimage" to the place of everlasting rest and eternal farewell. There were but four of us, for Amos Monkhouse had not yet arrived, though it was within a few minutes of the appointed time to start – quite a small party, for the deceased had but few relatives, and no outsiders had been bidden.

We were all rather silent. Intimate as we were, there was no need to make conversation. Each, no doubt, was busy with his or her own thoughts, and as I recall my own they seem to have been rather trivial and not very suitable to the occasion. Now and again I stole a look at Barbara and thought what a fine, handsome woman she was, and dimly wondered why, in all the years that I had known her, I had never fallen in love with her. Yet so it was. I had always admired her, we had been intimate friends, with a certain amount of quiet affection, but nothing more – at any rate on my part. Of her I was not so sure. There had been a time, some years before, when I had had an uneasy feeling that she looked to me for something more than friendship. But she was always a reticent girl, very self-reliant and self-contained. I never knew a woman better able to keep her own counsel or control her emotions.

She was now quite herself again, quiet, dignified, rather reserved and even a little inscrutable. Seated between Wallingford and Madeline, she seemed unconscious of either and quite undisturbed by the secretary's incessant nervous fidgeting and by his ill-concealed efforts to bring himself to her notice.

From Barbara my glance turned to the woman who sat by her side, noting with dull interest the contrast between the two, a contrast as marked in their bearing as in their appearance. For whereas Barbara was a rather big woman, dark in colouring, quiet and resolute in manner, Madeline Norris was somewhat small and slight, almost delicately fair, rather shy and retiring, but yet with a suggestion of mental alertness under the diffident manner. If Barbara gave an impression of quiet strength, Madeline's pretty, refined face was rather expressive of subtle

260

intelligence. But what chiefly impressed me at this moment was the curious inversion of their attitudes towards the existing circumstances, for whereas Barbara, the person mainly affected, maintained a quiet, untroubled demeanour, Madeline appeared to be overcome by the sudden catastrophe. Looking at her set, white face and the dismay in her wide, grey eyes, and comparing her with the woman at her side, a stranger would at once have assumed the bereavement to be hers.

My observations were interrupted by Wallingford once more dragging out his watch.

"What on earth can have happened to Mr. Amos?" he exclaimed "We are due to start in three minutes. If he isn't here by then we shall have to start without him. It is perfectly scandalous! Positively indecent! But there, it's just like a parson."

"My experience of parsons," said I, "is that they are, as a rule, scrupulously punctual. But certainly, Mr. Amos is unpardonably late. It will be very awkward if he doesn't arrive in time. Ah, there he is," I added as the bell rang and a muffled knock at the street door was heard.

At the sound, Wallingford sprang up as if the bell had actuated a hidden spring in the chair and darted over to the window, from which he peered out through the chink beside the blind.

"It isn't Amos," he reported. "It's a stranger, and a fool at that, I should say, if he can't see that all the blinds are down."

We all listened intently. We heard the housemaid's hurried footsteps, though she ran on tip-toe, the door opened softly, and then, after an interval, we heard someone ushered along the hall to the drawing room. A few moments later, Mabel entered with an obviously scandalized air.

"A gentleman wishes to speak to you, ma'am," she announced.

"But, Mabel," said Barbara, "did you tell him what is happening in this house?"

"Yes, ma'am, I explained exactly how things were and told him that he must call tomorrow. But he said that his business was urgent and that he must see you at once."

"Very well," said Barbara. "I will go and see what he wants. But it is very extraordinary."

She rose and nearly colliding with Wallingford, who had rushed to open the door – which was, in fact, wide open – walked out quickly, closing the door after her. After a short interval – during which Wallingford paced the room excitedly, peered out of the window, sat down, got up again and looked at his watch – she came back and, standing in the doorway, looked at me.

"Would you come here for a minute, Rupert," she said, quietly.

I rose at once and walked back with her to the drawing room, on entering which I became aware of a large man, standing monumentally on the hearth-rug and inspecting the interior of his hat. He looked to me like a plainclothes policeman, and my surmise was verified by a printed card which he presented and which bore the inscription "*Sergeant J. Burton*".

"I am acting as coroner's officer," he explained in reply to my interrogatory glance, "and I have come to notify you that the funeral will have to be postponed as the coroner has decided to hold an inquest, I have seen the undertakers and explained matters to them."

"Do you know what reason there is for an inquest?" I asked. "The cause of death was certified in the regular way."

"I know nothing beyond my instructions, which were to notify Mrs. Monkhouse that the funeral is put off and to serve the summonses for the witnesses. I may as well do that now."

With this he laid on the table six small blue papers, which I saw were addressed respectively to Barbara, Madeline, Wallingford, the housemaid, the cook, and myself.

"Have you no idea at all why an inquest is to be held?" I asked as I gathered up the papers.

"I have no information," he replied, cautiously, "but I expect there is some doubt about the exact cause of death. The certificate may not be quite clear or it may be that some interested party has communicated with the coroner. That is what usually happens, you know, sir. But at any rate," he added, cheerfully, "you will know all about it the day after tomorrow, which, you will observe, is the day fixed for the inquest."

"And what have we to do meanwhile?" Barbara asked. "The inquest will not be held in this house, I presume."

"Certainly not, Madam," the sergeant replied. "A hearse will be sent round tonight to remove the body to the mortuary, where the *post mortem* examination will be carried out, and the inquest will be held in the parish hall, as is stated on the summons. I am sorry that you should be put to this inconvenience," he concluded, moving tentatively towards the door, "but – er – it couldn't be helped, I suppose. Good morning, Madam."

I walked with him to the door and let him out, while Barbara waited for me in the hall, not unobserved by Wallingford, whose eye appeared in a chink beside the slightly open dining room door. I pointedly led her back into the drawing room and closed the door audibly behind us. She turned a pale and rather shocked face to me but she spoke quite composedly as she asked, "What do you make of it, Rupert? Is it Amos?"

I had already reluctantly decided that it must be. I say, reluctantly, because, if this were really his doing, the resigned tone of his last words to me would appear no less than sheer, gross hypocrisy.

"I don't know who else it could be," I answered. "The fact that he did not come this morning suggests that he at least knew what was happening. If he did, I think he might have warned us."

"Yes, indeed. It will be a horrid scandal, most unpleasant for us all, and especially for me. Not that I am entitled to any sympathy. Poor Harold! How he would have hated the thought of a public fuss over his body. I suppose we must go in now and tell the others. Do you mind telling them, Rupert?"

We crossed the hall to the dining room where we found the two waiting impatiently, Madeline very pale and agitated while Wallingford was pacing the room like a wild beast. Both looked at us with eager interrogation as we entered, and I made the announcement bluntly and in a dozen words.

The effect on both was electrical. Madeline, with a little cry of horror, sank, white-faced and trembling, into a chair. As for Wallingford, his behaviour was positively maniacal. After staring at me for a few moments with starting eyes and mouth agape, he flung up his arms and uttered a hoarse shout.

"This," he yelled, "is the doing of that accursed parson! Now we know why he kept out of the way – and it is well for him that he did!"

He clenched his fists and glared around him, showing his tobacco-stained teeth in a furious snarl while the sweat gathered in beads on his livid face. Then, suddenly, his mood changed and he dropped heavily on a chair, burying his face in his shaking hands. Barbara admonished him, quietly.

"Do try to be calm, Tony. There is nothing to get so excited about. It is all very unpleasant and humiliating, of course, but at any rate you are not affected. It is I who will be called to account."

"And do you suppose that doesn't affect me?" demanded Wallingford, now almost on the verge of tears.

"I am sure it does, Tony," she replied, gently, "but if you want to be helpful to me you will try to be calm and reasonable. Come, now," she added, persuasively, "let us put it away for the present. I must tell the servants. Then we had better have lunch and go our several ways to think the matter over quietly each of us alone. We shall only agitate one another if we remain together."

I agreed emphatically with this sensible suggestion. "Not," I added, "that there is much for us to think over. The explanations will have to come from Dimsdale. It was he who failed to grasp the seriousness of poor Harold's condition."

While Barbara was absent, breaking the news to the servants, I tried to bring Madeline to a more composed frame of mind. With Wallingford I had no patience. Men should leave hysterics to the other sex. But I was sorry for Madeline, and even if she seemed more overwhelmed by the sudden complications than the occasion justified, I told myself that the blow had fallen when she was already shaken by Harold's unexpected death.

The luncheon was a silent and comfortless function – indeed it was little more than an empty form. But it had the merit of brevity. When the last dish had been sent away almost intact, Wallingford drew out his cigarette case and we all rose.

"What are you going to do, Madeline?" Barbara asked.

"I must go to the school, I suppose, and let the secretary know that – that I may have to be absent for a day or two. It will be horrid. I shall have to tell him all about it – after having got leave for the funeral. But it will sound so strange, so extraordinary. Oh! It is horrible!"

"It is!" exclaimed Wallingford, fumbling with tremulous fingers at his cigarette case. "It is diabolical! A fiendish plot to disgrace and humiliate us. As to that infernal parson, I should like – "

"Never mind that. Tony," said Barbara, "and we had better not stay here, working up one another's emotions. What are you doing, Rupert?"

"I shall go to my chambers and clear off some correspondence."

"Then you might walk part of the way with Madeline and see if you can't make her mind a little more easy."

Madeline looked at me eagerly. "Will you, Rupert?" she asked.

Of course I assented, and a few minutes later we set forth together.

For a while she walked by my side in silence with an air of deep reflection, and I refrained from interrupting her thoughts, having no very clear idea as to what I should say to her. Moreover, my own mind was pretty busily occupied. Presently she spoke, in a tentative way, as if opening a discussion.

"I am afraid you must think me very weak and silly to be so much upset by this new trouble."

"Indeed, I don't," I replied. "It is a most disturbing and humiliating affair and it will be intensely unpleasant for us all, but especially for Barbara – to say nothing of Dimsdale."

"Dr. Dimsdale is not our concern," said she, "but it will be perfectly horrible for Barbara. For she really has been rather casual, poor girl, and they are sure to make things unpleasant for her. It will be a most horrid scandal. Don't you think so?"

To be candid, I did. Indeed, I had just been picturing to myself the possibilities with an officious coroner – and he would not need to be so very officious, either – and one or two cross-grained jurymen. Barbara might be subjected to a very unpleasant examination. But I did not think it necessary to say this to Madeline. Sufficient for the day is the evil thereof. I contented myself with a vague agreement.

There was another interval of silence. Then, a little to my surprise, she drew closer to me, and, slipping her hand under my arm, said very earnestly, "Rupert, I want you to tell me what you really think. What is it all about?"

I looked down, rather disconcerted, into the face that was turned up to me so appealingly, and suddenly – and rather irrelevantly – it was borne in on me that it was a singularly sweet and charming face. I had never quite realized it before. But then she had never before looked at me quite in this way, with this trustful, coaxing, appealing expression.

"I don't quite understand you, Madeline," I said, evasively. "I know no more about it than you do."

"Oh, but you do, Rupert. You are a lawyer and you have had a lot of experience. You must have formed some opinion as to why they have decided to hold an inquest. Do tell me what you think."

The coaxing, almost wheedling tone, and the entreaty in her eyes, looking so earnestly into mine, nearly conquered my reserve. But not quite. Once more I temporized.

"Well, Madeline, we all realize that what Dimsdale has written on the certificate is little more than a guess, and quite possibly wrong, and even Detling couldn't get much farther."

"Yes, I realize that. But I didn't think that inquests were held just to find out whether the doctors' opinions were correct or not."

Of course she was perfectly right, and I now perceived that her thoughts had been travelling along the same lines as my own. An inquest would not be held merely to clear up an obscure diagnosis. There was certainly something more behind this affair than Dimsdale's failure to recognize the exact nature of the illness. There was only one simple explanation of the coroner's action, and I gave it – with a strong suspicion that it was not the right one.

"They are not, as a rule, excepting in hospitals. But this is a special case. Amos Monkhouse was obviously dissatisfied with Dimsdale, and with Barbara, too. He may have challenged the death certificate and asked for an inquest. The coroner would be hardly likely to refuse, especially if there were a hint of negligence or malpractice."

"Did Mr. Amos say anything to you that makes you think he may have challenged the certificate?"

"He said very little to me at all," I replied, rather casuistically and suppressing the fact that Amos had explicitly accepted the actual circumstances and deprecated any kind of recrimination.

"I can hardly believe that he would have done it," said Madeline, "just to punish Barbara and Dr. Dimsdale. It would be so vindictive, especially for a clergyman."

"Clergymen are very human sometimes," I rejoined and, as, rather to my relief, we now came in sight of Madeline's destination, I adverted to the interview which she seemed to dread so much. "There is no occasion for you to go into details with the secretary," I said. "In fact you can't. The exact cause of death was not clear to the doctors and it has been considered advisable to hold an inquest. That is all you know, and it is enough. You are summoned as a witness and you are legally bound to attend, so you are asking no favour. Cut the interview dead short, and when you have done with it try, like a sensible girl, to forget the inquest for the present. I shall come over tomorrow and then we can reconstitute the history of the case, so that we may go into the witness-box, or its equivalent, with a clear idea of what we have to tell. And now, good-bye, or rather *au revoir*!"

"Good-bye, Rupert." She took my proffered hand and held it as she thanked me for walking with her. "Do you know, Rupert," she added, "there is something strangely comforting and reassuring about you. We all feel it. You seem to carry an atmosphere of quiet strength and security. I don't wonder that Barbara is so fond of you. Not," she concluded, "that she holds a monopoly."

With this she let go my hand, and, with a slightly shy smile and the faintest suspicion of a blush, turned away and walked quickly and with an air quite cheerful and composed towards the gateway of the institution. Apparently, my society had had a beneficial effect on her nervous condition.

I watched her until she disappeared into the entry, and then resumed my journey eastward, rather relieved, I fear, at having disposed of my companion. For I wanted to think – of her among other matters, and it was she who first occupied my cogitations. The change from her usual matter-of-fact friendliness had rather taken me by surprise, and I had to admit that it was not a disagreeable surprise. But what was the explanation? Was this intimate, clinging manner merely a passing phase due to an emotional upset, or was it that the special circumstances had allowed feelings hitherto concealed to come to the surface? It was an interesting question, but one that time alone could answer, and as there were other questions, equally interesting and more urgent, I consigned this one to the future and turned to consider the others.

266

What could be the meaning of this inquest? The supposition that Amos had suddenly turned vindictive and resolved to expose the neglect to which he probably attributed his brother's death I could not entertain, especially after what he had said to me. It would have written him down the rankest of hypocrites. And yet he was in some way connected with the affair as was proved by his failure to appear at the funeral. As to the idea that the inquiry was merely to elucidate the nature of the illness, that was quite untenable. A private autopsy would have been the proper procedure for that purpose.

I was still turning the question over in my mind when, as I passed the Griffin at Temple Bar, I became aware of a tall figure some distance ahead walking in the same direction. The build of the man and his long, swinging stride seemed familiar. I looked at him more attentively, and just as he turned to enter Devereux Court I recognized him definitely as a fellow-Templar named Thorndyke.

The chance encounter seemed a singularly fortunate one, and at once I quickened my pace to overtake him. For Dr. Thorndyke was a medical barrister and admittedly the greatest living authority on medical jurisprudence. The whole subject of inquests and Coroners' Law was an open book to him. But he was not only a lawyer. He had, I understood, a professional and very thorough knowledge of pathology and of the science of medicine in general, so that he was the very man to enlighten me in my present difficulties.

I overtook him at the Little Gate of the Middle Temple and we walked through together into New Court. I wasted no time, but, after the preliminary greetings, asked him if he had a few minutes to spare. He replied, in his quiet, genial way, "But, of course, Mayfield. I always have a few minutes to spare for a friend and a colleague."

I thanked him for the gracious reply, and, as we slowly descended the steps and sauntered across Fountain Court, I opened the matter without preamble and gave him a condensed summary of the case, to which lie listened with close attention and evidently with keen interest.

"I am afraid," he said, "that your family doctor will cut rather a poor figure. He seems to have mismanaged the case rather badly, to judge by the fact that the death of the patient took him quite by surprise. By the way, can you give me any idea of the symptoms – as observed by yourself, I mean?"

"I have told you what was on the certificate."

"Yes. But the certified cause of death appears to be contested. You saw the patient pretty often, I understand. Now what sort of appearance did he present to you?"

The question rather surprised me. Dimsdale's opinion might not be worth much, but the casual and inexpert observations of a layman would have seemed to me to be worth nothing at all. However, I tried to recall such details as I could remember of poor Monkhouse's appearance and his own comments on his condition and recounted them to Thorndyke with such amplifications as his questions elicited. "But," I concluded, "the real question is, who has set the coroner in motion and with what object?"

"That question," said Thorndyke, "will be answered the day after tomorrow, and there is not much utility in trying to guess at the answer in advance. The real question is whether any arrangements ought to be made in the interests of your friends. We are quite in the dark as to what may occur in the course of the inquest."

"Yes, I had thought of that. Someone ought to be present to represent Mrs. Monkhouse. I suppose it would not be possible for you to attend to watch the case on her behalf?"

"I don't think it would be advisable," he replied. "You will be present and could claim to represent Mrs. Monkhouse so far as might be necessary to prevent improper questions being put to her. But I do think that you should have a complete record of all that takes place. I would suggest that I send Holman, who does most of my shorthand reporting, with instructions to make a verbatim report of the entire proceedings. It may turn out to be quite unnecessary, but if any complications should arise, we shall have the complete depositions with the added advantage that you will have been present and will have heard all the evidence. How will that suit you?"

"If you think it is the best plan there is nothing more to say, excepting to thank you for your help."

"And give me a written note of the time and place to hand to Holman when I give him his instructions."

I complied with this request at once, and having by this time reached the end of the Terrace, I shook hands with him and walked slowly to my chambers in Fig Tree Court. I had not got much out of Thorndyke excepting a very useful suggestion and some valuable help – indeed, as I turned over his extremely cautious utterances and speculated on what he meant by "complications". I found myself rather more uncomfortably puzzled than I had been before I met him.

Chapter IV
"How, When, and Where – "

It was on the second day after the interrupted funeral that the thunderbolt fell. I cannot say that it found me entirely unprepared, for my reflections during the intervening day had filled me with forebodings, and by Thorndyke that catastrophe was pretty plainly foreseen. But on the others the blow fell with devastating effect. However, I must not anticipate. Rather let me get back to a consecutive narration of the actual events.

On the day after the visit of the coroner's officer we had held, at my suggestion, a sort of family committee to consider what we knew of the circumstances and antecedents of Harold's death, so that we might be in a position to give our evidence clearly and readily and be in agreement as to the leading facts. Thus we went to the coroners court prepared, at least, to tell an intelligible and consistent story.

As soon as I entered the large room in which the inquest was to be held, my forebodings deepened. The row of expectant reporters was such as one does not find where the proceedings are to be no more than a simple, routine inquiry. Something of public interest was anticipated, and these gentlemen of the Press had received a hint from some well-informed quarter. I ran my eye along the row and was somewhat relieved to observe Mr. Holman, Thorndyke's private reporter, seated at the table with a large notebook and a half-dozen well-sharpened pencils before him. His presence – as, in a sense, Thorndyke's deputy – gave me the reassuring feeling that, if there were to be "complications", I should not have to meet them with my own limited knowledge and experience, but that there were reserves of special knowledge and weighty counsel on which I could fall back.

The coroner's manner seemed to me ominous. His introductory address to the jury was curt and ambiguous, setting forth no more than the name of the deceased and the fact that circumstances had seemed to render an inquiry advisable, and having said this, he proceeded forthwith (the jury having already viewed the body) to call the first witness, the Reverend Amos Monkhouse.

I need not repeat the clergyman's evidence in detail. When he had identified the body as that of his brother, Harold, he went on to relate the events which I have recorded: His visit to his sick brother, his alarm at the patient's appearance, his call upon Dr. Dimsdale and his subsequent interview with Sir Robert Detling. It was all told in a very concise, matter-of-fact manner, and I noted that the coroner did not seek to amplify the condensed statement by any questions.

"At about nine o'clock in the morning of the thirteenth," the witness continued, "I received a telegram from Miss Norris informing me that my brother had died in the night. I went out at once and sent a telegram to Sir Robert Detling informing him of what had happened. I then went to number 16 Hilborough Square, where I saw the body of the deceased lying in his bed quite cold and stiff. I saw nobody at the house excepting the housemaid and Mr. Mayfield. After leaving the house, I walked about the streets for several hours and did not return to my hotel until late in the afternoon. When I arrived there, I found awaiting me a telegram from Sir Robert Detling asking me to call on him without delay. I set forth at once and arrived at Sir Robert's house at half-past-five, and was shown into his study immediately. Sir Robert then told me that he had come to the conclusion that the circumstances of my brother's death called for some investigation, and that he proposed to communicate with the coroner. He urged me not to raise any objections and advised me to say nothing to anyone but to wait until the coroner's decision was made known. I asked him for his reasons for communicating with the coroner, but he said that he would rather not make any statement. I heard no more until the morning of the fifteenth, the day appointed for the funeral, when the coroner's officer called at my hotel to inform me that the funeral would not take place and to serve the summons for my attendance here as a witness."

When Amos had concluded his statement, the coroner glanced at the Jury, and as no one offered to put any questions, he dismissed the witness and called the next – Mabel Withers – who, at once, came forward to the table. Having been sworn and having given her name, the witness deposed that she had been housemaid to the deceased and that it was she who had discovered the fact of his death, relating the circumstances in much the same words as I have recorded. When she had finished her narrative, the coroner said, "You have told us that the candle in the deceased's lamp was completely burnt out. Do you happen to know how long one of those candles would burn?"

"Yes. About four hours."

"When did you last see the deceased alive?"

"At half-past-ten on Tuesday night, the twelfth. I looked in at his room on my way up to bed to see if he wanted anything, and I gave him a dose of medicine."

"What was his condition then?"

"He looked very ill, but he seemed fairly comfortable. He had a book in his hand but was not reading."

"Was the candle alight then?"

"No, the gas was alight. I asked him if I should turn it out but he said 'No.' He would wait until Miss Norris or Mr. Wallingford came."

"Did you notice how much candle there was in the lamp then?"

"There was a whole candle. I put it in myself in the afternoon and it had not been lit. He used to read by the gas as long as it was alight. He only used the candle-lamp if he couldn't sleep and the gas was out."

"Could you form any opinion as to how long the candle had been burnt out?"

"It must have been out some time, for there was no smell in the room as there would have been if it had only been out a short time. The window was hardly open at all, only just a small crack."

"Do you know when the deceased last took food?"

"Yes, he had his supper at eight o'clock, an omelette and a tiny piece of toast with a glass of milk."

"Who cooked the omelette?"

"Miss Norris."

"Why did Miss Norris cook it? Was the cook out?"

"No. But Miss Norris usually cooked his supper and sometimes made little dishes for his lunch. She is a very expert cook."

"Who took the omelette up to the deceased?"

"Miss Norris. I asked if I should take his supper up, but she said she was going up and would take it herself."

"Was anyone else present when Miss Norris was cooking the omelette?"

"Yes, I was present and so was the cook."

"Did the deceased usually have the same food as the rest of the household?"

"No, he usually had his own special diet."

"Who prepared his food, as a rule?"

"Sometimes the cook, but more often Miss Norris."

"Now, with regard to his medicine. Did the deceased usually take it himself?"

"No, he didn't like to have the bottle on the bedside table, as it was rather crowded with his books and things. The bottle and the medicine-glass were kept on the mantelpiece, and the medicine was given to him by whoever happened to be in the room when a dose was due. Sometimes I gave it to him, at other times Mrs. Monkhouse or Miss Norris or Mr. Wallingford."

"Do you remember when the last bottle of medicine came?"

271

"Yes. It came early in the afternoon of the day before he died. I took it in and carried it up at once."

When he had written down this answer, the coroner ran his eye through his previous notes and then glanced at the jury.

"Do any of you gentlemen wish to ask the witness any questions?" he enquired, and as no one answered, he dismissed the witness with the request that she would stay in the court in case any further testimony should be required of her. He then announced that he would take the evidence of Sir Robert Detling next in order to release him for his probably numerous engagements. Sir Robert's name was accordingly called and a grave-looking, elderly gentleman rose from near the doorway and walked up to the table. When the new witness had been sworn and the formal preliminaries disposed of, the coroner said, "I will ask you, Sir Robert, to give the jury an account of the circumstances which led to your making a certain communication to me."

Sir Robert bowed gravely and proceeded at once to make his statement in the clear, precise manner of a practised speaker.

"On Friday, the eighth instant, the Reverend Amos Monkhouse called on me to arrange a consultation with Dr. Dimsdale who was in attendance on his brother, the deceased. I met Dr. Dimsdale by appointment the following afternoon, the ninth, and with him made a careful examination of the deceased. I was extremely puzzled by the patient's condition. He was obviously very seriously – I thought, dangerously – ill, but I was unable to discover any signs or symptoms that satisfactorily accounted for his grave general condition. I could not give his disease a name. Eventually, I took a number of blood-films and some specimens of the secretions to submit to a pathologist for examination and to have them tested for micro-organisms. I took them that night to Professor Garnett's laboratory, but the professor was unfortunately absent and not returning until the following night – Sunday. I therefore kept them until Sunday night when I took them to him and asked him to examine them with as little delay as possible. He reported on the following day that microscopical examination had not brought to light anything abnormal, but he was making cultures from the secretions and would report the result on Wednesday morning. On Wednesday morning at about half-past-nine, I received a telegram from the Reverend Amos Monkhouse informing me that his brother had died during the night. A few minutes later, a messenger brought Professor Garnett's report, which was to the effect that no disease-bearing organisms had been found, nor any thing abnormal excepting a rather singular scarcity of micro-organisms of any kind.

"This fact, together with the death of the patient, suddenly aroused my suspicions. For the absence of the ordinary micro-organisms suggested the presence of some foreign chemical substance. And now, as I recalled the patient's symptoms, I found them consistent with the presence in the body of some foreign substance. Instantly, I made my way to Professor Garnett's laboratory and communicated my suspicions to him. I found that he shared them and had carefully preserved the remainder of the material for further examination. We both suspected the presence of a foreign substance, and we both suspected it to be arsenic.

"The professor had at hand the means of making a chemical test, so we proceeded at once to use them. The test that we employed was the one known as Reinsch's Test. The result showed a very appreciable amount of arsenic in the secretions tested. On this, I sealed up what was left of the specimens and, after notifying Mr. Monkhouse of my intention, reported the circumstances to the coroner."

When Sir Robert ceased speaking, the coroner bowed, and having written down the last words, reflected for a few moments. Then he turned to the Jury and said, "I don't think we need detain Sir Robert any longer unless there are any questions that you would like to ask."

At this point the usual over-intelligent juryman interposed.

"We should like to know whether the vessels in which the specimens were contained were perfectly clean and free from chemicals."

"The bottles," Sir Robert replied, "were clean in the ordinary sense. I rinsed them out with clean water before introducing the material. But, of course, they could not be guaranteed to be chemically clean."

"Then doesn't that invalidate the analysis?" the juror asked.

"It was hardly an analysis," the witness replied. "It was just a preliminary test."

"The point which you are raising, sir," said the coroner, "is quite a sound one but it is not relevant to this inquiry. Sir Robert's test was made to ascertain if an inquiry was necessary. He decided that it was, and we are now holding that inquiry. You will not form your verdict on the results of Sir Robert's test but on those of the *post mortem* examination and the special analysis that has been made."

This explanation appeared to satisfy the juror and Sir Robert was allowed to depart. The coroner once more seemed to consider awhile and then addressed the jury.

"I think it will be best to take next the evidence relating to the examination of the body. When you have heard that you will be better able to weigh the significance of what the other witnesses have to tell us. We will now take the evidence of Dr. Randall."

As the new witness, a small, dry, eminently professional-looking man, stepped briskly up to the table, I stole a quick, rather furtive glance at my companions and saw my own alarm plainly reflected in their faces and bearing. Barbara, on my left hand, sat up stiffly, rigid as a statue, her face pale and set, but quite composed, her eyes fixed on the man who was about to be sworn. Madeline, on my right, was ghastly. But she, too, was still and quiet, sitting with her hands tightly clasped, as if to restrain or conceal their trembling, and her eyes bent on the floor. As to Wallingford, who sat on the other side of Barbara, I could not see his face, but by his foot, which I could see and hear, tapping quickly on the floor as if he were working a spinning-wheel, and his incessantly moving hands, I judged that his nerves were at full tension.

The new witness deposed that his name was Walter Randall, that he was a Bachelor of Medicine and police surgeon of the district, and that he had made a careful examination of the body of the deceased and that, with Dr. Barnes, he had made an analysis of certain parts of that body.

"To anticipate a little," said the coroner, "did you arrive at an opinion as to the cause of death?"

"Yes. From the *post mortem* examination and the analysis taken together, I came to the conclusion that the deceased died from the effects of arsenic poisoning."

"Have you any doubt that arsenic poisoning was really the cause of the deceased's death?"

"No, I have no doubt whatever."

The reply, uttered with quiet decision, elicited a low murmur from the jury and the few spectators, amidst which I heard Madeline gasp in a choking whisper, "Oh! God!" and even Barbara was moved to a low cry of horror. But I did not dare to look at either of them. As for me, the blow had fallen already. Sir Robert's evidence had told me all.

"You said," the coroner resumed, "that the *post mortem* and the analysis, taken together, led you to this conclusion. What did you mean by that?"

"I meant that the appearance of the internal organs, taken alone, would not have been conclusive. The conditions that I found were suggestive of arsenic poisoning but might possibly have been due to disease. It was only the ascertained presence of arsenic that converted the probability into certainty."

"You are quite sure that the conditions were not due to disease?"

"Not entirely. I would rather say that the effects of arsenical poisoning were added to and mingled with those of old-standing disease."

"Would you tell us briefly what abnormal conditions you found?"

274

"The most important were those in the stomach, which showed marked signs of inflammation."

"You are aware that the death certificate gives old-standing chronic gastritis as one of the causes of death?"

"Yes, and I think correctly. The arsenical gastritis was engrafted on an already existing chronic gastritis. That is what made the appearances rather difficult to interpret, especially as the *post mortem* appearances in arsenical poisoning are extraordinarily variable."

"What else did you find?"

"There were no other conditions that were directly associated with the poison. The heart was rather fatty and dilated, and its condition probably accounts for the sudden collapse which seems to have occurred."

"Does not collapse usually occur in poisoning by arsenic?"

"Eventually it does, but it is usually the last of a long train of symptoms. In some cases, however, collapse occurs quite early and may carry the victim off at once. That is what appears from the housemaid's evidence to have happened in this case. Death seems to have been sudden and almost peaceful."

"Were there any other signs of disease?"

"Yes, the lungs were affected. There were signs of considerable bronchial catarrh, but I do not regard this as having any connection with the effects of the poison. It appeared to be an old-standing condition."

"Yes," said the coroner. "The certificate mentions chronic bronchial catarrh of several years' standing. Did you find any arsenic in the stomach?"

"Not in the solid form, and only a little more than a hundredth-of-a-grain altogether. The stomach was practically empty. The other organs were practically free from disease, excepting, perhaps, the kidneys, which were congested but not organically diseased."

"And as to the amount of arsenic present?"

"The analysis was necessarily a rather hasty one and probably shows less than the actual quantity, but we found, as I have said, just over a hundredth-of-a-grain in the stomach, one-and-a-half grains in the liver, nearly a fifth-of-a-grain in the kidneys and small quantities, amounting in all to two grains, in the blood and tissues. The total amount actually found was thus a little over three-and-a-half grains – a lethal dose."

"What is the fatal dose of arsenic?"

"Two grains may prove fatal if taken in solution, as it appears to have been in this case. Two-and-a-half grains, in a couple of ounces of

275

fly-paper water, killed a strong, healthy girl of nineteen in thirty-six hours."

"And how long does a poisonous dose take to produce death?"

"The shortest period recorded is twenty minutes, the longest, over three weeks."

"Did you come to any general conclusion as to how long the deceased had been suffering from the effects of arsenic and as to the manner in which it had been administered?"

"From the distribution of the poison in the organs and tissues and from the appearance of the body, I inferred that the administration of arsenic had been going on for a considerable time. There were signs of chronic poisoning which led me to believe that for quite a long time – perhaps months – the deceased had been taking repeated small doses of the poison, and that the final dose took such rapid effect by reason of the enfeebled state of the deceased at the time when it was administered."

"And as to the mode of administration? Did you ascertain that?"

"In part, I ascertained it quite definitely. When the bearers went to the house to fetch the body, I accompanied them and took the opportunity to examine the bedroom. There I found on the mantelpiece a bottle of medicine with the name of the deceased on the label and brought it away with me. It was an eight-ounce bottle containing when full eight doses, of which only one had been taken. Dr. Barnes and I, together, analyzed the remaining seven ounces of the medicine and obtained from it just over eleven grains of arsenic, that is a fraction over a grain-and-a-half in each ounce dose. The arsenic was in solution and had been introduced into the medicine in the form of the solution known officially as *Liquor Arsenicalis*, or Fowler's Solution."

"That is perfectly definite," said the coroner. "But you said that you ascertained the mode of administration in part. Do you mean that you inferred the existence of some other vehicle?"

"Yes. A single dose of this medicine contained only a grain-and-a-half of arsenic, which would hardly account for the effects produced or the amount of arsenic which was found in the body. Of course, the preceding dose from the other bottle may have contained the poison, too, or it may have been taken in some other way."

"What other way do you suggest?"

"I can merely suggest possibilities. A meal was taken about eight o'clock. If that meal had contained a small quantity of arsenic – even a single grain – that, added to what was in the medicine, would have been enough to cause death. But there is no evidence whatever that the food did contain arsenic."

"If the previous dose of medicine had contained the same quantity of the poison as the one that was last taken, would that account for the death of the deceased?"

"Yes. He would then have taken over three grains in four hours – more than the minimum fatal dose."

"Did you see the other – the empty medicine bottle?"

"No. I looked for it and should have taken possession of it, but it was not there."

"Is there anything else that you have to tell us concerning your examination?"

"No, I think I have told you all I know about the case."

The coroner cast an interrogatory glance at the jury, and when none of them accepted the implied invitation, he released the witness and named Dr. Barnes as his successor.

I need not record in detail the evidence of this witness. Having deposed that he was a Doctor of Science and lecturer in Chemistry at St. Martha's Medical College, he proceeded to confirm Dr. Randall's evidence as to the analysis, giving somewhat fuller and more precise details. He had been present at the autopsy, but he was not a pathologist and was not competent to describe the condition of the body. He had analyzed the contents of the medicine bottle with Dr. Randall's assistance and he confirmed the last witness's statement as to the quantity of arsenic found and the form in which it had been introduced – Fowler's Solution.

"What is the strength of Fowler's Solution?"

"It contains four grains of arsenic – or, more strictly, of *arsenious acid* – to the fluid ounce. So that, as the full bottle of medicine must have contained just over twelve-and-a-half grains of arsenious acid, the quantity of Fowler's Solution introduced must have been a little over three fluid ounces, three-point-fourteen, to be exact."

"You are confident that it was Fowler's Solution that was used?"

"Yes, the chemical analysis showed that, but in addition, there was the colour and the smell. Fowler's Solution is coloured red with Red Sandalwood and scented with Tincture of Lavender as a precaution against accidents. Otherwise it would be colourless, odourless, and tasteless, like water."

On the conclusion of Dr. Barnes' evidence, the coroner remarked to the jury, "I think we ought to be clear on the facts with regard to this medicine. Let Mabel Withers be recalled."

Once more the housemaid took her place by the table and the coroner resumed the examination.

"You say that the last bottle of medicine came early in the afternoon. Can you tell us the exact time?"

"It was about a quarter-to-three. I remember that because when I took up the new bottle, I asked Mr. Monkhouse if he had had his medicine and he said that his brother, Mr. Amos Monkhouse, had given him a dose at two o'clock just before he left."

"Did you open the fresh bottle?"

"I took off the paper wrapping and the cap but I didn't take the cork out."

"Was the old bottle empty then?"

"No, there was one dose left in it. That would be due at six o'clock."

"Do you know what became of the old bottle?"

"Yes. When I had given him his last dose – that was out of the new bottle – I took the old bottle away and washed it at once."

"Why did you wash the bottle?"

"The used medicine bottles were always washed and sent back to Dr. Dimsdale."

"Did you send back the corks, too?"

"No, the corks were usually burned in the rubbish destructor."

"Do you know what happened to this particular cork?"

"I took it down with me in the morning and dropped it in the bin which was kept for the rubbish to be taken out to the destructor. The cork must have been burned with the other rubbish the same day."

"When you gave the deceased that last dose of medicine from the new bottle, did you notice anything unusual about it? Any smell, for instance?"

"I noticed a very faint smell of lavender. But that was not unusual. His medicine often smelt of lavender."

"Do you know if the previous bottle of medicine smelt of lavender?"

"Yes, it did. I noticed it when I was washing out the bottle."

"That, gentlemen," said the coroner, as he wrote down the answer, "is a very important fact. You will notice that it bears out Dr. Randall's opinion that more than one dose of the poison had been given, that, in fact, a number of repeated small doses had been administered. And, so far as we can see at present, the medicine was, at least, the principal medium of its administration. The next problem that we have to solve is how the poison got into the medicine. If none of you wish to put any questions to the very intelligent witness whom we have just been examining, I think we had better call Dr. Dimsdale and hear what he has to tell us."

The jury had no questions to put to Mabel but were manifestly all agog to hear Dr. Dimsdale's evidence. The housemaid was accordingly sent back to her seat, and the doctor stepped briskly – almost too briskly, I thought – up to the table.

Chapter V
Madeline's Ordeal

I was rather sorry for Dimsdale. His position was a very disagreeable one and he fully realized it. His patient had been poisoned before his very eyes and he had never suspected even grave illness. In a sense, the death of Harold Monkhouse lay at his door and it was pretty certain that every one present would hold him accountable for the disaster. Indeed, it was likely that he would receive less than justice. Those who judged him would hardly stop to reflect on the extraordinary difficulties that beset a busy medical man whose patient is being secretly poisoned, would fail to consider the immense number of cases of illness presented to him in the course of years of practice, and the infinitely remote probability that any one of them is a case of poison. The immense majority of doctors pass through the whole of their professional lives without meeting with such a case, and it is not surprising that when the infinitely rare contingency arises, it nearly always takes the practitioner unawares. My own amazement at this incredible horror tended to make me sympathetic towards Dimsdale, and it was with some relief that I noted the courteous and considerate manner that the coroner adopted in dealing with the new witness.

"I think," the former observed, "that we had better, in the first place, pursue our inquiries concerning the medicine. You have heard the evidence of Dr. Randall and Dr. Barnes. This bottle of medicine, before any was taken from it, contained twelve-and-a-half grains of arsenious acid, in the form of just over three fluid ounces of Fowler's Solution. Can you suggest any explanation of that fact?"

"No," replied Dimsdale, "I cannot."

"What should the bottle have contained? What was the composition of the medicine?"

"The medicine was just a simple, very mild tonic and alternative. The bottle contained twenty-four minims of Tincture of *Nux Vomica*, sixteen minims of *Liquor Arsenicalis*, half-a-fluid ounce of Syrup of Bitter Orange to cover the taste of the *Nux Vomica*, and half-an-ounce of Compound Tincture of Cardamoms. So that each dose contained three minims of Tincture of *Nux Vomica* and two minims of *Liquor Arsenicalis*."

"*Liquor Arsenicalis* is another name for Fowler's Solution, I understand?"

"Yes, it is the official name, the other is the popular name."

"Who supplied this medicine?"

"It was supplied by me."

"Do you usually supply your patients with medicine?"

"No. Only a few of my old patients who prefer to have their medicine from me. Usually, I write prescriptions which my patients have made up by chemists."

"This bottle, then, was made up in your own dispensary?"

"Yes."

"Now, I put it to you, Dr. Dimsdale: This medicine did actually contain Fowler's Solution, according to the prescription. Is it not possible that some mistake may have occurred in the amount put into the bottle?"

"No, it is quite impossible."

"Why is it impossible?"

"Because I made up this particular bottle myself. As my dispenser is not a qualified pharmacist, I always dispense, with my own hands, any medicines containing poisons. All dangerous drugs are kept in a poison cupboard under lock and key, and I carry the key on my private bunch. This is the key, and as you see, the lock is a Yale lock."

He held up the bunch with the little flat key separated, for the coroner's and the jurymen's inspection.

"But," said the coroner, "you have not made it clear that a mistake in the quantity was impossible."

"I was coming to that." replied Dimsdale. "The poisons in the cupboard are, of course, powerful drugs which are given only in small doses, and a special measure-glass is kept in the cupboard to measure them. This glass holds only two drachms – a hundred-and-twenty minims – that is, a quarter-of-an-ounce. Now, the analysts found in this bottle three fluid ounces of Fowler's Solution. But to measure out that quantity, I should have had to fill the measure-glass twelve times! That is impossible. No one could do such a thing as that inadvertently, especially when he was dispensing poisons.

"But that is not all. The poison bottles are all quite small. The one in which the *Liquor Arsenicalis* is kept is a four ounce bottle. It happened that I had refilled it a few days previously and it was full when I dispensed this medicine. Now, obviously, if I had put three ounces of the Liquor into the medicine bottle, there would have remained in the dispensing bottle only one ounce. But the dispensing bottle is still practically full. I had occasion to use it this morning and I found it full save for the few minims that had been taken to make up the deceased's medicine.

"And there is another point. This medicine was coloured a deepish pink by the Tincture of Cardamoms. But if it had contained three ounces of Fowler's Solution in addition, it would have been a deep red of quite a different character. But I clearly remember the appearance of the bottle as it lay on the white paper when I was wrapping it up. It had the delicate pink colour that is imparted by the cochineal in the Tincture of Cardamoms."

The coroner nodded as he wrote down the reply, and enquired, "Would any of you gentlemen like to ask any questions concerning the bottle of medicine?"

"We should like to know. sir," said the foreman, "whether this bottle of medicine ever left the doctor's hands before it was sent to the deceased?"

"No, it did not," replied Dimsdale. "As the dispenser was absent, I put up the bottle entirely myself. I put in the cork, wrote the label, tied on the paper cap, wrapped the bottle up, sealed the wrapping, addressed it, and gave it to the boy to deliver."

The foreman expressed himself as fully satisfied with this answer and the coroner then resumed. "Well, we seem to have disposed of the medicine so far as you are concerned, Doctor. We will now go on to consider the condition of the deceased during the last few days. Did no suspicion of anything abnormal ever occur to you?"

"No, I neither perceived nor suspected anything abnormal."

"Is that not rather remarkable? I realize that poisoning would be the last thing that you would be looking for or expecting. But when it occurred, is it not a little strange that you did not recognize the symptoms?"

"Not at all," replied Dimsdale. "There was nothing to recognize. The classical symptoms of arsenic poisoning were entirely absent. You will remember that Sir Robert Detling had no more suspicion than I had."

"What are the classical symptoms, as you call them, of arsenic poisoning?"

"The recognized symptoms – which are present in the immense majority of cases – are acute abdominal pain and tenderness, intense thirst, nausea, vomiting, and purging – the symptoms, in fact, of extreme irritation of the stomach and intestines. But in the case of the deceased, these symptoms were entirely absent. There was, in my opinion, nothing whatever in his appearance or symptoms to suggest arsenic poisoning. His condition appeared in no way different from what I had known it to be on several previous occasions, just a variation for the worse of his ordinary ill-health."

"You do not doubt that arsenic poisoning was really the cause of his death?"

"The analysis seems to put the matter beyond question. Otherwise – I mean apart from the analysis – I would not have entertained the idea of arsenic poisoning for a moment."

"But you do not dispute the cause of death?"

"No. Arsenic is extraordinarily variable in its effects, as Dr. Randall mentioned, both on the dead body and on the living. Very anomalous cases of arsenic poisoning have been mistaken, during life, for opium poisoning."

The coroner wrote down the answer and having glanced over his notes, asked, "What was the condition of the deceased when his wife went away from home?"

"He was much better. In fact his health seemed to be improving so much that I hoped he would soon be about again."

"And how soon after his wife's departure did his last attack begin?"

"I should hardly call it an attack. It was a gradual change for the worse. Mrs. Monkhouse went away on the twenty-ninth of August. On the second of September, the deceased was not so well and was extremely depressed and disappointed at the relapse. From that time his condition fluctuated, sometimes a little better and sometimes not so well. On the eighth he appeared rather seriously ill and was no better on the ninth, the day of the consultation with Sir Robert Detling After that he seemed to improve a little, and the slight improvement was maintained up to the twelfth. His death came, at least to me, as quite a surprise."

"You spoke just now of several previous occasions on which attacks – or, if you prefer it, relapses – of a similar kind occurred. Looking back on those relapses by the light of what we now know, do you say that they were quite similar, in respect of the symptoms, to the one which ended in the death of the deceased?"

"I should say they were identically similar. At any rate, I can recall no difference."

"Did any of them seem to be as severe as the fatal one?"

"Yes, in fact the last of them – which occurred in June – seemed to be more severe, only that it was followed by improvement and recovery. I have here the section of my card-index which relates to the deceased. In the entry dated June nineteenth, you will see that I have noted the patient's unsatisfactory condition."

He handed a small pack of index-cards to the coroner, who examined the upper card intently and then, with a sudden raising of the eyebrows, addressed the jury.

"I had better read out the entry. The card is headed '*Harold Monkhouse*' and this entry reads: '*June 19. Patient very low and feeble. No appetite. Considerable gastric discomfort and troublesome cough. Pulse 90, small, thready. Heart sounds weak. Sending report to Mrs. Monkhouse.*'"

He laid the cards down on the table, and, looking fixedly at Dimsdale, repeated, "'*Sending report to Mrs. Monkhouse*'. Where was Mrs. Monkhouse?"

"Somewhere in Kent, I believe. I sent the report to the headquarters of the Women's Freedom League in Knightrider Street, Maidstone, from whence I supposed it would be forwarded to her."

For some seconds after receiving this answer the coroner continued to gaze steadily at the witness. At length he observed, "This is a remarkable coincidence. Can you recall the condition of the deceased when Mrs. Monkhouse went away on that occasion?"

"Yes. I remember that he was in comparatively good health. In fact, his improved condition furnished the opportunity for Mrs. Monkhouse to make her visit to Maidstone."

"Can you tell us how soon after her departure on that occasion the relapse occurred?"

"I cannot say definitely, but my impression is that the change for the worse began a few days after she went away. Perhaps I might be able to judge by looking at my notes."

The coroner handed him back the index-cards, which he looked through rapidly. "Yes," he said, at length, "here is an entry on June eleventh of a bottle of tonic medicine for Mrs. Monkhouse. So she must have been at home on that date and, as it was a double-sized bottle, it was probably for her to take away with her."

"Then," said the coroner, "it is clear that, on the last two occasions, the deceased was comparatively well when his wife left home, but had a serious relapse soon after she went away. Now, what of the previous relapses?"

"I am afraid I cannot remember. I have an impression that Mrs. Monkhouse was away from home when some of them occurred, but at this distance of time, I cannot recollect clearly. Possibly Mrs. Monkhouse, herself, may be able to remember."

"Possibly," the coroner agreed, rather drily, "but as the point is of considerable importance, I should be glad if you would presently look through your case cards and see if you can glean any definite information on the subject. Meanwhile we may pass on to one or two other matters. First as to the medicine which you prescribed for the deceased, it contained, as you have told us, a certain amount of Fowler's Solution, and you considered the deceased to be suffering from chronic gastritis. Is Fowler's Solution usually given in cases of gastritis?"

"No. It is usually considered rather unsuitable. But the deceased was very tolerant of small doses of arsenic. I had often given it to him before as a tonic and it had always seemed to agree with him. The dose was extremely small – only two minims."

"How long have you known the deceased?"

"I have known and attended him professionally about twenty years."

"From your knowledge of him, should you say that he was a man who was likely to make enemies?"

"Not at all. He was a kindly, just, and generous man, amiable and even-tempered, rather reserved and aloof – not very human, perhaps, and somewhat self-contained and solitary. But I could not imagine him making an enemy and, so far as I know, he never did."

The coroner reflected awhile after writing down this answer and then turned to the jury.

"Are there any questions that you wish to put to the witness, gentlemen?"

The jury consulted together for a few moments, and the foreman then replied, "We should like to know, sir, if possible, whether Mrs. Monkhouse was or was not away from home when the previous relapses occurred."

"I am afraid," said Dimsdale, "that I cannot be more explicit as the events occurred so long ago. The other witnesses – the members of the household – would be much more likely to remember. And I would urge you not to detain me from my professional duties longer than is absolutely necessary."

Hereupon a brief consultation took place between the coroner and the jury, with the result that Dimsdale was allowed to go about his business and Barbara was summoned to take his place. I had awaited this stage of the proceedings with some uneasiness and was now rather surprised and greatly relieved at the coroner's manner towards her, which was courteous and even sympathetic. Having expressed his and the jury's regret at having to trouble her in the very distressing circumstances, he proceeded at once to clear off the preliminaries, eliciting the facts that she was thirty-two years of age and had been married a little over three years, and then said, "Dr. Dimsdale has told us that on the occasion of the attack or relapse in June last you were away from home, but he is not certain about the previous ones. Can you give us any information on the subject?"

"Yes," she replied, in a quiet, steady voice, "I recall quite clearly at least three previous occasions on which I went away from home leaving

285

my husband apparently well – as well as he ever was – and came back to find him quite ill. But I think there were more than three occasions on which this happened, for I remember having once accused him, facetiously, of saving up his illnesses until I was out of the house."

"Can you remember if a serious relapse ever occurred when you were at home?"

"Not a really serious one. My husband's health was always very unstable and he often had to rest in bed for a day or two. But the really bad attacks of illness seem always to have occurred when I was away from home."

"Did it never strike you that this was a very remarkable fact?"

"I am afraid I did not give the matter as much consideration as I ought to have done. He was always ailing, more-or-less, and those about him came to accept ill-health as his normal condition."

"But you see the significance of it now?"

Barbara hesitated and then replied in a low voice and with evident agitation, "I see that it may have some significance, but I don't in the least understand it. I am quite overwhelmed and bewildered by the dreadful thing that has happened."

"Naturally, you are," the coroner said in a sympathetic tone, "and I am most reluctant to trouble you with questions under circumstances that must be so terrible to you. But we must find out the truth if we can."

"Yes, I realize that," she replied, "and thank you for your consideration."

The coroner bowed, and after a brief pause, asked, "Did it never occur to you to engage a nurse to attend to the deceased?"

"Yes. I suggested it more than once, but he wouldn't hear of it. And I think he was right. There was nothing that a nurse could have done for him. He was not helpless and he was not continuously bed-ridden. He had a bell-push by his bedside and his secretary or the servants were always ready to do anything that he wanted done. The housemaid was most attentive to him. But he did not want much attention. He kept the books that he was reading on his bedside table and he liked to be left alone to read in peace. He felt that the presence of a nurse would have been disturbing."

"And at night?"

"At night his bell-push was connected with a bell in the secretary's bedroom. But he hardly ever used it. If his candle-lamp burned out, he could put in a fresh candle from the box on his table, and he never seemed to want anything else."

"Besides the deceased and yourself, who were the inmates of the house?"

286

"There was my husband's secretary, Mr. Wallingford, Miss Norris, the cook, Anne Baker, the housemaid, Mabel Withers, and the kitchen-maid, Doris Brown."

"Why did the deceased need a secretary? Did he transact much business?"

"No. The secretary wrote his few business letters, kept the accounts and executed any commissions, besides doing the various things that the master of the house would ordinarily have done. He is the son of an old friend of my husband's, and he came to us when his father died."

"And Miss Norris? What was her position in the household?"

"She lived with us as a guest at my husband's invitation. She was the daughter of his first wife's sister, and he, more-or-less informally, adopted her as he had no children of his own."

"The deceased was a widower, then, when you married him?"

"Yes. His wife had been dead about two years."

"What was his age when he died?"

"He had just turned fifty-seven."

"On what sort of terms was the deceased with the members of his household?"

"On the best of terms with them all. He was an undemonstrative man and rather cool and reserved with strangers, and distinctly solitary and self-contained. But he was a kind and generous man and all the household, including the servants, were devoted to him."

"Was the deceased engaged in any business or profession?"

"No, he had independent means, inherited from his father."

"Would you describe him as a wealthy man?"

"I believe he was quite well off, but he never spoke of his financial affairs to me, or to anybody but his lawyers."

"Do you know how his property is disposed of?"

"I know that he made a will, but I never enquired about the terms of it and he never told me."

"But surely you were an interested party."

"It was understood that some provision would be made for me if I survived him. That was all that concerned me. He was not a man with whom it was necessary to make conditions, and I have some small property of my own. Mr. Mayfield, who is present, of course, knows what the provisions of the will are, as he is one of the executors."

Once more the coroner paused to look over his notes. Then he glanced inquiringly at the jury and, when the foreman shook his head, he thanked Barbara and dismissed her, and as she walked back to her chair, pale and grave but perfectly composed, I found myself admiring her calm dignity and only hoping that the other witnesses would make as good a figure. But this hope was no sooner conceived than it was shattered. The next name that was called was Madeline Norris, and for a few moments there was no response. At length Madeline rose slowly, ashen and ghastly of face, and walked unsteadily to the table. Her appearance – her deathly pallor and her trembling hands – struck me with dismay, and what increased my concern for the unfortunate girl was the subtle change in manner that I detected in the jury and the coroner. The poor girl's manifest agitation might surely have bespoken their sympathy, but not a sign of sympathy was discernible in their faces – nothing but a stony curiosity.

Having been sworn – on a testament which shook visibly in her grasp – she deposed that her name was Madeline Norris and her age twenty-seven.

"Any occupation?" the coroner enquired drily without looking up.

"I am a teacher at the Westminster College of Domestic Science."

"Teacher of what?"

"Principally of cookery and kitchen management – especially invalid cookery."

"Are you, yourself, a skilled cook?"

"Yes. It is my duty to demonstrate to the class."

"Have you ever cooked or prepared food for the deceased?"

"Yes. I usually cooked his meals when I was in the house at meal times."

"It has been stated that you prepared the last meal that the deceased took. Is that correct?"

"Yes. I cooked an omelette for his supper."

"Will you describe to us the way in which you prepared that omelette?"

Madeline considered for a few moments and then replied in a low, shaky voice, "It was just a simple omelette. I first rubbed the pan with a cut clove of garlic and put in the butter to heat. Then I broke an egg into a cup, separated the yolk from the white, and, having beaten them up separately, mixed them and added a very small portion of pounded anchovy, a pinch or two of finely chopped parsley, and a little salt. I cooked it in the usual way and turned it out on a hot plate which I covered at once."

"Who took it up to the deceased?"

"I did. I ran straight up with it and sat and talked to him while he ate it."

"Did you meet anyone on your way up or in the bedroom?"

"No. There was nobody on the stairs, and, he was alone."

"Did he take anything to drink with his supper?"

"Yes. He had a glass of chablis. I fetched the bottle and the glass from the dining room and poured out the wine for him."

"Did you meet anybody in the dining room or coming or going?"

"No, I met nobody."

"Can you think of any way in which any poison could have got into the omelette or into the wine?"

"No. Nothing could possibly have got into the omelette. As to the wine, I poured it from the bottle into a clean glass. But the bottle was already open and had been in the cellaret since lunch."

"Now, with regard to the medicine: Did you give the deceased any on the day before his death?"

"Yes. I gave him a dose soon after I came in – about six o'clock. That was the last dose in the bottle."

"Did you notice anything unusual about the medicine?"

"No. It was similar to what he had been taking for some days past."

"What was the medicine like?"

"It was nearly colourless with the faintest tinge of red, and smelled slightly of lavender and bitter orange."

"Was there anything that caused you to notice particularly, on this occasion, the appearance and smell of the medicine?"

"No. I noticed the colour and the smell when I opened the bottle on the previous morning to give him a dose."

"Did you examine the new bottle which had just been sent?"

"Yes, I looked at it and took out the cork and smelled it and tasted it."

"What made you do that?"

"I noticed that it seemed to contain Tincture of Cardamoms, and I smelled and tasted it to find out if the other ingredients had been changed."

"And what conclusion did you arrive at?"

"That they had not been changed. I could taste the *Nux Vomica* and smell the orange and the *Liquor Arsenicalis* – at least the lavender."

"Did you realize what the lavender smell was due to?"

"Yes. I recognized it as the smell of *Liquor Arsenicalis*. I knew that he was taking *Liquor Arsenicalis* because I had asked Dr. Dimsdale about it when I first noticed the smell."

The coroner wrote down this answer and then, raising his head, looked steadily at Madeline for some seconds without speaking, and the jury looked harder still. At length the former spoke – slowly, deliberately, emphatically.

"You have told us that you examined this medicine to find out what it contained, and that you were able to recognize Tincture of Cardamoms by its colour and *Liquor Arsenicalis* by its smell. It would seem, then, that you know a good deal about drugs. Is that so?"

"I know something about drugs. My father was a doctor and he taught me simple dispensing so that I could help him."

The coroner nodded. "Was there any reason why you should have taken so much interest in the composition of the deceased's medicine?"

Madeline did not answer immediately. And as she stood trembling and hesitating in evident confusion, the coroner gazed at her stonily, and the jury craned forward to catch her reply.

"I used to examine his medicine," she replied at length, in a low voice and a reluctant and confused manner, "because I knew that it often contained *Liquor Arsenicalis*, and I used to wonder whether that was good for him. I understood from my father that it was a rather irritating drug, and it did not seem very suitable for a patient who suffered from gastritis."

There was a pause after she had spoken, and something in the appearance of the inquisitors, almost as if they had been a little disappointed by this eminently reasonable answer. At length the coroner broke the silence by asking, with a slight softening of manner, "You have said that the change in colour of the last medicine led you to taste and smell it to ascertain if the other ingredients had been changed. You have said that you decided that they had not been changed. Are you sure of that? Can you swear that the smell of lavender was not stronger in this bottle than in the previous ones?"

"It did not seem to me to be stronger."

"Supposing the bottle had then contained as much *Liquor Arsenicalis* as was found in it by the analysts – would you have been able to detect it by the smell or otherwise?"

"Yes, I feel sure that I should. The analysts found three ounces of *Liquor Arsenicalis*. That would be nearly half the bottle. I am sure I should have detected that amount, not only by the strong smell, but by the colour, too."

"You are sure that the colour of this medicine was due to Cardamoms only?"

"Yes, that is to cochineal. I recognized it at once. It is perfectly unmistakable and quite different from the colour of Red Sandalwood, with which *Liquor Arsenicalis* is coloured. Besides, this medicine was only a deepish pink in colour. But if three ounces of *Liquor Arsenicalis* had been in the bottle, the medicine would have been quite a dark red."

"You have had some experience in dispensing. Do you consider it possible that the *Liquor Arsenicalis* could have been put into the medicine by mistake when it was being made up?"

"It would be quite impossible if a minim measure-glass was used, as the glass would have had to be filled twelve times. But this is never done. One does not measure large quantities in small measures. Three ounces would be measured out in a four or five ounce measure, as a rule, or, possibly in a two ounce measure, by half refilling it."

"Might not the wrong measure-glass have been taken up by mistake?"

"That is, of course, just possible. But it is most unlikely, for the great disproportion between the large measure-glass and the little stock-bottle would be so striking that it could hardly fail to be noticed."

"Then, from your own observation and from Dr. Dimsdale's evidence, you reject the idea that a mistake may have been made in dispensing this bottle of medicine?"

"Yes, entirely. I have heard Dr. Dimsdale's evidence and I examined the medicine. I am convinced that he could not have made a mistake under the circumstances that he described, and I am certain that the medicine that I saw did not contain more than a small quantity – less than a drachm – of *Liquor Arsenicalis*."

"You are not forgetting that the analysts actually found the equivalent of three ounces of *Liquor Arsenicalis* in the bottle?"

"No. But I am sure it was not there when I examined the bottle."

The coroner wrote down this answer with a deliberate air, and, when he had finished, turned to the jury.

"I think we have nothing more to ask this witness, unless there is any point that you want made more clear."

There was a brief silence. Then the super-intelligent juryman interposed.

"I should like to know if this witness ever had any *Liquor Arsenicalis* in her possession."

The coroner held up a warning hand to Madeline, and replied, "That question, sir, is not admissible. It is a principle of English law that a witness cannot be compelled to make a statement incriminating him – or herself. But an affirmative answer to this question would be an incriminating statement."

"But I am perfectly willing to answer the question," Madeline said eagerly. "I have never had in my possession any *Liquor Arsenicalis*, or any other preparation of arsenic."

"That answers your question, sir," said the coroner, as he wrote down the answer, "and if you have nothing more to ask, we can release the witness."

He handed his pen to Madeline, and when she had signed her depositions – a terribly shaky signature it must have been – she came back to her chair, still very pale and agitated, but obviously relieved at having got through the ordeal. I had taken her arm as she sat down and was complimenting her on the really admirable way in which she had given her evidence, when I heard the name of Anthony Wallingford called and realized that another unpleasant episode had arrived.

Chapter VI
The Verdict

I had not been taking much notice of Wallingford, my attention being occupied with the two women when it strayed from the proceedings. Beyond an irritated consciousness of his usual restless movements, I had no information as to how the soul-shaking incidents of this appalling day were affecting him. But when he rose drunkenly and, grasping the back of his chair, rolled his eyes wildly round the Court, I realized that there were breakers ahead.

When I say that he rose drunkenly, I use the word advisedly. Familiar as I was with his peculiarities – his jerkings, twitchings, and grimacings – I saw, at once, that there was something unusual both in his face and in his bearing, a dull wildness of expression and an uncertainty of movement that I had never observed before. He had not come to the Court with the rest of us, preferring, for some reason, to come alone. And I now suspected that he had taken the opportunity to fortify himself on the way.

I was not the only observer of his condition. As he walked, with deliberate care, from his seat to the table, I noticed the coroner eyeing him critically and the jury exchanging dubious glances and whispered comments. He made a bad start by dropping the book on the floor and sniggering nervously as he stooped to pick it up, and I could see plainly, by the stiffness of the coroner's manner, that he had made an unfavourable impression before he began his evidence.

"You were secretary to the deceased?" said the coroner, when the witness had stated his name, age (33), and occupation. "What was the nature of your duties?"

"The ordinary duties of a secretary," was the dogged reply.

"Will you kindly give us particulars of what you did for the deceased?"

"I opened his business letters and answered them and some of his private ones. And I kept his accounts and paid his bills."

"What accounts would those be? The deceased was not in business, I understand?"

"No, they were his domestic accounts – his income from investments and rents and his expenditure."

"Did you attend upon the deceased personally, I mean in the way of looking after his bodily comfort and supplying his needs?"

"I used to look in on him from time to time to see if he wanted anything done. But it wasn't my business to wait on him. I was his secretary, not his valet."

"Who did wait on him, and attend to his wants?"

"The housemaid, chiefly, and Miss Norris, and of course, Mrs. Monkhouse. But he didn't usually want much but his food, his medicine, a few books from the library, and a supply of candles for his lamp. His bell-push was connected with a bell in my room at night, but he never rang it."

"Then, practically, the housemaid did everything for him?"

"Not everything. Miss Norris cooked most of his meals. We all used to give him his medicine. I used to put out his books and keep his fountain pen filled, and Mrs. Monkhouse kept his candle-box supplied. That was what he was most particular about, as he slept badly and used to read at night."

"You give us the impression, Mr. Wallingford," the coroner said, drily, "that you must have had a good deal of leisure."

"Then I have given you the wrong impression. I was kept constantly on the go, doing jobs, paying tradesmen, shopping and running errands."

"For whom?"

"Everybody. The deceased, Mrs. Monkhouse, Miss Norris, and even Dr. Dimsdale. I was everybody's servant."

"What did you do for Mrs. Monkhouse?"

"I don't see what that has got to do with this inquest."

"That is not for you to decide," the coroner said, sternly. "You will be good enough to answer my question."

Wallingford winced as if he had had his ears cuffed. In a moment, his insolence evaporated and I could see his hands shaking as he, evidently, cudgelled his brains for a reply. Suddenly he seemed to have struck an idea.

"Shopping of various kinds," said he. "For instance, there were the candles for the deceased. His lamp was of German make and English lamp-candles wouldn't fit it. So I used to have to go to a German shop at Sparrow Corner by the Tower, to get packets of Schneider's stearine candles. That took about half-a-day."

The coroner, stolidly and without comment, wrote down the answer, but my experience as a counsel told me that it had been a dummy question, asked to distract the witness's attention and cover a more significant one that was to follow. For that question I waited expectantly, and when it came my surmise was confirmed.

"And Dr. Dimsdale? What did you have to do for him?"

294

"I used to help him with his books sometimes when he hadn't got a dispenser. I am a pretty good accountant and he isn't."

"Where does Dr. Dimsdale do his bookkeeping?"

"At the desk in the surgery."

"And is that where you used to work?"

"Yes."

"Used Dr. Dimsdale to work with you or did you do the books by yourself?"

"I usually worked by myself."

"At what time in the day used you to work there?"

"In the afternoon, as a rule."

"At what hours does Dr. Dimsdale visit his patients?"

"Most of the day. He goes out about ten and finishes about six or seven."

"So that you would usually be alone in the surgery?"

"Yes, usually."

As the coroner wrote down the answer, I noticed the super-intelligent juryman fidgeting in his seat. At length he burst out, "Is the poison cupboard in the surgery?"

The coroner looked interrogatively at Wallingford, who stared at him blankly in sudden confusion.

"You heard the question? Is the poison cupboard there?"

"I don't know. It may be. It wasn't any business of mine."

"Is there any cupboard in the surgery? You must know that."

"Yes, there is a cupboard there, but I don't know what is in it."

"Did you never see it open?"

"No. Never."

"And you never had the curiosity to look into it?"

"Of course I didn't. Besides, I couldn't. It was locked."

"Was it always locked when you were there?"

"Yes, always."

"Are you certain of that?"

"Yes, perfectly certain."

Here the super-intelligent juror looked as if he were about to spring across the table as he demanded eagerly, "How does the witness know that that cupboard was locked?"

The coroner looked slightly annoyed. He had been playing his fish carefully and was in no wise helped by this rude jerk of the line. Nevertheless, he laid down his pen and looked expectantly at the witness. As for Wallingford, he was struck speechless. Apparently his rather muddled brain had suddenly taken in the import of the question, for he stood with dropped jaw and damp, pallid face, staring at the juryman in utter consternation.

"Well?" said the coroner, after an interval. "How did you know that it was locked?"

Wallingford pulled himself together by an effort and replied, "Why, I knew – I knew, of course, that it must be locked."

"Yes, but the question is, *how* did you know?"

"Why, it stands to reason that it must have been locked."

"Why does it stand to reason? Cupboards are not always locked."

"Poison cupboards are. Besides, you heard Dimsdale say that he always kept this cupboard locked. He showed you the key."

Once more the coroner, having noted the answer, laid down his pen and looked steadily at the witness.

"Now, Mr. Wallingford," said he, "I must caution you to be careful as to what you say. This is a serious matter, and you are giving evidence on oath. You said just now that you did not know whether the poison cupboard was or was not in the surgery. You said that you did not know what was in that cupboard. Now you say that you knew the cupboard must have been locked because it was the poison cupboard. Then it seems that you *did* know that it was the poison cupboard. Isn't that so?"

"No. I didn't know then. I do now because I heard Dimsdale say that it was."

"Then, you said that you were perfectly certain that the cupboard was always locked whenever you were working there. That meant that you knew positively, as a fact, that it was locked. Now you say that you knew that it must be locked. But that is an assumption, an opinion, a belief. Now, a man of your education must know the difference between a mere belief and actual knowledge. Will you, please, answer definitely: Did you, or did you not, know as a fact whether that cupboard was or was not locked?"

"Well, I didn't actually know, but I took it for granted that it was locked."

"You did not try the door?"

"Certainly not. Why should I?"

"Very well. Does any gentleman of the jury wish to ask any further questions about this cupboard?"

There was a brief silence. Then the foreman said, "We should like the witness to say what he means and not keep contradicting himself."

"You hear that, sir," said the coroner. "Please be more careful in your answers in future. Now, I want to ask you about that last bottle of medicine. Did you notice anything unusual in its appearance?"

"No. I didn't notice it at all. I didn't know that it had come."

"Did you go into the deceased's room on that day – the Wednesday?"

"Yes, I went to see him in the morning about ten o'clock and gave him a dose of his medicine, and I looked in on him in the evening about nine o'clock to see if he wanted anything, but he didn't."

"Did you give him any medicine then?"

"No. It was not due for another hour."

"What was his condition then?"

"He looked about the same as usual. He seemed inclined to doze, so I did not stay long."

"Is that the last time you saw him alive?"

"No. I looked in again just before eleven. He was then in much the same state – rather drowsy – and, at his request, I turned out the gas and left him."

"Did you light the candle?"

"No, he always did that himself, if he wanted it."

"Did you give him any medicine?"

"No. He had just had a dose."

"Did he tell you that he had?"

"No. I could see that there was a dose gone."

"From which bottle was that?"

"There was only one bottle there. It must have been the new bottle, as only one dose had been taken."

"What colour was the medicine?"

Wallingford hesitated a moment or two as if suspecting a trap. Then he replied, doggedly, "I don't know. I told you I didn't notice it."

"You said that you didn't notice it at all and didn't know that it had come. Now you say that you observed that only one dose had been taken from it and that you inferred that it was the new bottle. Which of those statements is the true one?"

"They are both true," Wallingford protested in a whining tone. "I meant that I didn't notice the medicine particularly, and that I didn't know when it came."

"That is not what you said," the coroner rejoined. "However, we will let that pass. Is there anything more that you wish to ask this witness, gentlemen? If not, we will release him and take the evidence of Mr. Mayfield."

I think the jury would have liked to bait Wallingford but apparently could not think of any suitable questions. But they watched him malevolently as he added his – probably quite illegible – signature to his depositions and followed him with their eyes as he tottered shakily back to his seat. Immediately afterwards my name was called and I took my place at the table, not without a slight degree of nervousness for, though I was well enough used to examinations, it was in the capacity of examiner, not of witness, and I was fully alive to the possibility of certain pitfalls which the coroner might, if he were wide enough awake, dig for me. However, when I had been sworn and had given my particulars (*Rupert Mayfield, 35, Barrister-at-Law, of No. 64 Fig Tree Court, Inner Temple*) the coroner's conciliatory manner led me to hope that it would be all plain sailing.

"How long have you known the deceased?" was the first question.

"About two-and-a-half years," I replied.

"You are one of the executors of his will, Mrs. Monkhouse has told us."

"Yes."

"Do you know why you were appointed executor after so short an acquaintance?"

"I am an old friend of Mrs. Monkhouse. I have known her since she was a little girl. I was a friend of her father – or rather, her stepfather."

"Was it by her wish that you were made executor?"

"I believe that the suggestion came from the deceased's family solicitor, Mr. Brodribb, who is my co-executor. But probably he was influenced by my long acquaintance with Mrs. Monkhouse."

"Has probate been applied for?"

"Yes."

"Then there can be no objections to your disclosing the provisions of the will. We don't want to hear them in detail, but I will ask you to give us a general idea of the disposal of the deceased's property."

"The gross value of the estate is about fifty-five thousand pounds, of which twelve-thousand represents real property and forty-three thousand personal. The principal beneficiaries are: Mrs. Monkhouse, who receives a house valued at four-thousand pounds and twenty-thousand pounds in money and securities, the Reverend Amos Monkhouse, land of the value of five-thousand and ten-thousand invested money, Madeline Norris, a house and land valued at three-thousand and five-thousand in securities, Anthony Wallingford, four-thousand pounds. Then there are legacies of a thousand pounds each to the two executors, and of three-hundred, two-hundred, and one-hundred respectively to the housemaid, the cook, and the kitchen-maid. That accounts for the bulk of the estate. Mrs. Monkhouse is the residuary legatee."

The coroner wrote down the answer as I gave it and then read it out slowly for me to confirm, working out, at the same time, a little sum on a spare piece of paper – as did also the intellectual juryman.

"I think that gives us all the information we want," the former remarked, glancing at the jury, and as none of them made any comment, he proceeded, "Did you see much of the deceased during the last few months?"

"I saw him usually once or twice a week. Sometimes oftener. But I did not spend much time with him. He was a solitary, bookish man who preferred to be alone most of his time."

"Did you take particular notice of his state of health?"

"No, but I did observe that his health seemed to grow rather worse lately."

"Did it appear to you that he received such care and attention as a man in his condition ought to have received?"

"It did not appear to me that he was neglected."

"Did you realize how seriously ill he was?"

"No. I am afraid not. I regarded him merely as a chronic invalid."

"It never occurred to you that he ought to have had a regular nurse?"

"No, and I do not think he would have consented. He greatly disliked having anyone about his room."

"Is there anything within your knowledge that would throw any light on the circumstances of his death?"

"No. Nothing."

"Have you ever known arsenic in any form to be used in that household for any purpose – any fly-papers, weed-killer or insecticides, for instance?"

"No, I do not remember ever having seen anything used in that household which, to my knowledge or belief, contained arsenic."

"Do you know of any fact or circumstance which, in your opinion, ought to be communicated to this Court or which might help the jury in arriving at their verdict?"

"No, I do not."

This brought my examination to an end. I was succeeded by the cook and the kitchen-maid but, as they had little to tell, and that little entirely negative, their examination was quite brief. When the last witness was dismissed, the coroner addressed the jury.

"We have now, gentlemen," said he, "heard all the evidence that is at present available, and we have the choice of two courses, which are either to adjourn the inquiry until further evidence is available, or to find a verdict on the evidence which we have heard. I incline strongly to the latter plan. We are now in a position to answer the questions, how, when, and where the deceased came by his death, and when we have done that, we shall have discharged our proper function. What is your feeling on the matter, gentlemen?"

The jury's feeling was very obviously that they wished to get the inquiry over and go about their business, and when they had made this clear, the coroner proceeded to sum up.

"I shall not detain you, gentlemen, with a long address. All that is necessary is for me to recapitulate the evidence very briefly and point out the bearing of it.

"First as to the cause of death. It has been given in evidence by two fully qualified and expert witnesses that the deceased died from the effects of poisoning by arsenic. That is a matter of fact which is not disputed and which you must accept, unless you have any reasons for rejecting their testimony, which I feel sure you have not. Accepting the fact of death by poison, the question then arises as to how the poison came to be taken by the deceased. There are three possibilities: He may have taken it himself, voluntarily and knowingly. He may have taken it by accident or mischance, or it may have been administered to him knowingly and maliciously by some other person or persons. Let us consider those three possibilities.

"The suggestion that the deceased might have taken the poison voluntarily is highly improbable in three respects. First, since he was mostly bed-ridden, it would have been almost impossible for him to have obtained the poison. Second, there is the nature of the poison. Arsenic has often been used for homicidal poisoning but seldom for suicide, for an excellent reason. The properties of arsenic which commend it to poisoners – its complete freedom from taste and the indefinite symptoms that it produces – do not commend it to the suicide. He has no need to conceal either the administration or its results. His principal need is rapidity of effect. But arsenic is a relatively slow poison and one which usually causes great suffering. It is not at all suited to the suicide. Then there is the third objection that the mode of administration was quite unlike that of a suicide. For the latter usually takes his poison in one large dose, to get the business over, but here it was evidently given in repeated small doses over a period that may have been anything from a week to a year. And, finally, there is not a particle of evidence in favour of the supposition that the deceased took the poison himself.

"To take the second case, that of accident: The only possibility known to us is that of a mistake in dispensing the medicine. But the evidence of Dr. Dimsdale and Miss Norris must have convinced you that the improbability of a mistake is so great as to be practically negligible. Of course, the poison might have found its way accidentally into the medicine or the food or both in some manner unknown to us. But while we admit this, we have, in fact, to form our decision on what is known to us, not what is conceivable but unknown.

300

"When we come to the third possibility, that the poison was administered to the deceased by some other person or persons with intent to compass his death, we find it supported by positive evidence. There is the bottle of medicine for instance. It contained a large quantity of arsenic in a soluble form. But two witnesses have sworn that it could not have contained, and, in fact, *did not* contain, that quantity of arsenic when it left Dr. Dimsdale's surgery or when it was delivered at the deceased's house. Moreover, Miss Norris has sworn that she examined this bottle of medicine at six o'clock in the evening and that it did not then contain more than a small quantity – less than a drachm – of *Liquor Arsenicalis*. She was perfectly positive. She spoke with expert knowledge. She gave her reasons, and they were sound reasons. So that the evidence in our possession is to the effect that at six o'clock in the afternoon, that bottle of medicine did not contain more than a drachm – about a teaspoonful – of *Liquor Arsenicalis*, whereas at half-past-ten, when a dose from the bottle was given to the deceased by the housemaid, it contained some three ounces – about six tablespoonfuls. This is proved by the discovery of the poison in the stomach of the deceased and by the exact analysis of the contents of the bottle. It follows that, between six o'clock and half-past-ten, a large quantity of arsenical solution must have been put into the bottle. It is impossible to suppose that it could have got in by accident. Somebody must have put it in, and the only conceivable object that the person could have had in putting that poison into the bottle would be to cause the death of the deceased.

"But further, the evidence of the medical witnesses proves that arsenic had been taken by the deceased on several previous occasions. That, in fact, he had been taking arsenic in relatively small doses for some time past – how long we do not know – and had been suffering from chronic arsenical poisoning. The evidence, therefore, points very strongly and definitely to the conclusion that some person or persons had been, for some unascertained time past, administering arsenic to him.

"Finally, as to the identity of the person or persons who administered the poison, I need not point out that we have no evidence. You will have noticed that a number of persons benefit in a pecuniary sense by the deceased's death. But that fact establishes no suspicion against any of them in the absence of positive evidence, and there is no positive evidence connecting any one of them with the administration of the poison. With these remarks, gentlemen, I leave you to consider the evidence and agree upon your decision."

The jury did not take long in arriving at their verdict. After a few minutes' eager discussion, the foreman announced that they had come to an unanimous decision.

301

"And what is the decision upon which you have agreed?" the coroner asked.

"We find," was the reply, "that the deceased died from the effects of arsenic, administered to him by some person or persons unknown, with the deliberate intention of causing his death."

"Yes," said the coroner, "that is, in effect, a verdict of wilful murder against some person or persons unknown. I agree with you entirely. No other verdict was possible on the evidence before us. It is unfortunate that no clue has happened as to the perpetrator of this abominable crime, but we may hope that the investigations of the police will result in the identification and conviction of the murderer."

The conclusion of the coroner's address brought the proceedings to an end and, as he finished speaking, the spectators rose and began to pass out of the Court. I remained for a minute to speak a few words to Mr. Holman and ask him to transcribe his report in duplicate. Then, I, too, went out to find my three companions squeezing into a taxicab which had drawn up opposite the entrance, watched with ghoulish curiosity by a quite considerable crowd. The presence of that crowd informed me that the horrible notoriety which I had foreseen had even now begun to envelop us. The special editions of the evening papers were already out, with, at least, the opening scenes of the inquest in print. Indeed, during the short drive to Hilborough Square, I saw more than one news-vendor dealing out papers to little knots of eager purchasers, and once, through the open window, a stentorian voice was borne in with hideous distinctness, announcing, "Sensational Inquest! Funeral stopped!"

Chapter VII
The Search Warrant

The consciousness of the horrid notoriety that had already attached itself to us was brought home to me once more when the taxi drew up at the house in Hilborough Square. I stepped out first to pay the driver, and Barbara following, with the latch-key ready in her hand, walked swiftly to the door, looking neither to the right nor left, opened it and disappeared into the hall, while the other two, lurking in the cab until the door was open, then darted across the pavement, entered and disappeared also. Nor was their hasty retreat unjustified. Lingering doggedly and looking about me with a sort of resentful defiance, I found myself a focus of observation. In the adjoining houses, not a window appeared to be unoccupied. The usually vacant foot-way was populous with loiterers whose interest in me and in the ill-omened house was undissembled, while mucous voices, strange to those quiet precincts, told me that the astute news-vendors had scented and exploited a likely market.

With ill-assumed indifference I entered the house and shut the door – perhaps rather noisily – and was about to enter the dining room when I heard hurried steps descending the stairs and paused to look up. It was the woman – the cook's sister, I think – who had been left to take care of the house while the servants were absent, and something of eagerness and excitement in her manner caused me to walk to the foot of the stairs to meet her.

"Is anything amiss?" I asked in a low voice as she neared the bottom of the flight.

She held up a warning finger, and coming close to me, whispered hoarsely: "There's two gentlemen upstairs. sir – leastways they look like gentlemen, but they are really policemen."

"What are they doing upstairs?" I asked.

"Just walking through the rooms and looking about. They came about a quarter-of-an-hour ago, and when I let them in they said they were police officers and that they had come to search the premises."

"Did they say anything about a warrant?"

"Oh, yes, sir. I forgot about that. One of them showed me a paper and said it was a search warrant. So of course I couldn't do anything. And then they started going through the house with their notebooks like auctioneers getting ready for a sale."

"I will go up and see them," said I, "and meanwhile you had better let Mrs. Monkhouse know. Where did you leave them?"

"In the large back bedroom on the first floor," she replied. "I think it was Mr. Monkhouse's."

On this I began quickly to ascend the stairs, struggling to control a feeling of resentment which, though natural enough, I knew to be quite unreasonable. Making my way direct to the dead man's room, I entered and found two tall men standing before an open cupboard. They turned on hearing me enter and the elder of them drew a large wallet from his pocket.

"Mr. Mayfield, I think, sir," said he. "I am Detective Superintendent Miller and this is Detective-Sergeant Cope. Here is my card and this is the search warrant, if you wish to see it."

I glanced at the document and returning it to him asked, "Wouldn't it have been more in order if you had waited to show the warrant to Mrs. Monkhouse before beginning your search?"

"That is what we have done," he replied, suavely. "We have disturbed nothing yet. We have just been making a preliminary inspection. Of course," he continued, "I understand how unpleasant this search is for Mrs. Monkhouse and the rest of your friends, but you, sir, as a lawyer will realize the position. That poor gentleman was poisoned with arsenic in this house. Somebody in this house had arsenic in his or her possession, and we have got to see if any traces of it are left. After all, you know, sir, we are acting in the interests of everybody but the murderer."

This was so obviously true that it left me nothing to say. Nor was there any opportunity, for, as the superintendent concluded, Barbara entered the room. I looked at her a little anxiously as I briefly explained the situation. But there was no occasion. Pale and sombre of face, she was nevertheless perfectly calm and self-possessed and greeted the two officers without a trace of resentment – indeed, when the superintendent was disposed to be apologetic, she cut him short by exclaiming energetically, "But, surely, who should be more anxious to assist you than I? It is true that I find it incredible that this horrible crime could have been perpetrated by any member of my household. But it was perpetrated by somebody. And if, either here or elsewhere, I can help you in any way to drag that wretch out into the light of day, I am at your service, no matter who the criminal may be. Do you wish anyone to attend you in your search?"

"I think, Madam, it would be well if you were present, and perhaps Mr. Mayfield. If we want any of the others, we can send for them. Where are they now?"

"Miss Norris and Mr. Wallingford are in the dining room. The servants have just come in and I think have gone to the kitchen or their sitting room."

"Then," said Miller, "we had better begin with the dining room."

We went down the stairs, preceded by Barbara, who opened the dining room door and introduced the visitors to the two inmates in tones as quiet and matter-of-fact as if she were announcing the arrival of the gas-fitter or the upholsterer. I was sorry that the other two had not been warned, for the announcement took them both by surprise and they were in no condition for surprises of this rather alarming kind. At the word "search", Madeline started up with a smothered exclamation and then sat down again, trembling and pale as death, while as for Wallingford, if the two officers had come to pinion him and lead him forth to the gallows, he could not have looked more appalled.

Our visitors were scrupulously polite, but they were also keenly observant and I could see that each had made a mental note of the effect of their arrival. But, of course, they made no outward sign of interest in any of us but proceeded stolidly with their business, and I noticed that, before proceeding to a detailed inspection, they opened their notebooks and glanced through what was probably a rough inventory, to see that nothing had been moved in the interval since their preliminary inspection.

The examination of the dining room was, however, rather perfunctory. It contained nothing that appeared to interest them, and after going through the contents of the sideboard cupboards methodically, the superintendent turned a leaf of his notebook and said, "I think that will do, Madam. Perhaps we had better take the library next. Who keeps the keys of the bureau and the cupboard?"

"Mr. Wallingford has charge of the library," replied Barbara. "Will you give the superintendent your keys, Tony?"

"There's no need for that," said Miller. "If Mr. Wallingford will come with us, he can unlock the drawers and cupboard and tell us anything that we want to know about the contents."

Wallingford rose with a certain alacrity and followed us into the library, which adjoined the dining room. Here the two officers again consulted their notebooks and, having satisfied themselves that the room was as they had left it, began a detailed survey, watched closely and with evident anxiety by Wallingford. They began with a cupboard, or small armoire, which formed the upper member of a large, old-fashioned bureau. Complying with Miller's polite request that it might be unlocked, Wallingford produced a bunch of keys, and, selecting from it, after much nervous fumbling, a small key, endeavoured to insert it into the keyhole,

305

but his hand was in such a palsied condition that he was unable to introduce it.

"Shall I have a try, sir?" the superintendent suggested, patiently, adding with a smile, "I don't smoke quite so many cigarettes as you seem to."

His efforts, however, also failed, for the evident reason that it was the wrong key. Thereupon he looked quickly through the bunch, picked out another key and had the cupboard open in a twinkling, revealing a set of shelves crammed with a disorderly litter of cardboard boxes, empty ink-bottles, bundles of letters and papers, and the miscellaneous rubbish that accumulates in the receptacles of a thoroughly untidy man. The superintendent went through the collection methodically, emptying the shelves, one at a time, on to the flap of the bureau, where he and the sergeant sorted the various articles and, examining each, returned it to the shelf. It was a tedious proceeding and, so far as I could judge, unproductive, for when all the shelves had been looked through and every article separately inspected, nothing was brought to light, save an empty foolscap envelope which had apparently once contained a small box and was addressed to Wallingford, and two pieces of what looked like chemist's wrapping-paper, the creases in which showed that they had been small packets. These were not returned to the shelves, but, without comment, enclosed in a large envelope on which the superintendent scribbled a few words with a pencil and which was then consigned to a large handbag that the sergeant had brought in with him from the hall.

The large drawers of the bureau were next examined. Like the shelves, they were filled with a horrible accumulation of odds-and-ends which had evidently been stuffed into them to get them out of the way. From this collection nothing was obtained which interested the officers, who next turned their attention to the small drawers and pigeonholes at the back of the flap. These, however, contained nothing but stationery and a number of letters, bills, and other papers, which the two officers glanced through and replaced. When all the small drawers and pigeonholes had been examined, the superintendent stood up, fixing a thoughtful glance at the middle of the range of drawers, and I waited expectantly for the next development. Like many old bureaus, this one had as a central feature a nest of four very small drawers enclosed by a door. I knew the arrangement very well, and so, apparently, did the superintendent, for, once more opening the top drawer, he pulled it right out and laid it on the writing flap. Then, producing from his pocket a folding foot-rule, he thrust it into one of the pigeonholes, showing a depth of eight-and-a-half inches, and then into the case of the little drawer, which proved to be only a fraction over five inches deep.

"There is something more here than meets the eye," he remarked pleasantly. "Do you know what is at the back of those drawers, Mr. Wallingford?"

The unfortunate secretary, who had been watching the officer's proceedings with a look of consternation, did not reply for a few moments, but remained staring wildly at the aperture from which the drawer had been taken out.

"At the back?" he stammered, at length. "No, I can't say that I do. It isn't my bureau, you know. I only had the use of it."

"I see," said Miller. "Well, I expect we can soon find out."

He drew out a second drawer and, grasping the partition between the two, gave a gentle pull, when the whole nest slid easily forward and came right out of its case. Miller laid it on the writing flap, and, turning it round, displayed a sliding lid at the back, which he drew up, when there came into view a set of four little drawers similar to those in front but furnished with leather tabs instead of handles. Miller drew out the top drawer and a sudden change in the expression on his face told me that he had lighted on something that seemed to him significant.

"Now I wonder what this is?" said he, taking from the drawer a small white-paper packet. "Feels like some sort of powder. You say you don't know anything about it, Mr. Wallingford?"

Wallingford shook his head but made no further reply, whereupon the superintendent laid the packet on the flap and very carefully unfolded the ends – it had already been opened – when it was seen that the contents consisted of some two or three teaspoonfuls of a fine, white powder.

"Well," said Miller, "we shall have to find out what it is. Will you pass me that bit of sealing-wax, Sergeant?"

He reclosed the packet with the greatest care and having sealed both the ends with his signet-ring, enclosed it in an envelope and put it into his inside breast pocket. Then he returned to the little nest of drawers. The second drawer was empty, but on pulling out the third, he uttered an exclamation.

"Well, now! Look at that! Somebody seems to have been fond of physic. And there's no doubt as to what this is. *Morphine hydrochlor*, a quarter-of-a-grain."

As he spoke, he took out of the drawer a little bottle filled with tiny white discs or tablets and bearing on the label the inscription which the superintendent had read out. Wallingford gazed at it with a foolish expression of surprise as Miller held it up for our – and particularly

Wallingford's – inspection, and Barbara, I noticed, cast at the latter a side-long inscrutable glance which I sought in vain to interpret.

"Morphine doesn't seem much to the point," Miller remarked as he wrapped the little bottle in paper and bestowed it in his inner pocket, "but, of course, we have only got the evidence of the label. It may turn out to be something else, when the chemical gentlemen come to test it."

With this he grasped the tab of the bottom drawer and drew the latter out, and in a moment his face hardened. Very deliberately, he picked out a small, oblong envelope which appeared once to have contained a box or hard packet, but was now empty. It had evidently come through the post and was addressed in a legible business hand to "*A. Wallingford Esq., 16 Hilborough Square*". Silently the superintendent held it out for us all to see, as he fixed a stern look on Wallingford. "You observe, sir," he said, at length, "that the post-mark is dated the twentieth of August, only about a month ago. What have you to say about it?"

"Nothing," was the sullen reply. "What comes to me by post is my affair. I am not accountable to you or anybody else."

For a moment, the superintendent's face took on a very ugly expression. But he seemed to be a wise man and not unkindly, for he quickly controlled his irritation and rejoined without a trace of anger, though gravely enough, "Be advised by me, Mr. Wallingford, and don't make trouble for yourself. Let me remind you what the position is. In this house a man has died from arsenic poisoning. The police will have to find out how that happened and if anyone is open to the suspicion of having poisoned him. I have come here today for that purpose with full authority to search this house. In the course of my search, I have asked you for certain information, and you have made a number of false statements. Believe me, sir, that is a very dangerous thing to do. It inevitably raises the question why those false statements should have been made. Now, I am going to ask you one or two questions. You are not bound to answer them, but you will be well-advised to hold nothing back, and, above all, to say nothing that is not true. To begin with that packet of powder. What do you say that packet contains?"

Wallingford, who, characteristically, was now completely cowed by the superintendent's thinly-veiled threats, hung his head for a moment and then replied, almost inaudibly, "Cocaine."

"What were you going to do with cocaine?" Miller asked.

"I was going to take a little of it for my health."

The superintendent smiled faintly as he demanded, "And the morphine tablets?"

"I had thought of taking one of them occasionally to – er – to steady my nerves."

Miller nodded, and casting a swift glance at the sergeant, asked, "And the packet that was in this envelope? What did that contain?"

Wallingford hesitated and was so obviously searching for a plausible lie that Miller interposed, persuasively, "Better tell the truth and not make trouble," whereupon Wallingford replied in a barely audible mumble that the packet had contained a very small quantity of cocaine.

"What has become of that cocaine?" the superintendent asked.

"I took part of it, the rest got spilt and lost."

Miller nodded rather dubiously at this reply and then asked, "Where did you get this cocaine and the morphine?"

Wallingford hesitated for some time and at length, plucking up a little courage again, replied, "I would rather not answer that question. It really has nothing to do with your search. You are looking for arsenic."

Miller reflected for a few moments and then rejoined, quietly, "That isn't quite correct, Mr. Wallingford. I am looking for anything that may throw light on the death of Mr. Monkhouse. But I don't want to press you unduly, only I would point out that you could not have come by these drugs lawfully. You are not a doctor or a chemist. Whoever supplied you with them was acting illegally and you have been a party to an illegal transaction in obtaining them. However, if you refuse to disclose the names of the persons who supplied them, we will let the matter pass, at least for the present, but I remind you that you have had these drugs in your possession and that you may be, and probably will be compelled to give an account of the way in which you obtained them."

With that he pocketed the envelope, closed the drawers, and turned to make a survey of the room. There was very little in it, however, for the bureau and its surmounting cupboard were the only receptacles in which anything could be concealed, the whole of the walls being occupied by open book-shelves about seven feet high. But even these the superintendent was not prepared to take at their face value. First, he stood on a chair and ran his eye slowly along the tops of all the shelves, then he made a leisurely tour of the room, closely inspecting each row of books, now and again taking one out or pushing one in against the back of the shelves. A set of box-files was examined in detail, each one being opened to ascertain that it contained nothing but papers, and even one or two obvious portfolios were taken out and inspected. Nothing noteworthy, however, was brought to light by this rigorous search until the tour of inspection was nearly completed. The superintendent was, in fact, approaching the door when his attention was attracted by a row of books which seemed to be unduly near the front edge of the shelf. Opposite this he halted and began pushing the books back, one at a time. Suddenly I noticed that one of the books, on being pushed, slid back about half-an-inch and stopped, as if there were something behind it. And there was. When the superintendent grasped the book and drew it out, there came into view, standing against the back of the shelf, a smallish bottle, apparently empty, and bearing a white label.

"Queer place to keep a bottle," Miller remarked, adding, with a smile, "unless it were a whisky bottle, which it isn't." He drew it out and, after looking at it suspiciously and holding it up to the light, took out the cork and sniffed at it. "Well," he continued, "it is an empty bottle and it is labelled 'Benzine.' Do you know anything about it, Mr. Wallingford?"

"No, I don't," was the reply. "I don't use benzine, and if I did I should not keep it on a book-shelf. But I don't see that it matters much. There isn't any harm in benzine, is there?"

"Probably not," said Miller, "but, you see, the label doesn't agree with the smell. What do you say, Mrs. Monkhouse?"

He once more drew out the cork and held the bottle towards her. She took it from him and having smelled at it, replied promptly, "It smells to me like lavender. Possibly the bottle has had lavender water in it, though I shouldn't, myself, have chosen a benzine bottle to keep a perfume in."

"I don't think it was lavender water," said the superintendent. "That, I think, is nearly colourless. But the liquid that was in this bottle was red. As I hold it up to the light, you can see a little ring of red round the edge of the bottom. I daresay the chemists will be able to tell us what was in the bottle, but the question now is, who put it there? You are sure you can't tell us anything about it, Mr. Wallingford?"

"I have never seen it before, I assure you," the latter protested almost tearfully. "I know nothing about it, whatsoever. That is the truth, Superintendent, I swear to God it is."

"Very well, sir," said Miller, writing a brief note on the label and making an entry in his notebook. "Perhaps it is of no importance after all. But we shall see. I think we have finished this room. Perhaps, Sergeant, you might take a look at the drawing room while I go through Mr. Monkhouse's room. It will save time. And I needn't trouble you anymore just at present, Mr. Wallingford."

The secretary retired, somewhat reluctantly, to the dining room while Barbara led the way to the first floor. As we entered the room in which that unwitnessed tragedy had been enacted in the dead of the night, I looked about me with a sort of shuddering interest. The bed had been stripped, but otherwise nothing seemed to be changed since I had seen the room but a few days ago when it was still occupied by its dread tenant. The bedside table still bore its pathetic furnishings – the water-bottle, the little decanter, the books, the candle-box, the burnt-out lamp, the watch – though that ticked no longer, but seemed, with its motionless hands, to echo the awesome stillness that pervaded that ill-omened room.

As the superintendent carried out his methodical search, joined presently by the sergeant, Barbara came and stood by me with her eyes fixed gloomily on the table.

"Were you thinking of him, Rupert?" she whispered. "Were you thinking of that awful night when he lay here, dying, all alone, and – Oh! The thought of it will haunt me every day of my life until my time comes, too, however far off that may be."

I was about to make some reply, as consolatory as might be, when the superintendent announced that he had finished and asked that Wallingford might be sent for to be present at the examination of his room. I went down to deliver the message and, as it would have appeared intrusive for me to accompany him, I stayed in the dining room with Madeline who, though she had recovered from the shock of the detectives' arrival, was still pale and agitated.

"Poor Tony seemed dreadfully upset when he came back just now." she said. "What was it that happened in the library?"

"Nothing very much," I answered. "The superintendent unearthed his little stock of dope, which, of course, was unpleasant for him, but it would not have mattered if he had not been fool enough to lie about it. That was a fatal thing to do, under the circumstances."

As Wallingford seemed not to have said anything about the bottle, I made no reference to it, but endeavoured to distract her attention from what was going on in the house by talking of other matters. Nor was it at all difficult, for the truth is that we all, with one accord, avoided any reference to the horrible fact which was staring us in the face, and of which we must all have been fully conscious. So we continued a somewhat banal conversation, punctuated by pauses in which our thoughts stole secretly back to the hideous realities, until, at length, Wallingford returned, pale and scowling, and flung himself into an armchair. Madeline looked at him inquiringly, but as he offered no remark and sat in gloomy silence, smoking furiously, she asked him no questions, nor did I.

A minute or two later, Barbara came into the room, quietly and with an air of calm self-possession that was quite soothing in the midst of the general emotional tension.

"Do you mind coming up, Madeline?" she said. "They are examining your room and they want you to unlock the cupboard. You have your keys about you, I suppose?"

"Yes," Madeline replied, rising and taking from her pocket a little key-wallet. "That is the key. Will you take it up to them?"

"I think you had better come up yourself," Barbara replied. "It is very unpleasant but, of course, they have to go through the formalities, and we must not appear unwilling to help them."

"No, of course," said Madeline. "Then I will come with you, but I should like Rupert to come, too, if he doesn't mind. Will you?" she asked, looking at me appealingly. "Those policemen make me feel so nervous."

Of course, I assented at once, and as Wallingford, muttering "Damned impertinence! Infernal indignity!" rose to open the door for us, we passed out and took our way upstairs.

"I am sorry to trouble you, Miss Norris," said Miller, in a suave tone, as we entered, "but we must see everything if only to be able to say that we have. Would you be so kind as to unlock this cupboard?"

He indicated a narrow cupboard which occupied one of the recesses by the chimney-breast, and Madeline at once inserted the key and threw open the door. The interior was then seen to be occupied by shelves, of which the lower ones were filled, tidily enough, with an assortment of miscellaneous articles – shoes, shoe-trees, brushes, leather bags, cardboard boxes, notebooks, and other "oddments" – while the top shelf seemed to have been used as a repository for jars, pots, and bottles, of which several appeared to be empty. It was this shelf which seemed to attract the superintendent's attention and he began operations by handing out its various contents to the sergeant, who set them down on a table in orderly rows. When they were all set out and the superintendent had inspected narrowly and swept his hand over the empty shelf, the examination of the jars and bottles began.

The procedure was very methodical and thorough. First, the sergeant picked up a bottle or jar, looked it over carefully, read the label if there was one, uncovered or uncorked it, smelled it and passed it to the superintendent, who, when he had made a similar inspection, put it down at the opposite end of the table.

"Can you tell us what this is?" Miller asked, holding out a bottle filled with a thickish, nearly black liquid.

"That is caramel," Madeline replied. "I use it in my cookery classes and for cooking at home, too."

The superintendent regarded the bottle a little dubiously but set it down at the end of the table without comment. Presently he received from the sergeant a glass jar filled with a brownish powder.

"There is no label on this," he remarked, exhibiting it to Madeline.

"No," she replied. "It is turmeric. That also is used in my classes, and that other is powdered saffron."

"I wonder you don't label them," said Miller. "It would be easy for a mistake to occur with all these unlabelled bottles."

"Yes," she admitted, "they ought to be labelled. But I know what each of them is, and they are all pretty harmless. Most of them are materials that are used in cookery demonstrations, but that one that you have now is French chalk, and the one the sergeant has is pumice-powder."

"Hmm," grunted Miller, dipping his finger into the former and rubbing it on his thumb. "What would happen if you thickened a soup with French chalk or pumice-powder? Not very good for the digestion, I should think."

"No, I suppose not," Madeline agreed, with the ghost of a smile on her pale face. "I must label them in future."

During this colloquy, I had been rapidly casting my eye over the collection that still awaited examination, and my attention had been almost at once arrested by an empty bottle near the end of the row. It looked to me like the exact counterpart of the bottle which had been found in the library, a cylindrical bottle of about the capacity of half-a-pint, or rather less, and like the other, labelled in printed characters *'Benzine'*.

But mine was not the only eye that had observed it. Presently, I saw the sergeant pick it up – out of its turn – scrutinize it suspiciously, – hold it up to the light, take out the cork and smell both it and the bottle, and then, directing the latter, telescope-fashion, towards the window, inspect the bottom by peering in through the mouth. Finally, he clapped in the cork with some emphasis, and with a glance full of meaning handed the bottle to the superintendent.

The latter repeated the procedure in even more detail. When he had finished, he turned to Madeline with a distinctly inquisitorial air.

"This bottle, Miss Norris," said he, "is labelled *'Benzine'*. But it was not benzine that it contained. Will you kindly smell it and tell me what you think it did contain. Or perhaps you can say off-hand."

"I am afraid I can't," she replied. "I have no recollection of having had any benzine and I don't remember this bottle at all. As it is in my cupboard I suppose I must have put it there, but I don't remember having ever seen it before. I can't tell you anything about it."

313

"Well, will you kindly smell it and tell me what you think it contained?" the superintendent persisted, handing her the open bottle. She took it from him apprehensively and, holding it to her nose, took a deep sniff, and instantly her already pale face became dead white to the very lips.

"It smells of lavender," she said in a faint voice.

"So I thought," said Miller. "And now, Miss Norris, if you will look in at the mouth of the bottle against the light, you will see a faint red ring round the bottom. Apparently, the liquid that the bottle contained was a red liquid. Moreover, if you hold the bottle against the light and look through the label, you can see the remains of another label under it. There is only a tiny scrap of it left, but it is enough for us to see that it was a red label. So it would seem that the liquid was a poisonous liquid – poisonous enough to require a red poison label. And then you notice that this red poison label seems to have been scraped off and the benzine label stuck on over the place where it had been, although, as the lavender smell and the red stain clearly show, the bottle never had any benzine in it at all. Now, Miss Norris, bearing those facts in mind, I ask you if you can tell me what was in that bottle."

"I have told you," Madeline replied with unexpected firmness, "that I know nothing about this bottle. I have no recollection of ever having seen it before. I do not believe that it ever belonged to me. It may have been in the cupboard when I first began to use it. At any rate, I am not able to tell you anything about it."

The superintendent continued to look at her keenly, still holding the bottle. After a few moments' silence he persisted. "A red, poisonous liquid which smells of lavender. Can you not form any idea as to what it was?"

I was about to enter a protest – for the question was really not admissible – when Madeline, now thoroughly angry and quite self-possessed, replied stiffly, "I don't know what you mean. I have told you that I know nothing about this bottle. Are you suggesting that I should try to guess what it contained?"

"No," he rejoined hastily, "certainly not. A guess wouldn't help us at all. If you really do not know anything about the bottle, we must leave it at that. You always keep this cupboard locked, I suppose?"

"Usually. But I am not very particular about it. There is nothing of value in the cupboard, as you see, and the servants are quite trustworthy. I sometimes leave the key in the door, but I don't imagine that anybody ever meddles with it."

The superintendent took the key out of the lock and regarded it attentively. Then he examined the lock itself, and I also took the

314

opportunity of inspecting it. Both the lock and the key were of the simplest kind, just ordinary builder's fittings, which, so far as any real security was concerned, could not be taken seriously. In the absence of the key, a stiff wire or a bent hair-pin would probably have shot that little bolt quite easily, as I took occasion to remark to the superintendent, who frankly agreed with me.

The bottle having been carefully wrapped up and deposited in the sergeant's hand-bag, the examination was resumed, but nothing further of an interesting or suspicious character was discovered among the bottles or jars. Nor did the sorting-out of the miscellaneous contents of the lower shelves yield anything remarkable with a single exception. When the objects on the lowest shelf had been all taken out, a small piece of white paper was seen at the back, and on this Miller pounced with some eagerness. As he brought it out I could see that it was a chemist's powder paper, about six-inches-square (when Miller had carefully straightened it out), and the creases which marked the places where it had been folded showed that it had contained a mass of about the bulk of a dessert-spoonful. But what attracted my attention – and the superintendent's – was the corner of a red label which adhered to a torn edge in company with a larger fragment of a white label on which the name or description of the contents had presumably been written or printed. Miller held it out towards Madeline, who looked at it with a puzzled frown.

"Do you remember what was in this paper, Miss Norris?" the former asked.

"I am afraid I don't," she replied.

"Hmm," grunted Miller, "I should have thought you would. It seems to have been a good-sized powder and it had a poison label in addition to the descriptive label. I should have thought that would have recalled it to your memory."

"So should I," said Madeline. "But I don't remember having bought any powder that would be labelled 'Poison'. It is very odd, and it is odd that the paper should be there. I don't usually put waste paper into my cupboard."

"Well, there it is," said Miller, "but if you can't remember anything about it, we must see if the analysts can find out what was in it." With which he folded it and having put it into an envelope, bestowed it in his pocket in company with his other treasures.

This was the last of the discoveries. When they had finished their inspection of Madeline's room the officers went on to Barbara's, which they examined with the same minute care as they had bestowed on the others, but without bringing anything of interest to light. Then they inspected the servants' bedrooms and finally the kitchen and the other premises appertaining to it, but still without result. It was a tedious affair and we were all relieved when, at last, it came to an end. Barbara and I escorted the two detectives to the street door, at which the superintendent paused to make a few polite acknowledgments.

"I must thank you, Madam," said he, "for the help you have given us and for the kind and reasonable spirit in which you have accepted a disagreeable necessity. I assure you that we do not usually meet with so much consideration. A search of this kind is always an unpleasant duty to carry out and it is not made any more pleasant by a hostile attitude on the part of the persons concerned."

"I can understand that," replied Barbara, "but really the thanks are due from me for the very courteous and considerate way in which you have discharged what I am sure must be a most disagreeable duty. And of course, it had to be, and I am glad that it has been done so thoroughly. I never supposed that you would find what you are seeking in this house. But it was necessary that the search should be made here if only to prove that you must look for it somewhere else."

"Quite so, Madam," the superintendent returned, a little drily, "and now I will wish you good afternoon and hope that we shall have no further occasion to trouble you."

As I closed the street door and turned back along the hall, the dining room door – apparently already ajar – opened and Madeline and Wallingford stepped out, and I could not help reflecting, as I noted their pale, anxious faces and shaken bearing, how little their appearance supported the confident, optimistic tone of Barbara's last remarks. But, at any rate, they were intensely relieved that the ordeal was over, and Wallingford even showed signs of returning truculence.

Whatever he was going to say, however, was cut short by Barbara, who, passing the door and moving towards the staircase, addressed me over her shoulder.

"Do you mind coming up to my den, Rupert? I want to ask your advice about one or two things."

The request seemed a little inopportune, but it was uttered as a command and I had no choice but to obey. Accordingly, I followed Barbara up the stairs, leaving the other two in the hall, evidently rather disconcerted by this sudden retreat. At the turn of the stairs I looked down on the two pale faces. In Madeline's I seemed to read a new apprehensiveness, tinged with suspicion, on Wallingford's a scowl of furious anger which I had no patience to seek to interpret.

Chapter VIII
Thorndyke Speaks Bluntly

When I had entered the little sitting room and shut the door, I turned to Barbara, awaiting with some curiosity what she had to say to me. But for a while she said nothing, standing before me silently, and looking at me with a most disquieting expression. All her calm self-possession had gone. I could read nothing in her face but alarm and dismay.

"It is dreadful, Rupert!" she exclaimed, at length, in a half-whisper. "It is like some awful dream! What can it all mean? I don't dare to ask myself the question."

I shook my head, for I was in precisely the same condition. I did not dare to weigh the meaning of the things that I had seen and heard.

Suddenly, the stony fixity of her face relaxed and with a little smothered cry she flung her arm around my neck and buried her face on my shoulder.

"Forgive me, Rupert, dearest, kindest friend," she sobbed. "Suffer a poor lonely woman for a few moments. I have only you, dear, faithful one, only your strength and steadfastness to lean upon. Before the others I must needs be calm and brave, must cloak my own fears to support their flagging courage. But it is hard, Rupert, for they see what we see and dare not put it into words. And the mystery, Rupert, the horrible shadow that is over us all! In God's name, what can it all mean?"

"That is what I ask myself, Barbara, and dare not answer my own question."

She uttered a low moan and clung closer to me, sobbing quietly. I was deeply moved, for I realized the splendid courage that enabled her to go about this house of horror, calm and unafraid, to bear the burden of her companions' weakness as well as her own grief and humiliation. But I could find nothing to say to her. I could only offer her a silent sympathy, holding her head on my shoulder and softly stroking her hair while I wondered dimly what the end of it all would be.

Presently she stood up, and, taking out her handkerchief, wiped her eyes resolutely and finally.

"Thank you, dear Rupert," she said, "for being so patient with me. I felt that I had come to the end of my endurance and had to rest my burden on you. It was a great relief. But I didn't bring you up here for that. I wanted to consult you about what has to be done. I can't look to poor Tony in his present state."

"What is it that has to be done?" I asked.

"There is the funeral. That has still to take place."

"Of course it has," I exclaimed, suddenly taken aback, for amidst all the turmoils and alarms, I had completely lost sight of this detail. "I suppose I had better call on the undertaker and make the necessary arrangements."

"If you would be so kind, Rupert, and if you can spare the time. You have given up the whole day to us already."

"I can manage," said I. "And as to the time of the funeral, I don't know whether it could be arranged for the evening. It gets dark pretty early."

"No, Rupert," she exclaimed, firmly. "Not in the evening. Certainly not. I will not have poor Harold's body smuggled away in the dark like the dishonoured corpse of some wretched suicide. The funeral shall take place at the proper time, if I go with it alone."

"Very well, Barbara. I will arrange for us to start at the time originally fixed. I only suggested the evening because – well, you know what to expect."

"Yes, only too well! But I refuse to let a crowd of gaping sight-seers intimidate me into treating my dead husband with craven disrespect."

"Perhaps you are right," said I with secret approval of her decision, little as I relished the prospect that it opened. "Then I had better go and make the arrangements at once. It is getting late. But I am loath to leave you alone with Madeline and Wallingford."

"I think, perhaps, we shall be better alone for the present, and you have your own affairs to attend to. But you must have some food before you go. You have had nothing since the morning, and I expect a meal is ready by now."

"I don't think I will wait, Barbara," I replied. "This affair ought to be settled at once. I can get some food when I have dispatched the business."

She was reluctant to let me go. But I was suddenly conscious of a longing to escape from this house into the world of normal things and people, to be alone for a while with my own thoughts, and, above all, to take counsel with Thorndyke. On my way out I called in at the dining room to make my *adieux* to Madeline and Wallingford. The former looked at me as she shook my hand, very wistfully and I thought a little reproachfully.

"I am sorry you have to go, Rupert," she said. "But you will try to come and see us tomorrow, won't you? And spend as much time here as you can."

I promised to come at some time on the morrow and, having exchanged a few words with Wallingford, took my departure, escorted to the street door by the two women.

The closing of the door, sounding softly in my ears, conveyed a sense of relief of which I felt ashamed. I drew a deep breath and stepped forward briskly with a feeling of emancipation that I condemned as selfish and disloyal, even as I was sensible of its intensity. It was almost with a sense of exhilaration that I strode along, a normal, unnoticed wayfarer among ordinary men and women, enveloped by no cloud of mystery, overhung by no shadow of crime. There was the undertaker, indeed, who would drag me back into the gruesome environment, but I would soon have finished with him, and then, for a time, at least, I should be free.

I finished with him, in fact, sooner than I had expected, for he had already arranged the procedure of the postponed funeral and required only my assent, and when I had given this, I went my way breathing more freely but increasingly conscious of the need for food.

Yet, after all, my escape was only from physical contact. Try as I would to forget for a while the terrible events of this day of wrath, the fresh memories of them came creeping back in the midst of those other thoughts which I had generated by a deliberate effort. They haunted me as I walked swiftly through the streets, they made themselves heard above the rumble of the train, and even as I sat in a tavern in Devereux Court, devouring with ravenous appreciation a well-grilled chop, accompanied by a pint of claret, black care stood behind the old-fashioned, high-backed settle, an unseen companion of the friendly waiter.

The lighted windows of Thorndyke's chambers were to my eyes as the harbour lights to the eyes of a storm-beaten mariner. As I emerged from Fig Tree Court and came in sight of them, I had already the feeling that the burden of mystery and vague suspicion was lightened, and I strode across King's Bench Walk with the hopeful anticipation of one who looks to shift his fardel on to more capable shoulders.

The door was opened by Thorndyke himself, and the sheaf of papers in his hand suggested that he was expecting me. "Are those the depositions?" I asked as we shook hands.

"Yes," he replied. "I have just been reading through them and making an abstract. Holman has left the duplicate at your chambers."

"I suppose the medical evidence represents the 'complications' that you hinted at? You expected something of the kind?"

319

"Yes. An inquest in the face of a regular death certificate suggested some pretty definite information, and then your own account of the illness told one what to expect."

"And yet," said I, "neither of the doctors suspected anything while the man was alive."

"No, but that is not very remarkable. I had the advantage over them of knowing that a death certificate had been challenged. It is always easier to be wise after than before the event."

"And now that you have read the depositions, what do you think of the case? Do you think, for instance, that the verdict was justified?"

"Undoubtedly," he replied. "What other verdict was possible on the evidence that was before the court? The medical witness swore that the deceased died from the effects of arsenic poisoning. That is an inference, it is true. The facts are that the man died and that a poisonous quantity of arsenic was found in the body. But it is the only reasonable inference and we cannot doubt that it is the true one. Then again as to the question of murder as against accident or suicide, it is one of probabilities. But the probabilities are so overwhelmingly in favour of murder that no others are worth considering. No, Mayfield, on the evidence before us, we have to accept the verdict as expressing the obvious truth."

"You think it impossible that there can be any error or fallacy in the case?"

"I don't say that," he replied. "I am referring exclusively to the evidence which is set forth in these depositions. That is all the evidence that we possess. Apart from the depositions we have no knowledge of the case at all – at least I have none – and I don't suppose you have any."

"I have not. But I understand that you think it at least conceivable that there may be, after all, some fallacy in the evidence of wilful murder?"

"A fallacy," he replied, "is always conceivable. As you know, Mayfield, complete certainty, in the most rigorous sense, is hardly ever attainable in legal practice. But we must be reasonable. The law has to be administered, and if certainty, in the most extreme, academic sense, is unattainable, we must be guided in our action by the highest degree of probability that is within our reach."

"Yes, I realize that. But still you admit that a fallacy is conceivable. Can you, for the sake of illustration, suggest any such possibility in the evidence that you have read?"

"Well," he replied, "as a matter of purely academic interest, there is the point that I mentioned just now. The body of this man contained a lethal quantity of arsenic. With that quantity of poison in his body, the man died. The obvious inference is that those two facts were connected as cause and effect. But it is not absolutely certain that they were. It is conceivable that the man may have died from some natural cause overlooked by the pathologist – who was already aware of the presence of arsenic, from Detling's information, or again it is conceivable that the man may have been murdered in some other way – even by the administration of some other, more rapidly acting poison, which was never found because it was never looked for. These are undeniable possibilities. But I doubt if any reasonable person would entertain them, seeing that they are mere conjectures unsupported by any sort of evidence. And you notice that the second possibility leaves the verdict of wilful murder unaffected."

"Yes, but it might transfer the effects of that verdict to the wrong person."

"True," he rejoined with a smile. "It might transfer them from a poisoner who had committed a murder to another poisoner who had only *attempted* to commit one, and the irony of the position would be that the latter would actually believe himself to be the murderer. But as I said, this is mere academic talk. The coroner's verdict is the reality with which we have to deal."

"I am not so sure of that, Thorndyke," said I, inspired with a sudden hope by his "illustration". "You admit that fallacies are possible, and you are able to suggest two off-hand. You insist, very properly, that our opinions at present must be based exclusively on the evidence given at the inquest. But, as I listened to that evidence, I had the feeling – and I have it still – that it did not give a credible explanation of the facts that were proved. I had – and have – the feeling that careful and competent investigation might bring to light some entirely new evidence."

"It is quite possible," he admitted, rather drily.

"Well, then," I pursued, "I should wish some such investigation to be made. I can recall a number of cases in which the available evidence, as in the present case, appeared to point to a certain definite conclusion, but in which investigations undertaken by you brought out a body of new evidence pointing in a totally different direction. There was the Hornby case, the case of Blackmore, deceased, the Bellingham case, and a number of others in which the result of your investigations was to upset completely a well-established case against some suspected individual."

He nodded but made no comment, and I concluded with the question, "Well, why should not a similar result follow in the present case?"

He reflected for a few moments and then asked, "What is it that is in your mind, Mayfield? What, exactly do you propose?"

"I am proposing that you should allow me to retain you on my own behalf and that of other interested parties to go thoroughly into this case."

"With what object?"

"With the object of bringing to light the real facts connected with the death of Harold Monkhouse."

"Are you authorized by any of the interested parties to make this proposal?"

"No, and perhaps I had better leave them out and make the proposal on my own account only."

He did not reply immediately, but sat looking at me steadily with a rather inscrutable expression which I found a little disturbing. At length he spoke, with unusual deliberation and emphasis.

"Are you sure, Mayfield, that you *want* the real facts brought to light?"

I stared at him, startled and a good deal taken aback by his question, and especially by the tone in which it was put. "But, surely," I stammered, in reply. "Why not?"

"Don't be hasty, Mayfield," said he. "Reflect calmly and impartially before you commit yourself to any course of action of which you cannot foresee the consequences. Perhaps I can help you. Shall we, without prejudice and without personal bias, take a survey of the *status quo* and try to see exactly where we stand?"

"By all means," I replied, a little uncomfortably.

"Well," he said, "the position is this. A man has died in a certain house, to which he has been confined as an invalid for some considerable time. The cause of his death is stated to be poisoning by arsenic. That statement is made by a competent medical witness who has had the fullest opportunity to ascertain the facts. He makes the statement with complete confidence that it is a true statement, and his opinion is supported by those of two other competent professional witnesses. It is an established fact, which cannot be contested, that the body of the deceased contained sufficient arsenic to cause his death. So far as we can see, there is not the slightest reason to doubt that the man died from arsenical poisoning.

"When we come to the question, 'How did the arsenic find its way into the man's body?' there appears to be only one possible answer. Suicide and accident are clearly excluded. The evidence makes it practically certain that the poison was administered to him by some person or persons with the intent to compass his death, and the circumstances in which the poisoning occurred make it virtually certain that the arsenic was administered to this man by some person or persons customarily and intimately in contact with him.

"The evidence shows that there were eight persons who would answer this description, and we have no knowledge of the existence of any others. Those persons are: Barbara Monkhouse, Madeline Norris, Anthony Wallingford, the housemaid, Mabel Withers, the cook, the kitchen-maid, Dr. Dimsdale and Rupert Mayfield. Of these eight persons, the police will assume that one, or more, administered the poison, and, so far as we can see, the police are probably right."

I was rather staggered by his bluntness. But I had asked for his opinion and I had got it. After a brief pause, I said, "We are still, of course, dealing with the depositions. On those, as you say, a presumption of guilt lies against these eight persons collectively. That doesn't carry us very far in a legal sense. You can't indict eight persons as having among them the guilty party. Do you take it that the presumption of guilt lies more heavily on some of these persons than on others?"

"Undoubtedly," he replied. "I enumerated them merely as the body of persons who fulfilled the necessary conditions as to opportunity and among whom the police will – reasonably – look for the guilty person. In a sense, they are all suspect until the guilt is fixed on a particular person. They all had, technically, a motive, since they all benefited by the death of the deceased. Actually, none of them has been shown to have any motive at all in an ordinary and reasonable sense. But for practical purposes, several of them can almost be put outside the area of suspicion – the kitchen-maid, for instance, and Dr. Dimsdale, and yourself."

"And Mrs. Monkhouse," I interposed, "seeing that she appears to have been absent and far away on each occasion when the poison seems to have been administered."

"Precisely," he agreed. "In fact, her absence would seem to exclude her from the group of possible suspects. But apart from its bearing on herself, her absence from home on these occasions has a rather important bearing on some of the others."

"Indeed!" said I, trying rapidly to judge what that bearing might be.

"Yes, it is this: The fact that the poisoning occurred – as it appears – only when Mrs. Monkhouse was away from home, suggests not only that the poisoner was fully cognizant of her movements, which all the household would be, but that her presence at home would have hindered that poisoner from administering the poison. Now, the different persons in the house would be differently affected by her presence. We need not pursue the matter any further just now, but you must see that the hindrance to the poisoning caused by Mrs. Monkhouse's presence would be determined by the nature of the relations between Mrs. Monkhouse and the poisoner."

"Yes, I see that."

"And you see that this circumstance tends to confirm the belief that the crime was committed by a member of the household?"

"I suppose it does," I admitted, grudgingly.

"It does, certainly," said Thorndyke, "and that being so, I ask you again: Do you think it expedient that you should meddle with this case? If you do, you will be taking a heavy responsibility, for I must remind you that you are not proposing to employ me as a counsel, but as an investigator who may become a witness. Now, when I plead in court, I act like any other counsel, I plead my client's case frankly as an advocate, knowing that the judge is there to watch over the interests of justice. But as an investigator or witness I am concerned only with the truth. I never give *ex parte* evidence. If I investigate a crime and discover the criminal, I denounce him, even though he is my employer, for otherwise I should become an accessory. Whoever employs me as an investigator of crime does so at his own risk.

"Bear this in mind, Mayfield, before you go any further in this matter. I don't know what your relations are to these people, but I gather that they are your friends, and I want you to consider very seriously whether you are prepared to risk the possible consequences of employing me. It is actually possible that one or more of these persons may be indicted for the murder of Harold Monkhouse. That would, in any case, be extremely painful for you. But if it happened through the action of the police, you would be, after all, but a passive spectator of the catastrophe. Very different would be the position if it were your own hand that had let the axe fall. Are you prepared to face the risk of such a possibility?"

I must confess that I was daunted by Thorndyke's blunt statement of the position. There was no doubt as to the view that he took of the case. He made no secret of it. And he clearly gauged my own state of mind correctly. He saw that it was not the crime that was concerning me, that I was not seeking justice against the murderer, but that I was looking to secure the safety of my friends.

I turned the question over rapidly in my mind. The contingency that Thorndyke had suggested was horrible. I could not face such a risk. Rather, by far, would I have had the murderer remain unpunished than be, myself, the agent of vengeance on any of these suspects. Hideous as the crime was, I could not bring myself to accept the office of executioner if one of my own friends was to be the victim.

I had almost decided to abandon the project and leave the result to Fate or the police. But then came a sudden revulsion. From the grounds of suspicion my thoughts flew to the persons suspected – to gentle, sympathetic Madeline, so mindful of the dead man's comfort, so solicitous about his needs, so eager to render him the little services that mean so much to a sick man. Could I conceive of her as hiding under this appearance of tender sympathy the purposes of a cruel and callous murderess? The thing was absurd. My heart rejected it utterly. Nor could I entertain for a moment such a thought of the kindly, attentive housemaid, and even Wallingford, much as I disliked him, was obviously outside the area of possible suspicion. An intolerable coxcomb he certainly was, but a murderer – never!

"I will take the risk, Thorndyke," said I. He looked at me with slightly raised eyebrows, and I continued. "I know these people pretty intimately and I find it impossible to entertain the idea that any of them could have committed this callous, deliberate crime. At the moment, I realize circumstances seem to involve them in suspicion, but I am certain that there is some fallacy – that there are some facts which did not transpire at the inquest, but which might be brought to the surface if you took the case in hand."

"Why not let the police disinter those facts?"

"Because the police evidently suspect the members of the household and they will certainly pursue the obvious probabilities."

"So should I, for that matter," said he, "and in any case, we can't prevent the police from bringing a charge if they are satisfied that they can support it. And your own experience will tell you that they will certainly not take a case into the Central Criminal Court unless they have enough evidence to make a conviction a virtual certainty. But I remind you, Mayfield, that they have got it all to do. There is grave suspicion in respect of a number of persons, but there is not, at present, a particle of positive evidence against any one person. It looks to me as if it might turn out to be a very elusive case."

"Precisely," said I. "That is why I am anxious that the actual perpetrator should be discovered. Until he is, all these people will be under suspicion, with the peril of a possible arrest constantly hanging over them. I might even say, 'hanging over us', for you, yourself, have included me in the group of possible suspects."

He reflected for a few moments. At length he replied, "You are quite right, Mayfield. Until the perpetrator of a crime is discovered and his guilt established, it is always possible for suspicion to rest upon the innocent and even for a miscarriage of justice to occur. In all cases it is most desirable that the crime should be brought home to the actual perpetrator without delay for that reason, to say nothing of the importance, on grounds of public policy, of exposing and punishing

325

wrong-doers. You know these people and I do not. If you are sufficiently confident of their innocence to take the risk of associating yourself with the agencies of detection, I have no more to say on that point. I am quite willing to go into the case so far as I can – though, at present, I see no prospect of success."

"It seems to you a difficult case, then?"

"Very. It is extraordinarily obscure and confused. Whoever poisoned that unfortunate man seems to have managed most skilfully to confuse all the issues. Whatever may have been the medium through which the poison was given, that medium is associated equally with a number of different persons. If the medicine was the vehicle, then the responsibility is divided between Dimsdale, who prepared it, and the various persons who administered it. If the poison was mixed with the food, it may have been introduced by any of the persons who prepared it or had access to it on its passage from the kitchen to the patient's bedroom. There is no one person of whom we can say that he or she had any special opportunity that others had not. And it is the same with the motive. No one had any really, adequate motive for killing Monkhouse, but all the possible suspects benefited by his death, though they were apparently not aware of it."

"They all knew, in general terms, that they had been mentioned in the will, though the actual provisions and amounts were not disclosed. But I should hardly describe Mrs. Monkhouse as benefiting by her husband's death. She will not be as well off now as she was when he was alive and the whole of his income was available."

"No. But we were not including her in the group since she was not in the house when the poison was being administered. We were speaking of those who actually had the opportunity to administer the poison, and we see that the opportunity was approximately equal in all. And you see, Mayfield, the trouble is that any evidence incriminating any one person would be in events which are past and beyond recall. The depositions contain all that we know and all that we are likely to know, unless the police are able to ascertain that someone of the parties has purchased arsenic from a chemist, which is extremely unlikely considering the caution and judgment that the poisoner has shown. The truth is that, if no new evidence is forthcoming, the murder of Harold Monkhouse will take its place among the unsolved and insoluble mysteries."

"Then I take it that you will endeavour to find some new evidence? But I don't see, at all, how you will go about it."

"Nor do I," said he. "There seems to be nothing to investigate. However, I shall study the depositions and see if a careful consideration of the evidence offers any suggestion for a new line of research. And as the whole case now lies in the past, I shall try to learn as much as possible about everything and everybody concerned. Perhaps I had better begin with you. I don't quite understand what your position is in this household."

"I will tell you with pleasure all about my relations with the Monkhouses, but it is a rather long story, and I don't see that it will help you in any way."

"Now, Mayfield." said Thorndyke, "don't begin by considering what knowledge may or may not be helpful. We don't know. The most trivial or seemingly irrelevant fact may offer a most illuminating suggestion. My rule is, when I am gravelled for lack of evidence, to collect, indiscriminately, all the information that I can obtain that is in the remotest way connected with the problem that I am dealing with. Bear that in mind. I want to know all that you can tell me, and don't be afraid of irrelevant details. They may not be irrelevant, after all, and if they are, I can sift them out afterwards. Now, begin at the beginning and tell me the whole of the long story."

He provided himself with a notebook, uncapped his fountain pen, and prepared himself to listen to what I felt to be a perfectly useless recital of facts that could have no possible bearing on the case.

"I will take you at your word," said I, "and begin at the very beginning, when I was quite a small boy. At that time, my father, who was a widower, lived at Highgate and kept the chambers in the Temple which I now occupy. A few doors away from us lived a certain Mr. Keene, an old friend of my father's – his only really intimate friend, in fact – and, of course, I used to see a good deal of him. Mr. Keene, who was getting on in years, had married a very charming woman, considerably younger than himself, and at this time there was one child, a little girl about two years old. Unfortunately, Mrs. Keene was very delicate, and soon after the child's birth she developed symptoms of consumption. Once started, the disease progressed rapidly in spite of the most careful treatment, and in about two years from the outset of the symptoms, she died.

"Her death was a great grief to Mr. Keene, and indeed to us all, for she was a most lovable woman, and the poor little motherless child made the strongest appeal to our sympathies. She was the loveliest little creature imaginable and as sweet and winning in nature as she was charming in appearance. On her mother's death, I adopted her as my little sister, and devoted myself to her service. In fact, I became her slave, but a very willing slave, for she was so quick and intelligent, so affectionate and so amiable that, in spite of the difference in our ages – some eight or nine years – I found her a perfectly satisfying companion.

327

She entered quite competently into all my boyish sports and amusements, so that our companionship really involved very little sacrifice on my part but rather was a source of constant pleasure.

"But her motherless condition caused Mr. Keene a good deal of anxiety. As I have said, he was getting on in life and was by no means a strong man, and he viewed with some alarm the not-very-remote possibility of her becoming an orphan with no suitable guardian, for my father was now an elderly man, and I was, as yet, too young to undertake the charge. Eventually, he decided, for the child's sake, to marry again, and about two years after his first wife's death he proposed to and was accepted by a lady named Ainsworth whom he had known for many years, who had been left a widow with one child, a girl some two years younger than myself.

"Naturally, I viewed the advent of the new Mrs. Keene with some jealousy. But there was no occasion. She was a good, kindly woman who showed from the first that she meant to do her duty by her little stepdaughter. And her own child, Barbara, equally disarmed our jealousy. A quiet, rather reserved little girl, but very clever and quickwitted, she not only accepted me at once with the frankest friendliness but, with a curious tactfulness for such a young girl, devoted herself to my little friend, Stella Keene, without in the least attempting to oust me from my position. In effect, we three young people became a most united and harmonious little coterie in which our respective positions were duly recognized. I was the head of the firm, so to speak, Stella was my adopted sister, and Barbara was the ally of us both.

"So our relations continued as the years passed, but presently the passing years began to take toll of our seniors. My father was the first to go. Then followed Mr. Keene, and after a few more years, Barbara's mother. By the time my twenty-fifth birthday came round, we were all orphans."

"What were your respective ages then?" Thorndyke asked.

Rather surprised at the question, I paused to make a calculation. "My own age," I replied, "was, as I have said, twenty-five. Barbara would then be twenty-two and Stella sixteen."

Thorndyke made a note of my answer and I proceeded. "The death of our elders made no appreciable difference in our way of living. My father had left me a modest competence and the two girls were fairly provided for. The houses that we occupied were beyond our needs, reduced as we were in numbers, and we discussed the question of sharing a house. But, of course, the girls were not really my sisters and the scheme was eventually rejected as rather too unconventional, so we continued to live in our respective houses."

"Was there any trustee for the girls?" Thorndyke asked.

"Yes, Mr. Brodribb. The bulk of the property was, I believe, vested in Stella, but, for reasons which I shall come to in a moment, there was a provision that, in the event of her death, it should revert to Barbara."

"On account, I presume, of the tendency to consumption?"

"Exactly. For some time before Mr. Keene's death there had been signs that Stella inherited her mother's delicacy of health. Hence the provisions for Barbara. But no definite manifestations of disease appeared until Stella was about eighteen. Then she developed a cough and began to lose weight, but, for a couple of years the disease made no very marked progress. In fact, there were times when she seemed to be in a fair way to recovery. Then, rather suddenly, her health took a turn for the worse. Soon she became almost completely bed-ridden. She wasted rapidly and, in fact, was now the typical consumptive – hectic, emaciated, but always bright, cheerful and full of plans for the future and enthusiasm for the little hobbies that I devised to keep her amused.

"But all the time, she was going down the hill steadily, although as I have said, there were remissions and fluctuations, and in short, after about a year's definite illness, she went the way of her mother. Her death was immediately caused, I understand, by an attack of hemorrhage."

"You understand?" Thorndyke repeated, interrogatively.

"Yes. To my lasting grief, I was away from home when she died. I had been recently called to the bar and was offered a brief for the Chelmsford Assizes, which I felt I ought not to refuse, especially as Stella seemed, just then, to be better than usual. What made it worse was that the telegram which was sent to recall me went astray. I had moved on to Ipswich and had only just written to give my new address, so that I did not get home until just before the funeral. It was a fearful shock, for no one had the least suspicion that the end was so near. If I had supposed that there was the slightest immediate danger, nothing on earth would have induced me to go away from home."

Thorndyke had listened to my story not only with close attention, but with an expression of sympathy which I noted gratefully and perhaps with a little surprise. But he was a strange man, as impersonal as Fate when he was occupied in actual research, and yet showing at times unexpected gleams of warm human feeling and the most sympathetic understanding. He now preserved a thoughtful silence for some time after I had finished. Presently he said, "I suppose this poor girl's death caused a considerable change in your way of living?"

"Yes, indeed! Its effects were devastating both on Barbara and me. Neither of us felt that we could go on with the old ways of life. Barbara let her house and went into rooms in London, where I used to visit her as

329

often as I could, and I sold my house, furniture and all, and took up residence in the Temple. But even that I could not endure for long. Stella's death had broken me up completely. Right on from my boyhood, she had been the very hub of my life. All my thoughts and interests had revolved around her. She had been to me friend and sister in one. Now that she was gone, the world seemed to be a great, chilly void, haunted everywhere by memories of her. She had pervaded my whole life, and everything about me was constantly reminding me of her. At last I found that I could bear it no longer. The familiar things and places became intolerable to my eyes. I did not want to forget her. On the contrary, I loved to cherish her memory. But it was harrowing to have my loss thrust upon me at every turn. I yearned for new surroundings in which I could begin a new life, and in the end, I decided to go to Canada and settle down there to practise at the Bar.

"My decision came as a fearful blow to Barbara, and indeed, I felt not a little ashamed of my disloyalty to her, for she, too, had been like a sister to me and, next to Stella, had been my dearest friend. But it could not be helped. An intolerable unrest had possession of me. I felt that I must go, and go I did, leaving poor Barbara to console her loneliness with her political friends.

"I stayed in Canada nearly two years and meant to stay there for good. Then one day, I got a letter from Barbara telling me that she was married. The news rather surprised me, for I had taken Barbara for an inveterate spinster with a tendency to avoid male friends other than myself. But the news had another, rather curious effect. It set my thoughts rambling amidst the old surroundings. And now I found that they repelled me no longer – that, on the contrary, they aroused a certain feeling of home-sickness, a yearning for the fuller, richer life of London and a sight of the English countryside. In not much more than a month, I had wound up my Canadian affairs and was back in my old chambers in the Temple, which I had never given up, ready to start practice afresh."

"That," said Thorndyke, "would be a little less than three years ago. Now we come to your relations with the Monkhouse establishment."

"Yes, and I drifted into them almost at once. Barbara received me with open arms, and of course, Monkhouse knew all about me and accepted me as an old friend. Very soon I found myself, in a way, a member of the household. A bedroom was set apart for my use, whenever I cared to occupy it, and I came and went as if I were one of the family. I was appointed a trustee, with Brodribb, and dropped into the position of general family counsellor."

"And what were your relations with Monkhouse?"

330

"We were never very intimate. I liked the man and I think he liked me. But he was not very approachable, a self-contained, aloof, undemonstrative man, and an inveterate book-worm. But he was a good man and I respected him profoundly, though I could never understand why Barbara married him, or why he married Barbara. I couldn't imagine him in love. On the other hand, I cannot conceive any motive that anyone could have had for doing him any harm. He seemed to me to be universally liked in a rather lukewarm fashion."

"It is of no use, I suppose," said Thorndyke, "to ask you if these reminiscences have brought anything to your mind that would throw any light on the means, the motive or the person connected with the crime?"

"No," I answered, "nor can I imagine that they will bring anything to yours. In fact, I am astonished that you have let me go on so long dribbling out all these trivial and irrelevant details. Your patience is monumental."

"Not at all," he replied. "Your story has interested me deeply. It enables me to visualize very clearly at least a part of the setting of this crime, and it has introduced me to the personalities of some of the principal actors, including yourself. The details are not in the least trivial, and whether they are or are not irrelevant we cannot judge. Perhaps, when we have solved the mystery – if ever we do – we may find connections between events that had seemed to be totally unrelated."

"It is, I suppose, conceivable as a mere speculative possibility. But what I have been telling you is mainly concerned with my own rather remote past, which can hardly have any possible bearing on comparatively recent events."

"That is perfectly true," Thorndyke agreed. "Your little autobiography has made perfectly clear your own relation to these people, but it has left most of them – and those in whom I am most interested – outside the picture. I was just wondering whether it would be possible for you to amplify your sketch of the course of events after Barbara's marriage – I am, like you, using the Christian name, for convenience. What I really want is an account of the happenings in that household during the last three years, and especially during the last year. Do you think that, if you were to turn out the garrets of your memory, you could draw up a history of the house in Hilborough Square and its inmates from the time when you first made its acquaintance? Have you any sort of notes that would help you?"

"By Jove!" I exclaimed. "Of course I have. There is my diary."

"Oh," said Thorndyke, with obviously awakened interest. "You keep a diary. What sort of diary is it? Just brief jottings, or a full record?"

"It is a pretty full diary. I began it more than twenty years ago as a sort of schoolboy hobby. But it turned out so useful and entertaining to refer to that I encouraged myself to persevere. Now, I am a confirmed diarist, and I write down not only facts and events, but also comments, which may be quite illuminating to study by the light of what has happened. I will read over the last three years and make an abstract of everything that has happened in that household. And I hope the reading of that abstract will entertain you, for I can't believe that it will help you to unravel the mystery of Harold Monkhouse's death."

"Well," Thorndyke replied, as I rose to take my leave, "don't let your scepticism influence you. Keep in your mind the actual position. In that house a man was poisoned, and almost certainly feloniously poisoned. He must have been poisoned either by someone who was an inmate of that house or by someone who had some sort of access to the dead man from without. It is conceivable that the entries in your diary may bring one or other such person into view. Keep that possibility constantly before you, and fill your abstract with irrelevancies rather than risk omitting anything from which we could gather even the most shadowy hint."

Chapter IX
Superintendent Miller is Puzzled

O_n arriving at my chambers after my conference with Thorndyke, I found awaiting me a letter from a Maidstone solicitor offering me a brief for a case of some importance that was to be tried at the forthcoming assizes. At first, I read it almost impatiently, so preoccupied was my mind with the tragedy in which I was involved. It seemed inopportune, almost impertinent. But, in fact it was most opportune, as I presently realized, in that it recalled me to the realities of normal life. My duties to my friends I did, indeed, take very seriously. But I was not an idle man. I had my way to make in my profession and could not afford to drop out of the race, to sacrifice my ambitions entirely, even on the altar of friendship.

I sat down and glanced through the instructions. It was a case of alleged fraud, an intricate case which interested me at once and in which I thought I could do myself credit, which was also the opinion of the solicitor, who was evidently anxious for me to undertake it. Eventually, I decided to accept the brief, and having written a letter to that effect, I set myself to spend the remainder of the evening in studying the instructions and mastering the rather involved details. For time was short, since the case was down for hearing in a couple of days' time and the morrow would be taken up by my engagements at Hilborough Square.

I pass over the incidents of the funeral. It was a dismal and unpleasant affair, lacking all the dignity and pathos that relieve the dreariness of an ordinary funeral. None of us could forget, as we sat back in the mourning coach as far out of sight as possible, that the corpse in the hearse ahead was the corpse of a murdered man, and that most of the bystanders knew it. Even in the chapel, the majestic service was marred and almost vulgarized by the self-consciousness of the mourners, and at the grave-side we found one another peering furtively around for signs of recognition. To all of us it was a profound relief, when we were once more gathered together in the drawing room, to hear the street door close firmly and the mourning carriage rumble away down the square.

I took an early opportunity of mentioning the brief and I could see that to both the women the prospect of my departure came as a disagreeable surprise.

"How soon will you have to leave us?" Madeline asked, anxiously.

"I must start for Maidstone tomorrow morning," I replied.

"Oh, dear!" she exclaimed. "How empty the place will seem and how lost we shall be without you to advise us."

"I hope," said I, "that the occasions for advice are past, and I shall not be so very far away, if you should want to consult me."

"No," said Barbara, "and I suppose you will not be away for very long. Shall you come back when your case is finished, or shall you stay for the rest of the assizes?"

"I shall probably have some other briefs offered, which will detain me until the assizes are over. My solicitor hinted at some other cases, and of course there is the usual casual work that turns up on circuit."

"Well," she rejoined, "we can only wish you good luck and plenty of work, though we shall be glad when it is time for you to come back, and we must be thankful that you were here to help us through the worst of our troubles."

The general tenor of this conversation, which took place at the lunch table, was not, apparently, to Wallingford's taste, for he sat glumly consuming his food and rather ostentatiously abstaining from taking any part in the discussion. Nor was I surprised, for the obvious way in which both women leant on me was a reproach to his capacity, which ought to have made my advice and guidance unnecessary. But though I sympathized in a way with his displeasure, it nevertheless made me a little uneasy. For there was another matter that I wanted to broach, one in which he might consider himself concerned – namely, my commission to Thorndyke. I had, indeed, debated with myself whether I should not be wiser to keep my own counsel on the subject, but I had decided that they were all interested parties and that it would seem unfriendly and uncandid to keep them in the dark. But, for obvious reasons, I did not propose to acquaint them with Thorndyke's views on the case.

The announcement, when I made it, was received without enthusiasm, and Wallingford, as I had feared, was inclined to be resentful.

"Don't you think, Mayfield," said he, "that you ought to have consulted the rest of us before putting this private inquiry agent, or whatever he is, on the case?"

"Perhaps I ought," I admitted. "But it is important to us all that the mystery should be cleared up."

"That is quite true," said Barbara, "and for my part, I shall never rest until the wretch who made away with poor Harold is dragged out into the light of day – that is, if there is really such a person, I mean, if Harold's death was not, after all, the result of some ghastly accident. But is it wise for us to meddle? The police have the case in hand. Surely, with all their

334

experience and their machinery of detection, they are more likely to be successful than a private individual, no matter how clever he may be."

"That," I replied, "is, in fact, Dr. Thorndyke's own view. He wished to leave the inquiry to the police, and I may say that he will not come into the case unless it should turn out that the police are unable to solve the mystery."

"In which case," said Wallingford, "it is extremely unlikely that an outsider, without their special opportunities, will be able to solve it. And if he should happen to find a mare's nest, we shall share the glory and the publicity of his discovery."

"I don't think," said I, "that you need have any anxiety on that score. Dr. Thorndyke is not at all addicted to finding mare's nests and still less to publicity. If he makes any discovery he will probably keep it to himself until he has the whole case cut and dried. Then he will communicate the facts to the police, and the first news we shall have on the subject will be the announcement that an arrest has been made. And when the police make an arrest on Thorndyke's information, you can take it that a conviction will follow inevitably."

"I don't think I quite understand Dr. Thorndyke's position." said Madeline. "What is he? You seem to refer to him as a sort of superior private detective."

"Thorndyke," I replied, "is a unique figure in the legal world. He is a barrister and a doctor of medicine. In the one capacity he is probably the greatest criminal lawyer of our time. In the other he is, among other things, the leading authority on poisons and on crimes connected with them, and so far as I know, he has never made a mistake."

"He must be a very remarkable man," Wallingford remarked, drily.

"He is," I replied, and in justification of my statement, I gave a sketch of one or two of the cases in which Thorndyke had cleared up what had seemed to be a completely and helplessly insoluble mystery. They all listened with keen interest and were evidently so far impressed that any doubts as to Thorndyke's capacity were set at rest. But yet I was conscious, in all three, of a certain distrust and uneasiness. The truth was, as it seemed to me, that none of them had yet recovered from the ordeal of the inquest. In their secret hearts, what they all wanted – even Barbara, as I suspected – was to bury the whole dreadful episode in oblivion. And seeing this, I had not the courage to remind them of their – of *our* position as the actual suspected parties whose innocence it was Thorndyke's function to make clear.

In view of my impending departure from London, I stayed until the evening was well advanced, though sensible of a certain impatience to be gone, and when, at length, I took my leave and set forth homeward, I was conscious of the same sense of relief that I had felt on the previous day. Now, for a time, I could dismiss this horror from my mind and let my thoughts occupy themselves with the activities that awaited me at Maidstone, which they did so effectually that by the time I reached my chambers, I felt that I had my case at my fingers' ends. I had just set to work making my preparations for the morrow when my glance happened to light on the glazed bookcase in which the long series of my diaries was kept, and then I suddenly bethought me of the abstract which I had promised to make for Thorndyke. There would be no time for that now, and yet, since he had seemed to attach some importance to it, I could not leave my promise unfulfilled. The only thing to be done was to let him have the diary, itself. I was a little reluctant to do this for I had never yet allowed any-one to read it. But there seemed to be no alternative, and, after all, Thorndyke was a responsible person, and if the diary did contain a certain amount of confidential matter, there was nothing in it that was really secret or that I need object to anyone reading. Accordingly, I took out the current volume, and, dropping it into my pocket, made my way round to King's Bench Walk.

My knock at the door was answered by Thorndyke himself, and as I entered the room, I was a little disconcerted at finding a large man seated in an easy chair by the fire with his back to me, and still more so when, on hearing me enter, he rose and turned to confront me. For the stranger was none other than Mr. Superintendent Miller.

His gratification at the meeting seemed to be no greater than mine, though he greeted me quite courteously and even cordially. I had the uncomfortable feeling that I had broken in on a conference and began to make polite preparations for a strategic retreat. But Thorndyke would have none of it.

"Not at all, Mayfield," said he. "The superintendent is here on the same business as you are, and when I tell him that you have commissioned me to investigate this case, he will realize that we are colleagues."

I am not sure that the superintendent realized this so very vividly, but it was evident that Thorndyke's information interested him. Nevertheless he waited for me and Thorndyke to make the opening moves and only relaxed his caution by slow degrees.

"We were remarking when you came in," he said, at length, "what a curiously baffling case this is, and how very disappointing. At first it looked all plain sailing. There was the lady who used to prepare the special diet for the unfortunate man and actually take it up to him and watch him eat it. It seemed as if we had her in the hollow of our hand. And then she slipped out. The arsenic that was found in the stomach

336

seemed to connect the death with the food, but then there was that confounded bottle of medicine that seemed to put the food outside the case. And when we came to reckon up the evidence furnished by the medicine, it proved nothing. Somebody put the poison in. All of them had the opportunity, more-or-less, and all about equally. Nothing pointed to one more than another. And that is how it is all through. There is any amount of suspicion, but the suspicion falls on a group of people, not on anyone in particular."

"Yes," said Thorndyke, "the issues are most strangely confused."

"Extraordinarily," said Miller. "This queer confusion runs all through the case. You are constantly thinking that you have got the solution, and just as you are perfectly sure, it slips through your fingers. There are lots of clues – fine ones, but as soon as you follow one up it breaks off in the middle and leaves you gaping. You saw what happened at the search, Mr. Mayfield."

"I saw the beginning – the actual search – but I don't know what came of it."

"Then I can tell you in one word: Nothing. And yet we seemed to be right on the track every time. There was that secret drawer of Mr. Wallingford's. When I saw that packet of white powder in it, I thought it was going to be a walk-over. I didn't believe for a moment that the stuff was cocaine. But it was. I went straight to our analyst to have it tested."

As the superintendent was speaking I caught Thorndyke's eye, fixed on me with an expression of reproachful inquiry. But he made no remark and Miller continued, "Then there were those two empty bottles. The one that I found in the library yielded definite traces of arsenic. But then, whose bottle was it? The place was accessible to the entire household. It was impossible to connect it with any one person.

"On the other hand, the bottle that I found in Miss Norris' cupboard, and that was presumably hers – though she didn't admit it – contained no arsenic, at least the analyst said it didn't, though as it smelt of lavender and had a red stain at the bottom, I feel convinced that it had had Fowler's Solution in it. What do you think, Doctor? Don't you think the analyst may have been mistaken?"

"No," Thorndyke replied, decidedly. "If the red stain had been due to Fowler's Solution there would have been an appreciable quantity of arsenic present, probably a fiftieth-of-a-grain at least. But Marsh's Test would detect a much smaller quantity than that. If no arsenic was found by a competent chemist who was expressly testing for it, you can take it that no arsenic was there."

"Well," Miller rejoined, "you know best. But you must admit that it is a most remarkable thing that one bottle which smelt of lavender and had a red stain at the bottom, should contain arsenic, and that another bottle, exactly similar in appearance and smelling of lavender and having a red stain at the bottom, should contain no arsenic."

"I am entirely with you, Miller," Thorndyke agreed. "It is a most remarkable circumstance."

"And you see my point," said Miller. "Every discovery turns out a sell. I find a concealed packet of powder – with the owner lying like Ananias – but the powder turns out not to be arsenic. I find a bottle that did contain arsenic, and there is no owner. I find another, similar bottle, which has an owner, and there is no arsenic in it. Rum, isn't it? I feel like the donkey with the bunch of carrots tied to his nose. The carrots are there all right, but he can never get a bite at 'em."

Thorndyke had listened with the closest attention to the superintendent's observations and he now began a cautious cross-examination – cautious because Miller was taking it for granted that I had told him all about the search, and I could not but admire his discretion in suppressing the fact that I had not. For while Thorndyke himself would not suspect me of any intentional concealment, Miller undoubtedly would, and what little confidence he had in me would have been destroyed. Accordingly, he managed the superintendent so adroitly that the latter described, piecemeal, all the incidents of the search.

"Did Wallingford say how he came to be in possession of all this cocaine and morphine?" he asked.

"No," replied Miller, "I asked him, but he refused to say where he had got it."

"But he could be made to answer," said Thorndyke. "Both of these drugs are poisons. He could be made to account for having them in his possession and could be called upon to show that he came by them lawfully. They are not ordinarily purchasable by the public."

"No, that's true," Miller admitted. "But is there any object in going into the question? You see, the cocaine isn't really any affair of ours."

"It doesn't seem to be," Thorndyke agreed, "at least, not directly, but indirectly it may be of considerable importance. I think you ought to find out where he got that cocaine and morphine, Miller."

The superintendent reflected with the air of having seen a new light.

"I see what you mean, Doctor," said he. "You mean that if he got the stuff from some Chinaman or common dope merchant, there wouldn't be much in it, whereas, if he got it from someone who had a general stock of drugs, there might be a good deal in it. Is that the point?"

338

"Yes. He was able to obtain poisons from somebody, and we ought to know exactly what facilities he had for obtaining poisons and what poisons he obtained."

"Yes, that is so," said Miller. "Well, I will see about it at once. Fortunately he is a pretty easy chappie to frighten. I expect, if I give him a bit of a shake-up, he will give himself away, and if he won't, we must try other means. And now, as I think we have said all that we have to say at present, I will wish you two gentlemen good night."

He rose and took up his hat, and having shaken our hands, was duly escorted to the door by Thorndyke, who, when he had seen his visitor safely on to the stairs, returned and confronted me with a look of deep significance.

"You never told me about that cocaine," said he.

"No," I admitted. "It was stupid of me, but the fact is that I was so engrossed by your rather startling observations on the case that this detail slipped my memory. And it really had not impressed me as being of any importance. I accepted Wallingford's statement that the stuff was cocaine and that, consequently, it was no concern of ours."

"I don't find myself able to agree to that 'consequently', Mayfield. How did you know that the cocaine was no concern of ours?"

"Well, I didn't see that it was, and I don't know. Do you?"

"No, I know very little about the case at present. But it seems to me that the fact that a person in this house had a considerable quantity of a highly poisonous substance in his possession is one that at least requires to be noted. The point is, Mayfield, that until we know all the facts of this case we cannot tell which of them is or is not relevant. Try to bear that in mind. Do not select particular facts as important and worthy of notice. Note everything in any way connected with our problem that comes under your observation and pass it on to me without sifting or selection."

"I ought not to need these exhortations," said I. "However, I will bear them in mind should I ever have anything more to communicate. Probably I never shall. But I will say that I think Miller is wasting his energies over Wallingford. The man is no favourite of mine. He is a neurotic ass. But I certainly do not think he has the makings of a murderer."

Thorndyke smiled a little drily. "If you are able," said he, "to diagnose at sight a potential murderer, your powers are a good deal beyond mine. I should have said that every man has the makings of a murderer, given the appropriate conditions."

"Should you really?" I exclaimed "Can you, for instance, imagine either of us committing a murder?"

339

"I think I can," he replied "Of course, the probabilities are very unequal in different cases. There are some men who may be said to be prone to murder. A man of low intelligence, of violent temper, deficient in ordinary self-control, may commit a murder in circumstances that would leave a man of a superior type unmoved. But still, the determining factors are motive and opportunity. Given a sufficient motive and a real opportunity, I can think of no kind of man who might not commit a homicide which would, in a legal sense, be murder."

"But is there such a thing as a sufficient motive for murder?"

"That question can be answered only by the individual affected. If it seems to him sufficient, it is sufficient in practice."

"Can you mention a motive that would seem to you sufficient?"

"Yes, I can. Blackmail. Let us take an imaginary case. Suppose a man to be convicted of a crime of which he is innocent. As he has been convicted, the evidence, though fallacious, is overwhelming. He is sentenced to a term of imprisonment – say penal servitude. He serves his sentence and is in due course discharged. He is now free, but the conviction stands against him. He is a discharged convict. His name is in the prison books, his photograph and his fingerprints are in the Habitual Criminals' Register. He is a marked man for life.

"Now suppose that he manages to shed his identity and in some place where he is unknown begins life afresh. He acquires the excellent character and reputation to which he is, in fact, entitled. He marries and has a family, and he and his family prosper and enjoy the advantages that follow deservedly from his industry and excellent moral qualities.

"And now suppose that at this point his identity is discovered by a blackmailer who forthwith fastens on him, who determines to live on him in perpetuity, to devour the products of his industry, to impoverish his wife and children and to destroy his peace and security by holding over his head the constant menace of exposure. What is such a man to do? The law will help him so far as it can, but it cannot save him from exposure. He can obtain the protection of the law only on condition that he discloses the facts. But that disclosure is precisely the evil that he seeks to avoid. He is an innocent man, but his innocence is known only to himself. The fact, which must transpire if he prosecutes, is that he is a convicted criminal.

"I say, Mayfield, what can he do? What is his remedy? He has but one, and since the law cannot really help him, he is entitled to help himself. If I were in that man's position and the opportunity presented itself, I would put away that blackmailer with no more qualms than I should have in killing a wasp."

"Then I am not going to blackmail you. Thorndyke, for I have a strong conviction that an opportunity would present itself."

"I think it very probable," he replied with a smile. "At any rate, I know a good many methods that I should not adopt, and I think arsenic poisoning is one of them. But don't you agree with me?"

"I suppose I do, at least in the very extreme case that you have put. But it is the only case of justifiable premeditated homicide that I can imagine, and it obviously doesn't apply to Wallingford."

"My dear Mayfield," he exclaimed. "How do we know what does or does not apply to Wallingford? How do we know what he would regard as an adequate motive? We know virtually nothing about him or his affairs or about the crime itself. What we do know is that a man has apparently been murdered, and that, of the various persons who had the opportunity to commit the murder (of whom he is one) none had any intelligible motive at all. It is futile for us to argue back-and-forth on the insufficient knowledge that we possess. We can only docket and classify all the facts that we have and follow up each of them impartially with a perfectly open mind. But, above all, we must try to increase our stock of facts. I suppose you haven't had time to consider that abstract of which we spoke?"

"That is really what brought me round here this evening. I haven't had time, and I shan't have just at present as I am starting tomorrow to take up work on the Southeastern Circuit. But I have brought the current volume of the diary, itself, if you would care to wade through it."

"I should, certainly. The complete document is much preferable to an abstract which might leave me in the dark as to the context. But won't you want to have your diary with you?"

"No, I shall take a short-hand notebook to use while I am away. That is, in fact, what I usually do."

"And you don't mind putting this very confidential document into the hands of a stranger?"

"You are not a stranger, Thorndyke. I don't mind you, though I don't think I would hand it to anybody else. Not that it contains anything that the whole world might not see, for I am a fairly discreet diarist. But there are references to third parties with reflections and comments that I shouldn't care to have read by Thomas, Richard, and Henry. My only fear is that you will find it rather garrulous and diffuse."

"Better that than over-condensed and sketchy," said he, as he took the volume from me. He turned the leaves over, and having glanced at one or two pages exclaimed, "This is something like a diary, Mayfield! Quite in the classical manner. The common, daily jottings such as most of us make are invaluable if they are kept up regularly, but this of yours is immeasurably superior. In a hundred years' time it will be a priceless historical work. How many volumes of it have you got?"

"About twenty – and I must say that I find the older ones quite interesting reading. You may perhaps like to look at one or two of the more recent volumes."

"I should like to see those recording the events of the last three years."

"Well, they are all at your service. I have brought you my duplicate latchkey and you will find the volumes of the diary in the glazed book-case. It is usually kept locked, but as nobody but you will have access to the chambers while I am away, I shall leave the key in the lock."

"This is really very good of you, Mayfield," he said, as I rose to take my departure. "Let me have your address, wherever you may be for the time being, and I will keep you posted in any developments that may occur. And now, good-bye and good luck!" He shook my hand cordially and I betook myself to my chambers to complete my preparations for my start on the morrow.

Chapter X
A Greek Gift

The incidents of my life while I was following the Southeastern Circuit are no part of this history, and I refer to this period merely by way of marking the passage of time. Indeed, it was its separateness, its detachment from the other and more personal aspects of my life, that specially commended it to me. In the cheerful surroundings of the Bar Mess I could forget the terrible experiences of the last few weeks, and even in the grimmer and more suggestive atmosphere of the courts, the close attention that the proceedings demanded kept my mind in a state of wholesome preoccupation.

Quite a considerable amount of work came my way, and though most of the briefs were small – so small, often, that I felt some compunction in taking them from the more needy juniors – yet it was all experience and what was more important just now, it was occupation that kept my mind employed.

That was the great thing: To keep my mind busy with matters that were not my personal concern. And the intensity of my yearning for distraction was the measure of the extent to which my waking thoughts tended to be pervaded by the sinister surroundings of Harold Monkhouse's death. That dreadful event and the mystery that encompassed it had shaken me more than I had at first realized. Nor need this be a matter for surprise. Harold Monkhouse had apparently been murdered – at any rate that was the accepted view. And who was the murderer? Evade the answer as I would, the fact remained that the finger of suspicion pointed at my own intimate friends – nay, even at me. It is no wonder, then, that the mystery haunted me. Murder has an ominous sound to any ears, but to a lawyer practising in criminal courts the word has connotations to which his daily experiences impart a peculiarly, hideous vividness and realism. Once, I remember that, sitting in court, listening to the evidence in a trial for murder, as my glance strayed to the dock where the prisoner stood, watched and guarded like a captured wild beast, the thought suddenly flashed on me that it was actually possible – and to the police actually probable – that thus might yet stand Wallingford or Madeline, or even Barbara or myself.

It would have been possible for me to run home from time to time at weekends but I did not. There was nothing that called for my presence in London and it was better to stick close to my work. Still, I was not quite

343

cut off from my friends, for Barbara wrote regularly and I had an occasional letter from Madeline. As to Thorndyke, he was too busy to write unnecessary letters and his peculiar circumstances made a secretary impossible, so that I had from him no more than one or two brief notes reporting the absence of any new developments. Nor had Barbara much to tell excepting that she had decided to let or sell the house in Hilborough Square and take up her residence in a flat. The decision did not surprise me. I should certainly have done the same in her place, and I was only faintly surprised when I learned that she proposed to live alone and that Madeline had taken a small flat near the school. The two women had always been on excellent terms, but they were not specially devoted to one another, and Barbara would now probably pursue her own special interests. Of Wallingford I learned only that, on the strength of his legacy, he had taken a set of rooms in the neighbourhood of Jermyn Street and that his nerves did not seem to have benefited by the change.

Such was the position of affairs when the Autumn Assizes came to an end and I returned home. I remember the occasion very vividly, as I have good reason to do – indeed, I had better reason than I knew at the time. It was a cold, dark, foggy evening, though not densely foggy, and my taxicab was compelled to crawl at an almost funereal pace (to the exasperation of the driver) through the murky streets, though the traffic was now beginning to thin out. We approached the Temple from the east and eventually entered by the Tudor Street Gate, whence we crept tentatively across Kings Bench Walk to the end of Crown Office Row. As we passed Thorndyke's chambers I looked up and had a momentary glimpse of lighted windows glimmering through the fog. Then they faded away and I looked out on the other side where the great shadowy mass of Paper Buildings loomed above us. A man was standing at the end of the narrow passage that leads to Fig Tree Court – a tallish man wearing a preposterous wide-brimmed hat and a long overcoat with its collar turned up above his ears. I glanced at him incuriously as we approached but had no opportunity to inspect him more closely, if I had wished – which I did not – for, as the cab stopped he turned abruptly and walked away up the passage. The suddenness of his retirement struck me as a little odd and, having alighted from the cab, I stood for a moment or two watching his receding figure. But he soon disappeared in the foggy darkness and I saw him no more. By the time that I had paid my fare and carried my portmanteau to Fig Tree Court, he had probably passed out into Middle Temple Lane.

When I had let myself into my chambers, switched on the light, and shut the door, I looked round my little domain with somewhat mixed feelings. It was very silent and solitary. After the jovial Bar Mess and the bright, frequented rooms of the hotels, or the excellent lodgings which I had just left, these chambers struck me as just a shade desolate. But yet there were compensations. A sense of peace and quiet pervaded the place and all around were my household gods – my familiar and beloved pictures, the little friendly cabinet busts and statuettes, and, above all, the goodly fellowship of books. And at this moment my glance fell on the long range of my diaries and I noticed that one of the series was absent. Not that there was anything remarkable in that since I had given Thorndyke express permission to take them away to read. What did surprise me a little was the date of the missing volume. It was that of the year before Stella's death. As I noted this I was conscious of a faint sense of annoyance. I had, it is true, given him the free use of the diary, but only for purposes of reference. I had hardly bargained for his perusal of the whole series for his entertainment. However, it was of no consequence. The diary enshrined no secrets. If I had, in a way, emulated Pepys in respect of fullness, I had taken warning from his indiscretions – nor, in fact, was I quite so rich in the material of indiscreet records as the vivacious Samuel.

I unpacked my portmanteau – the heavier *impedimenta* were coming on by rail – lit the gas fire in my bedroom, boiled a kettle of water – partly for a comfortable wash and partly to fill a hot water bottle wherewith to warm the probably damp bed – and then, still feeling a little like a cat in a strange house, decided to walk along to Thorndyke's chambers and hear the news, if there were any.

The fog had grown appreciably denser when I turned out of my entry and, crossing the little quadrangle, strode quickly along the narrow passage that leads to the Terrace and King's Bench Walk. I was approaching the end of the passage when there came suddenly into view a shadowy figure which I recognized at once as that of the man whom I had seen when I arrived. But again I had no opportunity for a close inspection, for he had already heard my footsteps and he now started to walk away rapidly in the direction of Mitre Court. For a moment I was disposed to follow him, and did, in fact, make a few quick steps towards him – which seemed to cause him to mend his pace, but it was not directly my business to deal with loiterers, and I could have done nothing even if I had overtaken him. Accordingly I changed my direction, and crossing King's Bench Walk, bore down on Thorndyke's entry.

As I approached the house, I was a little disconcerted to observe that there were now no lights in his chambers, though the windows above were lighted. I ran up the stairs, and finding the oak closed, pressed the electric bell, which I could hear ringing on the floor above. Almost immediately footsteps became audible descending the stairs and were followed by the appearance of a small gentleman whom I recognized as Thorndyke's assistant, artificer, or familiar spirit, Mr. Polton. He recognized me at the same moment and greeted me with a smile that seemed to break out of the corners of his eyes and spread in a network of wrinkles over every part of his face, a sort of compound smile, inasmuch as every wrinkle seemed to have a smile of its own.

"I hope, Mr. Polton," said I, "that I haven't missed the doctor."

"No, sir," he replied. "He is up in the laboratory. We are just about to make a little experiment."

"Well, I am in no hurry. Don't disturb him. I will wait until he is at liberty."

"Unless, sir," he suggested, "you would like to come up. Perhaps you would like to see the experiment."

I closed with the offer gladly. I had never seen Thorndyke's laboratory and had often been somewhat mystified as to what he did in it. Accordingly I followed Mr. Polton up the stairs, at the top of which I found Thorndyke waiting.

"I thought it was your voice, Mayfield," said he, shaking my hand. "You are just in time to see us locate a mare's nest. Come in and lend a hand."

He led me into a large room, around which I glanced curiously and not without surprise. One side was occupied by a huge copying camera, the other by a joiner's bench. A powerful back-geared lathe stood against one window, a jeweller's bench against the other, and the walls were covered with shelves and tool-racks, filled with all sorts of strange implements. From this room we passed into another which I recognized as a chemical laboratory, although most of the apparatus in it was totally unfamiliar to me.

"I had no idea," said I, "that the practice of Medical Jurisprudence involved such an outfit as this. What do you do with it all? The place is like a factory."

"It is a factory," he replied with a smile, "a place where the raw material of scientific evidence is worked up into the finished product suitable for use in courts of law."

"I don't know that that conveys much to me," said I. "But you are going to perform some sort of experiment, perhaps that will enlighten me."

"Probably it will, to some extent," he replied, "though it is only a simple affair. We have a parcel here which came by post this evening and we are going to see what is in it before we open it."

"The devil you are!" I exclaimed. "How in the name of Fortune are you going to do that?"

346

"We shall examine it by means of the X-rays."

"But why? Why not open it and find out what is in it in a reasonable way?"

Thorndyke chuckled softly. "We have had our little experiences, Mayfield, and we have grown wary. We don't open strange parcels nowadays until we are sure that we are not dealing with a 'Greek gift' of some sort. That is what we are going to ascertain now in respect of this."

He picked up from the bench a parcel about the size of an ordinary cigar-box and held it out for my inspection. "The overwhelming probabilities are," he continued, "that this is a perfectly innocent package. But we don't know. I am not expecting any such parcel and there are certain peculiarities about this one that attract one's attention. You notice that the entire address is in rough Roman capitals – what are commonly called 'block letters'. That is probably for the sake of distinctness, but it might possibly be done to avoid a recognizable handwriting or a possibly traceable typewriter. Then you notice that it is addressed to '*Dr. Thorndyke*' and conspicuously endorsed '*Personal*'. Now, that is really a little odd. One understands the object of marking a letter '*Personal*' – to guard against its being opened and read by the wrong person. But what does it matter who opens a parcel?"

"I can't imagine why it should matter," I admitted without much conviction, "but I don't see anything in the unnecessary addition that need excite suspicion. Do you?"

"Perhaps not, but you observe that the sender was apparently anxious that the parcel should be opened by a particular person."

I shrugged my shoulders. The whole proceeding and the reasons given for it struck me as verging on farce. "Do you go through these formalities with every parcel that you receive?" I asked.

"No," he replied. "Only with those that are unexpected or offer no evidence as to their origin. But we are pretty careful. As I said just now, we have had our experiences. One of them was a box which, on being opened, discharged volumes of poisonous gas."

"The deuce!" I exclaimed, rather startled out of my scepticism and viewing the parcel with a newborn respect, not unmixed with apprehension. "Then this thing may actually be an infernal machine! Confound it all, Thorndyke! Supposing it should have a clockwork detonator, ticking away while we are talking. Hadn't you better get on with the X-rays?"

He chuckled at my sudden change of attitude. "It is all right, Mayfield. There is no clockwork. I tried it with the microphone as soon as it arrived. We always do that. And, of course, it is a thousand-to-one that it is just an innocent parcel. But we will just make sure and then I shall be at liberty for a chat with you."

He led the way to a staircase leading to the floor above where I was introduced to a large, bare room surrounded by long benches or tables occupied by various uncanny-looking apparatus. As soon as we entered, he placed the parcel on a raised stand while Polton turned a switch connected with a great coil, the immediate result of which was a peculiar, high-pitched, humming sound as if a gigantic mosquito had got into the room. At the same moment a glass globe that was supported on an arm behind the parcel became filled with green light and displayed a bright red spot in its interior.

"This is a necromantic sort of business, Thorndyke," said I, "only you and Mr. Polton aren't dressed for the part. You ought to have tall pointed caps and gowns covered with cabalistic signs. What is that queer humming noise?"

"That is the interrupter," he replied. "The green bulb is the Crookes's tube and the little red-hot disc inside it is the anti-cathode. I will tell you about them presently. That framed plate that Polton has is the fluorescent screen. It intercepts the X-rays and makes them visible. You shall see, when Polton has finished his inspection."

I watched Polton – who had taken the opportunity to get the first innings – holding the screen between his face and the parcel. After a few moments' inspection he turned the parcel over on its side and once more raised the screen, grazing at it with an expression of the most intense interest. Suddenly he turned to Thorndyke with a smile of perfectly incredible wrinkliness and, without a word, handed him the screen, which he held up for a few seconds and then silently passed to me.

I had never used a fluorescent screen before and I must confess that I found the experience most uncanny. As I raised it before the parcel behind which was the glowing green bulb, the parcel became invisible but in its place appeared the shadow of a pistol, the muzzle of which seemed to be inserted into a jar. There were some other, smaller shadows, of which I could make nothing, but which seemed to be floating in the air.

"Better not look too long, Mayfield," said Thorndyke. "X-rays are unwholesome things. We will take a photograph and then we can study the details at our leisure, though it is all pretty obvious."

"It isn't to me," said I. "There is a pistol and what looks like a jar. Do you take it that they are parts of an infernal machine?"

"I suppose," he replied, "we must dignify it with that name. What do you say, Polton?"

"I should call it a booby-trap, sir," was the reply. "What you might expect from a mischievous boy of ten – rather backward for his age."

Thorndyke laughed. "Listen to the artificer," said he, "and observe how his mechanical soul is offended by an inefficient and unmechanical attempt to blow us all up. But we won't take the inefficiency too much for granted. Let us have a photograph and then we can get to work with safety."

It seemed that this part also of the procedure was already provided for in the form of a large black envelope which Polton produced from a drawer and began forthwith to adjust in contact with the parcel, in fact the appearance of preparedness was so striking that I remarked, "This looks like part of a regular routine. It must take up a lot of your time."

"As a matter of fact," he replied, "we don't often have to do this. I don't receive many parcels and of those that are delivered, the immense majority come from known sources and are accompanied by letters of advice. It is only the strange and questionable packages that we examine with the X-rays. Of course, this one was suspect at a glance, with that disguised handwriting and the special direction as to who should open it."

"Yes, I see that now. But it must be rather uncomfortable to live in constant expectation of having bombs or poison-gas handed in by the postman."

"It isn't as bad as that," said he. "The thing has happened only three or four times in the whole of my experience. The first gift of the kind was a poisoned cigar, which I fortunately detected and which served as a very useful warning. Since then I have kept my weather eyelid lifting, as the mariners express it."

"But don't you find it rather wearing to be constantly on the lookout for some murderous attack?"

"Not at all," he answered with a laugh. "It rather adds to the zest of life. Besides, you see, Mayfield, that on the rare occasions when these trifles come my way, they are so extremely helpful."

"Helpful!" I repeated. "In the Lord's name, how?"

"In a number of ways. Consider my position, Mayfield. I am not like an Italian or Russian politician who may have scores of murderous enemies. I am a lawyer and an investigator of crime. Whoever wants to get rid of me has something to fear from me, but at any given time, there will not be more than one or two of such persons. Consequently, when I receive a gift such as the present one, it conveys to me certain items of information. Thus it informs me that someone is becoming alarmed by some proceedings on my part. That is a very valuable piece of information, for it tells me that someone of my inquiries is at least

349

proceeding along the right lines. It is virtually an admission that I have made, or am in the way of making, a point. A little consideration of the cases that I have in hand will probably suggest the identity of the sender. But on this question the thing itself will in most cases yield quite useful information, as well as telling us a good deal about the personality of the sender. Take the present case. You heard Polton's contemptuous observations on the crudity of the device. Evidently the person who sent this is not an engineer or mechanician of any kind. There is an obvious ignorance of mechanism, and yet there is a certain simple ingenuity. The thing is, in fact, as Polton said, on the level of a schoolboy's booby-trap. You must see that if we had in view two or more possible senders. These facts might enable us to exclude one and select another. But here is Polton with the photograph. Now we can consider the mechanism at our leisure."

As he spoke, Polton deposited on the bench a large porcelain dish or tray in which was a very odd-looking photograph, for the whole of it was jet-black excepting the pistol, the jar, the hinges, and a small, elongated spot, which all stood out in clear, white silhouette.

"Why," I exclaimed as I stooped over it, "that is a muzzle-loading pistol!"

"Yes," Thorndyke agreed, "and a pocket pistol, as you can tell by the absence of a trigger-guard. The trigger is probably hinged and folds forward into a recess. I daresay you know the kind of thing. They were usually rather pretty little weapons – and useful, too, for you could carry one easily in your waistcoat pocket. They had octagon barrels, which screwed off for loading, and the butts were often quite handsomely ornamented with silver mounts. They were usually sent out by the gunsmiths in little baize-lined mahogany cases with compartments for a little powder-flask and a supply of bullets."

"I wonder why he used a muzzle-loader?" said I.

"Probably because he had it. It answers the purpose as well as a modern weapon and, as it was probably made more than a hundred years ago, it would be useless to go round the trade enquiring as to recent purchases."

"Yes, it was safer to use an old pistol than to buy a new one and leave possible tracks. But how does the thing work? I can see that the hammer is at full cock and that there is a cap on the nipple. But what fires the pistol?"

"Apparently a piece of string, which hasn't come out in the photograph except, faintly, just above that small mark – string is not dense enough to throw a shadow at the full exposure – but you see, about an inch behind the trigger, an elongated shadow. That is probably a screw-eye seen end-ways. The string is tied to the trigger, passed through the screw-eye and fastened to the lid of the box. I don't see how. There is no metal fastening, and you see that the lid is not screwed or nailed down. As to how it works, you open the lid firmly, that pulls the string tight, that pulls back the trigger and fires the pistol into the jar, which is presumably full of some explosive, the jar explodes and – up goes the donkey. There is a noble simplicity about the whole thing. How do you propose to open it, Polton?"

"I think, sir," replied the latter, "we had better get the paper off and have a look at the box."

"Very well," said Thorndyke, "but don't take anything for granted. Make sure that the paper isn't part of the joke."

I watched Polton with intense – and far from impersonal – interest, wishing only that I could have observed him from a somewhat greater distance. But for all his contempt for the "booby-trap", he took no unnecessary risks. First, with a pair of scissors, he cut out a piece at the back and enlarged the opening so that he could peer in and inspect the top of the lid. When he had made sure that there were no pitfalls, he ran the scissors round the top and exposed the box, which he carefully lifted out of the remainder of the wrapping and laid down tenderly on the bench. It was a cigar-box of the flat type and presented nothing remarkable excepting that the lid, instead of being nailed or pinned down, was secured by a number of strips of stout adhesive paper, and bore, near the middle, a large spot of sealing-wax.

"That paper binding is quite a happy thought," remarked Thorndyke, "though it was probably put on because our friend was afraid to knock in nails. But it would be quite effective. An impatient man would cut through the front strips and then wrench the lid open. I think that blob of sealing-wax answers our question about the fastening of the string. The end of it was probably drawn through a bradawl hole in the lid and fixed with sealing wax. But it must have been an anxious business drawing it just tight enough and not too tight. I suggest, Polton, that an inch-and-a-half centre-bit hole just below and to the right of the sealing-wax would enable us to cut the string. But you had better try it with the photograph first."

Polton picked the wet photograph out of the dish and carefully laid it on the lid of the box, adjusting it so that the shadows of the hinges were opposite the actual hinges. Then with a marking-awl he pricked through the shadow of the screw-eye, and again about two inches to the right and below it.

"You are quite right, sir," said he as he removed the photograph and inspected the lid of the box. "The middle of the wax is exactly over the screw-eye. I'll just get the centre-bit."

He bustled away down the stairs and returned in less than a minute with a brace and a large centre-bit, the point of which he inserted into the second awl-hole. Then, as Thorndyke grasped the box (and I stepped back a pace or two), he turned the brace lightly and steadily, stopping now and again to clear away the chips and examine the deepening hole. A dozen turns carried the bit through the thin lid and the remaining disc of wood was driven into the interior of the box. As soon as the hole was clear, he cautiously inserted a dentist's mirror, which he had brought up in his pocket, and with its aid examined the inside of the lid.

"I can see the string, sir," he reported, "a bit of common white twine and it looks quite slack. I could reach it easily with a small pair of scissors."

He handed the mirror to Thorndyke, who, having confirmed his observations, produced a pair of surgical scissors from his pocket. These Polton cautiously inserted into the opening, and as he closed them there was an audible snip. Then he slowly withdrew them and again inserted the mirror.

"It's all right," said he. "The string is cut clean through. I think we can open the lid now." With a sharp penknife he cut through the paper binding-strips and then, grasping the front of the lid, continued, "Now for it. Perhaps you two gentlemen had better stand a bit farther back, in case of accidents."

I thought the suggestion an excellent one, but as Thorndyke made no move, I had not the moral courage to adopt it. Nevertheless, I watched Polton's proceedings with my heart in my mouth. Very slowly and gently did that cunning artificer raise the lid until it had opened some two inches, when he stooped and peered in. Then, with the cheerful announcement that it was "All clear", he boldly turned it right back.

Of course, the photograph had shown us, in general, what to expect, but there were certain details that had not been represented. For instance, both the pistol and the jar were securely wedged between pieces of cork – sections of wine-bottle corks, apparently – glued to the bottom of the box.

"How is it," I asked, "that those corks did not appear in the photograph?"

"I think there is a faint indication of them," Thorndyke replied, "but Polton gave a rather full exposure. If you want to show bodies of such low density as corks, you have to give a specially short exposure and cut

352

short the development, too. But I expect Polton saw them when he was developing the picture, didn't you, Polton?"

"Yes," the latter replied, "they were quite distinct at one time, but then I developed up to get the pistol out clear."

While these explanations were being given, Polton proceeded methodically to "draw the teeth" of the infernal apparatus. First, he cut a little wedge of cork which he pushed in between the threatening hammer and the nipple and having thus fixed the former he quietly removed the percussion-cap from the latter, on which I drew a deep breath of relief. He next wrenched away one of the corks and was then able to withdraw the pistol from the jar and lift it out of the box. I took it from him and examined it curiously, not a little interested to note how completely it corresponded with Thorndyke's description. It had a blued octagon barrel, a folding trigger which fitted snugly into a recess, a richly-engraved lock-plate and an ebony butt, decorated with numbers of tiny silver studs and a little lozenge-shaped scutcheon-plate on which a monogram had been engraved in minute letters, which, however, had been so thoroughly scraped out that I was unable to make out or even to guess what the letters had been.

My investigations were cut short by Thorndyke who, having slipped on a pair of rubber gloves, now took the pistol from me, remarking, "You haven't touched the barrel, I think, Mayfield?"

"No," I answered, "but why do you ask?"

"Because we shall go over it and the jar for fingerprints. Not that they will be much use for tracing the sender of this present, but they will be valuable corroboration if we catch him by other means, for whoever sent this certainly had a guilty conscience."

With this he delicately lifted out the jar – a small, dark-brown stoneware vessel such as is used as a container for the choicer kinds of condiments – and inverted it over a sheet of paper, upon which its contents, some two or three tablespoonfuls of black powder, descended and formed a small heap.

"Not a very formidable charge," Thorndyke remarked, looking at it with a smile.

"Formidable!" repeated Polton. "Why, it wouldn't have hurt a fly! Common black powder such as old women use to blow out the copper flues. He must be an innocent, this fellow – if it is a he," he added reflectively.

Polton's proviso suddenly recalled to my mind the man whom I had seen lurking at the corner of Fig Tree Court. It was hardly possible to avoid connecting him with the mysterious parcel, as Thorndyke agreed when I had described the incident.

"Yes," exclaimed Polton, "of course. He was waiting to hear the explosion. It is a pity you didn't mention it sooner, sir. But he may be waiting there still. Hadn't I better run across and see?"

"And suppose he is there still," said Thorndyke. "What would you propose to do?"

"I should just pop up to the lodge and tell the porter to bring a policeman down. Why, we should have him red-handed."

Thorndyke regarded his henchman with an indulgent smile. "Your handicraft, Polton," said he, "is better than your law. You can't arrest a man without a warrant unless he is doing something unlawful. This man was simply standing at the corner of Fig Tree Court."

"But," protested Polton, "isn't it unlawful to send infernal machines by parcel post?"

"Undoubtedly it is," Thorndyke admitted, "but we haven't a particle of evidence that this man has any connection with the parcel or with us. He may have been waiting there to meet a friend."

"He may, of course," said I, "but seeing that he ran off like a lamplighter on both the occasions when I appeared on the scene, I should suspect that he was there for no good. And I strongly suspect him of having some connection with this precious parcel."

"So do I," said Thorndyke. "As a matter of fact, I have once or twice, lately, met a man answering to your description, loitering about King's Bench Walk in the evening. But I think it much better not to appear to notice him. Let him think himself unobserved and presently he will do something definite that will enable us to take action. And remember that the more thoroughly he commits himself, the more valuable his conduct will be as indirect evidence on certain other matters."

I was amused at the way in which Thorndyke sank all considerations of personal safety in the single purpose of pursuing his investigations to a successful issue. He was the typical enthusiast. The possibility that this unknown person might shoot at him from some ambush, he would, I suspected, have welcomed as offering the chance to seize the aggressor and compel him to disclose his motives. Also, I had a shrewd suspicion that he knew or guessed who the man was and was anxious to avoid alarming him.

"Well." he said when he had replaced the pistol and the empty jar in the box and closed the latter, "I think we have finished for the present. The further examination of these interesting trifles can be postponed until tomorrow. Shall we go downstairs and talk over the news?"

"It is getting rather late," said I, "but there is time for a little chat. Though as to news, they will have to come from you, for I have nothing to tell."

We went down to the sitting room where, when he had locked up the box, we took each an armchair and filled our pipes.

"So you have no news of any kind?" said he.

"No, excepting that the Hilborough Square household has been broken up and the inmates scattered into various flats."

"Then the house is now empty?" said he, with an appearance of some interest.

"Yes, and likely to remain so with this gruesome story attached to it. I suppose I shall have to make a survey of the premises with a view to having them put in repair."

"When you do," said he, "I should like to go with you and look over the house."

"But it is all dismantled. Everything has been cleared out. You will find nothing there but empty rooms and a litter of discarded rubbish."

"Never mind," said he. "I have occasionally picked up some quite useful information from empty rooms and discarded rubbish. Do you know if the police have examined the house?"

"I believe not. At any rate, nothing has been said to me to that effect."

"So much the better." said he. "Can we fix a time for our visit?"

"It can't be tomorrow," said I, "because I must see Barbara and get the keys if she has them. Would the day after tomorrow do, after lunch?"

"Perfectly," he replied. "Come and lunch with me. And by the way, Mayfield, it would be best not to mention to anyone that I am coming with you, and I wouldn't say anything about this parcel."

I looked at him with sudden suspicion, recalling Wallingford's observations on the subject of mare's nests. "But my dear Thorndyke!" I exclaimed, "you don't surely associate that parcel with any of the inmates of that house!"

"I don't associate it with any particular person," he replied. "I know only what you know, that it was sent by someone to whom my existence is, for some reason, undesirable, and whose personality is to some extent indicated by the peculiarities of the thing itself."

"What peculiarities do you mean?"

"Well," he replied, "there is the nature and purpose of the thing. It is an appliance for killing a human being. That purpose implies either a very strong motive or a very light estimate of the value of human life. Then, as we have said, the sender is fairly ingenious, but yet quite unmechanical and apparently unprovided with the common tools which

355

ordinary men possess and are more-or-less able to use. You notice that the combination of ingenuity with non-possession of tools is a rather unusual one."

"How do you infer that the sender possessed no tools?"

"From the fact that none were used, and that such materials were employed as required no tools, though these were not the most suitable materials. For instance, common twine was used to pull the trigger, though it is a bad material by reason of its tendency to stretch. But it can be cut with a knife or a pair of scissors, whereas wire, which was the really suitable material, requires cutting pliers to divide it. Again, there were the corks. They were really not very safe, for their weakness and their resiliency might have led to disaster in the event of a specially heavy jerk in transit. A man who possessed no more than a common keyhole saw, or a hand-saw and a chisel or two, would have roughly shaped up one or two blocks of wood to fit the pistol and jar, which would have made the thing perfectly secure. If he had possessed a glue-pot, he would not have used seccotine. But every one has waste corks, and they can be trimmed to shape with an ordinary dinner-knife, and seccotine can be bought at any stationer's. But, to return to what we were saying. I had no special precautions in my mind. I suggested that we should keep our own counsel merely on the general principle that it is always best to keep one's own counsel. One may make a confidence to an entirely suitable person, but who can say that that person may not, in his or her turn, make a confidence? If we keep our knowledge strictly to ourselves, we know exactly how we stand, and that if there has been any leakage, it had been from some other source. But I need not platitudinize to an experienced and learned counsel."

I grinned appreciatively at the neat finish, for "experienced counsel" as I certainly was not, I was at least able to realize, with secret approval, how adroitly Thorndyke had eluded my leading question.

And at that I left it, enquiring in my turn, "I suppose nothing of interest has transpired since I have been away?"

"Very little. There is one item of news, but that can hardly be said to have 'transpired' unless you can associate the process of transpiration with a suction-pump. Superintendent Miller took my advice and applied the suctorial method to Wallingford, with results of which he possibly exaggerates the importance. He tells me – this is, of course, in the strictest confidence – that under pressure, Wallingford made a clean breast of the cocaine and morphine business. He admitted that he had obtained those drugs fraudulently by forging an order in Dimsdale's name, written on Dimsdale's headed note-paper, to the wholesale druggists to deliver to bearer the drugs mentioned. He had possessed himself of the note-paper at the time when he was working at the account books in Dimsdale's surgery."

"But how was it that Dimsdale did not notice what had happened when the accounts were sent in?"

"No accounts were ever sent in. The druggists whom Wallingford patronized were not those with whom Dimsdale had an account. The order stated, in every case, that bearer would pay cash."

"Quite an ingenious little plan of Wallingford's," I remarked. "It is more than I should have given him credit for. And you say that Miller attaches undue importance to this discovery. I am not surprised at that. But why do you think he exaggerates its importance?"

Thorndyke regarded me with a quizzical smile. "Because," he answered, "Miller's previous experiences have been repeated. There has been another discovery. It has transpired that Miss Norris also had dealings with a wholesale druggist. But in her case there was no fraud or irregularity. The druggist with whom she dealt was the one who used to supply her father with *materia medica* and to whom she was well known."

"Then, in that case, I suppose she had an account with him?"

"No, she did not. She also paid cash. Her purchases were only occasional and on quite a small scale, too small to justify an account."

"Has she made any statement as to what she wanted the drugs for?"

"She denies that she ever purchased drugs, in the usual sense – that is substances having medicinal properties. Her purchases were, according to her statement, confined to such pharmaceutical and chemical materials as were required for purposes of instruction in her classes. Which is perfectly plausible, for, as you know, academic cookery is a rather different thing from the cookery of the kitchen."

"Yes, I know that she had some materials in her cupboard that I shouldn't have associated with cookery, and I should accept her statement without hesitation. In fact, the discovery seems to me to be of no significance at all."

"Probably you are right," said he, "but the point is that, in a legal sense, it confuses the issues hopelessly. In her case, as in Wallingford's, materials have been purchased from a druggist, and, as no record of those purchases has been kept, it is impossible to say what those materials were. Probably they were harmless, but it cannot be proved that they were. The effect is that the evidential value of Wallingford's admission is discounted by the fact that there was another person who is known to have purchased materials some of which may have been poisons."

"Yes," said I, "that is obvious enough. But doesn't it strike you, Thorndyke, that all this is just a lot of futile logic-chopping such as you might hear at a debating club? I can't take it seriously. You don't imagine that either of these two persons murdered Harold Monkhouse, do you? I certainly don't, and I can't believe Miller does."

"It doesn't matter very much what he believes, or, for that matter, what any of us believe. 'He discovers who proves.' Up to the present, none of us has proved anything, and my impression is that Miller is becoming a little discouraged. He is a genius in following up clues. But where there are no clues to follow up, the best of detectives is rather stranded."

"By the way," said I, "did you pick up anything from my diary that threw any light on the mystery?"

"Very little," he replied. "In fact, nothing that gets us any farther. I was able to confirm our belief that Monkhouse's attacks of severe illness coincided with his wife's absence from home. But that doesn't help us much. It merely indicates, as we had already observed, that the poisoner was so placed that his or her activities could not be carried on when the wife was at home. But I must compliment you on your diary, Mayfield. It is quite a fascinating work, so much so that I have been tempted to encroach a little on your kindness. The narrative of the last three years was so interesting that it lured me on to the antecedents that led up to them. It reads like a novel."

"How much of it have you read?" I asked, my faint resentment completely extinguished by his appreciation.

"Six volumes," he replied, "including the one that I have just borrowed. I began by reading the last three years for the purposes of our inquiry, and then I ventured to go back another three years for the interest of tracing the more remote causation of recent events. I hope I have not presumed too much on the liberty that you were kind enough to give me."

"Not at all," I replied, heartily. "I am only surprised that a man as much occupied as you are should have been willing to waste your time on the reading of what is, after all, but a trivial and diffuse autobiography."

"I have not wasted my time, Mayfield," said he. "If it is true that 'the proper study of mankind is man', how much more true is it of that variety of mankind that wears the wig and gown and pleads in Court. It seems to me that to lawyers like ourselves, whose professional lives are largely occupied with the study of motives of human actions and with the actions themselves viewed in the light of their antecedents and their consequences, nothing can be more instructive than a full, consecutive diary in which, over a period of years, events may be watched growing out of those that went before and in their turn developing their consequences and elucidating the motives of the actors. Such a diary is a synopsis of human life."

I laughed as I rose to depart. "It seems," said I, "that I wrought better than I knew. In fact, I am disposed, like Pendennis, to regard myself with respectful astonishment. But perhaps I had better not be too puffed up. It may be that I am, after all, no more than a sort of literary Strasburg goose, an unconscious provider of the food of the gods."

Thorndyke laughed in his turn and escorted me down the stairs to the entry where we stood for a few moments looking out into the fog.

"It seems thicker than ever," said he. "However, you can't miss your way. But keep a look-out as you go, in case our friend is still waiting at the corner. Good night!"

I returned his farewell and plunged into the fog, steering for the left corner of the library, and was so fortunate as to strike the wall within just a few yards of it. From thence I felt my way without difficulty to the Terrace where I halted for a moment to look about and listen, and as there was no sign, visible or audible of any loiterer at the corner, I groped my way into the passage and so home to my chambers without meeting a single human creature.

Chapter XI
The Rivals

The warmth with which Barbara greeted me when I made my first appearance at her flat struck me as rather pathetic, and for the first time I seemed to understand what it was that had induced her to marry Harold Monkhouse. She was not a solitary woman by nature and she had never been used to a solitary existence. When Stella's death had broken up her home and left her with no intimate friend in the world but me, I had been too much taken up with my own bereavement to give much consideration to her. But now, as she stood before me in her pretty sitting room, holding both my hands and smiling her welcome, it was suddenly borne in on me that her state was rather forlorn, in spite of her really comfortable means. Indeed, my heart prompted me to some demonstrations of affection and I was restrained only by the caution of a confirmed bachelor. For Barbara was now a widow, and even while my sympathy with my almost life-long friend tempted me to pet her a little, some faint echoes of Mr. Tony Weller's counsels bade me beware.

"You are quite an anchoress here, Barbara," I said, "though you have a mighty comfortable cell. I see you have a new maid, too. I should have thought you would have brought Mabel with you."

"She wouldn't come – naturally. She said she preferred to go and live among strangers and forget what had happened at Hilborough Square. Poor Mabel! She was very brave and good, but it was a terrible experience for her."

"Do you know what has become of her?"

"No. She has disappeared completely. Of course, she has never applied for a reference."

"Why 'of course'?"

"My dear Rupert," she replied a little bitterly, "do you suppose that she would want to advertise her connection with Mrs. Harold Monkhouse?"

"No, I suppose she would be likely to exaggerate the publicity of the affair, as I think you do. And how is Madeline? I rather expected that you and she would have shared a flat. Why didn't you?"

Barbara was disposed to be evasive. "I don't know," she replied, "that the plan commended itself to either of us. We have our separate interests, you know. At any rate, she never made any such suggestion and neither did I."

"Do you ever see Wallingford now?" I asked.

"Indeed, I do," she replied. "In fact, I have had to hint to him that he mustn't call too frequently. One must consider appearances and, until I spoke, he was here nearly every day. But I hated doing it."

"Still, Barbara, it was very necessary. It would be so in the case of any young woman, but in your case – er – especially so."

I broke off awkwardly, not liking to say exactly what was in my mind. For, of course, in the atmosphere of suspicion which hung about him, his frequent visits would be a source of real danger. No motive for the murder had yet been suggested. It would be a disaster if his folly were to create the false appearance of one. But, as I have said, I shrank from pointing this out, though I think she understood what was in my mind, for she discreetly ignored the abrupt finish of my sentence and continued, "Poor Tony! He is so very self-centred and he seems so dependent on me. And really, Rupert, I am a good deal concerned about him."

"Why?" I asked, rather unsympathetically.

"He is getting so queer. He was always rather odd, as you know, but this trouble seems to be quite upsetting his balance. I am afraid he is getting delusions – and yet, in a way, I hope that he is."

"What do you mean? What sort of delusions?"

"He imagines that he is being followed and watched. It is a perfect obsession, especially since that superintendent man called on him and cross-questioned him. But I don't think I told you about that."

"No, you did not," said I, quite truthfully, but with an uncomfortable feeling that I was indirectly telling a lie.

"Well, it seems that this man, Miller, called at his rooms – so you see he knew where Tony was living – and, according to Tony's account, extracted by all sorts of dreadful threats, a full confession of the means by which he obtained that cocaine."

"And how did he obtain it?"

"Oh, he just bought it at a wholesale druggist's. Rather casual of the druggist to have supplied him, I think, but still, he needn't have made such a secret of it. However, since then he has been possessed by this obsession. He imagines that he is constantly under observation. He thinks that some man hangs about near his rooms and watches his comings and goings and follows him about whenever he goes abroad. I suppose there can't be anything in it?"

"Of course not. The police have something better to do than spend their time shadowing harmless idiots. Why on earth should they shadow him? If they have any suspicions of him, those suspicions relate to the past, not to the present."

361

"But I don't think Tony connects these watchers with the police. I fancy he suspects them of being agents of Dr. Thorndyke. You remember that he was suspicious and uneasy about Dr. Thorndyke from the first, and I know that he suspects him of having set the superintendent on him about the cocaine."

"The deuce he does!" I exclaimed, a little startled. "Have you any idea what makes him suspect Thorndyke of that?"

"He says that the superintendent accepted his statement at the time when the cocaine was found, or at least, did not seem disposed to press him on the question as to where he obtained it, and that this inquisition occurred only after you had put the case in Dr. Thorndyke's hands."

I reflected on this statement with some surprise. Of course, Wallingford was quite right, as I knew from first-hand knowledge. But how had he arrived at this belief? Was it a mere guess, based on his evident prejudice against Thorndyke? Or had he something to go on? And was it possible that his other suspicions might be correct? Could it be that Thorndyke was really keeping him under observation? I could imagine no object for such a proceeding. But Thorndyke's methods were so unlike those of the police or of anyone else that it was idle to speculate on what he might do, and his emphatic advice to Miller showed that he regarded Wallingford at least with some interest.

"Well, Barbara," I said, mentally postponing the problem for future consideration, "let us forget Wallingford and everybody else. What are we going to do this afternoon? Is there a matinee that we could go to, or shall we go and hear some music?"

"No, Rupert," she replied. "I don't want any theatres or music. I can have those when you are not here. Let us go and walk about Kensington Gardens and gossip as we used to in the old days. But we have a little business to discuss first. Let us get that finished and then we can put it away and be free. You were going to advise me about the house in Hilborough Square. My own feeling is that I should like to sell it and have done with it once for all."

"I shouldn't do that, Barbara," said I. "It is a valuable property, but just at present its value is depreciated. It would be difficult to dispose of at anything like a reasonable price until recent events have been forgotten. The better plan would be to let it at a low rent for a year or two."

"But would anybody take it?"

"Undoubtedly, if the rent were low enough. Leave it to Brodribb and me to manage. You needn't come into the matter at all beyond signing the lease. Is the house in fairly good repair?"

"Most of it is, but there are one or two rooms that will need redecorating, particularly poor Harold's. That had to be left when the other rooms were done because he refused to be disturbed. It is in a very dilapidated state. The paint is dreadfully shabby and the paper is positively dropping off the walls in places. I daresay you remember its condition."

"I do, very well, seeing that I helped Madeline to paste some of the loose pieces back in their places. But we needn't go into details now. I will go and look over the house and see what is absolutely necessary to make the place presentable. Who has the keys?"

"I have the latch-keys. The other keys are inside the house."

"And I suppose you don't wish to inspect the place yourself?"

"No. I do not. I wish never to set eyes upon that house again." She unlocked a little bureau, and taking a bunch of latch-keys from one of the drawers, handed it to me. Then she went away to put on her outdoor clothes.

Left alone in the room, I sauntered round and inspected Barbara's new abode, noting how, already, it seemed to reflect in some indefinable way the personality of the tenant. It is this sympathetic quality in human dwelling-places which gives its special charm and interest to a room in which some person of character has lived and worked, and which, conversely, imparts such deadly dullness to the "best room" in which no one is suffered to distribute the friendly, humanizing litter, and which is jealously preserved, with all its lifeless ornamentation – its unenjoyed pictures and its unread books – intact and undefiled by any traces of human occupation. The furniture of this room was mostly familiar to me, for it was that of the old boudoir. There was the little piano, the two cosy armchairs, the open bookshelves with their array of well-used books, the water-colours on the walls, and above the chimney-piece, the little portrait of Stella with the thin plait of golden hair bordering the frame.

I halted before it and gazed at the beloved face which seemed to look out at me with such friendly recognition, and let my thoughts drift back into the pleasant old times and stray into those that might have been if death had mercifully passed by this sweet maid and left me the one companion that my heart yearned for. Now that time had softened my passionate grief into a tender regret, I could think other with a sort of quiet detachment that was not without its bitter-sweet pleasure. I could let myself speculate on what my life might have been if she had lived, and what part she would have played in it – questions that, strangely enough, had never arisen while she was alive.

I was so immersed in my reverie that I did not hear Barbara come into the room, and the first intimation that I had of her presence was when I felt her hand slip quietly into mine. I turned to look at her and met her eyes, brimming with tears, fixed on me with an expression of such unutterable sadness that, in a moment, my heart leaped out to her, borne on a wave of sympathy and pity which swept away all my caution and reserve. Forgetful of everything but her loneliness and the grief which we shared, I drew her to me and kissed her. It seemed the natural thing to do and I felt that she understood, though she flushed warmly and the tears started from her eyes so that she must needs wipe them away. Then she looked at me with the faintest, most pathetic little smile and without a word, we turned together and walked out of the room.

Barbara was, as I have said, a rather inscrutable and extremely self-contained woman, but she could be, on occasions, a very delightful companion. And so I found her today. At first a little pensive and silent, she presently warmed up into a quite unwonted gaiety and chatted so pleasantly and made so evident her pleasure at having me back that I yearned no more for the Bar Mess, but was able to forget the horrors and anxieties of the past and give myself up to the very agreeable present.

I have seldom spent a more enjoyable afternoon. Late autumn as it was, the day was mild and sunny, the sky of that wonderful tender, misty blue that is the peculiar glory of London. And the gardens, too, though they were beginning to take on their winter garb, had not yet quite lost their autumnal charm. Still, on the noble elms, thin as their raiment was growing, the golden and russet foliage lingered, and the leaves that they had already shed remained to clothe the earth with a many-coloured carpet.

We had crossed the gardens by some of the wider paths and had turned into one of the pleasant by-paths when Barbara, spying a seat set back between a couple of elms, suggested that we should rest for a few minutes before recrossing the gardens to go forth in search of tea. Accordingly we sat down, sheltered on either side by the great boles of the elms and warmed by the rays of the late afternoon sun. But we had been seated hardly a minute when the peace and forgetfulness that had made our ramble so delightful were dissipated in a moment by an apparition on the wide path that we had just left.

I was the first to observe it. Glancing back through the interval between the elm on my left and another at a little distance, I noticed a man coming toward us. My attention was first drawn to him by his rather singular behaviour. He seemed to be dividing his attention between something that was ahead of him and something behind. But I had taken no special note of him until I saw him step, with a rather absurd air of secrecy and caution, behind a tree-trunk and peer round it along the way that he had come. After keeping a look-out in this fashion for nearly a minute, apparently without result, he backed away from the tree and came forward at a quick pace, peering eagerly ahead and on both sides and pausing now and again to cast a quick look back over his shoulder. I drew Barbara's attention to him, remarking, "There is a gentleman who seems to be afflicted with Wallingford's disease. He is trying to look all round the compass at once."

Barbara looked at the man, watching his movements for a time with a faint smile. But suddenly the smile faded and she exclaimed, "Why, I believe it is Tony! Yes, I am sure it is."

And Tony it was. I recognized him almost as soon as she spoke. He came on now at a quick pace and seemed in a hurry either to escape from what he supposed to be behind him or to overtake whatever was in front. He had apparently not seen us, for though we must have been visible to him – or we could not have seen him – we were rendered inconspicuous by the two trees between which we sat. Presently he disappeared as the nearer elm-trunk hid him from our view, and I waited with half-amused annoyance for him to reappear.

"What a nuisance he is!" said Barbara. "Disturbing our peaceful *tete-a-tete*. But he won't freeze on to us. He would rather forego my much desired society than put up with yours." She laughed softly and added in a thoughtful tone, "I wonder what he is doing here."

I had been wondering that, myself. Kensington Gardens were quite near to Barbara's flat, but they were a long way from Jermyn Street. It was certainly odd that he should be here and on this day of all days. But at this point my reflections were interrupted by the appearance of their subject from behind the big elm-trunk.

He came on us suddenly and was quite close before he saw us. When he did see us, however, he stopped short within a few paces of us, regarding us with a wild stare. It was the first time that I had seen him since the funeral, and certainly his appearance had not improved in the interval. There was something neglected and dishevelled in his aspect that was distinctly suggestive of drink or drugs. But what principally struck me was the expression of furious hate with which he glared at me. There was no mistaking it. Whatever might be the cause, there could be no doubt that he regarded me with almost murderous animosity. He remained in this posture only for a few seconds. Then, as Barbara had begun to utter a few words of greeting, he raised his hat and strode away without a word.

Barbara looked at his retreating figure with a vexed smile.

"Silly fellow!" she exclaimed. "He is angry that I have come out to spend a few hours with my oldest friend, and shows it like a bad-mannered child. I wish he would behave more like an ordinary person."

"You can hardly expect him to behave like what he is not," I said. "Besides, a very ordinary man may feel jealous at seeing another man admitted to terms of intimacy, which are denied to him, with the woman to whom he is specially attached. For I suppose, Barbara, we may take it that that is the position?"

"I suppose so," she admitted. "He is certainly very devoted to me, and I am afraid he is rather jealous of you."

As she spoke, I looked at her and could not but feel a faint sympathy with Wallingford. She was really a very handsome woman, and today she was not only looking her best – she seemed, in some mysterious way to have grown younger, more girlish. The rather sombre gravity of the last few years seemed to be quite dissipated since we had left the flat, and much of the charm of her youth had come back to her.

"He looked more than rather jealous," said I. "Venomous hatred was what I read in his face. Do you think he has anything against me other than my position as his rival in your affections?"

"Yes, I do. He is mortally afraid of you. He believes that you suspect him of having at least had a hand in poor Harold's death, and that you have set Dr. Thorndyke to track him down and bring the crime home to him. And his terror of Dr. Thorndyke is positively an insane obsession."

I was by no means so sure of this, but I said nothing, and she continued, "I suppose you don't know whether Dr. Thorndyke does really look on him with any suspicion? To me the idea is preposterous. Indeed, I find it impossible to believe that there was any crime at all. I am convinced that poor Harold was the victim of some strange accident."

"I quite agree with you, Barbara. That is exactly my own view. But I don't think it is Thorndyke's. As to whom he suspects – if he suspects anybody – I have not the faintest idea. He is a most extraordinarily close and secretive man. No one ever knows what is in his mind until the very moment when he strikes. And he never does strike until he has his case so complete that he can take it into court with the certainty of getting a conviction, or an acquittal, as the case may be."

"But I suppose there are mysteries that elude even his skill?"

"No doubt there are, and I am not sure that our mystery is not one of them. Even Thorndyke can't create evidence, and as he pointed out to me, the evidence in our case lies in the past and is mostly irrecoverable."

"I hope it is not entirely irrecoverable," said she, "for until some reasonable solution of the mystery is reached, an atmosphere of suspicion will continue to hang about all the inmates of that house. So let us wish Dr. Thorndyke his usual success, and when he has proved that no one was guilty – which I am convinced is the fact – perhaps poor Tony will forgive him."

With this, we dismissed the subject, and, getting up from the seat, made our way out of the gardens just as the sun was setting behind the trees, and went in search of a suitable tea-shop. And there we lingered gossiping until the evening was well advanced and it was time for me to see Barbara home to her flat and betake myself to Fig Tree Court and make some pretence of doing an evening's work.

Chapter XII
Thorndyke Challenges
the Evidence

My relations with Thorndyke were rather peculiar and a little inconsistent. I had commissioned him, somewhat against his inclination, to investigate the circumstances connected with the dead of Harold Monkhouse. I was, in fact, his employer. And yet, in a certain subtle sense, I was his antagonist. For I held certain beliefs which I, half-unconsciously, looked to him to confirm. But apparently he did not share those beliefs. As his employer, it was clearly my duty to communicate to him any information which he might think helpful or significant, even if I considered it irrelevant. He had, in fact, explicitly pointed this out to me, and he had specially warned me to refrain from sifting or selecting facts which might become known to me according to my view of their possible bearing on the case.

But yet this was precisely what I felt myself constantly tempted to do, and as we sat at lunch in his chambers on the day after my visit to Barbara, I found myself consciously suppressing certain facts which had then come to my knowledge. And it was not that those facts appeared to me insignificant. On the contrary, I found them rather surprising. Only I had the feeling that they would probably convey to Thorndyke a significance that would be erroneous and misleading.

There was, for instance, the appearance of Wallingford in Kensington Gardens. Could it have been sheer chance? If so, it was a most remarkable coincidence, and one naturally tends to look askance at remarkable coincidences. In fact, I did not believe it to be a coincidence at all. I felt little doubt that Wallingford had been lurking about the neighbourhood of Barbara's flat and had followed us, losing sight of us temporarily, when we turned into the by-path. But, knowing Wallingford as I did, I attached no importance to the incident. It was merely a freak of an unstable, emotional man impelled by jealousy to make a fool of himself. Again, there was Wallingford's terror of Thorndyke and his ridiculous delusions on the subject of the "shadowings." How easy it would be for a person unacquainted with Wallingford's personality to read into them a totally misleading significance! Those were the thoughts that drifted half-consciously through my mind as I sat opposite my friend at the table. So, not without some twinges of conscience, I held my peace.

368

But I had not allowed for Thorndyke's uncanny capacity for inferring what was passing in another person's mind. Very soon it became evident to me that he was fully alive to the possibility of some reservations on my part, and when one or two discreet questions had elicited some fact which I ought to have volunteered, he proceeded to something like definite cross-examination.

"So the household has broken up and the inmates scattered?" he began, when I had told him that I had obtained possession of the keys. "And Mabel Withers seems to have vanished, unless the police have kept her in view. Did you hear anything about Miss Norris?"

"Not very much. Barbara and she have exchanged visits once or twice, but they don't seem to see much of each other."

"And what about Wallingford? Does he seem to have been much disturbed by Miller's descent on him?"

I had to admit that he was in a state bordering on panic.

"And what did Mrs. Monkhouse think of the forged orders on Dimsdale's headed paper?"

"He hadn't disclosed that. She thinks that he bought the cocaine at a druggist's in the ordinary way, and I didn't think it necessary to undeceive her."

"No. The least said the soonest mended. Did you gather that she sees much of Wallingford?"

"Yes, rather too much. He was haunting her flat almost daily, until she gave him a hint not to make his visits too noticeable."

"Why do you suppose he was haunting her flat? So far as you can judge, Mayfield – that is in the strictest confidence, you understand – does there seem to be anything between them beyond ordinary friendliness?"

"Not on her side, certainly, but on his – yes, undoubtedly. His devotion to her amounts almost to infatuation, and has for a long time past. Of course, she realizes his condition, and though he is rather a nuisance to her, she takes a very kindly and indulgent view of his vagaries."

"Naturally, as any well-disposed woman would. I suppose you didn't see anything of him yesterday?"

Of course I had to relate the meeting in Kensington Gardens, and I could see by the way Thorndyke looked at me that he was wondering why I had not mentioned the matter before.

"It almost looks," said he, "as if he had followed you there. Was there anything in his manner of approach that seemed to support that idea?"

369

"I think there was, for I saw him at some distance," and here I felt bound to describe Wallingford's peculiar tactics.

"But," said Thorndyke, "why was he looking about behind him? He must have known that you were in front."

"It seems," I explained, feebly, "that he has some ridiculous idea that he is being watched and followed."

"Ha!" said Thorndyke. "Now I wonder who he supposes is watching and following him."

"I fancy he suspects you," I replied. And so the murder was out, with the additional fact that I had not been very ready with my information.

Thorndyke, however, made no comment on my reticence beyond a steady and significant look at me.

"So," said he, "he suspects me of suspecting him. Well, he is giving us every chance. But I think, Mayfield, you would do well to put Mrs. Monkhouse on her guard. If Wallingford makes a public parade of his feelings towards her, he may put dangerous ideas into the head of Mr. Superintendent Miller. You must realize that Miller is looking for a motive for the assumed murder. And if it comes to his knowledge that Harold Monkhouse's secretary was in love with Harold Monkhouse's wife, he will think that he has found a motive that is good enough."

"Yes, that had occurred to me, and in fact, I did give her a hint to that effect, but it was hardly necessary. She had seen it for herself."

As we now seemed to have exhausted this topic, I ventured to make a few enquiries about the rather farcical infernal machine.

"Did your further examination of it," I asked, "yield any new information?"

"Very little," Thorndyke replied, "but that little was rather curious. There were no finger-prints at all. I examined both the pistol and the jar most thoroughly, but there was not a trace of a finger-mark, to say nothing of a print. It is impossible to avoid the conclusion that the person who sent the machine wore gloves while he was putting it together."

"But isn't that a rather natural precaution in these days?" I asked.

"A perfectly natural precaution, in itself," he replied, "but not quite consistent with some other features. For instance, the wadding with which the pistol-barrel was plugged consisted of a little ball of knitting-wool of a rather characteristic green. I will show it to you, and you will see that it would be quite easy to match and therefore possible to trace. But you see that there are thus shown two contrary states of mind. The gloves suggest that the sender entertained the possibility that the machine might fail to explode, whereas the wool seems to indicate that no such possibility was considered."

He rose from the table – lunch being now finished – and brought from a locked cabinet a little ball of wool of a rather peculiar greenish blue. I took it to the window and examined it carefully, impressed by the curious inconsistency which he had pointed out.

"Yes," I agreed, "there could be no difficulty in matching this. But as to tracing it, that is a different matter. There must have been thousands of skeins of this sold to, at least, hundreds of different persons."

"Very true," said he. "But I was thinking of it rather as a corroborating item in a train of circumstantial evidence."

He put the "corroborating item" back in the cabinet and as, at this moment a taxi was heard to draw up at our entry, he picked up a large attaché case and preceded me down the stairs.

During the comparatively short journey I made a few not very successful efforts to discover what was Thorndyke's real purpose in making this visit of inspection to the dismantled house. But his reticence and mine were not quite similar. He answered all my questions freely. He gave me a wealth of instances illustrating the valuable evidence obtained by the inspection of empty houses. But none of them seemed to throw any light on his present proceedings. And when I pointed this out, he smilingly replied that I was in precisely the same position as himself.

"We are not looking for corroborative evidence," said he. "That belongs to a later stage of the inquiry. We are looking for some suggestive fact which may give us a hint where to begin. Naturally we cannot form any guess as to what kind of fact that might be."

It was not a very illuminating answer, but I had to accept it, although I had a strong suspicion that Thorndyke's purpose was not quite so vague as he represented it to be, and determined unobtrusively to keep an eye on his proceedings.

"Can I give you any assistance?" I enquired, craftily, when I had let him into the hall and shut the outer door.

"Yes," he replied, "there is one thing that you can do for me which will be very helpful. I have brought a packet of cards with me . . . ." Here he produced from his pocket a packet of stationer's postcards. "If you will write on each of them the description and particulars of one room with the name of the occupant in the case of bedrooms, and lay the card on the mantelpiece of the room which it describes, I shall be able to reconstitute the house as it was when it was inhabited. Then we can each go about our respective businesses without hindering one another."

I took the cards – and the fairly broad hint – and together we made a preliminary tour of the house, which, now that the furniture, carpets, and pictures were gone, looked very desolate and forlorn, and as it had not been cleaned since the removal, it had a depressingly dirty and squalid appearance. Moreover, in each room, a collection of rubbish and discarded odds-and-ends had been roughly swept up on the hearth, converting each fireplace into a sort of temporary dust-bin.

After a glance around the rooms on the ground floor, I made my way up to the room in which Harold Monkhouse had died, which was my principal concern as well as Thorndyke's.

"Well, Mayfield," the latter remarked, running a disparaging eye round the faded, discoloured walls and the blackened ceiling, "you will have to do something here. It is a shocking spectacle. Would you mind roughly sketching out the position of the furniture? I see that the bedstead stood by this wall with the head, I presume, towards the window, and the bedside table about here, I suppose, at his right hand. By the way, what was there on that table? Did he keep a supply of food of any kind for use at night?"

"I think they usually put a little tin of sandwiches on the table when the night preparations were made."

"You say 'they'. Who put the box there?"

"I can't say whose duty it was in particular. I imagine Barbara would see to it when she was at home. In her absence it would be done by Madeline or Mabel."

"Not Wallingford?"

"No. I don't think Wallingford ever troubled himself about any of the domestic arrangements excepting those that concerned Barbara."

"Do you know who made the sandwiches?"

"I think Madeline did, as a rule. I know she did sometimes."

"And as to drink? I suppose he had a water-bottle, at any rate."

"Yes, that was always there, and a little decanter of whisky. But he hardly ever touched that. Very often a small flagon of lemonade was put on the table with the sandwiches."

"And who made the lemonade?"

"Madeline. I know that, because it was a very special brand which no one else could make."

"And supposing the sandwiches and the lemonade were not consumed – do you happen to know what became of the remainder?"

"I have no idea. Possibly the servants consumed them, but more probably they were thrown away. Well-fed servants are not partial to remainders from a sick-room."

"You never heard of any attacks of illness among any of the servants?"

"Not to my knowledge. But I shouldn't be very likely to, you know."

"No. You notice, Mayfield, that you have mentioned one or two rather material facts that were not disclosed at the inquest?"

"Yes. I was observing that. And it is just as well that they were not disclosed. There were enough misleading facts without them."

Thorndyke smiled indulgently. "You seem to have made up your mind pretty definitely – on the negative side, at least," he remarked, and then, looking round once more at the walls with their faded, loosened paper, he continued, "I take it that Mr. Monkhouse was not a fresh-air enthusiast."

"He was not," I replied. "He didn't much care for open windows, especially at night. But how did you arrive at that fact?"

"I was looking at the wallpaper. This is not a damp house, but yet the paper on the walls of this room is loosening and peeling off in all directions. And if you notice the distribution of this tendency you get the impression that the moisture which loosened the paper proceeded from the neighbourhood of the bed. The wall which is most affected is the one against which the bed stood, and the part of that wall that has suffered most is that which was nearest to the occupant of the bed, and especially to his head. That large piece, hanging down, is just where the main stream of his breath would have impinged."

"Yes, I see the connection now you mention it, and yet I am surprised that his breath alone should have made the air of the room so damp. All through the winter season, when the window would be shut most closely, the gas was burning, and at night, when the gas was out, he commonly had his candle-lamp alight. I should have thought that the gas and the candle together would have kept the air fairly dry."

"That," said Thorndyke, "is a common delusion. As a matter of fact, they would have quite the opposite effect. You have only to hold an inverted tumbler over a burning candle to realize, from the moisture which immediately condenses on the inside of the tumbler, that the candle, as it burns, gives off quite a considerable volume of steam. But of course, the bulk of the moisture which has caused the paper to peel in this room came from the man's own breath. However, we didn't come here for debating purposes. Let us complete our preliminary tour, and when we have seen the whole house we can each make such more detailed inspection as seems necessary for our particular purposes."

We accordingly resumed our perambulation (but I noticed that Thorndyke deposited his attaché case in Monkhouse's room with the evident intention of returning thither), both of us looking about narrowly – Thorndyke, no doubt, in search of the mysterious "traces" of which he had spoken, and I with an inquisitive endeavour to ascertain what kind of objects or appearances he regarded as "traces".

373

We had not gone very far before we encountered an object that even I was able to recognize as significant. It was in a corner of the long corridor that we came upon a little heap of rubbish that had been swept up out of the way, and at the very moment when Thorndyke stopped short with his eyes fixed on it, I saw the object – a little wisp of knitting-wool of the well-remembered green colour. Thorndyke picked it up and, having exhibited it to me, produced from his letter-case a little envelope such as seedsmen use, in which he put the treasure trove, and as he uncapped his fountain pen, he looked up and down the corridor.

"Which is the nearest room to this spot?" he asked.

"Madeline's," I replied. "That is the door of her bedroom, on the right. But all the principal bedrooms are on this floor and Barbara's boudoir as well. This heap of rubbish is probably the sweepings from all the rooms."

"That is what it looks like," he agreed as he wrote the particulars on the envelope and slipped the latter in his letter-case. "You notice that there are some other trifles in this heap – some broken glass, for instance. But I will go through it when we have finished our tour, though I may as well take this now."

As he spoke, he stooped and picked up a short piece of rather irregularly shaped glass rod with a swollen, rounded end.

"What is it?" I asked.

"It is a portion of a small glass pestle and it belongs to one of those little glass mortars such as chemists use in rubbing up powders into solutions or suspensions. You had better not touch it, though it has probably been handled pretty freely. But I shall test it on the chance of discovering what it was last used for."

He put it away carefully in another seed-envelope and then looked down thoughtfully at the miniature dust-heap, but he made no further investigations at the moment and we resumed the perambulation, I placing the identification card on the mantelpiece of each room while he looked sharply about him, opening all cupboards and receptacles and peering into their, usually empty, interiors.

When we had inspected the servants' bedrooms and the attics – leaving the indispensable cards – we went down to the basement and visited the kitchen, the scullery, the servants' parlour, and the cellars, and this brought our tour to an end.

"Now," said Thorndyke, "we proceed from the general to the particular. While you are drawing up your schedule of dilapidations, I will just browse about and see if I can pick up any stray crumbs in which inference can find nourishment. It isn't a very hopeful quest, but you observe that we have already lighted on two objects which may have a meaning for us."

"Yes, we have ascertained that someone in this house used a particular kind of wool and that someone possessed a glass mortar. Those do not seem to me very weighty facts."

"They are not," he agreed, "indeed, they are hardly facts at all. The actual fact is that we have found the things here. But trifles light as air sometimes serve to fill up the spaces in a train of circumstantial evidence. I think I will go and have another look at that rubbish-heap."

I was strongly tempted to follow him, but could hardly do so in face of his plainly expressed wish to make his inspection alone. Moreover, I had already seen that there was more to be done than I had supposed. The house was certainly not in bad repair, but neither did it look very fresh nor attractive. Furniture and especially pictures have a way of marking indelibly the walls of a room, and the paintwork in several places showed disfiguring traces of wear. But I was anxious to let this house, even at a nominal rent, so that, by a few years' normal occupation its sinister reputation might be forgotten and its value restored.

As a result, I was committed to a detailed inspection of the whole house and the making of voluminous notes on the repairs and re-decorations which would be necessary to tempt even an impecunious tenant to forget that this was a house in which a murder had been committed. For that was the current view, erroneous as I believed it to be. Notebook in hand, I proceeded systematically from room to room and from floor to floor, and became so engrossed with my own business that I almost forgot Thorndyke, though I could hear him moving about the house, and once I met him – on the first floor, with a couple of empty medicine bottles and a small glass jar in his hands, apparently making his way to Harold's room, where, as I have said, he had left his *attache* case.

That room I left to the last, as it was already entered in my list and I did not wish to appear to spy upon Thorndyke's proceedings. When at length I entered the room, I found that he, like myself, had come to the end of his task. On the floor his *attache* case lay open, crammed with various objects, several of which appeared to be bottles, wrapped in oddments of waste paper (including some pieces of wallpaper which he had apparently stripped off *ad hoc* when the other supplies failed) and among which I observed a crumpled fly-paper. Respecting this I remarked, "I don't see why you are burdening yourself with this. A fly-paper is in no sense an incriminating object, even though such things have, at times, been put to unlawful use."

"Very true," he replied as he peeled off the rubber gloves which he had been wearing during the search. "A fly-paper is a perfectly normal domestic object. But, as you say, it can on occasion be used as a source of arsenic for criminal purposes, and a paper that has been so used will be found to have had practically the whole of the arsenic soaked out of it. As I happened to find this in the servants' parlour, it seemed worthwhile to take it to see whether its charge of arsenic had or had not been extracted."

"But," I objected, "why on earth should the poisoner – if there really is such a person – have been at the trouble of soaking out fly papers when apparently he was able to command an unlimited supply of Fowler's Solution?"

"Quite a pertinent question, Mayfield," he rejoined. "But may I ask my learned friend whether he found the evidence relating to the Fowler's Solution perfectly satisfactory?"

"But surely!" I exclaimed. "You had the evidence of two expert witnesses on the point. What more would you require? What is the difficulty?"

"The difficulty is this. There were several witnesses who testified that when they saw the bottle of medicine, the Fowler's Solution had not yet been added, but there was none who saw the bottle after the addition had been made."

"But it must have been added before Mabel gave the patient the last dose."

"That is the inference. But Mabel said nothing to that effect. She was not asked what colour the medicine was when she gave the patient that dose."

"But what of the analysts and the *post mortem*?"

"As to the *post mortem*, the arsenic which was found in the stomach was not recognized as being in the form of Fowler's Solution, and as to the analysts, they made their examination three days after the man died."

"Still, the medicine that they analysed was the medicine that the deceased had taken. You don't deny that, do you?"

"I neither deny it nor affirm it. I merely say that no evidence was given that proved the presence of Fowler's Solution in that bottle before the man died, and that the bottle which was handed to the analysts was one that had been exposed for three days in a room which had been visited by a number of persons, including Mrs. Monkhouse, Wallingford, Miss Norris, Mabel Withers, Amos Monkhouse, Dr. Dimsdale, and yourself."

"You mean to suggest that the bottle might have been tampered with or changed for another? But, my dear Thorndyke, why in the name of God should anyone want to change the bottle?"

"I am not suggesting that the bottle actually was changed. I am merely pointing out that the evidence of the analysts is material only subject to the conditions that the bottle which they examined was the bottle from which the last dose of medicine was given, and that its contents were the same as on that occasion, and that no conclusive proof exists that it was the same bottle or that the contents were unchanged."

"But what reason could there be for supposing that it might have been changed?"

"There is no need to advance any reason. The burden of proof lies on those who affirm that it was the same bottle with the same contents. It is for them to prove that no change was possible. But obviously a change was possible."

"But still," I persisted, "there seems to be no point in this suggestion. Who could have had any motive for making a change? And what could the motive have been? It looks to me like mere logic-chopping and hair-splitting."

"You wouldn't say that if you were for the defence," chuckled Thorndyke. "You would not let a point of first-rate importance pass on a mere assumption, no matter how probable. And as to a possible motive, surely a most obvious one is staring us in the face. Supposing some person in this household had been administering arsenic in the food. If it could be arranged that a poisonous dose could be discovered in the medicine, you must see that the issue would be at once transferred from the food to the medicine, and from those who controlled the food to those who controlled the medicine. Which is, in fact, what happened. As soon as the jury heard about the medicine, their interest in the food became extinct."

I listened to this exposition with a slightly sceptical smile. It was all very ingenious but I found it utterly unconvincing.

"You ought to be pleading in court, Thorndyke," I said, "instead of grubbing about in empty houses and raking over rubbish-heaps. By the way, have you found anything that seems likely to yield any suggestions?"

"It is a little difficult to say," he replied. "I have taken possession of a number of bottles and small jars for examination as to their contents, but I have no great expectation in respect of them. I also found some fragments of the glass mortar – an eight-ounce mortar it appears to have been."

"Where did you find those?" I asked.

"In Miss Norris' bedroom, in a little pile of rubbish under the grate. They are only tiny fragments, but the curvature enables one to reconstruct the vessel pretty accurately."

It seemed to me a rather futile proceeding, but I made no comment. Nor did I give utterance to a suspicion which had just flashed into my mind, that it was the discovery of these ridiculous fragments of glass that had set my learned friend splitting straws on the subject of the medicine bottle. I had not much liked his suggestion as to the possible motive of that hypothetical substitution, and I liked it less now that he had discovered the remains of the mortar in Madeline's room. There was no doubt that Thorndyke had a remarkable constructive imagination, and, as I followed him down the stairs and out into the square, I found myself faintly uneasy lest that lively imagination should carry him into deeper waters than I was prepared to navigate in his company.

Chapter XIII
Rupert Makes Some Discoveries

By a sort of tacit understanding Thorndyke and I parted in the vicinity of South Kensington Station, to which he had made a bee line on leaving the square. As he had made no suggestion that I should go back with him, I inferred that he had planned a busy evening examining and testing the odds-and-ends that he had picked up in the empty house, while I had suddenly conceived the idea that I might as well take the opportunity of calling on Madeline, who might feel neglected if I failed to put in an appearance within a reasonable time after my return to town. Our researches had taken up most of the afternoon and it was getting on for the hour at which Madeline usually left the school, and as the latter was less than half-an-hour's walk from the station, I could reach it in good time without hurrying.

As I walked at an easy pace through the busily populated streets, I turned over the events of the afternoon with rather mixed feelings. In spite of my great confidence in Thorndyke, I was sensible of a chill of disappointment in respect alike of his words and his deeds. In this rather farcical grubbing about in the dismantled house there was a faint suggestion of charlatanism – of the vulgar, melodramatic sleuth, nosing out a trail, while, as to his hair-splitting objections to a piece of straightforward evidence, they seemed to me to be of the kind at which the usual hard-headed judge would shake his hard head while grudgingly allowing them as technically admissible.

But whither was Thorndyke drifting? Evidently he had turned a dubious eye on Wallingford, and that egregious ass seemed to be doing all that he could to attract further notice. But today I had seemed to detect a note of suspicion in regard to Madeline, and even making allowance for the fact that he had not my knowledge of her gentle, gracious personality, I could not but feel a little resentful. Once more, Wallingford's remarks concerning a possible mare's nest and a public scandal recurred to me and, not for the first time, I was aware of faint misgivings as to my wisdom in having set Thorndyke to stir up these troubled waters. He had, indeed, given me fair warning, and I was half-inclined to regret that I had not allowed myself to be warned off. Of course, Thorndyke was much too old a hand to launch a half-prepared prosecution into the air. But still, I could not but ask myself uneasily whither his over-acute inferences were leading him.

These reflections brought me to the gate of the school, where I learned from the porter that Madeline had not yet left and accordingly sent up my card. In less than a minute she appeared, dressed in her out-of-door clothes and wreathed in smiles, looking, I thought, very charming.

"How nice of you, Rupert!" she exclaimed, "to come and take me home. I was wondering how soon you would come to see my little spinster lair. It is only a few minutes' walk from here. But I am sorry I didn't know you were coming, for I have arranged to make a call – a business call – and I am due in about ten minutes. Isn't it a nuisance?"

"How long will you have to stay?"

"Oh, a quarter-of-an-hour, at least. Perhaps a little more."

"Very well. I will wait outside for you and do sentry-go."

"No, you won't. I shall let you into my flat – I should have to pass it – and you can have a wash and brush-up, and then you can prowl about and see how you like my little mansion – I haven't quite settled down in it yet, but you must overlook that. By the time you have inspected everything, I shall be back and then we can consider whether we will have a late tea or an early supper. This is the way."

She led me into a quiet by-street, one side of which was occupied by a range of tall, rather forbidding buildings whose barrack-like aspect was to some extent mitigated by signs of civilized humanity in the tastefully curtained windows. Madeline's residence was on the second floor, and when she had let me in by the diminutive outer door and switched on the light, she turned back to the staircase with a wave of her hand.

"I will be back as soon as I can," she said. "Meanwhile, go in and make yourself at home."

I stood at the door and watched her trip lightly down the stairs until she disappeared round the angle, when I shut the door and proceeded to follow her injunctions to the letter by taking possession of the bathroom, in which I was gratified to find a constant supply of hot water. When I had refreshed myself by a wash, I went forth and made a leisurely survey of the little flat. It was all very characteristic of Madeline, the professional exponent of Domestic Economy, in its orderly arrangement and its evidences of considered convenience. The tiny kitchen reminded one of a chemical laboratory or a doctor's dispensary with its labelled jars of the cook's materials set out in ordered rows on their shelves, and the two little mortars, one of Wedgewood ware and the other of glass. I grinned as my eye lighted on this latter and I thought of the fragments carefully collected by Thorndyke and solemnly transported to the

Temple for examination. Here, if he could have seen it, was evidence that proved the ownership of that other mortar and at the same time demolished the significance of that discovery.

I ventured to inspect the bedroom, and a very trim, pleasant little room it was, but the feature which principally attracted my attention was an arrangement for switching the electric light off and on from the bed – an arrangement suspiciously correlated to a small set of bookshelves also within easy reach of the bed. What interested me in it was what Thorndyke would have called its "unmechanical ingenuity", for it consisted of no more than a couple of lengths of stout string, of each of which one end was tied to the light-switch and the other end led by a pair of screw-eyes to the head of the bed. No doubt the simple device worked well enough in spite of the friction at each screw-eye, but a man of less intelligence than Madeline would probably have used levers or bell-cranks, or at least pulleys to diminish the friction in changing the direction of the pull.

There was a second bedroom, at present unoccupied and only partially furnished and serving, apparently, as a receptacle for such of Madeline's possessions as had not yet had a permanent place assigned to them. Here were one or two chairs, some piles of books, a number of pictures, and several polished wood boxes and cases of various sizes, evidently the residue of the goods and chattels that Madeline had brought from her home and stored somewhere while she was living at Hilborough Square. I ran my eye along the range of boxes, which were set out on the top of a chest of drawers. One was an old-fashioned tea-caddy, another an obvious folding desk of the same period, while a third, which I opened, turned out to be a work-box of mid-Victorian age. Beside it was a little flat rosewood case which looked like a small case of mathematical instruments. Observing that the key was in the lock, I turned it and lifted the lid, not with any conscious curiosity as to what was inside it, but in the mere idleness of a man who has nothing in particular to do. But the instant that the lid was up my attention awoke with a bound and I stood with dropped jaw staring at the interior in utter consternation.

There could be not an instant's doubt as to what this case was, for its green-baize-lined interior showed a shaped recess of the exact form of a pocket pistol and, if that were not enough, there, in its own compartment was a little copper powder-flask, and in another compartment about a dozen globular bullets.

I snapped down the lid and turned the key and walked guiltily out of the room. My interest in Madeline's flat was dead. I could think of nothing but this amazing discovery. And the more I thought, the more overpowering did it become. The pistol that fitted that case was the exact counterpart of the pistol that I had seen in Thorndyke's laboratory, and the case, itself, corresponded, exactly to his description of the case from which that pistol had probably been taken. It was astounding, and it was profoundly disturbing. For it admitted of no explanation that I could bring myself to accept other than that of a coincidence. And coincidences are unsatisfactory things, and you can't do with too many of them at once.

Yet, on reflection, this was the view that I adopted. Indeed, there was no thinkable alternative. And really, when I came to turn the matter over, it was not quite so extraordinary as it had seemed at the first glance. For what, after all, was this pistol with its case? It was not a unique thing. It was not even a rare thing. Thorndyke had spoken of these pistols and cases as comparatively common things with which he expected me to be familiar. Thousands of them must have been made in their time, and since they were far from perishable, thousands of them must still exist. The singularity of the coincidence was not in the facts, it was the product of my own state of mind.

Thus I sought – none too successfully – to rid myself of the effects of the shock that I had received on raising the lid of the case, and I was still moodily gazing out of the sitting room window and arguing away my perturbation when I heard the outer door shut and a moment later Madeline looked into the room.

"I haven't been so very long, have I?" she said, cheerily. "Now I will slip off my cloak and hat and we will consider what sort of meal we will have – or perhaps you will consider the question while I am gone."

With this she flitted away, and my thoughts, passing by the problem submitted, involuntarily reverted to the little rosewood case in the spare room. But her absence was of a brevity suggesting the performance of the professional quick-change artist. In a minute or two I heard her approach and open the door, and I turned-to receive a real knock-out blow.

I was so astonished and dismayed that I suppose I must have stood staring like a fool, for she asked in a rather disconcerted tone, "What is the matter, Rupert? Why are you looking at my jumper like that? Don't you like it?"

"Yes," I stammered, "of course I do. Most certainly. Very charming. Very – er – becoming. I like it – er – exceedingly."

"I don't believe you do," she said, doubtfully. "You looked so surprised when I first came in. You don't think the colour too startling, do you? Women wear brighter colours than they used to, you know, and I do think this particular shade of green is rather nice. And it is rather unusual, too."

"It is," I agreed, recovering myself by an effort. "Quite distinctive." And then, noting that I had unconsciously adopted Thorndyke's own expression, I added, hastily, "And I shouldn't describe it as startling, at all. It is in perfectly good taste."

"I am glad you think that," she said, "for you certainly did look rather startled at first, and I had some slight misgivings about it myself when I had finished it. It looked more brilliant in colour as a garment than it did in the form of mere skeins."

"You made it yourself, then?"

"Yes. But I don't think I would ever knit another. It took me months to do, and I could have bought one for very little more than the cost of the wool, though, of course, I shouldn't have been able to select the exact tint that I wanted. But what about our meal? Shall we call it tea or supper?"

She could have called it breakfast for all I cared, so completely had this final shock extinguished my interest in food. But I had to make some response to her eager hospitality.

"Let us split the difference or strike an average," I replied. "We will call it a 'swarry'-tea and unusual trimmings."

"Very well," said she, "then you shall come to the kitchen and help. I will show you the raw material of the feast and you shall dictate the bill of fare."

We accordingly adjourned to the kitchen where she fell to work on the preparations with the unhurried quickness that is characteristic of genuine efficiency, babbling pleasantly and pausing now and then to ask my advice (which was usually foolish and had to be blandly rejected) and treating the whole business with a sort of playful seriousness that was very delightful. And all the time I looked on in a state of mental chaos and bewilderment for which I can find no words. There she was, my friend, Madeline, sweet, gentle, feminine – the very type of gracious womanhood, and the more sweet and gracious by reason of these homely surroundings. For it is an appalling reflection, in these days of lady professors and women legislators, that to masculine eyes a woman never looks so dignified, so worshipful, so entirely desirable, as when she is occupied in the traditional activities that millenniums of human experience have associated with her sex. To me, Madeline, flitting about the immaculate little kitchen, neat-handed, perfect in the knowledge of her homely craft, smiling, dainty, fragile, with her gracefully flowing hair and the little apron that she had slipped on as a sort of ceremonial garment, was a veritable epitome of feminine charm. And yet, but a few feet away was a rosewood case that had once held a pistol, and even now, in Thorndyke's locked cabinet – but my mind staggered under the

383

effort of thought and refused the attempt to combine and collate a set of images so discordant.

"You are very quiet, Rupert," she said, presently, pausing to look at me. "What is it? I hope you haven't any special worries."

"We all have our little worries, Madeline," I replied, vaguely.

"Yes, indeed," said she, still regarding me thoughtfully, and for the first time I noticed that she seemed to have aged a little since I had last seen her and that her face, in repose, showed traces of strain and anxiety. "We all have our troubles and we all try to put them on you. How did you think Barbara was looking?"

"Extraordinarily well. I was agreeably surprised."

"Yes. She is wonderful. I am full of admiration of the way she has put away everything connected with – with that dreadful affair. I couldn't have done it if I had been in her place. I couldn't have let things rest. I should have wanted to know."

"I have no doubt that she does. We all want to know. But she can do no more than the rest of us. Do you ever see Wallingford now?"

"Oh, dear, yes. He was inclined to be rather too attentive at first, but Barbara gave him a hint that spinsters who live alone don't want too many visits from their male friends, so now he usually comes with her."

"I must bear Barbara's words of wisdom in mind," said I.

"Indeed you won't!" she exclaimed. "Don't be ridiculous. Rupert. You know her hint doesn't apply to you. And I shouldn't have troubled about the proprieties in Tony's case if I had really wanted him. But I didn't, though I felt awfully sorry for him."

"Yes, he seems to be in a bad way mentally, poor devil. Of course you have heard about his delusions?"

"If they really are delusions, but I am not at all sure that they are. Now help me to carry these things into the sitting room and then I will do the omelette and bring it in."

I obediently took up the tray and followed her into the sitting room, where I completed the arrangement of the table while she returned to the kitchen to perform the crowning culinary feat. In a minute or two she came in with the product under a heated cover and we took our seats at the table.

"You were speaking of Wallingford," said I. "Apparently you know more about him than I do. It seemed to me that he was stark mad."

"He is queer enough, I must admit – don't let your omelette get cold – but I think you and Barbara are mistaken about his delusions. I suspect that somebody is really keeping him under observation, and if that is so, one can easily understand why his nerves are so upset."

384

"Yes, indeed. But when you say you suspect that we are mistaken, what does that mean? Is it just a pious opinion, or have you something to go upon?"

"Oh, I shouldn't offer a mere pious opinion to a learned counsel," she replied, with a smile. "I have something to go upon, and I will tell you about it, though I expect you will think I am stark mad, too. The fact is that I have been under observation, too."

"Nonsense, Madeline!" I exclaimed. "The thing is absurd. You have let Wallingford infect you."

"There!" she retorted. "'What did I say? You think I am qualifying for an asylum now. But I am not. Absurd as the thing seems – and I quite agree with you on that point – it is an actual fact. I haven't the slightest doubt about it."

"Well," I said, "I am open to conviction. But let us have your actual facts. How long do you think it has been going on?"

"That I can't say, and I don't think it is going on now at all. At any rate, I have seen no signs of any watcher for more than a week, and I keep a pretty sharp lookout. The way I first became aware of it was this: I happened one day at lunch time to be looking out of this window through the chink in the curtains when I saw a man pass along slowly on the other side of the street and glance up, as it seemed, at this window. I didn't notice him particularly, but still I did look at him when he glanced up, and of course, his face was then directly towards me. Now it happened that, a few minutes afterwards, I looked out again, and then I saw what looked like the same man pass along again, at the same slow pace and in the same direction. And again he looked up at the window, though he couldn't have seen me because I was hidden by the curtain. But this time I looked at him very closely and made careful mental notes of his clothing, his hat and his features, because, you see, I remembered what Tony had said and I hadn't forgotten the way I was treated at the inquest or the way in which that detective man had turned out my cupboard when he came to search the house. So I looked this man over very carefully indeed so that I should recognize him without any doubt if I should see him again.

"Well, before I went out after lunch I had a good look out of the window, but I couldn't see anything of him, nor did I see him on my way to the school, though I stopped once or twice and looked back. When I got to the school, I stopped at the gate and looked along the street both ways, but still there was no sign of him. Then I ran up to a class-room window from which I could see up and down the street, and presently I saw him coming along slowly on the school side and I was able to check him off point-by-point, and though he didn't look up this time, I could

385

see his face and check that off, too. There was no doubt whatever that it was the same man.

"When I came out of school that afternoon I looked round but could not see him, so I walked away quickly in the direction that I usually take when going home, but suddenly turned a corner and slipped into a shop. I stayed there a few minutes buying some things, then I came out, and, seeing no one, slipped round the corner and took my usual way home but kept carefully behind a man and a woman who were going the same way. I hadn't gone very far before I saw my man standing before a shop window but evidently looking up and down the street. I was quite close to him before he saw me and of course I did not appear to notice him, but I hurried home without looking round and ran straight up to this window to watch for him. And sure enough, in about a couple of minutes I saw him come down the street and walk slowly past."

"And did you see him again after that?"

"Yes, I saw him twice more that same day. I went out for a walk in the evening on purpose to give him a lead. And I saw him from time to time every day for about ten days. Then I missed him, and I haven't seen a sign of him for more than a week. I suppose he found me too monotonous and gave me up."

"It is very extraordinary," I said, convinced against my will by her very circumstantial description. "What possible object could anyone have in keeping a watch on you?"

"That is what I have wondered," said she. "But I suppose the police have to do something for their pay."

"But this doesn't quite look like a police proceeding. There is something rather feeble and amateurish about the affair. With all due respect to your powers of observation, Madeline, I don't think a Scotland Yard man would have let himself be spotted quite so easily."

"But who else could it be?" she objected, and then, after a pause, she added with a mischievous smile, "unless it should be your friend, Dr. Thorndyke. That would really be a quaint situation – if I should, after all, be indebted to you, Rupert, for these polite attentions."

I brushed the suggestion aside hastily but with no conviction. And once more I recalled Wallingford's observations on mare's nests. Obviously this clumsy booby was not a professional detective. And if not, what could he be but some hired agent of Thorndyke's? It was one more perplexity, and added to those with which my mind was already charged, it reduced me to moody silence which must have made me the very reverse of an exhilarating companion. Indeed, when Madeline had rallied me once or twice on my gloomy preoccupation, I felt that the position was becoming untenable. I wanted to be alone and think things out, but as it would have been hardly decent to break up our little party and take my departure, I determined, if possible, to escape from this oppressive *tete-a-tete*. Fortunately, I remembered that a famous pianist was giving a course of recitals at a hall within easy walking distance and ventured to suggest that we might go and hear him.

"I would rather stay here and gossip with you," she replied, "but as you don't seem to be in a gossiping humour, perhaps the music might be rather nice. Yes, let us go. I don't often hear any good music nowadays."

Accordingly we went, and on the way to the hall Madeline gave me a few further details of her experiences with her follower, and I was not a little impressed by her wariness and the ingenuity with which she had lured that guileless sleuth into exposed and well-lighted situations.

"By the way," said I, "what was the fellow like? Give me a few particulars of his appearance in case I should happen to run across him."

"Good Heavens, Rupert!" she exclaimed, laughing mischievously, "you don't suppose he will take to haunting you, do you? That would really be the last straw, especially if he should happen to be employed by Dr. Thorndyke."

"It would," I admitted with a faint grin, "though Thorndyke is extremely thorough and he plumes himself on keeping an open mind. At any rate, let us have a few details."

"There was nothing particularly startling about him. He was a medium-sized man, rather fair, with a longish, sharp, turned-up nose and a sandy moustache, rather bigger than men usually have nowadays. He was dressed in a blue serge suit, without an overcoat, and he wore a brown soft felt hat, a turn-down collar, and a dark green necktie with white spots. He had no gloves but he carried a walking-stick – a thickish yellow cane with a crooked handle."

"Not very distinctive," I remarked, disparagingly.

"Don't you think so?" said she. "I thought he was rather easy to recognize with that brown hat and the blue suit and the big moustache and pointed nose. Of course, if he had worn a scarlet hat and emerald-green trousers and carried a brass fire-shovel instead of a walking-stick he would have been still easier to recognize, but you mustn't expect too much, even from a detective."

I looked with dim surprise into her smiling face and was more bewildered than ever. If she were haunted by any gnawing anxieties, she had a wonderful way of throwing them off. Nothing could be less suggestive of a guilty conscience than this quiet gaiety and placid humour. However, there was no opportunity for moralizing, for her little retort had brought us to the door of the hall, and we had barely time to find desirable seats before the principal musician took his place at the instrument.

It was a delightful entertainment, and if the music did not "soothe my savage breast" into complete forgetfulness, it occupied my attention sufficiently to hinder consecutive thought on any other subject. Indeed, it was not until I had said "Good night" to Madeline outside her flat and turned my face towards the neighbouring station that I was able to attempt a connected review of the recent startling discoveries.

What could they possibly mean? The pistol alone could have been argued away as a curious coincidence, and the same might have been possible even in the case of the wool. But the two together! The long arm of coincidence was not long enough for that. The wisp of wool that we had found in the empty house was certainly – admittedly – Madeline's. But that wisp matched identically the ball of wool from the pistol, and here was a missing pistol which was certainly the exact counterpart of that which had contained the wool plug. The facts could not be disputed. Was it possible to escape from the inferences which they yielded?

The infernal machine, feeble as it was, gave evidence of a diabolical intention – an intention that my mind utterly refused to associate with Madeline. And yet, even in the moment of rejection, my memory suddenly recalled the arrangement connected with the electric light switch in Madeline's bedroom. Its mechanism was practically identical with that of the infernal machine, and the materials used – string and screw-eyes – were actually the same. It seemed impossible to escape from this proof piled on proof.

But if the machine itself declared an abominable intention, what of that which lay behind the machine? The sending of that abomination was not an isolated or independent act. It was related to some antecedent act, as Thorndyke had implied. Whoever sent it, had a guilty conscience.

But guilty of what?

As I asked myself this question, and the horrid, inevitable answer framed itself in my mind, I turned automatically from Middle Temple Lane and passed into the deep shadow of the arch that gives entrance to Elm Court.

Chapter XIV
Rupert Confides in Thorndyke

Although few of its buildings (excepting the Halls) are of really great antiquity, the precinct of the Temples shares with the older parts of London at least one medieval characteristic: It abounds in those queer little passages and alleys which, burrowing in all directions under the dwelling-houses, are a source of endless confusion and bewilderment to the stranger, though to the accustomed denizen they offer an equally great convenience. For by their use the seasoned Templar makes his way from any one part of the precinct to any other, if not in an actual bee-line, at least in an abbreviated zig-zag that cuts across the regular thoroughfares as though they were mere paths traversing an open meadow. Some of these alleys do, indeed, announce themselves, even to unaccustomed eyes, as public passage-ways, by recognizable entrance arches, but many of them scorn even this degree of publicity, artfully concealing their existence from the uninitiated by an ordinary doorway, which they share with a pair of houses. Whereby the unsuspecting stranger, entering what, in his innocence, he supposes to be the front doorway of a house, walks along the hall and is presently astonished to find himself walking out of another front door into another thoroughfare.

The neighbourhood of Fig Tree Court is peculiarly rich in these deceptive burrows – indeed, excepting from the Terrace, it has no other avenue of approach. On the present occasion I had the choice of two, and was proceeding along the narrow lane of Elm Court to take the farther one, which led to the entry of my chambers, when I caught sight of a man approaching hurriedly from the direction of the Cloisters. At the first glance, I thought I recognized him – though he was a mere silhouette in the dim light – as the loiterer whom I had seen on the night of my return. And his behaviour confirmed my suspicion, for as he came in sight of me, he hesitated for a moment and then, quickening his pace forward, disappeared suddenly through what appeared to be a hole in the wall but was, in fact, the passage for which I was making.

Instantly, I turned back and swiftly crossing the square of Elm Court, dived into the burrow at its farther corner and came out into the little square of Fig Tree Court at the very moment when the mysterious stranger emerged from the burrow at the other side, so that we met face to face in the full light of the central lamp.

Naturally, I was the better prepared for the encounter and I pursued my leisurely way towards my chambers with the air of not having observed him, while he, stopping short for a moment with a wild stare at me, dashed across the square and plunged into the passage from which I had just emerged.

I did not follow him. I had seen him and had thereby confirmed a suspicion that had been growing upon me, and that was enough. For I need hardly say that the man was Anthony Wallingford. But though I was prepared for the identification, I was none the less puzzled and worried by it. Here was yet another perplexity, and I was just stepping into my entry to reflect upon it at my leisure when I became aware of hurrying footsteps in the passage through which Wallingford had come. Quickly drawing back into the deep shadow of the vestibule, I waited to see who this new-comer might be. In a few seconds he rushed out of the passage and came to a halt in the middle of the square, nearly under the lamp, where he stood for a few moments, looking to right and left and listening intently. And now I realized the justice of what Madeline had said for, commonplace as the man was, I recognized him in an instant. Brown hat, blue serge suit, big, sandy moustache and concave, pointed nose – they were not sensational characteristics, but they identified him beyond a moment's doubt.

Apparently, his ear must have caught the echoes of Wallingford's footsteps, for, after a very brief pause, he started off at something approaching a trot and disappeared into the passage by which I had come and Wallingford had gone. A sudden, foolish curiosity impelled me to follow and observe the methods of this singular and artless sleuth. But I did not follow directly. Instead, I turned and ran up the other passage, which leads into the narrow part of Elm Court, and as I came flying out of the farther end of it I ran full tilt into a man who was running along the court towards the Cloisters. Of course the man was Wallingford. Who else would be running like a lunatic through the Temple at night, unless it were his pursuer?

With muttered curses but no word of recognition, he disengaged himself and pursued his way, disappearing at length round the sharp turn in the lane which leads towards the Cloisters. I did not follow him, but drew back into the dark passage and waited. Very soon another figure became visible, approaching rapidly along the dimly lighted lane. I drew farther back and presently from my hiding-place I saw the brown-hatted shadower steal past with a ridiculous air of secrecy and caution, and when he had passed, I peered out and watched his receding figure until it disappeared round the angle of the lane.

I felt half-tempted to join the absurd procession and see what eventually became of these two idiots, but I had really seen enough. I now knew that Wallingford's "delusions" were no delusions at all and that Madeline's story set forth nothing but the genuine, indisputable truth. And with these new facts to add to my unwelcome store of data, I walked slowly back to my chambers, cogitating as I went.

In truth, I had abundant material for reflection. The more I turned over my discoveries in Madeline's flat, the more did the incriminating evidence seem to pile up. I recalled Polton's plainly expressed suspicion that the sender of the infernal machine was a woman, and I recalled Thorndyke's analysis of the peculiarities of the thing with the inferences which those peculiarities suggested, and read into them a more definite meaning. I now saw what the machine had conveyed to him, and what he had been trying to make it convey to me. The unmechanical outlook combined with evident ingenuity, the unfamiliarity with ordinary mechanical appliances, the ignorance concerning the different kinds of gun-powder, the lack of those common tools which nearly every man, but hardly any woman, possesses and can use – all these peculiarities of the unknown person were feminine peculiarities. And finally, there had been the plug of knitting-wool – a most unlikely material for a man to use for such a purpose – or, indeed, to possess at all.

So my thoughts went over and over the same ground, and every time finding escape from the obvious conclusion more and more impossible. The evidence of Madeline's complicity – at the very least – in the sending of the infernal machine appeared overwhelming. I could not reject it. Nor could I deny what the sending of it implied. It was virtually a confession of guilt. And yet, even as I admitted this to myself, I was strangely enough aware that my feelings towards Madeline remained unaltered. The rational, legal side of me condemned her. But somehow, in some incomprehensible way, that condemnation had a purely technical, academic quality. It left my loyalty and affection for her untouched.

But what of Thorndyke? Had his reasoning travelled along the same lines? If it had, there would be nothing sentimental in his attitude. He had warned me, and I knew well enough that whenever there should be evidence enough to put before a court, the law would be set in motion. What, then, was his present position? And even as I asked myself the question, there echoed uncomfortably in my mind the significant suggestion that he had thrown out only a few hours ago concerning the bottle of medicine. Evidently, he at least entertained the possibility that the Fowler's Solution had been put into that bottle after Monkhouse's death, and that for the express purpose of diverting suspicion from the food. The manifest implication was that he entertained the possibility that the poison had been administered in the food. But to suspect this was to suspect the person who prepared the food of being the poisoner. And the person who prepared the food was Madeline.

The question, therefore, as to Thorndyke's state of mind was a vital one. He had expressed no suspicion of Madeline. But then he had expressed no suspicion of anybody. On the other hand, he had exonerated nobody. He was frankly observant of every member of that household. Then there was the undeniable fact that Madeline had been watched and followed. Somebody suspected her. But who? The watcher was certainly not a detective. Amateur was writ large all over him. Then it was not the police who suspected her. Apparently there remained only Thorndyke, though one would have expected him to employ a more efficient agent.

But Wallingford was also under observation, and more persistently. Then he, too, was suspected. But here there was some show of reason. For what was Wallingford doing in the Temple? Evidently he had been lurking about, apparently keeping a watch on Thorndyke, though for what purpose I could not imagine. Still, it was a suspicious proceeding and justified some watch being kept on him. But the shadowing of Madeline was incomprehensible.

I paced up and down my sitting room turning these questions over in my mind and all the time conscious of a curious sense of unreality in the whole affair, in all this watching and following and dodging which looked so grotesque and purposeless. I felt myself utterly bewildered. But I was also profoundly unhappy and, indeed, overshadowed by a terrible dread. For out of this chaos one fact emerged clearly: There was a formidable body of evidence implicating Madeline. If Thorndyke had known what I knew, her position would have been one of the gravest peril. My conscience told me that it was my duty to tell him, and I knew that I had no intention of doing anything of the kind. But still the alarming question haunted me: How much did he really know? How much did he suspect?

In the course of my perambulations I passed and repassed a smallish deed box which stood on a lower book-shelf, and which was to me what the Ark of the Covenant was to the ancient Israelites – the repository of my most sacred possessions. Its lid bore the name "*Stella*", painted on it by me, and its contents were a miscellany of trifles, worthless intrinsically, but to me precious beyond all price as relics of the dear friend who had been all in all to me during her short life and who, though she had been lying in her grave for four long years, was all in all to me still. Often, in the long, solitary evenings, had I taken the relics out of their abiding-place and let the sight of them carry my thoughts back to the golden days of our happy companionship, filling in the pleasant pictures with the aid of my diary – but that was unnecessary now, since I knew the entries by heart – and painting other, more shadowy, pictures of a future that might have been. It was a melancholy pleasure, perhaps, but yet, as the years rolled on, the bitterness of those memories grew less bitter and still the sweet remained.

Presently, as for the hundredth time the beloved name met my eye, there came upon me a yearning to creep back with her into the sunny past, to forget, if only for a short hour, the hideous anxieties of the present and in memory to walk with her once more "along the meads of asphodel".

Halting before the box, I stood and lifted it tenderly to the table and, having unlocked it, raised the lid and looked thoughtfully into the interior. Then, one by one, I lifted out my treasures, set them out in order on the table, and sat down to look at them and let them speak to me their message of peace and consolation.

To a stranger's eye they were a mere collection of odds-and-ends. Some would have been recognizable as relics of the more conventional type. There were several photographs of the dead girl, some taken by myself, and a tress of red-gold hair – such hair as I had been told often glorifies the victims whom consumption had marked for its own. It had been cut off for me by Barbara when she took her own tress, and tied up with a blue ribbon. But it was not these orthodox relics that spoke to me most intimately. I had no need of their aid to call up the vision of her person. The things that set my memory working were the records of actions and experiences, the sketch-books, the loose sketches, and the little plaster plaques and medallions that she had made with my help after she had become bed-ridden and could go no more abroad to sketch. Every one of these had its story to tell, its vision to call up.

I turned over the sketches – simple but careful pencil drawings for the most part, for Stella, like me, had more feeling for form than for colour – and recalled the making of them, the delightful rambles across the sunny meadows or through the cool woodlands, the solemn planting of sketching-stools and earnest consultation on the selection and composition of the subjects. These were the happiest days, before the chilly hand of the destroyer had been laid on its chosen victim and there was still a long and sunny future to be vaguely envisaged.

And then I turned to the little plaques and medallions which she had modelled under my supervision and of which I had made the plaster moulds and casts. These called up sadder memories, but yet they spoke of an even closer and more loving companionship, for each work was, in a way, a joint achievement over which we had triumphed and rejoiced together. So it happened that, although the shadow of sickness, and at last of death, brooded over them, it was on these relics that I tended to linger most lovingly.

Here was the slate that I had got for her to stick the clay on and which she used to hold propped up against her knees as she worked with never-failing enthusiasm through the long, monotonous days, and even, when she was well enough, far into the night by the light of the shaded candle. Here were the simple modelling-tools and the little sponge and the camelhair brush with which she loved to put the final finish on the damp clay reliefs. Here was Lanterri's priceless textbook, over which we used to pore together and laud that incomparable teacher. Here were the plaques, medals, and medallions that we had prised out, with bated breath, from their too-adherent moulds. And here – the last and saddest relic – was the wax mould from which no cast had ever been made, the final, crowning work of those deft, sensitive fingers.

For the thousandth time, I picked it up and let the light fall obliquely across its hollows. The work was a medal some three inches across, a portrait of Stella, herself, modelled from a profile photograph that I had taken for the purpose. It was an excellent likeness and unquestionably the best piece of modelling that she had ever done.

Often, I had intended to take the cast from it, but always had been restrained by a vague reluctance to disturb the mould. Now, as I looked at the delicate, sunken impression, I had again the feeling that this, her last work, ought to be finished, and I was still debating the matter with the mould in my hand when I heard a quick step upon the stair, followed by a characteristic knock on my door.

My first impulse was to hustle my treasures back into their box before answering the summons. But this was almost instantly followed by a revulsion. I recognized the knock as Thorndyke's, and somehow there came upon me a desire to share my memories with him. He had shown a strangely sympathetic insight into my feelings towards Stella. He had read my diary. He now knew the whole story, and he was the kindest, the most loyal and most discreet of friends. Gently laying down the mould I went to the door and threw it open.

"I saw your light burning as I passed just now," said Thorndyke as he entered and shook my hand warmly, "so I thought I would take the opportunity to drop in and return your diary. I hope I am not disturbing you. If I am, you must treat me as a friend and eject me."

"Not at all, Thorndyke," I replied. "On the contrary, you would be doing me a charity if you would stay and smoke a companionable pipe."

"Good," said he. "Then I will give myself the pleasure of a quiet gossip. But what is amiss, Mayfield?" he continued, laying a friendly hand on my shoulder and looking me over critically. "You look worn, and worried and depressed. You are not letting your mind dwell too much, I hope, on the tragedy that has come unbidden into your life?"

"I am afraid I am," I replied. "The horrible affair haunts me. Suspicion and mystery are in the very air I breathe. A constant menace seems to hang over all my friends, so that I am in continual dread of some new catastrophe. I have just ascertained that Wallingford is really being watched and shadowed, and not only Wallingford, but even Miss Norris."

He did not appear surprised or seek for further information. He merely nodded and looked into my face with grave sympathy.

"Put it away, Mayfield," said he. "That is my counsel to you. Try to forget it. You have put the investigation into my hands. Leave it there and wash your own of it. You did not kill Harold Monkhouse. Whoever did must pay the penalty if ever the crime should be brought home to the perpetrator. And if it never can be, it were better that you and all of us should let it sink into oblivion rather than allow it to remain to poison the lives of innocent persons. Let us forget it now. I see you were trying to."

I had noticed that when he first entered the room, he cast a single, swift glance at the table which, I was sure, had comprehended every object on it. Then he had looked away and never again let his eyes stray in that direction. But now, as he finished speaking, he glanced once more at the table, and this time with undisguised interest.

"Yes," I admitted. "I was trying to find in the memories of the past an antidote for the present. These are the relics of that past. I daresay you have read of them in the diary and probably have written me down a mawkish sentimentalist."

"I pray you, my friend, not to do me that injustice!" he exclaimed. "Faithful friendship, that even survives the grave, is not a thing that any man can afford to despise. But for the disaster of untimely death, your faithfulness and hers would have created for two persons the perfect life. I assure you, Mayfield, that I have been deeply moved by the story of your delightful friendship and your irreparable loss. But don't let us dwell too much on the sad aspects of the story. Show me your relics. I see some very charming little plaques among them."

He picked up one with reassuring daintiness of touch and examined it through a reading-glass that I handed to him.

"It really is a most admirable little work," said he. "Not in the least amateurish. She had the makings of a first-class medallist, the appreciation of the essential qualities of a miniature relief. And she had a fine feeling for composition and spacing."

Deeply gratified by his appreciation and a little surprised by his evident knowledge of the medallist's art, I presented the little works, one after another, and we discussed their merits with the keenest interest. Presently he asked, "Has it never occurred to you, Mayfield, that these charming little works ought to be finished?"

"Finished?" I repeated. "But, aren't they finished?"

"Certainly not. They are only on the plaster. But a plaster cast is an intermediate form. Just a mere working model. It is due to the merits of these plaques and medals that they should be put into permanent material – silver or copper or bronze. I'll tell you what, Mayfield," he continued, enthusiastically. "You shall let Polton make replicas of some of them – he could do it with perfect safety to the originals. Then we could hand the casts to an electrotyper or a founder – I should favour the electrotype process for such small works – and have them executed in whichever metal you preferred. Then you would be able to see, for the first time, the real quality of the modelling."

I caught eagerly at the idea, but yet I was a little nervous.

"You think it would be perfectly safe?" I asked.

"Absolutely safe. Polton would make gelatine moulds which couldn't possibly injure the originals."

That decided me. I fell in with the suggestion enthusiastically, and forthwith we began an anxious consultation as to the most suitable pieces with which to make a beginning. We had selected half-a-dozen casts when my glance fell on the wax mould. That was Stella's masterpiece and it certainly ought to be finished, but I was loath to part with the mould for fear of an accident. Very dubiously, I handed it to Thorndyke and asked, "What do you think of this? Could it be cast without any risk of breaking it?"

He laid the mould on the table before him so that the light fell obliquely across it and looked down on it reflectively.

"So," said he, "this is the wax mould. I was reading about it only yesterday and admiring your resourcefulness and ingenuity. I must read the entry again with the actual object before me."

He opened the diary, which he had laid on the table, and when he had found the entry, read it to himself in an undertone:

> "Dropped in to have tea with Stella and found her bubbling with excitement and triumph. She had just finished the portrait medal and though her eyes were red and painful from the strain of the close work, in spite of her new

spectacles, she was quite happy and as proud as a little peacock. And well she might be. I should like Lanterri to see his unknown pupil's work. We decided to make the mould of it at once, but when I got out the plaster tin, I found it empty. Most unfortunate, for the clay was beginning to dry and I didn't dare to damp it. But something had to be done to protect it. Suddenly I had a brilliant idea. There was nearly a whole candle in Stella's candlestick, quite enough for a mould, and good, hard wax that wouldn't warp. I took off the reflector and lighted the candle, which I took out of the candlestick and held almost upside down over the clay medal and let the wax drip on to it. Soon the medal was covered by a film of wax which grew thicker and thicker, until, by the time I had used up practically the whole of the candle, there was a good, solid crust of wax, quite strong enough to cast from. When I went home, I took the slate with me with the wax mould sticking to it, intending to cover it with a plaster shell for extra safety. But my plaster tin was empty, too, so I put the slate away in a safe place until I should get some fresh plaster to make the cast, which will not happen until I get back from Chelmsford.

"Busy evening getting ready for tomorrow, hope I shall feel less cheap then than I do now."

As Thorndyke finished reading he looked up and remarked, "That was an excellent plan of yours. I have seen Polton use the same method. But how was it that you never made the cast?"

"I was afraid of damaging the mould. As you know, when I came back from Ipswich, Stella was dead, and as the medal was her last work and her best, I hardly dared to risk the chance of destroying it."

"Still," Thorndyke urged, "it was the medal that was her work. The mould was your own, and the medal exists only potentially in the mould. It will come into actual existence only when the cast is made."

I saw the force of this, but I was still a little uneasy, and said so,

"There is no occasion," said he. "The mould is amply strong enough to cast from. It might possibly break in separating the cast, but that would be of no consequence, as you would then have the cast, which would be the medal, itself. And it could then be put into bronze or silver."

"Very well," I said, "if you guarantee the safety of the operation, I am satisfied. I should love to see it in silver, or perhaps it might look even better in gold."

Having disposed of the works, themselves, we fell to discussing the question of suitable settings or frames, and this led us to the subject of the portraits. Thorndyke glanced over the collection, and picking up one, which happened to be my own favourite, looked at it thoughtfully.

"It is a beautiful face," said he, "and this seems to have been a singularly happy portrait. In red chalk autotype, it would make a charming little picture. Did you take it?"

"Yes, and as I have the negative I am inclined to adopt your suggestion. I am surprised that I never thought of it myself, for red chalk is exactly the right medium."

"Then let Polton have the negative. He is quite an expert in autotype work."

I accepted the offer gladly and we then came back to the question of framing. Thorndyke's suggestion was that the portrait should be treated as a medallion and enclosed in a frame to match that of the medal. The idea appealed to me rather strongly, and presently a further one occurred to me, though it was suggested indirectly by Thorndyke, who had taken up the tress of Stella's hair and was looking at it admiringly as he drew it softly between his fingers.

"Human hair," he remarked, "and particularly a woman's hair, is always a beautiful material, no matter what its colour may be, but this red-gold variety is one of the most gorgeous of Nature's productions."

"Yes," I agreed, "it is extremely decorative. Barbara had her tress made up into a thin plait and worked into the frame of a miniature of Stella. I liked the idea, but somehow the effect is not so very pleasing. But it is an oblong frame."

"I don't think," said Thorndyke, "that a plait was quite the best form. A little cable would look better, especially for a medallion portrait, indeed I think that if you had a plain square black frame with a circular opening, a little golden cable, carried round concentrically with the opening would have a rather fine effect."

"So it would," I exclaimed. "I think it would look charming. I had no idea, Thorndyke, that you were a designer. Do you think Polton could make the cable?"

"Polton," he replied, impressively, "can do anything that can be done with a single pair of human hands. Let him have the hair, and he will make the cable and the frame, too, and he will see that the glass cover is an airtight fit – for, of course, the cable would have to be under the glass."

To this also I agreed with a readiness that surprised myself. And yet it was not surprising. Hitherto I had been accustomed secretly and in solitude to pore over these pathetic little relics of happier days and lock up my sorrows and my sense of bereavement in my own breast. Now, for the first time, I had a confidant who shared the knowledge of my shattered hopes and vanished happiness, and so wholeheartedly, with such delicate sympathy and perfect understanding had Thorndyke entered into the story of my troubled life that I found in his companionship not only a relief from my old self-repression but a sort of subdued happiness. Almost cheerfully I fetched an empty cigar-box and a supply of cotton wool and tissue paper and helped him tenderly and delicately to pack my treasures for their first exodus from under my roof. And it was with only a faint twinge of regret that I saw him, at length, depart with the box under his arm.

"You needn't be uneasy, Mayfield," he said, pausing on the stairs to look back. "Nothing will be injured, and as soon as the casting is successfully carried through, I shall drop a note in your letter-box to set your mind at rest. Good night."

I watched him as he descended the stairs, and listened to his quick foot-falls, fading away up the court. Then I went back to my room with a faint sense of desolation to repack the depleted deed-box and thereafter to betake myself to bed.

Chapter XV
A Pursuit and a Discovery

More than a week had passed since that eventful evening – how eventful I did not then realize – when I had delivered my simple treasures into Thorndyke's hands. But I was not uneasy, for, within twenty-four hours, I had found in my letter-box the promised note, assuring me that the preliminary operations had been safely carried through and that nothing had been damaged. Nor was I impatient. I realized that Polton had other work than mine on hand and that there was a good deal to do. Moreover, a little rush of business had kept me employed and helped me to follow Thorndyke's counsel and forget, as well as I could, the shadow of mystery and peril that hung over my friends, and, by implication, over me.

But on the evening of which I am now speaking I was free. I had cleared off the last of the day's work, and, after dining reposefully at my club, found myself with an hour or two to spare before bed-time, and it occurred to me to look in on Thorndyke to smoke a friendly pipe and perchance get a glimpse of the works in progress.

I entered the Temple from the west, and, threading my way through the familiar labyrinth, crossed Tanfield Court, and passing down the narrow alley at its eastern side, came out into King's Bench Walk. I crossed the Walk at once and was sauntering down the pavement towards Thorndyke's house when I noticed a large, closed car drawn up at its entry, and, standing on the pavement by the car, a tall man whom I recognized by the lamplight as Mr. Superintendent Miller.

Now I did not much want to meet the superintendent, and in any case it was pretty clear to me that my visit to Thorndyke was not very opportune. The presence of Miller suggested business, and the size of the car suggested other visitors. Accordingly I slowed down and was about to turn back when my eye caught another phenomenon. In the entry next to Thorndyke's a man was standing, well back in the shadow, but not so far that he could not get a view of the car, on which he was quite obviously keeping a watchful eye. Indeed, he was so preoccupied with his observation of it that he had not noticed my approach, his back being turned towards me.

Naturally, the watchful attitude and the object of his watchfulness aroused my suspicions as to his identity. But a movement backward on his part which brought him within range of the entry lamp, settled matter. He was Anthony Wallingford.

I turned and walked quietly back a few paces. What was this idiot doing here within a few yards of Thorndyke's threshold? Was he merely spying fatuously and without purpose? Or was it possible that he might be up to some kind of mischief? As I framed the question my steps brought me opposite another entry. The walk was in darkness save for the few lamps and the place was practically deserted. After a moment's reflection, I stepped into the entry and decided thence to keep a watch upon the watcher.

I had not long to wait. Hardly had I taken up my rather undignified position when three men emerged from the house and walked slowly to the car. By the light of the lamp above Thorndyke's entry, I could see them quite plainly and I recognized them all. One was Thorndyke, himself, another was Dr. Jervis, Thorndyke's colleague, now in the employ of the Home Office, and the third was Dr. Barnwell, well-known to me as the analyst and toxicologist to the Home Office. All three carried substantial bags and Dr. Barnwell was encumbered with a large case, like an out-size suit-case, suggestive of chemical apparatus. While they were depositing themselves and their impedimenta in the car, Superintendent Miller gave directions to the driver. He spoke in clear, audible tones, but though (I have to confess) I listened intently, I caught only the question: "Do you know the way?" The words which preceded and followed it were just audible but not intelligible to me. It appeared, however, that they were intelligible to Wallingford, for, as soon as they were spoken and while the superintendent still held the open door of the car, he stepped forth from his lurking-place and walked boldly and rapidly across to the narrow passage by which I had come.

Realizing instantly what his intention was, I came out of the entry and started in pursuit. As I reached the entrance to the passage, my ear caught the already faint sound of his receding footsteps, by which I learned that he was running swiftly and as silently as he could. Since I did not intend to lose him, I had no choice but to follow his example, and I raced across Tanfield Court, past the Cloisters, and round by the church as if the Devil were after me instead of before. Half-way up Inner Temple Lane he slowed down to a walk – very wisely, for otherwise the night porter would certainly have stopped him – and was duly let out into Fleet Street, whither I followed him at a short interval.

When I stepped out of the gate I saw him some little distance away to the west, giving directions to the driver of a taxi. I looked round desperately, and, to my intense relief, perceived an apparently empty taxi approaching from the east. I walked quickly towards it, signalling as I

401

went, and the driver at once drew in to the kerb and stopped. I approached him, and, leaning forward, said in a low voice – though there was no one within earshot – "There is a taxi just in front. It will probably follow a big car which is coming up Middle Temple Lane. I want you to keep that taxi in sight, wherever it may go. Do you understand?"

The man broke into a cynical grin – the nearest approach to geniality of which a taxi-driver is capable – and replied that he understood and, as at this moment the nose of the car appeared coming through the arched entrance gate of Middle Temple Lane, I sprang into the taxi and shut the door. From the off-side window, but keeping well back out of sight, I saw the car creep across Fleet Street, turn eastward, and then sweep round into Chancery Lane. Almost immediately, Wallingford's taxi moved off and followed, and then, after a short interval, my own vehicle started, and, crossing directly to Chancery Lane, went ahead in the wake of the others.

It was an absurd affair. Now that the pursuit was started and its conduct delegated for the time to the driver, I leaned back in the shadow and was disposed to grin a little sheepishly at my own proceedings. I had embarked on them in obedience to a sudden impulse without reflection – for which, indeed, there had been no time. But was there anything to justify me in keeping this watch on Wallingford? I debated the question at some length and finally decided that, although he was probably only playing the fool, still it was proper that I should see what he was really up to. Thorndyke was my friend and it was only right that I should stand between him and any possible danger. Well as he was able to take care of himself, he could not be always on his guard. And I could not forget the infernal machine. Someone at least had the will to do him an injury.

But what about the brown-hatted man? Why had he not joined in this novel sport? Or had he? I put my head out of the window and looked along the street in our rear, but there was no sign of any pursuing taxi. The ridiculous procession was limited to three vehicles, which was just as well, since we did not want a police cyclist bringing up the rear.

From my own proceedings my thoughts turned to those of Thorndyke and his companions, though they were no affair of mine, or of Wallingford's either, for that matter. Apparently the three men were going somewhere to make a *post mortem* examination. The presence of Dr. Barnwell suggested an analysis in addition, and the presence of Miller hinted at a criminal case of some kind. But it was not my case or Wallingford's. For both of us the analyst had already done his worst.

While I reflected, I kept an eye on the passing landmarks, checking our route and idly trying to forecast our destination. From Chancery Lane we crossed Holborn and entered Gray's Inn Road, at the bottom of which we swept round by King's Cross into Pancras Road. At the end of this we turned up Great College Street, crossed Camden Road, and presently passed along the Kentish Town Road. So far I had noted our progress with no more than a languid interest. It did not matter to me whither we were going. But when, at the Bull and Gate, we swept round into Highgate Road, my attention awoke, and when the taxi turned sharply at the Duke of St. Albans and entered Swain's Lane, I sat up with a start. In a moment of sudden enlightenment, I realized what our destination must be, and the realization came upon me with the effect of a palpable blow. This lane, with its precipitous ascent at the upper end, was no ordinary thoroughfare. It was little more than an approach to the great cemetery whose crowded areas extended on either side of it, its traffic was almost completely limited to the mournful processions that crept up to the wide gates by the mortuary chapel. Indeed, on the very last occasion when I had ridden up this lane, my conveyance had been the mourning carriage which followed poor little Stella to her last home.

Before I had recovered from the shock of this discovery sufficiently to consider what it might mean, the taxi came to a sudden halt. I stepped out, and, looking up the lane, made out the shadowy form of Wallingford's vehicle, already backing and manoeuvring to turn round.

"Bloke in front has got out," my driver announced in a hoarse whisper, and as he spoke, I caught sight of Wallingford – or at least of a human figure – lurking in the shadow of the trees by the railings on the right-hand side of the road. I paid off my driver (who, thereupon, backed on to the footway, turned and retired down the hill) and, having waited for the other taxi to pass down, began slowly to ascend the lane, keeping in the shadow of the trees. Now that the two taxis were gone, Wallingford and I had the lane to ourselves, excepting where, in the distance ahead, the reflected light from the headlamps of the car made a dim halo and the shape of the gothic chapel loomed indistinctly against the murky sky. I could see him quite plainly, and no doubt he was aware of my presence – at any rate, I did not propose to attempt any concealment, so far as he was concerned. His movements had ceased to be of any interest to me. My entire concern was with the party ahead and with the question as to what Thorndyke was doing at this time of night in Highgate Cemetery.

The burial ground is divided, as I have said, into two parts, which lie on either side of the lane, the old cemetery with its great gates and the large mortuary chapel, on the left or west side, and the newer part on the right. To which of these two parts was Thorndyke bound? That was the question that I had to settle.

I continued to advance up the lane, keeping in the shadow, though it was a dark night and the precaution was hardly necessary. Presently I overtook Wallingford and passed him without either concealment or recognition on either side. I could now clearly make out the gable and pinnacles of the chapel and saw the car turn in the wide sweep and then extinguish its headlights. Presently, from the gate-house there emerged a party of men of whom some carried lanterns, by the light of which I could recognize Thorndyke and his three companions, and I noted that they appeared to have left their cases either in the car or elsewhere for they now carried nothing. They lingered for a minute or two at the wicket by the great gates. Then, accompanied by a man whom I took to be the gate-keeper, they crossed the road to the gate of the eastern cemetery and were at once followed by another party of men, who trundled two wheel-barrows, loaded with some bulky objects the nature of which I could not make out. I watched them with growing anxiety and suspicion as they passed in at the gate, and when they had all entered and moved away along the main path, I came forth from the shadow and began to walk quickly up the lane.

The eastern cemetery adjoins Waterlow Park, from which it is separated by a low wall surmounted by tall railings, and this was my objective. The park was now, of course, closed for the night, locked up and deserted. So much the better. Locks and bars were no hindrance to me. I knew the neighbourhood of old. Every foot of the lane was familiar to me, though the houses that had grown up at the lower end had changed its aspect from that which I remembered when as a boy I had rambled through its leafy shades. On I strode, past the great gates on the left and the waiting car, within which I could see the driver dozing, past the white gatehouse on the right, up the steep hill until I came to the place where a tall oak fence encloses the park from the lane. Here I halted and took off my overcoat, for the six-foot fence is guarded at the top by a row of vicious hooks. Laying the folded overcoat across the top of the fence, I sprang up, sat for a moment astride and then dropped down into the enclosure.

I now stood in a sort of dry ditch between the fence and a steep bank, covered with bushes which rose to the level of the park. I had just taken down my overcoat and was putting it on before climbing the bank when its place was taken by another overcoat cast over from without. Then a pair of hands appeared, followed by the clatter of feet against the fence and the next moment I saw Wallingford astride of the top and looking down at me.

I still affected to be unaware of him, and, turning away, began to scramble up the bank, at the summit of which I pushed my way through

404

the bushes and, stepping over a three-foot fence, came out upon a by-path overshadowed by trees. Pausing for a moment to get my bearings and to mark out a route by which I could cross the park without coming into the open, where I might be seen by some watchful keeper, I started off towards a belt of trees just as Wallingford stepped over the dwarf fence and came out upon the path behind me.

The position was becoming absurd, though I was too agitated to appreciate its humour. I could not protest against his following me, seeing that I had come in the first place to spy upon him, and was now, like himself, engaged in spying upon Thorndyke. However, he soon solved the difficulty by quickening his pace and overtaking me, when he asked in a quite matter-of-fact tone, "What is Thorndyke up to, Mayfield?"

"That is what I want to find out," I replied.

"He is not acting on your instructions, then?"

"No, and the probability is that what he is doing is no concern of mine or of yours either. But I don't know, and I have come here to make sure. Keep in the shadow. We don't want the keeper to see us prowling about here."

He stepped back into the shade and we pursued our way in silence – and even then, troubled and agitated as I was, I noted that he asked me no question as to what was in my mind. He was leaving the initiative entirely to me.

When we had crossed the park in the shelter of the trees and descended into the hollow by the little lake where we were out of sight of the gate-house, I led the way towards the boundary between the park and the cemetery. The two enclosures were separated, as I have said, by a low wall surmounted by a range of high, massive railings, and the wall and the cemetery beyond were partially concealed by an irregular hedge of large bushes. Pushing through the bushes, I moved along the wall until I came to the place which I intended to watch, and here I halted in the shade of a tall mass of bushes and, resting my arms on the broad coping of the wall, took up my post of observation with Wallingford, silently attentive at my side.

The great burial ground was enveloped in darkness so profound that the crowded headstones and monuments conveyed to the eye no more than a confused glimmer of ghostly pallor that was barely distinguishable from the general obscurity. One monument only could be separately identified – a solitary stone cross that rose above a half-seen grave some sixty yards from the wall. But already the mysterious procession could be seen threading its way in and out by the intricate, winding paths, the gleam of the lanterns lighting up now a marble figure and now a staring headstone or urn or broken column, and as it drew ever nearer, the glare of the lanterns, the rumble of the barrow-wheels on the hard paths, and the spectral figures of the men grew more and more distinct. And still Wallingford watched and spoke never a word.

At length, a turn of the path brought the procession into full view, and as it approached I could make out a man – evidently by his uniform, the cemetery keeper – leading, lantern in hand and showing the way. Nearer and nearer the procession drew until at last, close by the stone cross, the leader halted. Then, as Thorndyke and his companions – now clearly visible – came up, he lifted his lantern and let its light fall full on the cross. And even at this distance I could read with ease – though it was unnecessary – the single name: *STELLA*.

As that name – to me so sacred – flashed out of the darkness, Wallingford gripped my arm. "Great God!" he exclaimed. "It is Stella Keene's grave! I came here once with Barbara to plant flowers on it."

He paused, breathing hard and still clutching my arm. Then, in a hoarse whisper, lie demanded, "What can that devil be going to do?"

There was little need to ask. Even as he spoke, the labourers began to unload from the first barrow its lading of picks, shovels, and coils of rope. And when these were laid on the ground, the second barrow yielded up its cargo, a set of rough canvas screens which the men began to set up around the grave. And even as the screens were being erected, another lantern slowly approaching along the path, revealed two men carrying a long, bedstead-like object – a bier – which they at length set down upon its stunted legs just outside the screens.

With set teeth I stared incredulously between the railings at these awful preparations while Wallingford, breathing noisily, held fast to my arm with a hand that I could feel shaking violently. The lanterns inside the screens threw a weird, uncertain light on the canvas, and monstrous, distorted shadows moved to-and-fro. Presently, amidst these flitting, spectral shapes, appeared one like an enormous gnome, huge, hideous and deformed, holding an up-raised pick. The shadowy implement fell with an audible impact, followed by the ring of a shovel.

At the sight and the sound – so dreadfully conclusive – Wallingford sprang up with a stifled cry.

"God Almighty! That devil is going to dig her up!"

He stood motionless and rigid for a few moments. Then, turning suddenly, without another word, he burst through the bushes, and I heard him racing madly across the park.

I had half-a-mind to follow him. I had seen enough. I now knew the shocking truth. Why stay and let my soul be harrowed by the sight of these ghouls? Every stroke of pick or shovel seemed to knock at my

406

heart. Why not go and leave them to their work of desecration? But I could not go. I could not tear myself away. There was the empty bier. Presently she would be lying on it. I could not go until I had seen her borne away.

So I stayed there gazing between the railings, watching the elfin shapes that flitted to-and-fro on the screen, listening to the thud of pick and the ring and scrape of shovel and letting my confused thoughts wander obscurely through a maze of half-realized pain and anger. I try in vain to recall clearly what was my state of mind. Out of the confusion and bewilderment little emerges but a dull indignation, and especially a feeling of surprised resentment against Thorndyke.

The horrible business went on methodically. By degrees a shadowy mound grew up at the bottom of the screen. And then of her movements and other sounds, a hollow, woody sound that seemed to bring my heart into my mouth. At last, the screens were opened at the end and then the coffin was borne out and laid on the bier. By the light of the lanterns I could see it distinctly. I was even able to recognize it, shabby and earth-stained as it now was. I saw Thorndyke help the keeper to spread over it some kind of pall, and then two men stepped between the handles of the bier, stooped and picked it up, and then the grim procession re-formed and began slowly to move away.

I watched it until it had passed round a turn of the path and was hidden from my view. Then I stood up, pushed my way through the bushes, and stole away across the park by the way I had come. In the ditch inside the fence I stood for a few moments listening, but the silence was as profound as the darkness. As quietly as I could I climbed over the fence and dropped down into the lane. There seemed to be not a soul moving anywhere near. Nevertheless, when I had slipped on my overcoat, instead of retracing my steps down the lane past the entrance-gates of the cemetery, I turned to the right and toiled up the steep hill to its termination in South Grove, where I bore away westward and, descending the long slope of West Hill, passed the Duke of St. Albans and re-entered the Highgate Road.

It did not occur to me to look out for any conveyance. My mind was in a whirl that seemed to communicate itself to my body and I walked on and on like one in a dream.

The dreary miles of deserted streets were consumed unreckoned – though still, without conscious purpose, I followed the direct road home as a well-constructed automaton might have done. But I saw nothing. Nor, for a time, could I be said to think coherently. My thoughts seethed and eddied in such confusion that no product emerged. I was conscious only of an indignant sense of shocked decency and a loathing of Thorndyke and all his works.

Presently, however, I grew somewhat more reasonable and my thoughts began to take more coherent shape. As a lawyer, I could not but perceive that Thorndyke must have something definite in his mind. He could not have done what I had seen him do without a formal authority from the Home Secretary, and before any such authority would have been given, he would have been called upon to show cause why the exhumation should be carried out. And such licences are not lightly granted. Nor, I had to admit, was Thorndyke likely to have made the application without due consideration. He must have had reasons for this outrageous proceeding which not only appeared sufficient to him but which must have appeared sufficient to the Home Secretary.

All this became by degrees clear enough to me. But yet I had not a moment's doubt that he had made some monstrous mistake. Probably he had been misled by something in my diary. That seemed to be the only possible explanation. Presently he would discover his error – by means which I shudderingly put aside. But when the error was discovered, the scandal would remain. It is impossible to maintain secrecy in a case like this. In twenty-four hours or less, all the world would know that the body of Mrs. Monkhouse's step-sister had been exhumed, and no subsequent explanation would serve to destroy the effect of that announcement. Wallingford's dismal prophecy was about to be fulfilled.

Moreover, Thorndyke's action amounted in effect to an open accusation – not of Madeline or Wallingford, but of Barbara, herself. And this indignity she would suffer at my hands – at the hands of her oldest friend! The thought was maddening. But for the outrageous lateness of the hour, I would have gone to her at once to put her on her guard and crave her pardon. It was the least that I could do. But it could not he done tonight, for she would have been in bed hours ago and her flat locked up for the night. However, I would go in the morning at the earliest possible hour. I knew that Barbara was an early riser and it would not be amiss if I arrived at the flat before the maid. She must be warned at the earliest possible moment and by me, who was the author of the mischief.

Thus, by the time that I reached my chambers I had decided clearly what was to be done. At first, I was disposed to reject altogether the idea of sleep. But presently, more reasonable thoughts prevailing, I decided at least to lie down and sleep a little if I could. But first I made a few indispensable preparations for the morning, filled the kettle and placed it on the gas-ring, set out the materials for a hasty breakfast, and cleaned my shoes. Then, when I had wound the alarm clock and set it for five, I partially undressed and crept into bed.

Chapter XVI
Barbara's Message

The routine of modern life creates the habit of dividing the day into a series of definite phases which we feel impelled to recognize even in circumstances to which they have no real application. Normally, the day is brought formally to an end by retirement to bed, a process that – also normally – leads to a lapse into unconsciousness, the emergence from which marks the beginning of another day. So, in mere obedience to the call of habit, I had gone to bed, though, in spite of bodily fatigue, there had been no hint of any tendency to sleep. But I might have saved myself the trouble. True, my tired limbs stretched themselves out restfully and mere muscular fatigue slowly wore off, but my brain continued, uselessly and chaotically, to pursue its activities only the more feverishly when the darkness and the silence closed the avenues of impressions from without.

Hour after hour crept by with incredible slowness, marked at each quarter by the gentle undertone of the Treasury clock, voicing its announcement, as it seemed, in polite protest (surely there was never a clock that hinted so delicately and unobtrusively at the passage of the irrevocable minutes "that perish for us and are reckoned"). Other sound there was none to break the weary silence of the night, but by the soft, mellow chime I was kept informed of the birth of another day and the progress of its infancy, which crawled so tardily in the wake of my impatience.

At last, when half-past-four had struck, I threw back the bedclothes and, stepping out, switched on the light and put a match to the gas under the kettle. I had no occasion to hurry, but rather sought to make my preparations with studied deliberation. In spite of which I had shaved, washed, and dressed and was sitting down to my frugal breakfast when the alarm clock startled me by blurting out with preposterous urgency its unnecessary reminder.

It had just turned a quarter-past-five when I set forth to take my way on foot towards Kensington. No conveyance was necessary, nor would it have been acceptable, for though throughout the wearisome hours that I had spent in bed my thoughts had never ceased to revolve around the problem that Thorndyke had set, I still seemed to have the whole matter to debate afresh.

What should I say to Barbara? How should I break to her the news that my own appointed agent had made an undissembled accusation and

410

was holding over her an unconcealed menace? I knew well enough what her attitude would be. She would hold me blameless and she would confront the threat against her reputation – even against her liberty – calmly and unafraid. I had no fear for her either of panic or recrimination. But how could I excuse myself? What could I say in extenuation of Thorndyke's secret, hostile manoeuvre?

The hands of the church clock were approaching half-past-six when I turned the corner and came in sight of the entrance to her flat. And at the same moment, I was made to realize the imminence and the actuality of the danger which threatened her. In a narrow street nearly opposite to the flat, a closed car was drawn up in such a position that it could move out into the main road either to the right or left without turning round, and a glance at the alert driver and a watchful figure inside – both of whom looked at me attentively as I passed – at once aroused my suspicions. And when, as I crossed to the flat, I observed a tall man perambulating the pavement, those suspicions were confirmed. For this was no brown-hatted neophyte. The hard, athletic figure and the calm, observant face were unmistakable. I had seen too many plain-clothes policemen to miss the professional characteristics. And this man also took unobtrusive note of me as my destination became apparent.

The church clock was chiming half-past-six as I pressed the button of the electric bell by Barbara's front door. In the silence that still wrapped the building, I could hear the bell ring noisily, though far away, and I listened intently for some sounds of movement within. The maid would not arrive for another half-hour, but I knew that Barbara was usually up at this hour. But I could hear no sign of any one stirring in the flat. Then I rang again, and yet again, and as there was still no sound from within, a vague uneasiness began to creep over me. Could Barbara be away from home? That might be as well in some respects. It might give time for the discovery of the error and save some unpleasantness. On the other hand – but at this moment I made a singular discovery myself. The latch-key was in the door! That was a most remarkable circumstance. It was so very unlike the methodical, self-possessed Barbara. But probably it had been left there by the maid. At any rate, there it was, and as I had now rung four times without result, I turned the key, pushed open the door, and entered.

When I had closed the door behind me, I stood for some seconds in the dark hall, listening. There was not a sound. I was astonished that the noise of the bell had not aroused Barbara. Indeed, I was surprised that she was not already up and about. Still vaguely uneasy, I felt for the light-switch, and when I had turned it on, stole along the hall and peered into the sitting room. Of course there was no one in it, nor was there any one in the kitchen, or in the spare bedroom. Finally, I went to Barbara's bedroom and knocked loudly, at the same time calling her by name. But still there was no response or sound of movement.

At last, after one or two more trials, I turned the handle and opening the door a few inches, looked in. The room was nearly dark, but the cold, wan light of the early morning was beginning to show on the blind, and in that dim twilight I could just make out a figure lying on the bed. With a sudden thrill of alarm, I stepped into the room and switched on the light. And then I stood, rooted to the spot, as if I had been turned into stone.

She was there, lying half-dressed upon the bed and as still as a bronze effigy upon a tomb. From where I stood I could see that her right hand, resting on the bed, lightly held a hypodermic syringe, and that her left sleeve was rolled up nearly to the shoulder. And when, approaching stealthily on tip-toe, I drew near, I saw upon the bare arm a plainly visible puncture and close by it a little blister-like swelling.

The first glance had made plain the dreadful truth. I had realized instantly that she was dead. Yet still, instinctively, I put my fingers to her wrist in the forlorn hope of detecting some lingering trace of life, and then any possible doubt was instantly dispelled, for the surface was stone-cold and the arm as rigid as that of a marble statue. Not only was she dead, she had been lying here dead while I, in my bed in the Temple, had lain listening to the chimes and waiting for the hour when I could come to her.

For quite a long time I stood by the bed looking down on her in utter stupefaction. So overwhelming was the catastrophe that for the moment my faculties seemed to be paralysed, my power of thought suspended. In a trance of amazement I gazed at her, and, with the idle irrelevancy of a dreamer, noted how young, how beautiful she looked, how lissom and graceful was the pose of the figure, how into the waxen face with its drowsy eyes and parted lips, there had come a something soft and youthful, almost girlish, that had not been there during life. Dimly and dreamily I wondered what the difference could be.

Suddenly my glance fell on the syringe that still rested in her hand. And with that my faculties awoke. She had killed herself! But why? Even as I asked myself the question, the terrible, the incredible answer stole into my mind only to be indignantly cast out. But yet – I lifted my eyes from the calm, pallid face, so familiar and yet so strange, and cast a scared glance round the room, and then I observed for the first time a small table near the bed on which beside a flat candle-stick containing the remains of a burnt-out candle, lay two unstamped letters. Stepping over to the table, I read their superscriptions. One was addressed to me, the other to Superintendent Miller, CID, and both were in Barbara's handwriting.

With a shaking hand I snatched up the one addressed to me, tore open the envelope and drew out the letter, and this is what I read:

Thursday, 1 a.m.

My dearest Rupert,

This letter is to bid you farewell. When you receive it you will curse and revile me, but I shall not hear those curses. Now, as I write, you are my darling Rupert and I am your dear friend, Barbara. With what will be when I am gone, I have no concern. It would be futile to hope that any empty words of mine could win your forgiveness. I have no such thought and do not even ask for pardon. When you think of me in the future it will be with hatred and loathing. It cannot be otherwise. But I have no part in the future. In the present – which runs out with every word that I write – I love you, and you, at least, are fond of me. And so it will be to the end, which is now drawing near.

But though this which I write to you in love will be read by you in hatred, yet I have a mind to let you know the whole truth. And that truth can be summed up in three words. I love you. I have always loved you, even when I was a little girl and you were a boy. My desire for you has been the constant, consuming passion of my life, and to possess you for my own has been the settled purpose from which I have never deviated but once – when I married Harold.

As I grew up from girlhood to womanhood, my love grew from a girl's to a woman's passion and my resolution became more fixed. I meant to have you for my own. But there was Stella. I could see that you worshipped her, and I knew that I should never have you while she lived. I was fond of poor Stella. But she stood as an insuperable obstacle between you and me. And – I suppose I am not quite as other women. I am a woman of a single purpose. Stella stood in the way of that purpose. It was a terrible necessity. But it had to be.

And after all, I seemed to have failed. When Stella was gone, you went away and I thought I had lost you forever.

For I could not follow you. I knew that you had understood me, at least partly, and that you had fled from me.

Then I was in despair. It seemed that I had dismissed poor Stella to no purpose. For once, I lost courage, and, in my loneliness, committed myself to a marriage with poor Harold. It was a foolish lapse. I ought to have kept my courage and lived in hope, as I realized almost as soon as I had married him.

But when you came back, I could have killed myself. For I could see that you were still the same old Rupert and my love flamed up more intensely than ever. And once more I resolved that you should be my own, and so you would have been in the end but for Dr. Thorndyke. That was the fatal error that I fell into, the error of under-valuing him. If I had only realized the subtlety of that man, I would have made a serious effort to deal with him. He should have had something very different from the frivolous make-believe that I sent him.

Well, Rupert, my darling, I have played my hand and I have lost. But I have lost only by the merest mischance. As I sit here with the ready-filled syringe on the table at my side, I am as confident as ever that it was worthwhile. I regret nothing but the bad luck that defeated skilful play, and the fact that you, my dear one, have had to pay so large a proportion of my losings.

I will say no more. You know everything now, and it has been a melancholy pleasure to me to have this little talk with you before making my exit.

Your loving friend,
Barbara

I have just slipped the key into the latch on the chance that you may come to me early. From what Tony said and what I know of you, I think it just possible. I hope you may. I like to think that we may meet, for the last time, alone.

To say that this astounding letter left me numb and stupefied with amazement would be to express but feebly its effect on me. The whole episode presented itself to me as a frightful dream from which I should presently awaken and come back to understandable and believable realities. For I know not how long I stood, dazed by the shock, with my

414

eyes riveted on that calm, comely figure on the bed, trying to grasp the incredible truth that this dead woman was Barbara, that she had killed herself, and that she had murdered Stella – murdered her callously, deliberately, and with considered intent.

Suddenly, the deathly silence of the flat was broken by the sound of an opening, and then of a closing door. Then a strong masculine voice was borne to my ear saying, in a not unkindly tone. "Now, my girl, you had better run off to the kitchen and shut yourself in."

On this I roused, and, walking across to the door, which was still ajar, went out into the hall, where I confronted Superintendent Miller and Barbara's maid. Both stared at me in astonishment and the maid uttered a little cry of alarm as she turned and hurried into the kitchen. The superintendent looked at me steadily and with obvious suspicion, and, after a moment or two, asked, gruffly, nodding at the bedroom door, "Is Mrs. Monkhouse in there?"

"Mrs. Monkhouse is dead," I answered.

"Dead!" he repeated, incredulously. Then, pushing past me, he strode into the room, and as I followed, I could hear him cursing furiously in a not very low undertone. For a few moments he stood looking down on the corpse, gently touching the bare arm and apparently becoming aware of its rigidity. Suddenly he turned, and, glaring fiercely at me, demanded, "What is the meaning of this, Mr. Mayfield?"

"The meaning?" I repeated, looking at him inquiringly.

"Yes. How came you to let her do this – that is, if she did it herself?"

"I found her dead when I arrived here," I explained.

"And when did you arrive here?"

"About half-an-hour ago."

He shook his head and rejoined in an ominously quiet tone, "That won't do, sir. The maid has only just come and the dead woman couldn't have let you in."

I explained that I had found the key in the outer door but he made no pretence of accepting the explanation.

"That is well enough," said he, "if you can prove that the key was in the door. Otherwise it is a mere statement which may or may not be true. The actual position is that I have found you alone in this flat with the body of a woman who has died a violent death. You will have to account satisfactorily for your presence here at this time in the morning, and for your movements up to the time of your arrival here."

The very equivocal, not to say perilous, position in which I suddenly found myself served to steady my wits. I realized instantly how profoundly suspicious the appearances really were and that if I could not produce evidence of my recent arrival I should quite probably have to meet the charge of being an accessory to the suicide. And an accessory to suicide is an accessory to murder. It was a very serious position.

"Have you seen your man yet?" I asked. "The men, I mean, who were on observation duty outside."

"I have seen them, but I haven't spoken to them. They are waiting out on the landing now. Why do you ask?"

"Because I think they saw me come in here."

"Ah, well, we can see about that presently. Is that letter that you have in your hand from Mrs. Monkhouse? Because, if it is, I shall want to see it."

"I don't want to show it unless it is necessary, and I don't think it will be. There is a letter addressed to you which will probably tell you all that you need know."

He snatched up the letter, and, tearing it open, glanced through it rapidly. Then, without comment, he handed it to me. It was quite short and ran as follows:

Thursday, 1:35 a.m.

Mr. Superintendent Miller, CID

> *This is to inform you that I alone am responsible for the death of my late husband, Harold Monkhouse, and also for that of the late Miss Stella Keene. I had no confidants or accomplices and no one was aware of what I had done.*
>
> *As my own death will occur in about ten minutes (from an injection of morphine which I shall administer to myself) this statement may be taken as my dying declaration.*
>
> *I may add that no one is aware of my intention to take my life.*

Yours very truly,

Barbara Monkhouse

"Well," said Miller, as I returned the letter to him, "that supports your statement, and if my men saw you enter the flat, that will dispose of the matter so far as the suicide is concerned. But there is another question. It is evident that she knew that a discovery had been made. Now, who told her? Was it you, Mr. Mayfield?"

"No," I replied, "it was not. I found her dead when I arrived, as I have told you."

"Do you know who did tell her?"

"I do not, and I am not disposed to make any guesses."

"No, it's no use guessing. Still, you know, Mr. Mayfield. You knew, and you came here to tell her, and you know who knew besides yourself. But there," he added, as we moved out into the hall, "it is no use going into that now. I've acted like a fool – too punctilious by half. I oughtn't to have let her slip through my fingers. I should have acted at once on Dr. Thorndyke's hint without waiting for confirmation."

He was still speaking in an angry, reproachful tone, but suddenly his manner changed. Looking at me critically but with something of kindly sympathy, he said, "It has been a trying business for you, Mr. Mayfield – the whole scandalous affair, and this must have given you a frightful shock, though I expect you would rather have it as it is than as it ought to have been. But you don't look any the better for it."

He escorted me politely but definitely to the outer door, and when he opened it, I saw his two subordinates waiting on the landing, to both of whom collectively Miller addressed the inquiry. "Did you see Mr. Mayfield enter this flat?"

"Yes, sir," was the reply of one, confirmed by the other. "He went up the stairs at exactly half-past-six."

Miller nodded, and wishing me "Good morning," beckoned to the two officers, and as I turned to descend the stairs, I saw the three enter and heard the door shut.

Once more in the outer world, walking the grey, half-lighted streets, to which the yet unextinguished lamps seemed only to impart an added chill, my confused thoughts took up the tangled threads at the point at which the superintendent's appearance had broken them off. But I could not get my ideas arranged into any intelligible form. Each aspect of the complex tragedy conflicted with all the others. The pitiful figure that I had left lying on the bed made its appeal in spite of the protest of reason, for the friendship of a lifetime cannot easily be extinguished in a moment. I knew now that she was a wretch, a monster, and when I reminded myself of what she had done, I grudged the easy, painless death by which she had slipped away so quietly from the wreckage that her incredible wickedness had created. When I contrasted that death – a more gentle lapsing into oblivion – with the long, cheerfully endured sufferings of brave, innocent little Stella, I could have cursed the faithful friendship of Wallingford which had let her escape from the payment to the uttermost farthing other hideous debt. And yet the face that haunted me – the calm, peaceful, waxen face – was the face of Barbara, my

417

friend, almost my sister, who had been so much to me, who had loved me with that strange, tenacious, terrible passion.

It was very confusing. And the same inconsistency pervaded my thoughts of Thorndyke. Unreasonably, I found myself thinking of him with a certain repulsion, almost of dislike, as the cause of this catastrophe. Yet my reason told me that he had acted with the highest motives of justice, that he had but sought retribution for Stella's sufferings and death, and those of poor, harmless Harold Monkhouse. That as a barrister, even as a citizen, he could do no less than denounce the wrong-doer. But my feelings were too lacerated, my emotions too excited to allow my reason to deal with the conflicting elements of this tragedy.

In this confused state of mind, I walked on, hardly conscious of direction, until I found myself at the entry of my chambers. I went in and made a futile attempt to do some work. Then I paced the room for an hour or more, alternately raging against Barbara and recalling the lonely figure that I had seen in the twilight of that darkened room, until my unrest drove me forth again to wander through the streets, away into the squalid east, among the docks and the rookeries from Whitechapel to Limehouse.

It was evening when, once more, I dragged myself up my stairs, and, spent with fatigue and exhausted by lack of food – for during the whole day I had taken but a few cups of tea, hastily snatched in the course of my wanderings – re-entered my chamber. As I closed the door, I noticed a letter in the box, and taking it out, listlessly opened the envelope. It was from Thorndyke, a short note, but very cordially worded, begging me "like a good fellow" to go round to have a talk with him.

I flung the note down impatiently on the table, with an immediate resurgence of my unreasonable sense of resentment. But in a few minutes I experienced a sudden revulsion of feeling. A sense of profound loneliness came upon me, a yearning for human companionship, and especially for the companionship of Thorndyke, from whom I had no secrets, and who knew the whole dreadful story even to its final culmination.

Once more, foot-sore as I was, I descended my stairs and a couple of minutes later was ascending the "pair" that led up to Thorndyke's chambers.

Chapter XVII
Thorndyke Retraces the Trail

Apparently Thorndyke had seen me from the window as I crossed the Walk for, when I reached the landing, I found him standing in the open doorway of his chambers, and at the sight of him, whatever traces of unreasonable resentment may have lingered in my mind melted away instantly. He grasped my hand with almost affectionate warmth, and looking at me earnestly and with the most kindly solicitude said, "I am glad you have come, Mayfield. I couldn't bear to think of you alone in your chambers, haunted by this horrible tragedy."

"You have heard, then – about Barbara, I mean?"

"Yes. Miller called and told me. Of course, he is righteously angry that she has escaped, and I sympathize with him. But for us – for you and me – it is a great deliverance. I was profoundly relieved when I heard that she was gone – that the axe had fallen once for all."

"Yes," I admitted, "it was better than the frightful alternative of a trial and what would have followed. But still, it was terrible to see her, lying dead, and to know that it was my hand – the hand of her oldest and dearest friend – that had struck the blow."

"It was *my* hand, Mayfield, not yours, that actually struck the blow. But even if it had been yours instead of your agent's, what could have been more just and proper than that retribution should have come through the hand of the friend and guardian of that poor murdered girl?"

I assented with a shudder to the truth of what he had said, but still my mind was too confused to allow me to see things in their true perspective. Barbara, my friend, was still more real to me than Barbara the murderess. He nodded sympathetically enough when I explained this, but rejoined, firmly, "You must try, my dear fellow, to see things as they really are. Shocking as this tragedy is, it would have been immeasurably worse if that terrible woman had not received timely warning. As it is, the horrible affair has run its course swiftly and is at an end. And do not forget that if the axe has fallen on the guilty, its menace has been lifted from the innocent. Madeline Norris and Anthony Wallingford will sleep in peace tonight, free from the spectre of suspicion that has haunted them ever since Harold Monkhouse died. As to the woman whose body you found this morning, she was a monster. She could not have been permitted to live. Her very existence was a menace to the lives of all who came into contact with her."

Again, I could not but assent to his stern indictment and his impartial statement of the facts.

"Very well, Mayfield," said he. "Then try to put it to yourself that, for you, the worst has happened and is done with. Try to put it away as a thing that now belongs to the past and is, in so far as it is possible, to be forgotten."

"As far as is possible," I repeated. "Yes, of course, you are quite right, Thorndyke. But forgetfulness is not a thing which we can command at will."

"Very true," he replied. "But yet we can control to a large extent the direction of our thoughts. We can find interests and occupations. And, speaking of occupations, let me show you some of Polton's productions."

He rose and, putting a small table by the side of my chair, placed on it one or two small copper plaques and a silver medallion which he had taken from a drawer. The medallion was the self-portrait of Stella which had lain dormant in the wax mould through all the years which had passed since her death, and as I took it in my hand and gazed at the beloved face, I found it beautiful beyond my expectations.

"It is a most charming little work," I said, holding it so that the lamp light fell most favourably on the relic, "I am infinitely obliged to you, Thorndyke."

"Don't thank me," said he. "The whole credit is due to Polton. Not that he wants any thanks, for the work has yielded him hours of perfect happiness. But here he is with the products of another kind of work."

As he spoke, Polton entered with a tray and began in his neat, noiseless way, to lay the table. I don't know how much he knew, but when I caught his eye and his smile of greeting, it seemed to me that friendliness and kindly sympathy exuded from every line of his quaint, crinkly face. I thanked him for his skilful treatment of my treasures and then, observing that he was apparently laying the table for supper, would have excused myself. But Thorndyke would hear of no excuses.

"My dear fellow," said he, "you are the very picture of physical exhaustion. I suspect that you have had practically no food today. A meal will help you to begin to get back to the normal. And, in any case, you mustn't disappoint Polton, who has been expecting you to supper and has probably made a special effort to do credit to the establishment."

I could only repeat my acknowledgments of Polton's goodness (noting that he certainly must have made a special effort, to judge by the results which began to make themselves evident) and, conquering my repugnance to the idea of eating, take my place at the table.

It is perhaps somewhat humiliating to reflect that our emotional states, which we are apt to consider on a lofty spiritual plane, are controlled by matters so grossly material as the mere contents of our stomachs. But such is the degrading truth, as I now realized. For no sooner had I commenced a reluctant attack on the products of Polton's efforts and drunk a glass of Burgundy – delicately warmed by that versatile artist to the exact optimum temperature – than my mental and physical unrest began to subside and allow a reasonable, normal outlook to develop, with a corresponding bodily state. In effect, I made quite a good meal and found myself listening with lively interest to Thorndyke's account of the technical processes involved in converting my little plaster plaques and the wax mould into their final states in copper and silver.

Nevertheless, in the intervals of conversation the unforgettable events of the morning and the preceding night tended to creep back into my consciousness, and now a question which I had hitherto hardly considered began to clamour for an answer. Towards the end of the meal, I put it into words. Apropos of nothing in our previous conversation, I asked, "How did you know, Thorndyke?" and as he looked up inquiringly, I added, "I mean, how were you able to make so confident a guess, for, of course, you couldn't actually know?"

"When do you mean?" he asked.

"I mean that when you applied for a Home Office authority, you must have had something to go on beyond a mere guess."

"Certainly I had," he replied. "It was not a guess at all. It was a certainty. When I made the application, I was able to say that I had positive knowledge that Stella Keene had been poisoned with arsenic. The examination of the poor child's body was not for my information. I would have avoided it if that had been possible. But it was not. As soon as my declaration was made, the exhumation became inevitable. The Crown could not have prosecuted on a charge of poisoning without an examination of the victim's body."

"But, Thorndyke," I expostulated, "how could you have been certain – I mean certain in a legal sense? Surely it could have been no more than a matter of inference."

"It was not," he replied. "It was a matter of demonstrated fact. I could have taken the case into court and proved the fact of arsenical poisoning. But, of course, the jury would have demanded evidence from an examination of the body, and quite properly, too. Every possible corroboration should be obtained in a criminal trial."

"Certainly," I agreed. "But still I find your statement incomprehensible. You speak of demonstrated fact. But what means of demonstration had you? There was my diary. I take it that that was the principal source of your information, in fact I can't think of any other. But the diary could only have yielded documentary evidence, which is quite a different thing from demonstrated fact."

"Quite," he agreed. "The diary contributed handsomely to the train of circumstantial evidence that I had constructed. But the demonstration – the final, positive proof – came from another source. A very curious and unexpected source."

"I suppose," said I, "as the case is finished and dealt with, there would be no harm in my asking how you arrived at your conclusion?"

"Not at all," he replied. "The whole investigation is a rather long story, but I will give you a summary of it if you like."

"Why a summary?" I objected. "I would rather have it *in extenso* if it will not weary you to relate it."

"It will be more likely to weary you," he replied. "But if you are equal to a lengthy exposition, let us take to our easy chairs and combine bodily comfort with forensic discourse."

We drew up the two armchairs before the hearth and, when Polton had made up the fire and placed between us a small table furnished with a decanter and glasses, Thorndyke began his exposition.

"This case is in some respects one of the most curious and interesting that I have met with in the whole of my experience of medico-legal practice. At the first glance, as I told you at the time, the problem that it presented seemed hopelessly beyond solution. All the evidence appeared to be in the past and utterly irrecoverable. The vital questions were concerned with events that had passed unrecorded and of which there seemed to be no possibility that they could ever be disinterred from the oblivion in which they were buried. Looking back now on the body of evidence that has gradually accumulated, I am astonished at the way in which the apparently forgotten past has given up its secrets, one after another, until it has carried its revelation from surmise to probability and from probability at last to incontestable proof.

"The inquiry divides itself into certain definite stages, each of which added new matter to that which had gone before. We begin, naturally, with the inquest on Harold Monkhouse, and we may consider this in three aspects: The ascertained condition of the body, the evidence of the witnesses, and the state of affairs disclosed by the proceedings viewed as a whole.

"First, as to the body: There appeared to be no doubt that Monkhouse died from arsenical poisoning, but there was no clear evidence as to how the poison had been administered. It was assumed that it had been taken in food or in medicine – that it had been swallowed – and no alternative method of administration was suggested or considered. But on studying the medical witnesses' evidence, and comparing it with the descriptions of the patient's symptoms, I was disposed to doubt whether the poison had actually been taken by the mouth at all."

"Why," I exclaimed, "how else could it have been taken?"

"There are quite a number of different ways in which poisonous doses of arsenic can be taken. Finely powdered arsenic is readily absorbed by the skin. There have been several deaths from the use of 'violet powder' contaminated with arsenic, and clothing containing powdered arsenic would produce poisonous effects. Then there are certain arsenical gases – notably arsine, or arseniureted hydrogen – which are intensely poisonous and which possibly account for a part of the symptoms in poisoning from arsenical wallpapers. There seemed to me to be some suggestion of arsenical gas in Monkhouse's case, but it was obviously not pure gas poisoning. The impression conveyed to me was that of a mixed poisoning, that the arsenic had been partly inhaled and partly applied to the skin, but very little, if any, taken by the mouth."

"You are not forgetting that arsenic was actually found in the stomach?"

"No. But the quantity was very minute, and a minute quantity is of no significance. One of the many odd and misleading facts about arsenic poisoning is that, in whatever way the drug is taken, a small quantity is always found in the stomach and there are always some signs of gastric irritation. The explanation seems to be that arsenic which has got into the blood in any way – through the skin, the lungs, or otherwise – tends to be eliminated in part through the stomach. At any rate, the fact is that the presence of minute quantities of arsenic in the stomach affords no evidence that the poison was swallowed."

"But," I objected, "what of the Fowler's Solution which was found in the medicine?"

"Exactly," said he. "That was the discrepancy that attracted my attention. The assumption was that the deceased had taken in his medicine a quantity of Fowler's Solution representing about a grain-and-a-half of arsenious acid. If that had been so we should have expected to find a very appreciable quantity in the stomach – much more than was actually found. The condition of the body did not agree with the dose that was assumed to have been taken, and when one came to examine the evidence of the various witnesses there was further room for doubt. Two of them had noticed the medicine at the time when the Fowler's Solution had not been added, but no witness had noticed it after the alleged change and before the death of the deceased. The presence of the Fowler's Solution was not observed until several days after his death.

Taking all the facts together, there was a distinct suggestion that the solution had been added to the medicine at some time after Monkhouse's death. But this suggestion tended to confirm my suspicion that the poison had not been swallowed. For the discovery of the Fowler's Solution in the medicine would tend to divert inquiry – and did, in fact, divert it – from any other method of administering the poison.

"To finish with the depositions: Not only was there a complete lack of evidence even suggesting any one person as the probable delinquent, there was not the faintest suggestion of any motive that one could consider seriously. The paltry pecuniary motive applied to all the parties and could not be entertained in respect of any of them. The only person who could have had a motive was Barbara. She was a young, attractive woman, married to an elderly, unattractive husband. If she had been attached to another man, she would have had the strongest and commonest of all motives. But there was nothing in the depositions to hint at any other man, and since she was absent from home when the poisoning occurred, she appeared to be outside the area of possible suspicion.

"And now to look at the evidence as a whole, you remember Miller's comment. There was something queer about the case, something very oddly elusive. At the first glance it seemed to bristle with suspicious facts. But when those facts were scrutinized they meant nothing. There were plenty of clues but they led nowhere. There was Madeline Norris who prepared the victim's food – an obvious suspect. But then it appeared that the poison was in the medicine, not in the food. There was Wallingford who actually had poison in his possession. But it was the wrong poison. There was the bottle that had undoubtedly contained arsenic. But it was nobody's bottle. There was the bottle that smelled of lavender and had red stains in it and was found in Miss Norris' possession, but it contained no arsenic. And so on.

"Now all this was very strange. The strongest suspicion was thrown on a number of people collectively. But it failed every time to connect itself with any one individually. I don't know precisely what Miller thought of it, but to me it conveyed the strong impression of a scheme – of something arranged, and arranged with extraordinary skill and ingenuity, I had the feeling that, behind all these confusing and inconsistent appearances, was a something quite different, with which they had no real connection, that all these apparent clues were a sort of smoke-screen thrown up to conceal the actual mechanism of the murder.

"What could the mechanism of the murder have been? That was what I asked myself. And by whom could the arrangements have been made and carried out? Here the question of motive became paramount.

What motive could be imagined? And who could have been affected by it? That seemed to be the essential part of the problem, and the only one that offered the possibility of investigation.

"Now, as I have said, the most obvious motive in cases of this kind is that of getting rid of a husband or wife to make room for another. And ignoring moral considerations, it is a perfectly rational motive, for the murder of the unwanted spouse is the only possible means of obtaining the desired release. The question was, could such a motive have existed in the present case, and the answer was that, on inspection, it appeared to be a possible motive, although there was no evidence that it actually existed. But, assuming its possibility for the sake of argument, who could have been affected by it? At once, one saw that Madeline Norris was excluded. The death of Harold Monkhouse did not affect her, in this respect, at all. There remained only Barbara and Wallingford. To take the latter first: He was a young man, and the wife was a young, attractive woman. He had lived in the same house with her, appeared to be her social equal, and was apparently on terms of pleasant intimacy with her. If he had any warmer feelings towards her, her husband's existence formed an insuperable obstacle to the realization of his wishes. There was no evidence that he had any such feelings, but the possibility had to be borne in mind. And there were the further facts that he evidently had some means of obtaining poisons and that he had ample opportunities for administering them to the deceased. All things considered, Wallingford appeared, *prima facie*, to be the most likely person to have committed the murder.

"Now to take the case of Barbara. In the first place, there was the possibility that she might have had some feeling towards Wallingford, in which case she would probably have been acting in collusion with him and her absence from home on each occasion when the poisoning took place would have been part of the arrangement. But, excluding Wallingford, and supposing her to be concerned with some other man, did her absence from home absolutely exclude the possibility of her being the poisoner? There were suggestions of skilful and ingenious arrangements to create false appearances. Was it possible that those arrangements included some method by which the poison could be administered during her absence without the connivance or knowledge of any other person?

"I pondered this question carefully by the light of all the details disclosed at the inquest, and the conclusion that I reached was that, given a certain amount of knowledge, skill, and executive ability, the thing was possible. But as soon as I had admitted the possibility, I was impressed by the way in which the suggestion fitted in with the known facts and served to explain them. For all the arranged appearances pointed to the use of Fowler's Solution, administered by the mouth. But this could not possibly have been the method if the poisoner were a hundred miles away. And as I have said, I was strongly inclined to infer, from the patient's symptoms and the condition of the body, that the poison had *not* been administered by the mouth.

"But all this, as you will realize, was purely hypothetical. None of the assumptions was supported by a particle of positive evidence. They merely represented possibilities which I proposed to bear in mind in the interpretation of any new evidence that might come into view.

"This brings us to the end of the first stage, the conclusions arrived at by a careful study of the depositions. But following hard on the inquest was your visit to me when you gave me the particulars of your past life and your relations with Barbara and Monkhouse. Now your little autobiographical sketch was extremely enlightening and, as it has turned out, of vital importance. In the first place, it made clear to me that your relations with Barbara were much more intimate than I had supposed. You were not merely friends of long standing, you were virtually in the relation of brother and sister. But with this very important difference – that you were *not* brother and sister. An adopted brother is a possible husband, an adopted sister is a possible wife. And when I considered your departure to Canada with the intention of remaining there for life, and your unexpected return. I found that the bare possibility that Barbara might wish to be released from her marriage had acquired a certain measure of probability.

"But further, your narrative brought into view another person who had died. And the death of that person presented a certain analogy with the death of Monkhouse. For if Barbara had wished to be your wife, both these persons stood immovably in the way of her wishes. Of course there was no evidence that she had any such wish, and the death of Stella was alleged to have been due to natural causes. Nevertheless, the faint, hypothetical suggestions offered by these new facts were strikingly similar to those offered by the previous facts.

"The next stage opened when I read your diary, especially the volume written during the last year of Stella's life. But now one came out of the region of mere speculative hypothesis into that of very definite suspicion. I had not read very far when, from your chance references to the symptoms of Stella's illness, I came to the decided conclusion that, possibly mingled with the symptoms of real disease, were those of more-or-less chronic arsenical poisoning. And what was even more impressive, those symptoms seemed to be closely comparable with Monkhouse's symptoms, particularly in the suggestion of a mixed poisoning partly due

426

to minute doses of arsine. I need not go into details, but you will remember that you make occasional references to slight attacks of jaundice (which is very characteristic of arsine poisoning) and to 'eye-strain' which the spectacles failed to relieve. But redness, smarting, and watering of the eyes is an almost constant symptom of chronic arsenic poisoning. And there were various other symptoms of a decidedly suspicious character to which you refer and which I need not go into now.

"Then a careful study of the diary brought into view another very impressive fact. There were considerable fluctuations in Stella's condition. Sometimes she appeared to be so far improving as to lead you to some hopes of her actual recovery. Then there would be a rather sudden change for the worse and she would lose more than she had gained. Now, at this time Barbara had already become connected with the political movement which periodically called her away from home for periods varying from one to four weeks, and when I drew up a table of the dates other departures and returns, I found that the periods included between them – that is the periods during which she was absent from home – coincided most singularly with Stella's relapses. The coincidence was so complete that, when I had set the data out in a pair of diagrams in the form of graphs, the resemblance of the two diagrams was most striking. I will show you the diagrams presently.

"But there was something else that I was on the look-out for in the diary, but it was only quite near the end that I found it. Quite early, I learned that Stella was accustomed to read and work at night by the light of a candle. But I could not discover what sort of candle she used, whether it was an ordinary household candle or one of some special kind. At last I came on the entry in which you describe the making of the wax mould, and then I had the information that I had been looking for. In that entry you mention that you began by lifting the reflector off the candle, by which I learned that the receptacle used was not an ordinary candlestick. Then you remark that the candle was of 'good hard wax', by which I learned that it was not an ordinary household candle – these being usually composed of a rather soft paraffin wax. Apparently, it was a stearine candle, such as is made for use in candle-lamps."

"But," I expostulated, "how could it possibly matter what sort of candle she used? The point seems to be quite irrelevant."

"The point," he replied, "was not only relevant, it was of crucial importance. But I had better explain. When I was considering the circumstances surrounding the poisoning of Monkhouse, I decided that the probabilities pointed to Barbara as the poisoner. But she was a hundred miles away when the poisoning occurred. Hence, the question that I asked myself was this: Was there any method that was possible and practicable in the existing circumstances by which Barbara could have arranged that the poisoning could be effected during her absence? And the answer was that there *was* such a method, but only one. The food and the medicine were prepared and administered by those who were on the spot. But the candles were supplied by Barbara, and by her put into the bedside candle-box before she went away. And they would operate during her absence."

"But," I exclaimed, "do I understand you to suggest that it is possible to administer poison by means of a *candle*?"

"Certainly," he replied. "It is quite possible and quite practicable. If a candle is charged with finely powdered arsenious acid – 'white arsenic' – when that candle is burnt, the arsenious acid will be partly vaporized and partly converted into arsine, or arseniureted hydrogen. Most of the arsine will be burnt in the flame and reconverted into arsenious acid, which will float in the air, as it condenses, in the form of an almost invisible white cloud. The actual result will be that the air in the neighbourhood of the candle will contain small traces of arsine – which is an intensely poisonous gas – and considerable quantities of arsenious acid, floating about in the form of infinitely minute crystals. This impalpable dust will be breathed into the lungs of any person near the candle and will settle on the skin, from which it will be readily absorbed into the blood and produce all the poisonous effects of arsenic.

"Now, in the case of Harold Monkhouse, not only was there a special kind of candle, supplied by the suspected person, but, as I have told you, the symptoms during life and the appearances of the dead body, all seemed to me to point to some method of poisoning through the lungs and skin rather than by way of the stomach, and also suggested a mixed poisoning in which arsine played some part. So that the candle was not only a possible medium of the poisoning, it was by far the most probable.

"Hence, when I came to consider Stella's illness and noted the strong suggestion of arsenic poisoning, and when I noted the parallelism of her illness with that of Monkhouse, I naturally kept a watchful eye for a possible parallelism in the method of administering the poison. And not only did I find that parallelism, but in that very entry, I found strong confirmation of my suspicion that the candle was poisoned. You will remember that you mention the circumstance that on the night following the making of the wax mould you were quite seriously unwell. Apparently you were suffering from a slight attack of acute arsenical poisoning, due to your having inhaled some of the fumes from the burning candle."

"Yes, I remember that," said I. "But what is puzzling me is how the candles could have been obtained. Surely it is not possible to buy arsenical candles?"

"No," he replied, "it is not. But it is possible to buy a candle-mould, with which it is quite easy to make them. Remember that, not so very long ago, most country people used to make their own candles, and the hinged moulds that they used are still by no means rare. You will find specimens in most local museums and in curio shops in country towns and you can often pick them up in farmhouse sales. And if you have a candle-mould, the making of arsenical candles is quite a simple affair. Barbara, as we know, used to buy a particular German brand of stearine candles. All that she had to do was to melt the candles, put the separated wicks into the mould, stir some finely-powdered white arsenic into the melted wax and pour it into the mould. When the wax was cool, the mould would be opened and the candles taken out-these hinged moulds usually made about six candles at a time. Then it would be necessary to scrape off the seam left by the mould and smooth the candles to make them look like those sold in the shops."

"It was a most diabolically ingenious scheme," said I.

"It was," he agreed. "The whole villainous plan was very completely conceived and most efficiently carried out. But to return to our argument. The discovery that Stella had used a special form of candle left me in very little doubt that Barbara was the poisoner and that poisoned candles had been the medium used in both crimes. For we were now out of the region of mere hypothesis. We were dealing with genuine circumstantial evidence. But that evidence was still much too largely inferential to serve as the material for a prosecution. We still needed some facts of a definite and tangible kind, and as soon as you came back from your travels on the Southeastern Circuit, fresh facts began to accumulate. Passing over the proceedings of Wallingford and his follower and the infernal machine – all of which were encouraging, as offering corroboration, but of no immediate assistance – the first really important accretion of evidence occurred in connection with our visit to the empty house in Hilborough Square."

"Ha!" I exclaimed. "Then you *did* find something significant, in spite of your pessimistic tone at the time? I may say, Thorndyke, that I had a feeling that you went to that house with the definite expectation of finding some specific thing. Was I wrong?"

"No. You were quite right. I went there with the expectation of finding one thing and a faint hope of finding another, and both the expectation and the hope were justified by the event. My main purpose in that expedition was to obtain samples of the wallpaper from

429

Monkhouse's room, but I thought it just possible that the soot from the bedroom chimneys might yield some information. And it did.

"To begin with, the wallpaper: The condition of the room made it easy to secure specimens. I tore off about a dozen pieces and wrote a number on each, to correspond with numbers that I marked on a rough sketch-plan of the room which I drew first. My expectation was that if – as I believed – arsenical candles had been burnt in that room, arsenic would have been deposited on all the walls, but in varying amounts, proportionate to the distance of the wall from the candle. The loose piece of paper on the wall by the bed was, of course, the real touchstone of the case, for if there were no arsenic in it, the theory of the arsenical candle would hardly be tenable. I therefore took the extra precaution of writing a full description of its position on the back of the piece and deposited it for greater safety in my letter-case.

"As soon as I reached home that day I spread out the torn fragment on the wide stage of a culture microscope and examined its outer surface with a strong top light. And the very first glance settled the question. The whole surface was spangled over with minute crystals, many of them hardly a ten-thousandth-of-an-inch in diameter, sparkling in the strong light like diamonds and perfectly unmistakable, the characteristic octahedral crystals of arsenious acid.

"But distinctive as they were, I took nothing for granted. Snipping off a good-sized piece of the paper, I submitted it to the Marsh-Berzelius Test and got a very pronounced 'arsenical mirror', which put the matter beyond any possible doubt or question. I may add that I tested all the other pieces and got an arsenic reaction from them all, varying, roughly, according to their distance from the table on which the candle stood.

"Thus the existence of the arsenical candle was no longer a matter of hypothesis or even of mere probability. It was virtually a demonstrated fact. The next question was, who put the arsenic into the candle? All the evidence, such as it was, pointed to Barbara. But there was not enough of it. No single fact connected her quite definitely with the candles, and it had to be admitted that they had passed through other hands than hers and that the candle-box was accessible to several people, especially during her absence. Clear evidence, then, was required to associate her – or someone else – with those poisoned candles, and I had just a faint hope that such evidence might be forthcoming. This was how I reasoned:

"Here was a case of poisoning in which the poison was self-administered and the actual poisoner was absent. Consequently it was impossible to give a calculated dose on a given occasion, nor was it possible to estimate in advance the amount that would be necessary to produce the desired result. Since the poison was to be left within reach of

430

the victim, to be taken from time to time, it would be necessary to leave a quantity considerably in excess of the amount actually required to produce death on any one occasion. It is probable that all the candles in the box were poisoned. In any case, most of them must have been, and as the box was filled to last for the whole intended time of Barbara's absence, there would be a remainder of poisoned candles in the box when Monkhouse died. But the incident of the 'faked' medicine showed that the poisoner was fully alive to the possibility of an examination of the room. It was not likely that so cautious a criminal would leave such damning evidence as the arsenical candles in full view. For if, by chance, one of them had been lighted and the bearer had developed symptoms of poisoning, the murder would almost certainly have been out. In any case, we could assume that the poisoner would remove them and destroy them after putting ordinary candles in their place.

"But a candle is not a very easy thing to destroy. You can't throw it down a sink, or smash it up and cast it into the rubbish-bin. It must be burnt, and owing to its inflammability, it must be burnt carefully and rather slowly, and if it contains a big charge of arsenic, the operator must take considerable precautions. And finally, these particular candles had to be burnt secretly.

"Having regard to these considerations, I decided that the only safe and practicable way to get rid of them was to burn them in a fireplace with the window wide open. This would have to be done at night when all the household was asleep, so as to be safe from interruption and discovery, and a screen would have to be put before the fireplace to prevent the glare from being visible through the open window. If there were a fire in the grate, so much the better. The candles could be cut up into small pieces and thrown into the fire one at a time.

"Of course the whole matter was speculative. There might have been no surplus candles, or if there were, they might have been taken out of the house and disposed of in some other way. But one could only act on the obvious probabilities and examine the chimneys, remembering that whereas a negative result would prove nothing for or against any particular person, a positive result would furnish very weighty evidence. Accordingly I collected samples of soot from the various bedroom chimneys and from that of Barbara's boudoir, labelling each of them with the aid of the cards which you had left in the respective rooms.

"The results were, I think, quite conclusive. When I submitted the samples to analysis I found them all practically free from arsenic – disregarding the minute traces that one expects to find in ordinary soot – with one exception. The soot from Barbara's bedroom chimney yielded, not mere traces, but an easily measurable quantity – much too large to have been attributable to the coal burnt in the grate.

"Thus, you see, so far as the murder of Monkhouse was concerned, there was a fairly conclusive case against Barbara. It left not a shadow of doubt in my mind that she was the guilty person. But you will also see that it was not a satisfactory case to take into court. The whole of the evidence was scientific and might have appeared rather unconvincing to the ordinary juryman, though it would have been convincing enough to the judge. I debated with myself whether I should communicate my discoveries to the police and leave them to decide for or against a prosecution, or whether I should keep silence and seek for further evidence. And finally I decided, for the present, to keep my own counsel. You will understand why."

"Yes," said I. "You suspected that Stella, too, had been poisoned."

"Exactly. I had very little doubt of it. And you notice that in this case there was available evidence of a kind that would be quite convincing to a jury – evidence obtainable from an examination of the victim's body. But here again I was disposed to adopt a waiting policy for three reasons.

"First, I should have liked to avoid the exhumation if possible. Second, if the exhumation were unavoidable, I was unwilling to apply for it until I was certain that arsenic would be found in the body, and third, although the proof that Stella had been poisoned would have strengthened the case enormously against Barbara, it would yet have added nothing to the evidence that a poisoned candle had been used.

"But the proof of the poisoned candle was the kernel of the case against Barbara. If I could prove that Stella had been poisoned by means of a candle, that would render the evidence absolutely irresistible. This I was not at present able to do. But I had some slight hopes that the deficiency might be made up, that some new facts might come into view if I waited. And, as there was nothing that called for immediate action, I decided to wait, and in due course, the deficiency was made up and the new facts did come into view."

As he paused, I picked up Stella's medallion and looked at it with a new and sombre interest Holding it up before him, I said, "I am assuming, Thorndyke, that the new facts were in some way connected with this. Am I right?"

"Yes," he replied, "you are entirely right. The connection between that charming little work and the evidence that sent that monster of wickedness to her death is one of the strangest and most impressive circumstances that has become known to me in the whole of my experience. It is no exaggeration to say that when you and Stella were working on that medallion, you were forging the last link in the chain of evidence that could have dragged the murderess to the gallows."

He paused, and, having replenished my glass, took the medallion in his hand and looked at it thoughtfully. Then he knocked out and refilled his pipe and I waited expectantly for the completion of this singular story.

Chapter XVIII
The Final Proof

"We now," Thorndyke resumed, "enter the final stage of the inquiry. Hitherto we have dealt with purely scientific evidence which would have had to be communicated to the jury and which they would have had to take on trust with no convincing help from their own eyes. We had evidence, conclusive to ourselves, that Monkhouse had been murdered by means of a poisoned candle. But we could not produce the candle or any part of it. We had nothing visible or tangible to show to the jury to give them the feeling of confidence and firm conviction which they rightly demand when they have to decide an issue involving the life or death of the accused. It was this something that could be seen and handled that I sought, and sought in vain until that momentous evening when I called at your chambers to return your diary.

"I remember that as I entered the room and cast my eyes over the things that were spread out on the table, I received quite a shock. For the first glance showed me that, amongst those things were two objects that exactly fulfilled the conditions of the final test. There was the wax mould – a part, and the greater part, of one of the suspected candles – and there was the tress of hair – a portion of the body of the person suspected to have been poisoned. With these two objects, it was possible to determine with absolute certainty whether that person had or had not been poisoned with arsenic, and if she had, whether the candle had or had not been the medium by which the poison was administered."

"But," I said, "you knew from the diary of the existence of the wax mould."

"I knew that it had existed. But I naturally supposed that the cast had been taken and the mould destroyed years ago, though I had intended to ask you about it. However, here it was, miraculously preserved, against all probabilities, still awaiting completion. Of course, I recognized it instantly, and began to cast about in my mind for some means of making the necessary examination without disclosing my suspicions. For you will realize that I was unwilling to say anything to you about Stella's death until the question was settled one way or the other. If the examination had shown no arsenic either in the candle or in the hair, it would not have been necessary to say anything to you at all.

"But while I was debating the matter, the problem solved itself. As soon as I came to look at Stella's unfinished works, I saw that they cried

434

aloud to be completed and that Polton was the proper person to carry out the work. I made the suggestion, which I should have made in any case, and when you adopted it, I decided to say nothing but to apply the tests when the opportunity offered."

"I am glad," said I, "to hear you say that you would have made the suggestion in any case. It looked at first like a rather cold-blooded pretext to get possession of the things. But you were speaking of the hair. Can you depend on finding recognizable traces of arsenic in the hair of a person who has been poisoned?"

"Certainly, you can," he replied. "The position is this: When arsenic is taken, it becomes diffused throughout the whole body, including the blood, the bones, and the skin. But as soon as a dose of arsenic is taken, the poison begins to be eliminated from the body and, if no further dose is taken, the whole of the poison is thrown off in a comparatively short time until none remains in the tissues – with one exception. That exception is the epidermis, or outer skin, with its appendages – the finger and toe nails and the hair. These structures differ from all others in that, instead of growing interstitially and being alive throughout, they grow at a certain growing-point and then become practically dead structures. Thus a hair grows at the growing-point where the bulb joins the true skin. Each day a new piece of hair is produced at the living root, but when once it has come into being it grows no more, but is simply pushed up from below by the next portion. Thenceforward it undergoes no change, excepting that it gradually moves upwards as new portions are added at the root. It is virtually a dead, unchanging structure.

"Now suppose a person were to take a considerable dose of arsenic. That arsenic becomes diffused throughout all the living tissues and is for a time deposited in them. The growing-point of the hair is a living tissue and of course the arsenic becomes deposited in it. Then the process of elimination begins and the arsenic is gradually removed from the living tissues. But in twenty-four hours, what was the growing-point of the hair has been pushed up about the fiftieth-of-an-inch and is no longer a growing structure. It is losing its vitality. And as it ceases to be a living tissue, it ceases to be affected by the process of elimination. Hence the arsenic, which was deposited in it when it was a living tissue, is never removed. It remains as a permanent constituent of that part of the hair, slowly moving up as the hair grows from below, until at last it is snipped off by the barber, or, if the owner is a long-haired woman, it continues to creep along until the hair is full-grown and drops out."

"Then the arsenic remains always in the same spot?"

"Yes. It is a local deposit at a particular point in the hair. And this, Mayfield, is a most important fact, as you will see presently. For observe

435

what follows. Hair grows at a uniform rate – roughly, a fiftieth-of-an-inch in twenty-four hours. It is consequently possible, by measurement, to fix nearly exactly the age of any given point on a hair. Thus, if we have a complete hair and we find at any point in it a deposit of arsenic, by measuring from that point to the root we can fix, within quite narrow limits, the date on which that dose of arsenic was taken."

"But is it possible to do this?" I asked.

"Not in the case of a single hair," he replied. "But in the case of a tress, in which all the hairs are of the same age, it is perfectly possible. You will see the important bearing of this presently.

"To return now to my investigation. I had the bulk of a candle and a tress of Stella's hair. The questions to be settled were:

"1. Was there arsenic in the candle? and

"2. Had Stella been poisoned with arsenic?

"I began by trimming the wax mould in readiness for casting, and then I made an analysis of the trimmings. The result was the discovery of considerable quantities of arsenic in the wax.

"That answered the first question. Next, as the tress of hair was larger than was required for your purpose, I ventured to sacrifice a portion of it for a preliminary test. That test also gave a positive result. The quantity of arsenic was, of course, very minute, but still it was measurable by the delicate methods that are possible in dealing with arsenic, and the amount that I found pointed either to one large dose or to repeated smaller ones.

"The two questions were now answered definitely. It was certain – and the certainty could be demonstrated to a jury – that Stella had been poisoned by arsenic, and that the arsenic had been administered by means of poisoned candles. The complete proof in this case lent added weight to the less complete proof in the case of Monkhouse, and the two cases served to corroborate one another in pointing to Barbara as the poisoner. For she was the common factor in the two cases. The other persons – Wallingford, Madeline, and the others – who appeared in the Monkhouse case, made no appearance in the case of Stella, and the persons who were associated with Stella were not associated with Monkhouse. But Barbara was associated with both. And her absence from home was no answer to the charge if death was caused by the candles which she had admittedly supplied.

"But complete as the proof was, I wished, if possible, to make it yet more complete – to associate Barbara still more definitely with the crime.

In the case of Monkhouse, it was clear that the poisoning always occurred when she was absent from home. But this was not so clear in the case of Stella. Your diary showed that Stella's relapses coincided pretty regularly with Barbara's absences, but it was not certain (though obviously probable) that the relapses coincided with the periods of poisoning. If it could be proved that they did coincide, that proof would furnish corroboration of the greatest possible weight. It would show that the two cases were parallel in all respects.

"But could it be proved? If the tress of Stella's hair had been at my disposal, I had no doubt that I could have decided the question. But the tress was yours, and it had to be preserved. Whatever was to be done must be done without destroying or injuring the hair, and I set myself the task of finding some practicable method. Eventually, I decided, without much hope of success, to try the X-rays. As arsenic is a fairly dense metal and the quantity of it in the deposits quite considerable, it seemed to me possible that it might increase the density of the hairs at those points sufficiently to affect the X-ray shadow. At any rate, I decided to give the method a trial.

"Accordingly, Polton and I set to work at it. First, in order to get the densest shadow possible, we made the tress up into a close cylinder, carefully arranging it so that all the cut ends were in exactly the same plane. Then we made a number of graduated exposures on 'process' plates, developing and intensifying with the object of getting the greatest possible degree of contrast. The result was unexpectedly successful. In the best negative, the shape of the tress was faintly visible and was soon to be crossed by a number of perfectly distinct pale bands. Those bands were the shadows of the deposits of arsenic. There could be no doubt on the subject. For, apart from the fact that there was nothing else that they could be, their appearance agreed exactly with what one would have expected. Each band presented a sharp, distinct edge towards the tips of the hairs and faded away imperceptibly towards the roots. The sharp edge corresponded to the sudden appearance of arsenic in the blood when the poisoning began. The gradual fading-away corresponded to the period of elimination when the poisoning had ceased and the quantity of arsenic in the blood was becoming less and less from day to day.

"Now, since hair grows at a known, uniform rate, it was possible to convert the distances between these arsenical bands into periods of time, not with perfect exactness, because the rate of growth varies slightly in different persons, but with sufficient exactness for our present purpose. As soon as I looked at those bands, I saw that they told the whole story. But let us follow the method of proof.

"Assuming the rate of growth to be one fiftieth of an inch in twenty-four hours – which was probably correct for a person of Stella's age – I measured off on the photograph seven-inches-and-a-quarter from the cut ends as representing the last year of her life. Of course, I did not know how close to the head the hair had been cut, but, judging by the bands, I assumed that it had been cut quite close to the skin-within a quarter-of-an-inch."

"I happen to know that you were quite right," said I, "but I can't imagine how you arrived at your conclusion."

"It was quite a simple inference," he replied, "as you will see, presently. But to return to the photograph. Of the measured space of seven-inches-and-a-quarter I took a tracing on sheet celluloid, marking the sharp edges of the bands, the points at which the fading began and the points at which the band ceased to be visible. This tracing I transferred to paper ruled in tenths-of-an-inch – a tenth-of-an-inch representing five days – and I joined the points where the fading began and ended by a sloping line. I now had a diagram, or chart, which showed, with something approaching to accuracy, the duration of each administration of arsenic and the time which elapsed between the successive poisonings. This is the chart. The sloping lines show the fading of the bands."

He handed me a paper which he had just taken from a drawer and I looked at it curiously, but with no great interest. As I returned it after a brief inspection, I remarked, "It is quite clear and intelligible, but I don't quite see why you took the considerable trouble of making it. Does it show anything that could not be stated in a few words?"

"Not by itself," he replied. "But you remember that I mentioned having made two other charts, one showing the fluctuations in Stella's illness and the other showing Barbara's absences from home during the same period. Here are those other two charts, and now, if you put the three together, your eye can take in at a glance a fact of fundamental importance, which is that the relapses, the absences, and the poisonings all coincided in time. The periodicity is strikingly irregular, but it is identical in all three charts. I made these to hand to the jury, and I think they would have been quite convincing, since any juryman could check them by the dates given in evidence, and by inspection of the radiograph of the hair."

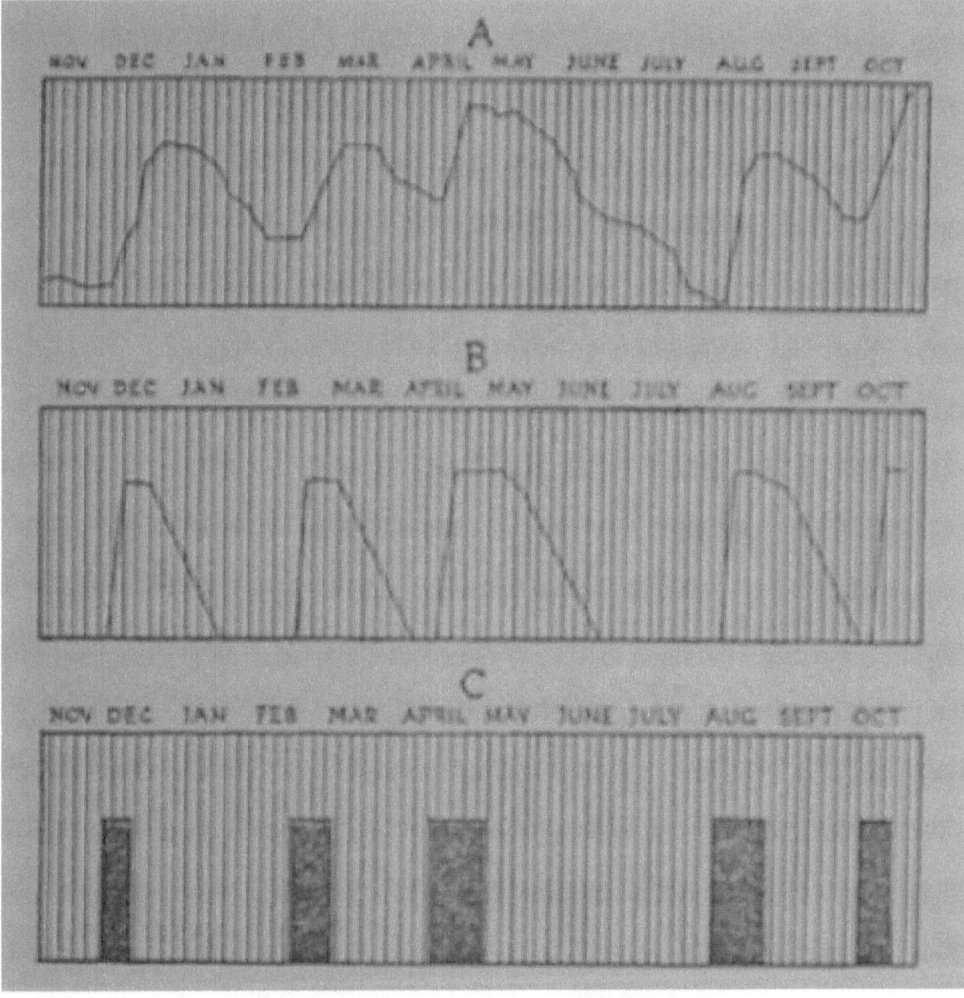

EXPLANATION OF THE CHARTS

CHART A – *Shows the fluctuations in the illness of Stella Keene during the year preceding her death in October. Divided into intervals of five days.*

CHART B – *Shows the distribution of the arsenical bands in Stella Keene's hair. The steep sides of the curves, towards the tips of the hairs, show the sudden appearance of the deposit, and the sloping sides, towards the roots of the hairs, represent its more gradual fading. Each of the narrow divisions represents five days' growth.*

439

CHART C – *Shows the periods during which Barbara was absent from home, each absence being represented by a black column. Divided into intervals of five days.*

I gazed at the three charts and was profoundly impressed by the convincing way in which they demonstrated the connection between Barbara's movements and the results of her diabolical activities. But what impressed me still more was the amazing ingenuity with which Thorndyke had contrived to build up a case of the most deadly precision and completeness out of what seemed, even to my trained intelligence, no more than a few chance facts, apparently quite trivial and irrelevant.

"It seems," I said, "that, so far as you were concerned, the exhumation was really unnecessary."

"Quite," he replied. "It proved nothing that was not already certain. Still, the Commissioner was quite right. For the purposes of a trial, evidence obtained from the actual body of the victim is of immeasurably more weight than indirect scientific evidence, no matter how complete. An ordinary juryman might have difficulty in realizing that the hair is part of the body and that proof of arsenical deposit in the hair is proof of arsenic in the body. But the mistake that he made, as events turned out, was in refusing to make the arrest until my statements had been confirmed by the autopsy and the analysis. That delay allowed the criminal to escape. Not that I complain. To me, personally, her suicide came as a blessed release from an almost intolerable position. But if I had been in his place, I would have taken no chances. She would have gone to trial and to the gallows."

"Yes," I admitted, "that was what justice demanded. But I cannot be thankful enough for the delay that let her escape. Fiend as she was, it would have been a frightful thing to have had to give the evidence that would have hanged her."

"It would," he agreed, "and the thought of it was a nightmare to me. However, we have escaped that, and after all, justice has been done."

We were silent for a few minutes, during which Thorndyke smoked his pipe with a certain air of attention as it he expected me to put some further questions. And, in fact, there were one or two questions that I wanted to have answered. I began with the simplest.

"I am still a little puzzled by some of the circumstances in this case. The infernal machine I happen to know to have been sent by Barbara, though I don't understand why she sent it. But Wallingford's proceedings are a complete mystery to me. What do you suppose induced him to keep a watch on you in that extraordinary fashion? And who was the man who shadowed him? There certainly was such a man, for I saw him, myself. And the same man had been shadowing Miss Norris. What do you make of it all?"

"One can only reason from past experiences," he replied. "It seems to be a rule that a person who has committed a crime cannot remain quiet and let things take their course. There appears to be an irresistible impulse to lay down false clues and create misleading appearances. It is always a mistake, unless the false clues are laid down in advance, and even then it is apt to fail and unexpectedly furnish a real clue.

"Now Barbara, with all her astonishing cleverness, made that mistake. She laid down a false clue in advance by her absences from home, and the trick certainly worked successfully at the inquest. But it was precisely those absences that put me on the track of the candle, which otherwise might have passed unsuspected. The faked medicine was another false clue which attracted my attention and added to my suspicion concerning the candle. Then, after the event came these other endeavours to mislead. They did neither harm nor good, as it happened, since I had already marked her down as the principal suspect. But if I had been in doubt, I should have followed up those clues and found her at the end of them.

"As to Wallingford, I imagine that she led him to believe that I was employed by you to fix the crime on him and that he was advised to watch me and be ready to anticipate any move on my part, her actual object being to cause him to behave in such a manner as to attract suspicious attention. The function of the private detective – for that is what he must have been – would be to keep Wallingford's nerves – and Miss Norris' too – in such a state that they would appear anxious and terrified and tend to attract attention. The infernal machine was primarily intended, I think, to cast suspicion on one or both of them.

"That was what I inferred from the total absence of finger-prints and the flagrantly identifiable character of the pistol and the wool.

"But the greatest, the most fatal mistake that Barbara made was the one that is absolutely characteristic of the criminal. She repeated the procedure of a previous crime that had been successful. It was that repetition that was her undoing. Either crime, separately, might have been difficult to fix on her. As it was, each crime was proof of the other."

Once more we fell silent, and still Thorndyke had the air of expecting some further question from me. I looked at him nervously, for there was something that I wanted to ask and yet I hardly dared to put it into words. For, as I had looked at those charts, a horrid suspicion had taken hold of me. I feared to have it confirmed, and yet I could not let it rest. At last, I summoned courage enough to put the question.

"Thorndyke," I said, "I want you to tell me something. I expect you know what it is."

He looked up and nodded gravely.

"You mean about Stella?" said he.

"Yes. How long would she have lived if she had not been poisoned?"

He looked away for a few moments, and, impassive as his face was, I could see that he was deeply moved. At length he replied, "I was afraid you were going to ask me that. But since you have, I can only answer you honestly. So far as I can judge, but for that accursed ghoul, the poor girl might have been alive and well at this moment."

I stared at him in amazement. "Do you mean," I demanded, "that she was not really suffering from consumption at all?"

"That is what it amounts to," he replied. "There were signs of old tubercular trouble, but there was nothing recent. Evidently she had good powers of resistance, and the disease had not only become stationary, but was practically extinct. The old lesions had undergone complete repair, and there is no reason to suppose that any recurrence would have taken place under ordinary conditions."

"But," I exclaimed, hardly able to believe that the disaster had been so overwhelmingly complete, "what about the cough? I know that she always had a more-or-less troublesome cough."

"So had Monkhouse," he replied, "and so would anyone have had whose lungs were periodically irritated by inhaling particles of arsenious acid. But the tubercular mischief was quite limited and recovery must have commenced early. And Barbara, watching eagerly the symptoms of the disease which was to rid her of her rival, must have noted with despair the signs of commencing recovery and at last resolved to do for herself what nature was failing to do. Doubtless, the special method of poisoning was devised to imitate the symptoms of the disease, which it did well enough to deceive those whose minds were prepared by the antecedent illness to receive the suggestion. It was a horribly, fiendishly ingenious crime – calmly, callously devised and carried out to its appalling end with the most hideous efficiency."

After he had finished speaking, I remained gazing at him dumbly, stupefied, stunned by the realization of the enormity of this frightful thing that had befallen. He, too, seemed quite overcome, for he sat silently, grasping his extinct pipe and looking sternly and fixedly into the fire. At length he spoke, but without removing his gaze from the bright embers.

"I am trying, Mayfield," he said, gently, "to think of something to say to you. But there is nothing to say. The disaster is too complete, too

442

irretrievable. This terrible woman has, so far, wrecked your life, and I recognize that you will carry the burden of your loss so long as you live. It would be a mere impertinence to utter futile and banal condolences. You know what I, your friend, am feeling and I need say no more of that, and I have too much confidence in your wisdom and courage to think of exhortations.

"But, though you have been robbed of the future that might have been, there is still a future that may be. It remains to you now only to shoulder your fardel and begin your pilgrimage anew, and if the road shall seem at first a dreary one, you need not travel it alone. You have friends, and one of them will think it a privilege to bear you company and try to hearten you by the way."

He held out his hand and I grasped it silently and with a full heart. And the closer friendship that was inaugurated in that hand-clasp has endured through the passing years, ever more precious and more helpful.

The End

1927 Hodder & Stoughton, London Cover

Prologue

The afternoon of a sultry day near the end of July was beginning to merge into evening. The crimson eye of the declining sun peered out through chinks in a bank of slaty cloud as if taking a last look at the great level of land and water before retiring for the night, while already, in the soft, greenish grey of the eastern sky, the new-risen moon hung like a globe of pearl.

It was a solitary scene – desolate, if you will, or peaceful. On the one hand the quiet waters of a broad estuary, on the other a great stretch of marshes, and between them the sea wall, following faithfully the curves and indentations of the shore and fading away at either end into invisibility.

A great stillness brooded over the place. On the calm water, far out beyond the shallows, one or two coasting craft lay at anchor, and yet farther out a schooner and a couple of barges crept up on the flood tide. On the land side in the marshy meadows a few sheep grazed sedately, and in the ditch that bordered the seawall the water-voles swam to and fro or sat on the banks and combed their hair. Sound there was none save the half-audible wash of the little waves upon the shore and now and again the querulous call of a sea-gull.

In strange contrast to the peaceful stillness that prevailed around was the aspect of the one human creature that was visible. Tragedy was written in every line of his figure, tragedy and fear and breathless haste. He was running – so far as it was possible to run among the rough stones and the high grass – at the foot of the seawall on the seaward side, stumbling onward desperately, breathing hard, and constantly brushing away with his hand the sweat that streamed down his forehead into his eyes. At intervals he paused to scramble up the slope of the wall among the thistles and ragwort and, with infinite caution, to avoid even showing his head on the skyline, peering over the top backwards and forwards, but especially backwards where, in the far distance, the grey mass of a town loomed beyond the marshes.

There was no mystery about the man's movements. A glance at his clothing explained everything. For he was dressed in prison grey, branded with the broad arrow and still bearing the cell number. Obviously, he was an escaped convict.

Criminologists of certain Continental schools are able to give us with remarkable exactness the facial and other characteristics by which the criminal may be infallibly recognized. Possibly these convenient

447

"stigmata" may actually occur in the criminals of those favoured regions. But in this backward country it is otherwise, and we have to admit the regrettable fact that the British criminal inconsiderately persists in being a good deal like other people. Not that the criminal class is, even here, distinguished by personal beauty or fine physique. The criminal is a low-grade man, but he is not markedly different from other low-grade men.

But the fugitive whose flight in the shelter of the sea wall we are watching did not conform even to the more generalized type. On the contrary, he was a definitely good-looking young man, rather small and slight, yet athletic and well-knit, with a face not only intelligent and refined but, despite his anxious and even terrified expression, suggestive of a courageous, resolute personality. Whatever had brought him to a convict prison, he was not of the rank-and-file of its inmates.

Presently, as he approached a bluff which concealed a stretch of the sea wall ahead, he slowed down into a quick walk, stooping slightly and peering forward cautiously to get a view of the shore beyond the promontory, until, as he reached the most projecting point of the wall, he paused for a moment and then crept stealthily forward, alert and watchful for any unexpected thing that might be lurking round the promontory.

Suddenly he stopped dead and then drew back a pace, craning up to peer over the high, rushy grass, and casting a glance of intense scrutiny along the stretch of shore that had come into view. After a few moments he again crept forward slowly and silently, still gazing intently along the shore and the face of the sea wall that was now visible for nearly a mile ahead. And still he could see nothing but that which had met his eyes as he crept round the bluff. He drew himself up and looked down at it with eager interest.

A little heap of clothes, evidently the shed raiment of a bather, as the completeness of the outfit testified. And in confirmation, just across the narrow strip of "saltings" on the smooth expanse of muddy sand, the prints of a pair of naked feet extended in a line towards the water. But where was the bather? There was only a single set of footprints, so that he must be still in the water or have come ashore farther down. Yet neither on the calm water nor on the open, solitary shore was any sign of him to be seen.

It was very strange. On that smooth water a man swimming would be a conspicuous object, and a naked man on that low, open shore would be still more conspicuous. The fugitive looked around with growing agitation. From the shore and the water his glance came back to the line of footprints, and now, for the first time, he noticed something very remarkable about them. They did not extend to the water. Starting from the edge of the saltings, they took a straight line across the sand, every footprint deep and distinct, to within twenty yards of the water's edge, and there they ended abruptly. Between the last footprint and the little waves that broke on the shore was a space of sand perfectly smooth and untouched.

What could be the meaning of this? The fugitive gazed with knitted brows at that space of smooth sand, and even as he gazed, the explanation flashed upon him. The tide was now coming in, as he could see by the anchored vessels. But when these footprints were made, the tide was going out. The spot where the footprints ended was the spot where the bather had entered the water. Then – since the tide had gone out to the low-water mark and had risen again to nearly half-tide – some five hours must have passed since that man had walked down into the water.

All this flashed through the fugitive's brain in a matter of seconds. In those seconds he realized that the priceless heap of clothing was derelict. As to what had become of the owner, he gave no thought but that in some mysterious way he had apparently vanished for good. Scrambling up the slope of the sea wall, he once more scanned the path on its summit in both directions, and still there was not a living soul in sight. Then he slid down, and breathlessly and with trembling hands stripped off the hated livery of dishonour and, not without a certain incongruous distaste, struggled into the derelict garments.

A good deal has been said – with somewhat obvious truth – about the influence of clothes upon the self-respect of the wearer. But surely there could be no more extreme instance than the present one, which, in less than one brief minute, transformed a manifest convict into a respectable artisan. The change took effect immediately. As the fugitive resumed his flight he still kept off the skyline, but he no longer hugged the base of the wall, he no longer crouched, nor did he run. He walked upright out on the more-or-less level saltings, swinging along at a good pace but without excessive haste. And as he went, he explored the pockets of the strange clothes to ascertain what bequests the late owner had made to him, and brought up at the first cast a pipe, a tobacco-pouch, and a box of matches. At the first he looked a little dubiously, but could not resist the temptation, and when he had dipped the mouthpiece in a little salt pool and scrubbed it with a handful of grass, he charged the bowl from the well-filled pouch, lighted it, and smoked with an ecstasy of pleasure born of long deprivation.

Next, his eye began to travel over the abundant jetsam that the last spring-tide had strewn upon the saltings. He found a short length of old rope, and then he picked up from time to time a scrap of driftwood. Not that he wanted the fuel, but that a bundle of driftwood seemed a convincing addition to his make-up and would explain his presence on the shore if he should be seen. When he had made up a small bundle with the aid of the rope, he swung it over his shoulder and collected no more.

He still climbed up the wall now and again to keep a look-out for possible pursuers, and at length, in the course of one of these observations, he espied a stout plank set across the ditch and connected with a footpath that meandered away across the marshes. In an instant he decided to follow that path, whithersoever it might lead. With a last glance towards the town, he boldly stepped up to the top of the wall, crossed the path at its summit, descended the landward side, walked across the little bridge and strode away swiftly along the footpath across the marshes.

He was none too soon. At the moment when he stepped off the bridge, three men emerged from the waterside alley that led to the sea wall and began to move rapidly along the rough path. Two of them were prison warders, and the third, who trundled a bicycle, was a police patrol.

"Pity we didn't get the tip a bit sooner," grumbled one of the warders. "The daylight's going fast, and he's got a devil of a start."

"Still," said the constable cheerfully, "it isn't much of a place to hide in. The wall's a regular trap, sea one side and a deep ditch the other. We shall get him all right, or else the patrol from Clifton will. I expect he has started by now."

"What did you tell the sergeant when you spoke to him on the 'phone?"

"I told him there was a runaway coming along the wall. He said he would send a cyclist patrol along to meet us."

The warder grunted. "A cyclist might easily miss him if he was hiding in the grass or in the rushes by the ditch. But we must see that we don't miss him. Two of us had better take the two sides of the wall so as to get a clear view."

His suggestion was adopted at once. One warder climbed down and marched along the saltings, the other followed a sort of sheep-track by the side of the ditch, while the constable wheeled his bicycle along the top of the wall. In this way they advanced as quickly as was possible to the two men stumbling over the rough ground at the base of the wall, searching the steep sides, with their rank vegetation, for any trace of the lost sheep, and making as little noise as they could. So for over a mile they toiled on, scanning every foot of the rough ground as they passed but uttering no word. Each of the warders could see the constable on the path above, and thus the party was enabled to keep together.

Suddenly the warder on the saltings stopped dead and emitted a shout of triumph. Instantly the constable laid his bicycle on the path and slithered down the bank, while the other warder came scrambling over the wall, twittering with excitement. Then the three men gathered together and looked down at the little heap of clothes, from which the discoverer had already detached the jacket and was inspecting it.

"They're his duds all right," said he. "Of course, they couldn't be anybody else's. But here's his number. So that's that."

"Yes," agreed the other, "they're his clothes right enough. But the question is, Where's my nabs himself?"

They stepped over to the edge of the saltings and gazed at the line of footprints. By this time the rising tide had covered up the strip of smooth, unmarked sand and was already eating away the footprints, winch now led directly to the water's edge.

"Rum go," commented the constable, looking steadily over the waste of smooth water. "He isn't out there. If he was, you'd see him easily, even in this light. The water's as smooth as oil."

"Perhaps he's landed farther down," suggested the younger warder.

"What for?" demanded the constable.

"Might mean to cross the ditch and get away over the marshes."

The constable laughed scornfully. "What, in his birthday suit? I don't think. No, I reckon he had his reasons for taking to the water, and those reasons would probably be a barge sailing fairly close inshore. They'd have to take him on board, you know, and from my experience of bargees, I should say they'd probably give him a suit of togs and keep their mouths shut."

The elder warder looked meditatively across the water.

"Maybe you are right," said he, "but barges don't usually come in here very close. The fairway is right out the other side. And, for my part, I should be mighty sorry to start on a swim out to a sailing vessel."

"You might think differently if you'd just hopped out of the jug," the constable remarked as he lit a cigarette.

"Yes, I suppose I should be ready to take a bit of a risk. Well," he concluded, "if that was his lay, I hope he got picked up. I shouldn't like to think of the poor beggar drifting about the bottom of the river. He was a decent, civil little chap."

There was silence for a minute or two as the three men smoked reflectively. Then the constable proposed, as a matter of form, to cycle along the wall and make sure that the fugitive was not lurking farther down. But before he had time to start, a figure appeared in the distance, apparently mounted on a bicycle and advancing rapidly towards them. In a few minutes he arrived and dismounted on the path above them glancing down curiously at the jacket which the warder still held.

"Those his togs?" he asked.

"Yes," replied the constable. "I suppose you haven't seen a gent bathing anywhere along here?"

The newcomer shook his head. "No," said he. "I have patrolled the whole wall from Clifton to here and I haven't seen a soul excepting old Barnett, the shepherd."

The elder warder gathered up the rest of the clothes and handed them to his junior. "Well," he said, "we must take it that he's gone to sea. All that we can do is to get the Customs people to give us a passage on their launch to make the round of all the vessels anchored about here. And if we don't find him on any of them, we shall have to hand the case over to the police."

The three men climbed to the top of the wall and turned their faces towards the town, and the Clifton patrol, having turned his bicycle about, mounted expertly and pedalled away at a smart pace to get back to his station before the twilight merged into night.

At that very moment, the fugitive was stepping over a stile that gave access from the marshes to a narrow, tree-shaded lane. Here he paused for a few moments to fling away the bundle of driftwood into the hedge and refill and light his pipe. Then, with a springy step, be strode away into the gathering moonlit dusk.

Chapter I
Mr. Pottermack Makes
a Discovery

A conscientious desire on the part of the present historian to tell his story in a complete and workmanlike fashion from the very beginning raises the inevitable question: What was the beginning? Not always an easy question to answer offhand, for if we reflect upon certain episodes in our lives and try to track them to their beginnings, we are apt, on further cogitation, to discover behind those beginnings antecedents yet more remote which have played an indispensable part in the evolution of events.

As to this present history, the whole train of cause and consequence might fairly be supposed to have been started by Mr. Pottermack's singular discovery in his garden. Yet, when we consider the matter more closely, we may doubt if that discovery would ever have been made if it had not been for the sun-dial. Certainly it would not have been made at that critical point in Mr. Pottermack's life, and if it had not – but we will not waste our energies on vain speculations. We will take the safe and simple course. We will begin with the sun-dial.

It stood, when Mr. Pottermack's eyes first beheld it, in a mason's yard at the outskirts of the town. It was obviously of some age, and therefore could not have been the production of Mr. Gallett, the owner of the yard, and standing amidst the almost garishly new monuments and blocks of freshly hewn stone, it had in its aspect something rather downfallen and forlorn. Now Mr. Pottermack had often had secret hankerings for a sun-dial. His big walled garden seemed to cry out for some central feature, and what more charming ornament could there be than a dial which, like the flowers and trees amidst which it would stand, lived and had its being solely by virtue of the golden sunshine?

Mr. Pottermack halted at the wide-open gate and looked at the dial (I use the word, for convenience to include the stone support). It was a graceful structure with a twisted shaft like that of a Norman column, a broad base and a square capital. It was nicely lichened and weathered, and yet in quite good condition. Mr. Pottermack found something very prepossessing in its comely antiquity. It had a motto, too, incised on the sides of the capital, and when he had strolled into the yard, and, circumnavigating the sun-dial, had read it, he was more than ever pleased. He liked the motto. It struck a sympathetic chord. *Sole orto, spes, decedente pax.* It might have been his own personal motto: *At the rising of the sun, hope, at the going down thereof, peace.* On his life the sun had risen in hope, and peace at eventide was his chief desire. And the motto was discreetly reticent about the intervening period. So, too, were there passages in the past which he was very willing to forget so that the hope of the morning might be crowned by peace when the shadows of life were lengthening.

"Having a look at the old dial, Mr. Pottermack?" said the mason, crossing the yard and disposing himself for conversation. "Nice bit of carving, that, and wonderful well preserved. He's counted out a good many hours in his time, he has. Seventeen thirty-four. And ready to count out as many again. No wheels to go rusty. All done with a shadder. No wear and tear about a shadder. And never runs down and never wants winding up. There's points about a sun-dial."

"Where did it come from?"

"I took it from the garden of Apsley Manor House, what's being rebuilt and brought up to date. New owner told me to take it away. Hadn't any use for sun-dials in these days, he said. More hasn't anybody else. So I've got him on my hands. Wouldn't like him for your garden, I suppose? He's going cheap."

It appeared, on enquiry, that he was going ridiculously cheap. So cheap that Mr. Pottermack closed with the offer there and then,

"You will bring it along and fix it for me?" said he.

"I will, sir. Don't want much fixing. If you will settle where he is to stand, I'll bring him and set him up. But you'd better prepare the site. Dig well down into the subsoil and make a level surface. Then I can put a brick foundation and there will be no fear of his settling out of the upright."

That was how it began. And on the knife-edge of such trivial chances is human destiny balanced. From the mason's yard Mr. Pottermack sped homeward with springy step, visualizing the ground-plan of his garden as he went, and by the time that he let himself into his house by the front door within the rose-embowered porch he was ready to make a bee-line for the site of his proposed excavation.

He did not, however, for, as he opened the door, he became aware of voices in the adjacent room and his housekeeper came forth to inform him that Mrs. Bellard had called to see him, and was waiting within. Apparently the announcement was not unwelcome, for Mr. Pottermack's cheerfulness was in nowise clouded thereby. We might even go far as to say that his countenance brightened.

Mrs. Bellard was obviously a widow. That is not to say that she was arrayed in the hideous "weeds" with which, a generation ago, women

454

used to make their persons revolting and insult the memory of the deceased. But she was obviously a widow. More obviously than is usual in these latter days. Nevertheless, her sombre raiment was well-considered, tasteful, and becoming. Indeed, the severity of her dress seemed rather to enhance her quiet, dignified comeliness. She greeted Mr. Pottermack with a frank smile, and as they shook hands she said in a singularly pleasant, musical voice, "It is too bad of me to come worrying you like this. But you said I was to."

"Of course I did," was the hearty response, and as the lady produced from her basket a small tin box, he enquired, "Snails?"

"Snails," she replied, and they both laughed.

"I know," she continued, "it is very silly of me. I quite believe that, as you say, they die instantaneously when you drop them into boiling water. But I really can't bring myself to do it."

"Very natural, too," said Pottermack. "Why should you, when you have a fellow conchologist to do it for you? I will slaughter them this evening and extract them from their shells, and you shall have their empty residences to-morrow. Shall I leave them at your house?"

"You needn't trouble to do that. Give them to your housekeeper and I will call for them on my way home from the shops. But I really do impose on you most shamefully. You kill the poor little beasts, you clean out the shells, you find out their names, and you leave me nothing to do but stick them on card, write their names under them, and put them in the cabinet. I feel a most horrid impostor when I show them at the Naturalists' Club as my own specimens."

"But, my dear Mrs. Bellard," protested Pottermack, "you are forgetting that you collect them, that you discover them in their secret haunts, and drag them out to the light of day. That is the really scientific part of conchology. The preparation of the shells and their identification are mere journeyman's work. The real naturalist's job is the field work, and you are a positive genius in finding these minute shells – the pupas and cochlicopas and such like."

The lady rewarded him with a grateful and gratified smile and, opening the little box, exhibited her "catch" and recounted some of the thrilling incidents of the chase, to which Pottermack listened with eager interest. And as they chatted, but half seriously, an observer would have noted that they were obviously the best of friends, and might have suspected that the natural history researches were, perhaps, somewhat in the nature of a plausible and convenient pretext for their enjoying a good deal of each other's society. These little precautions are sometimes necessary in a country district where people take an exaggerated interest in one another and tongues are apt to wag rather freely.

But a close observer would have noted certain other facts. For instance, these two persons were curiously alike in one respect: They both looked older to the casual stranger than they appeared on closer inspection. At a first glance, Mr. Pottermack, spectacled, bearded, and grave, seemed not far short of fifty. But a more critical examination showed that first impression to be erroneous. The quick, easy movements and the supple strength that they implied in the rather small figure, as well as the brightness of the alert, attentive eyes behind the spectacles, suggested that the lines upon the face and the white powdering of the hair owed their existence to something other than the mere effluxion of time. So, too, with Mrs. Bollard. On a chance meeting she would have passed for a well-preserved middle-aged woman. But now, as she chatted smilingly with her friend, the years dropped from her until, despite the white hairs that gleamed among the brown and a faint hint of crow's-feet, she seemed almost girlish.

But there was something else, something really rather odd. Each of the two cronies seemed to have a way of furtively examining the other. There was nothing unfriendly or suspicious in these regards. Quite the contrary, indeed. But they conveyed a queer impression of curiosity and doubt, differently manifested, however, in each. In Mr. Pottermack's expression there was something expectant. He had the air of waiting for some anticipated word or action, but the expression vanished instantly when his companion looked in his direction. The widow's manner was different, but it had the same curious furtive quality. When Pottermack's attention was occupied, she would cast a steady glance at him, and then the lines would come back upon her forehead, her lips would set, and there would steal across her face a look at once sad, anxious, and puzzled. Especially puzzled. And if the direction of her glance had been followed, it would have been traced more particularly to his profile and his right ear. It is true that both these features were a little unusual. The profile was almost the conventional profile of the Greek sculptors – the nose continuing the line of the forehead with no appreciable notch – a character very seldom seen in real persons. As to the ear, it was a perfectly well-shaped, proportionate ear. It would have been of no interest to Lombroso. But it had one remarkable peculiarity: On its lobule was what doctors call a "*diffuse naevus*" and common folk describe as a "port-wine mark". It was quite small, but very distinct, as if the lobule had been dipped into damson juice. Still, it hardly seemed to justify such anxious and puzzled consideration.

"What a dreadful pair of gossips we are!" Mrs. Bellard exclaimed, taking her basket up from the table. "I've been here half-an-hour by the clock, and I know I have been hindering you from some important work. You looked full of business as you came up the garden path."

"I have been full of business ever since – land and fresh-water *mollusca*. We have had a most instructive talk."

"So we have," she agreed, with a smile. "We are always instructive, especially you. But I must really take myself off now and leave you to your other business."

Mr. Pottermack held the door open for her and followed her down the hall to the garden path, delaying her for a few moments to fill her basket with roses from the porch. When he had let her out at the gate, he lingered to watch her as she walked away towards the village, noting how the dignified, matronly bearing seemed to contrast with the springy tread and youthful lissomness of movement.

As he turned away to re-enter the house he saw the postman approaching, but as he was not expecting any letters, and his mind was still occupied with his late visitor, he did not wait. Nor when, a minute later, he heard the characteristic knock, did he return to inspect the letter-box, which was just as well in the circumstances. Instead, he made his way out by the back door into the large kitchen garden and orchard and followed the long, central path which brought him at length to a high red brick wall, in which was a door furnished with a knocker and flanked by an electric bell. This he opened with a latchkey of the Yale pattern and, having passed through, carefully shut it behind him.

He was now in what had probably been originally the orchard and kitchen garden of the old house in which he lived, but which had since been converted into a flower garden, though many of the old fruit trees still remained. It was a large oblong space, more than a quarter-of-an-acre in extent, and enclosed on all sides by a massive old wall nearly seven feet high, in which were only two openings: The door by which he had just entered and another door at one side, also fitted with a Yale lock and guarded, in addition, by two bolts.

It was a pleasant place if quiet and seclusion were the chief desire of the occupant – as they apparently were, to judge by Mr. Pottermack's arrangements. The central space was occupied by a large, smooth grass plot, surrounded by well-made paths, between which and the wall were wide flower borders. In one corner was a brick-built summer-house, quite a commodious affair, with a good tiled roof, a boarded floor, and space enough inside for a couple of armchairs and a fair-sized table. Against the wall opposite to the summer-house was a long shed or outhouse with glass lights in the roof, evidently a recently built structure and just a little unsightly – but that would be remedied when the yew hedge that had been planted before it grew high enough to screen it from view. This was the workshop, or rather a range of workshops, for Mr. Pottermack was a man of many occupations, and, being also a tidy, methodical man, he liked to keep the premises appertaining to those occupations separate.

On the present occasion he made his way to the end compartment, in which were kept the gardening tools and appliances and, having provided himself with a spade, a mallet, a long length of cord, and a half-dozen pointed stakes, walked out to the grass plot and looked about him. He was quite clear in his mind as to where the sun-dial was to stand, but it was necessary to fix the spot with precision. Hence the stakes and the measuring-line, which came into use when he had paced out the distances approximately and enabled him, at length, to drive a stake into the ground and thereby mark the exact spot which would be occupied by the centre of the dial.

From this centre, with the aid of the cord, he drew a circle some four yards in diameter and began at once to take up the turf, rolling it up tidily and setting it apart ready for relaying. And now he came to the real job. He had to dig right down to the subsoil. Well, how far down was that? He took off his coat and, grasping the spade with a resolute air, gave a vigorous drive into the soil at the edge of the circle. That carried him through the garden mould down into a fine, yellowish, sandy loam, a small quantity of which came up on the spade. He noted its appearance with some interest but went on digging, opening up a shallow trench round the circumference of the circle.

By the time that he had made a second complete circuit and carried his trench to a depth of some eight inches, the circle was surrounded by a ring of the yellow loam, surprisingly bulky in proportion to the shallow cavity from which it had been derived. And once more his attention was attracted by its appearance. For Mr. Pottermack, amongst his various occupations, included occasionally that of sand-casting. Hitherto he had been in the habit of buying his casting-sand by the bag. But this loam, judging by the sharp impressions of his feet where he had trodden in it, was a perfect casting-sand, and to be had for the taking at his very door. By way of testing its cohesiveness, he took up a large handful and squeezed it tightly. When he opened his hand the mass remained hard and firm and showed the impressions of his fingers perfectly to the very creases of the skin.

Very pleased with his discovery, and resolving to secure a supply of the loam for his workshop, he resumed his digging, and presently came down to a stratum where the loam was quite dense and solid and came up on the spade in definite coherent lumps like pieces of a soft rock. This, he decided, was the true subsoil and was as deep as he need go, and having decided this, he proceeded to dig out the rest of the circle to the same depth.

The work was hard and, after a time, extremely monotonous. Still Mr. Pottermack laboured steadily with no tendency to slacking. But the monotony exhausted his attention, and while he worked on mechanically with unabated vigour his thoughts wandered away from his task, now in the direction of the sun-dial, and now – at, perhaps, rather more length – in that of his pretty neighbour and her spoils, which were still awaiting his attentions in the tin box.

He was getting near the centre of the circle when his spade cut through and brought up a piece of spongy, fungus-eaten wood. He glanced at it absently, and having flung it outside the circle, entered his spade at the same spot and gave a vigorous drive. As the spade met with more than usual resistance, he threw a little extra weight on it. And then, suddenly, the resistance gave way, the spade drove through, apparently into vacant space. Mr. Pottermack uttered a startled cry, and after an instant's precarious balancing saved himself by a hair's breadth from going through after it.

For a moment he was quite shaken – and no wonder. He had staggered back a pace or two and now stood, still grasping the spade, and gazing with horror at the black, yawning hole that had so nearly swallowed him up. But as, after all, it had not, he presently pulled himself together and began cautiously to investigate. A very little tentative probing with the spade made everything clear. The hole which he had uncovered was the mouth of an old well, one of those pernicious wells which have no protective coping but of which the opening, flush with the surface of the ground, is ordinarily closed by a hinged flap. The rotten timber that he had struck was part of this flap, and he could now see the rusty remains of the hinges. When the well had gone out of use, some one, with incredible folly, had simply covered it up by heaping earth on the closed flap.

Mr. Pottermack, having made these observations, proceeded methodically to clear away the soil until the entire mouth of the well was exposed. Then, going down on hands and knees, he approached, and cautiously advancing his head over the edge, peered down into the dark cavity. It was not quite dark, however, for though the slimy brick cylinder faded after a few feet into profound gloom, Mr. Pottermack could see, far down, as it seemed in the very bowels of the earth, a little circular spot of light on which was the dark silhouette of a tiny head. He picked up a pebble, and, holding it at the centre of the opening, let it drop. After a brief interval the bright spot grew suddenly dim and the little head vanished, and after another brief interval there came up to his ear a hollow "plop" followed by a faint, sepulchral splash.

There was, then, water in the well, not that it mattered to him, as he was going to cover it up again. But he was a man with a healthy curiosity and he felt that he would like to know all about this well before he once more consigned it to oblivion. Walking across to the workshop, he entered the metalwork section and cast his eye around for a suitable sinker. Presently, in the "oddments" drawer, he found a big iron clock-weight. It was heavier than was necessary, but he took it in default of anything more suitable, and going back to the well, he tied it to one end of the measuring-cord. The latter, being already marked in fathoms by means of a series of knots, required no further preparation. Lying full-length by the brink of the well, Mr. Pottermack dropped the weight over and let the cord slip through his hands, counting the knots as it ran out and moving it up and down as the weight neared the water.

The hollow splash for which he was listening came to his ear when the hand that grasped the cord was between the fourth and fifth knots. The depth, therefore, of the well to the surface of the water was about twenty-seven feet. He made a mental note of the number and then let the cord slip more rapidly through his hands. It was just after the seventh knot had passed that the tension of the cord suddenly relaxed, telling him that the weight now rested on the bottom. This gave a depth of sixteen feet of water and a total depth of about forty-three feet. And to think that, but for the merest chance, he would now have been down there where the clock-weight was resting!

With a slight shudder he rose, and, hauling up the cord, coiled it neatly and laid it down, with the weight still attached, a few feet away on the cleared ground. The question that he now had to settle was how far the existence of the well would interfere with the placing of the sun-dial. It did not seem to him that it interfered at all. On the contrary, the well had to be securely covered up in any case, and the sun-dial on top of the covering would make it safe for ever. For it happened that the position of the well coincided within a foot with the chosen site of the dial, which seemed quite an odd coincidence until one remembered that the position of both had probably been determined by identical sets of measurements, based on the ground-plan of the garden.

One thing, however, was obvious. Mr. Gallett would have to be informed of the discovery without delay, for something different from me proposed brickwork foundation would be required. Accordingly, Mr. Pottermack slipped on his coat and, having sought out a hurdle and laid it over the well – for you can't be too careful in such a case – set off without delay for the mason's yard. As he opened the front door, he observed the letter still lying in the wire basket under the letter-slit. But he did not take it out. It could wait until he came back.

Mr. Gallett was deeply interested, but he was also a little regretful. The altered arrangements would cause delay and increase the cost of the job. He would want two biggish slabs of stone, which would take some time to prepare.

"But why cover the well at all?" said he. "A good well with sixteen feet of water in it is not to be sneezed at if you gets a hard frost and all the pipes is bunged up and busted."

But Mr. Pottermack shook his head. Like most town-bred men, he had rather a dislike to wells, and his own recent narrow escape had done nothing to diminish his prejudice. He would have no open well in his garden.

"The only question is," he concluded, "whether the sun-dial will be safe right over the well. Will a stone slab bear the weight?"

"Lor' bless you," replied Gallett, "a good thick slab of flagstone would bear St. Paul's Cathedral. And we are going to put two, one on top of the other to form a step, and the base of the dial itself a good two foot wide. It will be as strong as a house."

"And when do you think you'll be able to fix it?"

Mr. Gallett reflected. "Let's see. To-day's Toos-day. It will take a full day to get them two slabs sawn off the block and trimmed to shape. Shall we say Friday?"

"Friday will do perfectly. There is really no hurry, though I shall be glad to get the well covered and made safe. But don't put yourself out."

Mr. Gallett promised that he would not, and Pottermack then departed homeward to resume his labours.

As he re-entered his house, he picked the letter out of the letter-cage, and, holding it unopened in his hand, walked through to the garden. Emerging into the open air, he turned the letter over and glanced at the address, and in an instant a most remarkable change came over him. The quiet gaiety faded from his face and he stopped dead, gazing at the superscription with a frown of angry apprehension. Tearing open the envelope, he drew out the letter, unfolded it and glanced quickly through the contents. Apparently it was quite short, for, almost immediately, he refolded it, returned it to its envelope and slipped the latter into his pocket.

Passing through into the walled garden, he took off his coat, laid it down in the summer-house, and fell to work on the excavation, extending the circle into a square and levelling the space around the well to make a bed for the stone slab. But all his enthusiasm had evaporated. He worked steadily and with care, but his usually cheerful face was

461

gloomy and stern, and a certain faraway look in his eyes hinted that his thoughts were not on what he was doing but on something suggested by the ill-omened missive.

When the light failed, he replaced the hurdle, cleaned and put away the spade, and then went indoors with his coat on his arm to wash and take his solitary supper, of which he made short work, eating and drinking mechanically and gazing before him with gloomy preoccupation. Supper being finished and cleared away, he called for a kettle of boiling water and a basin and, taking from a cupboard a handled needle, a pair of fine forceps, and a sheet of blotting-paper, laid them on the table with Mrs. Bellard's tin box. The latter he opened and very carefully transferred the imprisoned snails to the basin, which he then filled with boiling water, whereupon the unfortunate molluscs each emitted a stream of bubbles and shrank instantly into the recesses of its shell.

Having deposited the kettle in the fireplace, Mr. Pottermack drew a chair up to the table and seated himself with the basin before him and the blotting-paper at his right hand. But before beginning his work he drew forth the letter, straightened it out and, laying it on the table, read it through slowly. It bore no address and no signature, and though the envelope was addressed to Marcus Pottermack, Esq., it began, oddly enough:

Dear Jeff,

I send you this little billy-doo (it ran on) *with deep regret, which I know you will share. But it can't be helped. I had hoped that the last one would be in fact, the last one, whereas it turns out to have been the last but one. This is positively my final effort, so keep up your pecker. And it is only a small affair this time. A hundred – in notes, of course. Fivers are safest. I shall call at the usual place on Wednesday at 8 p.m. ('In the gloaming, O! My darling!') This will give you time to hop up to town in the morning to collect the rhino. And mind I've got to have it. No need to dwell on unpleasant alternatives. Necessity knows no law. I am in a devil of a tight corner and you have got to help me out. So* adieu *until Wednesday evening.*

Mr. Pottermack turned from the letter and, taking up the mounted needle, with the other hand picked out of the basin a snail with a delicate yellow shell (*Helix hortensis, var. arenicola*) and, regarding it

462

reflectively, proceeded with expert care to extract the shrivelled body of the mollusc. But though his attention seemed to be concentrated on his task, his thoughts were far away, and his eyes strayed now and again to the letter at his side.

"*I am in a devil of a tight corner.*" Of course he was. The incurable plunger is always getting into tight corners. "*And you have got to help me out*". Exactly. In effect, the money that you have earned by unstinted labour and saved by self-denial has got to be handed to me that I may drop it into the bottomless pit that swallows up the gambler's losings. "*This is positively my final effort.*" Yes. So was the last one, and the one before that, and so would be the next, and the one that would follow it, and so on without end. Mr. Pottermack saw it all clearly, realized, as so many other sufferers have realized, that there is about a blackmailer something hopelessly elusive. No transaction with him has any finality. He has something to sell, and he sells it, but behold! Even as the money passes the thing sold is back in the hand of the vendor, to be sold again and yet again. No covenant with him is binding, no agreement can be enforced. There can be no question of cutting a loss, for, no matter how drastic the sacrifice, it is no sooner made than the *status quo ante* reappears.

On these truths Mr. Pottermack cogitated gloomily and asked himself, as such victims often do, whether it would not have been better in the first place to tell this ruffian to go to the devil and do his worst. Yet that had hardly seemed practicable, for the fellow would probably have done his worst – and his worst was so extremely bad. On the other hand, it was impossible that this state of affairs should be allowed to go on indefinitely. He was not by any means a rich man, though this parasite persisted in assuming that he was. At the present rate he would soon be sucked dry – reduced to stark poverty. And even then he would be no safer.

The intensity of his revolt against his intolerable position was emphasized by his very occupation. The woman for whom he was preparing these specimens was very dear to him. In any pictures that his fancy painted of the hoped-for future, hers was the principal figure. His fondest wish was to ask her to be his wife, and he felt a modest confidence that she would not say him nay. But how could he ask any woman to marry him while this vampire clung to his body? Marriage was not for him – a slave to-day, a pauper to-morrow, at the best, and at the worst . . . .

The evening had lapsed into night by the time that all the specimens had been made presentable for the cabinet. It remained to write a little name-ticket for each with the aid, when necessary, of a handbook of the

British *Mollusca*, and then to wrap each separate shell, with its ticket, in tissue paper and pack it tenderly in the small tin box. Thus was he occupied when his housekeeper, Mrs. Gadby, "reported off duty" and retired, and the clock in the hall was striking eleven when, having packed the last of the shells, he made the tin box into a neat little parcel with the consignee's name legibly written on the cover.

The house was profoundly quiet. Usually Mr. Pottermack was deeply appreciative of the restful silence that settles down upon the haunts of men when darkness has fallen upon field and hedgerow and the village has gone to sleep. Very pleasant it was then to reach down from the bookshelves some trusty companion and draw the big easy-chair up to the fireplace, even though, as to-night, the night was warm and the grate empty. The force of habit did, indeed, even now, lead him to the bookshelves. But no book was taken down. He had no inclination for reading to-night. Neither had he any inclination for sleep. Instead, he lit a pipe and walked softly up and down the room, stem and gloomy of face, yet with a look of concentration as if he were considering a difficult problem.

Up and down, up and down he paced, hardly making a sound. And as the time passed, the expression of his face underwent a subtle change. It lost none of its sternness, but yet it seemed to clear, as if a solution of the problem were coming into sight.

The striking of the clock in the hall, proclaiming the end of the day, brought him to a halt. He glanced at his watch, knocked out his empty pipe, lit a candle, and blew out the lamp. As he turned to pass out to the stairs, something in his expression seemed to hint at a conclusion reached. All the anxiety and bewilderment had passed out of his face. Stern it was still, but there had come into it a certain resolute calm, the calm of a man who has made up his mind.

Chapter II
The Secret Visitor

The following morning found Mr. Pottermack in an undeniably restless mood. For a time he could settle down to no occupation, but strayed about the house and garden with an air of such gravity and abstraction that Mrs. Gadby looked at him askance and inwardly wondered what had come over her usually buoyant and cheerful employer.

One thing, however, was clear. He was not going to "hop up to town". Of the previous expeditions of that kind he had a vivid and unpleasant recollection, the big "bearer" cheque sheepishly pushed across the counter, the cashier's astonished glance at it, the careful examination of books, and then the great bundle of five-pound notes, which he counted, at the cashier's request, with burning cheeks, and his ignominious departure with the notes buttoned into an inside pocket and an uncomfortable suspicion in his mind that the ostentatiously unobservant cashier had guessed at once the nature of the transaction. Well, that experience was not going to be repeated on this occasion. There was going to be a change of procedure.

As he could fix his mind at nothing more definite, he decided to devote the day to a thorough clear-up of his workshops – a useful and necessary work, which had the added advantage of refreshing his memory as to the abiding-places of rarely used appliances and materials. And an excellent distraction he found it, so much so that several times, in the interest of rediscovering some long-forgotten tool or stock of material, he was able to forget for a while the critical interview that loomed before him.

So the day passed. The mid-day meal was consumed mechanically – under the furtive and disapproving observation of Mrs. Gadby – and dispatched with indecent haste. He was conscious of an inclination to lurk about the house on the chance of a brief gossip with his fair friend, but he resisted it, and, when he came in to tea, the housekeeper reported that the little package had been duly collected.

He lingered over his tea as if he were purposely consuming time, and when at last he rose from the table, he informed Mrs. Gadby that he had some important work to do and was under no circumstances to be disturbed. Then once more he retired to the walled garden and, having shut himself in, dropped the key into his pocket. He did not, however, resume his labours in the workshop. He merely called in there for an eight-inch steel bolt and a small electric lamp, both of which he bestowed in his pockets. Then he came out and walked slowly up and down the grass plot with his hands behind him and his chin on his breast as if immersed in thought, but glancing from time to time at his watch. At a quarter-to-eight he took off his spectacles and put them in his pocket, stepped across to the well and, picking up the hurdle that still lay over the dark cavity, carried it away and stood it against the wall. Then he softly unbolted the side gate, turned the handle of the latch, drew the gate open a bare inch, and, leaving it thus ajar, walked to the summer-house, and, entering it, sat down in one of the chairs.

His visitor, if deficient in some of the virtues, had at least that of punctuality, for the clock of the village church had barely finished striking the hour when the gate opened noiselessly and the watcher in the summer-house saw, through the gathering gloom, a large, portly man enter with stealthy step, close the gate silently behind him and softly shoot the upper bolt.

Pottermack rose as his visitor approached, and the two men met just outside the summer-house. There was a striking contrast between them in every respect, in build, in countenance, and in manner. The newcomer was a big, powerful man, heavy and distinctly over-fat, whose sly, shifty face – at present exhibiting an uneasy smile – showed evident traces of what is commonly miscalled "good living", especially as to the liquid element thereof, whereas his host, smallish, light, spare, with clean-cut features expressive of lively intelligence, preserved a stony calm as he looked steadily into his visitor's evasive eyes.

"Well, Jeff," the latter began in a deprecating tone, "you don't seem overjoyed to see me. Not an effusive welcome. Aren't you going to shake hands with an old pal?"

"It doesn't seem necessary," Pottermack replied coldly.

"Oh, very well," the other retorted. "Perhaps you'd like to kiss me instead". He sniggered foolishly and, entering the summer-house, dropped into one of the armchairs and continued, "What about a mild refresher while we discuss our little business? Looks like being a dry job, to judge by your mug."

Without replying, Pottermack opened a small cupboard, and taking out a decanter, a siphon, and a tumbler, placed them on the table by his guest. It was not difficult to see that the latter had already fortified himself with one or two refreshers, mild or otherwise, but that was not Pottermack's affair. He was going to keep his own brain clear. The other might do as he pleased.

466

"Not going to join me, Jeff?" the visitor protested. "Oh, buck up, old chap! It's no use getting peevish about parting with a few pounds. You won't miss a little donation to help a pal out of a difficulty."

As Pottermack made no reply but sat down and gazed stonily before him, the other poured out half-a-tumblerful of whisky, filled up with soda, and took a substantial gulp. Then he, too, sat silent for a time, gazing out into the darkening garden. And gradually the smile faded from his face, leaving it sullen and a little anxious.

"So you've been digging up your lawn," he remarked presently. "What's the game? Going to set up a flagstaff?"

"No. I am going to have a sun-dial there."

"A sun-dial, hey? Going to get your time on the cheap? Good. I like sun-dials. Do their job without ticking. Suppose you'll have a motto on it. *Tempus fugit* is the usual thing. Always appropriate, but especially so in the case of a man who has 'done time' and fugitted. It will help to remind you of olden days, 'the days that are no more'." He finished with a mirthless cackle and cast a malignant glance at the silent and wooden-faced Pottermack. There was another interval of strained, uncomfortable silence, during which the visitor took periodic gulps from his tumbler and eyed his companion with sullen perplexity. At length, having finished his liquor, he set down the empty tumbler and turned towards Pottermack. "You got my letter, I suppose, as you left the gate ajar?"

"Yes," was the laconic reply.

"Been up to town to-day?"

"No."

"Well, I suppose you have got the money?"

"No, I have not."

The big man sat up stiffly and stared at his companion in dismay.

"But, damn it, man!" he exclaimed, "didn't I tell you it was urgent? I'm in a devil of a fix. I've got to pay that hundred to-morrow. Must pay it, you understand. I'm going up to town in the morning to pay. As I hadn't got the money myself, I've had to borrow it from – you know where, and I was looking to you to enable me to put it back at once. I must have that money to-morrow at the latest. You'd better run up to town in the morning and I'll meet you outside your bank."

Pottermack shook his head. "It can't be done, Lewson. You'll have to make some other arrangements."

Lewson stared at him in mingled amazement and fury. For a moment he was too astonished for speech. At length he burst out, "Can't be done! What the devil do you mean? You've got the money in your bank and you are going to hand it over, or I'll know the reason why. What do you imagine you are going to do?"

467

"I am going," said Pottermack, "to hold you to your agreement, or at least to part of it. You demanded a sum of money – a large sum – as the price of your silence. It was to be a single payment, once for all, and I paid it. You promised solemnly to make no further demands, yet, within a couple of months, you did make further demands, and I paid again. Since then you have made demands at intervals, regardless of your solemn undertaking. Now this has got to stop. There must be an end to it, and this has got to be the end."

As he spoke, quietly but firmly, Lewson gazed at him as if he could not trust the evidence of his senses. This was quite a new Pottermack. At length, suppressing his anger, he replied in a conciliatory tone, "Very well, Jeff. It shall be the end. Help me out just this time and you shall hear no more from me. I promise you that on my word of honour."

At this last word Pottermack smiled grimly. But he answered in the same quiet, resolute manner. "It is no use, Lewson. You said that last time and the time before that, and, in fact, time after time. You have always sworn that each demand should be positively the last. And so you will go on, if I let you, until you have squeezed me dry."

On this Lewson threw off all disguise. Thrusting out his chin at Pottermack, he exclaimed furiously, "If you let me! And how do you think you are going to prevent me? You are quite right. I've got you, and I'm going to squeeze you, so now you know. And look here, young fellow, if that money isn't handed out to me to-morrow morning, something is going to happen. A very surprised gentleman at Scotland Yard will get a letter informing him that the late Jeffrey Brandon, runaway convict, is not the late J. B., but is alive and kicking, and that his present name and address is Marcus Pottermack, Esquire, of The Chestnuts, Borley, Bucks. How will that suit you?"

"It wouldn't suit me at all," Mr. Pottermack replied, with unruffled calm, "but before you do it, let me remind you of one or two facts. First, the run-away convict, once your closest friend, was to your knowledge an innocent man – "

"That's no affair of mine," Lewson interrupted. "He was a convict, and is one still. Besides, how do I know he was innocent? A jury of his fellow-countrymen found him guilty – "

"Don't talk rubbish, Lewson," Pottermack broke in impatiently. "There is no one here but ourselves. We both know that I didn't do those forgeries and we both know who did."

Lewson grinned as he reached out for the decanter and poured out another half-tumblerful of whisky. "If you knew who did it," he chuckled, "you must have been a blooming mug not to say."

"I didn't know then," Pottermack rejoined bitterly. "I thought you were a decent, honest fellow, fool that I was."

"Yes," Lewson agreed, with a low, cackling laugh, "you were a blooming mug and that's a fact. Well, well, we live and learn."

Still sniggering foolishly, he took a long pull at the tumbler, leering into the flushed, angry face that confronted him across the table. Suddenly Pottermack rose from his chair, and, striding out into the garden, halted some dozen paces away and stood with his back to the summer-house, looking steadily across the lawn. It was now quite dark, though the moon showed dimly from time to time through a thinning of the overcast sky, but still, through the gloom, he could make out faintly the glimmer of lighter-coloured soil where it had been turned up to level the ground for the sun-dial. The well was invisible, but he knew exactly where the black cavity yawned, and his eye, locating the spot, rested on it with gloomy fixity.

His reverie was interrupted by Lewson's voice, now pitched in a more ingratiating key.

"Well, Jeff, thinking it over? That's right, old chap. No use getting pippy."

He paused, and as there was no reply he continued, "Come now, dear boy, let's settle the business amicably as old pals should. Pity for you to go back to the jug when there's no need. You just help me out of this hole, and I will give you my solemn word of honour that it shall be the very last time. Won't that satisfy you?"

Pottermack turned his head slightly, and speaking over his shoulder, replied, "Your word of honour! The honour of a blackmailer, a thief, and a liar. It isn't exactly what you would call a gilt-edged security."

"Well," the other retorted thickly, "gilt-edged or not, you had better take it and shell out. Now, what do you say?"

"I say," Pottermack replied with quiet decision, "that I am not going to give you another farthing on any condition whatever."

For several seconds Lewson gazed in silent dismay at the shadowy figure on the lawn. This final, definite refusal was a contingency that he had never dreamed of, and was utterly unprovided for, and it filled him, for the moment, with consternation. Then, suddenly, his dismay changed to fury. Starting up from his chair, he shouted huskily, "Oh, you won't, won't you? We'll see about that! You'll either pay up or I'll give you the finest hammering that you've ever had in your life. When I've done with you, they'll want your finger-prints to find out who you are."

He paused to watch the effect of this terrifying proposal and to listen for a reply. Then, as the dim figure remained unmoved and no

469

answer came, he bellowed, "D' you hear? Are you going to pay up or take a hammering?"

Pottermack turned his head slightly and replied in a quiet, almost a gentle tone, "I don't think I'm going to do either."

The reply and the quiet, unalarmed tone were not quite what Lewson had expected. Trusting to the moral effect of his greatly superior size and weight, he had bluffed confidently. Now it seemed that he had got to make good his threat, and the truth is that he was not eager for the fray. However, it had to be done, and done as impressively as possible. After pausing for another couple of seconds, he proceeded, with a formidable air (but unobserved by Pottermack, whose back was still turned to him), to take off his coat and fling it on the table, whence it slipped down on to the floor. Then, stepping outside the summer-house, he bent forward, and, with an intimidating roar, charged like an angry rhinoceros.

At the sound of his stamping feet Pottermack spun round and faced him, but then stood motionless until his assailant was within a yard of him, when he sprang lightly aside, and as the big, unwieldy bully lumbered past him, he followed him closely. As soon as Lewson could overcome the momentum of his charge, he halted and turned, and instantly a smart left-hander alighted on his cheek and a heavy right-hander impinged on his ribs just below the armpit. Furious with the pain, and utterly taken aback, he cursed and grunted, hitting out wildly with all the viciousness of mingled rage and fear for now he realized with amazement that he was hopelessly outclassed by his intended victim. Not one of his sledge-hammer blows took effect on that agile adversary, whereas his own person seemed to be but an unprotected target on which the stinging blows fell in endless and intolerable succession. Slowly at first, and then more quickly, he backed away from that terrific bombardment, followed inexorably by the calm and scientific Pottermack, who seemed to guide and direct his backward course as a skilful drover directs the movements of a refractory bullock.

Gradually the pair moved away from the vicinity of the summer-house across the dark lawn, the demoralized bully, breathing hard and sweating profusely, reduced to mere defence and evasion while his light-footed antagonist plied him unceasingly with feint or blow. Presently Lewson stumbled backward as his foot sank into the loose, heaped earth at the margin of the cleared space, but Pottermack did not press his advantage, renewing his attack only when Lewson had recovered his balance. Then the movement began again, growing faster as the big man became more and more terrified and his evasion passed into undissembled retreat, deviously and with many a zig-zag, but always tending towards the centre of the cleared area. Suddenly Pottermack's tactics changed. The rapid succession of light blows ceased for an instant and he seemed to gather himself up as if for a decisive effort. There was a quick feint with the left, then his right fist shot out like lightning and drove straight on to the point of the other man's jaw, and as his teeth clicked together with an audible snap, Lewson dropped like a pole-axed ox, falling with his body from the waist upwards across the mouth of the well and his head on the brick edge, on which it struck with a sickening thud.

So he lay for a second or two until the limp trunk began to sag and the chin came forward on to the breast. Suddenly the head slipped off the brick edge and dropped into the cavity, shedding its cap and carrying the trunk with it. The heavy jerk started the rest of the body sliding forward, slowly at first, then with increasing swiftness until the feet rose for an instant, kicked at the farther edge and were gone. From the black pit issued vague, echoing murmurs, followed presently by a hollow, reverberating splash, and after that, silence.

It had been but a matter of seconds. Even as those cavernous echoes were muttering in the unseen depths, Pottermack's knuckles were still tingling from the final blow. From the moment when that blow had been struck he had made no move. He had seen his enemy fall, had heard the impact of the head on the brick edge, and had stood looking down with grim composure on the body as it sagged, slid forward, and at last made its dreadful dive down into the depths of its sepulchre. But he had moved not a muscle. It was a horrible affair. But it had to be. Not he, but Lewson, had made the decision.

As the last reverberations died away he approached the forbidding circle of blackness, and kneeling down at its edge, peered into the void. Of course, he could see nothing, and when he listened intently, not a sound came to his ear. From his pocket he brought out his little electric lamp and threw a beam of light down into the dark cavity. The effect was very strange and uncanny. He found himself looking down a tube of seemingly interminable length while from somewhere far away, down in the very bowels of the earth, a tiny spark of light glowed steadily. So even the last ripples had died away and all was still down in that underworld.

He replaced the lamp in his pocket, but nevertheless he remained kneeling by the well-mouth, resting on one hand, gazing down into the black void and unconsciously listening for some sound from below. Despite his outward composure, he was severely shaken. His heart still raced, his forehead was damp with sweat, his body and limbs were pervaded by a fine, nervous tremor.

471

Yet he was sensible of a feeling of relief. The dreadful thing that he had nerved himself to do, that he had looked forward to with shuddering horror, was done. And the doing of it might have been so much worse. He was relieved to feel the screw-bolt in his pocket – unused, to think that the body had slipped down into its grave without the need of any hideous dragging or thrusting. Almost, he began to persuade himself that it had been more-or-less of an accident. At any rate, it was over and done with. His merciless enemy was gone. The menace to his liberty, the constant fear that had haunted him were no more. At last – at long last – he was free.

Fear of discovery he had none, for Lewson, in his own interests, had insisted on strict secrecy as to their acquaintance with each other. In his own words, "he preferred to sit on his own nest-egg". Hence to all the world they were strangers, not necessarily even aware of each other's existence. And the blackmailer's stealthy arrival and his care in silently shutting the gate gave a guarantee that no one had seen him enter.

While these thoughts passed somewhat confusedly through his mind, he remained in the same posture, still unconsciously listening and still gazing, as if with a certain expectancy, into the black hole before him, or letting his eyes travel, now and again, round the dark garden. Presently an opening in the dense pall of cloud that obscured the sky uncovered the moon and flooded the garden with light. The transition from darkness to brilliant light – for it was full moon – was so sudden that Pottermack looked up with a nervous start, as though to see who had thrown the light on him, and in his overwrought state he even found something disquieting in the pale, bright disc with its queer, dim, impassive face that seemed to be looking down on him through the rent in the cloud like some secret watcher peeping from behind a curtain. He rose to his feet and, drawing a deep breath, looked around him, and then his glance fell on something more real and more justly disquieting. From the edge of the grass to the brink of the well was a double track of footprints, meandering to and fro, zig-zagging hither and thither, but undeniably ending at the well.

Their appearance was sinister in the extreme. In the bright moonlight they stared up from the pale buff soil, and they shouted of tragedy. To the police eye they would have been the typical "signs of a struggle", the tracks of two men facing one another and moving towards the well with, presently, a single track coming away from it. No one could mistake the meaning of those tracks, nothing could explain them away – especially in view of what was at the bottom of the well.

The first glance at those tracks gave Pottermack a severe shock. But he recovered from it in a moment. For they were mere transitory marks that could be obliterated in a minute or two by a few strokes of a rake and a few sweeps of a besom, and meanwhile he stooped over them, examining them with a curious interest not unmixed with a certain vague uneasiness. They were very remarkable impressions. He had already noted the peculiar quality of this loamy soil, its extraordinary suitability for making casting-moulds. And here was a most striking illustration of this property. The prints of his own feet were so perfect that the very brads in his soles were quite clear and distinct, while as to Lewson's, they were positively ridiculous. Every detail of the rubber soles and the circular rubber heels came out as sharply as if the impressions had been taken in moulding-wax. There was the prancing horse of Kent – the soles were of the Invicta brand and practically new – with the appropriate legend and the manufacturers' name, and in the central star-shaped space of the heels was the perfect impression of the screw. No doubt the singular sharpness of the prints was due to the fact that a heavy shower in the previous night had brought the loam to that particular state of dampness that the professional moulder seeks to produce with his watering-pot.

However, interesting as the prints were to the mechanic's eye, the sooner they were got rid of the better. Thus reflecting, Pottermack strode away towards the workshop in quest of a rake and a besom, and he was, in fact, reaching out to grasp the handle of the door when he stopped dead and stood for some seconds rigid and still with outstretched arm and dropped jaw. For in that moment a thought which had, no doubt, been stirring in his subconscious mind had come to the surface, and for the first time the chill of real terror came over him. Suddenly he realized that he had no monopoly of this remarkable loam. It was the soil of the neighbourhood – and incidentally of the little lane that led from the town and passed along beside his wall. In that lane there must be a single track of footprints – big, staring footprints, and every one of them as good as a signature of James Lewson – leading from the town and stopping at his gate!

After a few moments of horror-stricken reflection he darted into the tool-house and brought out a short ladder. His first impulse had been to open the gate and peer out, but an instant's reflection had shown him the folly of exposing himself to the risk of being seen – especially at the very gate to which the tracks led. He now carried the ladder across to an old pear tree which thrust its branches over the wall, and, planting it silently where the foliage was densest, crept softly up and listened awhile. As no sound of footsteps was audible, and as the moon had for the moment retired behind the bank of cloud, he cautiously advanced his head over the wall and looked down into the lane. It was too dark to see far in either direction, but apparently there was no one about, and as the country quiet was unbroken by any sound, he ventured to crane farther forward to inspect the path below.

The light was very dim, but even so he could make out faintly a single track of footprints – large footprints, widely spaced, the footprints of a tall man. But even as he was peering down at them through the darkness, trying to distinguish in the vaguely seen shapes some recognizable features, the moon burst forth again and the light became almost as that of broad day. Instantly the half-seen shapes started up with a horrid distinctness that made him catch his breath. There was the preposterous prancing horse with the legend "*Invicta*", there was the makers' name, actually legible from the height of the wall, and there were the circular heels with their raised central stars and the very screws clearly visible even to their slots!

Pottermack was profoundly alarmed. But he was not a panicky man. There, in those footprints, was evidence enough to hang him. But he was not hanged yet, and he did not mean to be, if the unpleasantness could be avoided. Perched on the ladder, with his eyes riveted on the tracks of the man who had come to "squeeze" him, he reviewed the situation with cool concentration, and considered the best way to deal with it.

The obvious thing was to go out and trample on those footprints until they were quite obliterated. But to this plan there were several objections. In the first place, those enormous impressions would take a deal of trampling out. Walking over them once would be quite useless, for his own feet were comparatively small, and even a fragment of one of Lewson's footprints would be easily recognizable. Moreover, the trampling process would involve the leaving of his own footprints in evidence, which might be disastrous if it should happen – as it easily might – that Lewson had been seen starting along the footpath. For this path, unfrequented as it was, turned off from the main road at the outskirts of the town where wayfarers were numerous enough. The reason that it was unfrequented was that it led only to a wood and a stretch of heath which were more easily approached by a by-road. Finally, he himself might quite possibly be seen performing the trampling operations, and that would never do. In short, the trampling scheme was not practicable at all.

But what alternative was there? Something must be done. Very soon the man would be missed and there would be a search for him, and as things stood there was a set of tracks ready to guide the searchers from the town to his – Pottermack's – very gate. And inside the gate was the open well. Clearly, something must be done, and done at once. But what?

As he asked himself this question again and again he was half-consciously noting the conditions. Hitherto, no one had seen Lewson's footprints at this part of the path. That was evident from the fact that there were no other fresh footprints – none that trod on Lewson's. Then, in half-an-hour at the most, the shadow of the wall would be thrown over the path and the tracks would then be quite inconspicuous. And, again, it was now past nine o'clock and his neighbours were early folk. It was extremely unlikely that any one would pass along that path until the morning. So there was still time. But time for what?

One excellent plan occurred to him, but, alas! He had not the means to carry it out. If only he had possession of Lewson's shoes he could put them on, slip out at the gate and continue the tracks to some distant spot well out of his neighbourhood. That would be a perfect solution of the problem. But Lewson's shoes had vanished for ever from human ken – at least, he hoped they had. So that plan was impracticable.

And yet, was it? As he put the question to himself his whole demeanour changed. He stood up on his perch with a new eagerness in his face, the eagerness of a man who has struck a brilliant idea. For that was what he had done. This excellent plan, which yielded the perfect solution, was practicable after all. Lewson's shoes were indeed beyond his reach. But he had a fine assortment of Lewson's footprints. Now footprints are made by the soles of shoes. That is the normal process. But by the exercise of a little ingenuity the process could be reversed, shoe-soles could be made from footprints.

He descended the ladder, thinking hard, and as the cloud once more closed over the moon, he fetched the hurdle and placed it carefully over the mouth of the well. Then he walked slowly towards the workshop – avoiding the now invaluable footprints – shaping his plan as he went.

Chapter III
Mr. Pottermack Goes
A-Sugaring

The efficient workman saves a vast amount of time by so planning out his job in advance that intervals of waiting are eliminated. Now Mr. Pottermack was an eminently methodical man and he was very sensible that, in the existing circumstances, time was precious. Accordingly, although his plan was but roughly sketched out in his mind, he proceeded forthwith to execute that part of it which could be clearly visualized, filling in the further details mentally as he worked.

The first thing to be done was, obviously, to convert the perishable, ephemeral footprints, which a light shower would destroy, into solid, durable models. To this end, he fetched from the workshop the tin of fine plaster of Paris which he kept for making small or delicate moulds. By the aid of his little lamp he selected a specially deep and perfect impression of Lewson's right foot, and into this he lightly dusted the fine powder, continuing the process until the surface was covered with an even layer of about half-an-inch thick. This he pressed down very gently with the flat end of the lamp, and then went in search of a suitable impression of the left foot, which he treated in like manner. He next selected a second pair of prints, but instead of dusting the dry plaster into them he merely dropped into each a pinch to serve as a mark for identifying it. His reason for thus varying the method was that he was doubtful whether it was possible to pour liquid plaster into a loam mould (for that was what the footprint actually was) without disturbing the surface and injuring the pattern.

Returning to the workshop, he mixed a good-sized bowl of plaster, stirring and beating the creamy liquid with a large spoon. Still stirring, he carried it out, and, going first to the prints which contained the dry plaster, he carefully ladled into them with the spoon small quantities of the liquid plaster until they were well filled. By this time the liquid was growing appreciably thicker and more suitable for the unprotected prints, to which he accordingly hastened, and proceeded quickly, but with extreme care, to fill them until the now rapidly thickening plaster was well heaped up above the surface.

He had now at least, a quarter-of-an-hour to wait while the plaster was setting, but this he occupied in cleaning out the bowl and spoon ready for the next mixing, placing the brush and plaster tools in readiness, and pouring out a saucerful of soap-size. When he had made these preparations, he filled a small jug with water and, making his way to the first two impressions, poured the water on to them to make up for that which would have been absorbed by the dry plaster underneath. In the second pair of impressions, which he ventured to test by a light touch of the finger, the plaster was already quite solid, and he was strongly tempted to raise them and see what luck he had had, but he resisted the temptation and went back to the workshop, leaving them to harden completely.

All this time, although he had given the closest attention to what he was doing, his mind had been working actively, and already the sketch-plan was beginning to shape into a complete and detailed scheme, for he had suddenly remembered a supply of sheet gutta-percha which he had unearthed when he turned out the workshop, and this discovery disposed of what had been his chief difficulty. Now, in readiness for a later stage of his work, he lighted his Primus stove and, having filled a good-sized saucepan with water, placed it on the stove to heat. This consumed the rest of the time that he had allotted for the hardening of the plaster, and he now went forth with no little anxiety to see what the casts were like, for they were the really essential element of his plan on which success or failure depended. If he could get a perfect reproduction of the footprints, the rest of his task, troublesome as it promised to be, would be plain sailing.

Very gingerly he insinuated his finger under one of the casts of the second pair and gently turned it over. And then, as he threw the light of his lamp on it, all his misgivings vanished in respect of that foot – the right. The aspect of the cast was positively ridiculous. It was just the sole of a shoe, snow-white, but otherwise completely realistic, and perfect in every detail and marking, even to the makers' name. And the second cast was equally good, so his special precautions had been unnecessary. Nevertheless, he went on to the first pair, and they proved to be, if anything, sharper and cleaner, more free from adherent particles of earth than the others. With a sigh of relief he picked up the four casts and bore them tenderly to the workshop, where he deposited them on the bench. There, under the bright electric light, their appearance was even more striking. But he did not stop to gloat. He could do that while he was working.

The first proceeding was to trim off the ragged edges with a scraper, and then came the process of "sizing" – painting with a boiled solution of soft soap – which also cleaned away the adherent particles of loam. When the soap had soaked in and "stopped" the surface, the surplus was washed away under the tap, and then, with a soft brush, an infinitesimal

477

coating of olive oil was applied. The casts were now ready for the next stage – the making of the moulds. First, Pottermack filled a shallow tray with loam from the garden, striking the surface level with a straight-edge. On this surface the two best casts were laid, sole upwards, and pressed down until they were slightly embedded. Then came the mixing of another bowl of plaster, and this was "gauged" extra stiff in order that it should set quickly and set hard. By the time this had been poured on – rapidly, but with infinite care to avoid bubbles, which would have marred the perfection of the moulds – the water in the saucepan was boiling. Having cleaned out the bowl and spoon, Pottermack fetched the pieces of gutta-percha from their drawer and dropped them into the saucepan, replacing the lid. Then he put on his spectacles, extinguished the lamp, switched off the light, and, passing out of the workshop, walked quickly towards the house.

As he let himself out of the walled garden and closed the door behind him, he had a strange feeling as of one awakening from a dream. The familiar orchard and kitchen garden through which he was now passing, and the lighted windows of the house which twinkled through the trees, brought him back to the realities of his quiet, usually uneventful life and made the tragic interlude of the past hour seem incredible and unreal. He pondered on it with a sort of dull surprise as he walked up the long path, on all that had happened since he had last walked along it a few hours ago. How changed since then was his world – and himself! Then, he was an innocent man over whom yet hung the menace of the convict prison. Now that menace was lifted, but he was an innocent man no more. Legally – technically, he put it to himself – he was a murderer, and the menace of the prison was exchanged for that of the rope. But there was this difference – the one had been an abiding menace that had been with him for the term of his life, the other was a temporary peril from which, when he had once freed himself, he would be free forever.

His appearance in the house was hailed by Mrs. Gadby with a sigh of relief. It seemed that she had made a special effort in the matter of supper and had feared lest her trouble should be wasted after all. Very complacently she inducted him into the dining-room and awaited, with confidence born of much experience, his appreciative comments.

"Why, bless my soul, Mrs. Gadby!" he exclaimed, gazing at the display on the table, "it's a regular banquet! Roses, too! And do I see a bottle under that shawl?"

Mrs. Gadby smilingly raised the shawl, revealing a small wooden tub in which a bottle of white wine stood embedded in ice. "I thought," she explained, "that a glass of Chablis would go rather well with the lobster."

"Rather well!" exclaimed Pottermack. "I should think it will. But why these extraordinary festivities?"

"Well, sir," said Mrs. Gadby, "you haven't seemed to be quite yourself the last day or two. Not in your usual spirits. So I thought a nice little supper and a glass of wine might pick you up a bit."

"And so it will, I am sure," affirmed Pottermack. "To-morrow you will find me as lively as a cricket and as gay as a lark. And, by the way, Mrs. Gadby, don't clear the table to-night. I am going out sugaring presently, and as I may be late getting back I shall probably be ready for another little meal before turning in. And of course you won't bolt the door – but I expect you will have gone to bed before I start."

Mrs. Gadby acknowledged these instructions and retired in sedate triumph. Particularly gratified was she at the evident satisfaction with which her employer had regarded the Chablis. A happy thought of hers that had been, in which she was right in general though mistaken in one particular. For it was not the wine that had brought that look of satisfaction to Pottermack's face. It was the ice. Mrs. Gadby's kindly forethought had disposed of the last of his difficulties.

Before sitting down to supper, he ran up to his bedroom, ostensibly for the necessary wash and brush up, but first he visited a spacious cupboard from the ground floor of which he presently took a pair of over-shoes that he was accustomed to wear in very rainy or snowy weather. Their upper parts were of strong waterproof cloth and their soles of balata, cemented on to leather inner soles. He had, in fact, cemented them on himself when the original soles had worn through, and he still had, in the workshop, a large tin nearly full of the cement. He now inspected the soles critically, and when, after having washed and made himself tidy, he went down to the dining-room, he carried the over-shoes down with him and slipped them out of sight under the table.

Although he was pretty sharp-set after his strenuous and laborious evening, he made but a hasty meal, for time was precious and he could dispose of the balance of the feast when he had finished his task. Rising from the table, he picked up the over-shoes and, stealing softly out into the garden, laid them down beside the path. Then he stole back to the dining-room, whence he walked briskly to the kitchen and tapped at the door.

"Good-night, Mrs. Gadby," he called out cheerfully. "I shall be starting when I've got my traps together. Leave everything as it is in the dining-room so that I can have a snack when I come in. Good-night!"

"Good-night, sir," the housekeeper responded cordially, presenting a smiling countenance at the door, "and good luck with the moths, though I must admit, sir, that they don't seem to me worth all the trouble of catching them."

"Ah, Mrs. Gadby," said Pottermack, "but you see, you are not a naturalist. You would think better of the moths, I expect, if they were good to eat." With this and a chuckle, in which the housekeeper joined, he turned away and went forth into the garden, where, having picked up the over-shoes, he made his way up the long path to the door of the walled garden. As he unlocked the door and let himself into the enclosure, he was again sensible of a change of atmosphere. The vision of that fatal combat rose before him with horrid vividness and once more he felt the menace of the rope hanging over him. He went to the ladder and looked over the wall to see if any new tracks had appeared on the path to tell of some wayfarer who might hereafter become a witness. But the path was shrouded in darkness so profound that he could not even see the tracks that he knew were there, so he descended, and, crossing the lawn by the well – where some unaccountable impulse led him to stop for a while and listen – re-entered the workshop, switched on the light and laid the over-shoes on the bench.

First, he assured himself by a touch that the saucepan was still hot. Then he turned his attention to the moulds. They were as hard as stone, and, as he had made them thick and solid, he ventured to use some little force in trying to separate them from the casts, but all his efforts failed. Then, since he could not prise them open with a knife for fear of marking them, he filled a bucket with water and in this immersed each of the moulds with its adherent cast, when, after a few seconds' soaking, they came apart quite easily.

He stood for a few moments with the cast of the right foot in one hand and its mould in the other, looking at them with a sort of amused surprise. They were so absurdly realistic in spite of their staring whiteness. The cast was simply a white shoe-sole, the mould an exact reproduction of the original footprint, and both were preposterously complete, not only in respect of the actual pattern and lettering but even of the little trivial accidental characters such as a clean cut – probably made by a sharp stone – across the neck of the prancing horse and a tiny angular fragment of gravel which had become embedded in the rubber heel. However, this was no time for contemplation. The important fact was that both the moulds appeared to be quite perfect. If the rest of the operations should be as successful, he would be in a fair way of winning through this present danger to find a permanent security.

480

He began with the right mould. Having first poured into it a little of the hot water from the saucepan, to take the chill off the surface, he laid it on a carefully folded towel, spread on the bench. Then with a pair of tongs he picked out of the saucepan one of the pieces of gutta-percha – now quite soft and plastic – and laid it in the mould, which it filled completely, with some overlap. As it was, at the moment, too hot to work comfortably with the fingers, he pressed it into the mould with a wet file-handle, replacing this as soon as possible with the infinitely more efficient thumb. It was a somewhat tedious process, for every part of the surface had to be pressed into the mould so that no detail should be missed, but it was not until the hardening of the gutta-percha as it cooled rendered further manipulation useless that Pottermack laid it aside as finished and proceeded to operate in like manner on the other mould.

When both moulds were filled, he immersed them in the cold water in the bucket in order to cool and harden the gutta-percha more quickly, and leaving them there, he turned his attention to the over-shoes. The important question was as to their size. How did they compare with Lewson's shoes? He had assumed that they were as nearly as possible alike in size, but now, when he placed one of the over-shoes, sole upwards, beside the corresponding cast, he felt some misgivings. However, a few careful measurements with a tape-measure reassured him. The over-shoes were a trifle larger – an eighth of an inch wider and nearly a quarter-of-an-inch longer than the casts, so that there would be a sixteenth overlap at the sides and an eighth at the toe and heel. That would be of no importance, or if it were, he could pare off the overlap.

Much encouraged, he fell to work on the over-shoes. He knew all about batata soles. The present ones – which were of one piece with the flat heels – he had stuck on with a powerful fusible cement. All that he had to do now was to warm them cautiously over the Primus stove until the cement was softened and then peel them off, and when he had done this, there were the flat leather soles, covered with the sticky cement, all ready for the attachment of the gutta-percha "squeezes."

There was still one possible snag ahead. The squeezes might have stuck to the moulds, for gutta-percha is a sticky material when hot. However, the moulds had been saturated with water and usually gutta-percha will not stick to a wet surface, so he hoped for the best. Nevertheless it was with some anxiety that he fished one of the moulds out of the bucket, and, grasping an overlapping edge of the squeeze with a pair of flat-nosed pliers, gave a cautious and tentative pull. As it showed no sign of yielding, he shifted to another part of the overlap and made gentle traction on that, with no better result. He then tried the piece of overlap that projected beyond the toe, and here he had better luck, for, as he gave a firm, steady pull, the squeeze separated visibly from the mould, and, with a little coaxing, came out bodily.

Pottermack turned it over eagerly to see what result his labours had yielded, and as his glance fell on the smooth, brown surface he breathed a sigh of deep satisfaction. He could have asked for no better result. The squeeze had not failed at a single point. There was the horse with the little gash in its neck, the inscription and the makers' mark, the circular heel with its sunk, five-pointed star, the little marks of wear, and the central screw showing its slot quite distinctly. Even the little grain of embedded gravel was there. The impression was perfect. He had never seen the soles of Lewson's shoes, but he knew now exactly what they looked like. For here before him was an absolutely faithful facsimile.

Handling it with infinite tenderness – for gutta-percha, when once softened, is slow to harden completely – he replaced it in the bucket, and taking out the other mould, repeated the extracting operation with the same patient care and with a similar happy result. It remained now only to pare off the overlap round the edges, shave off with a sharp knife one or two slight projections on the upper surface and wipe the latter perfectly dry. When this was done, the soles were ready for fixing on the over-shoes.

Placing the invaluable tin of cement on the bench near the Primus, Pottermack proceeded to warm the sole of one of the over-shoes over the flame. Then, scooping out a lump of tough cement, he transferred it to the warmed sole and spread it out evenly with a hot spatula. The next operation was more delicate and rather risky, for the upper surface of the gutta-percha sole had to be coated with cement without warming the mass of the sole enough to endanger the impression on its under surface. However, by loading the spatula with melted cement and wiping it swiftly over the surface, the perilous operation was completed without mishap. And now came the final stage. Fixing the over-shoe in the bench-vice, and once more passing the hot spatula over its cemented sole, Pottermack picked up the gutta-percha sole and carefully placed it in position on the over-shoe, adjusting it so that the overlaps at the sides and the toe were practically equal, the larger overlap at the heel being – by reason of the thickness of the latter – of no consequence.

When the second shoe had been dealt with in a similar manner and with a like success, and the pair placed on the bench, soles upward, to cool and harden, Pottermack emptied the bucket, and, carrying it in his hand, stole out of the workshop and made his way out of the walled garden into the orchard, where he advanced cautiously along the path. Presently the house came into view and he saw with satisfaction that the lower part was in darkness whereas lights were visible at two of the upper windows – those of the respective bedrooms of Mrs. Gadby and the maid. Thereupon he walked forward boldly, let himself silently into the house, and tiptoed to the dining-room, where, having closed the door, he proceeded at once to transfer the ice and the ice-cold water from the tub to the bucket. Then, in the same silent manner, he went out into the garden, softly closing the door after him, and took his way back to the workshop.

Here his first proceeding was to take down from a shelf a large, deep porcelain dish, such as photographers use. This he placed on the bench and poured into it the iced water from the bucket. Then, taking up the shoes, one at a time, he lowered them slowly and carefully, soles downward, into the iced water and finished by packing the ice round them. And there he left them to cool and harden completely while he attended to one or two other important matters.

The first of these was the line of tell-tale footprints leading to the well. They had served their invaluable purpose and now it was time to get rid of them, which he did forthwith with the aid of a rake and a hard broom. Then there must be one or two footprints outside the gate that would need to be obliterated. He took the broom and rake, and, crossing to the gate, listened awhile, then softly opened it, listened again and peered out. Having satisfied himself that there was no one in sight, he stooped to scrutinize the ground and finally went down on his hands and knees. Sure enough, there were four footprints that told the story much too plainly for safety: Two diverging from the main track towards the gate and two more pointing directly towards it. Their existence was a little disquieting at the first glance, for they might already have been seen, but a close scrutiny of the ground for signs of any more recent footprints reassured him. Evidently Lewson was the last person who had trodden that path. Having established this encouraging fact, Pottermack, still keeping inside his gate, passed the rake lightly over the four footprints and then smoothed the surface with the broom.

His preparations were now nearly complete. Re-closing the gate, he went back to the workshop to prepare his outfit. For though the 'sugaring' expedition was but a pretext, he intended to carry it through with completely convincing realism, on that realism it was quite conceivable that his future safety might depend. Accordingly, he proceeded to pack the large rucksack that he usually carried on these expeditions with the necessary appliances: A store of collecting-boxes, the killing-jar, a supply of pins, the folding-net, an air-tight metal pot which he filled with pieces of rag previously dipped into the sugaring mixture and reeking of beer and rum, and an electric inspection-lamp.

When he had packed it, he laid the net-stick by its side and then turned his attention to the shoes.

The gutta-percha soles were now quite cold and hard. He dried them carefully with a soft rag, and as he did so, the little surrounding overlap caught his eye. It seemed to be of no consequence. It was very unlikely that it would leave any mark on the ground, unless he should meet with an exceptionally soft patch. Still, there had been no overlap on Lewson's shoes, and it was better to be on the safe side. Thus reflecting, he took from the tool-rack a shoemaker's knife, and having given it a rub or two on the emery board, neatly shaved away the overlap on each sole to a steep bevel. Now the impression would be perfect no matter what kind of ground he met with.

This was the finishing touch, and he was now ready to go forth. Slipping his arms through the straps of the rucksack, he picked up the net-stick, took down from a peg his working apron, tucked the shoes under his arm, switched off the light, and went out, crossing the lawn direct to the side gate. Here he spread the apron on the ground and, stepping on to it, listened for a few moments and then softly opened the gate. Having taken a cautious peep out to assure himself that there was no one in sight, he slipped on and fastened the over-shoes and, taking the inspection-lamp from the rucksack, dropped the battery into his coat pocket and hooked the bulls-eye into a button-hole. Then, throwing the light for an instant on the path and marking the correct spot by his eye, he stepped out sideways, planting his right foot on the smoothly swept ground a pace in front of the last impression of Lewson's left foot.

Steadying himself with the net-stick, he pulled the gate to until the latch clicked. Then he put down his left foot a good pace in advance and set forth on his pilgrimage, carefully adapting the length of his stride to match, as well as he could judge, that of his long-legged predecessor.

The country was profoundly quiet, and, though the moon peeped out now and again, the night was for the most part so dark that he had occasionally to switch on his lamp to make sure that he was keeping to the path. The state of affairs, however, that these occasional flashes revealed was highly encouraging, for though the beaten surface of the path showed numerous traces of human feet, these were mostly faint and ill-defined, and none of them looked very recent. They suggested that few wayfarers used this path, and that the very striking tracks that he was laying down might remain undisturbed and plainly visible for many days unless a heavy rain should fall and wash them away.

So Pottermack trudged on, stepping out with conscious effort and keeping his attention fixed on the regulation of his stride. About half-a-mile from home the path entered a small wood, and here the aid of the lamp was needed continuously. Here, too, the sodden state of the path caused Pottermack to congratulate himself on his wise caution in shaving off the overlaps. For in this soft earth they would have shown distinctly and might have attracted undesirable notice – that is, if any one should give the footprints more than the passing glance that would suffice for recognition, which was in the highest degree unlikely.

Presently the path emerged from the wood and meandered across a rough common, covered with gorse and heather. Eventually, as Pottermack knew, it joined, nearly at a right angle, a by-road, which in its turn opened on the main London road. Here, he decided, the tracks could plausibly be lost, and as he drew near to the neighbourhood of the by-road he kept a sharp look-out for some indication of its whereabouts. At length he made out dimly a gate which he recognized as marking a little bridge across the roadside ditch. At once he stepped off the path into the heather, and, after walking on some twenty paces, halted, and unfastening the over-shoes, slipped them off. Then he took off the rucksack, turned out its contents and, having stowed the shoes at the bottom, repacked it and put it on again.

Hitherto he had not met or seen a soul since he started, and he was rather anxious not to meet any one until he was clear of this neighbourhood. His recent activities had perhaps made him a little over-conscious. Still, this was the night of the disappearance and here the tracks faded into the heather. If he were seen hereabouts, he might hereafter be questioned as to whether he had seen the missing man. No great harm in that, perhaps, but he had the feeling that it were much better for him not to be associated with the affair in any way. There were all sorts of possible snags. For instance, how did he get here without leaving any footprints on the path by which he would naturally have come? From which it will be seen that, if conscience was not making a coward of Mr. Pottermack, it was at least a little unduly stimulating his imagination. And yet it was as well to err on the right side.

Turning back, he strode on through the heather until he came once more to the path, which he crossed by a long jump that landed him in the heather on the farther side. He now struck across the common, making for a detached coppice that formed an outlier of the wood. As soon as he reached it he fell to work without delay on the completion of his programme, pinning the pieces of sugared rag on the trunks of half-a-dozen trees. Usually he gave the moths ample time to find the bait and assemble round it. But to-night, with that incriminating pair of shoes in his rucksack, his methods were more summary. By the time that he had pinned on the last rag, one or two moths had begun to flutter round the first, easily visible in the darkness by the uncanny, phosphorescent glow of their eyes. Pottermack unfolded his net, and, screwing it on to the stick switched on his lamp and proceeded to make one or two captures, transferring the captives from the net to the killing-jar, and, after the necessary interval, thence to the collecting-boxes.

He was not feeling avaricious to-night. He wanted to get home and bring his task definitely to an end. He was even disposed to resent the indecent way in which the moths began to swarm round the rags. They seemed to be inviting him to make a night of it, as they were doing amidst the fumes of the rum. But he was not to be tempted. When he had pinned a dozen specimens in his collecting-box and put a few more in the lethal jar, he considered that he had done enough to account plausibly for his nocturnal expedition. Thereupon he packed up and, leaving the lepidopterous revellers to the joys of intoxication, he turned away and strode off briskly in the direction of the by-road, carrying the net still screwed to the stick. A few minutes' rough walking brought him to the road, down which he turned in the direction of the town. In another ten minutes he reached the outskirts of the town and the road on which his house fronted. At this late hour it was as deserted as the country. Indeed in its whole length he encountered but a single person – a jovial constable who greeted him with an indulgent smile as he fixed a twinkling eye on the butterfly net, and, having playfully enquired what Mr. Pottermack had got in that bag, hoped that he had had good sport, and wished him good-night. So Pottermack went on his way, faintly amused at the flutter into which the constable's facetious question had put him, for if it had chanced that the guardian of the law had been a stranger and had insisted on examining the bag, nothing could have been more apparently innocent than its contents. But the guilty man finds it hard to avoid projecting into the minds of others the secret knowledge that his own mind harbours.

When Pottermack at last let himself in at his front door and secured it with bolt and chain, he breathed a sigh of relief. The horrible chapter was closed. Tomorrow he could clear away the last souvenirs of that hideous scene in the garden and then, in the peace and security of his new life, try to forget the price that he had paid for it. So he reflected as he carried the tub to the scullery and drew into it enough water to account for the vanished ice, as he washed at the sink, as he sat at the table consuming the arrears of his supper, and as, at length, he went up to bed, carrying the rucksack with him.

Chapter IV
The Placing of the Sun-Dial

When, after breakfast on the following morning, Mr. Pottermack betook himself, rucksack in hand, to the walled garden, he experienced, as he closed the door behind him and glanced round the enclosure, curiously mixed feelings. He was still shaken by the terrific events of the previous night and, in his disturbed state, disposed to be pessimistic and vaguely apprehensive. Not that he regretted what he had done. Lewson had elected to make his life insupportable, and a man who does that does it at his own risk. So Pottermack argued, and he reviewed the circumstances without the slightest twinge of remorse. Repugnant as the deed had been to him, and horrible as it had been in the doing – for he was by temperament a humane and kindly man – he had no sense of guilt. He had merely the feeling that he had been forced to do something extremely unpleasant.

When, however, he came to review the new circumstances, he was conscious of a vague uneasiness. Considered in advance, the making away with Lewson had been a dreadful necessity, accepted for the sake of the peace and security that it would purchase. But had that security been attained? The blackmailer, indeed, had gone forever with his threats and his exactions. But that thing in the well – It was actually possible that Lewson dead might prove more formidable even than Lewson living. It was true that everything seemed to be quite safe and secret. He, Pottermack, had taken every possible precaution. But supposing that he had forgotten something, that he had overlooked some small but vital detail. It was quite conceivable. The thing had frequently happened. The annals of crime, and especially of murder, were full of fatal oversights.

So Mr. Pottermack cogitated as, having picked up the apron, he made his way to the workshop, where he set to work at once on the tasks that remained to be done. First he dealt with the shoes. As it would have been difficult and was quite unnecessary to remove the gutta-percha soles, he simply shaved off the heels, heated the surface and then stuck on the original soles of balata.

Next he broke up the plaster moulds and casts into small fragments, which he carried out in the bucket and shot down the well. Those, he reflected with a sense of relief as he replaced the hurdle, were the last visible traces of the tragedy, but even as he turned away from the well, he saw that they were not. For, glancing at the summer-house, he observed the decanter, the siphon, and the tumbler still on the table. Of course, to no eye but his was there anything suspicious or unusual in their presence there. But the sight of them affected him disagreeably. Not only were they a vivid and unpleasant reminder of events which he wished to forget. They revived the doubts that had tended to fade away under the exhilarating influence of work. For here was something that he had overlooked. A thing of no importance, indeed, but still a detail that he had forgotten. Trivial as the oversight was, he felt his confidence in his foresight shaken.

He walked to the summer-house and, setting down the bucket outside, entered and proceeded to clear away these traces. Opening the cupboard, he caught up the siphon and the decanter and stepped behind the table to put them on the shelves. As he did so, he felt something soft under his foot, and when he had closed the cupboard door he looked down to see what it was. And then his heart seemed to stand still. For the thing under his foot was a coat – and it was not his coat.

There is a very curious phenomenon which we may describe as deferred visual sensation. We see something which is plainly before our eyes, but yet, owing to mental preoccupation, we are unaware of it. The image is duly registered on the retina, the retina passes on its record to the brain, but there the impression remains latent until some association brings it to the surface of consciousness.

Now, this was what had happened to Pottermack. In the moment in which his glance fell on the coat there started up before him the vision of a bulky figure flourishing its fists and staggering backwards towards the well – the figure of a man in shirt-sleeves. In spite of the darkness, he had seen that figure quite distinctly, he even recalled that the shirt-sleeves were of a dark grey. But so intense had been his preoccupation with the dreadful business of the moment that the detail, physically seen, had passed into his memory without conscious recognition.

He was literally appalled. Here, already, was a second oversight, and this time it was one of vital importance. Had any one who knew Lewson been present when the coat was discovered, recognition would have been almost certain, for the material was of a strikingly conspicuous and distinctive pattern. Then the murder would have been out, and all his ingenious precautions against discovery would have risen up to testify to his guilt.

All his confidence, all of the sense of security that he had felt on his return home on the previous night, had evaporated in an instant. Two obvious things he had forgotten, and one of them might have been fatal. Indeed, there were three, for he had been within an ace of overlooking those incriminating footprints that might have led the searchers to his very gate. Was it possible that there was yet some other important fact that he had failed to take into account? He realized that it was very possible indeed, that it might easily be that he should add yet another instance to the abundant records of murderers who, covering up their tracks with elaborate ingenuity, have yet left damning evidence plain for any investigator to see.

He picked up the coat, and, rolling it up loosely, considered what he should do with it. His first impulse was to drop it in the well. But he rejected the idea for several reasons. It would certainly float, and might possibly be seen by the mason when the sun-dial was fixed, especially if he should throw a light down. And then, if the well should, after all, be searched, the presence of a separate coat would be against the suggestion of accident. And it would be quite easy to burn it in the rubbish destructor. Moreover, in rolling the coat he had become aware of a bulky object in one of the pockets which recalled certain statements that Lewson had made. In the end, he tucked the coat under his arm and, catching up the bucket, took his way back to the workshop.

It was significant of Pottermack's state of mind that as soon as he was inside he locked the door, notwithstanding that he was alone in the walled garden and that both the gates were securely fastened. Moreover, before he began his inspection he unlocked a large drawer and left it open with the key in the lock, ready to thrust the coat out of sight in a moment. Then he unrolled the coat on the bench, and, putting his hand into the inside breast pocket, drew out a leather wallet. It bulged with papers of various kinds, mostly bills and letters, but to these Pottermack gave no attention. The one item in the contents that interested him was a compact bundle of banknotes. There were twenty of them, all five-pound notes, as he ascertained by going through the bundle, a hundred pounds in all – the exact sum that had been demanded of him. In fact, these notes were understudies of his expected contribution. They had been "borrowed" by Lewson out of the current cash to meet some sudden call, and his, Pottermack's, notes were to have been either paid in place of them or to have enabled Lewson to make good his loan in the morning.

It seemed a queer proceeding, and to Mr. Pottermack it was not very intelligible. But the motive was no concern of his, what was his concern was the train of consequences that would be set going. The obvious fact was that the little branch bank of which Lewson had had sole charge was now minus a hundred pounds in five-pound notes. That fact must inevitably come to light within a day or two, most probably this very day. Then the hue-and-cry would be out for the missing manager.

Well, that was all to the good. There would certainly be a hot search for Lewson. But the searchers would not be seeking the body of a murdered man. They would be on the look-out for an exceedingly live gentleman with a bundle of stolen notes in his pocket. As he considered the almost inevitable course of events, Pottermack's spirits rose appreciably. The borrowing of those notes had been most fortunate for him, for it turned what would have been an unaccountable disappearance into a perfectly accountable flight. It seemed an incredibly stupid proceeding, for if Pottermack had paid up, the borrowing would have been unnecessary, if he had not paid up, the "loan" could not have been made good. However, stupid or not, it had been done, and in the doing it Lewson had, for the first and last time, rendered his victim a real service.

When he had inspected the notes, Pottermack replaced them in the wallet, returned the latter to the pocket whence it had come, rolled up the coat and bestowed it in the drawer, which he closed and locked. The consumption of it in the rubbish destructor could be postponed for a time, and perhaps it might not come to that at all. For the finding of the notes had, to a great extent, restored Pottermack's confidence, and already there had appeared in his mind the germ of an idea – vague and formless at present – that the notes, and perhaps even the coat, might yet have further useful offices to perform.

As he had now completed his tasks and cleared away – as he hoped – the last traces of the previous night's doings, he thought it time that he should show himself to Mrs. Gadby in his normal, everyday aspect. Accordingly he took the rucksack, a setting-board, and a few other necessary appliances and made his way to the house, where he established himself in the dining-room at a table by the window and occupied the time in setting the moths which he had captured on the previous night. They were but a poor collection, with an unconscionable proportion of duplicates, but Pottermack pinned them all out impartially – even the damaged ones – on the setting-board. It was their number, not their quality, that would produce the necessary moral effect on Mrs. Gadby when she came in to lay the table for his mid-day dinner. So he worked away placidly with an outward air of complete absorption in his task, but all the while there kept recurring in his mind, like some infernal refrain, the disturbing question: Was there even now something that he had forgotten – something that his eye had missed but that other eyes might detect?

In the afternoon he strolled round to Mr. Gallett's yard to see if all was going well in regard to the preparations for setting up the sun-dial. He was anxious that there should be no delay, for though the presence of the dial would afford him no added security, he had an unreasonable feeling that the fixing of it would close the horrible incident. And he did very much want that sinister black hole hidden from sight for ever. Great therefore, was his relief when he discovered Mr. Gallett and two of his men in the very act of loading a low cart with what was obviously the material for the job.

The jovial mason greeted him with a smile and a nod. "All ready, you see, Mr. Pottermack," said he, indicating the dial-pillar, now swathed in a canvas wrapping, and slapping one of the stone slabs that stood on edge by its side. "Could almost have done it to-day, but it's getting a bit late and we've got one or two other jobs to finish up here. But we'll have him round by nine o'clock to-morrow morning, if that will do."

It would do admirably, Mr. Pottermack assured him, adding, "You will have to bring it in at the side gate. Do you know whereabouts that is?"

"I can't say as I do exactly," replied Gallett. "But I'll bring him to the front gate and then you can show me where he is to go."

To this Pottermack agreed, and they then strolled together to the gate, where Mr. Gallett halted, and, having looked up and down the street with a precautionary air, said in what he meant to be a low tone, "Rummy report going round the town. Have you heard anything of it?"

"No," replied Pottermack, all agog in a moment.

"What is it?"

"Why, they say that the manager of Perkins's Bank has hopped it. That's what they say, and I fancy there must be something in it, because I went there this morning to pay in a cheque and I found the place closed. Give me a rare turn, because I've got an account there. So I rang the bell and the caretaker he come and tells me that Mr. Lewson wasn't able to attend to-day but that there would be some one there later to carry on till he came back. And so there was, for I went round a couple of hours later and found the place open and business going on as usual. There was a youngish fellow at the counter, but there was an elderly gent – rather a foxy-looking customer – who seemed to be smelling round, taking down the books and looking into the drawers and cupboards. Looks a bit queer, don't you think?"

"It really does," Pottermack admitted. "The fact of the bank not being open at the usual time suggests that Mr. Lewisham – "

"Lewson is his name," Mr. Gallett corrected.

"Mr. Lewson. It suggests that he had absented himself without giving notice, which is really rather a remarkable thing for a manager to do."

"It is," said Gallett, "particularly as he lived on the premises."

"Did he, indeed?" exclaimed Pottermack. "That makes it still more remarkable. Quite mysterious, in fact."

"Very mysterious," said Gallett. "Looks as if he had mizzled, and if he has, why, he probably didn't go away with his pockets empty."

Pottermack shook his head gravely. "Still," he urged, "it is early to raise suspicions. He may possibly have been detained somewhere. He was at the bank yesterday?"

"Oh, yes, and seen in the town yesterday evening. Old Keeling, the postman, saw him about half-past-seven and wished him good-night. Says he saw him turn into the footpath that leads through Potter's Wood."

"Ha," said Pottermack. "Well, he may have lost his way in the wood, or been taken ill. Who knows? It is best not to jump at conclusions too hastily."

With this and a friendly nod he turned out of the yard and took his way homeward, cogitating profoundly. Events were moving even more quickly than he had anticipated, but they were moving in the right direction. Nevertheless, he recognized with something like a shudder how near he had been to disaster. But for the chance moonbeam that had lighted up the footprints in his garden, he would have overlooked those other tell-tale tracks outside. And again he asked himself uneasily if there could be something else that he had overlooked. He was tempted to take a walk into the country in the direction of the wood to see if there were yet any signs of a search, for, by Gallett's report, it appeared that the direction in which Lewson had gone, and even his route, was already known. But prudence bade him keep aloof and show no more than a stranger's interest in the affair. Accordingly he went straight home and, since in his restless state he could not settle down to read, he betook himself to his workshop and spent the rest of the day in sharpening chisels and plane-irons and doing other useful, time-consuming jobs.

True to his word, Mr. Gallett appeared on the following morning almost on the stroke of nine. Pottermack himself opened the door to him and at once conducted him through the house out into the orchard and thence to the walled garden. It was not without a certain vague apprehensiveness that he unlocked the gate and admitted his visitor, for since that fatal night no eye but his had looked on that enclosure. It is true that on this very morning he had made a careful tour of inspection and had satisfied himself that nothing was visible that all the world might not see. Nevertheless, he was conscious of a distinct sense of discomfort as he let the mason in, and still more when he led him to the well.

"So this is where you wants him planted?" said Mr. Gallett, stepping up to the brink of the well and looking down it reflectively. "It do seem a pity for to bung up a good well. And you say there's a tidy depth of water in him."

"Yes," said Pottermack, "a fair depth. But it's a long way down to it."

"So 'tis, seemingly," Gallett agreed. "The bucket would take a bit of histing up". As he spoke, he felt in his pocket and drew out a folded newspaper, and from another pocket he produced a box of matches. In leisurely fashion he tore off a sheet of the paper, struck a match, and, lighting a corner of the paper, let it fall, craning over to watch its descent. Pottermack also craned over, with his heart in his mouth, staring breathlessly at the flaming mass as it sank slowly, lighting up the slimy walls of the well, growing smaller and fainter as it descended, while a smaller, fainter spark rose from the depths to meet it. At length they met and were in an instant extinguished, and Pottermack breathed again. What a mercy he had not thrown the coat down!

"We'll have to bank up the earth a bit," said Mr. Gallett, "for the slabs to bed on. Don't want 'em to rest on the brickwork of the well or they may settle out of the level after a time. And if you've got a spade handy, we may as well do it now, 'cause we can't get to the side gate for a few minutes. There's a gent out there a-takin' photographs of the ground."

"Of the ground!" gasped Pottermack.

"Ay. The path, you know. Seems as there's some footmarks there – pretty plain ones they looked to me without a-photographin' of em. Well, it's them footmarks as he's a-takin'."

"But what for?" demanded Pottermack.

"Ah," said Mr. Gallett. "There you are. I don't know, but I've got my ideas. I see the police inspector a-watchin' of him – all on the broad grin he was too – and I suspect it's got something to do with that bank manager that I was tellin' you about."

"Ah, Mr. Lewis?"

"Lewson is his name. There's no news of him and he was seen coming this way on Wednesday night. Why, he must have passed this very gate."

"Dear me!" exclaimed Pottermack. "And as to his reasons for going away so suddenly. Is anything – er – ?"

"Well, no," replied Gallett. "Nothing is known for certain. Of course, the bank people don't let on. But there's some talk in the town about some cash that is missing. May be all bunkum, though it's what you'd expect. Now, about that spade. Shall I call in my men or can we do it ourselves?"

Pottermack decided that they could do it themselves, and, having produced a couple of spades, he fell to work under Gallett's direction, raising a low platform for the stone slabs to rest on. A few minutes' work saw it finished to the mason's satisfaction, and all was now ready for the fixing of the dial.

"I wonder if that photographer chap has finished," said Mr. Gallett. "Shall we go and have a look?"

This was what Pottermack had been bursting to do, though he had heroically suppressed his curiosity, and even now he strolled indifferently to the gate and held it open for the mason to go out first.

"There he is," said Gallett, "and blow me if he isn't a-takin' of 'em all the way along. What can he be doing that for? The cove had only got two feet."

Mr. Pottermack looked out and was no less surprised than the worthy mason. But he did not share the latter's purely impersonal interest. On the contrary, what he saw occasioned certain uncomfortable stirrings in the depths of his consciousness. Some little distance up the path a spectacled youth of sage and sober aspect had set up a tripod to which a rather large camera of the box type was attached by a goose-neck bracket. The lens was directed towards the ground, and when the young man had made his exposure by means of a wire release, he opened a portfolio and made a mark or entry of some kind on what looked like a folded map. Then he turned a key on the camera, and, lifting it with its tripod, walked away briskly for some twenty or thirty yards, when he halted, fixed the tripod and repeated the operation. It really was a most astonishing performance.

"Well," said Mr. Gallett, "he's finished here, at any rate, so we can get on with our business now. I'll just run round and fetch the cart along."

He sauntered away towards the road, and Pottermack, left alone, resumed his observation of the photographer. The proceedings of that mysterious individual puzzled him not a little. Apparently he was taking a sample footprint about every twenty yards, no doubt selecting specially distinct impressions. But to what purpose? One or two photographs would have been understandable as permanent records of marks that a heavy shower might wash away and that would, in any case, soon disappear. But a series, running to a hundred or more, could have no ordinary utility. And, yet it was not possible that that solemn young man could be taking all this trouble without some definite object. Now, what could that object be?

Pottermack was profoundly puzzled. Moreover, he was more than a little disturbed. Hitherto his chief anxiety had been lest the footprints should never be observed. Then he would have had all his trouble for nothing, and those invaluable tracks, leading suspicion far away from his own neighbourhood to an unascertainable destination, would have been lost. Well, there was no fear of that now. The footprints had not only been observed and identified, they were going to be submitted to minute scrutiny. He had not bargained for that. He had laid down his tracks expecting them to be scanned by the police or the members of a search party, to whom they would have been perfectly convincing. But how would they look in a photograph? Pottermack knew that photographs have an uncanny way of bringing out features that are invisible to the eye. Now could there be any such features in those counterfeit footprints? He could not imagine any. But then why was this young man taking all those photographs? With his secret knowledge of the real facts, Pottermack could not shake off an unreasoning fear that his ruse had been already discovered, or at least suspected.

His cogitations were interrupted by the arrival of the cart, which was halted and backed up against his gateway. Then there came the laying down of planks to enable the larger slab to be trundled on rollers to the edge of the platform. Pottermack stood by, anxious and restless, inwardly anathematizing the conscientious mason as he tried the surface of the platform again and again with his level. At last he was satisfied. Then the big base slab was brought on edge to the platform, adjusted with minute care and finally let down slowly into its place, and as it dropped the last inch with a gentle thud, Pottermack drew a deep breath and felt as if a weight, greater far than that of the slab, had been lifted from his heart.

In the remaining operations he had to feign an interest that he ought to have felt but did not. For him, the big base slab was what mattered. It shut that dreadful, yawning, black hole from his sight, as he hoped, for ever. The rest was mere accessory detail. But, as it would not do for him to let this appear, he assumed an earnest and critical attitude, particularly when it came to the setting up of the pillar on the centre of the upper slab.

"Now then," said Mr. Gallett as he spread out a thin bed of mortar on the marked centre, "how will you have him? Will you have the plinth parallel to the base or diagonal?"

"Oh, parallel, I think," replied Pottermack, "and I should like to have the word '*spes*' on the eastern side, which will bring the word '*pax*' to the western."

Mr. Gallett looked slightly dubious. "If you was thinking of setting him to the right time," said he, "you won't do it that way. You'll have to unscrew the dial-plate from the lead bed and have him fixed correct to time. But never mind about him now. We're a-dealing with the stone pillar."

"Yes," said Pottermack, "but I was considering the inscription. That is the way in which it was meant to be placed, I think", and here he explained the significance of the motto.

"There now," said Mr. Gallett, "see what it is to be a scholar. And you're quite right too, sir – you can see by the way the lichen grew on it that this here '*sole orto*' was the north side. So we'll put him round to the north again, and then I expect the dial will be about right, if you aren't partickler to a quarter-of-an-hour or so."

Accordingly the pillar was set up in its place and centred with elaborate care. Then, when the level of the slabs had been tested and a few slight adjustments made, the pillar was tried on all sides with the plumb-line and corrected to a hair's breadth.

"There you are, Mr. Pottermack," said Mr. Gallett, as he put the last touch to the mortar joint and stepped back to view the general effect of his work. "See that he isn't disturbed until the mortar has had time to set and he won't want touching again for a century or two. And an uncommon nice finish he'll give to the garden when you get a bit of smooth turf round him and a few flowers."

"Yes," said Pottermack, "you've made an extremely neat job of it, Mr. Gallett, and I'm very much obliged to you. When I get the turf laid and the flower borders set out, you must drop in and have a look at it."

The gratified mason, having suitably acknowledged these commendations of his work, gathered up his tools and appliances and departed with his myrmidons. Pottermack followed them out into the lane and watched the cart as it retired, obliterating the footprints which had given him so much occupation. When it had gone, he strolled up the path in the direction in which the photographer had gone, unconsciously keeping to the edge and noting with a sort of odd self-complacency the striking distinctness of the impressions of his gutta-percha soles. The mysterious operator was now out of sight, but he, too, had left his traces on the path, and these Pottermack studied with mingled curiosity and uneasiness. It was easy to see, by the marks of the tripod, which footprints had been photographed, and it was evident that care had been taken to select the sharpest and most perfect impressions. Pottermack had noticed, when he first looked out of the gate with Mr. Gallett, that the tripod had been set up exactly opposite the gateway and that the three marks surrounded the particularly fine impression that he had made when he stepped out sideways on to the smooth-swept path.

On these facts he reflected as he sauntered back to the gate, and entering, closed it behind him. What could be that photographer's object in his laborious proceeding? Who could it be that had set him to work? And what was it possible for a photograph to show that the eye might fail to see? These were the questions that he turned over uncomfortably in his mind and to which he could find no answer. Then his glance fell on the dial, resting immovable on its massive base, covering up the only visible reminder of the past, standing there to guard for ever his secret from the eyes of man. And at the sight of it he was comforted. With an effort he shook off his apprehensions and summoned his courage afresh. After all, what was there to fear? What could these photographs show that was not plainly visible? Nothing. There was nothing to show. The footprints were, it is true, counterfeits in a sense. But they were not imitations in the sense that a forged writing is an imitation. They were mechanical reproductions, necessarily true in every particular. In fact, they were actually Lewson's own footprints, though it happened that other feet than his were in the shoes. No. Nothing could be discovered for the simple reason that there was nothing to discover.

So Mr. Pottermack, with restored tranquillity and confidence, betook himself to the summer-house, and sitting down, looked out upon the garden and let his thoughts dwell upon what it should be when the little island of stone should be girt by a plot of emerald turf. As he sat, two sides of the sun-dial were visible to him, and on them he read the words "*decedente pax*". He repeated them to himself, drawing from them a new confidence and encouragement. Why should it not be so? The storms that had scattered the hopes of his youth had surely blown themselves out. His evil genius, who had first betrayed him and then threatened to destroy utterly his hardly earned prosperity and security, who had cast him into the depths and had fastened upon him when he struggled to the surface, the evil genius, the active cause of all his misfortunes, was gone forever and would certainly trouble him no more.

Then why should the autumn of his life not be an Indian summer of peace and tranquil happiness? Why not?

Chapter V
Dr. Thorndyke
Listens To a Strange Story

"And that," said Mr. Stalker, picking up a well-worn attaché case and opening it on his knees, "finishes our little business and relieves you of my society."

"Say 'deprives'." Thorndyke corrected. "That is, if you must really go."

"That is very delicate of you, Doctor," Stalker replied as he stuffed a bundle of documents into the attaché case, "and, by the way, it isn't quite the finish. There is another small matter which I had nearly forgotten, something that my nephew, Harold, asked me to hand to you. You have heard me speak of Harold – my sister's boy?"

"The inventive genius? Yes, I remember your telling me about him."

"Well, he asked me to pass this on to you – thought it might interest you."

He took from his case a flat disc which looked like a closely rolled coil of paper tape, secured with a rubber band, and passed it to Thorndyke, who took it, and, unrolling a few inches, glanced at it with a slightly puzzled smile.

"What is it?" he asked.

"I had better explain," replied Stalker. "You see, Harold has invented a recording camera which will take small photographs in a series and mark each one with its serial number, so that there can be no mistake about the sequence. It is a box camera and it takes quite a big roll of kinematograph film with a capacity of something like five-hundred exposures. And the mechanism not only marks each negative with its number but also shows the number which is being exposed on a little dial on the outside of the camera. Quite a useful instrument, I should think, for certain purposes, though I can't, at the moment, think of a case to which it would be applicable."

"I can imagine certain cases, however," said Thorndyke, "in which it would be quite valuable. But with regard to these particular photographs?"

"They are, as you see, a series of footprints – the footprints of a man who absconded from a country bank and has not been seen since."

"But why did Harold take so many? There must be about a couple-of-hundred on this strip."

Stalker chuckled. "I don't think," said he, "that we need go far for the reason. Harold had got a camera that would take a numbered series and he had never had a chance to try it. Now here was an undoubted series of footprints on a footpath and they were those of an absconding man. It was a chance to show what the camera would do, and he took it. He professes to believe that these photographs might furnish an important clue to an investigator like yourself. But, of course, that is all nonsense. He just wanted to try his new camera. Still, he did the job quite thoroughly. He took a twenty-five inch ordnance map with him and marked each exposure on it, showing the exact position of that particular footprint. He made an exposure about every twenty yards. You will see, if you look at the map. I have the three sheets here. He told me to give them to you with the photographs, so that you could examine them together if you wanted to – which I imagine you won't. Of course, the information they give is quite valueless. One or two photographs would have shown all that there was to show."

"I wouldn't say that," Thorndyke dissented. "The application of the method to the present case is, I must admit, not at all evident. One or two photographs would have been enough for simple identification. But I can imagine a case in which it might be of the highest importance to be able to prove that a man did actually follow a particular route, especially if a time factor were also available."

"Which it is, approximately, in the present instance. But it was already known that the man went that way at that time, so all this elaborate detail is merely flogging a dead horse. The problem is not which way did he go, but where is he now? Not that we care a great deal. He only took a hundred pounds with him – so far as we know at present – so the Bank is not particularly interested in him. Nor am I, officially, though I must confess to some curiosity about him. There are some rather odd features in the case. I am quite sorry that we can't afford to call you in to investigate them."

"I expect you are more competent than I am," said Thorndyke. "Banking affairs are rather out of my province."

"It isn't the banking aspect that I am thinking of," replied Stalker. "Our own accountants can deal with that. But there are some other queer features, and about one of them I am a little uncomfortable. It seems to suggest a miscarriage of justice in another case. But I mustn't take up your time with irrelevant gossip."

"But indeed you must," Thorndyke rejoined. "If you have got a queer case, I want to hear it. Remember, I live by queer cases."

499

"It is rather a long story," objected Stalker, evidently bursting to tell it nevertheless.

"So much the better," said Thorndyke. "We will have a bottle of wine and make an entertainment of it."

He retired from the room and presently reappeared with a bottle of Chambertin and a couple of glasses and having, filled the latter, he provided himself with a writing-pad, resumed his armchair, and disposed himself to listen at his ease.

"I had better begin," said Stalker, "with an account of this present affair. The man who has absconded is a certain James Lewson, who was the manager of a little branch of Perkins's Bank down at Borley. He ran it by himself, living on the premises and being looked after by the caretaker's wife. It is quite a small affair – just a nucleus with an eye for the future, for Meux's do most of the business at Borley, such as it is – and easily run by one man, and everything has gone on quite smoothly there until last Wednesday week. On that day Lewson went out at about a quarter-past-seven in the evening. The caretaker saw him go out at the back gate and thought that he looked as if he had been drinking, and on that account he sat up until past twelve o'clock to see him in safely. But he never came home, and as he had not returned by the morning, the caretaker telegraphed up to headquarters.

"Now I happened to be there when the telegram arrived – for I am still on the board of directors and do a bit of work there – and I suggested that old Jewsbury should go down to see what had been happening and take a young man with him to do the routine work while he was going through the books. And as Harold was the only one that could be spared, he was told off for the job. Of course, he fell in with it joyfully, for he thought he saw a possible chance of giving his camera a trial. Accordingly, down he went, with the camera in his trunk, all agog to find a series of some kind that wanted photographing. As soon as they arrived, Jewsbury saw at a glance that some of the cash was missing – a hundred pounds in five-pound Bank of England notes."

"And the keys?" asked Thorndyke.

"The safe key was missing too. But that had been anticipated, so Jewsbury had been provided with a master-key. The other keys were in the safe.

"Well, as soon as the robbery was discovered, Jewsbury had a talk with the caretaker and the police inspector, who had called to see him. From the caretaker, a steady old retired police sergeant, Jewsbury gathered that Lewson had been going to the bad for some time, taking a good deal more whisky than was good for him. But we needn't go into that. The police inspector reported that Lewson had been seen at about seven-thirty – that is, within a quarter-of-an-hour of his leaving the bank – turning into a footpath that leads out into the country and eventually to the main London road. The inspector had examined the path and found on it a track of very distinct and characteristic footprints, which he was able to identify as Lewson's, not only by the description given by the caretaker, who usually cleaned Lewson's shoes, but by one or two fairly clear footprints in the garden near the back gate, by which Lewson went out. Thereupon, he returned to the footpath and followed the tracks out into the country, through a wood and across a heath until he came to a place where Lewson had left the path and gone off through the heather, and there, of course all traces of him were lost. The inspector went on and searched a by-road and went on to the London road, but not a single trace of him could he discover. At that point where he stepped off the footpath into the heather, James Lewson vanished into thin air."

"Where is the railway station?" Thorndyke asked.

"In the town. There is a little branch station by the London road, but it is certain that Lewson did not go there, for there were no passengers at all on that evening. He must have gone off along the road on foot.

"Now, as soon as Harold heard of those footprints, he decided that his chance had come. The footprints would soon be trodden out or washed away by rain, and they ought to be recorded permanently. That was his view."

"And a perfectly sound one, too," remarked Thorndyke.

"Quite. But there was no need for a couple of hundred repetitions."

"Apparently not," Thorndyke agreed, "though it is impossible to be certain even of that. At any rate, a superabundance of evidence is a good deal better than a deficiency."

"Well, that is what Harold thought, or pretended to think, and in effect, he nipped off to the Post Office and got the large-scale ordnance maps that contained his field of operations. Then, on the following morning, he set to work, leaving Jewsbury to carry on. He began by photographing a pair of the footprints in the garden – they are numbers 1 and 2 – and marking them on the map. Then he went off to the footpath and took a photograph about every twenty yards, selecting the most distinct footprints and writing down the number of the exposure on the map at the exact spot on which it was made. And so he followed the track into the country, through the wood, across the heath to what we may call the vanishing point. Number 197 is the last footprint that Lewson made before he turned off into the heather.

"So much for Harold and his doings. Now we come to the queer features of the case, and the first of them is the amount taken. A hundred pounds! Can you imagine a sane man, with a salary of six-hundred a year, absconding with such a sum? The equivalent of two months' salary. The thing seems incredible. And why a hundred pounds only? Why didn't he take, at least, the whole of the available cash? It is incomprehensible. And in a few days his monthly salary would have been due. Why didn't he wait to collect that?

"But there is a partial explanation. Only the explanation is more incomprehensible than what it explains. By the evening post on the day on which Jewsbury arrived a letter was delivered, addressed to Lewson and, under the circumstances, Jewsbury felt justified in opening it. Its contents were to this effect:

Dear Lewson,

I expected you to come round last night, as you promised, to settle up. As you didn't come and have not written, I think it necessary to tell you plainly that this can't be allowed to go on. If the amount (£97 13s 4d.) is not paid within the next forty-eight hours, I shall have to take measures that will be unpleasant to both of us.

Yours faithfully,

Lewis Bateman

"Now this letter seemed to explain the small amount taken. It suggested that Lewson was being pressed for payment and that, as he had not got the wherewith to pay, he had taken the amount out of the cash, trusting to be able to replace it before the periodical audit. But if so, why had he not paid Bateman? And why had he absconded? The letter only deepens the mystery."

"Is it an ascertained fact that he had not the wherewithal to pay?"

"I think I may say that it is. His own current account at the bank showed a balance of about thirty shillings and he had no deposit account. Looking over his account, Jewsbury noticed that he seemed to spend the whole of his income and was often overdrawn at the end of the month.

"But this letter brought into view another queer feature of the case. On enquiring of the police inspector, Jewsbury found that the man, Bateman, is a member of a firm of outside brokers who have offices in Moorgate Street. Bateman lives at Borley, and he and Lewson seemed to have been on more-or-less friendly terms. Accordingly, Jewsbury and the inspector called on him and, under some pressure, he disclosed the nature of Lewson's dealing with his firm. It appeared that Lewson was a regular 'operator', and that he was singularly unfortunate in his speculations and that he had a fatal habit of carrying over when he ought to have cut his loss and got out. As a result, he dropped quite large sums of money from time to time, and had lost heavily during the last few months. On the transactions of the last twelve months, Bateman reckoned – he hadn't his books with him, of course, at Borley – that Lewson had dropped over six-hundred pounds, and in addition, he happened to know that Lewson had been plunging and losing on the turf.

"Now, where did Lewson get all this money? His account shows no income beyond his salary, and the debit side shows only his ordinary domestic expenditure. There are a good many cash drafts, some of which may have represented betting losses, but they couldn't represent the big sums that he lost through the bucket shop."

"He didn't pay the brokers by cheque, then?"

"No. Always in notes – five-pound notes – not that there is anything abnormal in that. As a bank manager, he would naturally wish to keep these transactions secret. It is the amount that creates the mystery. He spent the whole of his income in a normal though extravagant fashion, and he dropped over six-hundred pounds in addition. Now, where did he get that six-hundred pounds?"

"Is it certain that he had no outside source of income?" Thorndyke asked.

"Obviously he had. But since there is no sign of it on the credit side of his account, he must have received it in cash, which is a mighty queer circumstance when you consider the amount. Jewsbury is convinced that he must have been carrying on some kind of embezzlement, and I don't see what other explanation there can be. But if so, it has been done with extraordinary skill. Jewsbury has been through the books with the utmost rigour and with this suspicion in his mind, but he can't discover the slightest trace of any falsification. And mind you, Jewsbury is a first-class accountant and as sharp as a needle. So that is how the matter stands, and I must confess that I can make nothing of it."

Mr. Stalker paused, and, with a profoundly reflective air, took a sip from his glass, which Thorndyke had just refilled. The latter waited for some time with an expectant eye upon his guest and at length remarked, "You were saying something about a miscarriage of justice."

"So I was," said Stalker. "But that is another story – unless it is a part of this story, which I begin to be afraid it is. However, you shall judge. I should like to hear what you think. It carries us back some fifteen years, that was before I took up the Griffin Company, and I was then assistant manager of Perkins', at the Cornhill office. About that time it was discovered that quite a long series of forgeries had been

503

committed. They were very skilfully done and very cleverly managed, evidently by somebody who knew what customers' accounts it would be safe to operate on. It was found that a number of forged bearer cheques had been presented and paid over the counter, and it was further found that nearly all of them had been presented and paid at the counter of one man, a young fellow named Jeffrey Brandon. As soon as the discovery was made it was decided – seeing that the forger was almost certainly an employee of the bank – to muster the staff and invite them all to turn out their pockets. And this was done on the following morning. When they had all arrived, and before the bank opened, they were mustered in the hall and the position of affairs explained to them, whereupon all of them, without being invited, expressed the wish to be searched. Accordingly, a detective officer who was in attendance searched each of them in turn, without any result. Then the detective suggested that the office coats, which most of them used and which were hanging in the lobby, should be fetched by the detective and the porter and searched in the presence of their owners. This also was done. Each man identified his own coat, and the detective searched it in his presence. All went well until we came to nearly the last coat – that belonging to Jeffrey Brandon and identified by him as his. When the detective put his hand into the inside breast pocket, he found in it a letter-case, and on opening this and turning out its contents, he discovered in an inner compartment three bearer cheques. They were payable to three different – presumably fictitious – persons and were endorsed in the names of the payees in three apparently different handwritings.

"On the production of those cheques, Brandon showed the utmost astonishment. He admitted that the letter-case was his, but denied any knowledge of the cheques, declaring that they must have been put into the case by someone else – presumably the forger – while the coat was hanging in the lobby. Of course, this could not be accepted. No one but the senior staff knew even of the discovery of the forgery – at least, that was our belief at the time. And the search had been sprung on the staff without a moment's warning. Furthermore, there was the fact that nearly all the forged cheques had been paid at Brandon's counter. What followed was inevitable. Brandon was kept under observation at the bank until the ostensible drawers of the cheques had been communicated with by telegram or telephone, and when they had all denied having drawn any such cheques, he was arrested and charged before a magistrate. Of course, he was committed for trial, and when he was put in the dock at the Old Bailey, the only defence he had to offer was a complete denial of any knowledge of the cheques and a repetition of his statement that they must have been put into his pocket by some other person for the purpose of incriminating him. It was not a very convincing defence, and it is not surprising that the jury would not accept it."

"And yet," Thorndyke remarked, "it was the only defence that was possible if he was innocent. And there was nothing inherently improbable in it."

"No. That was what I felt, and when he was found guilty and sentenced to five years' penal servitude, I was decidedly unhappy about the affair. For Brandon was a nice, bright, prepossessing youngster, and there was nothing whatever against him but this charge. And, later, I was made still more uncomfortable when I had reason to believe that the discovery of the forgeries had in some way become known, on the day before the search, to some members of the junior staff. So that what Brandon had said might easily have been true.

"However, that is the old story. And now as to its connection with the present one. Brandon had one specially intimate friend at the bank, and that friend's name was James Lewson. Now, we have never had anything against Lewson in all these years, or he would never have been a branch manager. But, from what we know of him now, he is, at least, an unscrupulous rascal and, if Jewsbury is right, he is an embezzler and a thief. I can't rid myself of a horrible suspicion that James Lewson put those forged cheques into Brandon's pocket."

"If he did," said Thorndyke, "hanging would be a great deal too good for him."

"I quite agree with you," Stalker declared emphatically. "It would have been a dastardly crime. But I can't help suspecting him very gravely. I recall the look of absolute amazement on poor Brandon's face when those cheques were produced. It impressed me deeply at the time, but the recollection of it impresses me still more now. If Brandon was innocent, it was a truly shocking affair. It won't bear thinking of."

"No," Thorndyke agreed. "There is no tragedy more dreadful than the conviction of an innocent man. By the way, do you know what became of Brandon?"

"Indeed I do," replied Stalker. "The poor fellow is beyond the reach of any possible reparation, even if his innocence could be proved. He died in an attempt to escape from prison. I remember the circumstances only too clearly. Soon after his conviction he was sent to the convict prison at Colport. There, while he was working outside with a gang, he slipped past the civil guard and made off along the sea wall. He got quite a good start while they were searching for him in the wrong direction, but at last they picked up his tracks and set off in pursuit. And presently, on the seaward face of the wall, they found his clothes and the marks of his feet where he had walked out across the mud to the sea. They assumed that he had swum out to some passing vessel, and that is probably what he tried to do. But no tidings of him could be obtained from any of the anchored vessels or those that had passed up or down. Then, about six weeks later, the mystery was solved, for his body was found on the mud in a creek some miles farther down."

"About six weeks later," Thorndyke repeated. "What time of year was it?"

"He was found about the middle of August. Yes, I know what you are thinking. But, really, the question of identity hardly arose, although, no doubt, the corpse was examined as far as was possible. Still, the obvious facts were enough. A naked man was missing and the body of a nude man was found just where it was expected to wash ashore. I think we may take it that the body was Brandon's body. I only wish I could think otherwise."

"Yes," said Thorndyke. "It is a melancholy end to what sounds like a very tragic story. But I am afraid you are right. The body was almost certainly his."

"I think so," agreed Stalker. "And now, I hope I haven't taken up your time for nothing. You will admit that this Lewson case has some rather queer features."

"It certainly has," said Thorndyke. "It is most anomalous and puzzling from beginning to end."

"I suppose," said Stalker, "it would be hardly fair to ask for a few comments?"

"Why not?" demanded Thorndyke. "This is an entertainment, not a professional conference. If you want my views on the case, you are welcome to them, and I may say, in the first place, that I do not find myself quite in agreement with Jewsbury in regard to the embezzlement – of which, you notice, he can find no evidence. To me there is a strong suggestion of some outside source of income. We note that Lewson paid these large sums of money in cash – in five-pound notes. Now that may have been for secrecy. But where did he get all those notes? He paid no cheques into his account. He couldn't have stolen the notes from the bank's cash. There is a distinct suggestion that he received the money in the same form in which he paid it away. And his conduct on this occasion supports that view. He just baldly took a hundred pounds out of cash – in five-pound notes – to meet a sudden urgent call. One feels that he must have expected to be able to replace it almost at once. The idea that a man of his experience should have committed a simple, crude robbery like this is untenable. And then there is the amount – taken, almost certainly, for this specific purpose. The irresistible suggestion is that he merely borrowed this money in the confident expectation of obtaining the wherewith to put it back before it should be missed.

"Then there is the singular suggestion of a change of purpose. Apparently he started out to pay Bateman. Then why did he not pay him? He had the money. Instead, he suddenly turns off and walks out into the country. Why this change of plan? What had happened in the interval to cause him to change his plans in this remarkable manner? Had he discovered that he would not be able to replace the money? Even that would not explain his proceedings, for the natural thing would have been to return to the bank and put the notes back.

"Again, if he intended to abscond, why go away across the country on foot? He could easily have taken the train to town and disappeared there. But the idea of his absconding with that small amount of money is difficult to accept – and yet he undoubtedly did walk out into the country. And he has disappeared in a manner which is rather remarkable when one considers how easy a solitary pedestrian is to trace in the country. There is even something rather odd in his leaving the footpath and plunging into the heather, which must have been very inconvenient walking for a fugitive. Taking the case as a whole, I feel that I cannot accept the idea that he simply absconded with stolen money. Why he suddenly changed his plans and made off I am unable to guess, but I am certain that behind his extraordinary proceedings there is something more than meets the eye."

"That is precisely my feeling," said Stalker, "and the more so now that I have heard your summing-up of the case. I don't believe the man set out from home with the idea of absconding. I suspect that something happened after he left the house, that he got some sudden scare that sent him off into the country in that singular fashion. And now I must really take myself off. It has been a great pleasure to talk this case over with you. What about those things of Harold's? Shall I relieve you of them, now that you have seen them?"

"No," replied Thorndyke. "Leave them with me for the present. I should like to look them over before I hand them back."

"You don't imagine that Harold is right, do you? That these footprints may yield a clue to the man's disappearance?"

"No. I was not thinking of them in relation to the present case, but in regard to their general evidential bearing. As you know, I have given a great deal of attention and study to footprints. They sometimes yield a surprising amount of information, and as they can be accurately reproduced in the form of plaster casts, or even photographs, they can be produced in court and shown to the judge and the jury, who are thus able

507

to observe for themselves instead of having to rely on the mere statements of witnesses.

"But footprints, as one meets with them in practice, have this peculiarity: That, although they are made in a series, they have to be examined separately as individual things. If we try to examine them on the ground as a series, we have to walk from one to another and trust largely to memory. But in these photographs of Harold's we can take in a whole series at a glance and compare any one specimen with any other. So what I propose to do is to look over these photographs and see if, apart from the individual characters which identify a footprint, there are any periodic or recurring characters which would make it worthwhile to use a camera of this type in practice. I want to ascertain, in fact, whether a consecutive series of footprints is anything more than a number of repetitions of a given footprint."

"I see. Of course, this is not a continuous series. There are long intervals."

"Yes. That is a disadvantage. Still, it is a series of a kind."

"True. And the maps?"

"I may as well keep them too. They show the distances between the successive footprints, which may be relevant, since the intervals are not all equal."

"Very well," said Stalker, picking up his attaché case. "I admire your enthusiasm and the trouble you take, and I will tell Harold how seriously you take his productions. He will be deeply gratified."

"It was very good of him to send them, and you must thank him for me."

The two men shook hands, and when Thorndyke had escorted his guest to the landing and watched him disappear down the stairs, he returned to his chambers, closing the "oak" behind him and thereby secluding himself from the outer world.

Chapter VI
Dr. Thorndyke Becomes Inquisitive

Temperamentally, Dr. John Thorndyke presented a peculiarity which, at the first glance, seemed to involve a contradiction. He was an eminently friendly man, courteous, kindly and even genial in his intercourse with his fellow-creatures. Nor was his suave, amicable manner in any way artificial or consciously assumed. To every man his attitude of mind was instinctively friendly, and if he did not suffer fools gladly, he could, on occasion, endure them with almost inexhaustible patience.

And yet, with all his pleasant exterior and his really kindly nature, he was at heart a confirmed solitary. Of all company, his own thoughts were to him the most acceptable. After all, his case was not singular. To every intellectual man, solitude is not only a necessity, it is the condition to which his mental qualities are subject, and the man who cannot endure his own sole society has usually excellent reasons for his objection to it.

Hence, when Thorndyke closed the massive outer door and connected the bell-push with the laboratory floor above, there might have been detected in his manner a certain restfulness. He had enjoyed Stalker's visit. Particularly had he enjoyed the "queer case", which was to him what a problem is to an ardent chess player. But still, that was only speculation, whereas with the aid of Harold's photographs he hoped to settle one or two doubtful points relating to the characters of footprints which had from time to time arisen in his mind, and thereby to extend his actual knowledge.

With a leisurely and thoughtful air he moved a few things on the table to make a clear space, took out from a cupboard a surveyor's boxwood scale, a pair of needle-pointed spring dividers, a set of paper-weights, a note-block, and a simple microscope (formed of a watchmaker's doublet mounted on three legs) which he used for examining documents. Then he laid the three sheets of the ordnance map in their proper sequence on the table, with the roll of photographs by their side, drew up a chair and sat down to his task.

He began by running his eye along the path traversed by the fugitive, which was plainly marked by a row of dots, each dot having above it a microscopic number. Dots and numbers had originally been marked with a sharp-pointed pencil, but they had subsequently been

509

inked in with red ink and a fine-pointed pen. From the maps he turned his attention to the photographs, unrolling a length of about nine inches and fixing the strip with a paper-weight at each end. The strip itself was an inch wide, and each photograph was an inch and a half long, and every one of the little oblongs contained the image of a footprint which occupied almost its entire length and which measured – as Thorndyke ascertained by taking the dimensions with his dividers – one-inch-and-three-eighths. Small as the photographs were, they were microscopically sharp in definition, having evidently been taken with a lens of very fine quality, and in the corner of each picture was a minute number in white, which stood out clearly against the rather dark background.

Sliding the little microscope over one of the prints, Thorndyke examined it with slightly amused interest. For a fugitive's footprint it was a frank absurdity, so strikingly conspicuous and characteristic was it. If Mr. Lewson had had his name printed large upon the soles of his shoes, he could hardly have given more assistance to his pursuers. The impression was that of a rubber sole on which, near the toe, was a framed label containing the makers' name, *J. Dell and Co.* Behind this was a panel, occupied by a prancing horse, and the Kentish motto, "*Invicta*". beneath the panel, implied that this was the prancing horse of Kent. The circular rubber heel was less distinctive, though even this was a little unusual, for its central device was a five-pointed star, whereas most star-pattern heels present six points. But not only were all the details of the pattern distinctly visible – even the little accidental markings, due to wear and damage, could be plainly made out. For instance, a little ridge could be seen across the horse's neck, corresponding to a cut or split in the rubber sole, and a tiny speck on the heel, which seemed to represent a particle of gravel embedded in the rubber.

When he had made an exhaustive examination of the one photograph, he went back to Numbers *1* and *2* which represented the footprints near the back gate of the bank, and which were not for his purpose part of the series. After a brief inspection of them, he placed one of the paper-weights on them, and, by means of another, exposed about eighteen inches of the strip. Next, he drew a vertical line down the middle of the note-block, dividing it into two parts, which he headed respectively "*Right*" and "*Left*". Then he began his comparative study with a careful examination of Number *3*, the first print photographed on the footpath.

Having finished with Number *3*, which was a right foot, he wrote down the number at the top of the "*Right*" column, in the middle of the space. Then he passed to Number *5* – the next right foot – and having examined it, wrote down its number. Next, he took, with the dividers, the distance between the dots marked *3* and *5* on the map, and, transferring the dividers to the boxwood scale, took off the distance in yards – forty-three yards – and wrote this down on the note-block opposite and at the left side of the Number *5*. From *5* he passed on to *7*, *9*, *11*, *13*, and so on, following the right foot along the strip until he had dealt with a couple of yards (the total length of the strip was a little over twenty-four feet), occasionally turning back to verify his comparisons, writing down the numbers in the middle of the column with the distances opposite to them on the left and jotting down in the space at the right a few brief notes embodying his observations. Then he returned to the beginning of the strip and dealt with the prints of the left foot in the same manner and for the same distance along the strip.

One would not have regarded it as a thrilling occupation. Indeed there was rather a suggestion of monotony in the endless recurrence of examination, comparison, and measurements of things which appeared to be merely mechanical repetitions of one another. Nor did the brief and scanty jottings in the *"Notes"* column suggest that this tedious procedure was yielding any great wealth of information. Nevertheless, Thorndyke continued to work at his task methodically, attentively, and without any symptoms of boredom, until he had dealt with nearly half of the strip. But at this point his manner underwent a sudden and remarkable change. Hitherto he had carried on his work with the placid air of one who is engaged on a mildly interesting piece of routine work. Now he sat up stiffly, gazing at the strip of photographs before him with a frown of perplexity, even of incredulity. With intense attention, he re-examined the last half-dozen prints that he had dealt with, then, taking a right foot as a starting-point, he followed the strip rapidly, taking no measurements and making no notes, until he reached the end, where he found a slip of paper pasted to the strip and bearing the note: *"Footprints cease here. Track turned off to left into heather. Length of foot, 12 inches. Length of stride from heel to heel, 34 inches."*

Having rapidly copied this note on to his block, Thorndyke resumed his examination with eager interest. Returning to the starting-point, he again examined a print of the left foot and then followed its successive prints to the final one at the end of the strip. Again he came back to the starting-point, but now, taking this as a centre, he began to move backwards and forwards, at first taking a dozen prints in each direction, then, by degrees, reducing the distance of his excursions until he came down to a single print of the right foot – a specially clear impression, marked with the number 93. This he again examined through the little microscope with the most intense scrutiny. Then, with a like concentrated attention, he examined first the preceding right-foot print,

91, and then the succeeding one, *95*. Finally, he turned to the map to locate number *93*, which he found near the middle of a wall – apparently the enclosing wall of a large garden or plantation – and exactly opposite a gate in that wall.

From this moment Thorndyke's interest in his original investigations seemed to become extinct. The little microscope, the scale, even the photographs themselves, were neglected and unnoticed, while he sat with his eyes fixed on the map – yet seeming to look through it rather than at it – evidently immersed in profound thought. For a long time he sat thus, immovable as a seated statue. At length he rose from his chair and, mechanically filling his pipe, began slowly to pace up and down the room, and to any observer who knew him, had there been one, the intense gravity of his expression, the slight frown, the compressed lips, the downcast eyes, as well as the unlighted pipe that he grasped in his hand, would have testified that some problem of more than common intricacy was being turned over in his mind and its factors sorted out and collated.

He had been pacing the room for nearly half-an-hour when a key was softly inserted into the latch of the outer door. The door opened and closed quietly, and then a gentle tap on the knocker of the inner door heralded the entry of a small gentleman of somewhat clerical aspect and uncommon crinkliness of countenance, who greeted Thorndyke with a deprecating smile.

"I hope, sir," said he, "that I am not disturbing you, but I thought that I had better remind you that you have not had any supper."

"Dear me!" exclaimed Thorndyke. "What a memory you have, Polton. And to think that I, who am really the interested party, should have overlooked the fact. Well, what do you propose?"

Polton glanced at the table with a sympathetic eye. "You won't want your things disturbed, I expect, if you have got a job on hand. I had better put your supper in the little laboratory. It won't take more than five minutes."

"That will do admirably," said Thorndyke. "And, by the way, I think that adjourned inquest at Aylesbury is the day after to-morrow, isn't it?"

"Yes, sir, Thursday. I fixed the letter on the appointment board."

"Well, as there is nothing pressing on Friday, I think I will stay the night there and come back on Friday evening if nothing urgent turns up in the interval."

"Yes, sir. Will you want anything special in the research case?"

"I shall not take the research case," replied Thorndyke. "In fact, I don't know that I want anything excepting the one-inch ordnance map, unless I take that stick of yours."

Polton's face brightened. "I wish you would, sir," he said persuasively. "You have never tried it since I made it, and I am sure you will find it a most useful instrument."

"I am sure I shall," said Thorndyke, "and perhaps I might as well take the little telephoto camera, if you will have it charged."

"I will charge it to-night, sir, and overhaul the stick. And your supper will be ready in five minutes."

With this, Polton disappeared as silently as he had come, leaving his principal to his meditations.

On the following Friday morning, at about half-past ten. Dr. John Thorndyke might have been seen – if there had been any one to see him, which there was not – seated in a first-class smoking-compartment in the Aylesbury-to-London train. But he was evidently not going to London, for, as the train slowed down on approaching Borley Station, he pocketed the folded ordnance map which he had been studying, stood up, and took his stick down from the rack.

Now this stick was the only blot on Thorndyke's appearance. Apart from it, his "turn-out" was entirely satisfactory and appropriate to his country surroundings without being either rustic or sporting. But that stick, with a tweed suit and a soft hat, struck a note of deepest discord. With a frock-coat and a top-hat it might have passed, though even then it would have called for a Falstaffian bearer. But as a country stick it really wouldn't do at all.

In the first place it was offensively straight – as straight as a length of metal tube. It was of an uncomely thickness, a full inch in diameter. As to the material, it might, by an exceedingly bad judge, have been mistaken for ebony. In fact, it was, as to its surface, strongly reminiscent of optician's black enamel. And the handle was no better. Of the same funereal hue and an unreasonable thickness, it had the stark mechanical regularity of an elbow-joint on a gas pipe, and, to make it worse, its end was finished by a sort of terminal cap. Moreover, on looking down the shaft of the stick, a close observer would have detected, about fifteen inches from the handle, a fine transverse crack, suggestive of a concealed joint. A sharp-eyed rural constable would have "spotted" it at a glance as a walking-stick gun, and he would have been wrong.

However, despite its aesthetic shortcomings, Thorndyke seemed to set some store by it, for he lifted it from the rack with evident care, and with the manner of lifting something heavier than an ordinary walking-stick, and when he stepped forth from the station, instead of holding it by its unlovely handle with its ferrule on the ground, he carried it "at the trail", grasping it by its middle.

On leaving the station precincts, Thorndyke set forth with the confident air of one who is on familiar ground, though, as a matter of fact, he had never been in the district before. But he had that power, which comes by practice, of memorizing a map that makes unvisited regions familiar and is apt to cause astonishment to the aboriginal inhabitants. Swinging along at an easy but rapid pace, he presently entered a quiet, semi-suburban road which he followed for a quarter-of-a-mile, looking about him keenly, and identifying the features of the map as he went. At length he came to a kissing-gate which gave access to a footpath and, turning into this, he strode away along the path, looking closely at its surface, and once stopping and retracing his steps for a few yards to examine his own footprints.

A few hundred yards farther on he crossed another road, more definitely rural in character, and noted at the corner a pleasant-looking house of some age, standing back behind a well-kept garden, its front entrance sheltered by a wooden porch which was now almost hidden by a mass of climbing roses. The side wall of the garden abutted on the footpath and extended along it for a distance that suggested somewhat extensive grounds. At this point he reduced his pace to a slow walk, scrutinizing the ground – on which he could detect, even now, occasional fragmentary traces of the familiar footprints of Harold's photographs – and noting how, since crossing the road, he had passed completely out of the last vestiges of the town into the open country.

He had traversed rather more than half the length of the wall when he came to a green-painted wooden gate, before which he halted for a few moments. There were, however, no features of interest to note beyond the facts that its loop handle was unprovided with a latch and that it was secured with a Yale lock. But as he stood looking at it with a deeply reflective air, he was aware of a sound proceeding from within – a pleasant sound, though curiously out of key with his own thoughts – the sound of some one whistling, very skilfully and melodiously, the old-fashioned air, "Alice, Where Art Thou?" He smiled grimly, keenly appreciative of the whimsical incongruity of these cheerful, innocent strains with the circumstances that had brought him thither. Then he turned away and walked slowly to the end of the wall where it was joined by another, which enclosed the end of the grounds. Here he halted and looked along the path towards a wood which was visible in the distance. Then, turning, he looked back along the way by which he had come. In neither direction was there anyone in sight, and Thorndyke noted that he

514

had not met a single person since he had passed through the kissing-gate. Apparently this path was quite extraordinarily unfrequented.

Having made this observation, Thorndyke stepped off the path and walked a few paces along the end wall – which abutted on a field – to a spot where an apple tree in the grounds rose above the summit. Here he stopped and, having glanced up at the wall – which was nearly seven feet high – grasped the uncomely stick with both hands, one on either side of the concealed joint, and gave a sharp twist. Immediately the stick became divided into two parts, the lower of which – that bearing the ferrule – Thorndyke stood against the wall. It could now be seen that the upper part terminated in a blackened brass half-cylinder, the flat face of which was occupied by a little circular glass window, and when Thorndyke had unscrewed the cap from the end of the handle, the latter was seen to be a metal tube, within which was another little glass window – the eye-piece. In effect, Polton's hideous walking-stick was a disguised periscope.

Taking up a position close to the wall, Thorndyke slowly raised the periscope until its end stood an inch or so above the top of the wall, with the little window looking into the enclosure. The eye-piece being now at a convenient level, he applied his eye to it, and immediately had the sensation of looking through a circular hole in the wall. Through this aperture (which was, of course, the aperture of the object-glass above him, reflected by a pair of prisms) he looked into a large garden, enclosed on all sides by the high wall and having apparently only two doors or gates, the one at the side, which he had already seen, and another which appeared to open into another garden nearer the house, and which, like the side gate, seemed to be fitted with a night-latch of the Yale type. On one side, partly concealed by a half-grown yew hedge, was a long, low building which, by the windows in its roof, appeared to be some kind of workshop, and by rotating the periscope it was possible to catch a glimpse of part of what seemed to be a summer-house in the corner opposite the workshop. Otherwise, excepting a narrow flower border and a few fruit trees ranged along the wall, the whole of the enclosure was occupied by a large lawn, the wide expanse of which was broken only by a sun-dial beside which, at the moment, a man was standing, and on man and sun-dial, Thorndyke, after his swift preliminary survey, concentrated his attention.

The stone pillar of the dial was obviously ancient. Equally obviously the stone base on which it stood was brand new. Moreover, the part of the lawn immediately surrounding the base was yellow and faded as if it had been recently raised and relaid. The manifest inference was that the dial had but lately been placed in its present position, and this inference was supported by the occupation in which the man was

515

engaged. On the stone base stood a Windsor chair, the seat of which bore one or two tools and a pair of spectacles. Thorndyke noted the spectacles with interest, observing that they had "curl sides" and were therefore habitually worn, and since they had been discarded while their owner consulted a book that he held, it seemed to follow that he must be near-sighted.

As Thorndyke watched, the man closed the book and laid it on the chair, when by its shape and size, its scarlet back and apple-green sides, it was easily recognizable as *Whitaker's Almanack*. Having laid down the book, the man drew out his watch and, holding it in his hand, approached the pillar and grasped the gnomon of the dial, and now Thorndyke could see that the dial-plate had been unfixed from its bed, for it moved visibly as the gnomon was grasped. The nature of the operation was now quite clear. The man was re-setting the dial. He had taken out the Equation of Time from *Whitaker* and was now adjusting the dial-plate by means of his watch to show the correct Apparent Solar Time.

At this point – leaving the man standing beside the pillar, watch in hand – Thorndyke picked up the detached portion of the stick, and stepping along the wall, glanced up and down the path. So far as he could see – nearly a quarter-of-a-mile in each direction – he had the path to himself, and, noting with some surprise and no little interest the remarkable paucity of wayfarers, he returned to his post and resumed his observations.

The man had now put away his watch and taken up a hammer and bradawl. Thorndyke noted the workmanlike character of the former – a rather heavy ball-pane hammer such as engineers use – and when the bradawl was inserted into one of the screw-holes of the dial-plate and driven home into the lead bed with a single tap, he observed the deftness with which the gentle, calculated blow was delivered with the rather ponderous tool. So, too, with the driving of the screw, it was done with the unmistakable ease and readiness of the skilled workman.

Having rapidly made these observations, Thorndyke drew from his hip pocket the little camera and opened it, setting the focus by the scale to the assumed distance – about sixty feet – fixing the wire release and setting the shutter to half-a-second – the shortest exposure that was advisable with a telephoto lens. Another peep through the periscope showed the man in the act of again inserting the bradawl, and, incidentally, presenting a well-lighted right profile, whereupon Thorndyke raised the camera and placed it on the top of the wall with the wire release hanging down and the lens pointed, as well as he could judge, at the sun-dial. Then, as the man poised the hammer preparatory to striking, he pressed the button of the release and immediately took down the camera and changed the film.

Once more he went to the corner of the wall and looked up and down the path. This time a man was visible – apparently a labourer – coming from the direction of the town. But he was a long distance away and was advancing at a pace so leisurely that Thorndyke decided to complete his business, if possible, before he should arrive. A glance through the periscope showed the man in the garden driving another screw. When he had driven it home, he stepped round the pillar to deal with the screws on the other side. As he inserted the bradawl and balanced the hammer, presenting now his left profile, Thorndyke lifted the camera to the top of the wall, made the exposure, took down the camera, and having changed the film, closed it and put it in his pocket. Then he joined up the two parts of the stick, fixed the cap on the eye-piece and came out on to the path, turning towards the town to meet the labourer. But the latter had now disappeared, having apparently turned into the road on which the house fronted. Having the path once more to himself, Thorndyke walked along it to the gate, where he paused and rapped on it smartly with his knuckles.

After a short interval, during which he repeated the summons, the gate was opened a few inches and the man whom he had seen within looked out with an air of slightly irritable enquiry.

"I must apologize for disturbing you," Thorndyke said with disarming suavity, "but I heard someone within, and there was no one about from whom I could make my enquiry."

"You are not disturbing me in the least," the other replied, not less suavely. "I shall be most happy to give you any information that I can. What was the enquiry that you wished to make?"

As he asked the question, the stranger stepped out on the path, drawing the gate to after him, and looked inquisitively at Thorndyke.

"I wanted to know," the latter replied, "whether this footpath leads to a wood – Potter's Wood, I think it is called. You see, I am a stranger to this neighbourhood."

On this the man seemed to look at him with heightened interest as he replied, "Yes, it leads through the wood about half-a-mile farther on."

"And where does it lead to eventually?"

"It crosses a patch of heath and joins a by-road that runs from the town to the main London road. Was that where you wanted to go?"

"No," replied Thorndyke. "It is the path itself that I am concerned with. The fact is, I am making a sort of informal inspection in connection with the case of a man who disappeared a short time ago – the manager of a local branch of Perkins's Bank. I understand that he was last seen walking along this path."

"Ah," said the other, "I remember the affair. And is he still missing?"

"Yes. He has never been seen or heard of since he started along this path. What is the wood like? Is it a place in which a man might lose himself?"

The other shook his head. "No, it is only a small wood. A sound and sober man could not get lost in it. Of course, if a man were taken ill and strayed into the wood, he might die and lie hidden for months. Has the wood been searched?"

"I really can't say. It ought to have been."

"I thought," said the stranger, "that you might, perhaps, be connected with the police."

"No," replied Thorndyke. "I am a lawyer and I look after some of the affairs of the bank. One of the directors mentioned this disappearance to me a few days ago, and as I happened to be in the neighbourhood to-day, I thought I would come and take a look round. Perhaps you could show me where we are on my map. It is a little confusing to a stranger."

He drew out the folded map and handed it to his new acquaintance, who took it and pored over it as if he found it difficult to decipher. As he did so, Thorndyke took the opportunity to look him over with the most searching scrutiny, his face, his hair, his spectacles, his hands and his feet, and when he had inspected the left side of the face which was the one presented to him – he crossed as if to took over the man's right shoulder and examined the face from that side.

"This dotted line seems to be the footpath," said the stranger, tracing it with the point of a pencil. "This black dot must be my house, and here is the wood with the dotted line running through it. I think that is quite clear."

"Perfectly clear, thank you," said Thorndyke, as the other handed him back the map. "I am very greatly obliged to you and I must again apologize for having disturbed you."

"Not at all," the stranger returned genially, "and I hope your inspection may be successful."

Thorndyke thanked him again, and with mutual bows they separated, the one retiring into his domain, the other setting forth in the direction of the wood.

For some minutes Thorndyke continued to walk at a rapid pace along the path. Only when a sharp turn carried him out of sight of the walled garden did he halt to jot down in his note-book a brief summary of his observations while they were fresh in his mind. Not that the notes were really necessary for, even as he had made those observations, the significance of the facts that they supplied became apparent. Now, as he walked, he turned them over again and again.

What had he observed? Nothing very sensational, to be sure. He had seen a man who had recently set up in his garden a pillar dial on a broad stone base. The dial was old, but the base was new and seemed to have been specially constructed for its present purpose. The garden in which it had been set up was completely enclosed, was extremely secluded, was remote from its own or any other house, and was very thoroughly secured against any possible intrusion by two locked gates. The man himself was a skilled workman, or at least a very handy man – ingenious and resourceful, too, for he could time a sun-dial, a thing that not every handy man could do. Then he appeared to have some kind of workshop of a size suggesting good accommodation and facilities for work, and this workshop was in a secluded situation, very secure from observation. But in these facts there would seem to be nothing remarkable, only they were in singular harmony with certain other facts – very remarkable facts indeed – that Thorndyke had gleaned from an examination of Harold's absurd photographs.

And there was the man himself, and especially his spectacles. When Thorndyke had seen those spectacles lying on the chair while their owner drove in the screws, looked at his watch, and scrutinized the shadow on the dial, he had naturally assumed that the man was near-sighted, that he had taken off his "distance" glasses to get the advantage of his near sight for the near work. But when the man appeared at the gate, it was immediately evident that he was not near-sighted. The spectacles were convex bi-focal glasses, with an upper half of nearly plain glass and a lower segment distinctly convex, suited for long sight or "old sight". A near-sighted man could not have seen through them. But neither did their owner seem to need them, since he had taken them off just when they should have been most useful – for near work. Moreover, when Thorndyke had presented the map, the man had looked at it, not through the lower "reading" segment, but through the weak, upper, "distance" segment. In short, the man did not need those spectacles at all. So far from being a convenience, they were a positive inconvenience. Then, why did he wear them? Why had he put them on to come to the gate? There could be only one answer. People who wear useless and inconvenient spectacles do so in order to alter their appearance, as a species of disguise, in fact. Then it seemed as if this man had some reason for wishing to conceal his identity. But what could that reason be?

As to his appearance, he was a decidedly good-looking man, with an alert, intelligent face that was in harmony with his speech and bearing.

His mouth and chin were concealed by a moustache and a short beard, but his nose was rather handsome and very striking, for it was of that rare type which is seen in the classical Greek sculptures. His ears were both well-shaped, but one of them – the right – was somewhat disfigured by a small "port-wine mark" which stained the lobule a deep purple. But it was quite small and really inconspicuous.

This was the sum of Thorndyke's observations, to which may be added that the man appeared to be prematurely grey and that his face, despite its cheerful geniality, had that indefinable character that may be detected in the faces of men who have passed through long periods of stress and mental suffering. Only one datum remained unascertained, and Thorndyke added it to his collection when, having traversed the wood and the heath, he returned to the town by way of the by-road. Encountering a postman on his round, he stopped him and enquired, "I wonder if you can tell me who is living at The Chestnuts now? You know the house I mean. It stands at the corner – "

"Oh, I know The Chestnuts, sir. Colonel Barnett used to live there. But he went away nigh upon two years ago, and, after it had been empty for a month or two, it was bought by the gentleman who lives there now, Mr. Pottermack."

"That is a queer name," said Thorndyke. "How does he spell it?"

"$P - O - T - T - E - R - M - A - C - K$," the postman replied. "Marcus Pottermack, Esq. It is a queer name, sir. I've never met with it before. But he is a very pleasant gentleman, all the same."

Thorndyke thanked the postman for his information, on which he pondered as he made his way to the station. It was a very queer name. In fact, there was about it something rather artificial, something that was not entirely out of character with the unwanted spectacles.

Chapter VII
The Criminal Records

On each of the two men who parted at the gate the brief interview produced its appropriate effects, in each it generated a certain train of thought which, later, manifested itself in certain actions. In Mr. Pottermack, as he softly reopened the gate to listen to the retreating footsteps, once even venturing to peep out at the tall figure that was striding away up the path, the encounter was productive of a dim uneasiness, a slight disturbance of the sense of security that had been growing on him since the night of the tragedy. For the first few days thereafter he had been on wires. All seemed to be going well, but he was constantly haunted by that ever-recurring question, "Was there anything vital that he had overlooked?"

The mysterious photographer, too, had been a disturbing element, occasioning anxious speculations on the motive or purpose of his inexplicable proceedings and on the possibility of something being brought to light by the photographs that was beyond the scope of human vision. But as the days had passed with no whisper of suspicion, as the local excitement died down and the incident faded into oblivion, his fears subsided, and by degrees he settled down into a feeling of comfortable security.

And after all, why not? In the first few days his own secret knowledge had prevented him from seeing the affair in its true perspective. But now, looking at it calmly with the eyes of those who had not that knowledge, what did Lewson's disappearance amount to? It was a matter of no importance at all. A disreputable rascal had absconded with a hundred pounds that did not belong to him. He had disappeared and no one knew whither he had gone. Nor did any one particularly care. Doubtless the police would keep a look-out for him, but he was only a minor delinquent, and they would assuredly make no extraordinary efforts to trace him.

So Mr. Pottermack argued, and quite justly, and thus arguing came by degrees to the comfortable conclusion that the incident was closed and that he might now take up again the thread of his peaceful life, secure alike from the menace of the law and the abiding fear of impoverishment and treachery.

It was this new and pleasant feeling of security that had been disturbed by his encounter with the strange lawyer. Not that he was seriously alarmed. The man seemed harmless enough. He was not, apparently, making any real investigations but just a casual inspection of the neighbourhood, prompted, as it appeared, by a not-very-lively curiosity. And as a tracker he seemed to be of no account, since he could not even find his position on a one-inch map.

But for all that, the incident was slightly disquieting. Pottermack had assumed that the Lewson affair was closed. But now it seemed that it was not closed. And it was a curious coincidence that this man should have knocked at his gate, should have selected him for these enquiries. No doubt it was but chance, but still, there was the coincidence. Again, there was the man himself. He had seemed foolish about the map. But he did not look at all like a foolish man. On the contrary, his whole aspect and bearing had a suggestion of power, of acute intellect and quiet strength of character. As Pottermack recalled his appearance and manner, he found himself asking again and again: Was there anything behind this seemingly chance encounter? Had this lawyer seen those photographs, and if so, had he found in them anything more than met the eye? Could he have had any special reason for knocking at this particular gate? And what on earth could he be doing with that walking-stick gun?

Reflections such as these pervaded Mr. Pottermack's consciousness as he went about his various occupations. They did not seriously disturb his peace of mind, but still they did create a certain degree of unrest, and this presently revived in his mind certain plans which he had considered and rejected, plans for further establishing his security by shifting the field of possible inquiry yet farther from his own neighbourhood.

On Thorndyke the effects of the meeting were quite different. He had come doubting if a certain surmise that he had formed could possibly be correct. He had gone away with his doubts dispelled and his surmise converted into definite belief. The only unsolved question that remained in his mind was, "Who was Marcus Pottermack?" The answer that suggested itself was improbable in the extreme. But it was the only one that he could produce, and if it were wrong he was at the end of his unassisted resources.

The first necessity, therefore, was to eliminate the improbable – or else to confirm it. Then he would know where he stood and could consider what action he would take. Accordingly he began by working up the scanty material that he had collected. The photographs, when developed and enlarged by Polton, yielded two very fair portraits of Mr. Pottermack showing clearly the right and left profiles respectively, and while Polton was dealing with these, his principal made a systematic, but not very hopeful, inspection of the map in search of possible finger-prints. He had made a mental note of the way in which Pottermack had held the map, and even of the spots which his finger-tips had touched, and on these he now began cautiously to operate with two fine powders, a black and a white, applying each to its appropriate background.

The results were poor enough, but yet they were better than he had expected. Pottermack had held the map in his left hand, the better to manipulate the pencil with which he pointed, and his thumb had been planted on a green patch which represented a wood. Here the white powder settled and showed a print which, poor as it was, would present no difficulties to the experts and which would be more distinct in a photograph, as the background would then appear darker. The prints of the finger-tips which the black powder brought out on the white background were more imperfect and were further confused by the black lettering. Still, Thorndyke had them all carefully photographed and enlarged to twice the natural size, and, having blocked out on the negative the surrounding lettering (to avoid giving any information that might be better withheld), had prints made and mounted on card.

With these in his letter-case and the two portraits in his pocket, he set forth one morning for New Scotland Yard, proposing to seek the assistance of his old friend, Mr. Superintendent Miller, or, if he should not be available, that of the officer in charge of criminal records. However, it happened fortunately that the Superintendent was in his office, and thither Thorndyke, having sent in his card, was presently conducted.

"Well, Doctor," said Miller, shaking hands heartily, "here you are, gravelled as usual. Now what sort of mess do you want us to help you out of?"

Thorndyke produced his letter-case, and, extracting the photographs, handed them to the Superintendent.

"Here," he said, "are three finger-prints, apparently the thumb and first two fingers of the left hand."

"Ha," said Miller, inspecting the three photographs critically. "Why 'apparently'?"

"I mean," explained Thorndyke, "that that was what I inferred from their position on the original document."

"Which seems to have been a map," remarked Miller, with a faint grin. "Well, I expect you know. Shall I take it that they are the thumb and index and middle finger of the left hand?"

"I think you may," said Thorndyke.

"I think I may," agreed Miller. "And now the question is: What about it? I suppose you want us to tell you whose finger-prints they are, and you want to gammon us that you don't know already. And I suppose

– as I see you have been faking the negative – that you don't want to give us any information?"

"In effect," replied Thorndyke, "you have, with your usual acuteness, diagnosed the position exactly. I don't much want to give any details, but I will tell you this much. If my suspicions are correct, these are the finger-prints of a man who has been dead some years."

"Dead!" exclaimed Miller. "Good Lord, Doctor, what a vindictive man you are! But you don't suppose that we follow the criminal class into the next world, do you?"

"I have been assuming that you don't destroy records. If you do, you are unlike any government officials that I have ever met. But I hope I was right."

"In the main, you were. We don't keep the whole set of documents of a dead man, but we have a set of skeleton files on which the personal documents – the finger-prints, photographs, and description – are preserved. So I expect we shall be able to tell you what you want to know."

"I am sorry," said Thorndyke, "that they are such wretchedly poor prints. You don't think that they are too imperfect to identify, I hope."

Miller inspected the photographs afresh. "I don't see much amiss with them," said he. "You can't expect a crook to go about with a roller and inking-plate in his pocket so as to give you nice sharp prints. These are better than a good many that our people have to work from. And besides, there are three digits from one hand. That gives you part of the formula straight away. No, the experts won't make any trouble about these. But supposing these prints are not on the file?"

"Then we shall take it that I suspected the wrong man."

"Quite so. But, if I am not mistaken, your concern is to prove whose finger-prints they are in order that you can say whose finger-prints they are not. Now, supposing that we don't find them on the files of the dead men, would it help you if we tried the current files – the records of the crooks who are still in business? Or would you rather not?"

"If it would not be giving you too much trouble," said Thorndyke, "I should be very much obliged if you would."

"No trouble at all," said Miller, adding with a sly smile, "only it occurred to me that it might be embarrassing to you if we found your respected client's finger-prints on the live register."

"That would be a highly interesting development," said Thorndyke, "though I don't think it a likely one. But it is just as well to exhaust the possibilities."

"Quite," agreed Miller, and thereupon he wrote the brief particulars on a slip of paper which he put into an envelope with the photographs, and, having rung a bell, handed the envelope to the messenger who appeared in response to the summons.

"I don't suppose we shall have to keep you waiting very long," said the Superintendent. "They have an extraordinarily ingenious system of filing. Out of all the thousands of finger-prints that they have, they can pounce on the one that is wanted in the course of a few minutes. It seems incredible, and yet it is essentially simple – just a matter of classification and ringing the changes on different combinations of types."

"You are speaking of completely legible prints?" suggested Thorndyke.

"Yes, the sort of prints that we get sent in from local prisons for identification of a man who has been arrested under a false name. Of course, when we get a single imperfect print found by the police at a place where a crime has been committed, a bit more time has to be spent. Then we have not only got to place the print, but we've got to make mighty sure that it is the right one, because an arrest and a prosecution hangs on it. You don't want to arrest a man and then, when you come to take his finger-prints properly, find that they are the wrong ones. So, in the case of an imperfect print, you have got to do some careful ridge-tracing and counting and systematic checking of individual ridge-characters, such as bifurcations and islands. But, even so, they don't take so very long over it. The practised eye picks out at a glance details that an unpractised eye can hardly recognize even when they are pointed out."

The Superintendent was proceeding to dilate, with professional enthusiasm, on the wonders of finger-print technique and the efficiency of the Department when his eulogies were confirmed by the entrance of an officer carrying a sheaf of papers and Thorndyke's photographs, which he delivered into Miller's hands.

"Well, Doctor," said the Superintendent, after a brief glance at the documents, "here is your information. Jeffrey Brandon is the name of the late lamented. Will that do for you?"

"Yes," replied Thorndyke, "that is the name I expected to hear."

"Good," said Miller. "I see they have kept the whole of his papers for some reason. I will just glance through them while you are doing Thomas Didymus with the finger-prints. But it is quite obvious, if you compare your photographs with the rolled impressions, that the ridge-patterns are identical."

He handed Thorndyke the finger-print sheet, to which were attached the photograph and personal description, and sat down at the table to look over the other documents, while Thorndyke walked over to the window to get a better light. But he did not concern himself with the

525

finger-prints beyond a very brief inspection. It was the photograph that interested him. It showed, on the same print, a right profile and a full face, of which he concentrated his attention on the former. A rather remarkable profile it was, strikingly handsome and curiously classical in outline, rather recalling the head of Antinous in the British Museum. Thorndyke examined it minutely, and then – his back being turned to Miller – he drew from his waistcoat pocket the right profile of Mr. Pottermack and placed it beside the prison photograph.

A single glance made it clear that the two photographs represented the same face. Though one showed a clean-shaven young man with the full lips and strong, rounded chin completely revealed, while the other was a portrait of a bearded, spectacled, middle-aged man, yet they were unmistakably the same. The remarkable nose and brow and the shapely ear were identical in the two photographs, and in both, the lobe of the ear was marked at its tip by a dark spot.

From the photograph he turned to the description. Not that it was necessary to seek further proof, and he did, in fact, merely glance through the particulars. But that rapid glance gathered fresh confirmation. *"Height 5-feet-6-inches, hair chestnut, eyes darkish grey, small port-wine mark on lobe of right ear,"* etc. All the details of Jeffrey Brandon's personal characteristics applied perfectly to Mr. Marcus Pottermack.

"I don't quite see," said Miller, as he took the papers from Thorndyke and laid them on the others, "why they kept all these documents. The conviction doesn't look to me very satisfactory – I don't like these cases where the prosecution has all its eggs in one basket, with the possible chance that they may be bad eggs, and it was a devil of a sentence for a first offence. But as the poor beggar is dead, and no reconsideration of either the conviction or the sentence is possible, there doesn't seem much object in preserving the records. Still, there may have been some reason at the time."

In his own mind, Thorndyke was of opinion that there might have been a very good reason. But he did not communicate this opinion. He had obtained the information that he had sought and was not at all desirous of troubling still waters, and his experience having taught him that Mr. Superintendent Miller was an exceedingly "noticing" gentleman, he thought it best to avoid further discussion and take his departure, after having expressed his appreciation of the assistance that he had received.

Nevertheless, for some time after he had gone, the Superintendent remained wrapped in profound thought, and that his cogitations were in some way concerned with the departed visitor would have been suggested by the circumstance that he sauntered to the window and

526

looked down with a speculative eye on that visitor as he strode across the courtyard towards the Whitehall gate.

Meanwhile Thorndyke's mind was no less busy. As he wended his way Temple-wards he reviewed the situation in all its bearings. The wildly improbable had turned out to be true. He had made a prodigiously long shot and he had hit the mark – which was gratifying inasmuch as it justified a previous rather hypothetical train of reasoning. Marcus Pottermack, Esq., was undoubtedly the late Jeffrey Brandon. There was now no question about that. The only question that remained was what was to be done in the matter, and that question would have been easier to decide if he had been in possession of more facts. He had heard Mr. Stalker's opinion of the conviction, based on intimate knowledge of the circumstances, and he had heard that of the Superintendent, based on an immense experience of prosecutions. He was inclined to agree with them both, and the more so inasmuch as he had certain knowledge which they had not.

In the end, he decided to take no action at present, but to keep a watchful eye for further developments.

Chapter VIII
Mr. Pottermack Seeks Adventure

In the last chapter it was stated that one of the effects of Thorndyke's appearance at the side gate of The Chestnuts, Borley, was to revive in the mind of its tenant certain projects which had been considered and rejected. But perhaps the word "rejected" overstates the case. For the continued existence in a locked drawer in Mr. Pottermack's workshop of a coat which had once been James Lewson's and a bundle of twenty five-pound notes implied a purpose which had been abandoned only conditionally and subject to possible reconsideration.

Again and again, as the destructor which stood in the corner beyond the tool-shed smoked and flared as he fed it with combustible rubbish, had he been on the point of flinging into it the coat and the banknotes and thereby reducing to unrecognizable ash the last visible traces of the tragedy. And every time his hand had been stayed by the thought that possibly, in some circumstances as yet unforeseen, these mementoes of that night of horror might yet be made to play a useful part. So, not without many a twinge of uneasiness, he had let these incriminating objects lie hidden in the locked drawer. And now, as it seemed to him, the circumstances had arisen in which some of them, at least, might be turned to account.

What were those circumstances? Simply the state of mind of the strange lawyer. To the people of Borley, including the police, Lewson was a man who had absconded and vanished. His tracks had shown him striking out across country towards the London road. Those tracks, it is true, broke off short on the heath and had not reappeared elsewhere, but no one doubted that he had gone clear away from the vicinity of Borley and was now in hiding at a safe distance from his old haunts. The natives of the district had never given Mr. Pottermack a moment's anxiety. But with this lawyer the case was different. The disturbing thing about him was that his curiosity, tepid as it was, concerned itself, not with the man who had vanished, but with the locality from which he disappeared. But curiosity of that kind, Mr. Pottermack felt, was a thing that was not to be encouraged. On the contrary, it had better be diverted into a more wholesome channel. In short, the time had come when it would be desirable that James Lewson should make his appearance, if only by proxy, in some district as far removed as possible from the neighbourhood of The Chestnuts, Borley.

So it came about that Mr. Pottermack prepared to set forth along that perilous track beaten smooth by the feet of those who do not know when to let well alone.

For some days after having come to his decision in general terms, he was at a loss for a detailed plan. Somehow, the stolen notes had got to be put into circulation. But not by him. The numbers of those notes were known, and, as soon as they began to circulate, some, at least, of them would be identified and would be rigorously traced. The problem was how to get rid of them in a plausible manner without appearing in the transaction, and for some time he could think of no better plan than that of simply dropping them in a quiet London street, a plan which he summarily rejected as not meeting the necessities of the case. The fruitful suggestion eventually came from a newsboy who was roaring, "Egbert Bruce's Finals!" outside the station. In an instant, Mr. Pottermack realized that here was the perfect plan and, having purchased a paper, took it home to extract the details on which he proposed to base his strategic scheme.

The "finals" related to a somewhat unselect race-meeting which was to take place in a couple of days' time at Illingham in Surrey, a place conveniently accessible from Borley and yet remote enough to render it unlikely that he would be seen there by any of his fellow-townsmen. Not that his presence there would be in any way suspicious or incriminating, but still, the less people knew about his movements the better.

On the appointed day he set forth betimes, neatly but suitably dressed and all agog for the adventure, tame though it promised to be if it worked according to plan. To Mrs. Gadby he had explained – quite truthfully – that he was going to London, and if she had wanted confirmation of the statement, it could have been supplied by sundry natives of the town with whom he exchanged greetings on the platform as he waited for the London train.

But despite his geniality, he made a point of selecting an empty first-class compartment and shutting himself in. He had no hankering for human companionship. For beneath the exhilaration engendered by this little adventure was an appreciable tinge of nervousness. No foreseeable contingency threatened his safety, but it is an undeniable fact that a man who carries, buttoned up in his inside breast pocket, twenty stolen banknotes, of which the numbers are known to the police, and of his possession of which he could give no credible account, is not without some reason for nervousness. And that was Mr. Pottermack's position. Just before starting, he had disinterred the whole bundle of those fatal notes and stuffed them into a compartment of the letter-case which he usually carried in his breast pocket. He had also hunted up another letter-case, aged, outworn and shabby, into which he had put a half-dozen ten-shilling notes for the day's expenses and stowed it in the outside hip pocket of his jacket.

As soon as the train had fairly started, he proceeded to make certain rearrangements related to his plan of campaign. Taking out the two letter-wallets – which we may distinguish as the inner and the outer – he laid them on the seat beside him. From the inner wallet he took out five of the stolen notes and placed them loosely in a compartment of the other wallet with their ends projecting so that they were plainly visible when it was open, and from the outer wallet he transferred four of the ten-shilling notes to the inner. (He had paid for his ticket in silver.) Then he returned the two wallets to their respective pockets and buttoned up his coat.

From Marylebone Station he walked to Baker Street, where he took a train for Waterloo and arrived to find the great station filled with a seething crowd of racegoers. Not, on the whole, a prepossessing crowd, though all sorts and conditions of men were represented. But Mr. Pottermack was not hypercritical. At the over-smart, horsey persons, the raffish sporting men with race-glasses slung over their shoulders, the men of mystery with handbags or leather satchels, he glanced with benevolent interest. They had their uses in the economy of nature – in fact, he hoped to make use of some of them himself. So tolerant, indeed, was he that he even greeted with a kindly smile the notices pasted up urging passengers to beware of pickpockets, for in that respect his condition was unique. In spite of the wallet in his outside pocket, he enjoyed complete immunity, and as he joined the queue at the booking-office window, he reflected with grim amusement that, of all that throng, he was probably the only person who had come expressly to have his pocket picked.

As he approached the window, he drew the wallet from his outside pocket, and, opening it, inspected its interior with an air of indecision, took out one of the banknotes, put it back, and, finally dipping into the other compartment, fished out a ten-shilling note. Holding this in one hand and the open wallet in the other, he at last came opposite the window, where he purchased his ticket and moved on to make way for a large, red-faced man who seemed to be in a hurry. As he walked on slowly towards the barrier, pocketing the wallet as he went, the crowd surged impatiently past him, but watching that crowd as it swept on ahead, he could see no sign of the red-faced man. That gentleman's hurry seemed suddenly to have evaporated, and it was only when Pottermack was entering his carriage and turned to look back that he observed his roseate friend immediately behind him. Instantly he entered the nearly full compartment, and as he took his seat he was careful to leave a vacant place on his right hand, and when the red-faced man, closely following him, plumped down into the vacant space and at once began to exercise his elbows, he smiled inwardly with the satisfaction of the fortunate angler who "sees his quill or cork down sink". In short, he felt a comfortable certainty that he had "got a bite".

It was now a matter of deep regret to him that he had neglected to provide himself at the bookstall with something to read. A newspaper would have been so helpful to his friend on the right. However, the deficiency was made up to a practicable extent by a couple of men who faced each other from the two corners to his left, and who, having spread a small rug across their joint knees, were good enough to give a demonstration for the benefit of the company at large of the immemorial three-card trick. Towards them Pottermack craned with an expression of eager interest that aroused in them an unjustified optimism. With intense concentration, the operator continued over and over again to perform dummy turns, and the professional "mug", who sat opposite to Pottermack, continued with blatant perversity to spot the obviously wrong card every time, and pay up his losses with groans of surprise, while the fourth confederate, on Pottermack's left, nudged him from time to time and solicited in a whisper his opinion as to which was really the right card. It is needless to say that his opinion turned out invariably to be correct, but still he resisted the whispered entreaties of his neighbour to try his luck "seeing that he was such a dab at spotting 'em". Under other circumstances he would have invested the ten-shilling note for the sake of publicity. As things were, he did not dare to touch the wallet, or even put his hand to the pocket wherein it reposed. Premature discovery would have been fatal.

As the train sped on and consumed the miles of the short journey, the operator's invitations to Pottermack to try his luck became more urgent and less polite, until at length, as the destination drew near, they degenerated into mere objurgation and epithets of contempt. At length the train slowed down at the platform. Every one stood up and all together tried to squeeze through the narrow doorway, Pottermack himself emerging with unexpected velocity, propelled by a vigorous shove. At the same moment his hat was lightly flicked off his head and fell among the feet of the crowd. He would have stooped to recover it, but the necessity was forestalled by an expert kick which sent it soaring aloft, and hardly had it descended when it rose again and yet again until, having taken its erratic flight over the fence, it came at last to rest in the station-master's garden. By the time it had been retrieved with the aid of

531

the sympathetic station-master, the last of the passengers had filed through the barrier, and Pottermack brought up the extreme rear like a belated straggler.

As soon as he had had time to recover from these agitating experiences, his thoughts flew to the wallet and he thrust his hand into his outside pocket. To his unspeakable surprise, the wallet was still there. As he made the discovery, he was aware of a pang of disappointment, even of a sense of injury. He had put his trust in the red-faced man, and behold! That rubicund impostor had betrayed him. It looked as if this plan of his was not so easy as it had appeared.

But when he came to the turnstile of the enclosure and drew out the wallet to extract the ten-shilling note – and incidentally to display its other contents – he realized that he had done the red-faced man an injustice. The ten-shilling note, indeed, was there, tucked away at the bottom of its compartment, but otherwise the wallet was empty. Pottermack could hardly believe his eyes. For a few moments he stood staring at it in astonishment until an impatient poke in the back and an imperative command to "Pass along, please" recalled him to the present proceedings, when he swept up and pocketed his change and strolled away into the enclosure, meditating respectfully on the skill and tact of his red-faced acquaintance, and wishing that he had made the discovery sooner. For, now, the wallet would need to be recharged for the benefit of the next artist. This he could have done easily in the empty station, but in the crowd which surrounded him the matter presented difficulties. He could not do it unobserved, and it would appear a somewhat odd proceeding – especially to the eye of a plain-clothes policeman. There must be a good number of those useful officials in the crowd, and it was of vital importance that he should not attract the attention of any of them.

He looked round in some bewilderment, seeking a secluded spot in which he could refill the outer wallet unnoticed. A vain quest! Every part of the enclosure, excepting the actual course, was filled with a seething multitude, varying in density but all-pervading. Here and there a closely packed mass indicated some juggler, mountebank, thimble artist, or card expert, and some distance away a Punch-and-Judy show rose above the heads of the crowd, the sound of its drum and Pan's pipes and the unmistakable voice of the hero penetrating the general hub-bub. Towards this exhibition Pottermack was directing his course when shouts of laughter proceeding from the interior of a small but dense crowd suggested that something amusing was happening there, whereupon Pottermack, renouncing the delights of Punch-and-Judy, began cautiously to elbow his way towards the centre of attraction.

532

At this moment a bell rang in the distance, and instantly the whole crowd was in motion, surging towards the course. And then began a most singular hurly-burly in Pottermack's immediate neighbourhood. An unseen foot trod heavily on his toes, and at the same moment he received a violent shove that sent him staggering to the right against a seedy-looking person who thumped him in the ribs and sent him reeling back to the left. Before he could recover his balance, someone butted him in the back with such violence that he flew forward and impinged heavily on a small man in a straw hat – very much in it, in fact, for it had been banged down right over his eyes – who was beginning to protest angrily when some unseen force from behind propelled him towards Pottermack and another violent collision occurred. Thereafter, Pottermack had but a confused consciousness of being pushed, pulled, thumped, pinched, and generally hustled until his head swam. And then, quite suddenly, the crowd streamed away towards the course and Pottermack was left alone with the straw-hatted man, who stood a few yards away, struggling to extract himself from his hat and at the same time feverishly searching his pockets. By the well-known process of suggestion, this latter action communicated itself to Mr. Pottermack, who proceeded to make a hasty survey of his own pockets, which resulted in the discovery that, though the inside wallet, securely buttoned in, was still intact, the outside, empty one had this time disappeared, and most of his small change with it.

Strange are the inconsistencies of the human mind. But a little while ago he had been willing to make a free gift of that wallet to his red-faced fellow-traveller. Now that it was gone he was quite appreciably annoyed. He had planned to recharge it with a fresh consignment to be planted in a desirable quarter, and its loss left him with the necessity of making some other plausible arrangements, and at the moment he could not think of any. To put the notes loose in his pocket seemed to be but inviting failure, for, to the sense of touch from without, the pocket would appear to be empty.

As he was thus cogitating, he caught the eye of the straw-hatted gentleman fixed upon him with unmistakable and undissembled suspicion. This was unpleasant, but one must make allowances. The man was, no doubt, rather upset. With a genial smile, Mr. Pottermack approached the stranger and expressed the rather optimistic hope that he had not suffered any loss, but the only reply that his enquiry elicited was an inarticulate grunt.

"They have been through my pockets," said Mr. Pottermack cheerfully, "but I am glad to say that they took nothing of any value."

"Ha," said the straw-hatted gentleman.

"Yes," pursued Pottermack, "they must have found me rather disappointing."

"Oh," said the other in a tone of sour indifference.

"Yes," said Pottermack, "all they got from me was an empty letter-case and a little loose silver."

"Ah," said the straw-hatted man.

"I hope," Pottermack repeated, beginning slightly to lose patience, "that you have not lost anything of considerable value."

For a moment or two the other made no reply. At length, fixing a baleful eye on Pottermack, he answered with significant emphasis. "If you want to know what they took, you'd better ask them." And with this he turned away.

Pottermack also turned away – in the opposite direction, and some inward voice whispered to him that it were well to evacuate the neighbourhood of the man in the straw hat.

He strolled away, gradually increasing his pace, until he reached the outskirts of the crowd that had gathered at the margin of the course. By a sound of cheering, he judged that some ridiculous horses were careening along somewhere beyond the range of his vision. But they were of no interest to him. They did, however, furnish him with a pretext for diving into the crowd and struggling towards the source of the noise, and this he did, regardless of the unseemly comments that he provoked and the thumps and prods that he received in his progress. When, as it seemed, he had become immovably embedded, he drew a deep breath and turned to look back. For a few blissful moments he believed that he had effected a masterly retreat and escaped finally from his suspicious fellow-victim, but suddenly there emerged into view a too-familiar battered straw hat, moving slowly through the resisting multitude, and moving in a bee-line in his direction.

Then it was that Mr. Pottermack became seized with sudden panic. And no wonder. His previous experiences of the law had taught him that mere innocence is of no avail, and now, simply to be charged involved the risk of recognition and inevitable return to a convict prison. But apart from that, his position was one of extreme peril. On his person at this very moment were fifteen stolen notes of which he could give no account, but which connected him with that thing that reposed under the sun-dial. At the best, those notes might fairly send him to penal servitude. At the worst, to the gallows.

It is therefore no matter for surprise that the sight of that ominous straw hat sent a sudden chill down his spine. But Mr. Pottermack was no coward. Unforeseen as the danger was, he kept his nerve and made no outward sign of the terror that was clutching at his heart. Calmly he continued to worm his way through the crowd, glancing back now and again to note his distance from that relentless hat, and ever-looking for a chance to get rid of those fatal notes. For, if once he could get clear of those, he would be ready to face with courage and composure the lesser risk. But no chance ever came. Openly to jettison the notes in the midst of the crowd would have been fatal. He would have been instantly written down a detected and pursued pickpocket.

While his mind was busy with these considerations, his body was being skilfully piloted along the line of least resistance in the crowd. Now and again he made excursions into the less dense regions on the outskirts, thereby securing a gain in distance, only to plunge once more into the thick of the throng in the faint hope of being lost sight of. But this hope was never realized. On the whole, he maintained his distance from his pursuer and even slightly increased it. Sometimes for the space of a minute or more the absurd sleuth was lost to his view, but just as his hopes were beginning to revive, that accursed hat would make its reappearance and reduce him, if not to despair, at least to the most acute anxiety.

In the course of one of his excursions into the thinner part of the crowd, he noticed that, some distance ahead, a bold curve of the course brought it comparatively near to the entrance to the enclosure. He could see a steady stream of people still pouring in through the entrance turnstile, but that which gave exit from the ground was practically free. No one seemed to be leaving the enclosure at present, so the way out was quite unobstructed. Noting this fact with a new hope, he plunged once more into the dense crowd and set a course through it nearly parallel to the railings. When he had worked his way to a point nearly opposite to the entrance, he looked back to ascertain the whereabouts of his follower. The straw-hatted man was plainly visible, tightly jammed in the thickest part of the crowd and apparently not on amicable terms with his immediate neighbours. Pottermack decided that this was his chance and proceeded to take it. Skilfully extricating himself from the throng, he walked briskly towards the gates and made for the exit turnstile. As there was no one else leaving the ground, he passed out unhindered, pausing only for a moment to take a quick glance back. But what he saw in that glance was by no means reassuring. The straw-hatted man was, indeed, still tightly jammed in the thick of the crowd, but at his side was a policeman to whom he appeared to be making a statement as he pointed excitedly towards the turnstile. And both informer and constable seemed to be watching his departure.

Pottermack waited to see no more. Striding away from the entrance, he came to a road on which was a signpost pointing to the station. The

535

railway being the obvious means of escape, he turned in the opposite direction, which apparently led into the country. A short distance along the road, he encountered an aged man, engaged in trimming the hedge, who officiously wished him good-afternoon and whom he secretly anathematized for being there. A little farther on, round a sharp turn in the road, he came to a stile which gave access to a little-used footpath which crossed a small meadow. Vaulting over the stile, he set out along the footpath at a sharp walk. His impulse was to run, but he restrained it, realizing that a running man would attract attention where a mere walker might pass unobserved, or at least unnoticed. However, he quickly came to the farther side of the meadow, where another stile gave on a narrow by-lane. Here Pottermack paused for a moment, doubtful which way to turn, but the fugitive's instinct to get as far as possible from the pursuers decided the question. He turned in the direction that led away from the race-course.

Walking quickly along the lane for a minute or two, he came to a sudden turn and saw that, a short distance ahead, the lane opened into a road. At the same moment there rose among a group of elms on his right the tower of a church, and here the hedgerow gave place to a brick wall, broken by a wicket-gate, through which he looked into a green and pleasant churchyard. The road before him he surmised to be the one that he had left by the stile, and his surmise received most alarming confirmation. For, even at the very moment when he was entering the wicket, two figures walked rapidly across the end of the lane. One of them was a tall, military-looking man who swung along with easy but enormous strides, the other, who kept up with him with difficulty, was a small man in a battered straw hat.

With a gasp of horror, Pottermack darted in through the wicket and looked round wildly for possible cover. Then he saw that the church door was open, and, impelled, possibly, by some vague idea of sanctuary, bolted in. For a moment he stood at the threshold looking into the peaceful, silent interior, forgetting in his agitation even to take off his hat. There was no one in the church, but immediately confronting the intruder, securely bolted to a stone column, was a small iron-bound chest. On its front were painted the words "*Poor Box*", and above it, an inscription on a board informed Mr. Pottermack that "*The Lord Loveth a Cheerful Giver*".

Well, he had one that time. No sooner had Mr. Pottermack's eyes lighted on that box than he had whipped out his wallet and extracted the notes. With trembling fingers he folded them up in twos and threes and poked them through the slit, and when the final pair – as if protesting against his extravagant munificence – stuck in the opening and refused to

536

go in, he adroitly persuaded them with a penny, which he pushed through and dropped in by way of an additional thank-offering. As that penny dropped down with a faint, papery rustle, he put away his wallet and drew a deep breath. Mr. Pottermack was his own man again.

Of course, there was the straw-hatted man. But now that those incriminating notes were gone, so great was the revulsion that he could truly say, in the words of the late S. Pepys – or at least in a polite paraphrase of them – that he *"valued him not a straw"*. The entire conditions were changed. But as he turned with a new buoyancy of spirit to leave the church, there came to him a sudden recollection of the red-faced man's skill and ingenuity which caused him to thrust his hands into his pockets. And it was just as well that he did, for he brought up from his left-hand coat pocket a battered silver pencil-holder that was certainly not his and that advertised the identity of its legitimate owner by three initial letters legibly engraved on its flat end.

On this – having flung the pencil-holder out through the porch doorway into the high grass of the churchyard – he turned back into the building and made a systematic survey of his pockets, emptying each one in turn on to the cushioned seat of a pew. When he had ascertained beyond all doubt that none of them contained any article of property other than his own, he went forth with a light heart and retraced his steps through the wicket out into the lane, and, turning to the right, walked on towards the road. It had been his intention to return along it to the station, but when he came out of the lane, he found himself at the entrance to a village street and quite near to a comfortable-looking inn which hung out the sign of *"The Farmer's Boy"*. The sight of the homely hostelry reminded him that it was now well past his usual luncheon hour and made him aware of a fine, healthy appetite.

It appeared, on enquiry, that there was a cold sirloin in cut and a nice, quiet parlour in which to consume it. Pottermack smiled with anticipatory gusto at the report and gave his orders, and within a few minutes found himself in the parlour aforesaid, seated at a table covered with a clean white cloth on which was an abundant sample of the sirloin, a hunk of bread, a slab of cheese, a plate of biscuits, and a jovial, pot-bellied brown jug crowned with a cap of foam.

Mr. Pottermack enjoyed his lunch amazingly. The beef was excellent, the beer was of the best, and their combined effect was further to raise his spirits and lower his estimate of the straw-hatted man. He realized now that his initial panic had been due to those ill-omened notes, to the fact that a false charge might reveal the material for a real one of infinitely greater gravity. Now that he was clear of them, the fact that he was a man of substance and known position would be a sufficient answer to any mere casual suspicion. His confidence was completely restored, and he even speculated with detached interest on the possible chance of encountering his pursuers on his way back to the station.

He had finished the beef to the last morsel and was regarding with tepid interest the slab of high-complexioned cheese when the door opened and revealed two figures at the threshold, both of whom halted with their eyes fixed on him intently. After a moment's inspection, the shorter – who wore a battered straw hat – pointed to him and affirmed in impressive tones, "That's the man."

On this, the taller stranger took a couple of steps forward and said, as if repeating a formula, "I am a police officer." (It was a perfectly unnecessary statement. No one could have supposed that he was anything else). "This – er – gentleman informs me that you picked his pocket."

"Does he really?" said Pottermack, regarding him with mild surprise and pouring himself out another glass of beer.

"Yes, he does, and the question is, what have you got to say about it? It is my duty to caution you – "

"Not at all," said Pottermack. "The question is, what has *he* got to say about it? Has he given you any particulars?"

"No. He says you picked his pocket. That's all."

"Did he see me pick his pocket?"

The officer turned to the accuser. "Did you?" he asked.

"No, of course I didn't," snapped the other. "Pickpockets don't usually let you see what they are up to."

"Did he feel me pick his pocket?" Pottermack asked, with the air of a cross-examining counsel.

"Did you?" the officer asked, looking dubiously at the accuser.

"How could I," protested the latter, "when I was being pulled and shoved and hustled in the crowd?"

"Ha!" said Pottermack, taking a sip of beer. "He didn't *see* me pick his pocket, he didn't *feel* me pick his pocket. Now, how did he arrive at the conclusion that I *did* pick his pocket?"

The officer turned almost threateningly on the accuser.

"How did you?" he demanded.

"Well," stammered the straw-hatted man, "there was a gang of pickpockets and he was among them."

"But so were you," retorted Pottermack. "How do I know that you didn't pick my pocket? Somebody did."

"Oh!" said the officer. "Had your pocket picked too? What did they take of yours?"

"Mighty little – just a few oddments of small change. I kept my coat buttoned."

There was a slightly embarrassed silence, during which the officer, not for the first time, ran an appraising eye over the accused. His experience of pickpockets was extensive and peculiar, but it did not include any persons of Pottermack's type. He turned and directed a dubious and enquiring look at the accuser.

"Well," said the latter, "here he is. Aren't you going to take him into custody?"

"Not unless you can give me something to go on," replied the officer. "The station inspector wouldn't accept a charge of this sort."

"At any rate," said the accuser, "I suppose you will take his name and address?"

The officer grinned sardonically at the artless suggestion but agreed that it might be as well, and produced a large, funereal note-book.

"What is your name?" he asked.

"Marcus Pottermack," the owner of that name replied, adding "my address is The Chestnuts, Borley, Buckinghamshire."

The officer wrote down these particulars, and then closing the note-book, put it away with a very definite air of finality, remarking, "That's about all that we can do at present". But this did not at all meet the views of the straw-hatted man, who protested plaintively, "And you mean to say that you are going to let him walk off with my gold watch and my note-case with five pounds in it? You are not even going to search him?"

"You can't search people who haven't been charged," the officer growled, but here Pottermack interposed.

"There is no need," he said suavely, "for you to be hampered by mere technical difficulties. I know it is quite irregular, but if it would give you any satisfaction just to run through my pockets, I haven't the slightest objection."

The officer was obviously relieved. "Of course, sir, if you volunteer that is a different matter, and it would clear things up."

Accordingly, Pottermack rose and presented himself for the operation, while the straw-hatted man approached and watched with devouring eyes. The officer began with the wallet, noted the initials, M. P., on the cover, opened and considered the orderly arrangement of the stamps, cards and other contents, took out a visiting-card, read it and put it back, and finally laid the wallet on the table. Then he explored all the other pockets systematically and thoroughly, depositing the treasure trove from each on the table beside the wallet. When he had finished, he thanked Mr. Pottermack for his help, and turning to the accuser, demanded gruffly, "Well, are you satisfied now?"

"I should be better satisfied," the other man answered, "if I had got back my watch and my note-case. But I suppose he passed them on to one of his confederates."

Then the officer lost patience. "Look here," said he, "you are behaving like a fool. You come to a race-meeting, like a blooming mug, with a gold watch sticking out, asking for trouble, and when you get what you asked for, you let the crooks hop off with the goods while you go dandering about after a perfectly respectable gentleman. You bring me trapesing out here on a wild goose chase, and when it turns out that there isn't any wild goose, you make silly, insulting remarks. You ought to have more sense at your age. Now, I'll just take your name and address and then you'd better clear off."

Once more he produced the Black Maria note-book, and when he had entered the particulars he dismissed the straw-hatted man, who slunk off, dejected but still muttering.

Left alone with the late accused, the officer became genially and politely apologetic. But Pottermack would have none of his apologies. The affair had gone off to his complete satisfaction, and, in spite of some rather half-hearted protests, he insisted on celebrating the happy conclusion by the replenishment of the brown jug. Finally, the accused and the minion of the law emerged from the inn together and took their way back along the road to the station, beguiling the time by amicable converse on the subject of crooks and their ways and the peculiar mentality of the straw-hatted man.

It was a triumphant end to what had threatened to be a most disastrous incident. But yet, when he came to consider it at leisure, Pottermack was by no means satisfied. The expedition had been a failure, and he now wished, heartily, that he had left well alone and simply burnt the notes. His intention had been to distribute them in small parcels among various pickpockets, whereby they would have been thrown into circulation with the certainty that it would have been impossible to trace them. That scheme had failed utterly. There they were, fifteen stolen notes, in the poor-box of Illingham Church. When the reverend incumbent found them, he would certainly be surprised, and, no doubt, gratified. Of course, he would pay them into his bank, and then the murder would be out. The munificent gift would resolve itself into the dump of a hunted and hard-pressed pickpocket, and Mr. Pottermack's name and address was in the note-book of the plain-clothes constable.

Of course, there was no means of connecting him directly with the dump. But there was the unfortunate coincidence that both he and the stolen notes were connected with Borley, Buckinghamshire. That coincidence could hardly fail to be noticed, and, added to his known

540

proximity to the church, it might create a very awkward situation. In short, Mr. Pottermack had brought his pigs to the wrong market. He had planned to remove the area of investigation from his own neighbourhood to one at a safe and comfortable distance. Instead of which, he had laid down a clue leading straight to his own door.

It was a lamentable affair. As he sat in the homeward train with an unread evening paper on his knee, he found himself recalling the refrain of the old revivalist hymn and asking himself, "Oh, what shall the harvest be?"

Chapter IX
Providence Intervenes

In his capacity of medico-legal adviser to the Griffin Life Assurance Company, Thorndyke saw a good deal of Mr. Stalker, who, in addition to his connection with Perkins's Bank, held the post of Managing Director of the Griffin. For if the Bank had but rarely any occasion to seek Thorndyke's advice, the Assurance Office was almost daily confronted with problems which called for expert guidance. It thus happened that, about three weeks after the date of the Illingham Races, Thorndyke looked in at Mr. Stalker's office in response to a telephone message to discuss the discrepancies between a proposal form and the medical evidence given at an inquest on the late proposer. The matter of this discussion does not concern us and need not be detailed here. It occupied some considerable time, and when Thorndyke had stated his conclusions, he rose to take his departure. As he turned towards the door, Mr. Stalker held up a detaining hand.

"By the way, Doctor," said he, "I think you were rather interested in that curious case of disappearance that I told you about – one of our branch managers, you may remember."

"I remember," said Thorndyke, "James Lewson of your Borley branch."

"That's the man," Stalker assented, adding, "I believe you keep a card index in your head."

"And the best place to keep it," retorted Thorndyke. "But what about Lewson? Has he been run to earth?"

"No, but the notes that he took with him have. You remember that he went off with a hundred pounds – twenty five-pound notes, of all of which we were able to ascertain the numbers. Now, the numbers of those notes were at once given to the police, who circulated the information in all the likely quarters and kept a sharp look-out for their appearance. Yet in all this time, up to a week or two ago, there was not a sign of one of them. Then a most odd thing happened. The whole lot of them made their appearance almost simultaneously."

"Very remarkable," commented Thorndyke.

"Very," agreed Stalker. "But there is something still more queer about the affair. Of course, each note, as it was reported, was rigorously traced. As a rule there was no difficulty – up to a certain point. And at that point the trail broke off short, and that point was the possession of the note by a person known to the police. In every case in which tracing was possible, the trail led back to an unquestionable crook."

"And were the crooks unable to say where they got the notes?"

"Oh, not at all. They were able, in every case, to give the most lucid and convincing accounts of the way in which they came into possession of the notes. Only, unfortunately, not one of them could give 'a local habitation and a name'. They had all received the notes from total strangers."

"They probably had," said Thorndyke, "without the stranger's concurrence."

"Exactly. But you see the oddity of the affair – at least, I expect you do. Remember that, although the individual notes were reported at different times, on tracing them to their origin it looks almost as if the whole of them had come into circulation on the same day, about three weeks ago. Now, what does that suggest to you?"

"The obvious suggestion," replied Thorndyke, "seems to be that Lewson had been robbed, that some fortunate thief had managed to relieve him of the whole consignment at one coup. The only other explanation – and it is far less probable – is that Lewson deliberately jettisoned an incriminating cargo."

"Yes," Stalker agreed doubtfully, "that is a possibility, but, as you say, it is very much less probable. For if he had simply thrown them away, there would be no reason why they should have been so invariably traceable to a member of the criminal class, and surely, out of the whole lot, there would have been one or two honest persons who would admit to having found them. No, I feel pretty certain that Lewson has been robbed, and if he has, he must be in a mighty poor way. One is almost tempted to feel sorry for him."

"He has certainly made a terrible hash of his affairs," said Thorndyke, and with this, the subject having been exhausted, he picked up his hat and stick and took his departure.

But as he wended his way back to the Temple he cogitated profoundly on what Stalker had told him, and very surprised would Mr. Stalker have been if he could have been let into the matter of those cogitations. For, as to what had really happened, Thorndyke could make an approximate guess, though guesses were not very satisfying to a man of his exact habit of mind. But he had been expecting those notes to reappear, and he had expected that when they did reappear it would prove impossible to trace them to their real source.

Nevertheless, though events had befallen, so to speak, according to plan, he speculated curiously on the possible circumstances that had determined the issue of the whole consignment at once, and on arrival at his chambers he made certain notes in his private shorthand which he bestowed in a small portfolio labelled "*James Lewson*", which, in its turn, reposed, safely under lock and key, in the cabinet in which he kept his confidential documents.

Meanwhile, Mr. Pottermack was passing through a period of tribulation and gnawing anxiety. Again and again did he curse the folly that had impelled him, when everything seemed to have settled down so comfortably, to launch those notes into the world to start a fresh train of trouble. Again and again did he follow in imagination what appeared to be the inevitable course of events. With horrid vividness did his fancy reconstruct the scenes of that calamitous comedy, the astonished parson lifting the treasure with incredulous joy from the poor-box, the local bank manager carrying the notes round to the police station, the plain-clothes constable triumphantly producing his note-book and pointing to the significant word "*Borley*", and finally, the wooden-faced detective officer confronting him in his dining-room and asking embarrassing questions. Sometimes his imagination went farther, and, becoming morbid, pictured Mr. Gallett, the mason, volunteering evidence, with a resulting exploration of the well. But this was only when he was unusually depressed.

In his more optimistic moods he presented the other side of the case. If enquiries were made, he would, naturally, deny all knowledge of the notes. And who was to contradict him? There was not a particle of evidence that could connect him with them directly – at least, he believed there was not. But still, deep down in his consciousness was the knowledge that he *was* connected with them, that he had taken them from the dead man's pocket and he had dumped them in the church. And Mr. Pottermack was no more immune than the rest of us from the truth that "conscience does make cowards of us all".

So, in those troublous times, by day and by night, in his walks abroad and in his solitude at home, he lived in a state of continual apprehension. The fat was in the fire and he waited with constantly strained ears to catch the sound of its sizzling, and though, as the days and then the weeks went by and no sound of sizzling became audible, the acuteness of his anxiety wore off, still his peace of mind was gone utterly and he walked in the shadow of dangers unknown and incalculable. And so he might have gone on indefinitely but for one of those trivial chances that have befallen most of us and that sometimes produce results so absurdly disproportionate to their own insignificance.

The occasion of this fortunate chance was a long, solitary walk through the beautiful Buckinghamshire lanes. Of late, in his disturbed state of mind, which yielded neither to the charms of his garden nor the allurements of his workshop, Mr. Pottermack had developed into an inveterate pedestrian, and on this particular day he had taken a long round, which brought him at length, tired and hungry, to the town of Aylesbury, where, at a frowsy restaurant in a bystreet, he sat him down to rest and feed. It was a frugal meal that he ordered, for with the joy of living had gone his zest for food. Indeed, to such depths of despondency had he sunk that he actually scandalized the foreign proprietor by asking for a glass of water.

Now, it happened that on an adjacent chair was an evening paper. It was weeks old, badly crumpled and none too clean. Almost automatically, Mr. Pottermack reached out for it, laid it on the table beside him, and smoothed out its crumpled pages. Not that he had any hankering for news, but like most of us, he had contracted the pernicious habit of miscellaneous reading – which is often but an idle substitute for thought – and he scanned the ill-printed columns in mere boredom. He was not in the least interested in the Hackney man who had kicked a cat and been fined forty shillings. No doubt it served him right – and the cat too, perhaps – but it was no affair of his, Pottermack's. Nevertheless he let an inattentive eye ramble aimlessly up and down the page, lightly scanning the trivial vulgarities that headed the paragraphs, while in the background of his consciousness, hovering, as it were, about the threshold, lurked the everlasting theme of those accursed notes.

Suddenly his roving eye came to a dead stop, for it had alighted on the word "*Illingham*". With suddenly sharpened attention, he turned back to the heading and read:

Sacrilege in a Surrey Church

A robbery of a kind that is now becoming increasingly common occurred late in the afternoon of last Tuesday at the picturesque and venerable church of Illingham. This was the day of the races on the adjacent course, and it is believed that the outrage was committed by some of the doubtful characters who are always to be found at race-meetings. At any rate, when the sexton entered to close the church in the evening, he found that the lid of the poor-box had been wrenched open, and of course, the contents, whatever they may have been, abstracted. The rector is greatly distressed at the occurrence, not on account of what has been stolen – for he remarked, with a pensive smile, that the loss is probably limited to the cost of repairing the box – but because he holds strong opinions on the duty of a clergyman

545

to leave his church open for private prayer and meditation,
and he fears that he may be compelled to close it in future, at
least on race-days.

Mr. Pottermack read this paragraph through, first with ravenous haste and then again, slowly and with the minutest attention. It was incredible. He could hardly believe the evidence of his eyes. Yet there it was, a clear and unmistakable message, of which the marvellous significance was to be grasped by him alone of all the world. Providence – which is reported to make some queer selections for its favourites – had stepped in and mercifully repaired his error.

In a moment he was a new man, or rather the old man restored. For he was saved. Now could he go abroad with a confident step and look the world in the face. Now could he take his ease at home in peace and security, could return with gusto to his garden and know once more the joys of labour in his workshop. With a fresh zest he fell to upon the remainder of his meal. He even electrified the proprietor by calling for coffee and a green Chartreuse. And when he at length went forth refreshed to take the road homeward, he seemed to walk upon air.

Chapter X
A Retrospect

The fortunate ending of the great note adventure, which had at one time looked so threatening, had a profound effect on Mr. Pottermack's state of mind, and through this on his subsequent actions. Wherever the notes might be circulating, they were, he felt confident, well out of his neighbourhood, and since they had all fallen into the hands of thieves, he was equally confident that they would prove untraceable. So far as he was concerned, they had served their purpose. The field of inquiry concerning Lewson's disappearance was now shifted from Borley to the localities in which those notes had made their appearance.

Thus, to Mr. Pottermack it appeared that he was finally rid of Lewson, alive or dead. The incident was closed. He could now consign the whole horrible affair to oblivion, forget it if he could, or at least remember it only as a hideous experience which he had passed through and finished with, just as he might remember certain other experiences which belonged to the unhappy past. Now he might give his whole attention to the future. He was still a comparatively young man, despite the grizzled hair upon his temples. And Fortune was deeply in his debt. It was time that he began to collect from her some of the arrears.

Now, whenever Mr. Pottermack let his thoughts stray into the future, the picture that his fancy painted was wont to present a certain constant deviation from the present. It was not that the surroundings were different. Still in imagination he saw himself rambling through the lovely Buckinghamshire lanes, busying himself in his workshop, or whiling away the pleasant hours in the walled garden among his flowers and his fruit trees. But in those pictures of the sunny future that was to indemnify him for the gloomy past there were always two figures, and one of them was that of the comely, gracious young widow who had already brought so much sunshine into his rather solitary life.

During the last few strenuous weeks he had seen little of her – indeed he had hardly seen her at all. Now that he could put behind him for ever the events that had filled those weeks, now that he was free from the haunting menace of the blackmailer's incalculable actions and could settle down to a stable life with his future in his own hands, the time had arrived when he might begin to mould that future in accordance with his heart's desire.

Thus reflecting on the afternoon following his visit to Aylesbury, he proceeded to make the first move. Having smartened himself up in a modest way, he took down from his shelves a favourite volume to serve as a pretext for a call and set forth with it in his pocket towards the quiet lane on the fringe of the town wherein Mrs. Alice Bellard had her habitation. And a very pleasant habitation it was, though, indeed, it was no more than an old-fashioned country cottage, built to supply the simple needs of some rural worker or village craftsman. But houses, like dogs, have a way of reflecting the personalities of their owners, and this little dwelling, modest as it was, conveyed to the beholder a subtle sense of industry, of ordered care, and a somewhat fastidious taste.

Pottermack stood for a few moments with his hand on the little wooden gate, looking up with an appreciative eye at the ripe red brickwork, the golden tiles of the roof, and the little stone tablet with the initials of the first owners and the date, *1761*. Then he opened the latch and walked slowly up the path. Through the open window came the sound of a piano rendering, with no little skill and feeling, one of Chopin's *Preludes*. He waited at the door, listening, until the final notes of the piece were played. Then he turned and rapped out a flourish on the brightly burnished brass knocker.

Almost immediately the door opened, revealing a girl of about sixteen, who greeted him with a friendly smile, and forthwith, without question or comment inducted him to the sitting-room, where Mrs. Bellard had just risen from the piano-stool.

"I am afraid," said he, as they shook hands, "that I am interrupting your playing – in fact, I know I am. I was half-inclined to wait out in the garden and enjoy your performance without disturbing you."

"That would have been foolish of you," she replied, "when there is a nice, comfortable armchair in which you can sit and smoke your pipe and listen at your ease – if you want to."

"I do, most certainly," said he. "But first, lest I should forget it, let me hand you this book. I mentioned it to you once – *The Harvest of a Quiet Eye*. It is by a nice old west country parson and I think you will like it."

"I am sure I shall if you do," she said. "We seem to agree in most things."

"So we do," assented Pottermack, "even to our favourite brands of snail. Which reminds me that the pleasures of the chase seem to have been rather neglected of late."

"Yes, I have been quite busy lately furbishing up the house. But I have nearly finished. In a few days I shall have everything straight and tidy, and then a-snailing we will go."

"We will," he agreed, "and if we find that we are exhausting the subject of molluscs, we might, perhaps, give a passing thought to the question of beetles. They are practically inexhaustible, and they are not so hackneyed as butterflies and moths, and not so troublesome to keep. And they are really very beautiful and interesting creatures."

"I suppose they are," she said a little doubtfully, "when you have got over your prejudice against their undeniable tendency to crawliness. But I am afraid you will have to do the slaughtering. I really couldn't kill the poor little wretches."

"Oh, I will do that cheerfully," said Pottermack, "if you will make the captures."

"Very well, then, on that understanding I will consider the beetle question. And now, would you really like me to play to you a little?"

"I should like it immensely. I seem to hear so little music nowadays, and you play so delightfully. But are you sure you don't mind?"

She laughed softly as she sat down at the piano. "Mind, indeed!" she exclaimed. "Did you ever know a musician who wasn't only too delighted to play to a sympathetic listener? It is the whole joy and reward of the art. Now, you just sit in that chair and fill your pipe, and I will play to you some of the things that I like playing to myself and that you have got to like too."

Obediently Pottermack seated himself in the easy-chair and reflectively filled his pipe while he watched the skilful hands moving gracefully with effortless precision over the keyboard. At first she kept to regular *pianoforte* music, mostly that of Chopin: One or two of the shorter nocturnes, a prelude and a polonaise, and a couple of Mendelssohn's "*Lieder*". But presently she began to ramble away reminiscently among all sorts of unconventional trifles: Old-fashioned songs, country dances, scraps of church music, and even one or two time-honoured hymn tunes. And as she played these simple melodies, softly, tastefully, and with infinite feeling, she glanced furtively from time to time at her visitor until, seeing he was no longer looking at her but was gazing dreamily out of the window, she let her eyes rest steadily on his face. There was something very curious in that long, steady look, a strange mingling of sadness, of pity and tenderness, and of yearning affection with a certain vague anxiety, as if something in his face was puzzling her. The eyes that dwelt on him with such soft regard yet seemed to ask a question.

And Pottermack, sitting motionless as a statue, grasping his unlighted pipe, let the simple, homely melodies filter into his soul and deliver their message of remembrance. His thoughts were at once near and far away, near to the woman at his side, yet far away from the quiet room and the sunlit garden on which his eyes seemed to rest. Let us for a while leave him to his reverie, and if we may not follow his thoughts, at least – in order that we may the better enter into the inwardness of this history – transport ourselves into the scenes that memory is calling up before his eyes.

Fifteen years ago there was no such person as Marcus Pottermack. The sober, middle-aged man, greyheaded, bearded, spectacled, who sits dreaming in the widow's parlour, was a handsome, sprightly youth of twenty-two – Jeffrey Brandon by name – who, with his shapely, clean-shaven face and his striking Grecian nose, had the look and manner of a young Olympian. And his personality matched his appearance. Amiable and kindly by nature, with a gay and buoyant temperament that commended him alike to friends and strangers, his keen intelligence, his industry and energy, promised well for his worldly success in the future.

Young as he was, he had been, at this time, engaged for two years. And here again he was more than commonly fortunate. It was not merely that the maiden of his choice was comely, sweet-natured, clever and accomplished, or that she was a girl of character and spirit, or even that she had certain modest expectations. The essence of the good fortune lay in the fact that Jeffrey Brandon and Alice Bentley were not merely lovers, they were staunch friends and sympathetic companions, with so many interests in common that it was incredible that they should ever tire of each other's society.

One of their chief interests – perhaps the greatest – was music. They were both enthusiasts. But whereas Jeffrey's accomplishments went no farther than a good ear, a pleasant baritone voice, and the power of singing a part at sight, Alice was really a musician. Her skill at the piano was of the professional class, she was a fair organist, and in addition she had a good and well-trained contralto voice. Naturally enough, it happened that they drifted into the choir of the little friendly Evangelical church that they attended together, and this gave them a new and delightful occupation. Now and again Alice would take a service at the organ, and then there were practice nights and preparations for special services, musical festivals or informal sacred concerts which kept them busy with the activities that they both loved. And so their lives ran on, serenely, peacefully, filled with quiet enjoyment of the satisfying present, with the promise of a yet more happy future when they should be married and in full possession of each other.

And then, in a moment, the whole fabric of their happiness collapsed like a house of cards. As if in an incomprehensible nightmare, the elements of that tragedy unfolded – the amazing accusation, the still more amazing discovery, the trial at the Old Bailey Sessions, the

550

conviction, the sentence, the bitter, despairing farewell, and, last of all, the frowning portals of the convict prison.

Of course, Alice Bentley scouted the idea of her lover's guilt. She roundly declared that the whole affair was a plot, a wicked and foolish miscarriage of justice, and she announced her intention of meeting him at the prison gate when he should be set free, to claim him as her promised husband, that she might try to make up to him by her devotion and sympathy what he had suffered from the world's injustice. And when it was coldly pointed out to her that he had had a fair trial and had been found guilty by a jury of his fellow-countrymen, she broke away indignantly and thereafter withdrew herself from the society of these fair-weather friends.

Meanwhile, the unfortunate Jeffrey, meditating in his prison cell, had come with no less resolution to his decision. In so far as was possible, he would bear the burden of his misfortune alone. Deeply, passionately as he loved the dear girl who, almost alone of all the world, still believed in his innocence, he must cast her out of his life for ever. He gloried in her loyalty, but he could not accept her sacrifice. Alice – his Alice – should never marry a convict. For that was what he was: A convicted thief and forger, and nothing but a miracle could alter his position. The fact that he was innocent was beside the mark, since his innocence was known only to himself and one other – the nameless villain who had set this infamous trap for him. To all the rest of the world he was a guilty man, and the world was right according to the known facts. He had had a fair trial, a perfectly fair trial. The prosecution had not been vindictive, the judge had summed up fairly, and the jury had found him guilty, and the jury had been right. On the evidence before them, they could have found no other verdict. He had no complaint against them. No one could have guessed that all the evidence was false and illusory. From which it followed that he must go through life stamped as a convicted thief, and as such could never be a possible husband for Alice Bentley.

But he realized very clearly that Alice, certain as she was of his innocence, would utterly refuse to accept this view. To her he was a martyr, and as such she would proclaim him before all the world. On his release, she would insist on the restoration of the *status quo ante*. Of that he felt certain, and hour after hour, in his abundant solitude, he sought vainly a solution of the problem. How should he meet her demand? Letters he knew would be useless. She would wait for the day of his release, and then – The prospect of having, after all, to refuse her love, to repudiate her loyalty, was one that wrung his heart to contemplate.

And then, in the most unforeseen way, the problem was solved. His escape from the gang was totally unpremeditated. He just saw a chance, when the attention of the civil guard was relaxed, and took it instantly. When he found the absent bather's clothes upon the shore and hastily assumed them in place of his prison suit, he suspected that the bather was already dead, and the report which he read in the next day's paper confirmed this belief. But during the next few weeks, as he tramped across country to Liverpool – subsisting, not without qualms, on the little money that he had found in the unknown bather's pockets, eked out by an occasional odd job – he watched the papers eagerly for further news. For six long weeks he found nothing either to alarm or reassure him. Indeed, it was not until he had secured a job as deck-hand on an American tramp steamer and was on the point of departure that he learned the welcome tidings. On the very night before the ship was due to sail, he was sitting in the forecastle, watching an evening paper that was passing round from hand to hand, when the man who was reading it held it towards him, pointing with a grimy forefinger to a particular paragraph.

"I call that damned hard luck, I do," said he. "Just you read it, mate, and see what you think of it."

Jeffrey took the paper, and, glancing at the indicated paragraph, suddenly sat up with a start. It was the report of an inquest on the body of a man who had been found drowned, which body had been identified as that of Jeffrey Brandon, a convict who had recently escaped from Colport Gaol. He read it through slowly, and then, with an inarticulate mumble, handed the paper back to his sympathetic messmate. For some minutes he sat dazed, hardly able to realize this sudden change in his condition. That the bather's body would, sooner or later, be found he had never doubted. But he had expected that the finding of it and its identification would solve the mystery of his escape and immediately give rise to a hue-and-cry. Never had he dreamed that the body could be identified as his.

But now that this incredible thing had happened, he would be simply written off and forgotten. He was free. And not only was he free, Alice was free too. Now he would quietly pass out of her life without bitterness or misunderstanding – not forgotten, indeed, but cherished only, in the years to come, with loving remembrance.

Nevertheless, when at daybreak on the morrow the good ship *Potomac of New Orleans* crossed the Mersey bar, the new deck-hand, Joe Watson, looked back at the receding land with a heavy heart and a moistening eye. The world was all before him. But it was an empty world. All that could make life gracious and desirable was slipping away

552

farther with each turn of the propeller, and a waste of waters was stretching out between him and his heart's desire.

His life in America need not be followed in detail. He was of the type that almost inevitably prospers in that country. Energetic, industrious, handy, ready to put his heart into any job that offered, an excellent accountant with a sound knowledge of banking business and general finance, he was not long in finding a position in which he could prove his worth. And he had undeniably good luck. Within a year of his landing, almost penniless, he had managed, by hard work and the most drastic economy, to scrape together a tiny nest-egg of capital. Then he met with a young American, nearly as poor as himself but of the stuff of which millionaires are made, a man of inexhaustible energy, quick, shrewd and resolute, and possessed by a devouring ambition to be rich. But notwithstanding his avidity for wealth, Joseph Walden was singularly free from the vices of his class. He looked to become rich by work, good management, thrift, and a reputation for straight dealing. He was a man of strict integrity, and, if a little blunt and outspoken, was still a good friend and a pleasant companion.

With his shrewd judgment, Walden saw at once that his new friend would make an ideal collaborator in a business venture. Each had special qualifications that the other lacked, and the two together would form a highly efficient combination. Accordingly the two young men pooled forces and embarked under the style and title of the Walden Pottermack Company. (Jeffrey had abandoned the name of Joe Watson on coming ashore, and, moved by some whimsical sentiment, had adopted as his godparent the ship which had carried him away to freedom and the new life. With a slight variation of spelling, he was now Marcus Pottermack.)

For some time, the new firm struggled on under all the difficulties that attend insufficient capital. But the two partners held together in absolute unison. They neglected no chances, they spared no effort, they accepted willingly the barest profits, and they practised thrift to the point of penury. And slowly the tension of poverty relaxed. The little snowball of their capital began to grow, imperceptibly at first, but then with a constantly increasing acceleration – for wealth, like population, tends to increase by geometrical progression. In a year or two the struggles were over and the Company was a well-established concern. A few more years and the snowball had rolled up to quite impressive dimensions. The Walden Pottermack Company had become a leading business house, and the partners men of respectable substance.

It was at this point that the difference between the two men began to make itself apparent. To the American, the established prosperity of the firm meant the attainment of the threshold of big business with the prospect of really big money. His fixed intention was to push the success for all that it was worth, to march on to greater and yet greater things, even unto million-airedom. Pottermack, on the other hand, began to feel that he had enough. Great wealth held out no allurements for him. Nor did he, like Walden, enjoy the sport of winning and piling it up. At first he had worked hard for a mere livelihood, then for a competence that should presently enable him to live his own life. And now, as he counted up his savings, it seemed to him that he had achieved his end. With what he had, he could purchase all that he desired and that was purchasable.

It was not purchasable in America. Grateful as he was to the country that had sheltered him and taken him to her heart as one of her own sons, yet he found himself from time to time turning a wistful eye towards the land beyond the great ocean. More and more, as the time went on, he was conscious of a hankering for things that America could not give – for the sweet English countryside, the immemorial villages with their ancient churches, their oast-houses and thatched barns, for all the lingering remains of an older civilization.

And there was another element of unrest. All through the years the image of Alice had never ceased to haunt him. At first it was but as the cherished memory of a loved one who had died and passed out of his life for ever. But as the years ran on there came a subtle change. Gradually he began to think of their separation, not as something final and irretrievable but as admitting in a vague and shadowy way of the idea of reunion this side of the grave. It was very nebulous and indefinite, but it clung to him persistently, and ever the idea grew more definite. The circumstances were, indeed, changed utterly. When he left her, he was a convict, infamous in the eyes of all the world. But the convict, Jeffrey Brandon, was dead and forgotten, whereas he, Marcus Pottermack, was a man of position and repute. The case was entirely altered.

So he would argue with himself in moments of expansiveness. And then he would cast away his dreams, chiding himself for his folly and telling himself that doubtless she had long since married and settled down, that dead he was and dead he must remain, and not seek to rise again like some unquiet spirit to trouble the living.

Nevertheless, the leaven continued to work, and the end of it was that Mr. Pottermack wound up his business affairs and made arrangements for his retirement. His partner regretfully agreed to take over his interest in the company – which he did on terms that were not merely just but generous – and thus his commercial life came to an end. A week or two later he took his passage for England.

Now, nebulous and shadowy as his ideas had been with reference to Alice, partaking rather of the nature of day-dreams than of thoughts implying any settled purpose, no sooner had he landed in the Old Country than he became possessed by a craving, at least to hear of her, to make certain that she was still alive, if possible to see her. He could not conceal from himself some faint hope that she might still be unmarried. And if she were – well, then it would be time for him to consider what he would do.

His first proceeding was to establish himself in lodgings in the old neighbourhood, where he spent his days loitering about the streets that she had been used to frequent. On Sundays he attended the church with scrupulous regularity, modestly occupying a back seat and lingering in the porch as the congregation filed out. Many familiar faces he noted, changed more-or-less by the passage of time, but no one recognized in the grey-haired, bearded, spectacled stranger the handsome youth whom they had known in the years gone by. Indeed, how should they, when that youth had died, cut off in the midst of his career of crime?

He would have liked to make some discreet enquiries, but no enquiries would have been discreet. Above all things, it was necessary for him to preserve his character as a stranger from America. And so he could do no more than keep his vigil in the streets and at the church, watching with hungry eyes for the beloved face – and watching in vain.

And then at last, after weeks of patient searching with ever-dwindling hope, he had his reward. It was on Easter Sunday, a day which had, in old times, been kept as the chief musical festival of the year. Apparently the custom was still maintained, for the church was unusually full and there was evidently a special choir. Mr. Pottermack's hopes revived, though he braced himself for another disappointment. Surely, he thought, if she ever comes to this church, she will come to-day.

And this time he was not disappointed. He had not long been seated on the modest bench near the door when a woman, soberly dressed in black, entered and walked past him up the aisle, where she paused for a few moments looking about her somewhat with the air of a stranger. He knew her in a moment by her figure, her gait, and the poise of her head. But if he had had any doubt, it would have been instantly dispelled when she entered a pew, and, before sitting down, glanced back quickly at the people behind her.

For Pottermack it was a tremendous moment. It was as if he were looking on the face of one risen from the dead. For some minutes after she had sat down and become hidden from his sight by the people behind her he felt dazed and half-incredulous of the wonderful vision that he had seen. But as the effects of the shock passed, he began to consider the present position. That single instantaneous glance had shown him that she had aged a little more than the lapse of time accounted for. She

555

looked graver than of old, perhaps even a thought sombre, and something matronly and middle-aged in the fashion of her dress made disquieting suggestions.

When the long service was ended, Pottermack waited on his bench watching her come down the aisle and noting that she neither spoke to nor seemed to recognize any one. As soon as she had passed his bench, he rose and joined the throng behind her. His intention was to follow her and discover, if possible, where she lived. But as they came into the crowded porch he heard an elderly woman exclaim in a markedly loud tone, "Why, surely it is Miss Bentley!"

"Yes," was the reply in the well-remembered voice. "At least, I was Miss Bentley when you knew me. Nowadays I am Mrs. Bellard."

Pottermack, standing close behind her and staring at a notice-board, drew a deep breath. Only in that moment of bitter disappointment did he realize how much he had hoped.

"Oh, indeed," said the loud-spoken woman. "Mrs. Bennett – it was Bennett that you said?"

"No, *Bellard. B – E – L – L – A – R – D.*"

"Oh, Bellard. Yes. And so you are married. I have often wondered what became of you when you stopped coming to the church after – er – all those years ago. I hope your good husband is well."

"I lost my husband four years ago," Mrs. Bellard replied in a somewhat dry, matter-of-fact tone.

Pottermack's heart gave a bound and he listened harder than ever.

"Dear, dear!" exclaimed the other woman. "What a dreadfully sad thing! And are there any children?"

"No, no children."

"Ah, indeed. But perhaps it is as well, though it must be lonely for you. Are you living in London?"

"No," replied Mrs. Bellard, "I have only just come up for the week-end. I live at Borley in Buckinghamshire – not far from Aylesbury."

"Do you? It must be frightfully dull for you, living all alone right down in the country. I do hope you have found comfortable lodgings".

Mrs. Bellard laughed softly. "You are pitying me more than you need, Mrs. Goodman. I am not dull at all, and I don't have to live in lodgings. I have a house to myself. It is only a very small one, but it is big enough and it is my own, so I am secure of a shelter for the rest of my life."

Here the two women drifted out of distinct ear-shot, though their voices continued to be audible as they walked away, for they both spoke in raised tones, Mrs. Goodman being, apparently, a little dull of hearing. But Pottermack had heard enough. Drawing out his pocket-book, he carefully entered the name and the address, such as it was, glancing at the notice-board as if he were copying some particulars from it. Then he emerged from the porch and walked after the two women, and when they separated, he followed Mrs. Bellard at a discreet distance – not that he now had any curiosity as to her present place of abode, but merely that he might pleasure his eyes with the sight of her trim figure tripping youthfully along the dull suburban street.

Mr. Pottermack's joy and triumph were tempered with a certain curiosity, especially with regard to the late Mr. Bellard. But his cogitations were not permitted to hinder the necessary action. Having no time-table, it being Sunday, he made his way to Marylebone Station to get a list of the week-day trains, and at that station he presented himself on the following morning at an unearthly hour, suitcase in hand, to catch the first train to Borley. Arrived at the little town, he at once took a room at the Railway Inn, from whence he was able conveniently to issue forth and stroll down the station approach as each of the London trains came in.

It was late in the afternoon when, among the small crowd of passengers who came out of the station, he saw her, stepping forward briskly and carrying a good-sized handbag. He turned, and, walking back slowly up the approach, let her pass him and draw a good distance ahead. He kept her in sight without difficulty in the sparsely peopled streets until, at the outskirts of the town, she turned into a quiet by-lane and disappeared. Thereupon he quickened his pace and entered the lane just in time to see her opening the garden gate of a pleasant-looking cottage, at the open door of which a youthful maidservant stood, greeting her with a welcoming grin. Pottermack walked slowly past the little house, noting the name, "*Lavender Cottage*" painted on the gate, and went on to the top of the lane, where he turned and retraced his steps, indulging himself as he passed the second time with a long and approving look at the shrine which held the object of his worship.

On his return to the inn, he proceeded to make enquiries as to a reliable house-agent, in response to which he was given, not only the name of a recommended agent, but certain other more valuable information. For the landlord, interested in a prospective new resident, was questioning Pottermack as to the class of house that he was seeking when the landlady interposed.

"What about The Chestnuts, Tom, where Colonel Barnett used to live? That's empty and for sale – been empty for months. And it's a good house, though rather out-of-the-way. Perhaps that might suit this gentleman."

Further details convinced Mr. Pottermack that it would, and the upshot was that on the very next day, after a careful inspection, the deposit was paid to the agents, Messrs. Hook and Walker, and a local solicitor was instructed to carry out the conveyance. Within a week the principal builder of the town had sent in his estimates for repairs and decoration, and Mr. Pottermack was wrestling with the problem of household furnishing amidst a veritable library of catalogues.

But these activities did not distract him from his ultimate object. Realizing that, as a stranger to the town, his chance of getting a regular introduction to Mrs. Bellard was infinitely remote, he decided to waive the conventions and take a short-cut. But the vital question was, would she recognize him? It was a question that perplexed him profoundly and that he debated endlessly without reaching any conclusion. Of course, under normal circumstances there would be no question at all. Obviously, in spite of his beard, his spectacles, and his grey hair, she would recognize him instantly. But the circumstances were very far from normal. To her, he was a person who had died some fifteen years ago. And the news of his death would have come to her, not as a mere rumour or vague report, but as an ascertained fact. He had been found dead and identified by those who knew him well. She could never have had a moment's doubt that he was dead.

How, then, would she react to the conflict between her knowledge and the evidence of her senses? Which of the two alternate possibilities would she accept? That a dead man might come to life again or that one human being might bear so miraculous a resemblance to another? He could form no opinion. But of one thing he felt confident. She would certainly be deeply impressed by the resemblance, and that state of mind would easily cover anything unconventional in the manner of their meeting.

His plan was simple to crudeness. At odd times, in the intervals of his labours, he made it his business to pass the entrance of the lane – Malthouse Lane was its name – from whence he could see her house. For several days no opportunity presented itself. But one morning, a little more than a week after his arrival, on glancing up the lane, he perceived a manifestly feminine hat above the shrubs in her garden. Thereupon he turned boldly into the little thoroughfare and walked on until he was opposite the cottage, when he could see her, equipped with gardening gloves and a rather juvenile fork, tidying up the borders. Unobserved by her, he stepped up to the wooden palings, and, lifting his hat, enquired apologetically if she could inform him whether, if he followed the lane, he would come to the Aylesbury Road.

At the first sound of his voice she started up and gazed at him with an expression of the utmost astonishment, nor was her astonishment diminished when she looked at his face. For an appreciable time she stood quite still and rigid, with her eyes fixed on him and her lips parted as if she had seen a spectre. After an interval, Pottermack – who was more-or-less prepared, though his heart was thumping almost audibly – repeated his question, with apologies for intruding on her, whereupon, recovering herself with an effort, she came across to the palings and began to give him some directions in a breathless, agitated voice, while the gloved hand that she rested on the palings trembled visibly.

Pottermack listened deferentially and then ventured to explain his position – that he was a stranger, about to settle in the district, and anxious to make himself acquainted with his new surroundings. As this was received quite graciously, he went on to comment in admiring terms on the appearance of the cottage and its happy situation in this pleasant leafy lane. Through this channel they drifted into amicable conversation concerning the town and the surrounding country, and as they talked – Pottermack designedly keeping his face partially turned away from her – she continued to watch him with a devouring gaze and with a curious expression of bewilderment and incredulity mingled with something reminiscent, far away and dreamy. Finally, encouraged by his success, Pottermack proceeded to expound the embryonic state of his household, and enquired if by any chance she happened to know of a reliable middle-aged woman who would take charge of it.

"How many are you in family?" Mrs. Bellard asked with ill-concealed eagerness.

"My entire family," he replied, "is covered by one rather shabby hat."

"Then you ought to have no difficulty in finding a housekeeper. I do, in fact," she continued, "know of a woman who might suit you, a middle-aged widow named Gadby – quite a Dickens name, isn't it? I know very little about her abilities, but I do know that she is a pleasant, good-natured, and highly respectable woman. If you like, and will give me your address, I will send her to see you."

Mr. Pottermack jumped at the offer, and having written down his name and his address at the inn (at the former of which she glanced with eager curiosity) he thanked her warmly and, wishing her good-morning with a flourish of the shabby hat, went on his way rejoicing. That same evening, Mrs. Gadby called at the inn and was promptly engaged, and a very fortunate transaction the engagement proved. For not only did she turn out to be an incomparable servant, but she constituted herself a link between her employer and her patroness. Not that the link was extremely necessary, for whenever Pottermack chanced to meet Mrs. Bellard – and it was surprising how often it happened – she greeted him frankly as an acknowledged acquaintance, so that gradually – and not so very gradually either – their footing as acquaintances ripened into that of friends. And so, as the weeks passed and their friendship grew up into a pleasant, sympathetic intimacy, Mr. Pottermack felt that all was going well and that the time was at hand when he should collect some of the arrears that were outstanding in his account with Fortune.

But Fortune had not done with him yet. The card that she held up her sleeve was played a few weeks after he had entered into occupation of his new house and was beginning to be comfortably settled. He was standing by the counter of a shop where he had made some purchases when he became aware of some person standing behind him and somewhat to his left. He could not see the person excepting as a vague shadow, but he had the feeling that he was being closely scrutinized. It was not a pleasant feeling, for, altered as he was, some inopportune recognition was always possible, and when the person moved from the left side to the right, Mr. Pottermack began to grow distinctly apprehensive. His right ear bore a little purple birthmark that was highly distinctive, and the movement of the unknown observer associated itself very disagreeably in his mind with this mark. After enduring the scrutiny for some time with growing uneasiness, he turned and glanced at the face of the scrutinizer. Then he received a very distinct shock, but at the same time was a little reassured. For the stranger was not a stranger at all, but his old friend and fellow-clerk, James Lewson.

Involuntarily his face must have given some sign of recognition, but this he instantly suppressed. He had no fear of his old friend, but still, he had renounced his old identity and had no intention of acknowledging it. He had entered on a new life with a new personality. Accordingly, after a brief glance, as indifferent as he could make it, he turned back to the counter and concluded his business. And Lewson, for his part, made no outward sign of recognition, so that Pottermack began to hope that he had merely noticed an odd resemblance, without any suspicion of actual identity. After all, that was what one would expect, seeing that the Jeffrey Brandon whom he resembled had been dead nearly fifteen years.

But when he left the shop and went his way through the streets on other business, he soon discovered that Lewson was shadowing him closely. Once or twice he put the matter to the test by doubling back or darting through obscure passages and by-ways, and when he still found Lewson doggedly clinging to his skirts, he had to accept the conviction that he had been recognized and deal with the position to the best of his discretion. Accordingly, he made straight for home, but instead of

560

entering by the front door, he took the path that skirted the long wall of his garden and let himself in by the small side gate, which he left unlatched behind him. A minute later, Lewson pushed it open and looked in then, seeing that the garden was unoccupied save by Pottermack, he entered and shut the gate.

"Well, Jeff," he said genially, as he faced Pottermack, "so here you are. A brand – or shall we say a Brandon – snatched from the burning. I always wondered if you had managed to do a mizzle, you are such an uncommonly downy bird."

Pottermack made a last, despairing effort. "Pardon me," said he, "but I fancy you must be mistaking me for – "

"Oh, rats," interrupted Lewson. "Won't do, old chap. Besides, I saw that you recognized me. No use pretending that you don't know your old pal, and certainly no use pretending that he doesn't know you."

Pottermack realised the unwelcome truth and, like a wise man, bowed to the inevitable.

"I suppose it isn't," he admitted, "and, for that matter, I don't know that there is any reason why I should. But you will understand that – "

"Oh, I understand well enough," said Lewson. "Don't imagine that I am offended. Naturally you are not out for digging up your old acquaintances, especially as you seem to have feathered your nest pretty well. Where have you been all these years?"

"In the States. I only came back a few weeks ago."

"Ah, you'd have been wiser to stay there. But I suppose you made a pile and have come home to spend it."

"Well, hardly a pile," said Pottermack, "but I have saved enough to live on in a quiet way. I am not expensive in my habits."

"Lucky beggar!" said Lewson, glancing around with greedy eyes. "Is this your own place?"

"Yes, I have just bought it and moved in. Got it remarkably cheap, too."

"Did you? Well, I say again, lucky beggar. It's quite a lordly little estate."

"Yes, I am very pleased with it. There's a good house and quite a lot of land, as you see. I hope to live very comfortably here."

"You ought to, if you don't get blown on, and you never need be if you are a wise man."

"No, I hope not," said Pottermack, a little uneasily. He had been looking at his old friend and was disagreeably impressed by the change that the years had wrought. He was by no means happy to know that his secret was shared with this unprepossessing stranger – for such he, virtually, was. But still he was totally unprepared for what was to follow.

561

"It was a lucky chance for me," remarked Lewson, "that I happened to drop in at that shop. Best morning's work that I have done for a long time."

"Indeed!" said Pottermack, looking a little puzzled.

"Yes. I reckon that chance was worth a thousand pounds to me."

"Was it really? I don't quite see how."

"Don't you?" demanded Lewson, with a sudden change of manner. "Then I'll explain. I presume you don't want the Scotland Yard people to know that you are alive and living here like a lord?"

"Naturally I don't."

"Of course you don't. And if you show a proper and liberal spirit towards your old pal, they are never likely to know."

"But," gasped Pottermack, "I don't think I quite understand what you mean."

"You are devilish thick-headed if you don't," said Lewson. "Then I'll put in a nutshell. You hand me over a thousand pounds and I give you a solemn undertaking to keep my mouth shut forever."

"And if I don't?"

"Then I hop off to Scotland Yard and earn a small gratuity by giving them the straight tip."

Pottermack recoiled from him in horror. He was thunderstruck. It was appalling to find that this man, whom he had known as an apparently decent youth, had sunk so low. He had actually descended to blackmail – the lowest, the meanest, and the shabbiest of crimes. But it was not the blackmail alone that filled Pottermack's soul with loathing of the wretch who stood before him. In the moment in which Lewson made his demand, Pottermack knew the name of the villain who had forged those cheques and had set the dastardly trap in which he, Pottermack, was, in effect, still held.

For some moments he was too much shocked to reply. When at length he did, it was merely to settle the terms of the transaction. He had no choice. He realized that this was no empty threat. The gleam of malice in Lewson's eye was unmistakable. It expressed the inveterate hatred that a thoroughly base man feels towards one on whom he has inflicted an unforgivable injury.

"Will a crossed cheque do for you?" he asked.

"Good Lord! No!" was the reply, "nor an open one either. No cheques for me. Hard cash is what I should prefer, but as that might be difficult to manage I'll take it in notes – five-pound notes."

"What, a thousand pounds!" exclaimed Pottermack. "What on earth will the people at the bank think?"

Lewson sniggered. "What would they think, old chap, if I turned up with an open cheque for a thousand pounds? Wouldn't they take an interest in the endorsement? No, dear boy, you get the notes – fivers, mind. They know you. And look here, Jeff. This is a strictly private transaction. Neither of us wants it to leak out. It will be much safer for us both if we remain tee-total strangers. If we should meet anywhere, you needn't take off your hat. I shan't. We don't know one another. I don't even know your name. By the way, what is your name?"

"Marcus Pottermack."

"God, what a name! However, I'll forget it if I can. You agree with me?"

"Certainly," replied Pottermack with unmistakable sincerity. "But where and how am I to hand you over the money?"

"I was coming to that," said Lewson. "I will come along here and collect it on Thursday night – that will give you time to get the notes. I shall come after dark, about nine o'clock. You had better leave this gate unlatched, and then, if I see that the coast is clear, I can pop in unobserved. Will that do?"

Pottermack nodded. "But there is one thing more, Lewson," said he. "This is a single, final transaction. I pay you a thousand pounds to purchase your silence and secrecy for ever!"

"That is so. *In saecula saeculorum.*"

"There will be no further demands?"

"Certainly not," Lewson replied indignantly. "Do you think I don't know what a square deal is? I've given you my solemn promise and you can trust me to keep it."

Pottermack pursued the matter no farther, and as the calamitous business was now concluded, he softly opened the gate, and, having ascertained that no one was in sight, he let his visitor out and watched the big burly figure swaggering townwards along the little path that bordered his wall.

Closing the gate, he turned back into the garden, his heart filled with bitterness and despair. His dream was at an end. Never, while this horse-leech hung on to him, could he ask Alice Bellard to be his wife. For his prophetic soul told him only too truly that this was but a beginning, that the blackmailer would come again and again and yet again, always to go away still holding the thing that he had sold.

And so it befell, and so the pitiless extortion might have gone on to its end in the ruin and impoverishment of the victim but for the timely appearance of the sundial in Mr. Gallett's yard.

Chapter XI
Mr. Pottermack's Dilemma

The sound of the piano faded away in a gradual diminuendo and at last stopped. A brief interval of silence followed.

Then Mr. Pottermack, withdrawing his gaze from the infinite distance beyond the garden, turned to look at his hostess and found her regarding him with a slightly quizzical smile.

"You haven't lit your pipe after all, Mr. Pottermack," said she.

"No," he replied. "My savage breast was so effectually soothed by your music that tobacco would have been superfluous. Besides, my pipe would have gone out. It always does when my attention is very completely occupied."

"And was it? I almost thought you were dozing."

"I was dreaming," said he, "day-dreaming, but wide awake and listening. It is curious," he continued after a pause, "what power music has to awaken associations. There is nothing like it, excepting, perhaps, scents. Music and odours, things utterly unlike anything but themselves, seem to have a power of arousing dormant memories that is quite lacking in representative things such as pictures and statues."

"So it would seem," said Mrs. Bellard, "that I have been, in a fashion, performing the function of an opium pipe in successful competition with the tobacco article. But it is too late to mend matters now. I can hear Anne approaching with the tea-things."

Almost as she spoke, the door opened and the maid entered, carrying a tray with anxious care, and proceeded to set out the tea-things with the manner of one performing a solemn rite. When she had gone and the tea was poured out, Mrs. Bellard resumed the conversation.

"I began to think you had struck me off your visiting list. What have you been doing with yourself all this time?"

"Well," Pottermack replied evasively – for, obviously, he could not go into details – "I have been a good deal occupied. There have been a lot of things to do – the sun-dial, for instance. I told you about the sun-dial, didn't I?"

"Yes, but that was a long time ago. You said you were going to show it to me when it was set up, but you never have. You haven't even shown it to Mrs. Gadby. She is quite hurt about it."

"Dear me!" exclaimed Mr. Pottermack, "how self-centred we old bachelors get! But this neglect must be remedied at once. When can you come and see it? Could you come round and have tea with me tomorrow?"

"Yes. I should like to, but I can't come very early. Will a quarter-to-five do?"

"Of course it will. We can have tea first and then make a leisurely survey of the sun-dial and the various other things that I have to show you."

Thus the arrangement was made, very much to Mr. Pottermack's satisfaction, for it enabled him to postpone to the morrow a certain very momentous question which he had thought of raising this very afternoon, but which now appeared a little inopportune. For a delicate question must be approached cautiously through suitable channels, and no such means of approach had presented themselves or seemed likely to. Accordingly, relieved of the necessity of looking for an opening, Mr. Pottermack was able to give his whole attention to making himself agreeable, and eventually took his departure in the best of spirits, looking forward with confidence to the prospects of the morrow.

The tea, as arranged by Mrs. Gadby in the pleasant dining-room of The Chestnuts, was a triumphant success. It would have been an even greater success if the fair visitor had happened to have been on short commons for the preceding week. But the preposterous abundance at least furnished the occasion of mirth, besides serving as an outlet for Mrs. Gadby's feelings of regard and admiration towards the guest and a demonstration of welcome.

"It is really very nice of her," said Mrs. Bellard, glancing smilingly round the loaded table, "and tactful too. It is a compliment to us both. It implies that she has cause to be grateful to me for introducing her here, and you are that cause. I expect she has a pretty comfortable time."

"I hope so," said Pottermack. "I have, thanks to her and to you. And she keeps the house in the most perfect order. Would you like to look over it presently?"

"Naturally I should. Did you ever meet a woman who was not devoured by curiosity in regard to a bachelor's household arrangements? But I am really more interested in the part of the premises that is outside Mrs. Gadby's domain, the part that reflects your own personality. I want especially to see your workshop. Am I to be allowed to?"

"Undoubtedly you are. In fact, if we have finished, as it seems we have, you shall be introduced to it forthwith."

They rose, and, passing out at the back door, walked together up the long path through the kitchen garden and orchard until they came to the gate of the walled garden, which Pottermack unlocked with his Yale key.

"This is very impressive and mysterious," said Mrs. Bellard as the gate closed and the spring-latch snapped. "I am quite proud to be admitted into this Holy of Holies. It is a delightful garden," she continued, letting her eyes travel round the great oblong enclosure, "so perfectly peaceful and quiet and remote. Here one is cut off from all the world, which is rather restful at times."

Mr. Pottermack agreed, and reflected that the present was one of those times. "When I want to be alone," he remarked, "I like to be definitely alone and secure from interruption."

"Well, you are secure enough here, shut in from the sight of any human eye. Why, you might commit a murder and no one would be any the wiser."

"So I might," agreed Mr. Pottermack, rather taken aback. "I hadn't thought of that advantage, and, of course, you understand that the place wasn't laid out with that purpose in view. What do you think of the sun-dial?"

"I was just looking at it and thinking what a charming finish it gives to the garden. It is delightful, and will be still more so when the new stone has weathered down to the tone of the old. And I think you told me that there is a well underneath. That adds a sort of deliciously horrible interest to it."

"Why horrible?" Pottermack enquired uncomfortably.

"Oh, don't you think wells are rather gruesome things? I do. There is one in my garden, and it gives me the creeps whenever I lower the bucket and watch it sinking down, down that black hole and vanishing into the bowels of the earth."

"Yes," said Pottermack, "I have that feeling myself. Probably most town-bred people have. And they are really rather dangerous, especially when they are unguarded as this one was. That was why I took the opportunity to cover it up."

By this time they were close up to the dial, and Mrs. Bellard walked round it to read the motto. "Why do they always write these things in Latin?" she asked.

"Partly for the sake of brevity," he replied. "Here are five Latin words. The equivalent in English is: '*At the rising of the sun, hope, at the going down thereof, peace*'."

"It is a beautiful motto," she said, looking wistfully and a little sadly at the stone pillar. "The first part is what we all know by experience, the second is what we pray for to compensate us for the sorrows and disillusionments of the years that come between. But now let us go and look at the workshop."

Pottermack conducted her behind the yew hedge into the range of well-lighted workrooms, where he exhibited, not without a touch of pride, his very complete outfit. But the fair widow's enthusiastic interest in the tools and appliances rather surprised him, for women are apt to look on the instruments of masculine handicraft with a slightly supercilious eye. No general survey satisfied her. He had to display his "plant" in detail and explain and demonstrate the use of each appliance – the joiner's bench with its quick-grip vice, the metal-work bench with its anvil and stakes and the big brazing-jet, the miniature forge, the lathe, the emery-wheel, and the bench-drill. She examined them all with the closest attention and with a singularly intelligent grasp of their purposes and modes of action. Pottermack became so absorbed in the pleasure of exhibiting his treasures that, for the moment, he almost forgot his main purpose.

"I am glad I have seen the place where you work," she said, as they came out into the garden. "Now I can picture you to myself among your workshop gods, busy and happy. You are happy when you are working there, aren't you?"

She asked the question with so much concern that Pottermack was fain to reply, "Every workman, I think, is happy when he is working. Of course, I mean a skilled man, working with his hands and his brain, creating something, even if it is only a simple thing. Yes, I am happy when I am doing a job, especially if it is a little difficult."

"I understand, for a little extra planning and thought. But are you, in general, a happy man? Do you find life pleasant? You always seem very cheerful, and yet sometimes I wonder if you really enjoy life."

Pottermack reflected a few moments. "You are thinking," said he, "of my solitary and apparently friendless state, though I am not friendless at all, seeing that I have you – the dearest and kindest friend that a man could wish for. But in a sense you are right. My life is an incomplete affair, and these activities of mine, pleasant as they are, serve but as makeshifts to fill a blank. But it could easily be made complete. A word from you would be enough. If you were my wife, there would be nothing left in the world for me to covet. I should be a perfectly happy man."

He paused and looked at her, and was a little disconcerted to see that her eyes had filled and that she was looking down with an evident expression of distress. As she made no answer, he continued, more eagerly, "Why should it not be, Alice? We are the very best of friends – really devoted and affectionate friends. We like the same things and the same ways of life. We have the same interests, the same pleasures. We should try to make one another happy, and I am sure we should succeed.

Won't you say the word, dear, and let us join hands to go our ways together for the rest of our lives?"

She turned and looked in his face with brimming eyes and laid her hand on his arm.

"Dear friend," she said. "Dearest Marcus, I would say yes, joyfully, thankfully, if only it were possible. I have given you my friendship, my most loving friendship, and that is all I have to give. It is impossible for me to be your wife."

Pottermack gazed at her in dismay. "But," he asked huskily, "why is it impossible? What hinders?"

"My husband hinders," she replied in a low voice.

"Your husband!" gasped Pottermack.

"Yes. You have believed, as every one here believes, that I am a widow. I am not. My husband is still alive. I cannot and will not live with him or even acknowledge him. But he lives, to inflict one more injury on me by standing between you and me. Come," she continued, as Pottermack, numb with amazement, gazed at her in silence, "let us go and sit down in the summer-house and I will tell you the whole pitiful story."

She walked across the lawn, and Pottermack accompanied her with half-unconscious reluctance. Since that fatal night he had made little use of the summer-house. Its associations repelled him. Even now he would, by choice, have avoided it, and it was with a certain vague discomfort that he saw his beloved friend seat herself in the chair that had stood vacant since that night when Lewson had sat in it.

"I will tell you my story," she began, "from the time when I was a girl, or perhaps I should say a young woman. At that time I was engaged to a young man named Jeffrey Brandon. We were devotedly attached to each other. As to Jeffrey, I need say no more than that you are – allowing for the difference of age – quite extraordinarily like him – like in features, in voice, in tastes, and in nature. If Jeffrey had been alive now, he would have been exactly like you. That is what attracted me to you from the first.

"We were extremely happy – perfectly happy – in our mutual affection, and we were all-sufficient to one another. I thought myself the most fortunate of girls, and so I was, for we were only waiting until I should come into a small property that was likely to fall to me shortly, when we should have had enough to marry upon comfortably. And then, in a moment, our happiness was shattered utterly. A most dreadful thing happened. A series of forgeries was discovered at the bank where Jeffrey was employed. Suspicion was made to fall upon him. He was prosecuted, convicted – on false evidence, of course – and sentenced to a term of penal servitude.

"As soon as he was convicted, he formally released me from our engagement, but I need not say that I had no intention of giving him up. However, the question never arose. Poor Jeffrey escaped from prison, and in trying to swim out to some ship in the river was drowned. Later, his body was recovered and taken to the prison, where an inquest was held. I went down, and by special permission attended the funeral and laid a wreath on the grave in the prison cemetery. And that was the end of my romance.

"When Jeffrey died, I made up my mind that I was a spinster for life, and so I ought to have been. But things fell out otherwise. Besides me, Jeffrey had one intimate friend, a fellow-clerk at the bank named James Lewson. Of course, I knew him fairly intimately, and after Jeffrey's conviction I saw a good deal of him. Indeed, we became quite friendly – which we had hardly been before – by reason of the firm belief that he expressed in Jeffrey's innocence. Everyone else took the poor boy's guilt for granted, so, naturally, I was drawn to the one loyal friend. Then, when Jeffrey died and was lost to me forever, he took every opportunity of offering me comfort and consolation, and he did it so tactfully, was so filled with grief for our lost friend and so eager to talk of him and keep his memory green between us, that we became greater friends than ever.

"After a time, his friendship took on a more affectionate and demonstrative character, and finally he asked me plainly to marry him. Of course, I said no. In fact, I was rather shocked at the proposal, for I still felt that I belonged to Jeffrey. But he was quietly persistent. He took no offence, but he did not pretend to accept my refusal as final. Especially he urged on me that Jeffrey would have wished that I should not be left to go through life alone, but that I should be cherished and protected by his own loyal and devoted friend.

"Gradually his arguments overcame my repugnance to the idea of the marriage, though it was still distasteful to me, and when he asked for my consent as a recognition and reward of his loyalty to Jeffrey, I at last gave way. It appeared ungrateful to go on refusing him, and after all, nothing seemed to matter much now that Jeffrey was gone. The end of it was that we were married just before he started to take up an appointment in a branch of the bank at Leeds.

"It was not long before the disillusionment came, and when it did come, I was astonished that I could have been so deceived. Very soon I began to realize that it was not love of me that had made him such a persistent suitor. It was the knowledge that he had gathered of the little fortune that was coming to me. His greediness for money was incredible, and yet he was utterly unable to hold it. It ran through his hands like water. He had a fair salary, but yet we were always poor and usually in debt. For he was an inveterate gambler – a gambler of that hopeless type that must inevitably lose. He usually did lose at once, for he was a reckless plunger, but if by chance he made a coup, he immediately plunged with his winnings and lost them. It was no wonder that he was always in difficulties.

"When, at last, my little property came to me, he was deeply disappointed, for it was tied up securely in the form of a trust, and my uncle, who is a solicitor, was the managing trustee. And a very careful trustee he was, and not at all well impressed by my husband. James Lewson had hoped to get control of the entire capital, instead of which he had to apply to me for money when he was in difficulties and I had to manage my trustee as best I could. But in spite of this, most of the income that I received went to pay my husband's debts and losses.

"Meanwhile our relations grew more and more unsatisfactory. The disappointment due to the trust, and the irritation at having to ask me for money and explain the reasons for his need of it, made him sullen and morose, and even, at times, coarsely abusive. But there was something more. From the first I had been dismayed at his freedom in the matter of drink. But the habit grew upon him rapidly, and it was in connection with this that the climax of our disagreement came about and led to our separation.

"I understand that drink has different effects on different types of men. On James Lewson its effects began with the loss of all traces of refinement and a tendency to coarse facetiousness. The next stage was that of noisy swagger and boasting, and then he soon became quarrelsome and even brutal. There were one or two occasions when he threatened to become actually violent. Now it happened more than once that, when he had drunk himself into a state of boastful exaltation, he spoke of Jeffrey in a tone of such disrespect and even contempt that I had to leave the room to avoid an open, vulgar quarrel. But on the final occasion he went much farther. He began by jeering at my infatuation for 'that nincompoop', as he called him, and when I, naturally, became furiously angry and was walking out of the room, he called me back, and, laughing in my face, actually boasted to me – to me! – that his was the master-mind that had planned and carried out the forgeries and then set up that mug, Jeff, as the man of straw for the lawyers to knock down.

"I was absolutely thunderstruck. At first I thought that it was mere drunken fooling. But then he went on to give corroborative details, chuckling with idiotic self-complacency, until at last I realized that it was true, that this fuddled brute was the dastardly traitor who had sent my Jeffrey to his death.

"Then I left him. At once I packed a small suitcase and went out and took a room at an hotel in the town. The next day I returned and had an interview with him. He was mightily flustered and apologetic. He remembered quite well what he had said, but tried to persuade me that it was a mere drunken joke and that it was all a fabrication, invented to annoy me. But I knew better. In the interval I had thought matters over, and I saw how perfectly his confession explained everything and agreed with what I now knew of him, his insatiable greed for money, his unscrupulousness, his wild gambling, and the reckless way in which he contracted debts. I brushed aside his explanations and denials and presented my ultimatum, of which the terms were these: "We should separate at once and completely, and henceforth be as total strangers, not recognizing one another if we should ever meet. I should take my mother's maiden name, Bellard, and assume the status of a widow. He should refrain from molesting me or claiming any sort of acquaintance or relationship with me.

"If he agreed to these terms, I undertook to pay him a quarterly allowance and to take no action in respect of what I had learned. If he refused, I should instruct my uncle to commence proceedings to obtain a judicial separation and I should state in open court all that I knew. I should communicate these facts to the directors of the bank, and if, in my uncle's opinion, any prosecution were possible – for perjury or any other offence connected with the forgeries – I should instruct him to prosecute.

"My ultimatum took him aback completely. At first he tried to bluster, then he became pathetic and tried to wheedle. But in the end, when he saw that I was not to be moved from my resolution, he gave way. I could see that my threats had scared him badly – though, in fact, I don't believe that I could have done anything. But perhaps he knew better. There may have been some other matters of which I had no knowledge. At any rate, he agreed, with the one stipulation: That the quarterly allowance should be paid in notes and not by a cheque.

"As soon as I had settled the terms of the separation I moved to Aylesbury, where my mother's people had lived, and stayed there in lodgings while I looked for a small, cheap house. At length I found the cottage at Borley, and there I have lived ever since, as comfortably as my rather straitened means would let me. For, of course, the allowance has been rather a strain, though I have paid it cheerfully as the price of my freedom, and I may say that James Lewson has kept to the terms of our agreement with one exception – an exception that I expected. He has not been satisfied with the allowance. From time to time, and with increasing

571

frequency, he has applied for loans – which, of course, meant gifts – to help him out of some temporary difficulty, and sometimes – but not always – I have been weak enough to supply him.

"But I was not to be left completely in peace. When I had been settled in Borley for about a year, I received a letter from him informing me that 'by a strange coincidence' he had been appointed to the managership of the Borley branch of the Bank. Of course, I knew that it was no coincidence at all. He had engineered the transfer himself."

"With what object, do you suppose?" asked Pottermack.

"It may have been mere malice," she replied, "just to cause me annoyance without breaking the terms of the agreement. But my impression is that it was done with the deliberate purpose of keeping me in a state of nervous unrest so that I should be the more easily prevailed on to comply with his applications for money. At any rate, those applications became more frequent and more urgent after he came to live here, and once he threw out a hint about calling at my house for an answer. But I put a stop to that at once."

"Did you ever meet him in Borley?" Pottermack asked.

"Yes, once or twice. But I passed him in the street without a glance of recognition and he made no attempt to molest me. I think he had a wholesome fear of me. And, of course, I kept out of his way as much as I could. But it was an immense relief to me when he went away. You heard of his disappearance, I suppose? It was the talk of the town at the time."

"Oh yes," replied Pottermack. "My friend, Mr. Gallett, the mason, was the first to announce the discovery. But I little thought when I heard of it how much it meant to you – and to me. What do you suppose has become of him?"

"I can't imagine. It is a most mysterious affair. There is no reason that I can think of why he should have absconded at all. I can only suppose that he had done something which he expected to be found out but which has not come to light. Perhaps the most mysterious thing about it is that he has never applied to me for money. He would know quite well that I should at least have sent him his allowance, and that he could depend on me not to betray him, profoundly as I detest him."

Mr. Pottermack cogitated anxiously. He loathed the idea of deceiving this noble, loyal-hearted woman. Yet what could he do? He was committed irrevocably to a certain line of action, and in committing himself he had unconsciously committed her. He had embarked on a course of deception and had no choice but to follow it. And with regard to the future, he could honestly assure himself that whatever made for his happiness would make for hers.

"Do you think he may have gone abroad?" he asked.

"It is impossible to say," she replied. "I have no reason to suppose he has, excepting his extraordinary silence."

"It is even possible," Pottermack suggested in a slightly husky voice, "that he may be dead."

"Yes," she admitted, "that is possible, and it would certainly account for his silence. But is it any use guessing?"

"I was only thinking," said Pottermack, "that if he should happen to have died, that would – er – dispose of our difficulties."

"Not unless we knew that he was dead. On the contrary. If he should have died and his death should remain undiscovered, or, what is the same thing, if he should have died without having been identified, then I should be bound to him beyond any possible hope of release."

Pottermack drew a deep breath, and unconsciously his glance fell on the sun-dial.

"But," he asked in a low tone, "if it should ever become known as an ascertained fact that he was dead? Then, dear Alice, would you say yes?"

"But have I not said it already?" she exclaimed. "Did I not tell you that, if I were free, I would gladly, thankfully take you for my husband? Then, if that is not enough, I say it again. Not that it is of much use to say it, seeing that there is no reason to suppose that he is dead or likely to die. I only wish there were. It may sound callous to express such a wish, but it would be mere hypocrisy to pretend to any other feeling. He ruined poor Jeffrey's life and he has ruined mine."

"I wouldn't say that," Pottermack protested gently. "The sands of your life have yet a long time to run. There is still time for us both to salve some happy years from the wreckage of the past."

"So there is," she agreed. "I was wrong. It is only a part of my life that has been utterly spoiled. And if you, too, have been through stormy weather – as I, somehow, think you have – we must join forces and help one another with the salvage work. But we shall have to be content to be friends, since marriage is out of our reach."

"My dear," said Pottermack, "if you say that you would be willing to have me for your husband that is all I ask."

They went forth from the summer-house and walked slowly, hand in hand, round the old garden, and Pottermack, anxious to conceal his bitter disappointment, chatted cheerfully about his fruit trees and the flowers that he meant to plant in the sunny borders. Very soon they seemed to be back on the old footing, only with a new note of affection and intimacy which made itself evident when Pottermack, with his hand on the latch of

573

the gate, drew his companion to him and kissed her before they passed through together into the orchard.

He walked with her back to the cottage and said good-bye at the little wooden gate.

"I hope, dear," she whispered, as she held his hand for a moment, "that you are not very, very disappointed."

"I am not thinking of disappointments," he replied cheerily. "I am gloating over the blessings that I enjoy already and hoping that Fortune may have something to add to them later on."

But despite his assumed cheeriness of manner, Mr. Pottermack took his way homeward in a profoundly depressed state of mind. The dream of settled happiness that had haunted him for years, vague and unreal at first but ever growing more definite and vivid, had been shattered in the very moment when it seemed to have become a reality. He thought bitterly of the later years in America when his purpose of seeking his lost love had been forming, almost unrecognized by himself as a thing actually intended, of his long search in London with its ultimate triumph, of the patient pursuit of the beloved object to this place and the purchase of his house, of the long untiring effort, always bringing him nearer and nearer to success. And then, when he seemed to have conquered every difficulty, to have his treasure within his very grasp, behold an obstacle undreamed of and apparently insuperable.

It was maddening, and the most exasperating feature of it was that the obstacle was of his own creating. Like most men who have committed a fatal blunder, Mr. Pottermack was impelled to chew the bitter cud of the might-have-been. If he had only known! How easy it would have been to arrange things suitably! Looking back, he now saw how unnecessary had been all that laborious business of the gutta-percha soles. It had been the result of mere panic. He could see that now. And he could have met the conditions so much more simply and satisfactorily. Supposing he had just made a few footprints in the soft earth leading to the well – he could have done that with the plaster casts – flung down the coat by the brink and gone out on the following morning and informed the police. There would have been no risk of suspicion. Why should there have been? He would have told a perfectly convincing story. He could have related how he had gone out in the evening, leaving his gate unlocked, had returned in the dark and found it ajar, had discovered in the morning strange footprints and a coat, suggesting that some stranger had strayed into the garden and, in the darkness, had fallen down the well. It would have been a perfectly natural and straightforward story. Nobody would have doubted it or connected him with the accident. Then

574

the well would have been emptied, the body recovered and the incident closed for ever.

As it was, the situation was one of exasperating irony. He was in a dilemma from which there seemed to be no escape. He alone, of all the world, knew that Alice Bellard was free to marry him, and that knowledge he must carry locked up in his breast for the remainder of his life.

Chapter XII
The Understudy

$\mathbf{R}$eaders who have followed this history to its present stage will have realized by this time that Mr. Pottermack was a gentleman of uncommon tenacity of purpose. To the weaker vessels the sudden appearance of an apparently insuperable obstacle is the occasion for abandoning hope and throwing up the sponge. But Mr. Pottermack was of a tougher fibre. To him a difficulty was not a matter for wringing of hands but for active search for a solution.

Hence it happened that the black despair that enveloped and pervaded him after his proposal to Alice Bellard soon began to disperse under the influence of his natural resiliency. From profitless reflections on the might-have-been he turned to the consideration of the may-be. He began to examine the obstacle critically, not as a final extinguisher of his hopes, but as a problem to be dealt with.

Now what did that problem amount to? He, Marcus Pottermack, desired to marry Alice Bellard. That had been the darling wish and purpose of his life and he had no intention of abandoning it. She, on her side, wished to marry him, but she believed that her husband was still alive. He, Pottermack, knew that the said husband was dead, but he could not disclose his knowledge. Yet until the fact of the husband's death was disclosed, the marriage was impossible and must remain so for ever. For there is this unsatisfactory peculiarity about a dead man – that it is hopeless to look forward to the possibility of his dying. Thus the problem, put in a nutshell, amounted to this: That James Lewson, being dead *de facto*, had got to be made dead *de jure*.

But how was this to be done? It is hardly necessary to say that, at first, a number of wild-cat schemes floated through Mr. Pottermack's mind, though they found no lodgment there. For instance, he actually considered the feasibility of dismounting the sun-dial, fishing up the body and planting it in some place where it might be found. Of course, the plan was physically impossible even if he could have faced the horrors of its execution.

Then he turned his attention to the now invaluable coat. He conceived the idea of depositing it at the edge of a cliff or on the brink of a river or dock. But this would not have served the required purpose. Doubtless it would have raised a suspicion that the owner was dead. But suspicion was of no use. Absolute certainty was what was needed to turn the wife into a widow. In connection with this idea, he studied the law relating to Presumption of Death, but when he learned that, about 1850, the Court of Queen's Bench had refused to presume the death of a person who was known to have been alive in the year 1027, he decided that the staying power of the law was considerably greater than his own and finally abandoned the idea.

Nevertheless his resolution remained unshaken. Somehow James Lewson would have to be given the proper, recognized status of a dead man. Though no practicable scheme presented itself, the problem was ever present in his mind. By day and by night, in his work in the garden, in his walks through the quiet lanes, even in the fair widow's pleasant sitting-room, his thoughts were constantly busy with the vain search for some solution, and so they might have continued indefinitely but for a chance circumstance that supplied him with a new suggestion. And even then, the suggestion was so indirect and so little related to the nature of his problem that he had nearly missed it.

From time to time, Mr. Pottermack was in the habit of paying a visit to London for the purpose of making various purchases, particularly of tools and materials. On one of these occasions, happening to be in the neighbourhood of Covent Garden, and realizing suddenly that the day was Friday, it occurred to him to look in at the auction rooms in King Street, hard by, and see what was going, for the Friday sales of "miscellaneous property" are of special interest to those who use tools, appliances, or scientific instruments, and Pottermack had on one or two previous occasions picked up some very useful bargains.

But this time he seemed to have drawn a blank, for when he ran his eye over the catalogue which was fixed to the doorpost he found, to his disgust, that the principal feature was "*The valuable collection brought together by a well-known Egyptologist, lately deceased*". He was on the point of turning away when he noticed, near the end of the catalogue, "Another Property" consisting of a quantity of model-maker's tools and appliances, whereupon he entered the office and, having provided himself with a catalogue, made his way to the inner room where the tools were on view. These he looked over critically, marking here and there a "*Lot*" which might be worth buying if it should go cheaply enough. Then, having finished his actual business, he proceeded rather aimlessly to browse round the room, catalogue in hand, glancing at the various items of the Egyptologist's collection.

There is always something impressive about the relics of Ancient Egypt. Their vast antiquity, the evidence that they present of strange knowledge and a rather uncanny skill, with suggestions of a state of mind by no means primitive, yet utterly unlike our own, gives them a certain

577

weird quality that makes itself felt by most observers. Pottermack was distinctly aware of it. As he looked over the collection of venerable objects – the ushabti figures, the wooden head-rests, the pre-dynastic painted vases, the jar-sealings, the flint implements and copper tools and weapons – he had the feeling that the place was unworthy of them. Particularly in regard to the wooden and stone steles, the portrait statuettes, the canopic jars, and other pious memorials of the dead, did he feel that their presence here, offered for sale in the public market, was an affront to their sacred character. As to the coffins, and above all the mummies, their exposure here seemed to him positively indecent. Here were the actual bodies of deceased ladies and gentlemen, persons of rank and station in their day, as the inscriptions testified, catalogued as mere curios, with the auctioneer's ticket pasted on their very coffins or even on their funeral vesture.

Mr. Pottermack halted by a large open box into which a much-damaged mummy had been crammed and lay, partly doubled up, amidst a litter of broken wood. The ticket, stuck on the linen bandage in which the body was swathed, marked it as "*Lot 15*", and reference to the catalogue elicited the further particulars: "*Mummy of an official with portions of wooden coffin (a.f.)*", while a label attached to the mummy identified the deceased as "*Khama-Heru, a libationer of the 19th or 20th Dynasty*".

Mr. Pottermack stood by the box, looking down distastefully, almost resentfully, at the shapeless figure, wrapped in its bulky swathings, and looking like a gigantic rag doll that had been bundled into a rubbish-box. That great rag doll had once been a respected attendant at feasts and solemn ceremonials. Presently it would be put up "with all faults" and probably knocked down for a few shillings to some speculative curio dealer. And as he reflected thus, the words of Sir Thomas Browne floated through his mind: "*The Egyptian mummies which Time or Cambyses hath spared, Avarice now consumeth*". Vain, indeed, were the efforts of the pious Mizraim to achieve even physical immortality.

He had turned away and was beginning to move slowly towards the door. And then, suddenly, in a moment of time, two separate ideas, apparently unrelated, linked themselves together and evolved a third. And a very strange one that newly evolved idea was. Mr. Pottermack was quite startled. As it flashed into his mind, he stopped dead, and then, retracing his steps, halted once more beside the box. But now, as he looked down on the great rag doll that had once been Khama-Heru, no distaste or resentment was in his eye, but rather an eager curiosity that estimated and measured and sought for details. He inspected critically the fracture where the brittle corpse had been doubled up to jam it in the box, the spot where part of a shrivelled nose peeped through a hole in the rotten linen. The history of this thing interested him no more. What it had been was no concern of his. Its importance to him was in what it was now. It was a dead body – a dead human body, the body of a man, of a tall man, so far as he could judge.

He made a pencil mark on his catalogue opposite Lot 15, and then, having glanced at his watch, walked out into King Street, there to pace up and down until it should be time for the auction to begin, and meanwhile to try to fashion this startling but rather nebulous idea into a more definite shape – to decide, in short, the part which the late Khama-Heru could be given to play in his slightly involved affairs.

The actual acquirement of the gruesome relic presented no difficulties. It is true that the auctioneer made some conscientious efforts to invest Lot 15 with some semblance of value. But his plausible suggestions as to the "trifling restorations" that might be necessary aroused no enthusiasm. He had to start the bidding himself – at ten shillings, and at fifteen the hammer descended to confirm Mr. Pottermack in the lawful possession of a deceased libationer. Thereupon the money was handed in and the box handed out, and when it had its lid nailed on and a length of cord tied round it, it was conveyed out to the pavement, whence it was presently transferred to the roof of a cab and in due course transported to Marylebone Station to await the next train to Borley.

The advent of Khama-Heru, deceased, to The Chestnuts, Borley, inaugurated a radical change in Mr. Pottermack's habits and mental state. Gone was the restless indecision that had kept him mooning about, thinking everlastingly and getting nothing done. Now, his mind was, in a measure, at rest. He had a job, and if all the details of that job were not yet clear to him, still he could, as in any other job, get on with the part that he knew while he was planning out the remainder.

The first problem was to dispose of the box – and of the occupant when he should emerge. In the first place, it had been conveyed through the side gate to the workshop, where it at present reposed. But this would never do, especially when the emergence should take place. For, of late, Alice Bellard had taken to bringing him little commissions and sitting by him in the workshop babbling cheerfully while he carried them out. Which was exceedingly pleasant. But two is company, and, assuredly, Khama-Heru would have made a very undesirable third. And there was another point. At present, in his box with the fragments of the coffin and the auctioneer's ticket, *K.-H.*, was harmless enough, a mere fifteen shillings' worth of miscellaneous property. But after a few "trifling restorations" (of a rather different kind from those contemplated by the auctioneer) the said *K.-H.* would present a highly compromising appearance. Arrangements would have to be made for keeping him in strict retirement.

The conditions were met fairly well by emptying the tool-house. The roller and the lawn-mower could rest safely outside under a tarpaulin, and the garden tools could be stowed at the end of the metal-shop. When this had been done and the tool-house door fitted with a really safe lock, Pottermack dragged the box thither, and having taken off the lid, strengthened it, and fitted it with a pair of stout hinges and a good lever lock, he felt that he had made things secure for the present. The tool-house was furnished with a long bench for the storage of flower-pots, and, as it was lighted only by a window in the roof, he would be able to work there conveniently and safe from observation.

His first proceeding was to unroll the mummy, to unwind the countless yards of rotten linen bandage with which it had been covered. He wanted to see what the mummy itself was like and whether it was complete. But when he had got all the wrappings off and looked at the thing as it lay on the bench, he was appalled at its appearance. In its wrappings it had been gruesome enough – a great, horrible rag doll, but divested of those wrappings it was ghastly. For now it revealed itself frankly for what it was – a dead man, dry, shrivelled, unnatural, but still undeniably the dead body of a man.

Pottermack stood by the bench gazing at it distastefully and with something of the compunction that he had felt in the auction room. But it was of no use being squeamish. He had bought the thing for a specific and most necessary purpose, and that purpose had got to be carried into effect. Gulping down his qualms, therefore, he set himself to make a systematic examination.

Apparently the body was quite complete. The abdomen looked a little queer, but probably that was due to the drying, though there were unmistakable signs of its having been opened. Both legs were partially broken off at the hip-joints, just hanging on loosely by a few strings of dried flesh. But the bones seemed quite uninjured. The head was in the same condition as the legs, detached from the spine save for one or two strands of dry muscle, and at the moment rolled over on its side with its face turned towards Pottermack. And a grisly face it was, for despite the shrivelled nose, the papery ears, the sunken eyes, and the horrid sardonic grin, it had a recognizable human expression. Looking at it with shuddering interest, Pottermack felt that he could form a fairly clear idea as to what Khama-Heru must have looked like when alive.

Careful measurement with a two-foot rule showed that the body was just under five feet nine inches in length. Allowing for shrinkage in drying, his height had probably been well over five feet ten, enough to make him a passable understudy for James Lewson. Unfortunately, there was no facial resemblance whatever, but this, Pottermack hoped, would be of no consequence. The dimensions were what really mattered. But, of course, the body was useless for Pottermack's purpose in its present rigid, brittle state, and the important question was how far it could be softened and rendered flexible. Pottermack decided to make a tentative experiment on one shoulder by leaving it for an hour or two under several thicknesses of wet rag, which he did, with results that were, on the whole, satisfactory. The moistened flesh and skin swelled up appreciably and took on a much more natural appearance, and the arm now moved freely at the shoulder-joint. But it was evident that this treatment must not be applied prematurely, or other, less desirable changes would set in. He accordingly allowed the moistened area to dry thoroughly and then put the mummy away in its box, there to remain hidden until the other preparations had been completed.

These were of two kinds. First, the understudy had to be provided with a "make-up" which would be perfectly convincing under somewhat rigorous conditions, and secondly, a suitable setting had to be found for the little drama in which the understudy should play his part. Both gave Mr. Pottermack considerable occupation.

In connection with the make-up, it happened most fortunately that he had preserved the copy of the local paper containing the announcement of the disappearance with the description of the missing man issued by the police. With native caution, Mr. Pottermack had used the paper to line a drawer, and he now drew it forth and studied its remarkably full details. The coat was in his possession, most fortunately, since it was of a conspicuous pattern and would have been almost impossible to duplicate. The other clothing – the pin-head worsted waistcoat and trousers, the plain grey cotton shirt, the collar, neck-tie, and underclothing – was all of a kind that could be easily matched from the description, aided in some cases by his own memory, and the shoes, which were described minutely, could be duplicated with ease at any large shoe-retailers, while as to the rubber soles, they were of a pattern that were turned out by the thousand.

Nevertheless, the outfit for the deceased gave him endless trouble and occasioned numerous visits to London. The clothing called for tactful manoeuvring, since it was obviously not for his own wear. The "*Invicta*" sole manufacturers had to be found through the directory, and the circular heels, with their five-pointed stars, involved a long and troublesome search, for most of the star-pattern heels have six-pointed stars. And even when the outfit had been obtained the work was not at an end. For all the things were new. They had to be "conditioned" before they would be ready for the final act. The garments had to be worn, and worn roughly (in the garden and workshop, since their size made them entirely unpresentable), to produce marks of wear and convincing creases. The shoes, when the soles had been stuck on and a knife-cut made across the neck of the horse on the right sole, had to be taken out for long nocturnal walks on rough roads, having been previously fitted with two pairs of inner cork soles to prevent them from dropping off. The underclothing would require to be marked, but this Pottermack prudently put off until the last moment. Still, all these preparatory activities took up a good deal of time and gave a considerable amount of trouble. Not that time was of any importance. There was no hurry. Now that Pottermack had a plan his mind was at rest.

Moreover, he had certain distractions, besides his frequent visits to Lavender Cottage. For, in addition to these preparations connected with the costume of the actor, there were others concerned with the scene of the drama. A suitable setting had to be found for James Lewson's next – and, as Pottermack devoutly hoped, final – appearance.

The place must of necessity be close at hand and ought to be on the line of Lewson's known route. This left, practically, the choice between the heath and the wood. The former he rejected as too exposed for his purpose and too much frequented to be perfectly convincing. Of the wood he knew little excepting that few persons seemed ever to enter it, probably for the reason that had led him to avoid it, that, owing to its neglected state, it was choked by almost impenetrable undergrowth.

Now he decided to explore it thoroughly, and since the path which meandered through it divided it into two nearly equal parts, he proposed to make a systematic exploration of each part separately.

He began with the part that lay to the left of the path, which was, if possible, less frequented than the other. Choosing a place where the undergrowth was least dense, he plunged in and began to burrow through the bushes, stooping low to avoid the matted twigs and branches and keeping an eye on a pocket-compass that he held in his left hand. It was a wearisome and uncomfortable mode of progression, and had the disadvantage that, doubled up as he was, he could see little but the compass and the ground at his feet. And it nearly brought him to disaster, for he had been blundering along thus for about ten minutes in as near to a straight line as was possible, when he suddenly found himself at the edge of what looked like a low cliff. Another step forward and he would have been over the brink.

He stopped short, and, straightening his back, drew aside the branches of the tall bushes and looked down. Beneath him was what had evidently been a gravel-pit, but it must have been disused for many years, for its floor was covered, not only with bushes but trees of quite a respectable size. It seemed to him that this place was worth a closer examination. And since the pit had been produced by excavation, there must obviously be some passage-way to the bottom, up and down which the carts had passed when the gravel was being dug.

Accordingly he began to make his way cautiously along the brink, keeping a safe distance from the possibly crumbling edge. He had proceeded thus for a couple of hundred yards when he came to the edge of a sunken cart-track, and following this, soon reached the entrance. Walking down the rough track, in which the deep cart-ruts could still be made out, he reached the floor of the pit and paused to look around, but the trees that had grown up and the high bushes made it impossible to see across. He therefore embarked on a circumnavigation of the pit, wading through beds of tall nettles that grew luxuriantly right up to the cliff-like face of the gravel.

He had made nearly half the circuit of the pit when he perceived, some distance ahead, a large wooden gate which guarded the entrance to a tunnel or excavation of some kind. It had two leaves, in of which he could see, as he came nearer, a wicket which stood half open. Approaching and peering in through the opening, he found the cavity to be an artificial cave dug in the hard gravel, apparently to serve as a cart-shelter, for the floor was marked by a pair of wide ruts and the remains of a broken sway-bar lay close to one side.

Deeply interested in this excavation, Mr. Pottermack pulled open the wicket-gate – in the lock of which a rusty key still remained – and stepping in through the opening, looked critically around the interior. That it had been for many years disused, so far as its original purpose was concerned, followed from the state of the pit and the absence of any signs of recent digging. But yet the cave itself showed traces of comparatively recent occupation, and those traces threw considerable light on the character of the occupants. A sooty streak up one wall, fading away on the roof, and a heap of wood-ashes mixed with fragments of charcoal, told of not one fire but a series of fires lit on the same spot. Beside the long-extinct embers lay a rusty "billy," originally made from a bully-beef tin fitted with a wire handle, fragments of unsavoury rags and a pair of decayed boots spoke of changes of costume that could certainly not have been premature, while numbers of bird and rabbit bones strewn around hinted at petty poaching, with, perchance, a fortunate snatch now and again in the vicinity of a farmyard.

Mr. Pottermack viewed these relics of the unknown nomad with profound attention. Like most resourceful men, he was quick to take a suggestion. And here, in the pit, the cavern, and these unmistakable relics, was a ready-made story. His own scheme had hardly advanced beyond the stage of sketchy outline. He knew broadly what he intended, but the details had not yet been filled in. Now he could complete the sketch in such detail that nothing would remain but the bare execution, and even that had been robbed of its chief difficulties by the discovery of this cavern.

He paced slowly up and down the echoing chamber, letting his imagination picture the dramatic climax and congratulating himself on this fortunate discovery. How astonishingly well it all came together! The place and the circumstances might have been designed for the very purpose. No need now to puzzle out a plausible cause of death. The empty poison-bottle and the discharged pistol-bullet, which he had considered alternatively, could now be discarded. The cause of death would be obvious. He had nearly broken his own neck coming here in broad daylight. If he had come in the dark, he would have broken it to a certainty.

Then there were the vanished notes and the necessarily empty pockets – necessarily empty, since, as he did not know what they had contained, he would not dare to introduce contents. He had hoped that a reasonable inference would be drawn. But now no inference would be needed. Even the most guileless village constable, when he had seen those fowl and rabbit bones, would understand how the deceased's pockets came to be empty.

From reflections on the great denouement Pottermack recalled his thoughts to the practical details of procedure. He proposed forthwith to take over the reversion of the late resident's tenancy. But he could not leave it in its present unguarded state. When the time came for him to occupy it he would require "the use and enjoyment of the said messuage and premises" in the strictest privacy. It would never do to have casual callers dropping in there in his absence. He must see how the place could be made secure.

Inspection of the entrance showed that the large gates were fastened on the inside by massive bars of wood thrust through great iron staples. Consequently, when the wicket-gate was locked the cave was absolutely secure from intrusion. The important question now was as to the lock of the wicket-gate. Was it possible to turn the key? A few strenuous wrenches answered the question in the negative. It is true that, by a strong effort, the rusty key could be made to turn backwards, but by no effort whatever could it be made to shoot the bolt. Key and lock were both encrusted with the rust of years.

There was only one thing to be done. The key must be taken away and scraped clean. Then, with the aid of oil or paraffin, it would probably be possible to make the lock work. By putting out all his strength, Pottermack managed to turn the key backwards far enough to enable him to pull it out of the lock, whereupon, having dropped it in his pocket, he retraced his steps to the entrance to the pit and walked up the sloping cart-track until it emerged on the level, when he halted, and having consulted his compass, set forth, holding it in his hand, and trying by means of the ruts to find the track along which the carts used to pass to and fro across the road.

As the matter was of considerable importance (since the cave was to be the scene of some momentous operations and it was necessary for him to be able to find his way to it with ease and certainty), he took his time over the survey, tracing the ruts until they faded away into the younger undergrowth, and thereafter identifying the overgrown track by the absence of large bushes or trees. From time to time he jotted down a note of the compass-bearing and sliced off with his knife a piece of bark from one of the larger branches of a bush or the trunk of a sapling, and so proceeded methodically, leaving an inconspicuously blazed trail behind him until at last he came out on to the path. Here he paused and looked about him for a landmark, his natural caution restraining him from making an artificial mark, nor was this necessary, for exactly opposite to the point where he had emerged, a good-sized beech tree stood back only a few yards from the path.

Having taken a good look at the tree, that he might recognize it at the next visit, he pocketed his compass and started homewards, counting his paces as he went until he reached the place where the path entered the wood, when he halted and wrote down in his pocket-book the number of paces. That done, his exploration was finished for the time being. The rest of the day he devoted to cleaning the key, to drawing on a card a little sketch-map of his route from the notes in his pocket-book, and to one or two odd jobs connected with the great scheme.

We need not follow his proceedings in minute detail. On the following day, having furnished himself with the cleaned key, a small spanner, a bottle of paraffin mixed with oil, and one or two feathers, he returned to the cave, finding his way thither without difficulty by the aid of his map. There he made a determined attack on the rusty lock, oiling its interior parts freely and turning the key – also oiled – by means of the spanner. At length its corroded bolt shot out with a reluctant groan, and when this, too, had been oiled and shot back and forth a few times,

Pottermack shut the wicket, locked it, and carried off the key in his pocket, with the comfortable feeling that he now had a secure place in which the highly compromising final operations could be carried out in reasonable safety.

And now the time drew nigh for those final operations to be proceeded with. The costume was complete and its various items had been brought by wear and rough usage to a suitable condition. The waning summer hinted at the approach of autumn and the weather would presently be such as to render woodland expeditions, especially of a nocturnal kind, disagreeable and difficult. And then Pottermack, though not in any way hustled, was beginning to look forward a little eagerly to the end of this troublesome, secret business. He yearned to feel that the tableau was set and that he could wait quietly for the denouement. Also, he was getting to feel very strongly that he would be glad to be relieved of the society of Khama-Heru.

But meanwhile that ancient libationer became daily a more and more undesirable tenant. For the time had come for the course of treatment that should render him at once more convincing and more portable. His condition when first unrolled from his wrappings was that of a wooden effigy, hard and stiff as a board. In that state he could never be got into his clothes, nor could he be transported to the cave under the necessary conditions of secrecy, nor could he effectively impersonate the late James Lewson. The work that the embalmers had done so well would have to be undone. After all, he had had some four-thousand years of physical immortality, so the embalmers' fees would not have been thrown away.

There was no difficulty about the treatment. Pottermack simply wrapped the mummy in several thicknesses of wet rag, poured a can of water over it, and, having enclosed it in an outer covering of tarpaulin, left it to macerate for forty-eight hours. When, at the end of that time, he uncovered it, he was at once encouraged and appalled. The last trace of the museum atmosphere was dissipated. It was a mummy no more but just an unburied corpse. The dry muscles had absorbed the moisture and swelled up to an unexpected bulk, the parchment-like skin had grown soft and sodden, and the skeleton hands had filled out and looked almost natural save for the queer, dirty orange colour of the fingernails. And even that, when Pottermack had observed it with a strong suspicion that it was an artificial stain, disappeared almost completely after a cautious application of chlorinated soda. In short, Khama-Heru seemed already to call aloud for the coroner. All, then, was going well so far. But Pottermack realized only too clearly that the part that was done was the easy part. The real difficulties had now to be faced, and when he

586

considered those difficulties, when he reflected on the hideous risks that he would have to run, the awful consequences of a possible miscarriage of his plans, he stood aghast.

But still with unshaken resolution he set himself to plotting out the details of the next move.

Chapter XIII
The Setting of the Tableau

The task which confronted Mr. Pottermack in the immediate future involved a series of operations of greatly varying difficulty. The materials for the "tableau" had to be transported from the workshop and tool-house to the cave in the gravel-pit. Thither they would be conveyed in instalments and left safely under lock and key until they were all there, ready to be "assembled". In the case of the clothing, the conveyance would be attended by no difficulties and little risk. It could be done quite safely by daylight. But the instalments of Khama-Heru, particularly the larger ones, would have to be transported, not merely after dark, but so late as to make it practically certain that he would have the path and the wood to himself.

The latter fact had been evident from the beginning, and in view of it, Pottermack had provided himself with a night-marching compass (having a two-inch luminous dial and direction-pointer) and an electric lamp of the police pattern, so that he was now ready to begin, and as he had decided to convey the clothing first, he commenced operations by making a careful survey of the separate items and putting the necessary finishing touches to them.

It was now for the first time that he made a thorough examination of Lewson's coat and of the contents of the letter-case. And it was just as well that he did, for among those contents was a recent letter from Alice, refusing a "loan" (probably that letter had precipitated the catastrophe). It was unsigned and bore no address, but still it might have given trouble, even if no one but himself should have been able to identify the very characteristic handwriting. Accordingly he burned it forthwith and went still more carefully through the remaining papers, but there was nothing more that interested him. They consisted chiefly of tradesmen's bills, demands for money owing, notes of racing transactions, a letter from his broker, and a few visiting-cards – his own – all of which Pottermack returned to their receptacle. The other pockets contained only a handkerchief, marked "*J. Lewson*", a leather cigarette-case, and a loose key which looked like a safe key. The key he transferred to the trousers pocket, the cigarette-case he burned, and the handkerchief he retained as a guide to the next operation, that of marking the underclothing. This he did with great care, following his copy closely and placing the marks in accordance with the particulars in the police description, using a special ink of guaranteed durability.

When the "properties" were ready for removal, he considered the question of time. This need not be a nocturnal expedition. There would be nothing suspicious in his appearance, and he had, in fact, during his exploration of the wood, not met or seen a single person. Still, it might be better to make his visit to the pit after dusk, when, even if he should be seen, he would not be recognized, and the nature of his proceedings there would not be clearly observable.

Accordingly he prepared for his start with the first instalment as the sun was getting low in the west. Lewson's coat he put on *in lieu* of his own, covering it with a roomy showerproof overcoat. The trousers and waistcoat he stowed neatly at the bottom of his rucksack with his moth-collecting kit and folding-net above them. Then, with the net-staff in his hand, he let himself out of the side gate just as the crimson disc of the sun began to dive behind a bank of slaty cloud.

The expedition was quite uneventful. He tramped along the path in the gloaming, a solitary figure in the evening landscape, he followed it into the wood and along to the now familiar beech tree, and in all the way he met not a soul. He turned off on the almost indistinguishable track, finding no need for his sketch-map and only glancing at the inconspicuous blazings on bush and sapling. By the time he reached the entrance to the pit, the dusk had closed in but even now there was light enough for him to find his way down the sloping cart-track, and even to note that apparently since his last visit, inasmuch as he had not noticed it before, a small tree had toppled over the edge of the cliff, bringing down with it a little avalanche of stones and gravel. He looked up and made a slight detour, picking his way cautiously among the fallen stones, and, preoccupied as he was, that fallen tree and those heaped and scattered stones started a train of thought of which he was hardly conscious at the time.

When he had shed Lewson's coat and by the light of a little, dim pocket-lamp unpacked the trousers and waistcoat, he threw them down in a corner at the back of the cave. Apprehensively he glanced round for some trace of recent visitors (though he knew there could have been none), then he extinguished the lamp, passed out through the wicket, shut the little gate, locked it, and, having pocketed the key, turned away with a sigh of relief. The first instalment was delivered. It wasn't much, but still, he had made a beginning.

On his way back through the wood he made use of the night-compass, not that he seemed greatly to need it, for he found his way with an ease that surprised him. But it was obviously a useful instrument and

589

it was well that he should acquire experience in its management, for there were circumstances that might possibly arise in which it would be invaluable. It would be a fearsome experience to be lost at night in the wood – especially with one of the later instalments.

The easy success of this first expedition had a beneficial moral effect, and with each of the succeeding journeys the strangeness of the experience wore off more and more. Even in the twilight he threaded the blazed track through the wood quite readily without reference to the blazings, and the return in the dark, with the glowing compass in his hand, was hardly more difficult. Half-a-dozen of these evening jaunts found the entire costume – clothes, shoes, cap, socks, underclothing – stored under lock and key in the cave – waiting for the arrival of the wearer.

But now came the really formidable part of the undertaking, and as Pottermack contemplated those next few journeys he quailed. There was now no question of setting forth in the gloaming, these journeys would have to be made in the very dead of night. So he felt, and even as he yielded to the feeling as to something inevitable, he knew that the reason for it was largely psychological, that it was determined by his own mental state rather than by external circumstances. Admittedly, a human head is an awkward thing to pack neatly in a rucksack. Still, it is of no great size. Its longest diameter, including the lower jaw, is no more than nine or ten inches. A half-quarter loaf and a bottle of beer would make a bigger bulge. Yet with these, Pottermack would have gone abroad gaily, never dreaming of having his burden challenged.

He knew all this. And yet as he took up the head (it came off in his hands owing to the frayed-out condition of the softened muscle and ligament) a thrill of horror ran through him at the thought of that journey. The thing seemed to grin derisively in his face as he carried it from the tool-house to the workshop, and when he laid it down on the sheet of brown paper on the bench, the jaws fell open as if it were about to utter a yell.

He wrapped it up hastily and thrust it into the ruck-sack, and then, by way of feeble and futile precaution stuffed the sugaring-tin and collecting-box on top. With creeping flesh he slung the package on his back and, grasping the net-stick, went out across the garden to the gate. He was frankly terrified. When he had passed out of the gate, he stood for some seconds irresolute, unwilling to shut it behind him, and when at last he closed it softly, the click of the spring-latch shutting him out definitely gave him such a qualm that he could hardly resist the impulse to reopen the gate, or, at least, to leave the key in the lock ready for instant use.

Once started, he strode forward at a rapid pace, restraining himself by an effort from breaking into a run. It was a pitch-dark night, near to new moon and overcast as well, so dark that he could barely see the path in the open, and only a slightly intenser gloom told him when he had entered the wood. Here he began to count his paces and strain his eyes into the blackness ahead, for, anticipating some nervousness on this journey, he had taken the precaution when returning from the last to spread a sheet of newspaper at the foot of the beech tree (which formed his "departure" for the cart-track and the gravel-pit) and weight it with a large stone. For this patch of light on the dark background he looked eagerly as he stumbled forward, peering into utter blackness and feeling his way along the path with his feet, and when he had counted out the distance and still saw no sign of it, he halted, and, listening fearfully to the stealthy night sounds of the wood, looked anxiously both ahead and behind him.

Nothing whatever could be seen. But perhaps it was too dark for even a white object to show. Perhaps he had counted wrong, or possibly in his haste he had "stepped out" or "stepped short". Reluctantly he drew out his little pocket-lamp (he did not dare to use the powerful inspection-lamp, though he had it with him) and let its feeble glimmer travel around him. Somehow the trees and bushes looked unfamiliar, but doubtless everything would look unfamiliar in that deceptive glimmer. Still, he had begun to know this path pretty well, even by night. Eventually he turned back and slowly retraced his steps, throwing the dim lamplight on the path ahead. Presently, out of the greenish gloom with its bewildering shadows there sprang a spot of white, and hurrying forward, he recognized with a sigh of relief the sheet of paper lying at the foot of the beech.

From this point he had no more difficulty. Plunging forward into the cellar-like darkness, he went on confidently, guided by the trusty compass which glowed only the more brightly for the impenetrable gloom around. Now and again he stopped to let the swinging dial come to rest and to verify his position by a momentary flash of the lamp. Soon he felt the familiar ruts beneath his feet and came out into the mitigated obscurity of the open track, then, following it down the slope, found his way through the nettles under the cliff, over the remains of the avalanche, until he reached the gate of the cave. A few minutes more and he had discharged his ghastly cargo, locked it into its new abode, and started, free at last from his horrid incubus, on the homeward journey, noting with a certain exasperation how, now that it was of no consequence, he made his way through the wood almost as easily as he would have done by daylight.

But it had been a harrowing experience. Short as had been the journey and light the burden, he stumbled in at his gate as wearily as if he had tramped a dozen miles with a sack of flour on his back. And yet it was but the first and by far the easiest of these midnight expeditions. He realized that clearly enough as he stole silently into the house while a neighbouring church clock struck two. There were three more instalments, and of the last one he would not allow himself to think.

But events seldom fall out precisely as we forecast them. The next two "trips" gave Pottermack less trouble than had the first, though they were undeniably more risky. The safe conveyance of the first instalment gave him confidence, and the trifling, but disconcerting, hitch in finding the "departure" mark suggested measures to prevent its repetition. Still, it was as well that he had transported the easiest load first, for the two succeeding ones made call enough on his courage and resolution. For whereas the head had merely created a conspicuous bulge in the rucksack, the legs refused to be concealed at all. Doubled up as completely as the softened muscles and ligaments permitted, each made an unshapely, elongated parcel over twenty inches in length, of which nearly half projected from the mouth of the rucksack.

However, the two journeys were made without any mishap. As on the previous occasions, Pottermack met nobody either on the path or in the wood, and this circumstance helped him to brace up his nerves for the conveyance of the final instalment. Indeed, the chance of his meeting any person at one or two in the morning in this place, which was unfrequented even by day, was infinitely remote. At those hours one could probably have walked the whole length of the town without encountering a single human being other than the constables on night duty, and it was certain that no constable would be prowling about the deserted countryside or groping his way through the wood.

So Pottermack argued, and reasonably enough, but still he shied at that last instalment. The headless trunk alone was some twenty-six inches long, and, with the attached arms, was a bulky mass. No disguise was possible in its conveyance. It would have to be put into a sack and frankly carried on his shoulder. Of course, if he met nobody, this was of no consequence apart from the inconvenience and exertion, and again he assured himself that he would meet nobody. There was nobody to meet. But still – well, there was no margin for the unexpected. The appearance of a man carrying a sack at one o'clock in the morning was a good deal more than suspicious. No rural constable or keeper would let him pass. And a single glance into that sack –

However, it was useless to rack his nerves with disquieting suppositions. There was pretty certainly not a human creature abroad in the whole countryside, and at any rate the thing had got to be taken to the cave. Quivering with disgust and apprehension, he persuaded the limp torso into the sack that he had obtained for it, tied up the mouth, and, hoisting it on his shoulder, put out into the darkness.

As soon as he had closed the gate he set off at a quick walk. He had no inclination to run this time, for his burden was of a very substantial weight from the moisture that it had absorbed. From time to time he had to halt and transfer it from one shoulder to the other. He would have liked to put it down and rest for a few moments, but did not dare while he was in the open. An unconquerable terror urged him forward to the shelter of the wood and forbade him to slacken his pace, though his knees were trembling and the sweat trickled down his face. Yet he kept sufficient presence of mind to make sure of his "departure", counting his paces from the entrance to the wood and showing the glimmer of his little lamp as his counting warned him of his approach to the beech tree. Soon its light fell on the sheet of paper, and, with a sigh of relief, he turned off the path into the old cart-track.

Once off the path, his extreme terror subsided and he followed the track confidently with only an occasional flash of his lamp to pick up a blaze on bush or tree and verify his direction. He even contemplated a brief rest, and he had, in fact, halted and was about to lower his burden from his shoulders when his ear seemed to catch a faint sound of movement somewhere within the wood. Instantly all his terrors revived. His limbs trembled and his hair seemed to stir under his cap as he stood stock-still with mouth agape, listening with almost agonized intentness.

Presently he heard the sound again, the sound of something moving through the undergrowth. And then it became quite distinct and clearly recognizable as footfalls – the footsteps of two persons at least, moving rather slowly and stealthily, and by the increasing distinctness of the sounds, it was evident that they were coming in his direction. The instant that he recognized this, Pottermack stole softly off the track into the dense wood until he came to a young beech tree, at the foot of which he silently deposited the sack, leaning it against the bole of the tree. Then in the same stealthy manner he crept away a dozen paces or so and again halted and listened. But now the sounds had unaccountably ceased, and to Pottermack the profound silence that had followed them was sinister and alarming. Suddenly there came to him distinctly a hoarse whisper, "Joe, there's someone in the wood!"

Again the deathly silence descended. Then the sack, which must have been stood up insecurely, slipped from the bole of the tree and rolled over among the dead leaves.

"J'ear that?" came the hushed voice of the unseen whisperer.

Pottermack listened intently, craning forward in an effort to locate the owner of the voice. In fact, he craned a little too far and had to move one foot to recover his balance. But the toe of that foot caught against a straggling root and tripped him up, so that he staggered forward a couple of paces, not noisily, but still very audibly.

Instantly the silence of the wood was dissipated. A startled voice exclaimed, "Gawd! Look out!" and then Joseph and his companion took to undissembled flight, bursting through the undergrowth and crashing into the bushes like a couple of startled elephants. Pottermack made a noisy pretence of pursuit which accelerated the pace of the fugitives, then he stood still, listening with grateful ears to the hurried tramplings as they gradually grew faint in the distance.

When they had nearly died away, he turned, and re-entering the dense wood, made his way, with the aid of the little lamp, towards the beech where he had put down the sack. But the beech was not exactly where he had supposed it to be, and it took him a couple of minutes of frantic searching to locate it. At last the feeble rays of his lamp fell on the slender trunk, and he hurried forward eagerly to retrieve his treasure. But when he reached the tree and cast the light of his lamp on the buttressed roots, the sack was nowhere to be seen. He gazed in astonishment at the roots and the ground beyond, but the sack was certainly not there. It was very strange. He had heard the sack fall over and roll off the roots, but it could not have rolled out of sight. Was it possible that the poachers, or whatever they were, could have picked it up and carried it away? That seemed quite impossible, for the voice had come from the opposite direction. And then the simple explanation dawned on him. This was the wrong tree.

As he realized this, his self-possession forsook him completely. With frantic haste he began to circle round, thrusting through the undergrowth, peering with starting eyes at the ground carpeted with last year's leaves on which the light fell from his lamp. Again and again a tall, slender trunk lured him on to a fresh disappointment. He seemed to be bewitched. The place appeared to be full of beech trees – as in fact it was, being a beech wood. And with each failure he became more wildly terrified and distraught. All sense of direction and position was gone. He was just blindly seeking an unknown tree in a pitch-dark wood.

Suddenly he realized the horrid truth. He was lost. He had no idea whatever as to his whereabouts. He could not even guess in which direction the track lay, and as to his hideous but precious burden, he might have strayed half-a-mile away from it. He stopped short and tried to pull himself together. This sort of thing would never do. He might wander on, at this rate, until daylight or topple unawares into the pit and

594

break his neck. There was only one thing to be done. He must get back to the path and take a fresh departure.

As this simple solution occurred to him, his self-possession became somewhat restored and he was able to consider his position more calmly. Producing his compass and opening it, he stood quite still until the dial came to rest. Then he turned slowly, so as not to set it swinging again, until the luminous "lubber-line" pointed due west. He had only to keep it pointing in that direction and it would infallibly lead him to the path, which ran nearly north and south. So, with renewed confidence, he began to walk forward, keeping his eye fixed on that invaluable direction-line.

He had been walking thus some three or four minutes, progressing slowly of necessity since he had to push straight forward through the undergrowth, when he tripped over some bulky object and butted rather heavily into the trunk of a tree. Picking himself up, a little shaken by the impact, he snatched out his lamp and threw its light on the object over which he had stumbled. And then he could hardly repress a shout of joy.

It was the sack.

How differently do we view things under different circumstances. When Pottermack had started, the very touch of that sack with its damp, yielding inmate had sent shudders of loathing down his spine. Now he caught it up joyfully, he could almost have embraced it, and as he set forward in the new direction he steadied it fondly on his shoulder. For he had not only found the sack, he had recovered his position. A dozen paces to the north brought him to the spot from whence he had stepped off the track into the wood. Now he had but to turn east and resume his interrupted journey.

But the meeting with those two men had shaken his confidence. He stole on nervously along the cart-track, and when he reached the pit, he peered apprehensively into the darkness on every side, half-expecting to detect some lurking figure watching him from among the high nettles. Only when he had at last deposited his burden in the cave and locked and tried the wicket was his mind even moderately at rest, and even then throughout the homeward journey his thoughts occupied themselves in picturing, with perverse ingenuity, all the mischances that might possibly have befallen him and that might yet lie in wait to defeat his plans in the very moment of their accomplishment.

He arrived home tired, shaken, and dispirited, inclined rather to let his thoughts dwell on the difficulties and dangers that lay ahead than to congratulate himself on those that he had surmounted. As he crept noiselessly up to bed and thought of the gruesome task that had yet to be accomplished, he resolved to give himself a day or two's rest to steady his nerves before he embarked on it. But the following day saw a change of mind. Refreshed even by the short night's sleep, as soon as he had risen he began to be possessed by a devouring anxiety to finish this horrible business and be done with it. Besides which, common sense told him that the presence of the body and the clothes in the cave constituted a very serious danger. If they should be discovered, very awkward enquiries might be set on foot, and at the best his scheme would be "blown on" and rendered impossible forever after.

A long nap in the afternoon further revived him, and as the evening wore on he began to be impatient to get on the road. This time there were no special preparations to make and no risks in the actual journeys, either going or returning. The recollection of those two men occasioned some passing thoughts of means of defence, for they had obviously been out for no good, as their precipitate retreat showed. He even considered taking a revolver, but his thorough-going British dislike of lethal weapons, which his long residence in the States had accentuated rather than diminished, made him reject the idea. The net-staff was quite a good weapon, especially in the dark, and, in fact, he was not particularly nervous about those men, or any others, so long as he bore no incriminating burden.

When at last he started, just after midnight, he carried the rucksack slung from his shoulders and the stout net-stick in his hand. But the former contained nothing but a bona fide collecting outfit, including the inspection-lamp, so even a police patrol had no terrors for him. Naturally, it followed that he neither met, saw, nor heard a single person either on the path or in the wood. Swinging easily along the now familiar way, he made his departure almost by instinct and threaded the cart-track with hardly a glance at the compass. And all too soon – as it seemed to him – he found himself at the gate of the cave with the last horrid task immediately confronting him.

It was even worse than he had expected, for he had never dared to let his imagination fill in all the dreadful details. But now, when he had locked himself in and hung the inspection-lamp on a nail in the gate so that a broad beam of light fell on the grisly heap, he stood, shivering and appalled, struggling to brace up his courage to begin. And at last he brought himself to the sticking point and fell to work.

We need not share his agonies. It was a loathly business. The dismembered parts had to be inducted separately into their garments, leaving the 'assembling' for a later stage, and the sheer physical difficulty of persuading those limp, flabby, unhelpful members into the closer-fitting articles of clothing was at once an aggravation and a distraction from the horror of the task. And with it all, it was necessary to keep the attention wide awake. For there must be no mistakes. A time would come when the clothing would be submitted to critical examination and the slightest error might rouse fatal suspicions. So Pottermack told himself as, with trembling fingers, he buttoned the waistcoat on the headless, legless torso, only to discover, as he fastened the last button, that he had forgotten the braces.

At length the actual clothing was completed. The legs, encased in underclothing, trousers, socks and shoes, lay on the floor, sprawling in hideous, unnatural contortion, the trunk, fully dressed even to collar and neck-tie, reposed on its back with its arms flung out and the brown, claw-like hands protruding from the sleeves, while, hard by, the head seemed to grin with sardonic amusement at the cloth cap that sat incongruously on its ancient cranium. All was now ready for the 'assembling'.

This presented less difficulty, but the result was far from satisfactory. For no kind of fastening was permissible. The legs were joined to the trunk by the trousers only, secured precariously by the braces. As to the head, it admitted of no junction, but would have to be placed in position as best it could. However, bad as the "assemblage" was, it would answer well enough if there were no premature discovery.

Having seen everything ready for the final act, Pottermack switched off the lamp and stood awhile to let his eyes grow accustomed to the darkness before he should venture outside. It was not a situation that was helpful to a man whose nerves were already on edge. All sorts of sinister suggestions awakened in his mind in connection with the ghastly figure that sprawled unseen within a few inches of his feet. And then he became acutely sensible of the sepulchral silence of the place, a silence which was yet penetrated by sounds from without, especially by the hootings of a company of owls, whose derisive "hoo-hoos" seemed particularly addressed to him with something of a menacing quality. At length, finding the suspense unbearable, he unlocked the wicket and looked out. By now his eyes had recovered from the glare of the lamp sufficiently for him to be able to see the nearer objects distinctly and to make out the shadowy mass of the cliff close at hand. He peered into the gloom on all sides and listened intently. Nothing seemed to be moving, nor could his ear detect aught but the natural sounds of the woods.

He turned back into the cave, and, guided by a momentary glimmer of his small lamp, carefully gathered up the limp, headless effigy and lifted it with infinite precaution not to disturb the insecure fastenings that held its parts together. Thus he carried it tenderly out through the wicket, and, stepping cautiously over the rough ground and through the rank vegetation, bore it to "the appointed place" – the place where the fallen tree and the scattered stones and gravel marked the site of the "avalanche". Here, close by the tree, he laid it down, and, having inspected it rapidly by the light of the lamp and made a few readjustments, he went back and fetched out the head. This he laid in position by what was left of the neck and supported it in the chosen posture by packing handfuls of gravel round it. When the arrangement was completed he threw the feeble glimmer of the lamp on it once more and looked it over quickly. Then, satisfied that its appearance was as convincing as he could make it, he gathered a few stones and laid them on it, sprinkled over it a handful or two of gravel, and, finally, pulled the high nettles down over it until it was almost hidden from view.

And with that, his task was finished. Now, all he had to do was to get clear of the neighbourhood and wait for whatever might happen. With a sigh of relief he turned away and re-entered the cave, for the last time, as he hoped. Shutting himself in once more, he made a thorough examination of the place by the light of the inspection-lamp to make sure that he had left no traces of his tenancy. The remains of the tramp's fire, the billy, and the fowl and rabbit bones, he left intact, and, having satisfied himself that there was nothing else, he slipped on his rucksack, picked up his net-stick and went out, leaving the wicket gate ajar with the key in the outside of the lock as he had found it.

Very different were his feelings this night as he wended homewards through the woods from what they had been on the night before. Now he cared not whom he might meet – though he was better pleased that he met nobody. His task was done. All the troublesome secrecy and scheming was over, and all the danger was at an end. His premises were purged of every relic of that night of horror and release. Now he could go back to his normal life and resume his normal occupations. And as to the future, at the worst, a premature discovery might expose the fraud and spoil his plans. But no one would connect him with the fraud. He had given no name to the auctioneer. If suspicion fell on any one, it would fall on the fugitive, James Lewson.

But it was infinitely unlikely that the fraud would be detected. And if it were not, if all went well, James Lewson would be given a decent, reasonable death, and, in due course, a suitable burial. And – again in due course – Alice Bellard would become Mrs. Pottermack.

Chapter XIV
The Discovery

It will not appear surprising that for some days after his final expedition Mr. Pottermack's thoughts were almost exclusively occupied by the product of that night's labour. Indeed, his interest in it was so absorbing that on the very next day he was impelled to pay it a visit of inspection. He did not, however, go down to the gravel-pit, but, approaching it from above, found his way easily to that part of the brink from which the tree had fallen, carrying the "avalanche" with it. Here, going down on hands and knees, he crept to the extreme edge and peered over. There was not much to see. There lay the fallen tree, there was the great bed of nettles, and in the midst of it an obscure shape displaying at one end a pair of shoes and at the other, part of a shabby cap.

It was surprisingly inconspicuous. The tall nettles, which he had pulled down across it, concealed the face and broke the continuity of the figure so that its nature was not evident at the first glance. This was eminently satisfactory, for it multiplied the improbabilities of early discovery. It was unlikely that any one would come here at all, but if some person should chance to stray hither, still it was unlikely that the body would be observed.

Considerably reassured, Mr. Pottermack backed away from the insecure edge and went his way, and thereafter firmly resisted the strong impulse to repeat his visit. But, as we have said, that grim figure, though out of sight, was by no means out of mind, and for the next week or two Mr. Pottermack was uncomfortably on the *qui vive* for the rumour of discovery. But as the weeks went by and still the body lay undiscovered, his mind settled down more and more to a state of placid expectancy.

The summer came to an end with a month of steady rain that made the woods impossible for wayfarers despite the gravel soil. The autumn set in mild and damp. Hedgerow elms broke out into patches of yellow, and the beeches in the wood, after a few tentative changes, burst out into a glory of scarlet and crimson and orange. But their glory was short-lived. A sudden sharp frost held them in its grip for a day or two, and when it lifted, the trees were bare. Their gay mantles had fallen to form a carpet for the earth at their feet.

Then came the autumn gales, driving the fallen leaves hither and thither, but sooner or later driving most of them into the gravel-pit, whence there was no escape. And there they accumulated in drifts and mounds, moving restlessly round their prison as the winds eddied beneath the cliffs, and piling up in sheltered places, smothering the nettles and flattening them down by their weight.

Once, at this time, Mr. Pottermack was moved to call on the disguised libationer. But when he crawled to the edge of the pit and looked down, the figure was invisible. Even the nettles were hidden. All that was to be seen was a great russet bank, embedding the fallen tree, and revealing to the expert eye a barely perceptible elongated prominence.

These months of waiting were to Pottermack full of peace and quiet happiness. He was not impatient. The future was rich in promise and it was not so far ahead but that it seemed well within reach. He had no present anxieties, for the danger of premature discovery was past, and every month that rolled away added its contribution of security as to the final result. So he went his way and lived his life, care-free and soberly cheerful.

There were, indeed, times when he was troubled with twinges of compunction with regard to his beloved friend, for whom these Titanic labours had been undertaken. For Alice Bellard was acutely aware of the unsatisfactory nature of their relationship. She realized that simple, almost conventional friendship is no sort of answer to passionate love, and she made it clear to Pottermack that it was an abiding grief to her that she had no more to give. He yearned to disillusion her, to let her share his confident hopes that all would yet be well. But how could he? It was unavoidable that, in deceiving all the world, he must deceive her.

But, in fact, he was not deceiving her. He was merely conveying to her the actual truth by an indirect and slightly illusory method. So he argued in regard to his ultimate purpose, and as to this intervening period – well, obviously he could not make her an accessory to his illegal actions. So he had to put up, as best he could, with her grateful acknowledgments of his patience and resignation, his cheerful acceptance of the inevitable, feeling all the time an arrant humbug as he realized how far he had been from any such acceptance.

Thus, in quiet content and with rising hopes, he watched the seasons pass, saw the countryside mantled with snow, heard "the ring of gliding steel" on icebound ponds and streams, and walked with smoking breath on the hard-frozen roads. And still, as the sands of time trickled out slowly, he waited, now hardly expectant and not at all impatient but rather disposed to favour a little further delay. But presently the winter drew off her forces reluctantly, like a defeated army, with rear guard actions of rain and howling gales. And then the days began to lengthen, the sunbeams to shed a sensible warmth, the birds ventured on tentative twitterings and the buds made it clear that they were getting ready for business. In short, the spring was close at hand, and with the coming of spring, Mr. Pottermack's fancy lightly turned to thoughts of inquests.

For the time had come. The long months of waiting had been all to the good. They had given the crude understudy time to mature, to assimilate itself to its setting and to take on the style of the principal actor. But the preparatory stage must not be unduly prolonged or it might defeat its own end. There might come a stage at which the transformation would be so complete as not only to prevent the detection of the imposture but to render identification even of the counterfeit impossible. Hence, as the spring sunshine brightened and the buds began to burst, Mr. Pottermack's expectancy revived, not untinged with anxiety. Hopefully his thoughts dwelt on primrose-gatherers and rambling juveniles in search of birds' nests and eggs, and when still no news was heard from the gravel-pit, he began seriously to consider the abandonment of his purely passive attitude and the adoption of some active measures to bring about the discovery.

It was a difficult problem. The one thing that was quite clear to him was that he must on no account appear personally in the matter. He could not say exactly why. But he had that feeling, and probably he was right. But if he could not appear in it himself, how was the thing to be managed? That was the question that he put to himself a hundred times in a day, but to which he could find no answer. And as events fell out, no answer had, after all, to be found, for a contingency that he had never contemplated arose and solved his problem for him.

It happened that on a fine sunny day after a spell of wet he was moved to take a walk along the path through the wood, which he had not done for a week or two. He was conscious of a rather strong desire to pay a visit to the pit and see for himself how matters were progressing, but he had no intention of yielding to this weakness, for the nearer the discovery, the more necessary it was for him to keep well in the background. Accordingly he trudged on, propounding to himself again and again that seemingly unanswerable question, and meanwhile picking up half-unconsciously the old landmarks. He had approached within a few yards of the well-remembered 'departure' beech tree when he suddenly caught sight of a new feature that brought him instantly to a stand. Right across the path, cutting deep into the soft loam of the surface, was a pair of cart-ruts with a row of large hoof-marks between them. They were obviously quite fresh, and it was clear, by the depth and width of the ruts and by the number of hoof-prints and the fact that they pointed in both directions, that they had been made by more than one cart, or at least by more than one journey to and fro of a single cart.

As he was standing eagerly examining them and speculating on what they portended, a hollow rumbling on his right heralded the approach of an empty cart from the west. A few moments later it came into sight through an opening just beyond the beech, the carter, dismounted, leading his horse by the bridle. Seeing Pottermack, he touched his hat and civilly wished him good morning.

"Now, where might you be off to?" Pottermack enquired genially.

"To the old gravel-pit, sir," was the reply. "'Tis many a year since any gravel was dug there. But Mr. Barber he's a-makin' a lot of this here concrate stuff for to put into the foundations of the new houses what he's buildin', and he thought as it were foolishness to send for gravel to a distance when there's a-plenty close at hand. So we're a-openin' up the old pit."

"Where about is the pit?" asked Pottermack. "Is it far from here?"

"Far! Lor' bless yer, no, sir. Just a matter of a few hundred yards. If you like to walk along with me, I'll show you the place."

Pottermack accepted the offer promptly, and as the man started his horse with a friendly "gee-up," he walked alongside, following the new ruts down the familiar track – less familiar now that the great hoofs and the wide cart wheels had cleared an open space – until they came out at the top of the rough road that led down to the pit. Here Pottermack halted, wishing his friend "Good morning," and stood watching the cart as it rumbled down the slope and skirted the floor of the pit towards a spot where a bright-coloured patch on the weathered "face" showed the position of the new working.

Here Pottermack could see two men loosening the gravel with picks and two more shovelling the fallen stuff into a cart that was now nearly full. The place where they were at work was on the right side of the pit, as Pottermack stood, and nearly opposite to the cave, the gates of which he could see somewhat to his left. Standing there, he made a rapid mental note of the relative positions, and then, turning about, made his way back to the path, cogitating profoundly as he went.

How long would it be before one of those men made the momentous discovery? Or was it possible that they might miss it altogether? The British labourer is not by nature highly observant, nor has he an excessively active curiosity. Nearly the whole width of the pit separated them from the remains. No occasion need arise for them to stray away from the spot where their business lay. But it would be exasperating if they should work there for a week or two and then go away leaving the discovery still to be made.

However, it was of no use to be pessimistic. There was a fair probability that one of them would at least go round to the cave. Quite possibly it might again be put to its original use as a cart-shelter. For his part, he could do no more than wait upon the will of Fortune and meanwhile hold himself prepared for whatever might befall. But in spite of the latter discreet resolution, the discovery, when it came, rather took him by surprise. He was lingering luxuriously over his after-breakfast pipe some four or five days after his meeting with the carter, idly turning over the leaves of a new book, while his thoughts circled about the workers in the pit and balanced the chances of their stumbling upon that gruesome figure under the cliff, when a familiar knock at the front door dispelled his reverie in an instant and turned his thoughts to more pleasant topics. He had risen and was about to go to the door himself, but was anticipated by Mrs. Gadby, who, a few moments later, announced and ushered in Mrs. Bellard.

Pottermack advanced to greet her, but was instantly struck by something strange and disquieting in her appearance and manner. She stopped close by the door until the housekeeper's footsteps had died away. Then, coining close to him, exclaimed almost in a whisper, "Marcus, have you heard – about James, I mean?"

"James!" repeated Pottermack helplessly, his wits for the moment paralysed by the suddenness of the disclosure. Then, pulling himself together with a violent effort, he asked, "You don't mean to say that fellow has turned up again?"

"Then you haven't heard. He is dead, Marcus. They found his body yesterday evening. The news is all over the town this morning."

"My word!" exclaimed Pottermack. "This is news with a vengeance! Where was he found?"

"Quite near here. In a gravel-pit in Potter's Wood. He must have fallen into it the very night that he went away."

"Good gracious!" ejaculated Pottermack. "What an astonishing thing! Then he must have been lying there all these months! But – er – I suppose there is no doubt that it is Lewson's body?"

"Oh, not the least. Of course the body itself was quite unrecognizable. They say it actually dropped to pieces when they tried to pick it up. Isn't it horrible? But the police were able to identify it by the clothes and some letters and visiting-cards in the pockets. Otherwise there was practically nothing left but the bones. It makes me shudder to think of it."

"Yes," Pottermack admitted calmly, his self-possession being now restored, "it does sound rather unpleasant. But it might have been worse. He might have turned up alive. Now you are rid of him for good."

"Yes, I know," said she, "and I can't pretend that it isn't a great relief to know that he is dead. But still – what ought I to do, Marcus?"

603

"Do?" Pottermack repeated in astonishment.

"Yes. I feel that I ought to do something. After all, he was my husband."

"And a shocking bad husband at that. But I don't understand what you mean. What do you suppose you ought to do?"

"Well, don't you think that somebody – somebody belonging to him – ought to come forward to – to identify him?"

"But," exclaimed Pottermack, "you said that there is nothing left of him but his bones. Now, my dear, you know you can't identify his bones. You've never seen them. Besides, he has been identified already."

"Well, say, to acknowledge him."

"But, my dear Alice, why on earth should you acknowledge him, when you had, years ago, repudiated him, and even taken another name to avoid being in any way associated with him? No, no, my dear, you just keep quiet and let things take their course. This is one of those cases in which a still tongue shows a wise head. Think of all the scandal and gossip that you would start if you were to come forward and announce yourself as Mrs. Lewson. You would never be able to go on living here. I take it that no one in this place knows who you are?"

"Not a soul."

"And how many people altogether know that you were married to him?"

"Very few, and those practically all strangers. We lived a very solitary life at Leeds."

"Very well. Then the least said, the soonest mended. Besides," he added, as another highly important consideration burst on him, "there is our future to think of. You are still willing to marry me, dear, aren't you?"

"Yes, Marcus, of course I am. But please don't let us talk about it now."

"I don't want to, my dear, but we have to settle this other matter. The position now is that we can get married whenever we please."

"Yes, there is no obstacle now."

"Then, Alice dearest, don't let us make obstacles. But we shall if we make known the fact that you were Lewson's wife. Just think of the position. Here were you and your husband in the same town, posing as total strangers. And here were you and I, intimate friends and generally looked upon almost as an engaged couple. Now, suppose that we marry in the reasonably near future. That alone would occasion a good deal of comment. But suppose that it should turn out that Lewson met his death by foul means. What do you imagine people would say then?"

"Good heavens!" exclaimed Alice. "I had never thought of that. Of course, people – or at any rate, some people – would say that we had conspired to get him out of the way. And really, that is what it would look like. I am glad I came and consulted you."

Pottermack drew a deep breath. So that danger was past. Not that it had been a very obvious danger. But instinct warned him – and it was a perfectly sound instinct – to avoid at all costs having his personality in any way connected with that of James Lewson. Now he would be able to watch the course of events at his ease, and to all appearance from the detached standpoint of a total stranger. Nor was Alice less relieved. Some obscure sense of loyalty had seemed to impel her to proclaim her relationship to the dead wastrel. But she was not unwilling to be convinced of her mistake, and when presently she went away, her heart was all the lighter for feeling herself excused from the necessity of laying bare to the public gaze the sordid details of her domestic tragedy.

When she was gone, Pottermack reflected on the situation and considered what he had better do. Caution conflicted with inclination. He was on the very tiptoe of curiosity, but yet he felt that he must show no undue interest in the affair. Nevertheless, it was desirable that he should know, if possible, what had really happened and what was going to be done about it. Accordingly he decided to go forth and perambulate the town and passively permit the local quidnuncs to supply him with the latest details.

He did not, however, add much to his knowledge excepting in one important respect, which was that the date of the inquest was already fixed. It was to take place at three o'clock in the afternoon on the next day but one, and having regard to the public interest in the case, the inquiry was to be held in the Town Hall. When he had ascertained this fact, and that the public would have free access to the hall during the proceedings, he went home and resolved to manifest no further interest in the case until those proceedings should open.

But the interval was one of intense though suppressed excitement. He could settle to nothing either in the workshop or in the garden. He could only seek relief in interminable tramps along the country roads. His mind seethed with mingled anxiety and hope. For the inquest was the final scene of this strange drama of which he was at once author and stage manager, and it was the goal of all his endeavours. If it went off successfully, James Lewson would be finished with for ever, he would be dead, buried, and duly registered at Somerset House, and Marcus Pottermack could murmur "*Nunc dimittis*" and go his way in peace.

Naturally enough, he was punctual, and more than punctual, in his attendance at the Town Hall on the appointed day, for he arrived at the entrance nearly half-an-hour before the time announced for the opening of the inquiry. However, he was not alone. There were others still more punctual and equally anxious to secure good places. In fact, there was quite a substantial crowd of early place-seekers which grew from moment to moment. But their punctuality failed to serve its purpose, since the main doors were still closed and a constable stationed in front of them barred all access. Some of them strayed into the little square or yard adjoining, apparently for the satisfaction of looking at the closed door of the mortuary on its farther side.

Pottermack circulated among the crowd, speaking to no one but listening to the disjointed scraps of conversation that came his way. His state of mind was very peculiar. He was acutely anxious, excited, and expectant. But behind these natural feelings he had a queer sense of aloofness, of superiority to these simple mortals around him, including the coroner and the police. For he knew all about it, whereas they would presently grope their way laboriously to a conclusion, and a wrong conclusion at that. He knew whose were the remains lying in the mortuary. He could have told them that they were about to mistake the scanty vestiges of a libationer of the nineteenth or twentieth dynasty for the body of the late James Lewson. So it was that he listened with a sort of indulgent complacency to the eager discussions concerning the mysterious end of the deceased branch manager.

Presently a report began to circulate that a gentleman had been admitted to the mortuary by the sergeant and, as the crowd forthwith surged along in that direction, he allowed himself willingly to be carried with it. Arrived at the little square, the would-be spectators developed a regular gyratory movement down one side and up the other, being kept on the move by audible requests to "Pass along, please". In due course, Pottermack came in sight of the mortuary door, now half-open and guarded by a police-sergeant who struggled vainly to combine the incompatible qualities of majestic impassivity and a devouring curiosity as to what was going on inside.

At length Pottermack reached the point at which he could see in through the half-open door, and at the first glance his "superiority complex" underwent sudden dissolution. A tall man, whose back was partly turned towards him, held in his hand a shoe, the sole of which he was examining with concentrated attention. Pottermack stopped dead, gazing at him in consternation. Then the sergeant sang out his oft-repeated command and Pottermack was aware of increasing pressure from behind. But at the very instant when he was complying with the sergeant's injunction to "Pass along", the tall man turned his head to look out at the door and their eyes met. And at the sight of the man's face Pottermack could have shrieked aloud.

It was the strange lawyer.

For some moments Pottermack's faculties were completely paralysed by this apparition. He drifted on passively with the crowd in a state of numb dismay. Presently, however, as the effects of the shock passed off and his wits began to revive, some of his confidence revived with them. After all, what was there to be so alarmed about? The man was only a lawyer, and he had seemed harmless enough when they had talked together at the gate. True, he had seemed to be displaying an unholy interest in the soles of those shoes. But what of that? Those soles were all correct, even to the gash in the horse's neck. They were, in fact, the most convincing and unassailable part of the make-up.

But, encourage himself as he would, the unexpected appearance of this lawyer had given his nerves a nasty jar. It suggested a number of rather disquieting questions. For instance, how came this man to turn up at this "psychological moment" like a vulture sniffing from afar a dead camel in the desert? Why was he looking at those soles with such extraordinary interest? Was it possible that he had seen those photographs? And if so, might they have shown something that was invisible to the unaided eye?

These questions came crowding into Mr. Pottermack's mind, each one more disquieting than the others. But always he came back to the most disquieting one of all. How, in the name of Beelzebub, came this lawyer to make his appearance in the Borley Mortuary at this critical and most inopportune moment?

It was natural that Mr. Pottermack should ask himself this very pertinent question, for, in truth, it did appear a singular coincidence. And inasmuch as coincidences usually seem to demand some explanation, we may venture to pursue the question that the reader may attain to the enlightenment that was denied to Mr. Pottermack.

607

Chapter XV
Dr. Thorndyke's
Curiosity Is Aroused

The repercussions of Mr. Pottermack's activities made themselves felt at a greater distance than he had bargained for. By the agency of an enterprising local reporter, they became communicated to the daily press, and thereby to the world at large, including Number 5A King's Bench Walk, Inner Temple, London, E.C., and the principal occupant thereof. The actual purveyor of intelligence to the latter was Mr. Nathaniel Polton, and the communication took place in the afternoon of the day following the discovery. At this time, Dr. Thorndyke was seated at the table with an open brief before him, jotting down a few suggestions for his colleague, Mr. Anstey, when to him entered Nathaniel Polton aforesaid, with a tray of tea-things in one hand and the evening paper in the other. Having set down the tray, he presented the paper, neatly folded into a small oblong, with a few introductory words.

"There is a rather curious case reported in *The Evening Post*, sir. Looks rather like something in our line. I thought you might be interested to see it, so I've brought you the paper."

"Very good of you, Polton," said Thorndyke, holding out his hand with slightly exaggerated eagerness. "Curious cases are always worth our attention."

Accordingly, he proceeded to give his attention to the marked paragraph, but at the first glance at the heading, the interest which he had assumed out of courtesy to his henchman became real and intense. Polton noted the change, and his lined face crinkled up into a smile of satisfaction as he watched his employer reading the paragraph through with a concentration that, even to him, seemed hardly warranted by the matter. For, after all, there was no mystery about the affair, so far as he could see. It was just curious and rather gruesome. And Polton had a distinct liking for the gruesome. So, apparently, had the reporter, for he used that very word to lend attraction to his heading. Thus:

Gruesome Discovery at Borley

Yesterday afternoon some labourers who were digging gravel in a pit in Potter's Wood, Borley, near Aylesbury,

608

made a shocking discovery. When going round the pit to inspect a disused cart-shelter, they were horrified at coming suddenly upon the much-decomposed body of a man lying at the foot of the perpendicular "face", down which he had apparently fallen some months previously. Later it was ascertained that the dead man is a certain James Lewson, the late manager of the local branch of Perkins's Bank, who disappeared mysteriously about nine months ago. An inquest on the body is to be held at the Town Hall, Borley, on Thursday next at 3 p.m., when the mystery of the disappearance and death will no doubt be elucidated.

"A very singular case, Polton," said Thorndyke, as he returned the paper to its owner. "Thank you for drawing my attention to it."

"There doesn't seem to be any mystery as to how the man met his death," remarked Polton, cunningly throwing out this remark in the hope of eliciting some illuminating comments. "He seems to have just tumbled into the pit and broken his neck."

"That is what is suggested," Thorndyke agreed. "But there are all sorts of other possibilities. It would be quite interesting to attend the inquest and hear the evidence."

"There is no reason why you shouldn't, sir," said Polton. "You've got no arrangements for Thursday that can't easily be put off."

"No, that is true," Thorndyke rejoined. "I must think it over and consider whether it would be worth giving up the time."

But he did not think it over, for the reason that he had already made up his mind. Even as he read the paragraph, it was clear to him that here was a case that called aloud for investigation.

The call was twofold. In the first place, he was profoundly interested in all the circumstances surrounding the disappearance of James Lewson. In any event, he would have wished to make his understanding of the case complete. But there was another and a more urgent reason for inquiry. Hitherto his attitude had been simply spectatorial. Neither as a citizen nor as an officer of the law had he felt called upon to interfere. Now it became incumbent on him to test the moral validity of his position, to ascertain whether that detached attitude was admissible in these new circumstances.

The discovery had taken him completely by surprise. Some developments he had rather expected. The appearance of the stolen notes, for instance, had not surprised him at all. It had seemed quite "according to plan", just a manoeuvre to shift the area of inquiry. But this new development admitted of no such explanation, for if it was an "arrangement" of some kind, what could be the motive? There appeared to be none.

He was profoundly puzzled. If this was really James Lewson's body, then the whole of his elaborate scheme of reasoning was fallacious. But it was not fallacious. For it had led him to the conclusion that Mr. Marcus Pottermack was Jeffrey Brandon, deceased. And investigation had proved beyond a doubt that that conclusion was correct. But a hypothesis which, on being applied, yields a new truth – and one that is conditional upon its very terms – must be true. But again, if his reasoning was correct, this could not be Lewson's body.

But if it was not Lewson's body, whose body was it? And how came it to be dressed in Lewson's clothes – if they really were Lewson's clothes and not a carefully substituted make-up? It was here that the question of public policy arose. For here was undoubtedly a dead person. If that person proved to be James Lewson, there was nothing more to be said. But if he were *not* James Lewson, then it became his, Thorndyke's, duty as a citizen and a barrister to ascertain who he was and how his body came to be dressed in Lewson's clothes – or, at least, to set going inquiries to that effect.

That evening he rapidly reviewed the material on which his reasoning had been based. Then, unrolling the strip of photographs, he selected a pair of the most distinct – showing a right and a left foot – and, with the aid of the little document microscope, made an enlarged drawing of each on squared paper to a scale of three inches to the foot, *i.e.* a quarter of the natural size. The drawings, however, were little more than outlines, showing none of the detail of the soles, but the dimensions were accurately rendered, excepting those of the screws which secured the heels, which were drawn disproportionately large and the position of the slots marked in with special care and exactness.

With these drawings in his pocket and the roll of photographs in his attaché case for reference if any unforeseen question should arise, Thorndyke started forth on the Thursday morning en route for Borley. He did not anticipate any difficulties. An inquest which he had attended at Aylesbury some months previously had made him acquainted with the coroner who would probably conduct this inquiry, but in any case, the production of his card would secure him the necessary facilities.

It turned out, however, that his acquaintance was to conduct the proceedings, though he had not yet arrived when Thorndyke presented himself at the Town Hall nearly an hour before the time when the inquest was due to open. But the police officer on duty, after a glance at his card, showed him up to the coroner's room and provided him with a newspaper wherewith to while away the time of waiting, which

Thorndyke made a show of reading, as a precaution against possible attempts at conversation, until the officer had retired, when he brought forth the two drawings and occupied himself in memorizing the dimensions and other salient characteristics of the footprints.

He had been waiting close upon twenty minutes when he heard a quick step upon the stair and the coroner entered the room with extended hand.

"How do you do, Doctor?" he exclaimed, shaking Thorndyke's hand warmly. "This is indeed an unexpected pleasure. Have you come down to lend us a hand in solving the mystery?"

"Is there a mystery?" Thorndyke asked.

"Well, no, there isn't," was the reply, "excepting how the poor fellow came to be wandering about the wood in the dark. But I take it, from your being here, that you are in some way interested or concerned in the case."

"Not in the case," replied Thorndyke. "Only in the body. And my interest in that is rather academic. I understand that it is known to have been lying exposed in the open for nine months. Now, I have never had an opportunity of inspecting a body that has been exposed completely in the open for so long. Accordingly, as I happened to be in the neighbourhood, I thought that I would ask your kind permission just to look it over and make a few notes as to its condition."

"I see, so that you may know exactly what a nine-months-old exposed body looks like, with a view to due future contingencies. But of course, my dear Doctor, I shall be delighted to help you to this modest extent. Would you like to make your inspection now?"

"How will that suit you?"

"Perfectly. The jury will be going in to view the remains in about half-an-hour, but they won't interfere with your proceedings. But you will probably be finished by then. Are you coming to the inquest?"

"I may as well, as I have nothing special to do for an hour or two, and the evidence may help me to amplify my notes."

"Very well," said the coroner. "Then I will see that a chair is kept for you. And now I will tell Sergeant Tatnell to take you to the mortuary and see that you are not disturbed while you are making your notes."

Hereupon, the sergeant, being called in and given his instructions, took Thorndyke in custody and conducted him down a flight of stairs to a side door which opened on a small square, on the opposite side of which was the mortuary. A considerable crowd had already collected here, in front of the Town Hall and at the entrance of the square, and by its members Thorndyke's emergence with the sergeant by no means passed unnoticed, and when the latter proceeded to unlock the mortuary door

611

and admit the former, there was a general movement of the crowd into the square with a tendency to converge on the mortuary door.

The sergeant, having admitted Thorndyke, gazed at him hungrily as he pointed out the rather obvious whereabouts of the corpse and the clothing. Then, with evident reluctance, he retired, leaving the door half open and stationing himself on guard in a position which commanded an unobstructed view of the interior. Thorndyke would rather have had the door closed, but he realized the sergeant's state of mind and viewed it not unsympathetically. And a spectator or two was of no consequence since he was merely making an inspection.

As the sergeant had obligingly explained, the body was in the open shell or coffin which rested on one of the tables, while the clothing was laid out on an adjoining table in a manner slightly reminiscent of a rummage sale or a stall in the Petticoat Lane Market. Having put down his attaché case, Thorndyke began his inspection with the clothing and, bearing in mind the sergeant's eye, which was following his every movement, he first looked over the garments, one by one, until he came naturally to the shoes. These he inspected from various points of view, and when he had minutely examined the uppers he picked up the right shoe, and, turning it over, looked at the heel. And in the instant that his glance fell on it his question was answered.

It was not Lewson's shoe.

Putting it down, he picked up the left shoe and inspected it in the same manner. It gave the same answer as the right had done, and each confirmed the other with the force of cumulative evidence. These were not James Lewson's shoes. There was no need to apply the measurements that he had marked on his diagrams. The single fact which he had elicited settled the matter.

It was quite a plain and obvious fact, too, though it had escaped the police for the simple reason that they were not looking for a discrepancy in the position of the screws. But it was absolutely conclusive. For the central screw by which a circular rubber heel is secured is of necessity a fixture. When once it is driven in, it remains immovable so long as the heel continues in position. For if the screw turns in the slightest degree, its hold is loosened, it unscrews from its hole and the heel comes off. But these heels had not come off. They were quite firmly attached, as Thorndyke ascertained by grasping them and as was proved by the extent to which they were worn down. Therefore the screws could not have moved. But yet their slots were at a totally different angle from the slots of the screws in Lewson's shoes.

He was standing with the shoe in his hand when a sharply spoken command from the sergeant to "Pass along, please" caused him half-unconsciously to turn his head. As he did so, he became aware of Mr. Pottermack gazing at him through the half-open door with an expression of something very like consternation. The glance was only momentary, for, even as their eyes met, Pottermack moved away in obedience to the sergeant's command, reinforced by a vigorous *vis a tergo* applied by the spectators in his rear.

Thorndyke smiled grimly at the coincidence – which was hardly a coincidence at all – and then returned to the consideration of the shoes. He had thoroughly memorized his drawings, but still, his rigorously exact mind demanded verification. Accordingly he placed both shoes sole uppermost and – with his back to the sergeant – produced the drawings from his pocket for comparison with the shoes. Of course he had made no mistake. In the drawing of the right foot, the slot of the screw was at a right angle to the long axis of the shoe – in the position of the hands of a clock at a quarter-to-three. In the right shoe before him, the slot was oblique – in the position of the clock-hands at five-minutes-past-seven. So with the left, in the drawing it was in the position of ten-minutes-to-four, in the mortuary shoe it was in that of twenty-minutes-to-two.

The proof was conclusive, and it justified Thorndyke's forecast, for he had assumed that if the shoes on the discovered body were counterfeits, the one detail which the counterfeiter would overlook or neglect would be the position of the screw-slots, while, by the ordinary laws of probability, it was infinitely unlikely that the positions of the slots would happen to match in both feet by mere chance.

But, this point being settled, a more important one arose. If the shoes were *not* Lewson's shoes, the body was probably *not* Lewson's body. And if it were not, then it was the body of some other person, which conclusion would raise the further question. How was that body obtained? This was the vitally important issue, for it would appear that the having possession of a dead human body almost necessarily implies the previous perpetration of some highly criminal act.

So Thorndyke reflected, a little anxiously, as he stood by the open shell, looking down on the scanty remains of what had once been a man. His position was somewhat difficult, for since he had never seen Lewson and knew nothing of his personal characteristics beyond his approximate age and what he had inferred from the footprints – that he was a man approaching six feet in height, which appeared to be also true of the body in the shell – he had no effective means of identification. Nevertheless, it was possible that a careful examination might bring into view some distinctive characters that would furnish a basis for further inquiry when the witnesses should presently be called.

Thus encouraging himself, he began to look over the gruesome occupant of the shell more critically. And now, as his eye travelled over it, he began to be conscious of an indefinite something in its aspect that was not quite congruous with the ostensible circumstances. It seemed to have wasted in a somewhat unusual manner. Then his attention was attracted by the very peculiar appearance of the toe-nails. They showed a distinct orange-yellow coloration which was obviously abnormal, and when he turned for comparison to the finger-nails, traces of the same unnatural colour were detectable, though much less distinct.

Here was a definite suggestion. Following it up, he turned his attention to the teeth, and at once the suggestion was confirmed. These were the teeth of no modern civilized European. The crowns of the molars, cuspless and ground down to a level surface, spoke of the gritty meal from a hand-quern and other refractory food-stuffs beyond the powers of degenerate civilized man. Still following the clue, Thorndyke peered into the nasal cavities, the entrance to which had been exposed by the almost complete disappearance of the nose. With the aid of a tiny pocket electric lamp, he was able to make out on both sides extensive fractures of the inner bones – the turbinates and ethmoid. In the language of the children's game, he was "getting warm", and when he had made a close and prolonged examination of the little that was left of the abdomen, his last lingering doubts were set at rest.

He stood up, at length, with a grim but appreciative smile, and recapitulated his findings. Here was a body, found in a gravel-pit, clothed in the habiliments of one James Lewson. The toe and finger nails were stained with henna, the teeth were the characteristic teeth of somewhat primitive man, the ethmoid and turbinate bones were fractured in a manner incomprehensible in connection with any known natural agency, but in precisely the manner in which they would have been damaged by the embalmer's hook. There was not the faintest trace of any abdominal viscera, and there did appear to be – though this was not certain, owing to the wasted condition of the remains – some signs of an incision in the abdominal wall. And finally, the hair showed evidence of chemical corrosion, not to be accounted for by any mere exposure to the weather. In short, this body displayed a group of distinctive features which, taken collectively, were characteristic of, and peculiar to, an Egyptian mummy – and that it was an Egyptian mummy he felt no doubt whatever.

He hailed the conclusion with a sigh of relief. He had come here prepared to intervene at the inquest and challenge the identity of the corpse if he had found any evidence of the perpetration of a crime. But he would have been profoundly reluctant to intervene. Now there was no need to intervene, since there was no reason to suppose that any crime had been committed. Possession of an Egyptian mummy does not imply any criminal act. Admittedly, these proceedings of Mr. Pottermack's were highly irregular. But that was a different matter. Allowance had to be made for special circumstances.

Nevertheless, Thorndyke was not a little puzzled. Acting on his invariable principle, he had disregarded the apparent absence of motive and had steadily pursued the visible facts. But now the question of motive arose as a separate problem. What could be the purpose that lay behind this quaint and ingenious personation of a dead man? Some motive there must have been, and a powerful motive too. Its strength could be measured by the enormous amount of patient and laborious preparation that the result must have entailed, to say nothing of the risk. What could that motive have been? It did not, apparently, arise out of the original circumstances. There must be something else that had not yet come into view. Perhaps the evidence at the inquest might throw some light upon it.

At any rate, no crime had been committed, and as to this dummy inquest, there was no harm in it. On the contrary, it was all to the good. For it would establish and put on record a fact which otherwise would have-gone unascertained and unrecorded, but which ought, on public grounds, to be duly certified and recorded.

As Thorndyke reached this comfortable conclusion, the sergeant announced the approach of the jury to view the body, whereupon he picked up his attaché case and, emerging from the mortuary, made his way to the court-room and took possession of a chair which a constable was holding in reserve for him, close to that which was to be occupied by the coroner.

Chapter XVI
Exit Khama-Heru

Having taken his seat – and wished that it had been a little farther from the coroner's – Thorndyke glanced round the large court-room, noting the unusual number of spectators and estimating from it the intense local interest in the inquiry. And as his eye roamed round, it presently alighted on Mr. Pottermack, who had secured a seat in a favourable position near the front and was endeavouring, quite unsuccessfully, to appear unaware of Thorndyke's arrival. So unsuccessful, indeed, were his efforts that inevitably their eyes met, and then there was nothing for it but to acknowledge as graciously as he could the lawyer's friendly nod of recognition.

Pottermack's state of mind was one of agonized expectation. He struggled manfully enough to summon up some sort of confidence. He told himself that this fellow was only a lawyer, and that lawyers know nothing about bodies. Now, if he had been a doctor it might have been a different matter. But there was that accursed shoe. He had certainly looked at that as if he saw something unusual about it, and there was no reason why a lawyer shouldn't know something about shoes. Yet what could he have seen in it? There was nothing to see. It was a genuine shoe, and the soles and heels were unquestionably correct in every detail. He, Pottermack, could hardly have distinguished them from the originals himself.

So his feelings oscillated miserably between unreasonable hope and an all too reasonable alarm. He would have got up and gone out but that even his terrors urged him to stay at all costs and hear what this lawyer should say when his turn came to give evidence. And thus, though he longed to escape, he remained glued to his chair, waiting, waiting for the mine to blow up, and whenever his roving glance fell, as it constantly did from minute to minute, on the sphinx-like countenance of that inopportune lawyer, a cold chill ran down his spine.

Thorndyke, catching from time to time that wandering, apprehensive gaze, was alive to Mr. Pottermack's condition and felt a humane regret that it was impossible to reassure him and put an end to his sufferings. He realized how sinister a significance his unexpected arrival would seem to bear to the eyes of the self-conscious gamester, sitting there trembling for the success of his last venture. And the

616

position was made even worse when the coroner, re-entering with the jury, stopped to confer with him before taking his seat.

"You had a good look at the body, Doctor?" he asked, stooping and speaking almost in a whisper. "I wonder if it would be fair for me to ask you a question?"

"Let us hear the question," Thorndyke replied cautiously.

"Well, it is this – the medical witness that I am calling is the police surgeon's *locum tenens*. I don't know anything about him, but I suspect that he hasn't had much experience. He tells me that he can find nothing definite to indicate the cause of death, but that there are no signs of violence. What do you say to that?"

"It is exactly what I should have said myself if I had been in his place," Thorndyke replied. "I saw nothing that gave any hint as to the cause of death. You will have to settle that question on evidence other than medical."

"Thank you, thank you," said the coroner. "You have set my mind completely at rest. Now I will get on with the inquiry. It needn't take very long."

He retired to his chair at the head of the long table, on one side of which sat the jury and on the other one or two reporters, and having seen that his writing materials were in order, prepared to begin. And Thorndyke, once more meeting Mr. Pottermack's eye, found it fixed on him with an expression of expectant horror.

"The inquiry, gentlemen," the coroner began, "which we are about to conduct concerns the most regrettable death of a fellow-townsman of yours, Mr. James Lewson, who, as you probably know, disappeared rather mysteriously on the night of the 23rd of last July. Quite by chance, his dead body was discovered last Monday afternoon, and it will be our duty to inquire and determine how, when, and where he met with his death. I need not trouble you with a long preliminary statement, as the testimony of the witnesses will supply you with the facts and you will be entitled to put any questions that you may wish to amplify them. We had better begin with the discovery of the body and take events in their chronological order. Joseph Crick."

In response to this summons a massively built labourer rose and advanced sheepishly to the table. Having been sworn, he deposed that his name was Joseph Crick and that he was a labourer in the employ of Mr. Barber, a local builder.

"Well, Crick," said the coroner, "now tell us how you came to discover this body."

617

The witness cast an embarrassed glance at the eager jurymen, and, having wiped his mouth with the back of his hand, began, "'Twere last Monday afternoon – "

"That was the thirteenth of April," the coroner interposed.

"Maybe 'twere," the witness agreed cautiously, "I dunno. But 'twere last Monday afternoon. Me and Jim Wurdle had been workin' in the pit a-fillin' the carts with gravel. We'd filled the last cart and seen her off, and then, as it were gettin' on for knockin'-off time, we lights our pipes and goes for a stroll round the pit to have a look at the old shelter-place where they used to keep the carts in the winter. We'd got round to the gate and Jim Wurdle was a lookin'-in when I happened to notice a tree that had fell down from the top of the face. And then I see something layin' by the tree what had got a cap at one end and a pair of shoes at the other. Give me a regler start, it did. So I says to Jim Wurdle I says, Jim, I says, that's a funny-lookin' thing over yonder long-side the tree, I says. Looks like some one a-layin' down there, I says. So Jim Wurdle he looks at it and he says, 'Right you are, mate', he says, 'So it do', he says. So we walked over to have a look at it and then we see as 'twere a dead man, or leastways a man's skillinton. Give us a rare turn, it did, to see it a-layin' there in its shabby old clothes with the beedles a-crawlin' about on it."

"And what did you do then?" asked the coroner.

"We sung out to the other chaps t'other side of the pit and told them about it, and then we set off for the town as hard as we could go until we come to the police station, where we see Sergeant Tatnell and told him about it, and he sent us back to the pit to wait for him and show him where it were."

When the coroner had written down Crick's statement he glanced at the jury and enquired, "Do you wish to ask the witness any questions, gentlemen?" And as nobody expressed any such wish, he dismissed Crick and called James Wurdle, who, in effect, repeated the evidence of the previous witness and was in his turn dismissed.

The next witness was Inspector Barnaby of the local police force, a shrewd-looking man of about fifty, who gave his evidence in the concise, exact manner proper to a police officer.

"On Monday last, the thirteenth of April, at five twenty-one p.m., it was reported to me by Sergeant Tatnell that the dead body of a man had been discovered in the gravel-pit in Potter's Wood. I obtained an empty shell from the mortuary and, having put it on a wheeled stretcher, proceeded with Sergeant Tatnell to the gravel-pit, where the previous witnesses showed us the place where the body was lying. We found the body lying at the foot of the gravel-face close to a tree that had fallen

618

from the top. I examined it carefully before moving it. It was lying in a sprawling posture, not like that of a sleeping man but like that of a man who had fallen heavily. There were a few stones and some gravel on the body, but most of the gravel which had come down with the tree was underneath. The body was in an advanced stage of decay, so much so that it began to fall to pieces when we lifted it to put it into the shell. The head actually dropped off, and we had great trouble in preventing the legs from separating."

An audible shudder ran round the court at this description and the coroner murmured, "Horrible! Horrible!" But the inspector proceeded in matter-of-fact tones, "We conveyed the remains to the mortuary, where I removed the clothing from the body and examined it with a view to ascertaining the identity of the deceased. The underclothing was marked clearly '*J. Lewson*' and in the breast pocket of the coat I found a letter-case with the initials '*J.L.*' stamped on the cover. Inside it were a number of visiting-cards bearing the name '*Mr. James Lewson*' and the address '*Perkins's Bank, Borley, Bucks*', and some letters addressed to James Lewson, Esquire, at that address. In one of the trousers pockets I found a key, which looked like a safe key, and as there seemed to be no doubt that the body was that of Mr. Lewson, the late manager of the Borley branch of Perkin's Bank, I cleaned the rust off the key and showed it to Mr. Hunt, the present manager, who tried it in the lock of the safe and found that it entered and seemed to fit perfectly."

"Did it shoot the bolt of the lock?" one of the jurors asked.

"No," replied the inspector, "because, after Mr. Lewson went away and took the key with him, the manager had the levers of the lock altered and a pair of new keys made. But the old duplicate key was there, and when we compared it with the key from the body, it was obvious that the two keys were identical in pattern."

"Did you take any other measures to identify the body?" the coroner asked.

"Yes, sir. I checked the clothing carefully, garment by garment, by the description that we issued when Mr. Lewson disappeared, and it corresponded to the description in every respect. Then I got the caretaker from the bank to look it over, and he identified the clothes and shoes as those worn by Mr. Lewson on the night when he disappeared."

"Excellent," said the coroner. "Most thorough and most conclusive. I think, gentlemen, that we can fairly take it as an established fact that the body is that of Mr. James Lewson. And now. Inspector, to return to the clothing, you have mentioned two articles found by you in the deceased's pockets. What else did you find?"

619

"Nothing, sir. With the exception of those two articles – which I handed to you – the pockets were all completely empty."

"And the letter-case?"

"That contained nothing but letters, bills, cards, and a few stamps – nothing but what was in it when I gave it to you."

Here the coroner opened his attaché case and, taking from it the letter-wallet, the letters, cards, bills, and other contents, placed them, together with the key, on a wooden office tray which he pushed along the table for the jurymen's inspection. While they were curiously poring over the tray, he continued his examination.

"Then you found nothing of value on the person of the deceased?"

"With the exception of the stamps, nothing whatsoever. The pockets were absolutely empty."

"Do you happen to know if the deceased, at the time of his disappearance, had any valuable property about him?"

"Yes, sir. It is nearly certain that when he went away at about eight o'clock on the night of Wednesday, the twenty-third of last July, he had on his person one-hundred pounds in five-pound Bank of England notes."

"When you say that it is nearly certain, what does that certainty amount to?"

"It is based on the fact that after he had gone, banknotes to that amount were found to be missing from the bank."

"And is it known what became of those notes?"

"Yes, sir. Their numbers were known and they have now all been recovered. As soon as they appeared in circulation they were traced, and in nearly every case traced to some person who was known to the police."

"Is it certain that these notes were taken by the deceased and not by some other person?"

"Yes, practically certain. The deceased was in sole charge, and he had one key on his person and the other locked in the safe, where it was found when the lock was picked. But, if you will allow me, sir, I should like to say, in justice to the deceased, that he had, apparently, no intention of stealing these notes, as was thought at first. Certain facts came to light later which seemed to show that he had merely borrowed this money to meet a sudden urgent call and that he meant to replace it."

"I am sure everyone will be very glad to hear that," said the coroner. "We need not go into the circumstances that you mention, as they do not seem relevant to this inquiry. But these notes raise an important point. If they were on his person when he went away and they were not on his body when it was found, and if, moreover, they are known to have been in circulation since his death, the question of robbery arises, and with it the further question of possible murder. Can you give us any help in considering those questions?"

"I have formed certain opinions, sir, but, of course, it is a matter of guesswork."

"Never mind, Inspector. A coroner's court is not bound by the strict rules of evidence, and, besides, yours is an expert opinion. Let us hear what view you take of the matter."

"Well, sir, my opinion is that the deceased met his death by accident the night that he went away. I think that he fell into the pit in the dark, dislodging a lot of gravel and pulling the small tree down with him. Both the body and the tree were on top of the heap of gravel, but yet there was a good deal of gravel and some stones on the body."

The coroner nodded and the witness proceeded, "Then I think that, about a month later, some tramp found the body and went through the pockets, and when he discovered the notes, he cleared off and said nothing about having seen the body."

"Have you any specific reasons for this very definite theory?"

"Yes, sir. First, there is clear evidence that the pit has been frequented by one or more tramps. Quite close to where the body was discovered is an old cart-shelter, dug out of the gravel, and that shelter has been used from time to time by some tramp or tramps as a residence. I found in it a quantity of wood ashes and charcoal and large sooty deposits on the wall and roof, showing that many fires had been lit there. I also found an old billy, or boiling-can, a lot of rags and tramps' raffle, and a quantity of small bones – mostly rabbits' and fowls' bones. So tramps have certainly been there.

"Then the state of the deceased's pockets suggests a tramp's robbery. It was not only the valuables that were taken. He had made a clean sweep of everything. Not a thing was left. Not even a pipe or a packet of cigarettes or even a match-box."

"And as to the time that you mentioned?"

"I am judging by the notes. A sharp look-out was kept for them from the first. A very sharp look-out. But for fully a month after the disappearance not one of them came to light. And then, suddenly, they began to come in one after the other and even in batches, as if the whole lot had been thrown into circulation at once. But if it had been a case of robbery with violence, the robber would have got rid of the notes immediately, before the hue-and-cry started."

"So you consider that the possibility of robbery with murder may be ruled out?"

"On the facts known to me, sir, I do – subject, of course, to the medical evidence."

"Exactly," said the coroner. "But in any case you have given us most valuable assistance. Is there any point, gentlemen, that is not quite clear, or any question that you wish to put to the inspector? No questions? Very well. Thank you, Inspector."

The next witness called was the police surgeon's deputy, a youngish Irishman of somewhat convivial aspect. Having been sworn, he deposed that his name was Desmond M'Alarney, that he was a Doctor of Medicine, and at present acting as *locum tenens* for the police surgeon, who was absent on leave.

"Well, Doctor," said the coroner, "I believe that you have made a careful examination of the body of the deceased. Is that so?"

"I have made a most careful examination, sir," was the reply, "though as to calling it a body, I would rather describe it as a skeleton."

"Very well!" the coroner agreed good-humouredly, "call it what you like. Perhaps we may refer to it as the remains."

"Ye may," replied the witness, "and mighty small remains, by the same token. But such as they are, I have examined them with the greatest care."

"And did your examination enable you to form any opinion as to the cause of death?"

"It did not."

"Did you find any injuries or signs of violence?"

"I did not."

"Were any of the bones fractured or injured in any way?"

"They were not."

"Can you give us no suggestion as to the probable cause of death?"

"I would suggest, sir, that a twenty-foot drop into a gravel-pit is a mighty probable cause of death."

"No doubt," said the coroner. "But that is hardly a matter of medical evidence."

"Tis none the worse for that," the witness replied cheerfully.

"Can you say, definitely, that the deceased did not meet his death by any kind of homicidal violence?"

"I cannot. When a body is reduced to a skeleton, all traces of violence are lost so long as there has been no breaking of bones. He might have been strangled or smothered or stabbed or had his throat cut without leaving any marks on the skeleton. I can only say that I found no indications of any kind of homicidal violence or any violence whatsoever."

622

"The inspector has suggested that the deceased met his death by accident – that is, by the effects of the fall, and that appears to be your opinion too. Now, if that were the case, what would probably be the immediate cause of death?"

"There are several possible causes, but the most probable would be shock, contusion of the brain, or dislocation of the neck."

"Would any of those conditions leave recognizable traces?"

"Contusion of the brain and dislocation of the neck could be recognized in the fresh body, but not in a skeleton like this. Of course, if the dislocation were accompanied – as it very often is – by fracture of the little neck-bone known as the odontoid process of the axis, that could be seen in the skeleton. But there is no such fracture in the skeleton of the deceased. I looked for it particularly."

"Then we understand that you found nothing definite to indicate the cause of death?"

"That is so, sir."

"Do you consider that the appearance of the body, in a medical sense, is consistent with a belief that the deceased was killed by the effects of the fall?"

"I do, sir."

"Then," said the coroner, "that seems to be about all that we can say as to the cause of death. Do the jury wish to put any questions to the medical witness? If not, we need not detain the doctor any longer."

As Dr. M'Alarney picked up an uncommonly smart hat and retired, the coroner glanced quickly over his notes and then proceeded to address the jury.

"I need not occupy your time, gentlemen, with a long summing-up. You have heard the evidence and probably have already arrived at your conclusions. There are certain mysterious circumstances in the case – as, for instance, how the deceased came to be wandering about in the wood at night. But these questions do not concern us. We have to consider only how the deceased met his death, and as the doctor justly remarked, the fact that the body was found at the bottom of a gravel-pit, having evidently fallen some eighteen or twenty feet, offers a pretty obvious explanation. The only suspicious circumstance was that the deceased had clearly been robbed either before or after death. But you have heard the opinion of a very able and experienced police inspector, and the excellent reasons that he gave for that opinion. So I need say no more, but will now leave you to consider your verdict."

During the short interval occupied by the discussions of the jurymen among themselves, two members of the audience were engaged busily in reviewing the evidence in its relation to the almost inevitable verdict. To

Thorndyke, the proceedings offered an interesting study in the perverting effect upon the judgment of an unconscious bias, engendered by the suggestive power of a known set of circumstances. All the evidence that had been given was true. All the inferences from that evidence were sound and proper inferences, so far as they went. Yet the final conclusion which was going to be arrived at would be wildly erroneous, for the simple reason that all the parties to the inquiry had come to it already convinced as to the principal fact – the identity of the deceased person – which had accordingly been left unverified.

As to Pottermack, his state of mind at the close of the inquiry was one of astonished relief. All through the proceedings he had sat in tremulous expectancy, with a furtive eye on the strange lawyer, wondering when that lawyer's turn would come to give his evidence and what he would have to say. That the stranger had detected some part, at least, of the fraud he had at first little doubt, and he expected no less than to hear the identity of the body challenged. But, as the time ran on and witness after witness came forward guilelessly and disgorged the bait for the nourishment of the jury, his fears gradually subsided and his confidence began to revive. And now that the inquiry was really over and they had all gobbled the bait and got it comfortably into their gizzards, now that it was evident that this lawyer had nothing to say, after all, in spite of his preposterous porings over those admirable shoes, Mr. Pottermack was disposed just a little to despise himself for having been so easily frightened. The "superiority complex" began to reassert itself. Here he sat, looking upon a thoroughly bamboozled assembly, including a most experienced police inspector, a coroner, a lawyer, and a doctor. He alone of all that assembly, indeed of the whole world, knew all about it.

But perhaps his alarm had been excusable. We get into the habit too much importance to these lawyers and doctors. We credit them with knowing a great deal more than they do. But, at any rate, in this case it was all to the good. And as Mr. Pottermack summed up in this satisfactory fashion, the foreman of the jury announced that the verdict had been agreed on.

"And what is your finding, gentlemen, on the evidence that you have heard?" the coroner asked.

"We find that the deceased, James Lewson, met his death on the night of the twenty-third of last July by falling into a gravel-pit in Potter's Wood."

"Yes," said the coroner. "That amounts to a verdict of Death by Misadventure. And a very proper verdict, too, in my opinion. I must thank you, gentlemen, for your attendance and for the careful consideration which you have given to this inquiry, and I may take this opportunity of telling you what I am sure you will be glad to hear, that the directors of Perkins's Bank have generously undertaken to have the funeral conducted at their expense."

As the hall slowly emptied, Thorndyke lingered by the table to exchange a few rather colourless comments on the case with the coroner. At length, after a cordial handshake, he took his departure, and, joining the last stragglers, made his way slowly out of the main doorway, glancing among the dispersing crowd as he emerged, and presently his roving glance alighted on Mr. Pottermack at the outskirts of the throng, loitering irresolutely as if undecided which way to go.

The truth is that the elation at the triumphant success of his plan had begotten in that gentleman a spirit of mischief. Under the influence of the "superiority complex" he was possessed with a desire to exchange a few remarks with the strange lawyer, perhaps to 'draw' him on the subject of the inquest, possibly even to "pull his leg" – not hard, of course, which would be a liberty, but just a gentle and discreet tweak. Accordingly he hovered about opposite the hall, waiting to see which way the lawyer should go, and as Thorndyke unostentatiously steered in his direction, the meeting came about quite naturally, just as the lawyer was turning – rather to Mr. Pottermack's surprise – away from the direction of the station.

"I don't suppose you remember me," he began.

But Thorndyke interrupted promptly, "Of course I remember you, Mr. Pottermack, and am very pleased to meet you again."

Pottermack, considerably taken aback by the mention of his name, shook the proffered hand and cogitated rapidly. How the deuce did the fellow know that his name was Pottermack? He hadn't told him.

"Thank you," he said. "I am very pleased, too, and rather surprised. But perhaps you are professionally interested in this inquiry."

"Not officially," replied Thorndyke. "I saw a notice in the paper of what looked like an interesting case and, being in the neighbourhood, I dropped in to see and hear what was going on."

"And did you find it an interesting case?" Pottermack asked.

"Very. Didn't you?"

"Well," replied Pottermack, "I didn't bring an expert eye to it as you did, so I may have missed some of the points. But there did seem to be some rather queer features in it. I wonder which of them in particular you found so interesting?"

This last question he threw out by way of a tentative preliminary to of "drawing" the lawyer, and he waited expectantly for the reply.

Thorndyke reflected a few moments before answering it. At length he replied,

"There was such a wealth of curious matter that I find it difficult to single out any one point in particular. The case interested me as a whole, and especially by reason of the singular parallelism that it presented to another most remarkable case which was related to me in great detail by a legal friend of mine, in whose practice it occurred."

"Indeed," said Mr. Pottermack, still intent on tractive operations. "And what were the special features in that case?"

"There were many very curious features in that case," Thorndyke replied in a reminiscent tone. "Perhaps the most remarkable was an ingenious fraud perpetrated by one of the parties, who dressed an Egyptian mummy in a recognizable suit of clothes and deposited it in a gravel-pit."

"Good gracious!" gasped Pottermack, and the "superiority complex" died a sudden death.

"Yes," Thorndyke continued with the same reminiscent air, observing that his companion was for the moment speechless, "it was a most singular case. My legal friend used to refer to it, in a whimsical fashion, as the case of the dead man who was alive and the live man who was dead."

"B-but," Pottermack stammered, with chattering teeth, "that sounds like a c-contradiction."

"It does," Thorndyke agreed, "and of course it is. What he actually meant was that it was a case of a living man who was believed to be dead, and a dead man who was believed to be alive – until the mummy came to light."

Pottermack made no rejoinder. He was still dumb with amazement and consternation. He had a confused feeling of unreality as if he were walking in a dream. With a queer sort of incredulous curiosity he looked up at the calm, inscrutable face of the tall stranger who walked by his side and asked himself who and what this man could be. Was he, in truth, a lawyer – or was he the Devil? Stranger as he certainly was, he had some intimate knowledge of his – Pottermack's – most secret actions – knowledge which could surely be possessed by no mere mortal. It seemed beyond belief.

With a violent effort he pulled himself together and made an attempt to continue the conversation. For it was borne in on him that he must, at all costs, find out what those cryptic phrases meant and how much this person – lawyer or devil – really knew. After all, he did not seem to be a malignant or hostile devil.

626

"That must have been a most extraordinary case," he observed at length. "I am – er – quite intrigued by what you have told me. Would it be possible or admissible for you to give me a few details?"

"I don't know why not," said Thorndyke, "excepting that it is rather a long story, and I need not say highly confidential. But if you know of some place where we could discuss it in strict privacy, I should be pleased to tell you the story as it was told to me. I am sure it would interest you. But I make one stipulation."

"What is that?" Pottermack asked.

"It is that you, too, shall search your memory, and if you can recall any analogous circumstances as having arisen within your experience or knowledge, you shall produce them so that we can make comparisons."

Pottermack reflected for a few moments, but only a few. For his native common sense told him that neither secrecy nor reservation was going to serve him.

"Very well," he said, "I agree, though until I have heard your story I cannot judge how far I shall be able to match it from my limited experience. But if you will come and take tea with me in my garden, where we shall be quite alone, I will do my best to set my memory to work when I have heard what you have to tell."

"Excellent," said Thorndyke. "I accept your invitation with great pleasure. And I observe that some common impulse seems to have directed us towards your house, and even towards the very gate at which I had the good fortune to make your acquaintance."

In effect, as they had been talking, they had struck into the footpath and now approached the gate of the walled garden.

627

Chapter XVII
Dr. Thorndyke Relates a Queer Case

Mr. Pottermack inserted the small, thin key into the Yale lock of the gate and turned it while Thorndyke watched him with a faint smile.

"Admirable things, these Yale locks," the latter remarked as he followed his host in through the narrow gateway and cast a comprehensive glance round the walled garden, "so long as you don't lose the key. It is a hopeless job trying to pick one."

"Did you ever try?" asked Pottermack.

"Yes, and had to give it up. But I see you appreciate their virtues. That looks like one on the farther gate."

"It is," Pottermack admitted. "I keep this part of the garden for my own sole use, and I like to be secure from interruption."

"I sympathize with you," said Thorndyke. "Security from interruption is always pleasant, and there are occasions when it is indispensable."

Pottermack looked at him quickly but did not pursue the topic.

"If you will excuse me for a minute," he said, "I will run and tell my housekeeper to get us some tea. You would rather have it out here than in the house, wouldn't you?"

"Much rather," replied Thorndyke. "We wish to be private, and here we are with two good Yale locks to keep eavesdroppers at bay."

While his host was absent he paced slowly up and down the lawn, observing everything with keen interest but making no particular inspections. Above the yew hedge he could see the skylighted roof of what appeared to be a studio or workshop, and in the opposite corner of the garden a roomy, comfortable summer-house. From these objects he turned his attention to the sundial, looking it over critically and strolling round it to read the motto. He was thus engaged when his host returned with the news that tea was being prepared and would follow almost immediately.

"I was admiring your sun-dial, Mr. Pottermack," said Thorndyke. "It is a great adornment to the garden and a singularly happy and appropriate one, for the flowers, like the dial, number only the sunny hours. And it will look still better when time has softened the contrast between the old pillar and the new base."

"Yes," Pottermack agreed, a trifle uneasily, "the base will be all the better for a little weathering. How do you like the motto?"

"Very much," replied Thorndyke. "A pleasant, optimistic motto, and new to me. I don't think I have ever met with it before. But it is a proper sun-dial motto, '*Hope in the morning, Peace at eventide.*' Most of us have known the first and all of us look forward to the last. Should I be wrong if I were to assume that there is a well underneath?"

"N-no," stammered Pottermack, "you would not. It is an old well that had been disused and covered up. I discovered it by accident when I was levelling the ground for the sun-dial and very nearly fell into it. So I decided to put the sun-dial over it to prevent any accidents in the future. And mighty glad I was to see it safely covered up."

"You must have been," said Thorndyke. "While it was uncovered it must have been a constant anxiety to you."

"It was," Pottermack agreed, with a nervous glance at his guest.

"That would be about the latter part of last July," Thorndyke suggested with the air of one recalling a half-forgotten event, and Mr. Pottermack breathlessly admitted that it probably was.

Here they were interrupted by the arrival of Mrs. Gadby, for whom the gate had been left open, followed by a young maid, both laden with the materials for tea on a scale suggestive of a Sunday School treat. The housekeeper glanced curiously at the tall, imposing stranger, wondering inwardly why he could not come to the dining-room like a Christian. In due course, the load of provisions was transferred to the somewhat inadequate table in the summer-house and the two servants then retired, Mrs. Gadby ostentatiously shutting the gate behind her. As its lock clicked, Mr. Pottermack ushered his guest into the summer-house, offering him the chair once occupied by James Lewson and since studiously avoided by its owner.

When the hospitable preliminaries had been disposed of and the tea poured out, Thorndyke opened the actual proceedings with only the briefest preamble.

"I expect, Mr. Pottermack, you are impatient to hear about that case which seemed to pique your curiosity so much, and as the shadow is creeping round your dial, we mustn't waste time, especially as there is a good deal to tell. I will begin with an outline sketch of the case, in the form of a plain narrative, which will enable you to judge whether anything at all like it has ever come to your knowledge.

"The story as told to me by my legal friend dealt with the histories of two men, whom we will call respectively Mr. Black and Mr. White. At the beginning of the story they appear to have been rather intimate friends, and both were employed at a bank, which we will call Alsop's

Bank. After they had been there some time – I don't know exactly how long – a series of forgeries occurred, evidently committed by some member of the staff of the bank. I need not go into details. For our purpose the important fact is that suspicion fell upon Mr. White. The evidence against him was striking, and, if genuine, convincing and conclusive. But to my friend it appeared decidedly unsatisfactory. He was strongly disposed to suspect that the crime was actually committed by Mr. Black and that he fabricated the evidence against Mr. White. But, however that may have been, the Court accepted the evidence. The jury found Mr. White guilty and the judge sentenced him to five years' penal servitude.

"It was a harsh sentence, but that does not concern us, as Mr. White did not serve the full term. After about a year of it, he escaped and made his way to the shore of an estuary, and there his clothes were found and a set of footprints across the sand leading into the water. Some six weeks later a nude body was washed up on the shore and was identified as his body. An inquest was held and it was decided that he had been accidentally drowned. Accordingly he was written off the prison books and the records at Scotland Yard as a dead man.

"But he was not dead. The body which was found was probably that of some bather whose clothes Mr. White had appropriated in exchange for his own prison clothes. Thus he was able to get away without hindrance and take up a new life elsewhere, no doubt under an assumed name. Probably he went abroad, but this is only surmise. From the moment of his escape from prison he vanishes from our ken, and for the space of about fifteen years remains invisible, his existence apparently unknown to any of his former friends or acquaintances.

"This closes the first part of the history, the part which deals with the person whom my friend whimsically described as 'the dead man who was alive. And now, perhaps, Mr. Pottermack, you can tell me whether you have ever heard of a case in any way analogous to this one."

Mr. Pottermack reflected for a few moments. Throughout Thorndyke's recital he had sat with the feeling of one in a dream. The sense of unreality had again taken possession of him. He had listened with a queer sort of incredulous curiosity to the quiet voice of this inscrutable stranger, relating to him with the calm assurance of some wizard or clairvoyant the innermost secrets of his own life, describing actions and events which he, Pottermack, felt certain could not possibly be known to any human creature but himself. It was all so unbelievable that any sense of danger, of imminent disaster, was merged in an absorbing wonder. But one thing was quite clear to him: Any attempt to deceive or mislead this mysterious stranger would be utterly futile. Accordingly he replied:

"By a most strange coincidence it happens that a case came to my knowledge which was point by point almost identical with yours. But there was one difference. In my case, the guilt of the person who corresponds to your Mr. Black was not problematical at all. He admitted it. He even boasted of it, and of the clever way in which he had set up Mr. White as the dummy to take all the thumps."

"Indeed!" exclaimed Thorndyke. "That is extremely interesting. We must bear that point in mind when we come to examine the details. Now I go on to the second part of the narrative, the part that deals with the 'live man who was dead'.

"After the lapse of some fifteen years, Mr. White came to the surface, so to speak. He made his appearance in a small country town, and from his apparently comfortable circumstances he seemed to have prospered in the interval. But here he encountered a streak of bad luck. By some malignant chance, it happened that Mr. Black was installed as manager of the branch bank in that very town, and naturally enough they met. Even then all might have been well but for an unaccountable piece of carelessness on Mr. White's part. He had, by growing a beard and taking to the use of spectacles, made a considerable change in his appearance. But he had neglected one point: He had, it appears, on his right ear a small birth-mark. It was not at all conspicuous, but when once observed it was absolutely distinctive.

"But," exclaimed Pottermack, "I don't understand you. You say he neglected this mark. But what could he possibly have done to conceal it?"

"He could have had it obliterated," replied Thorndyke. "The operation is quite simple in the case of a small mark. The more widespread 'port-wine' mark is less easy to treat, but a small spot, such as I understand that this was, can be dealt with quite easily and effectively. Some skin surgeons specialize in the operation. One of them I happen to know personally: Mr. Julian Parsons, the dermatologist to St. Margaret's Hospital."

"Ha," said Mr. Pottermack.

"But," continued Thorndyke, "to return to our story. Mr. White had left his birth-mark untreated, and that was probably his undoing. Mr. Black would doubtless have been struck by the resemblance, but the birth-mark definitely established the identity. At any rate, Mr. Black recognized him and forthwith began to levy blackmail. Of course, Mr. White was an ideal subject for a blackmailer's operations. He was absolutely defenceless, for he could not invoke the aid of the law by

631

reason of his unexpired sentence. He had to pay, or go back to prison – or take some private measures.

"At first, it appears that he accepted the position and paid. Probably he submitted to be bled repeatedly, for there is reason to believe that quite considerable sums of money passed. But eventually Mr. White must have realized what most blackmailers' victims have to realize – that there is no end to this sort of thing. The blackmailer is always ready to begin over again. At any rate, Mr. White adopted the only practicable alternative to paying out indefinitely. He got Mr. Black alone in a secluded garden in which there was a disused well. Probably Mr. Black came there voluntarily to make fresh demands. But however that may have been, Mr. Black went, dead or alive, down into the well."

"In the case which came to my knowledge," said Pottermack, "it was to some extent accidental. He had become rather violent, and in the course of what amounted to a fight he fell across the opening of the well, striking his head heavily on the brick coping, and dropped down in a state of insensibility."

"Ah," said Thorndyke, "that may be considered, as you say, to some extent accidental. But probably to a rather small extent. I think we may take it that he would have gone down that well in any case. What do you say?"

"I think I am inclined to agree with you," replied Pottermack.

"At all events," said Thorndyke, "down the well he went. And there seemed to be an end of the blackmailer. But it was not quite the end, and the sequel introduces a most interesting feature into the case.

"It appears that the path by which Mr. Black approached Mr. White's premises was an earth path, and owing to the peculiar qualities of the soil in that locality, it took the most extraordinarily clear impressions of the feet that trod on it. Now, it happened that Mr. Black was wearing shoes with rubber soles and heels of a strikingly distinctive pattern, which left on the earth path impressions of the most glaringly conspicuous and distinctive character. The result was a set of footprints, obviously and certainly those of Mr. Black, leading directly to Mr. White's gate and stopping there. This was a most dangerous state of affairs, for as soon as the hue-and-cry was raised – which it would be immediately in the case of a bank manager – the missing Black would be traced by his footprints to Mr. White's gate. And then the murder would be out.

"Now what was Mr. White to do? He could not obliterate those footprints in any practicable manner. So he did the next best – or even better – thing. He continued them past his gate, out into the country and across a heath, on the farther side of which he allowed them discreetly to fade away into the heather.

"It was an admirable plan, and it succeeded perfectly. When the hue-and-cry was raised, the police followed those tracks like bloodhounds until they lost them on the heath. A photographer with a special camera patiently took samples of the footprints along the whole route, from the place where they started to where they were lost on the heath. But no one suspected Mr. White. He did not come into the picture at all. It seemed that he had now nothing to do but to lie low and let the affair pass into oblivion.

"But he did nothing of the kind. Instead, he embarked on a most unaccountable proceeding. Months after the disappearance of Mr. Black, when the affair had become nearly forgotten, he proceeded deliberately to revive it. He obtained an Egyptian mummy, and having dressed it in Mr. Black's clothes, or in clothes that had been specially prepared to counterfeit those of Mr. Black, he deposited it in a gravel-pit. His reasons for doing this are unknown to my legal friend and are difficult to imagine. But whatever the object may have been, it was attained, for in due course the mummy was discovered and identified as the body of Mr. Black, an inquest was held, and the mystery of the disappearance finally disposed of.

"That is a bare outline of the case, Mr. Pottermack, just sufficient to enable us to discuss it and compare it with the one that you have in mind."

"It is a very remarkable case," said Pottermack, "and the most remarkable feature in it is its close resemblance to the one of which I came to hear. In fact, they are so much alike that – "

"Exactly," interrupted Thorndyke. "The same thought had occurred to us both – that your case and the one related by my legal friend are in reality one and the same."

"Yes," agreed Pottermack, "I think they must be. But what is puzzling me is how your legal friend came by the knowledge of these facts, which would seem to have been known to no one but the principal actor."

"That is what we are going to consider," said Thorndyke. "But before we begin our analysis, there is one point that I should like to clear up. You said that Mr. Black had explicitly admitted his guilt in regard to those forgeries. To whom did he make that admission?"

"To his wife," replied Pottermack.

"His wife!" exclaimed Thorndyke. "But it was assumed that he was a bachelor."

"The facts," said Pottermack, "are rather singular. I had better fill in this piece of detail, which apparently escaped your legal friend's investigations.

"Mr. White, in the days before his troubles befell, was engaged to be married to a very charming girl to whom he was completely devoted and who was equally devoted to him. After Mr. White's reported death, Mr. Black sought her friendship and later tried to induce her to marry him. He urged that he had been Mr. White's most intimate friend and that their marriage was what the deceased would have wished. Eventually she yielded to his persuasion and married him, rather reluctantly, since her feeling towards him was merely that of a friend. What his feeling was towards her it is difficult to say. She had some independent means, and it is probable that her property was the principal attraction. That is what the subsequent history suggests.

"The marriage was a failure from the first. Black sponged on his wife, gambled with her money, and was constantly in debt and difficulties. Also he drank to an unpleasant extent. But she put up with all this until one day he let out that he had committed the forgeries, and even boasted of his smartness in putting the suspicion on White. Then she left him and, assuming another name, went away to live by herself, passing herself off as a widow."

"And as to her husband? How came he to allow this?"

"First, she frightened him by threatening to denounce him, but she also made him an allowance on condition that he should not molest her. He seems to have been rather scared by her threats and he wanted the money, so he took the allowance and as much more as he could squeeze out of her, and agreed to her terms.

"Later Mr. White returned to England from America. As he had now quite shed his old identity and was a man of good reputation and comfortably off, he sought her out in the hopes of possibly renewing their old relations. That, in fact, was what brought him to England. Eventually he discovered her, apparently a widow, and had no difficulty in making her acquaintance."

"Did she recognize him?"

"I think we must assume that she did. But nothing was said. They maintained the fiction that they were new acquaintances. So they became friends. Finally he asked her to marry him, and it was then that he learned, to his amazement, that she had married Mr. Black."

Thorndyke's face had suddenly become grave. He cast a searching glance at Mr. Pottermack and demanded, "When was this proposal of marriage made? I mean, was it before or after the incident of the well?"

634

"Oh, after, of course. No marriage could have been thought of by Mr. White while he was under the thumb of the blackmailer, with the choice of ruin or the prison before him. It was only when the affair was over and everything seemed to be settling down quietly that the marriage seemed to have become possible."

Thorndyke's face cleared and a grim smile spread over it. "I see," he chuckled. "A quaint situation for Mr. White. Now, of course, one understands the mummy. His function was to produce a death certificate. Very ingenious. And now I gather that you would like an exposition of the evidence in this case?"

"Yes," replied Pottermack. "Your legal friend seems to have had knowledge of certain actions of Mr. White's which I should have supposed could not possibly have been known to any person in the world but Mr. White himself. I should like to hear how he came by that knowledge if you would be so kind as to enlighten me."

"Very well," said Thorndyke, "then we will proceed to consider the evidence in this case, and I must impress on you, Mr. Pottermack, the necessity of discriminating clearly between what my legal friend knew and what he inferred, and of observing the point at which inference becomes converted into knowledge by verification or new matter.

"To begin with what my friend knew, on the authority of a director of Mr. Black's bank. He knew that Mr. Black had disappeared under very mysterious circumstances. That he had received an urgent and threatening demand from a creditor for the payment of a certain sum of money. That before starting that night, he had taken from the monies belonging to the bank a sum of money in notes exactly equal to the amount demanded from him. The reasonable inference was that he set out intending to call on that creditor and pay that money, instead of which, he appeared to have walked straight out of the town into the country, where all trace of him was lost.

"Then my friend learned from the director that, whereas the books of the bank showed Mr. Black's known income and ordinary expenditure, there was evidence of his having paid away large sums of money on gambling transactions, always in cash – mostly five-pound notes, that these sums greatly exceeded his known income, and that his account showed no trace of their having been received. Since he must have received that money before he could have paid it away, he must clearly have had some unknown source of income, and since he had paid it away in cash, and there was no trace of his having received any cheques to these amounts, the inference was that he had received it in cash. I need not remind you, Mr. Pottermack, that the receipt of large

635

sums of money in notes or specie is a very significant and rather suspicious circumstance."

"Might not these sums represent his winnings?" Pottermack asked.

"They might, but they did not, for all the transactions that were traced resulted in losses. Apparently he was the type of infatuated gambler who always loses in the end. So much for Mr. Black. Next, my friend learned from the director the circumstances of the forgeries, and he formed the opinion – which was also that of the director – that Mr. White had been a victim of a miscarriage of justice and that the real culprit had been Mr. Black. He also learned the particulars of Mr. White's escape from prison and alleged death. But he differed from the director in that, being a lawyer with special experience, he did not accept that death as an established fact, but only as a probability, reserving in his mind the possibility of a mistaken identity of the body and that Mr. White might have escaped and be still alive.

"Thus, you see, Mr. Pottermack, that my friend started with a good deal of knowledge of this case and the parties to it. And now we come to some facts of another kind which carry us on to the stage of inference. The director who furnished my friend with the information that I have summarized also put into his hands a long series of photographs of the footprints of Mr. Black, taken by an employee of the bank on the second morning after the disappearance."

"For what purpose?" asked Mr. Pottermack.

"Principally, I suspect, to try a new camera of a special type, but ostensibly to help the investigators to discover what had become of the missing man. They were handed to my friend for his inspection and opinion as to their value for this purpose. Of course, at the first glance they appeared to be of no value at all, but as my friend happens to be deeply interested in footprints as material for evidence, he retained them for further examination in relation to a particular point which he wished to clear up. That point was whether a series of footprints is anything more that a mere multiple of a single footprint, whether it might be possible to extract from a series any kind of evidence that would not be famished by an individual footprint.

"Evidently, those photographs offered an exceptional opportunity for settling this question. They were in the form of a long paper ribbon on which were nearly two-hundred numbered photographs of footprints, and they were accompanied by a twenty-five inch ordnance map on which each footprint was indicated by a numbered dot. The row of dots started at the bank, and then, after a blank interval, entered and followed a footpath which passed along a wall in which was a gate, and which enclosed a large garden or plantation. Beyond the wall the dots continued, still on the footpath, between some fields, through a wood, and across a heath, on the farther side of which they stopped. A note at the end of the ribbon stated that here the missing man had turned off the path into the heather and that no further traces of him could be found."

"Well," remarked Pottermack. "the police could see all that for themselves. It doesn't seem as if the photographs gave any further information."

"It does not," Thorndyke agreed. "And yet a careful examination of those photographs led my friend to the conviction that the missing man had entered the gate in the wall and had never come out again."

"But," exclaimed Pottermack, "I understood you to say that the footprints continued past the wall, through the wood, and out across the heath."

"So they did. But a careful scrutiny of the photographs convinced my friend that this was not a *single* series of footprints, made by one man but *two* series, made by *two different men*. The first series started from the bank and ended at the gate. The second series started from the gate and ended on the heath."

"Then the footprints were not all alike?"

"That," replied Thorndyke, "depends on what we mean by 'alike'. If you had taken any one footprint from any part of the whole series and compared it with any other corresponding footprint – right or left – in any other part of the series, you would have said that they were undoubtedly prints of the same foot."

"Do I understand you to mean that every footprint in the whole series was exactly like every other footprint of the same side?"

"Yes. Every right footprint was exactly like every other right footprint, and the same with the left. That is, considered as individual footprints."

"Then I don't see how your friend could have made out that the whole series of footprints, all indistinguishably alike, consisted of two different series, made by two different men."

Thorndyke chuckled. "It is quite a subtle point," he said, "and yet perfectly simple. I am a little surprised that it had not occurred to Mr. White, who seems to have been an acute and ingenious man. You see, the difference was not between the individual footprints but between certain periodic characters in the two series."

"I don't think I quite follow you," said Pottermack.

"Well, let us follow my legal friend's procedure. I have told you that his object in examining these photographs was to ascertain whether footprints in series present any periodic or recurrent characters that might be of evidential importance. Now, a glance at these photographs showed

637

him that these footprints must almost certainly present at least one such character. They were the prints of shoes with rubber soles of a highly distinctive pattern and circular rubber heels. Now, Mr. Pottermack, why does a man wear circular rubber heels?"

"Usually, I suppose, because if he wears ordinary leather heels he wears them down all on one side."

"And how do the circular heels help him?"

"In the case of circular heels," Pottermack replied promptly, "the wear does not occur all at one point, but is distributed round the whole circumf – "

He stopped abruptly with his mouth slightly open and looked at Thorndyke.

"Exactly," said the latter, "you see the point. A circular heel is secured to the shoe by a single, central screw. But it is not a complete fixture. As the wearer walks, the oblique impact as it meets the ground causes it to creep round, very slowly when the heel is new and tightly screwed on, more rapidly as it wears thinner and the central screw-hole wears larger. Of course, my friend knew this, but he now had an opportunity of making his knowledge more exact and settling certain doubtful points as to rapidity and direction of rotation. Accordingly he proceeded, with the ribbon of photographs and the ordnance map before him, to follow the track methodically, noting down the distances and the rate and direction of rotation of each heel.

"His industry was rewarded and justified within the first dozen observations, for it brought to light a fact of considerable importance, though it does not happen to be relevant to our case. He found that both heels revolved in the same direction – clock-wise – though, of course, since they were in what we may call 'looking-glass' relation, they ought to have revolved in opposite directions."

"Yes," said Pottermack, "it is curious, but I don't see what its importance is."

"Its importance in an evidential sense," replied Thorndyke, "is this: The anomaly of rotation was evidently not due to the shoes but to some peculiarity in the gait of the wearer. The same shoes on the feet of another person would almost certainly have behaved differently. Hence, the character of the rotation might become a test point in a question of personal identity. However, that is by the way. What concerns us is that my friend established the fact that both heels were rotating quite regularly and rather rapidly. Each of them made a complete rotation in about a hundred-and-fifty-yards.

"My friend, however, did not accept this result as final, but continued his observations to ascertain if this regular rate of rotation was maintained along the whole of the track. So he went on methodically until he had examined nearly half of the ribbon. And then a most astonishing thing happened. Both the heels suddenly ceased to revolve. They stopped dead, and both at the same place.

"Now, the thing being apparently an impossibility, my friend thought that he must have made some error of observation. Accordingly he went over this part of the ribbon again. But the same result emerged. Then, abandoning his measurements, he went rapidly along the whole remaining length of the ribbon to the very end, but still with the same result. Throughout the whole of that distance, neither heel showed the slightest sign of rotation. So it came to this: The photographs from number *1* to number *92* showed both heels rotating regularly about once in every hundred-and-fifty-yards, from number *93* to number *197*, showed the heels completely stationary.

"My friend was profoundly puzzled. On the showing of the photographs, the heels of this man's shoes which had been turning quite freely and regularly as he walked, had, in an instant, become immovably fixed. And both at the same moment. He tried to think of some possible explanation, but he could think of none. The thing was utterly incomprehensible. Then he turned to the ordnance map to see if anything in the environment could throw any light on the mystery. Searching along the row of dots for number *93* he at length found it – exactly opposite the gate in the wall.

"This was a decidedly startling discovery. It was impossible to ignore the coincidence. The position was that this man's heels had been turning freely until he reached the gate, after passing the gate his heels had become permanently fixed. The obvious suggestion was that this mysterious change in the condition of the heels was in some way connected with the gate. But what could be the nature of the connection? And what could be the nature of the change in the shoes?

"To the first question the suggested answer was that the man might have gone in at the gate, and while he was inside, something might have happened to his shoes which caused the heels to become fixed. But still the difficulty of the shoes remained. What could cause revolving heels to become fixed? To this question my friend could find no answer. The possibility that the heels had been taken off and screwed on again more tightly would not have explained their complete immobility, and, in fact, they had not been. The screws showed plainly in many of the photographs, and the position of their slots in all was identical. The footprints in the second series – those past the gate – were in every respect the exact counterparts of those in the first series – those from the town to the gate. The only condition that my friend could think of as agreeing with the physical facts was that which would have occurred if the prints in the second series had been made, not by the shoes themselves but by some sort of reproductions of them, such as plaster casts or casts in some other material."

"That sounds rather a far-fetched suggestion," remarked Pottermack.

"It does," Thorndyke agreed, "and in fact my friend did not entertain it seriously at first. He merely noted that the appearances were exactly such as would be produced by making impressions with casts, in which, of course, since the soles and heels would be all in one piece, no movement of the heels would be possible. But, Mr. Pottermack, we must bear in mind whose footprints these were. They were the footprints of a man who had disappeared in the most mysterious and unaccountable manner. The whole affair was highly abnormal. No reasonable explanation was possible either of the disappearance or of the singular character of the footprints. But in the absence of a reasonable explanation, it is admissible to consider an unreasonable one, if it agrees with the known facts. The cast theory did agree with the physical facts and, on reflection, my friend decided to adopt it as a working hypothesis and see what came of it.

"Now, if the footprints from the gate to the heath were counterfeits of Black's footprints, made with shoes the soles and heels of which were mechanical reproductions of the soles and heels of Black's shoes, it followed that the wearer of these shoes was not Black, but some other person, in which case Black's own footprints ended at the gate. This at once got rid of the most unaccountable feature of the disappearance – the nocturnal flight out into the country, for if his footprints ended at the gate he must have gone in. But there was nothing at all abnormal about his calling at a house quite close to, and, in fact, almost in the town, from which he could have easily gone to keep his appointment with his creditor. Thus far, the hypothesis seemed to simplify matters.

"But it not only followed that Black must have gone in at the gate, it followed that he could never have come out. For the footprints that went on were not his, and there were no footprints going back towards the town."

"He might have come out another way – by the front door, for instance," Pottermack suggested.

"So he might," Thorndyke agreed, "under different circumstances. But the counterfeit footprints showed that he did not. For if the continuing footprints were counterfeits, made by some other person, what could have been their purpose? Clearly their purpose could have been no other than that of concealing the fact that Black had gone in at the gate. But if he had come out of the premises, there could have been no reason for concealing the fact that he had gone in.

"If, however, he did not come out, then, obviously, he remained inside. But in what condition? Was he alive and in hiding? Evidently not. In the first place, he had no occasion to hide, since he could have gone back to the bank and replaced the money. But the conclusive evidence that he was not in hiding was the counterfeit footprints. No mechanical reproduction of the shoes would have been necessary if Black had been there. Black's own shoes would have been borrowed and used to make the false footprints. But, obviously, the whole set of circumstances was against the supposition that he could be alive. If the evidence was accepted that he went in and was never seen again, the most obvious inference was that he had been made away with. And this inference was strongly supported by the troublesome and elaborate measures that had been taken to conceal the fact that he had gone in at the gate. Accordingly my friend adopted the view, provisionally, that Mr. Black had been made away with by some person inside the gate, hereinafter referred to as the tenant.

"But the adoption of this view at once raised two questions. First, how came it to be necessary to make reproductions of the dead man's shoes? Why did not the tenant simply take the shoes off the corpse and put them on his own feet? If he had done this, if he had made the false footprints with the dead man's own shoes, the illusion would have been perfect. No detection would have been possible. Why had he not done it? The shoes themselves could have presented no difficulty. They were large shoes, and large shoes can, with suitable preparation, be worn even by a small man.

"The answer that suggested itself was that, for some reason, the shoes were not available, that by the time that the necessity for the false footprints had been perceived, the shoes had in some way become inaccessible. But how could they have become inaccessible? Could the body have been buried? Apparently not. For it would have been much less trouble to dig up a body and recover the shoes than to make a pair of reproductions of them. Could it have been burned? Evidently not. Apart from the extreme difficulty of the operation, there had not been time. The false footprints were made on the very night of the disappearance since they were traced by the police the next morning.

"The possibility that the body might have been conveyed away off the premises had to be borne in mind. But it was highly improbable, for many obvious reasons and it did not dispose of the difficulty. For it would surely have been easier and quicker to go – at night – and retrieve the shoes than to make the counterfeits. Indeed, when my friend considered the immense labour that the making of those reproductions must have entailed, to say nothing of the great expenditure of time, just when every moment was precious, he felt that nothing but the absolute physical impossibility of getting access to the original shoes would explain their having been made.

"Now, what conditions would have rendered those shoes totally inaccessible? Remember the circumstances. Inasmuch as the sham footprints were found on the following morning, they must have been made that night. But before they could be made, the counterfeit soles must have been made, and the making of them must have been a long and tedious piece of work. It therefore followed that the tenant must have begun work on them almost immediately after the death of Mr. Black. From this it followed that the body of Mr. Black must have been immediately disposed of in such a way as at once to become inaccessible.

"What methods of disposing of a body would fulfil these conditions? My friend could think of only three, all very much alike: The dropping of the body down a dene-hole, or into a cess-pit, or into a disused well. Any of these methods would at once put the body completely out of reach. And all these methods had a special probability in this particular case. The great difficulty that confronts the would-be murderer is the disposal of the body. Hence the knowledge that there was available a means of immediately, securely, and permanently hiding the body might be the determining factor of the murder. Accordingly, my friend was strongly inclined to assume that one of these three methods was the one actually employed.

"As to the particular method, the question was of no great importance. Still, my friend considered it. The idea of a dene-hole was at once excluded on geological grounds. Dene-holes are peculiar to the chalk. But this was not a chalk district.

"The cess-pit was possible but not very probable, for if in use, it would be subject to periodical clearance, which would make it quite unsuitable as a hiding-place, while cess-pits which become superseded by drainage are usually filled in and definitely covered up. A well, on the other hand, is often kept open for occasional and special use after the laying on of a pipe service."

"Your friend," remarked Pottermack, "seems to have taken it for granted that a well actually existed."

"Not entirely," said Thorndyke. "He looked up an older map and found that this house had formerly been a farm-house, so that it must once have had a well, and as it now fronts on a road in which other houses have been built and which is virtually a street, it is pretty certainly connected with the water-service. So that it was practically certain that there was a well, and that well would almost certainly be out of use.

"And now, having deduced a reason why the counterfeit soles should have been necessary, he had to consider another question. If the original shoes were inaccessible, how could it have been possible to make the counterfeits, which were, apparently, casts of the originals? At first it looked like an impossibility. But a little reflection showed that the footprints themselves supplied the answer. Mr. Black's own footprints on the path were such perfect impressions that a little good plaster poured into selected samples of them would have furnished casts which would have been exact reproductions of the soles and heels of Mr. Black's shoes. Possibly there were equally good footprints inside the premises, but that is of no consequence. Those on the footpath would have answered the purpose perfectly.

"I may say that my friend tested this conclusion and got some slight confirmation. For if the false footprints were impressions of reproductions, not of the original shoes but of some other footprints, one would expect to find the accidental characters of those particular footprints as well as those of the shoes which produced them. And this appeared to be the case. In one of the points of the star on the left heel a small particle of earth seemed to have adhered. This was not to be found in Black's own footprints, but it was visible in all the footprints of the second series, from the gate to the heath. And the fact that it never changed along the whole series suggested that it was really a part of the cast, due to an imperfection in the footprint from which it was made.

"That brings us to an end of my friend's train of reasoning in regard to the actual events connected with Mr. Black's disappearance. His conclusions were, you observe, that Mr. Black went in at the gate, that he was thereafter made away with by some person inside whom we have called the tenant, that his body was deposited by the tenant in some inaccessible place, probably a disused well, and that the tenant then made a set of false footprints to disguise the fact that Mr. Black had gone in at the gate.

"The questions that remained to be considered were, first, What could be the tenant's motive for making away with Mr. Black? And second, Who was the tenant? But before we deal with his inferences on those points, I should like to hear any observations which you may have to make on what I have told you."

Mr. Pottermack pondered awhile on what he had heard, and as he reflected, he laid a disparaging hand on the teapot.

"It is rather cool," he remarked apologetically, "but such as it is, can I give you another cup?"

"Prolonged exposition," Thorndyke replied with a smile, "is apt to have a cooling effect upon tea. But it also creates a demand for liquid refreshment. Thank you, I think another cup would cheer, and we can dispense with the inebriation."

Mr. Pottermack refilled both the cups and put down the teapot, still cogitating profoundly.

Chapter XVIII
The Sun-Dial Has the
Last Word

"**Y**our legal friend," Mr. Pottermack said at length, "must be a man of extraordinary subtlety and ingenuity if he deduced all that you have told me from the mere peculiarities of a set of footprints, and only photographs at that. But what strikes me about it is that his reconstruction was, after all, pure speculation. There were too many 'ifs'."

"But, my dear Mr. Pottermack," exclaimed Thorndyke, "it was all 'ifs'. The whole train of reasoning was on the plane of hypothesis, pure and simple. He did not, at this stage, assume that it was actually true, but merely true conditionally on the facts being what they appeared to be. But what does a scientific man do when he sets up a working hypothesis? He deduces from it its consequences, and he continues to pursue these so long as they are consistent with the facts known to him. Sooner or later, this process brings him either to an impossibility or a contradiction – in which case he abandons the hypothesis – or to a question of fact which is capable of being settled conclusively, yes or no.

"Well, this is what my friend did. So far we have seen him pursuing a particular hypothesis and deducing from it certain consequences. The whole thing might have been fallacious. But it was consistent, and the consequences were compatible with the known facts. Presently we shall come to the question of fact – the crucial experiment which determines yes or no, whether the hypothesis is true or false. But we have to follow the hypothetical method a little farther first.

"The questions that remained to be considered were: First, What could have been the tenant's motive for killing Mr. Black? And second, Who was the tenant? My friend took the questions in this order because the motive might be arrived at by reasoning, and, if so arrived at, might throw light on the personality of the tenant, whereas the identity of the tenant, taken by itself, was a matter of fact capable of being ascertained by enquiry, but not by reasoning apart from the motive.

"Now, what motives suggest themselves? First, we must note that my friend assumed that the homicide was committed by the tenant himself – that is, by the proprietor of the premises and not by a servant or other person. That is a reasonable inference from the facts that the person, whoever he was, appeared to have command of all the means and materials necessary for making the counterfeits, and also that he must have had full control of the premises, both at the time and in the future, in order to hide the body and ensure that it should remain hidden. Well, what motive could a man in this position have had to kill Mr. Black?

"There is the motive of robbery, but the circumstances seem to exclude it as not reasonably probable. It is true that Black had a hundred pounds on his person, but there is no reason to suppose that any one knew that he had, and in any case, so small a sum, relatively, furnishes a quite insufficient motive for murder in the case of an apparently well-to-do man such as the tenant. My friend decided that robbery, though possible, was highly improbable.

"The possibilities that Black's death might have been the result of a quarrel or of some act of private vengeance had to be borne in mind, but there were no means of forming any opinions for or against them. They had to be left as mere speculative possibilities. But there was another possibility which occurred to my friend, the probabilities of which were susceptible of being argued, and to this he turned his attention. It was based upon the application of certain facts actually known and which we will now consider.

"First, he noted that Mr. Black came to this place voluntarily, and that he came expressly to visit the premises within the gate is proved by the fact that this is the last house on that path. Beyond it is the country. There is no other human habitation to which he could have been bound. Now Mr. Black was, at this moment, in acute financial difficulties. He had borrowed a hundred pounds from the bank's money, and this hundred pounds he was about to pay away to meet an urgent demand. But that hundred pounds would have to be replaced, and it was of the utmost importance that it should be replaced without delay. For if a surprise inspection should have occurred before it was replaced, he stood to be charged with robbery. The circumstances, therefore, seemed to suggest that he had taken it with the expectation of being able to replace it almost immediately.

"Now, you will remember that it transpired after his disappearance that Mr. Black had some mysterious unknown source of income, that he had received on several occasions large sums of money, which had apparently come to him in the form of cash and had been paid away in the same form – always in five-pound notes. These monies did not appear in his banking account or in any other account. They were unrecorded – and, consequently, their total amount is not known. But the sums that he is known to have received were ascertained by means of the discovery of certain payments that he had made. I need not point out to you the great and sinister significance of these facts. When a man who has a banking account receives large payments in cash, and when, instead of paying them into his account, he pays them away in cash, it is practically certain that the monies that he has received are connected with some secret transaction, and that transaction is almost certainly an illicit one. But of all such transactions, by far the commonest is blackmail. In fact, one would hardly be exaggerating if one were to say that evidence of secret payments of large sums in coin or notes is presumptive evidence of blackmail. Accordingly, my friend strongly suspected Mr. Black of being a blackmailer.

"And now, assuming this to be correct, see how admirably the assumption fits the circumstances. Mr. Black is at the moment financially desperate. He has taken certain money, which is not his, to pay an urgent and threatening creditor. Instead of going direct to that creditor, he comes first to this house. But he does not enter by the front door. He goes to a gate which opens on an unfrequented lane and which gives entrance to a remote part of the grounds, and he does this late in the evening. There is a manifestly secret air about the whole proceeding.

"And now let us make another assumption."

"What, another!" protested Pottermack.

"Yes, another, just to see if it will fit the circumstances as the others have done. Let us assume that the tenant was the person from whom Mr. Black had been extorting those mysterious payments, the victim whom he had been blackmailing. That he had called in on his way to his creditor to see if he could squeeze him for yet another hundred, so that the notes could be replaced before they could be missed. That the victim, being now at the end of his patience and having an opportunity of safely making away with his persecutor, took that opportunity and made away with him. Is it not obvious that we have a perfectly consistent scheme of the probable course of events?"

"It is all pure conjecture," objected Pottermack.

"It is all pure hypothesis," Thorndyke admitted, "but you see that it all hangs together, it all fits the circumstances completely. We have not come to any inconsistency or impossibility. And it is all intrinsically probable in the special conditions, for you must not forget that we are dealing with a set of circumstances that admits of no normal explanation.

"And now for the last question. Assuming that Mr. Black was a blackmailer and that the tenant was his victim, was it possible to give that victim a name? Here my friend was handicapped by the fact that Mr. Black was a complete stranger, of whose domestic affairs and friends and acquaintances he had no knowledge. With one exception. He had knowledge of one of Mr. Black's friends. That friend, it is true, was alleged to be dead. But it was by no means certain that he was dead. And if he were not dead, he was a perfectly ideal subject for blackmail, for he was an escaped convict with a considerable term of penal servitude still to run. My friend was, of course, thinking of Mr. White. If he should have attained to something approaching affluence and should be living in prosperous and socially desirable circumstances, he would allow himself to be bled to an unlimited extent rather than suffer public disgrace and be sent back to prison. And the person who would be, of all others, the most likely to recognize him and in the best position to blackmail him would be his old friend Mr. Black.

"Bearing these facts in mind, my friend was disposed to waive the *prima facie* improbability and assume, provisionally, that the tenant was Mr. White. It was certainly rather a long shot."

"It was indeed," said Pottermack. "Your friend was a regular Robin Hood."

"And yet," Thorndyke rejoined, "the balance of probability was in favour of that assumption. For against the various circumstances that suggested that the tenant was Mr. White, there was to be set only one single improbability, and that not at all an impressive one: The improbability that a body – found drowned after six weeks' immersion and therefore really unrecognizable – should have been wrongly identified. However, my friend did feel that (to continue the metaphor, since you seem to approve of it) the time had come to step forward and have a look at the target. The long train of hypothetical reasoning had at length brought him to a proposition the truth of which could be definitely tested. The tenant's identity with Mr. White was a matter of fact which could be proved or disproved beyond all doubt. Of course, the test would not be a real *experimentum crucis*, because it would act in only one direction. If it should turn out that the tenant was not Mr. White, that would not invalidate the other conclusions, but if it should turn out that he *was* Mr. White, that fact would very strongly confirm those conclusions.

"My friend, then, left his photographs and his ordnance map and made a journey to the scene of these strange events to inspect the place and the man with his own eyes. First he examined the path and the exterior of the premises, and then he made a survey of the grounds enclosed by the wall."

"How did he do that?" enquired Pottermack. "It was a pretty high wall – at least, so I understand."

"He made use of an ancient optical instrument which has been recently revived in an improved form under the name of 'periscope'. The old instrument had two mirrors, the modern one has two total-reflection prisms in a narrow tube. By projecting the upper or objective end of the

648

tube above the top of the wall, my friend was able, on looking into the eye-piece, to get an excellent view of the premises. What he saw was a large garden, completely enclosed by four high walls in which were two small gates, each provided with a night-latch and therefore capable of being opened only from within or by means of a latch-key. A very secure and secluded garden. On one side of it was a range of out-buildings which, by the glazed lights in their roofs, appeared to be studios or workshops. Near one end of the lawn was a sun-dial on a very wide stone base. The width of the base was rather remarkable, being much greater than is usual in a garden dial. A glance at it showed that the dial had been quite recently set up, for, though the stone pillar was old, the base stones were brand new. Moreover, the turf around it had been very recently laid and some of the earth was still bare. Further proof of its newness was furnished by a gentleman who was, at the moment, engaged, with the aid of *Whitaker's Almanack* and his watch, in fixing the dial-plate in correct azimuth.

"This gentleman – the mysterious tenant – naturally engaged my friend's attention. There were several interesting points to be noted concerning him. The tools that he used were workmen's tools, not amateurs', and he used them with the unmistakable skill of a man accustomed to tools. Then he had laid aside his spectacles, which were 'curl-sided' and therefore habitually worn. It followed, then, that he was near-sighted, for if he had been old-sighted or long-sighted he would have needed the spectacles especially for the close and minute work that he was doing.

"When he had made these observations, my friend proceeded to take a couple of photographs – a right and a left profile."

"How did he manage that?" demanded the astonished Pottermack.

"By placing his camera on the top of the wall. It was a special, small camera, fitted with a four-point-five Ross-Zeiss lens and a cord release. Of course, he made the exposure with the aid of the periscope.

"When he had exposed the photographs, he decided to have a nearer view of the tenant. Accordingly he went round and knocked at the gate, which was presently opened by the gentleman of the sun-dial, who was now wearing his spectacles. Looking at those spectacles, my friend made a very curious discovery. The man was not near-sighted, for the glasses were convex bi-focals, the upper part nearly plain glass. Now, if he had not needed those spectacles for near work, he certainly could not need them for distance. Then, obviously, he did not need them at all. But, if so, why was he wearing them? The only possible explanation was that they were worn for their effect on his appearance, in short, for the purpose of disguise.

649

"As this gentleman was answering some questions about the locality, my friend handed him a folded map. This he did with two objects: That he might get a good look at him unobserved, and that he might possibly obtain some prints of his finger-tips. As to the first, he was able to make a mental note of the tenant's salient characteristics and to observe, among other peculiarities, a purplish mark on the lobe of the right ear of the kind known to surgeons as a *capillary naevus*."

"And the finger-prints?" Pottermack asked eagerly.

"They were rather a failure, but not quite. When my friend developed them up, though very poor specimens, they were distinct enough to be recognizable by an expert.

"Now you will have noticed that everything that my friend observed was consistent with, and tended to confirm, the conclusions that he had arrived at by hypothetical reasoning. But the actual test still remained to be applied. Was the tenant Mr. White or was he not? In order to settle this question, my friend made enlargements of the photographs of the tenant and also of the finger-prints, and, with these in his pocket, paid a visit to Scotland Yard."

At the mention of the ill-omened name Pottermack started and a sudden pallor spread over his face. But he uttered no sound, and Thorndyke continued, "There he presented the finger-prints as probably those of a deceased person, photographed from a document, and asked for an expert opinion on them. He gave no particulars and was not asked for any, but the experts made their examination and reported that the finger-prints were those of a convict named White who had died some fifteen years previously. My friend had, further, the opportunity of inspecting the prison photographs of the deceased White and of reading the personal description. Needless to say, they agreed completely in every particular, even to the *capillary naevus* on the ear.

"Here, then, my legal friend emerged from the region of hypothesis into that of established fact. The position now was that the person whom we have called 'the tenant' was undoubtedly the convict, White, who was universally believed to be dead. And since this fact had been arrived at by the train of reasoning that I have recited, there could be no doubt that the other, intermediate, conclusions were correct – that, in fact, the hypothesis as a whole was substantially true. Do you agree with that view?"

"There seems to be no escape from it," replied Pottermack, and after a brief pause he asked, a little tremulously, "And what action did your legal friend take?"

"In respect of the identity of the tenant? He took no action. He now considered it perfectly clear that Mr. White ought never to have been a convict at all. That unfortunate gentleman had been the victim of a miscarriage of justice. It would have been actually against public policy to disclose his existence and occasion a further miscarriage.

"With regard to the killing of Mr. Black, the position was slightly different. If it comes to the knowledge of any citizen – and especially a barrister, who is an officer of justice – that a crime has been committed, it is the duty of that citizen to communicate his knowledge to the proper authorities. But my friend had not come by any such knowledge. He had formed the opinion – based on certain inferences from certain facts – that Mr. Black had been killed. But a man is not under any obligation to communicate his opinions.

"This may seem a little casuistical. But my friend was a lawyer, and lawyers are perhaps slightly inclined to casuistry. And in this case there were certain features that encouraged this casuistical tendency. We must take it, I think, that a man who suffers a wrong for which the law provides a remedy and in respect of which it offers him protection is morally and legally bound to take the legal remedy and place himself under the protection of the law. But if the law offers him no remedy and no protection, he would appear to be entitled to resume the natural right to protect himself as best he can. That, at any rate, is my friend's view.

"Of course, the discovery of the alleged body of Mr. Black in the gravel-pit seemed to put an entirely new complexion on the affair. My friend was greatly perturbed by the news. It was hardly conceivable that it could really be Mr. Black's body. But it was some person's body, and the deliberate 'planting' of a dead human body seemed almost inevitably to involve a previous crime. Accordingly, my friend started off, hot-foot, to investigate. When the deceased turned out to be a mummy, his concern with the discovery came to an end. There was no need for him to interfere in the case. It was a harmless deception and even useful, for it informed the world at large that Mr. Black was dead.

"That, Mr. Pottermack, is the history of the dead man who was alive and the live man who was dead, and I think you will agree with me and my legal friend that it is a most curious and interesting case."

Pottermack nodded, but for some time remained silent. At length, in a tone the quietness of which failed to disguise the suppressed anxiety, he said, "But you have not quite finished your story."

"Have I not?" said Thorndyke. "What have I forgotten?"

"You have not told me what became of Mr. White."

"Oh, Mr. White. Well, I think we can read from here upon your sundial a few words that put his remaining history in a nutshell. '*Sole decedente pax*'. He had the mark removed from his ear, he married his old love, and lived happy ever after."

"Thank you," said Mr. Pottermack, and suddenly turned away his head.

The End

About the Author

Richard Austin Freeman was born on April 11th, 1862 in the Soho district of London. He was the son of a skilled tailor and the youngest of five children. As he grew, it was expected that he would become a tailor as well, but instead he had an interest in natural history and medicine, and so he obtained employment in a pharmacist's shop. While there, he qualified as an apothecary and could have gone on to manage the shop, but instead he began to study medicine at Middlesex Hospital.

Austin Freeman qualified as a physician in 1887, and in that same year he married. Faced with the twin facts of his new marital responsibilities and his very limited resources as a young doctor, he made the unusual decision to join the Colonial Service, spending the next seven years in Africa as an Assistant Colonial Surgeon. This continued until the early 1890's, when he contracted Blackwater Fever, an illness that eventually forced him to leave the service and return permanently to England.

For several years, he served as a *locum tenens* for various physicians, a bleak time in his life as he moved from job to job, his income low, and his health never quite recovered. However, he supplemented his meager income and exercised his creativity during these years by beginning to write. His early publications included *Travels and Live in Ashanti and Jaman* (1898), recounting some of his African sojourns.

In 1900, Freeman obtained work as an assistant to Dr. John James Pitcairn (1860-1936) at Holloway Prison. Although he wasn't there for very long, the association between the two men was enough to turn Freeman's attention toward writing mysteries. Over the next few years, they co-wrote several under the pseudonym *Clifford Ashdown*, including *The Adventures of Romney Pringle* (1902), *The Further Adventures of Romney Pringle* (1903), *From a Surgeon's Diary* (1904-1905), and *The Queen's Treasure* (written around 1905-1906, and published posthumously in 1975.)

In approximately 1904, Freeman began developing a mystery novella based on a short job that he had held at the Western Ophthalmic Hospital. This effort, "31 New Inn", was published in 1905, and it is the true first Dr. Thorndyke story. In 1907, the first Thorndyke novel, *The Red Thumb Mark*, was published.

From Thorndyke's creation until 1914, Freeman wrote four novels and two volumes of short stories. Then, with the commencement of the

First World War, he entered military service. In February 1915, at the age of fifty-two, he joined the Royal Army Medical Corps. Due to his health, which had never entirely recovered from his time in Africa, he spent the duration of the war involved with various aspects of the ambulance corps, having been promoted very early to the rank of Captain. He wrote nothing about Thorndyke during this period, but he did publish one book concerning the adventures of a scoundrel, *The Exploits of Danby Croker* (1916).

Following the war, he resumed his previous life, writing approximately one Thorndyke novel per year, as well as three more volumes of Thorndyke short stories and a number of other unrelated items, until his death on September 28th, 1943 – likely related to Parkinson's Disease, which had plagued him in later years. He is buried in Gravesend.

The MX Book of New Sherlock Holmes Stories
Edited by David Marcum
(MX Publishing, 2015-   )

Publishers Weekly says:

Part VI: *The traditional pastiche is alive and well . . . .*

Part VII: *Sherlockians eager for faithful-to-the-canon plots and characters will be delighted.*

Part VIII: *The imagination of the contributors in coming up with variations on the volume's theme is matched by their ingenious resolutions.*

Part IX: *The 18 stories . . . will satisfy fans of Conan Doyle's originals. Sherlockians will rejoice that more volumes are on the way.*

Part X: *. . . new Sherlock Holmes adventures of consistently high quality.*

Part XI: *. . . an essential volume for Sherlock Holmes fans.*

Part XII: *. . . continues to amaze with the number of high-quality pastiches . . .*

Part XIII: *. . . Amazingly, Marcum has found 22 superb pastiches . . . This is more catnip for fans of stories faithful to Conan Doyle's original*

Part XIV: *. . . this standout anthology of 21 short stories written in the spirit of Conan Doyle's originals.*

Part XV: *Stories pitting Sherlock Holmes against seemingly supernatural phenomena highlight Marcum's 15th anthology of superior short pastiches.*

Part XVI: *Marcum has once again done fans of Conan Doyle's originals a service.*

Part XVII: *This is yet another impressive array of new but traditional Holmes stories.*

Part XVIII: *Sherlockians will again be grateful to Marcum and MX for high-quality new Holmes tales.*

Part XIX: *Inventive plots and intriguing explorations of aspects of Dr. Watson's life and beliefs lift the 24 pastiches in Marcum's impressive 19th Sherlock Holmes anthology*

Part XX: *Marcum's reserve of high-quality new Holmes exploits seems endless.*

Part XXI: *This is another must-have for Sherlockians.*

The MX Book of New Sherlock Holmes Stories
Edited by David Marcum
(MX Publishing, 2015-   )

Also From MX Publishing

Traditional Canonical Sherlock Holmes Adventures by
David Marcum
Creator and editor of
The MX Book of New Sherlock Holmes Stories

 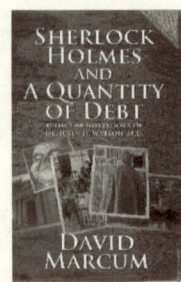 

The Papers of Sherlock Holmes
"The Papers of Sherlock Holmes by David Marcum contains nine intriguing mysteries . . . very much in the classic tradition . . . He writes well, too."
– Roger Johnson, Editor, *The Sherlock Holmes Journal,*
The Sherlock Holmes Society of London

"Marcum offers nine clever pastiches."
– Steven Rothman, Editor, *The Baker Street Journal*

Sherlock Holmes and A Quantity of Debt
"This is a welcome addendum to Sherlock lore that respectfully fleshes out Doyle's legendary crime-solving couple in the context of new escapades . . . ."
– Peter Roche, Examiner.com

"David Marcum is known to Sherlockians as the author of two short story collections . . . In Sherlock Holmes and A Quantity of Debt*, he demonstrates mastery of the longer form as well."*
– Dan Andriacco, Author

Sherlock Holmes – Tangled Skeins
(Included in Randall Stock's, 2015 Top Five Sherlock Holmes Books – Fiction)
"Marcum's collection will appeal to those who like the traditional elements of the Holmes tales"
– Randall Stock, BSI

"There are good pastiche writers, there are great ones, and then there is David Marcum who ranks among the very best . . . I cannot recommend this book enough."
– Derrick Belanger, Author and Publisher of Belanger Books

Sherlock Holmes in Montague Street
by Arthur Morrison
Edited, Holmes-ed, and with Original Material
by David Marcum

Separate Paperback Editions

Combined Hardcover Edition

*"It's been suggested that Hewitt was the young Mycroft Holmes,
but David Marcum has a more plausible and attractive theory
– that he was Sherlock, early in his career as an investigator
. . . these are remarkably convincing in their new guise."*
– Roger Johnson, Editor, *The Sherlock Holmes Journal*,
The Sherlock Holmes Society of London

MX Publishing

MX Publishing is the world's largest specialist Sherlock Holmes publisher, with several hundred titles and over a hundred authors creating the latest in Sherlock Holmes fiction and non-fiction.

From traditional short stories and novels to travel guides and quiz books, MX Publishing caters to all Holmes fans.

The collection includes leading titles such as *Benedict Cumberbatch In Transition* and *The Norwood Author*, which won the 2011 *Tony Howlett Award* (Sherlock Holmes Book of the Year).

MX Publishing also has one of the largest communities of Holmes fans on *Facebook*, with regular contributions from dozens of authors.

www.mxpublishing.co.uk (UK) and *www.mxpublishing.com* (USA)

www.ingramcontent.com/pod-product-compliance
Lightning Source LLC
Chambersburg PA
CBHW030738030726
47497CB00001B/28